Parallels

by

Cassandra Lynn King

CSJ King Publishing
Oregon, Wisconsin

DEDICATION

To my fourth grade teacher. Who's the lazy writer now?

CONTENTS

ACKNOWLEDGMENTS

First and foremost, I'd like to thank my parents, Didi and Jeff King for the outstanding amount of support and effort they've put into helping me finish this book. Both of them have full time jobs and on top of that, they spent their free time editing and publishing my work. This could not be a book without them. I'd also like to recognize four of my closest friends for their help. Natalie Wallace, you were with me when this all started, and you cheered me on to the end and even now give me support and encouragement. Katie Brown, even when I didn't deserve it, you supported me and gave me the motivation I needed to keep writing. Emma Brukner, your unicorn drawings in my notebooks were symbols of the enthusiasm you provided. James Halverson, your humor left a smile on my face and propelled me to the end.

Thanks to my great friend Ashley L. Steinberg, who set aside time in her busy college schedule to design my amazing cover page. Her artistic talent will get her far in life. Thanks and appreciations are sent to Deanna Blanchard for catching the final few errors during the editing process. Thanks to Amber Blanchard for the author photo. Thanks to all of my high school English teachers for helping me to improve upon my writing over the years, and thanks to all of my teachers who supported me through my writing process. A special thanks to my high school Spanish teacher Cynthia Ellestad for all the moral support she gave to me my senior year as I completed *Parallels*.

I want to thank my little brother Jackson for letting me borrow his name and for drawing the funny scenes of the book to give me a good laugh as I wrote. Also, thanks to my little sister Sydney for helping me type up the 866 pages of handwritten text. Thanks a lot for the help, Sista.

Thanks to all my family and friends who supported me throughout this long and occasionally tedious process.

I have one final thanks to send. Gordon Mennenga, an English professor at Coe College, took the time to read over the first few chapters of *Parallels*. He gave me great feedback to help me improve my writing. Thank you so much for your time.

For those of you who helped me to complete *Parallels*, I thank you for allowing me to pursue my dreams. You are some of the greatest people I will ever know.

With love,
Cassafrass

i

1

Hara's Beginning

April 2, 2008, began like any other day. The sun rose, birds sang in the trees, and the grand city of Philadelphia awoke. Children kissed their mothers goodbye before getting on the bus to go to school, people drank their coffee on their way to work, and the metropolitan area roared to life in no time.

Nothing out of the ordinary happened. The day would proceed with few worries of crime or other problems. The calm morning and afternoon deceived the city into believing that all would remain well.

The day that started out calm and peaceful would end with a bang. The events that would follow over the course of the next two days would bore a deep hole in the memories of the citizens of Philadelphia. They would go down as the most violent and devastating forty-eight hours in Philadelphia's history. Many innocent lives would be lost to a cause known only by a handful of people. The lives of these individuals would be altered forever. Those two days would cause the survivors to savor every day, to value their simple lives as much as they could, while they could.

* * *

At 5:47 p.m., one of Philadelphia's banks was closing for the day. The lone security guard who patrolled the premises throughout the day had already locked the front doors and was proceeding to check the locks on the emergency exit on the eastern side of the building. The hallway leading to the exit connected with the main lobby, a bright room whose ceiling, walls, and floor were constructed from peach, black, and turquoise colored marble that reflected sunlight around the room. The room shone until sunset when the light steadily flickered out and left it feeling as hollow and lifeless as a tomb, which was how the employees viewed the place. At the end of the hall, the amount of lighting was reduced to a bare minimum. The bright marble changed to dull concrete, and a sharp turn to the right led to a stairwell that went down to the exit, where a single light bulb and red EXIT sign lit up the dark and gloomy chamber.

Being a security guard in a bank wasn't Henry's highest goal in life. When he was a child and lived in L.A., he had dreamed of being a professional trombone player and an NBA star. It was an unlikely combination, but those were the two things at which he excelled: music and basketball. Those dreams were shattered when his parents were killed in a car accident when he was sixteen. His life took some wrong turns and he never seized upon the opportunity to pursue his dreams. He moved around working odd jobs here and there, never staying in one place for very long. A friend in Philadelphia hooked him up with the security guard position, which didn't require a college education, and he had been working at the bank for two years. It was the longest he had ever stayed in one spot. He hated the job and everyone else there, but his salary allowed him to live in a decent apartment.

Henry hesitated when he reached the side door that evening. There was something off about it that caused him to pause. Staring at it made him feel foolish, like he was a child scared of a monster behind his closet door. Part of him wanted to cautiously push it open to make sure the devil wasn't on the other side beckoning for Henry to come join him, but he knew that there was a camera behind his head taping his every move. He needed to shake off the uneasy feeling, so Henry unhooked the keychain from his belt and began unlatching the three locks on the door.

As Henry turned the key in the third lock, something happened that made him wish that he had just checked the locks and continued on his rounds. The door was thrown open with a hard kick from the outside, causing the heavy metal frame to strike Henry square in the forehead. Stunned and disoriented, Henry stumbled backward into the thick concrete wall. Confused by what was happening, he hesitated as a man dressed in all black with a ski mask suddenly entered. Henry had less than a second to react. His instincts directed his hand to the Taser at his side, but a blunt object was thrust into his face before he could get a grip on it. The force of the blow knocked Henry out cold before his body struck the floor. His last conscious thoughts left him wondering why he hadn't kept playing the trombone and promising himself that if he lived through the next half hour, he would start practicing again.

✳ ✳ ✳

Five men broke into the bank that evening. Each had spent at least three years in prison for a variety of crimes, including murder, grand theft auto, possession of drugs, physical assault, and sexual assault. For more than six months they had been carefully planning the break-in. They were not allowed to know each other's true names or faces lest one of them be caught and reveal the others' identities. Instead they were each given a fake name and disposable phone for communication purposes.

Lester was in charge of the operation. He had led several operations like this one, and he always went by the same alias. He had very pale skin and pale blue eyes. He was a quiet man who spoke with a sharp-tongued British accent. His ruthless reputation kept the others in line. Lester was not someone they had a desire to challenge. The only thing that suggested he had a soul was the gold Star of David he wore on a chain around his neck.

Westley was the second in command. The others feared him almost as much as Lester. Westley was a huge African American man with tree trunk arms and washboard abs, as described by the other three. He was about six-foot-five and looked like he could be a professional wrestler. His beady black eyes always seemed to be angry about something.

Zephyr was a squat little man in his mid-forties, with huge brown eyes that were constantly darting about. He was despised by everyone else in the group. He was obnoxious and had no idea when to shut his mouth. His vulgar and offensive language had nearly cost him his life several times when he had pushed it too far with Westley. He always wore a strip of red electrical tape around the left wrist of his jacket for good luck.

Mendeleev was a chemist who claimed to work at MIT. He was the one in charge of getting the group in and out of the building by eliminating any electronic barriers that they would encounter. His knowledge of computers and security systems was unsurpassed. He could manipulate them like no one else. So far, he had done an excellent job and Lester was impressed. Even so, Lester had been planning all along to eliminate him and Zephyr once the job was finished.

Juarez, the youngest of the group, was in charge of transportation. He barely spoke English but he was smart and was good in hand-to-hand combat. Juarez was quick tempered but trusted by Westley, so Lester allowed him on the team.

The men broke in at exactly 5:48 p.m., and after months of careful planning they were confident they could be out before the clock struck six. They knew exactly who was working and where they would be at that specific time thanks to Mendeleev and his mighty computer knowledge. So far, they had managed to take out the guard without any difficulty, and it appeared to them as if the rest of the operation would proceed quite smoothly. But they didn't realize how horribly wrong they were.

Lester and Westley headed for the manager's office while Juarez, Mendeleev, and Zephyr hurried to take care of the remaining people in the building. Westley took the door down with a single kick, and without hesitation he and Lester burst through the manager's door. The manager looked up in surprise from behind his desk at the automatic rifle that Lester pointed at his face.

"Good evening, Mr. Hamilton," Lester greeted cheerfully, cocking his weapon to prove to the manager that he had every intent to use the huge gun. "Don't bother notifying the police with the panic button beneath your desk. We've already disabled that."

Slowly, Mr. Hamilton raised his hands, nervously eyeing the gun not four inches from his nose. He swallowed hard and then looked back up at Lester. "What do you want?" he demanded, his low voice rising in pitch from fear.

Chuckling, Lester said, "Oh, I'm quite certain you knew why we were here the moment we stepped into the room." Getting down to business, he ordered, "Open your top desk drawer and take out your keys. I need to make a withdrawal. A very large withdrawal."

* * *

As Lester and Westley dealt with the manager, Zephyr sprinted as fast as his little legs could carry him down to another door at the end of the hallway where he knew the janitor—sixty-year-old Richard Merchant—would be vacuuming the back office. Richard heard the door being kicked down; he poked his head out of the back office with a puzzled look on his face as Zephyr approached.

Zephyr took hold of the back of the janitor's shirt and brought him out of the back room with a sharp yank. The janitor inhaled deeply in shock. "Do you want to die, old man?" Zephyr demanded, waving his automatic weapon in front of Richard. When the poor janitor didn't reply, Zephyr dragged him out to the lobby while his two remaining colleagues went to get the teller and her young son.

Richard didn't say a word as he was brought out into the lobby. Zephyr gave him a hard shove, and Richard cried out in agony as he hit the floor and something in his leg snapped.

"Shut your mouth or you're fucking dead!" Zephyr warned, pointing the gun at Richard. The old janitor clenched his jaw in an effort to contain his cries. He gazed pleadingly into Zephyr's eyes, but it was pointless. "Don't you fucking give me that pathetic look! I'll shoot you in the face and I'll still be able to sleep tonight!" He turned suddenly when he heard the sound of a door closing. The metal click had echoed from the hall in which they had entered. That meant either the guard had escaped, or someone else had entered. Either way, it was one of those unforeseen problems that the group had hoped they would not encounter. Knowing that the janitor wasn't about to go anywhere, Zephyr marched toward the hall to investigate.

* * *

It couldn't have been more than a few minutes before Henry finally awoke. At first, he couldn't quite remember why he was unconscious at the bottom of the stairwell. Then his heart began to pound in his chest as he realized what was happening. In a panic, he felt a burst of adrenaline course through his body, but when he attempted to get up he found that he was unable to. His head was spinning from the blow he had received from the first intruder, and when he made his move to rise he felt a horrible throbbing in the middle of his forehead. Dropping his body back against the floor, he moaned and reached for his cell phone to try to call the police. It wasn't in his belt, and he glanced around only to see that it was smashed into several small pieces a few inches from his knees. Groaning in anger and frustration, Henry tried to get up one last time but couldn't rise more than a few inches before falling back down again. He felt useless and angry for failing at his job. Praying that one of the others still in the bank had gotten away and would call for help, Henry sighed and waited for the spinning and the aching in his head to subside.

It was there, lying on the floor while he struggled through his pain, that Henry met Hara.

The exit door suddenly opened, but not as it had before. Instead of being thrown open, the door simply creaked open. Henry's heart began to pound again, fearing that another intruder was coming to finish him off. He had a gun in his belt, but he wasn't sure if he was strong enough to use it. Breathing hard and staring in terror, he watched as the new intruder came inside.

Something was different about this person. First of all, Henry could tell she was a female from the way she walked and also by the shape of her legs. She didn't seem to pose a threat to him, and almost appeared friendly. Still, he was on alert and wasn't about to let anybody fool him.

She was wearing all black like the previous intruders. Henry couldn't see her face until she cautiously approached and crouched down beside him. It was surprising to Henry to see just how young the girl really was. She couldn't have been older than twenty. Her young face had several scars. There was a patch of skin on her neck that looked like it had suffered some kind of acid or chemical burn. Her brown hair was long and wavy, and although it looked like it had been through hell, it somehow managed to look completely amazing. Her flowing hair fell in front of her face, and Henry had trouble seeing her eyes through the curtain of slight curls until she gave a graceful toss of her head and it fell down her back. Her eyes were the most amazing eyes Henry had ever seen. They were green, but they shone with a light so alive that they left him awestruck. They were beautiful. She was beautiful. Other than the few scars, her face was perfect, flawless. Her expression was blank, but

Henry felt that she was there to help him. Even so, there was something burning in her eyes that seemed dangerous, like a rage was bubbling up inside her and threatening to burst forth. Her eyes were the barrel of a gun aimed directly at Henry's face, and there was something else in them besides the rage, something that made Henry even more wary. There was something about them that seemed almost non-human.

Henry started to reach for his gun. Looking into the young girl's eyes frightened him more than the first intruders had.

The girl reached out a hand as well and she caught him by his wrist to stop him. Her grip wasn't urgent or forceful, but it was firm. She stared into Henry's eyes with her strange and beautiful eyes, and the intenseness of her gaze made Henry feel as if she were looking straight into his soul.

Henry stared back at her with a mixture of confusion, fear, and wonder, and he saw written across her face that she did not intend to hurt him. Still, he couldn't be entirely certain about her intent. Finding his voice, Henry asked quietly, "Are…are you with them?"

Her green eyes flashed, and it was such a peculiar thing to see that Henry thought at first that he was hallucinating. The right corner of her mouth turned up in a slight smile and she gave a small shake of her head. "No," she said softly. "I'm here to stop them."

Although the girl provoked fear and uncertainty in him, Henry knew that she was telling him the truth. For whatever the reason might have been, the young girl had shown up out of the blue—not necessarily to help him—but to stop whoever had entered uninvited and attacked him. Something was brewing deep inside of her that could very well be evil. At the moment, that didn't concern Henry. The enemy of his enemy was his friend.

She released his wrist, but Henry kept reaching for his gun. She didn't try to stop him this time.

"You should take this," he said, knowing that it wouldn't be helpful to anyone while he lay useless on the floor. It wasn't like him to hand over his firearm to just anyone, but she looked determined and he didn't want her to get hurt. "You shouldn't even be going in there."

"I don't need it," she replied in her quiet, smooth voice. She stood up as footsteps could be heard coming down the hall toward them from the lobby.

"What's this?" a man's voice asked.

Henry couldn't see the man and he didn't move to get a look at him, fearing that if he did he would be attacked again. Where he was, he could see that the girl hadn't moved either. She stood frozen, facing the man who Henry assumed was one of the men who had broken in.

The man whistled in a very rude way. "Well," he said with a perverted, piggish tone to his voice. "Aren't you pretty?"

Without responding, the girl continued to stand without moving a muscle in her body. Henry could hear the man's footsteps coming closer until he saw another pair of legs—also in black—step into view barely a foot from the girl's.

"Do you like my gun?" the man asked, clearly toying with her.

"I do, actually," the girl replied to Henry's surprise, and a moment later Henry heard something snap and then the pair of legs supporting the intruding man buckled beneath him. His body collapsed beside Henry and didn't move. Henry didn't have to look at him to know that the girl had snapped his neck.

Henry watched as she crouched down in front of him again. She was holding an automatic rifle in her left hand, as well as the man's jacket and ski mask. She stared into his eyes again before saying to him suddenly, "You should pick up the trombone again. You were pretty good."

Startled, Henry blinked up at her calm expression. "How did you know that?" Henry demanded.

"I know a lot of things," the girl said mysteriously. She put the jacket on and zipped it up.

Henry tried to raise his head to get a better look at the strange girl, but his head began to throb again and he lowered himself back down and winced in pain.

The girl cocked her head to one side and paused before reaching out a hand again and placing it gently on the side of his head. "You'll be okay," she murmured.

While the girl held her hand over his head, Henry felt something strange occurring. The floor tilted beneath him and he felt a numbing sensation where he had been struck. There was another presence inside his mind, forcing the pain out of him. It was all over within seconds and she pulled her hand away again, still gazing blankly into him.

Henry's pain had completely subsided. He had absolutely no idea how it had been done. Staring back at the girl in wonder, Henry whispered, "Who are you?"

The girl rose and stood over him for a moment and said, "If anyone asks, my name is Hara." She walked away from him, her footsteps silent as she headed down the hallway towards the lobby.

* * *

As Hara walked towards the lobby to join the rest of the criminals storming the bank, she pulled the ski mask over her head and tucked her hair into her jacket to hide it from the others. She was dressed in the same way that Zephyr had been dressed: black cargo pants, black jacket with the strip of red tape around the left wrist, and black shoes. The four others were too concerned with getting the money and getting out quickly to notice that her eyes were a different color.

Hara entered the marble lobby, and she eyed Juarez carefully. Juarez eyed her as well. Hara looked around the room at the people who had been herded in and were sitting on the floor huddled together. There was the old janitor, whose face was pained and whose leg appeared to have been broken. There was also a young woman, a teller, unfortunate enough to still be in the bank with her five-year-old son when the intruders entered.

The little brown-haired boy clung to his mother with a look of pure terror on his face, and for a moment an image of Hara's little brown-haired boy flashed into her mind. Her gaze softened at the sight of the boy and her mind began to wander back to her own family before it had been destroyed. She was only eighteen, but she had been a proud mother of five before a terrible war tore apart her society. Almost everyone she had ever loved had been killed. Now that she was free from the center of it, she would murder everyone responsible, along with the criminals in the bank who reminded her of those who had murdered her family.

"Hey!" Juarez snapped, causing Hara to look up in surprise. "Well? You gotta problem?"

Shaking her head quickly to avoid suspicion, Hara answered in a low voice, "No, no problems."

Juarez kept eyeing her suspiciously, but he looked back down at the hostages as the little boy began to cry softly in his mother's arms. "Hey, shut up," Juarez warned sharply. "I don't want to hear any of that. Shut up!" He kicked the boy in the back, and the boy cried out in pain.

The rage that had been bubbling up inside Hara for so long finally took control of her mind and body. Hearing the boy cry reminded her so much of her baby boy, and Juarez's kick reminded her of the abuse that her fourth child had received from people like him. She felt the wild fire raging inside of her. Her eyes narrowed at him, and then Juarez's eyes changed from irritation to terror. With a sick choking sound, he grabbed at his throat and gasped for air. Hara enjoyed the pain and fear she was causing him, and she caught herself smirking as she stepped around the hostages. She gazed into the terrified man's eyes in amusement, and he stared back at her in confusion.

"Do you like hurting people?" Hara asked him quietly, without disguising her voice. Juarez didn't answer her question, but he didn't need to. Hara could hear the answer ringing on the surface of his mind, a mind that was pathetic and not at all difficult to access. "That's okay," she told him, grinning at him even though he couldn't see it through her mask. "I do too."

"Who are you?" Juarez managed to choke out, but he didn't get an answer. Hara had let herself go. The wild fire inside of her, which had been begging to be set free, was allowed a short time out of its cage. His skin wasn't exposed because of the jacket and the ski mask, but if it had been, Hara would have been able to see the skin on his neck and face being slowly burned away. A moment before Juarez collapsed to the floor dead, Hara caught the pain in his eyes and his pleading look in them, but she didn't care. His body fell, and when it struck the ground it didn't move. As Hara and the three hostages stared down at the body, she felt no remorse

The young mother held her son to her as he continued to cry; she turned away from the body and squeezed her eyes shut. The old janitor stared at Hara confusion and disbelief.

Without another word, Hara turned and started for the second hall that led to the work stations for the employees. The door had been kicked in and it hung on the frame by its bottom hinge. Hara hadn't even gotten to the doorway before Westley came running out with a large black bag in each hand. He tossed one of the bags to Hara and snapped, "Make yourself useful."

The bag was heavy and swollen, but Hara had no trouble holding onto it; however, she didn't want to hang on to it. She had no desire to steal the useless green paper that was inside. As Westley brushed past her she threw the bag to the ground, making sure to put enough force into it to get his attention.

Westley had been saying, "Taking a nap, Juarez?" as Hara did so, and without waiting for a reply he turned back towards Hara in surprise. Glancing down at the bag and then back to her face, he studied her defiant body posture. "You got a problem, you red-neck bastard?" When Hara didn't move or reply, he growled, "If you want your share in this, then pick up the damn bag and take it to the car!"

"I don't want your worthless paper," Hara told him, kicking the bag back at him and tossing the automatic rifle at him as well.

Peering at her curiously, Westley started to realize that Hara wasn't who she appeared to be. He looked back at the crumpled body of Juarez and then back to her. "Did you kill him?" he demanded, the arm holding his weapon raising slightly.

Hara cocked her head to the side again. Westley already knew the answer to his own question, and Hara was preparing herself for what he was planning to do next.

He just stared at her for a few tense moments before he whipped his weapon up and aimed it at her head. He was almost able to pull the trigger before Hara reacted. Raising her arm as well, she waved her hand from Westley to the side of Juarez's body, sending his automatic rifle flying out of his hands and clattering to the floor several feet away. Then, she raised her hand towards Westley's neck and tightened her fingers as if she were actually holding his throat.

Westley's eyes widened and he grabbed at his throat just as Juarez had. He tried taking steps backwards to get away from Hara, but Hara had him completely immobilized.

"I'm sorry," Hara said sincerely, "that you have nothing in your life better than this. I'm sorry that you have nothing better to live for."

"What do you want?" Westley asked in a strangled voice, his troubled eyes pleading with hers.

"I want you to die," Hara told him simply, and she clenched her hand into a tight fist. She heard a small squeak in the back of his throat, followed by a sickening crunch as his windpipe was crushed. When he crumpled to the floor just as Juarez had, Hara said, "I want people like you gone from this world."

Mere seconds passed from when Hara killed Westley to when she heard a gunshot from down the hall. Hara had known the plan of the intruders from the very beginning: get the money and then kill any hostages. If she was not mistaken, Lester had just killed the bank manager now that he was no longer useful. That didn't matter to Hara. The bank manager was a selfish man of no use to the future or Hara. The three other hostages, however, were good people at heart. Hara would protect them from Lester and help them like she had helped Henry.

Since Lester was the mastermind behind the operation and the most heinous murderer of the group, Hara decided that it was only fitting that she played with him before she killed him. He had played with so many of his past victims before he had killed them. There had been a time when he had invaded the house of a young couple back in England, and killed the husband and two young children without much thought. Before he killed the wife and took all of the family's valuables, he made her watch as he murdered her children, and then he raped her before finally finishing the job. Lester's lack of morals reminded Hara of a man she knew, the same man who had made her watch as he killed so many of the people she loved. Hara would make him face the consequences of his past decisions before she finally wiped him off the face of the earth.

It felt like several minutes passed before Lester finally stepped into the lobby with two more loaded bags of cash in his hands. He stopped and stared at the gruesome scene. Calmly, he asked, "What happened here?"

"It was Mendeleev," Hara said immediately, precisely imitating Zephyr's Southern drawl. She knew very well that Mendeleev was cowering as he hid from her, watching the scene play out from the surveillance room. "He killed them all and left. I just came in and found this mess."

Lester stared at her. His cold, calm blue eyes made her so angry, and the fact that he didn't even seem bothered by the death of his colleagues made her want to harm him even more. He glanced at the two dead men once again before shrugging and sighing. "Well, that's a shame," he muttered, his curious eyes landing on hers again. "More for us, then. Why don't you grab the other bags and then we can get the hell out of here."

Hara nodded and made the mistake of turning her back on Lester. Somehow, she hadn't caught the thought on the edge of his mind. He was so calm; she hadn't realized that he was aware that she was an impostor.

"You know, if you really wanted to fool me, you should have picked someone quieter," Lester said. Hara heard the bags in his hands drop to the floor before hearing the sound of his weapon being cocked. "Put your hands above your head, kiddo," Lester instructed quietly.

Stopping where she was, Hara slowly raised her hands as she heard Lester approach her from behind. He had been right; Zephyr had been a stupid choice. She should have picked Juarez instead.

"Besides, you're too tall," Lester added from a few inches behind her. "Turn around, and if you make any sudden movements, I won't hesitate to shoot."

Hara turned around and looked up into Lester's eyes with a blank expression. She wasn't afraid of him. Even with a gun, she knew Lester was no match for her.

Lester looked down into her eyes as well, and he cocked his head in a familiar way that made Hara's anger begin to boil again. He was so close to her, and he only made their proximity more uncomfortable by smiling at her. His face wasn't visible due to the mask, but his eyes were betraying his every thought. "Has anyone ever told you that you have very nice eyes?" he asked her softly, unable to look away from her mesmerizing gaze.

Hara didn't answer.

Snickering, Lester reached up without a moment's hesitation and lifted the ski mask up and over her head so he could see her face. Hara's hair frizzed on the ends and fell over her face, but she gave a slight toss of her head so Lester would be able to see who she really was. When Lester got a good long look, he raised his eyebrows and searched her face for several seconds, taking in her unexpected beauty. Finally getting hold of himself, he asked her, "How old are you? Seventeen? Eighteen?"

"Eighteen," Hara replied, still not blinking or shifting her gaze.

Lester nodded and continued to stare at her face before smiling again. "You're very good for your age. So, you want a job, is that it? You want to work for me?"

It was Hara's turn to smile, but instead she took the opportunity to smirk at him, an expression so unnerving that it wiped the smile from Lester's eyes. Shaking her head ever so slowly, Hara said, "I actually just had an important question I needed to ask you." She didn't wait for his permission to ask. "All those people you've killed...all those women you've raped...did you, even once, feel a single shred of remorse for what you did?"

He didn't look surprised that Hara knew about his past crimes. With barely a pause, Lester replied, "No."

Hara smirked again and couldn't keep herself from giggling like a maniac. "Wrong answer," she said.

Lester's neck was snapped in several places half a second later, and he was dead before his body struck the floor. Hara started to turn and head for the hallway leading to the back offices, but she was stopped by the old janitor.

"You're so young," he whispered, his eyes sad when Hara looked back to him. "You're so young and you're already throwing your life away. You should be in school, not getting involved with people like him." He nodded to Lester.

Hara replied in a low voice, "I've barely gotten started."

"Go home," the old man pleaded, his eyes showing pure concern. Hara twitched angrily. No one should be feeling pity for her after the horrible things she had done, and the horrible things she would do. "Stay in school. You could have such a bright future. It's not too late to stop this."

Hara stared at him, and then slowly shook her head. "It's way too late for me now. I'm too far gone."

"It's never too late," the old man insisted, his eyes still pleading.

Hara shook her head harder and pursed her lips. "You haven't seen what I've seen!" she hissed, turning on her heel without waiting for another reply. She didn't need humans telling her what she should and shouldn't do. They had lost all rights to do that after they murdered her people.

Down the hallway, the second to last door on the right granted access to the room that Hara was looking for, the surveillance room. She knew it was locked before she entered the bank, but a locked door could never stop her. A single wave of a finger split the door in two vertically and caused it to collapse to the floor with a crunch. Stepping over it, her gaze landed on Mendeleev in the far corner of the room. His entire body was shaking in fear, and he held a nine-millimeter handgun aimed at her head. Hara couldn't take him seriously with his eyes widened like a little puppy's. She held out her hand. The weapon was wrenched from his hand, flew across the room, and landed in Hara's, who then turned the gun back on him.

The chemistry professor raised his hands, his eyes full of terror. "Please!" he begged helplessly. "I'm sorry! I'm not a bad person! I've never hurt anybody!"

"I know, Jack," Hara told him softly, clenching her hand in a fist and crushing the gun without any effort at all. Dropping the clump of metal to the floor with a clatter, she lowered her hand back to her side. "That's why I'm not going to hurt you. But you have to do exactly as I say, and you have to do it now."

"What do you want?" Jack asked quickly, lowering his hands as well.

"Don't delete the footage on the surveillance tapes like you planned to," Hara explained, walking over to the many computers sitting on a table between them. "I need the cops to see what I can do."

"Why?" Jack demanded in confusion. "What are you?"

"Must you ask so many questions?" Hara snapped

"Why are you sparing me when you killed everyone else?" Jack asked.

"Because you're not all that different from me. You're doing this because you lost your family, which is the same reason why I'm doing this. Plus, your buddy Lester was going to kill you once the job was finished. You should be thanking me."

Unsure of how to reply, Jack nodded slowly. "Okay. I won't delete the footage."

"Turn the camera in here back on," Hara ordered, pointing to the camera in the corner. Just so Jack wouldn't ask why, she added, "I need to get a message to someone."

Nodding again, Jack walked around to Hara's side of the table and typed something into a computer. A moment later, he told her, "It's back on. Do whatever you want with it."

Peering at him curiously, Hara said, "You know, I used to have a close friend named Jack. He was one of the good guys, but he died. You kind of remind me of him in a strange way."

Staring blankly back at her, Jack said, "Thank you for not killing me."

Hara snickered. "Get out. Go home, and stay out of business like this. You're a good person, Jack. Stuff like this isn't worth the consequences."

"You don't know what I've been through," Jack replied curtly.

Taking a step forward so they were very close, Hara said, "Believe me, I do."

Jack backed out of the room, stumbling over the door as he did so. Once he was out into the hallway, he turned and sprinted towards the lobby to get out. Hara knew that the young man would never flirt with crime again.

A newspaper sitting on the corner of the table caught Hara's eye, and the image on the front startled her. There was a large picture on the front page of a man about forty years old with wavy blonde hair, smiling for the camera. The picture was in black and white, but Hara knew that the man had deep blue eyes that shone like diamonds. She knew that because they had once been friends. Reaching down, she picked up the newspaper and read the headline.

MAYOR ALLAN BROWN CONTINUES TO REDUCE PHILADELPHIA'S CRIME RATE

"Huh," Hara muttered, unable to keep the corner of her mouth from turning up in a grin. "You've been putting the bad guys in jail, have you?" Snickering, she tossed the newspaper to the floor. "Be prepared to see that change, my friend." Shaking her head and smirking to herself, Hara looked around for some paper and a marker. She needed to get her message to her man quickly. Henry would be dialing 911 shortly, and Hara needed to be long gone by then. Hara really didn't feel like killing any more people that day.

2

The Case

The call came for him around 8:00 a.m. on April 3. A very troubled lieutenant in the Philadelphia police force had called the FBI and requested help investigating a high-profile case. Special Agent Rhett Long had then told Special Agent Shawn Perry that he, his partner Renee Michaels, and two other agents would be assigned to take on the new case in Philadelphia. Unfortunately, the others were wrapping up a case in Pittsburgh and would not be able to travel with him right away. Perry would have to report to Philadelphia ahead of the others and get a head start on the new case. Perry got into his black SUV and set off towards Philadelphia.

He didn't know what it was about that particular drive to Philadelphia—a path that he had taken numerous times before throughout his career—but it caused him to think a lot about his troubled past. He thought about his mother, Leah, and her death when he was only four years old. Memories of her had long since faded away, but Perry knew that if she had survived cancer, he would have had a much better childhood and a much easier life. After his mother's death, Perry's father Marco slowly and painfully withdrew into his misery. He drank himself into a stupor every night, and as the years wore on, Marco became very violent. He attacked Perry and three times beat him so severely that the he had ended up in the hospital. Finally, when Perry was sixteen and had had enough, he fought back. His father hadn't liked that. Fearing for his life, Perry had gotten the gun out of his father's bedside table and shot him in self-defense, killing him instantly. After seeing him in the hospital so many times before, the doctors and police both believed Perry when he insisted it was to protect himself, and charges were never brought against him. Still a minor, Perry then lived with his aunt and uncle. Because of his troubled and abusive childhood, Perry decided to go into law enforcement and eventually made it into the FBI. Perry had only shared his past with his partner Renee and his superior officer Agent Long.

Perry had held onto his grief for a long time, but over the past several years the feelings of guilt had finally begun to subside. The drive to Philadelphia seemed to draw them to the surface again. Maybe it was just the strangeness and horror of the new case that caused him to recall his own violent past, or maybe it was his lack of sleep. There could have been several reasons. All Perry was concerned with was blocking the memories out like he had before.

At one point in his life—when he was twenty-nine—his depression had gotten the better of him and he had resorted to drinking just like his father had. One night, he had been at a bar and was completely shit-faced. He met a woman there named Kira who was about the same age and was quite lovely at first glance. They had a one night stand. Kira called him about two months later claiming that she was pregnant. In their drunken stupor, protection hadn't crossed the minds of either of them. Kira told Perry that she didn't want anything to do with him and that a baby would never change anything. However, since neither of his parents had ever been there for him, Perry wanted to be there for his kids. He knew that he would be fighting for his child once she was born, whether Kira wanted him around or not.

Kira named their baby Jillian after her mother, and Perry had fought constantly with Kira to see his daughter whenever he could. It was a never-ending battle with the woman just to play with his child for a few hours every month and to show her that he really did love her. He would never give up on his child like his father had. He may have lost the custody battle, but he would never give her up. He barely knew his own child, but he loved her, and from what he saw she loved him too. Jillian was now five, and Perry hadn't seen her in nearly a year since Kira moved to Florida with her boyfriend. He could hear in his daughter's voice that she would rather be with him than with her obnoxious mother. When Perry was ready to raise his daughter in a stable environment, he would fight Kira once again for custody of his child and he would win, no matter the costs.

It had irritated Perry that his boss was separating him from his partner, but he understood why. Agent Long had seen something in him and had accepted him immediately after his training was complete. Before Renee, he'd had two other female partners. The first had been a woman in her mid-forties named Isabelle Walker. She had only worked with Perry for eight months before she had been gunned down during a drug bust in Philadelphia. Perry barely escaped with his life. His second partner was only a few months older than he was. She was a gorgeous brunette by the name of Whitney Lindert, and she had been his partner until his thirtieth birthday. The two of them had been in pursuit of three murder suspects when their SUV blew a tire and they ran off a bridge into a river. Whitney's neck broke upon impact with the water, and Perry once again escaped with nothing more than a few bumps and bruises.

Renee was his third partner and was about a year younger than Perry. She had been working with Perry for the past five years—about the same amount of time as he had with Whitney—but she was the first partner he had ever developed feelings for. She was beautiful—blonde haired and blue-eyed, the complete opposite of Perry. But that wasn't the reason he had fallen for her. She may have been beautiful, but she was so much more than that. Renee was the only person who could commiserate with him for his loss. Three years earlier, she had lost her older brother Josh, also an FBI agent, in a drug bust in the same area of Philadelphia where Perry had lost his first partner. She was the only person who knew how he felt and could sympathize with him. Not only that, Renee cared for him in a way that no one else in his life ever had. She was sweet and gentle and at the proper times stern and stubborn. She was the most amazing person he had ever met.

Agent Long had clearly seen that Perry and Renee had developed feelings for each other. He saw everything. He had confronted the two of them in private and had given them both "the talk" about how agents were not supposed to share feelings for each other. The distraction was a potential threat to their safety as well as the safety of other agents. Agent Long must have thought that a little time apart might do them both some good. So Perry thought about his future. He had spent his thirty-five years of life drowning in pain and misery and personal crises. If he had finally found the one person that could take that all away, and someone with whom he shared a mutual respect, then he wasn't going to let the fact that they were partners get in the way. Agent Long wouldn't be able to get his foot in between the two of them no matter what he threatened.

When he finally arrived at the scene of the crime, Perry parked his SUV alongside a line of squad cars. He didn't get out right away. He'd had to deal with the Philadelphia police force in the past, and his experience had not been pleasant. The police chief was not the easiest man to get along with. Their last encounter was the day that Renee's brother was killed; it ended in a brawl. Perry had no desire to deal with him again. Cops were not his specialty, but Agent Long had insisted that Perry be the one for the job and Perry didn't want to start his morning by getting into a heated argument with his superior officer. When he gathered himself enough to face the Chief of Police again, Perry took a deep breath and stepped out of his vehicle.

There were at least half a dozen camera crews surrounding the building, but Perry pushed past them easily. He was glad that none of the reporters tried to stop him on his way through, because if there was anything he hated more than dealing with cops, it was dealing with the press. He was surprised that no one tried to stop him. They were all desperate for answers, judging by the way they were yelling questions at the police officers working to keep people behind the yellow caution tape. Considering that Perry was wearing a black jacket with FBI in big bold letters on the back, most people would assume that he held a lot of the answers. He wasn't complaining, but it was a little peculiar considering the circumstances. A younger male officer about the same age as Perry with wavy brown hair and very lively baby blue eyes started to approach him, uncertainly, to see what he was up to. Perry opened his jacket to show the officer his credentials. The officer stopped, waved Perry inside, and quickly returned to his post. Perry did catch the strange look the officer gave him before he entered the bank, but he ignored it.

The inside of the bank was, to say the least, beautiful. But as lovely as the marble structure, the space had one flaw: it produced such a horrendous echo of voices that Perry could barely hear himself think. There was a door on the far left that led to a hallway. It had been kicked down and was lying on the floor with a large dent in the center of it.

Perry had been told that the body count stood at five. The bodies had since been removed. There were, however, forensic teams spread out in different areas throughout the large marble room, examining the places where the deaths had occurred. As Perry passed a group of three about halfway into the room, he couldn't see anything on the floor in front of them, but something was obviously of interest because they were talking quickly in hushed whispers.

Unsure of who to report to, Perry stopped and looked around at the others doing their jobs. Everyone was intent on their work and didn't take notice of him. Perry had been told to meet with a Lieutenant Odau, the officer who had contacted the Pittsburgh FBI, but alas, he had no idea where Lieutenant Odau was.

"Sir?" a female voice said off to his right.

Turning towards the sound of the voice, Perry saw an officer a few years older than him standing a few feet away, peering at him curiously. She was wearing the familiar dark blue police uniform with the gold badge on her left breast. She was about five-foot-ten, with dark brown eyes and long black hair. To Perry's relief she seemed to recognize him.

"Are you Agent Perry?" she asked, taking a step towards him.

"It's Special Agent, actually," Perry corrected, and he smiled at her pleasantly.

He caught the flash of annoyance in the officer's eyes before she smiled back and extended her hand. "I'm Detective Maggie Finchly. I work under the direction of Lieutenant Odau, so I suppose we'll be working together."

Perry nodded to her and shook her hand. "It's nice to meet you. I was just looking for the lieutenant, actually. Do you know where I could find him?"

"He's in the manager's office," Detective Finchly replied, pointing towards the broken down door and starting to walk in that direction.

Perry followed her. When they reached the door, Perry and the detective had to brush past a few forensics officers searching for fingerprints, and he was relieved to see that there were fewer people in the hallway. It was a lot quieter, with a lot less sound reverberating off the walls, a relief to his ringing ears.

Finchly led him to the first door on the left and called in, "Sir, Special Agent Perry is here to see you."

As Finchly stood aside for Perry to present himself, Perry stepped forward and entered the office, looking around the room as well as at the two men dressed in police uniforms. There were three laptops resting on the cherry wood desk in the center of the room. Against the right wall were three large file cabinets. Files and folders were strewn across the floor, the tops of the cabinets, and the cherry wood desk.

Perry knew right away that the man sitting in the black leather chair behind the desk was Lieutenant Graham Odau. He was older than both Detective Finchly and the other male detective in the room. The way that the male detective was standing beside the lieutenant suggested that he both feared and revered his boss. The way the lieutenant held himself and looked back at Perry showed authority, also. He sat tall in his chair and was gazing expectantly, almost impatiently, at Perry, as if he had been forced to wait too long for his arrival.

"You look a little young to have been in the bureau for ten years," were the first words out of Odau's mouth.

Perry may have been thirty-five, but his physical appearance made him look even younger. His dark brown hair had been growing out and now fell over his mahogany eyes—a trait that had won him many compliments in the past—in light curls. He had a handsome, friendly face that tended to draw people to him. This wasn't the first time that another officer had commented on his youthful appearance. Even so, the comment still irritated Perry.

Perry struggled to mask his irritation. Offering a fake smile, Perry told Odau as the lieutenant looked him up and down, "I get that a lot."

Nodding, Odau's eyes locked on Perry's and narrowed slightly. "Since when do agents not travel in pairs? I was told that three more agents would be accompanying you."

"Special Agents Michaels, Martinson, and Hersh are completing an assignment back in Pittsburgh," Perry explained. "Special Agent Long requested that I arrive ahead of the group to get started on this new case. They'll be arriving later today."

Odau nodded in satisfaction. The lieutenant looked to be in his mid-forties. He wore thick-framed glasses over his eyes and they actually made him appear rather intelligent despite his awkward first impression. Behind the glasses, he had eyes that were an icy shade of blue and looked as if they themselves could bite Perry. Odau's hair, which was wavy and a dusty brown color, wasn't graying at all. The corners of his eyes were beginning to wrinkle as well as the skin around his mouth, cheeks, and forehead.

"Where's Chief Monarsky?" Perry asked flatly, glad that he hadn't yet seen the police chief but wondering why that might be.

"He's on vacation," Odau replied. "He won't be back for another week. So you have to deal with me."

"Ah," Perry muttered, unsure of which cop he'd rather deal with.

As a moment of silence filled the room, the male detective standing beside Odau, a man about the same age as Finchly with brown eyes and curly black hair, took a step forward and smiled warmly before extending a hand. "I'm Garrick Aubrey," he said as Perry shook his hand. "Maggie's my partner."

"Shawn Perry," Perry said, glad that at least the detectives had a sense of respect and welcoming.

"Detectives Aubrey and Finchly will be assisting us as well as Detective Daniel Marcus, who you may have met on your way in," Odau explained, fishing through a large stack of papers on the desk in front of him.

"I'm afraid that I missed Detective Marcus," Perry replied.

"It would be pretty hard to," Aubrey told him. "His eyes aren't exactly something you miss."

"Oh, him," Perry said, recalling the baby blue-eyed officer who had tried to stop him on his way in. "Yeah, I bumped into him outside."

"Yes, he's handling crowd control right now," Odau said, glancing up at Aubrey as if he were a lingering pest. "Is there something else that you need, Detective?" When Aubrey looked back to him in surprise and confusion, Odau raised his eyebrows. "If not, then feel free to leave."

Shooting Perry a look as if to say "Good luck," Aubrey left the room. Perry stepped further in to allow him space to exit. Both detectives then gladly hurried away without another word.

In the bureau, Perry had been used to a mutual respect that was shared between each agent. They were all friends and were always fighting for the same cause, therefore they always treated each other courteously. There were superior officers in each area—in Perry's case it was Agent Long—and they tended to push the lower agents around a bit, but never in a way like Odau had just treated his detectives.

"You know, you really shouldn't speak to your detectives like that," Perry told him as he stepped up to the desk, already feeling a strong sense of resentment towards the lieutenant.

Odau looked up and raised his eyebrows again. "Excuse me?"

"From what I've observed, Aubrey and Finchly are very decent people and are most likely doing their absolute hardest to help solve this case and please you." Perry put his hands in his jacket pockets as he spoke to the lieutenant. "They don't deserve to be brushed aside in the way they just were, and if that's how you've always treated them, then it's time to change."

Setting the stack of papers back down on the desk, Odau folded his hands upon them and leaned forward. "I'm not exactly sure how things are run in the bureau," the lieutenant began in a quiet voice "but things are clearly run differently there than they are here."

"Clearly," Perry challenged, holding Odau's glare easily. The lieutenant may have been older, but Perry knew that his authority outranked Odau's by a long shot. Placing his hands on the desk and leaning closer to him, Perry said, "I can see how you run things here, but when you called for me, you handed over your authority to me. I'm in charge now. Things are going to change around here, starting with your attitude."

"Be careful of who you call next time," Perry replied curtly, standing up straight again and taking a step back.

His gaze never wavering, Odau paused before saying with great difficulty and a bit of sarcasm, "Yes, sir." He leaned back in his chair casually, but his eyes never left Perry's and his hard expression never changed. "Monarsky warned me that you were a stubborn one."

Cocking his head to the side slightly, a small smile suddenly came to Odau's lips. "It must be why he likes you so much."

Taken aback, Perry blinked at him in surprise. "What are you talking about? We can't stand each other. Did you hear about what happened the last time we met?"

"Oh, yes," Odau said, and his smile broadened. "The whole force knows about the infamous altercation between Liam Monarsky and Shawn Perry. However, despite the chief's negative feelings toward you, he claimed that you were the best at what you do. He told me that if there was anyone in the FBI who could get the job done, it was you."

Shocked by the fact the Chief Monarsky had anything positive to say about him, Perry nodded slowly, unsure of how to respond.

"So, since the chief obviously has respect for you, then that means I do too," Odau added, nodding back to him. "I'm sorry that I upset you and if you want something to change, then you can expect it to."

"Thank you. Now, can we pretend that none of this happened and just get to work?" Holding out his hand, Perry told him, "I'm Special Agent Shawn Perry."

Shaking it, Odau said, "Lieutenant Graham Odau."

"So what exactly happened here?" Perry asked.

"Well, the bank was robbed by five men, four of whom are now dead, and one hostage was killed."

"Where's the fifth intruder?"

"We don't know yet. He fled the scene unharmed and unarmed, and we're working on tracking him using security cameras spread around the city."

"I have a man who can help with that once he gets here," Perry told him, knowing that his colleague Andy Martinson could never get enough of the thrill of tracking a suspect through security footage. "How much money was taken from the vault?"

"Over eighty thousand," Odau declared. "But it's all here and accounted for. Not a dollar made it out of the building."

Perry's brow furrowed in confusion. "The fifth suspect didn't take any money with him when he left?"

Odau snickered. "He was probably too desperate to get out to even think about taking any money." Watching Perry closely, it was clear to Odau that Perry didn't know what had gone down the night before. "Didn't anyone tell you how the men were killed?"

"I wasn't told much," Perry replied. "I just assumed that the security guard had intervened and there had been a firefight, or the single man who escaped had attacked the others and killed them all."

Shaking his head slowly, Odau explained, "Henry Johnson was injured during the break-in and suffered a serious blow to the head, although the EMTs claimed he's perfectly fine. He wasn't capable of fighting five armed men on his own, and the fifth intruder wasn't around when the other four were killed."

"Maybe you can explain to me what exactly happened here," Perry said.

Odau stared at him uncertainly for a moment before saying, "I should warn you, what happened here is pretty disturbing."

"I think I can handle it," Perry assured him.

"This isn't one of your regular cases," Odau added. "This is like nothing any of us have ever seen before."

"Are you going to tell me what happened or not?" Perry demanded, growing more irritated.

Odau stood up and walked around the desk towards him. "I can't explain it in words. I have to show you. Come." He left the room and gestured for Perry to follow.

As Perry followed the lieutenant down the hall to the surveillance room, he was unable to fathom what could have happened in that bank that was so unusual. After having two partners killed right in front of him and almost dying several times, there wasn't much that Perry couldn't handle.

The security footage shocked him. He had thought the victims were killed by each other, but that was the case only for the manager. The four intruders that had been killed were taken out by what appeared to be a teenage girl. She had killed two of the four dead intruders by snapping their necks. The other two she somehow killed without even touching them. Perry was told that one of those two suffered a crushed windpipe, and the other had suffered third degree burns on his cranial and cervical regions. In the end the mask she had stolen from one of her victims was removed, but Perry didn't see her face until later. The girl went to the surveillance room where the fifth intruder had been hiding while he watched everything. She crushed his weapon in her bare hand and then seemed to be having a conversation with the man. Then, the last man hesitantly walked around the table full of computers to meet her and then typed something into a computer while the girl looked on. They spoke for a brief moment again before the man hastily left the room and then the building, leaving everything behind except for the black pickup truck that they had arrived in. The girl bustled about in the surveillance room for several minutes before she looked directly into the camera and held something up above her head for the camera to see as well. It was a sign written on a large sheet of paper, and all it said was 3 P.M. TOMORROW in big bold, capital letters.

Upon seeing the girl's face, Perry understood why the first intruder killed had paused when he had first looked at her. The girl was gorgeous. Her face was perfectly shaped, and she had big beautiful green eyes that shone like emeralds. Perry was glad that he'd had a chance to see the girl's face, considering that there was not a single trace of her left behind, not a hair, not a fingerprint, nothing. Although it was a relief to have some way of tracking her down, it seemed like odd behavior for someone to purposely look into the camera after murdering four people.

"Why would she look into the camera like that?" Odau asked him.

"I was just asking myself the same thing," Perry replied, pondering over what he had just witnessed. "You were right. This is like nothing I've ever seen before."

"You saw everything that she did, right?" Odau asked. "I'm not going completely crazy, am I?"

"I saw it," Perry confirmed, still lost in thought. "It has to be some kind of special effect. Everything she did is impossible."

"We checked the tapes," Odau said. "They're the original copies and they haven't been tampered with. We're planning to take them back to the station for further analysis, but I doubt we'll find anything different."

"She crushed an automatic rifle with her bare hands," Perry declared, looking at the lieutenant in confusion.

"And she killed two men without touching them," Odau added. "It's bizarre, isn't it?"

"That's one word for it," Perry muttered, looking back at the image of the girl holding up her sign, which was frozen on the computer screen. "Have you found out who this girl is yet?"

"We're running her face through our database, but so far we haven't found her. We haven't had any luck tracking her movements either. She disappeared into thin air once she left the building."

Perry glanced at him. "Are you being literal when you say that?" After seeing her performance, Perry wouldn't be too surprised to discover that she indeed had disappeared into thin air.

Chuckling, Odau answered, "No, we just haven't seen her on any security camera in the city after this incident." He glanced at Perry. "These aren't special effects, and I have the handgun that she crushed with the finger indentations to prove it. This girl is clearly not typical, and I wonder if this was the result of a top secret government test gone horribly wrong."

"Government experiments are out of my league," Perry informed him. "But now that you mention it, I might have to make some calls to check that out."

"If it's true, then maybe we can actually figure out how Hara can do those things."

"What did you just call her?" Perry asked in surprise, wondering if it was a code name that he used for her.

"Her name is Hara," Odau explained. "At least, that's what she's calling herself. I spoke with Mr. Johnson when I arrived, and the girl apparently told him her name. I highly doubt that's her real name, though. I've checked, and so far there's no match for the name Hara."

"Well, at least we have a name for her," Perry replied. "Why do you think she let the fifth guy go?"

"Not a clue," Odau stated.

"What about the guard? Hara seemed awfully friendly to him. Does she know him?"

"He claims that he's never met her before, but he could be lying."

Remembering that the bank had almost been robbed, Perry tried to shift his gaze away from Hara for a moment. "I understand that this new predicament is quite fascinating, but why exactly was I called down here? Was it because the bank was nearly robbed and you want to catch the fifth suspect, or was it because you want to catch this girl that can do bizarre things?"

"A bit of both," Odau responded immediately. "But mostly because we want to find the girl."

"Well, she obviously knew that the robbery was going to occur, so maybe she had connections to the men involved. Have you uncovered the identities of the four dead suspects yet?"

"Yes," Odau said. "All of them spent a great deal of time in prison, but so far we haven't found how she fits in." He cocked his head slightly again as he had before. "The leader of the group was a British man by the name of Neville Tyler."

Perry's heart skipped a beat at the name of the infamous drug dealer who had killed a number of his colleagues. "He was the last one killed, wasn't he?"

Odau nodded.

Raising an eyebrow at the image of Hara's calm face on the computer, Perry snickered. "Good riddance. I hope that we do find this girl, because then I can thank her for getting rid of that scum."

"What exactly happened between the two of you?" Odau asked. "If you don't mind me asking."

"He killed my first partner, Isabelle Walker," Perry explained. "A few years ago, he killed another colleague of mine by the name of Joshua Michaels, the older brother of my current partner. Those are only two of the many agents he has killed."

"Oh," Odau said, and smiled. "I suppose that you feel no sympathy for any of these men then."

"None whatsoever," Perry replied. He turned towards the door when he heard the sound of several papers falling to the floor. Standing just inside the door, with his mouth agape and his eyes wide in shock, was the brown-haired and blue-eyed detective from outside who had tried to stop him when he first arrived. If Perry remembered Aubrey's words correctly, his name was Daniel Marcus. The detective was staring at the computer screen with Hara's image, his hand held in front of him as if he had just been holding onto something. At his feet was a folder with a stack of papers that lay scattered about.

"Can I help you, Detective?" Odau asked in irritation when he saw Marcus's astonished expression. When he received no response, the lieutenant ordered, "Snap out of it, Marcus!" Still no response. "Daniel!"

Marcus's eyes snapped away from the computer screen and they locked on the lieutenant. Taking a deep breath, the detective said, "Yes, right. Sorry...um..." He stooped down and picked up his fallen papers and stuttered to explain himself. "I was just...I just came to..." Sighing, he handed the folder to the lieutenant. "Detective Pulaski just returned from the hospital with the statement from the janitor, Richard Merchant. You said that you wanted it as soon as it was available, and he was in a hurry to get somewhere, so..." He gestured to the folder.

"Right, thank you, Marcus," Odau said, opening it up to take a brief look. Shooting a glance at Perry, he introduced, "Agent Perry, this is Detective Marcus, the other detective that will be working with us."

Smiling at the flustered detective, Perry extended his hand, but he didn't get the reaction he had been expecting. Marcus's eyebrows came together as he gazed back at Perry with a mildly puzzled look on his face. It almost appeared as if he recognized Perry, but that was impossible because Perry knew that they had never encountered each other before. Finally, after a few awkward moments, Marcus reached out and shook Perry's waiting hand before pulling away quickly and looking back to the floor uncomfortably. Clearing his throat as Perry stared back at him perplexed, Marcus asked, "So...that's her?"

Odau looked up at him and raised an eyebrow. "Of course it's her. Who else would it be?"

"I know. It's just..." His voice trailed off for a moment. "I hadn't seen her face until now."

Perry peered at him curiously. "Do you recognize her?"

His eyes widening at the accusation, Marcus shook his head quickly. "No! Of course I don't! It's just..." He stared at Hara again for a few seconds before shaking his head, turning on his heel, and making his way hastily out of the room.

Befuddled by Marcus's odd behavior, Perry looked to Odau for an explanation.

The lieutenant only shook his head as he stared after his detective in disbelief. "There is something that is just not right with that boy. He is so unusual."

"Yes, I've noticed," Perry replied, shrugging off the strange encounter and focusing once again on the task at hand. Pointing to Hara's display on the monitor, he said, "We need to figure out what this sign means, and quickly. It's nearly three, and I'm not receiving a good vibe from this girl."

"I've been wondering the same thing, and I'm thinking that it's a warning," Odau said.

"Of another attack?" Perry asked him, not convinced.

"Well, she comes out of nowhere and then kills four people. Maybe this wasn't random. Maybe this is the beginning of something bigger. Maybe she's got a plan beyond killing a couple of burglars, and she's letting us know that she's just gotten started."

"Maybe, but I don't think that is what's going on. I know that murder, no matter who the victim is, is a terrible crime, but she didn't kill innocent people. I think she was trying to get a message to someone for a meeting."

"But why give the time and not a place?" Odau asked. "Why go through all this trouble to get a message to someone when she could just give the person a call?"

Perry shrugged. "As you said when I first arrived, this is like nothing we've ever seen before."

Nodding thoughtfully, Odau sighed in frustration. "But how will this get a message to someone?"

"She was trying to get our attention, and now she's got it," Perry reminded him. "We're interested in her now, and she probably thinks that we're going to try to use any means necessary to find her. Maybe she assumed that we would put this on the news so people could be on the lookout for her. Maybe she's got someone watching and waiting for her, knowing where to meet her, but just waiting for a time."

Odau nodded again. "Maybe…but just to be safe, I think we should be wary, just in case it is a warning and we need to prepare for something."

"Alright," Perry agreed. "Why don't you have one or two of your people keep an eye on the news for the next hour or two in case anything happens?"

Turning towards the door, Odau called, "Finchly!"

Finchly hurried inside. "Yes, sir?"

"I need you and Marcus to keep an eye on the major news stations until four o'clock. Something might be happening, and if so I want to know right away… what?"

Finchly, who was looking rather confused, had raised her hand slightly to stop the lieutenant. "Um…Marcus left not two minutes ago, sir."

"What?" Perry and Odau said in unison.

"Where?" Odau demanded angrily.

Looking frightened, Finchly explained, "He said he had a very important errand he had to attend to immediately, and he said that you said he could go."

"I didn't…" Odau started, looking to Perry for help.

Perry, however, had already figured it all out. Glancing at his watch, he saw that it was about 2:50 p.m. "He didn't tell you where he was going, I gather?"

Finchly shook her head. "He did say he would most likely be back within the hour, though."

Perry nodded slowly. "Well, when he does, tell him we would like to speak with him."

Giving him a single nod, Finchly left the room quicker than Marcus had.

Odau stared at him in disbelief. "You're just going to let this go?" he demanded.

Taking a seat, Perry replied, "For now."

"Why? He just left!"

"We're going to let this go until Marcus comes back," Perry said firmly, "because I know where he's going."

✳ ✳ ✳

Daniel Marcus had been a paranoid man for most of his life, more so for the past two years. He had chosen to live an isolated life ever since his family had been murdered two years earlier. So far it had been going okay. At first he was afraid to go outside or near anyone other than the two friends with whom he had fled the war. Not too long after he and his two colleagues settled down in Philadelphia, he forged papers about his past and received a job as a detective in the Philadelphia police force without much trouble. He had experience as a man of the law where he was originally from. No one else knew about his past or who or what he really was. As each day of his newly constructed life passed by, Marcus found that he was slowly beginning to heal from the terrible ordeal he had been through. His paranoia was still a limiting factor, but it had begun to lessen over the past couple of months. After two years spent in constant fear of being uncovered, it was nice to finally feel a sense of belonging. He was calmer and his disguise had been working. His true identity had remained hidden, and after a while he started to believe that the war really was behind him.

He left the bank as soon as he saw the familiar face of the girl. He had been praying that he would never see her face again, or at least not for a very long time. Upon seeing the message meant for him and him alone, Marcus made up a quick lie to his friend and colleague Maggie and rushed to the pre-determined meeting site. The girl had told him that once he traveled to Philadelphia, he should work his way into law enforcement, and then she would contact him there if she ever needed to. Killing four people and showing her face to the entire world was not exactly what Marcus had expected, nor was it very wise, but it had worked. She had certainly gotten Marcus's attention, along with the attention of higher government agencies. Marcus had a strong feeling that things were about to become very complicated for him and the two others hiding in the city, and possibly very dangerous as well.

When he finally arrived at his destination, his chest was so tight from anxiety that he felt as if it might implode. The paranoia that he had been so relieved to say farewell to was back. He could feel his life beginning to take the same downward spiral it had taken just two years earlier. He pulled his squad car into the small parking lot of the abandoned church, his hands sweating and his knuckles white from his tight grip on the steering wheel. He parked, took a deep breath, pulled the keys out of the ignition, but didn't get out right away. He gazed upon the church that had been abandoned for nearly six years. It was an old Presbyterian house of worship that looked about as inviting as the girl's expression had on the surveillance tape. It was broken and cracked, falling apart from the inside out. There were gaping holes in the sides and in the once beautiful stained glass windows. The brown shingles were barely held onto the roof by old rusted nails, and the white paint was chipping away to expose the weathered gray wood beneath.

It was peculiar just how much that church had in common with the girl. She too was caving in on herself because of what she had been through, and the happy, beautiful child had transformed into something hideous. The ugliness beneath the girl's perfectly tanned skin was beginning to spring forth, and knowing what she could do when angered only made Marcus's current fear of her heighten. He had seen her destroy entire towns and kill countless people because she lost control. Marcus had seen the rage inside her, just by looking into her eyes, and he had a sense that the deaths in the bank were only the beginning of something much, much worse.

Gripping his keys tightly in his hands, he carefully pushed his car door open and stepped out into the cool, moist April air, being certain to keep his mind receptive to any other presence nearby. Just like the girl, he had a talent as well: being able to sense the thoughts of others.

He paused and gazed upon the daunting structure before starting forward, knowing that every step he took led him closer to his fate. A part of him—the part from his past that had survived the transformation into a new life—propelled him forward. He had known that the day would come when he would need to face his past once again, but he had hoped that he would have a little more time to live a normal life. The part of him that had become human told him to turn and leave and forget that he ever had anything to do with the girl, but the part of him that clung to the memories of his dead family and friends told him to keep going and face the blackening shadow over his past and his future.

Even outside the church, he could feel her presence. Now that she was back and was even angrier than before, who knew what she would be like face to face? Who knew what she had in store for him? She could have transformed into something worse than anticipated. She could destroy him with a single thought. What if she had lost interest in his help and planned to rid the world of him?

"Those are some pretty negative thoughts, don't you think?"

Daniel was still in his uniform; it had been a quarter to three when he had received the message, so he had to hurry to make it there in time and hadn't had a chance to change into casual clothes. Still, he would have carried his nine-millimeter for protection, being the paranoid man he was. In a panic, he whipped out his gun and spun around, aiming it in the direction of her voice. His hands shook violently and he felt his face showing the terror that was overwhelming him, making him look more pathetic than threatening. His heart was pounding so hard that he could hear it in his ears and could feel it pulsing in his head.

The girl was standing beside the back bumper of Marcus's squad car with her hip resting against it and her arms folded across her chest. She didn't move when Marcus turned his gun on her, because she knew that he wouldn't pull the trigger. He had only pulled it out in fear. After waiting a moment to allow Marcus to recognize her, the girl slowly raised her hands and took a few steps toward him. She dropped her hands back down when she stopped six feet away from him and her eyes narrowed slightly at him. Her piercing green eyes had an eerie glow to them that made Marcus shudder inside and out. There was something about them that was off, something that had been visible on the security tape as well.

She had really changed. Not on the outside though. She still looked pretty much the same on the outside, just not as clean as he was used to seeing her. Her black pants and t-shirt looked like they hadn't been washed in weeks, and her hair was in tangles and was tossed about her head. Her eyes, though, clearly told Marcus that she was not the same girl he had left behind. He knew that she had been slipping away from reality, but he didn't think that it would get to the point where she would actually remind him of the man who had tortured her and killed her family. That man had completely turned her life upside down, and he had done some very sick and disturbing things to her. Her eyes told him that she might become as dangerous and deranged as the man who had hurt her. If that was the case then someone would have to do something to stop her. She was not the sweet, innocent, loving young mother he had first met and had grown quite fond of. She had become a monster, a cold-blooded killer.

"Cold-blooded killer," she repeated, having heard Marcus's anxious thoughts. It was the same talent that Marcus possessed, but coming from her in such a damaged state, it really made him uncomfortable. "Huh. That's a bit harsh."

"Stop it," Daniel whispered, lowering his gun and gazing at her with a deep sadness.

"Stop what?" the girl asked quietly, her eyes narrowing a little more.

"You know what," Daniel breathed, feeling his knees begin to weaken.

"Why?" she wanted to know. "Does it bother you? The last time I checked, you could do the same thing."

"What's happened to you?" Daniel asked her in disbelief. "You're not...you anymore. You're not right."

"People change over time, Marcus," she whispered coldly. "You ought to know that."

"Don't call me Marcus," Marcus told her. "It's Daniel to you." He paused as he was about to speak her true name, but he sensed in her mind that she would become very angry if he did, and he didn't want to upset her. "Hara," he said slowly. "Why did you kill those people in the bank? Why would you do something like that?"

Hara raised an eyebrow. "Why not? They all killed people too. I needed to get your attention somehow."

Marcus's mouth fell open and he took a step closer to her. "That's not you! Where's the noble girl I remember?"

"Gone!" Hara spat, becoming angry very fast. "Gone, gone, gone! I don't care about these people anymore! I'd kill them all if I could! We owe them that much for what they did to us!"

Shaking his head as he took in the sight of her angered, quivering form, Marcus told her softly, "You're not thinking this through clearly. You need help."

"I think I'm a little ways beyond help if you haven't noticed already," Hara muttered, glowering at him from where she stood.

"Why are you here?" Marcus asked her. "Why did you come back?"

"Our camp was destroyed," Hara whispered, looking at the cracked concrete beneath her feet as she recalled what had happened just before her departure from home. "It was wiped out in one single, bloody massacre. I had nowhere else to go, and nowhere else to hide." She looked back up to Marcus, a look of longing replacing her look of anger. "So I came here, knowing that the only people I had left would help me with what I had to do to bring an end to all of this. I had to come and be with the only people who still cared about me."

Marcus's heart melted at her words. It wasn't surprising that Hara's camp had been found and destroyed. They all knew that the man who was still searching for her would stop at nothing to catch her. He was very persistent, and he would do anything to get to her, including killing hundreds of refugees. Marcus knew that Hara was telling the truth when she said that he and the two others were the only people left alive who cared about her and could protect her, but he couldn't allow her to keep doing what she was doing, and he certainly wouldn't help her. "How did you escape?" he asked her.

"I ran," Hara said. "I ran, and I ran, and I didn't look back."

"How long has it been for you?" Marcus implored. "How long has it been since we last spoke?"

"Two weeks."

Only two weeks? Marcus felt like it was much longer than that, judging by how Hara had changed and how much it looked like she had been through. He would have guessed that it had been months.

Taking a deep breath, Hara started slowly, "I need your help with something."

Although Marcus knew that Hara was telling the truth about the massacre, he also knew that there was a more important reason for coming back to Philadelphia. She wouldn't have risked coming so far if it wasn't very important. "Why are you really here?" he demanded.

Hara didn't snap at him and shout, "I already told you!" like he expected. She knew exactly what Marcus was thinking, and she didn't need to listen into his mind for that. "Well, it wasn't so I could take a tour," she muttered, and wrinkled her nose. "This place is disgusting!"

Marcus said, "You're looking for him, aren't you?"

Hara didn't have to answer for Marcus to know he was right. "This city was our birthplace," she told him, but he already knew that. "But I didn't come back here to experience it for myself."

"You can't kill him," Marcus whispered, his dread pressing down on him. "He's just a boy!"

"No!" Hara shouted. "No! He's a monster! He's evil! I'll be doing the world a favor by getting rid of him!"

"You shouldn't have come back here," Marcus told her, his pulse and breathing quickening. "You should have stayed back home. Just a little longer, and things would have been okay. We would have changed things!"

"You didn't change anything!" Hara snapped. "Everything's the same as you left it! Nothing you can do will ever fix it, which is why I came back. I know what I have to do to make things right, and you're going to help me."

"I'm not going to help you with any of this," Marcus replied firmly.

Her eyebrow rising, Hara said quietly, "Excuse me?"

"I didn't sign up for this," Marcus told her. "And neither did you."

"We didn't sign up for what? Saving our families?"

"I signed up to save my family, yes, but not to murder innocent children!"

"He's not innocent!"

"Yes, he is!" Marcus cried breathlessly. "He hasn't done anything!"

"Not yet, he hasn't," Hara growled.

"I won't do this," Marcus repeated. "I won't resort to killing innocents. We swore we would never do that!"

"Things have changed, Daniel," Hara hissed, her eyes flashing dangerously. "You yourself said you were in this to the end, and now look at you."

"I am in this until the end," Marcus promised her, taking another step forward. "I said I wouldn't help you kill people, but I will help you finish this war, by any means necessary except for murder. And I will help you with whatever it is you are going through right now."

Hara glared menacingly at him. "If you're not going to help me kill that boy, then you're a traitor to your people!"

Marcus shook his head, his desperate eyes pleading with her enraged ones. "Murder of any sort is frowned upon in our society, and you know that."

"I don't care anymore!"

Sighing wearily, Marcus told her again, "I won't help you kill innocents, and I won't let you either. You are in serious pain right now, and I can see it as well as feel it. Come with me, and I can help you get better."

Hara shook her head and continued to glower at him. "You can't help me," she whispered. "No one can."

"Please," Marcus begged as he walked toward her and tried to take her gently by the arm. "I can help."

"Don't touch me!" she hissed, pulling her arm away from him while she bared her teeth. "I don't want that kind of help!"

"What do you want from me?"

"I want you to help me get rid of him!"

"I've already told you I won't do that."

"Then tell me where they are!" Hara ordered in exasperation.

"Who?" Marcus asked in perplexity. "The others?"

"Yes! If you're not going to help me, then I'll go to people who will!"

"They're not going to go for this either, kid."

"I didn't ask for your opinion, Daniel!" Hara snarled.

The air around Marcus suddenly grew very hot, and as he realized what was happening his heart skipped a beat. "Okay, okay," he told her, lowering his voice and raising his hands defensively. He knew that the poor girl was moments away from exploding and killing him in her anger. "They're not going to agree with you, but if you want to find them, then I'll try to help you."

Taking a deep breath as she understood how far her own anger was going, Hara managed to say to Marcus's surprise, "Thank you. I need their home addresses."

"I don't know where they live," Marcus apologized.

"How do you not know where they live?" Hara demanded, her temper flaring up again.

"You told us not to keep in contact, remember?" Marcus reminded her cautiously.

"Yes," Hara said, and sighed in frustration. "But I didn't think you would actually listen to that."

Nodding, Marcus paused to allow her a moment to calm herself. "I can, however, tell you where they work. We give each other a phone call every six months to share what we've accomplished, and Allan has managed to become the mayor of the city. You'll be able to find him at City Hall."

"Yes, I saw his mug shot in the newspaper," Hara muttered in disapproval.

"He's been doing a really good job," Marcus defended. "He's really cleaned up the city in the past few months."

"Whatever," Hara grumbled. She would much rather hear from Allan face to face why he had taken such a high-profile position. "What about Meg? Where can I find her?"

"She's a district attorney," Marcus explained. "I don't know precisely where her office is, but I accidentally bumped into her a few months ago and found out that she gets coffee every day at 4:30 p.m. at the Starbucks down on 4th Avenue. You could still catch her today if you wanted to."

"I have to talk to Allan first," Hara muttered, staring at the ground again. "I'm not happy with him about his position as mayor. Plus, he's the only one who can get us home. I have to figure out how we're going to do that."

Marcus's heart sank. He had wanted to go home for a long time, but to a free home, not to the horrifying home he would be returning to. "Are we really going home?"

Hara looked up yet again, her eyes narrowing slightly as she heard the tentative thought lingering in Marcus's mind. "You are, and so will the other two if they decide not to help. I'm staying here until I end this."

"Please don't make me go back there," Marcus pleaded, the pace of his heart beginning to quicken at the thought of returning to where his family was murdered and his life destroyed. "I can't go back there after what happened. I'll stay here until you figure things out."

Her eyes narrowing even more, Hara said, "You will do what I tell you to do, Daniel."

Marcus wanted to argue with her but knew that nothing good would come of it. He took a sideways step around her towards his car. "Yes, I will," he muttered, and walked around her to get to his driver's side door.

"And," Hara started, stopping Marcus in his tracks. "Since you're obviously in league with the police department, I need you to give them a message. If they don't want too many casualties, then they ought to stay out of my way. I honestly don't care how many people I kill, but I would prefer not to have too much of a struggle, and I have a feeling that you might care if some of your colleagues bite it because they get in my way."

Biting his lip, Marcus nodded. He knew that she wouldn't hesitate to kill a few officers who drew guns on her, but she was right when she said that he would feel remorse if one of his friends were hurt or killed. Even after what the human race had done to him and his people, he had grown very fond of a few people with whom he worked. His partner, Kali Nyman—who was currently on maternity leave with her first child—had shown a kindness he had never experienced from a member of the human race. She had known that he was jumpy because of something that had happened in his past. Marcus knew because he had heard her think it several times before. She had never given him a hard time about it and had never demanded an explanation. Kali was a very kind and thoughtful person, and although Marcus was aware that she wouldn't be participating in the upcoming fight against Hara, he would still be devastated if she was ever injured. There were also two others who had been kind to Marcus during his time in Philadelphia, and the two of them would be fighting against Hara. Hopefully they would take his advice and steer clear of the deadly teenage killing machine. The names of the two officers were Maggie Finchly and Garrick Aubrey, and although it would be difficult to get them to listen to him, Marcus's friendship with them might be enough to convince them to listen to his warning. Marcus would obey Hara's order and warn the others involved in the case, but he also had a warning he had to give to Hara. "There's something I need you to know before we leave here," he told her gravely. "The boy's father, Lieutenant Graham Odau, is in charge of this case. He's a very stubborn man, and I can assure you that he will give you plenty of trouble."

Hara shrugged nonchalantly. "It's nothing I can't handle."

"That's the thing though," Marcus said. "You can't kill him if he pisses you off. You know as well as I do that his death is fixed in time. Altering his destiny could be catastrophic."

Looking rather irritated, Hara sighed heavily. "Whatever. I'll deal with this cop when I'm in a better mood." She started to turn away and walk across the parking lot towards the highway.

"And," Marcus added, stopping Hara's retreat. "Since it is obvious that this is a bizarre and complex case due to the security footage, Odau phoned for the FBI to assist."

Hara shrugged again, looking dubious as to why that should matter. "So what? The FBI doesn't scare me."

Gazing back at her, Marcus explained, "The agent's name is Shawn Perry."

Hara's bemused expression was wiped clean from her face at the sound of the name. "Perry?" she repeated in astonishment.

Marcus nodded, his expression serious, knowing that Hara would be extremely careful around Perry to avoid injuring him.

"Are you sure?"

"Yes, I'm sure," Marcus insisted, nodding again. Looking her square in the eyes, he said, "Don't...hurt...him! You know what will happen if he's killed during this."

Nodding slowly, Hara said, "Okay. Perry's in the FBI. Thanks for telling me that. An interesting fact."

"They're going to ask questions about you," Marcus told her. "When I saw your face on the footage for the first time, I tuned into their minds to see what they thought of you, and they saw you using your abilities. They're curious as to how you can do what you do, and they're going to ask me questions about it. I'd be really surprised if they haven't figured out by now that your message was for me."

"Don't tell them anything about why I can do what I do," Hara ordered. "That's too complicated, and I don't want these people learning the truth about us. It's too soon, especially for Perry. Make up a story about me or just say that you don't know anything. I don't care what you say. Just don't tell them what I'm here to do or what I really am."

"Okay," Marcus said, and walked to his car door. As he opened it, he glanced back. "Good luck with your meetings with Allan and Meg. I'll be waiting for whatever new message you'll be getting to me soon."

"See you soon, my friend," Hara replied, turning her back on him and marching off in the direction of the highway.

Marcus thought about offering her a ride somewhere, but he doubted she would accept. He prayed that the grief-stricken girl wouldn't do anything too damaging to the city or its people. He knew that the results would be much worse than anything he was picturing in his head. The world had a twisted way of turning the odds against him and his people.

✳ ✳ ✳

Marcus arrived back at the bank at about quarter after three. Perry was studying the security footage, trying to catch anything they might have missed. Perry had only been alone in the surveillance room for about four minutes. Lieutenant Odau had stayed with him for a while, and during that time, Perry began to learn a little bit more about his new colleague. The lieutenant had graduated from the University of Philadelphia in 1975 with a degree in biology and criminal science and a desire to work in forensics. For some reason, Odau changed his mind and decided to work in law enforcement instead. He had been married to his wife Jane for twenty-three years. They had three children: Sarah, 14, Jackson, 10, and Caroline, 6.

Perry hadn't heard Marcus enter, but he sensed the uneasy presence cautiously approaching from behind and knew that his long-awaited guest had finally arrived. Swiveling his chair around to face the wide-eyed detective standing just inside the door, Perry smiled at him. "Welcome back, Detective Marcus," he said, a little overenthusiastically. He knew that Hara's message was for Marcus, and he was very eager to learn more about that very peculiar girl.

A thin layer of sweat was forming on Marcus's brow and hands, and his face had an almost gray shade to it. He swallowed when Perry's prying gaze landed on him, and he dried his hands on his pants and wrung them together before clearing his throat and muttering, "Maggie said that you wanted to see me."

"Yes, I do," Perry replied, still smiling. He gestured to a chair next to him at the table of computers. "Why don't you take a seat?"

Without looking at the chair, Marcus held Perry's gaze and took a tiny step back. He swallowed again before saying, "Look, I've got a lot of work to do, so if this isn't important then I'm afraid it's going to have to wait."

Leaning forward in his chair, Perry said in a deadly voice, "I'm only going to say this once before I start pulling out my cuffs." He gestured to the chair once more with his head. "Sit down."

Marcus knew he had been caught; it was written all over the terrified lines in his face. For an instant, Perry thought that the detective was going to try and make a desperate attempt to escape, but he sighed before hesitantly making his way over to Perry. Pulling out the vacant chair and sitting down, Marcus continued to wring his hands, but he was no longer holding Perry's intense gaze. He stared down at the floor, knowing that he was in deep trouble and wouldn't be able to worm his way out of it with simple excuses.

"Where's your partner?" Perry asked curiously.

"She's on maternity leave," Marcus said quietly, fidgeting uncomfortably in his chair.

"Ah," Perry replied, nodding.

Pausing for effect, Perry stared at the nervous man without speaking. It was disappointing that a man like Marcus was involved with such a cold-blooded killer as Hara. It was obvious that he was a jittery man, but Perry was a fairly good judge of character, and he had a strong feeling that Marcus wasn't one of the bad guys. Finally, Perry spoke to him. "If you had so much work to do, then why did you abandon your duties for the past half hour?" he demanded.

Still not glancing up, Marcus shrugged and muttered, "I forgot about an important errand I had to run today."

Raising an eyebrow, Perry challenged, "It was so important that you lied to your colleague and walked out on your job to do it?" He waited for Marcus to reply, but no reply was made. Perry leaned closer to him as he had before. "The last time you walked in here, it was right as the lieutenant was showing me the footage of the girl holding up her sign." Perry waited again, but still didn't receive any response. "You left to run your errand just before three o'clock, the time specified on the sign."

Marcus nodded slowly, but he still didn't say anything and he didn't look up.

"The message was for you, wasn't it?"

Marcus slowly lifted his eyes to meet Perry's, and he held his gaze for a few short moments before speaking. "I'm...not who you think I am," he said quietly, his shoulders becoming rigid.

A corner of his mouth rising to form a half smirk, Perry replied, "Well, that's apparent." Again, Perry paused to allow the detective a moment to speak, and yet again, the detective had nothing to say. "So who are you?"

Shrugging again, Marcus murmured, "I'm just a man who's trying to live his life as normally as possible."

"Why don't you tell me about your young friend?" Perry suggested.

"Her name is Hara," Marcus told him, returning his gaze to the floor.

"Everyone is aware of that much," Perry replied flatly. "I want to know about her. I want to know how she snapped two men's necks with her bare hands and killed two others without even touching them."

Again, Marcus shrugged. "I don't know."

Irritated, Perry snapped, "Look at me, Marcus!" When Marcus slowly raised his eyes, Perry lowered his voice again. "Your young friend is wanted for murder, and if you don't start talking to me right now, I'm afraid I'm going to have to detain you and interrogate you the proper way, and trust me, you don't want me as your interrogator."

Marcus opened his mouth, but for a few seconds no sound came out. He glanced up and looked over the top of Perry's head before exhaling loudly. "I'm sorry, but I can't tell you anything about her. You saw what she did to those men. She wouldn't hesitate to do it to me if I open my mouth."

Perry nodded slowly. "Alright," he said. "Then maybe I can get a few harmless answers out of you to satisfy my own curiosity. What did Hara's message mean? Was it a meeting time for the two of you?"

Marcus started to stand up. "I really have to get back to work," he said. "I'm sorry that I can't be of any help to you."

Right at that moment, Lieutenant Odau hurried into the room, out of breath. "Why didn't you call me when he got here?" he snapped at Perry before putting a firm hand on Marcus's shoulder and shoving him back into his chair. "Sit down! You're not going anywhere." Pulling out another chair beside Perry, he took a seat and stared intently at his detective. "You're staying in that chair until you answer his questions and a few of mine as well."

Perry shot an annoyed glance at Odau before turning back to the now petrified Marcus. "Listen, Daniel," Perry began, using his first name in the hope that Marcus would be more cooperative. "I'm not the bad guy here. I don't want to hurt you. If this girl is a threat to you and other people in this city, then I need you to give me some help in finding her. Okay?"

Marcus nodded but didn't return Perry's gaze.

Glad that Odau hadn't interrupted yet, Perry asked Marcus, "So the message for you was a meeting time?"

Marcus nodded again.

"How did you know where to meet?"

"We discussed the meeting place before we lost contact," Marcus whispered, his voice very small.

"Which was when?"

"More than two years ago. January of 2006."

"That was just months before you got a position here," Odau pointed out, talking more to himself than anyone else.

"How did you know this girl?" Perry asked Marcus, ignoring Odau's comment.

"I knew her father," Marcus explained, his voice gaining volume but not confidence. "He saved my life when I was just a toddler. The two of us worked together for a few years before…" His voice cut off as he said the word 'before,' but it was already out of his mouth and Perry knew there was a big story behind that single word.

"Before what?" Perry demanded, leaning forward once again.

Shaking his head, Marcus mumbled under his breath, "Nothing." He slouched back in his chair and crossed his arms tightly over his chest, putting up a defensive wall between himself and his interrogators. He stared at his knees as he tried to block out everything else.

Perry suddenly understood. Marcus was a very nervous man, and he had a reason for that. He had been through a terrible ordeal, and afterwards he had hidden in Philadelphia and had tried to rebuild a new life. Something awful had happened to this man, and he had been keeping himself safe with his undercover job and quiet personal life until Hara had shown up and had threatened everything. He was caught; maybe not by the people he was hiding from, but he was still in serious trouble. "Marcus, what happened to you?" Perry asked him softly, hoping that the traumatized officer would open up—even just a little.

A flash of pain crossed Marcus's face and his silence made Perry feel a guilt that he hadn't felt since the death of his father. After taking a moment to gather his thoughts, Marcus finally raised his eyes again. For once, Perry wished that he wouldn't have done so. "My family was murdered. My…my wife…and my nine-year-old daughter…they were murdered."

"By Hara?" Odau asked.

"No," Perry said before Marcus could. Gazing back at Marcus's grieving face, Perry said, "This happened before you lost contact with Hara. Hara's massacre was a result of what happened to you."

Marcus nodded slowly.

"What kind of business were you in with her father?" Perry asked curiously, thinking that maybe it was illegal activity and the death of Marcus's family was repayment for something he had done.

"It wasn't a business," Marcus muttered, shaking his head. "It's…complicated."

"Where is he now?" Perry asked. "I'd like to meet this man."

"He's dead, too."

Nodding slowly, Perry continued, "So you were involved in something big. Can I get the name of this man?"

Marcus shook his head.

"I'm guessing that means I'm not going to get a real name for Hara either?"

Marcus shook his head again. "She's just going by Hara."

"Okay," Perry said, leaning back in his chair and thinking. "I can see that we're going to have interesting conversations in an interrogation room later." Marcus groaned and dropped his head in his hands. Perry asked, "So you've been working with her, correct?"

"No!" Marcus cried immediately, snapping his face up to look back at him again. "I worked with her and her father a long time ago, but I wasn't a part of this! I didn't want to kill anybody!"

"But Hara did," Perry pointed out. "Why? Were they the ones who killed her father? Did she have a grudge against them?"

"No," Marcus sighed. "She only killed them because they were terrible criminals and she needed to get a message to me somehow."

"Oh," Odau muttered. "That's lovely."

"Just before we lost contact, she told me that if she ever needed my help again, she would get a message to me so we could meet," Marcus explained. "But I saw what she did to those men, and I don't want anything to do with it."

"What did she want your help with?" Perry asked, hoping it didn't involve any more murders.

Marcus shrugged. "Just some unfinished business she wanted to deal with. I don't really want to know what she's got planned."

"How old is Hara?"

"She should be eighteen by now."

"Are you really telling me that this kid has been involved in a murder conspiracy since she was sixteen?"

"No!" Marcus cried in disbelief. "It's not a conspiracy, and she hasn't killed anyone in cold blood...until now."

"But she has killed people?"

"You've seen what she can do. It can get a little out of control when she's under elevated levels of stress."

Perry wanted to push further the subject of Hara's peculiar capabilities, but he knew that Marcus wouldn't answer. Instead, he asked about things that could be affecting them at the present time. "Are there other people out there that she's trying to make contact with?"

"Just two," Marcus replied. "But neither of them is planning on helping her. They don't want to kill anyone, especially after what we've all been through. They won't be a problem for you."

"I would still like their names," Perry said sternly, not planning to let that one slide.

Marcus started to go on the defense again. "I'd rather not say."

"This isn't a question which you can choose to answer if you want to," Odau snapped at him. "You lied to your colleagues and put your job on hold to meet this girl who has plans to kill other people. You've been lying to everyone about your past all along. You are going to answer Agent Perry, right now."

Swallowing nervously at the lieutenant's harsh glare, Marcus sank lower in his chair. His voice quavering, he stammered, "Are…are you going to arrest them like you're going to arrest me?"

Blinking in surprise, Perry was glad that Marcus was aware of the gravity of his situation. "That depends," Perry replied.

"On what?"

"On how they respond to her arrival."

Marcus's face hardened, something that Perry hadn't expected, and it made him feel quite uneasy. His eyes seemed to give off a strange flash of light, and Perry stared back at him. Marcus growled, "They aren't bad people. Neither am I."

Perry opened his mouth to speak, but then hesitated. It wasn't until Odau looked to him impatiently that Perry stuttered, "I…I never said that you were."

"No," Marcus said, as his eyes narrowed and his harsh expression caused Odau to inhale sharply. "You didn't. But that's what you're thinking."

That *was* what Perry was thinking. How could they not be bad people? If whatever Marcus was involved with caused his family and his employer to be murdered, then how could they be good people? Perry bit his lip. He didn't want to judge Marcus or his colleagues based only on what he had seen so far, but it was difficult not to. He didn't know any of them personally and he didn't know anything about their pasts, but as Marcus continued talking, it was becoming harder and harder to see how his past involvement with Hara and her father could have been anything but bad.

Odau could see Perry's hesitance, but he didn't have any reason to be intimidated by Marcus—having been his superior officer for two years—and he seemed to have no trouble judging him himself. "Enough with the side conversations!" he snapped. "We have a criminal we have to catch, and I don't care how you defend yourself, Marcus! You're involved in this, and you should know that you're now in a hell of a lot of trouble. You're going to tell us who these two men are right now, or I'll turn you over to the FBI."

His eyes flickering at Odau in irritation before returning to Perry, Marcus cleared his throat. "They're not both men," he said flatly. "Why does your society always assume it's men first?"

"*My* society?" Odau repeated.

Gritting his teeth together, Marcus grumbled, "I meant ours."

Ignoring Marcus's comment, Perry demanded, "Their names! I need their names, Marcus."

"The first one Hara said she was going to see is Allan Brown."

"Allan Brown?" Odau said, bewildered.

"Who's he?" Perry asked.

"He's the mayor," Odau said, shocked by the sudden revelation. Directing his attention back to Marcus, he demanded, "So the mayor is compromised as well? He's been involved in this too?"

Marcus shrugged. "As I said, it was a long time ago."

"That doesn't make it any better!" Odau exclaimed, but after receiving a look from Perry he shook his head and took a deep breath. They didn't have time for arguments. "What about the woman? Who is she?"

"Her name is Meg Hopper," Marcus replied. "She's a..."

"District Attorney," Perry finished, nodding. "I heard about her. She replaced Harper Ziegler after she was murdered last year. I've never met her, but I've heard she's good at what she does."

"That's because she's had years of past experience," Marcus muttered, looking back down to the floor.

"Are you ever going to tell us who you people are?"

Marcus smirked lightly. "All in good time, my friend. And even if I don't, you'll still learn the truth. Eventually."

Perry quickly turned to Odau. "Get a unit to Allan Brown's location immediately, and send someone to bring Meg Hopper into custody as well. If we're lucky, we can catch this Hara with your mayor and bring her in before she has a chance to hurt any more people."

"There's no need to send another unit," Odau replied. "I'm going down there myself with my own unit."

"You really don't want to do that," Marcus warned.

Perry smirked back at him. "And why is that, Detective Marcus?"

"You've seen what she can do," Marcus said again. "She's extremely dangerous."

"So am I, Detective," Odau told him matter-of-factly. He glanced at Perry and said, "Are you coming?"

"Yes, but I can drive myself," Perry replied.

"You don't understand, sirs," Marcus said insistently, rising to his feet.

"What don't we understand, Detective?" Odau demanded, walking the space between them and getting right in Marcus's face. "That you've led a murderer to one of her conspirators?"

"Hara is not exactly what either of us would call normal," Marcus told him, his eyes hardening once again. "In case you haven't noticed."

"I have noticed," Odau replied, his eyes narrowing further. "But in case *you* haven't noticed, the only person I currently have as a link to the girl won't explain to me why she's not normal!"

"What you saw on the tape is barely a fraction of the damage she can cause!" Marcus shouted back. "She's in a very agitated state right now, and the angrier she is, the more dangerous she gets!"

"Yes, well, I'm in a very agitated state as well," Odau growled, getting his face even closer to Marcus's. "And I think the same conditions apply to me."

"If you go to Allan with your guns drawn, she could and will kill you all without a moment's hesitation!"

"The more you talk about Hara, the more I'm thinking that you're bluffing," Odau told him, giving him a shove backwards so he stumbled and fell back into his chair. "I think that Hara's just a freak who can do a few magic tricks, and you're just a liar who's covering for her to try to stall for time."

As Marcus's eyes let off another strange flash of light, Perry realized that he hadn't imagined it the first time. Odau suddenly stumbled back a few paces, a startled look on his face.

"Whoa!" Perry cried, jumping to his feet and catching the lieutenant as he started to fall. As Odau regained his balance—the confused look still plastered on his face—Perry asked, "Are you alright?"

"Y-yes," Odau stammered, reaching up with his hand and rubbing his eyes under his glasses. "I...I just..."

Perry's gaze snapped back to Marcus, whose face suddenly appeared afraid as well. "What did you do?" he demanded.

Marcus's eyes were terror-filled, and he stared at the lieutenant before looking up to Perry and crying, "Dr. Perry, please! You need to listen to me when I tell you that you can't confront her without getting someone hurt or killed!"

"What did you just call me?" Perry asked in surprise.

Confusion clouded his eyes, but then Marcus realized his mistake. "I-I'm sorry. Agent Perry." He lowered his eyes again and didn't move from his seat.

Odau was out of his sudden stupor, and he shook Perry off of him. "I'm going to get my people ready," he muttered before leaving the room, being sure to avoid Marcus's gaze.

Perry stared hard at Marcus, bewildered. Marcus was clearly frazzled by having been caught as a conspirator. He must have just blurted out the first thing that came to his head, and he had at least corrected himself. "What makes her so dangerous?" Perry asked him softly. "What exactly is it that she can do that has you so concerned?"

"She knows how you think," Marcus murmured, refusing to raise his eyes. It appeared as if the two men were about to have a repeat of their earlier conversation without Odau. "She's very smart. She can manipulate you and make you do things that you can't predict."

"And how can she do that?" Perry asked. "If you help me get to know our friend a little better, then maybe I can outsmart her."

"She just can," Marcus said, shrugging. "And trust me; there is no way that a man like you could outsmart someone like her. No offense. You have no idea of what you're up against."

Perry chuckled and rose to his feet. "What is she going to do, make me slit my wrists?"

"You never know," Marcus mumbled, his reply barely audible.

Perry shook his head and started to leave the room. "We're not finished yet," he called over his shoulder, leaving Marcus alone with his dread. At the end of the hallway, he turned into the manager's office to see if Odau was in there, but instead nearly ran into Finchly.

"Excuse me, sir," Finchly apologized as they both halted themselves quickly to prevent a collision.

"Excuse me," Perry apologized as well, stepping aside to allow her space to exit. "You said that your first name was Maggie, right?"

"Yes, sir," Finchly replied.

"You're accompanying us to the mayor's location, correct?"

Finchly nodded once.

Gesturing with his head back towards the surveillance room, he said, "Then I need you to get somebody else to take Marcus back to your station and place him in a holding cell until I have time to talk to him further."

"Come again?" Finchly said, her brow furrowing in confusion.

"Hara is an old companion of your pal Marcus," Perry explained. "He left his job earlier so he could go meet with her. Now, I need you to get someone who can escort him back to the station and place him in a holding cell, okay?"

Finchly gaped at him in astonishment and shook her head hard. "Daniel can't be a part of this! He's always been so good to us…"

Perry felt a small swell of pity for the woman, but he pushed it aside. "Is this going to be a problem for you?" he asked her.

Biting her lip, Finchly said with an air of guilt about her, "No, Agent Perry."

"Good," Perry said, giving her a comforting pat on the back as he walked past her and out into the lobby. Odau was already there, getting his unit together and shouting orders at others as they prepared to set up a perimeter around City Hall. As Perry left the bank to accompany the team, he couldn't help but think back to Marcus's words, and wonder whether or not confronting Hara—who had already clearly demonstrated that she was quite capable of taking down several grown men on her own—was a wise and fully thought out decision.

3

Bittersweet Reunions

Allan Brown, the current mayor of Philadelphia, Pennsylvania, hadn't had a decent night's sleep in over two years. No matter how hard he tried, or how many sleeping pills he took, he always ended up lying awake on his back in bed, thinking about his past. He didn't want to, but his thoughts always lingered on his people, and on his family. Just like his friends Daniel Marcus, Meg Hopper, and Hara, Allan had also lost his family to a cause that was unknown to the people around him. He had a beautiful wife named Harley—who had been blonde-haired and blue-eyed just like him—and three beautiful blonde children named Zander, Kendall, and Zane, who were all under the age of ten when they were murdered. He had loved them with all his heart, but he struggled to avoid thinking of them because of how much pain it caused. It was impossible to talk to anyone about it because the only people who knew were dead or in hiding, and if he told anyone he would risk being discovered. To keep from appearing suspicious, he would just put a smile on his face for the public and keep to himself when he wasn't performing his duties as mayor.

Allan was a handsome man, although he didn't think of himself that way. His colleagues called him modest, and it would always make him blush. He had turned forty-three the month before, but his round baby-face gave him a younger look. No one believed him when he told them his age, but he would just smile and accept the compliments.

Before he came to Philadelphia two years earlier, Hara had instructed him and his two friends to "stay out of the spotlight and lie low." Becoming the mayor of a major American city wasn't exactly following her instructions, but he thought that if he had such a position of leadership, he could eventually work his way up politically until he got to a position where he could protect and prepare the world for what was coming and what had already come. If he could influence the world to be a little more tolerant, then maybe the future wouldn't be as grisly, and maybe the past horrors wouldn't have been in vain.

The horrific events of his past life had been suppressed for the time being, however. He was still lacking sleep and a social life, but he had been finding it easier to block his memories from his conscious mind. His objective in Philadelphia was still clear to him, but that didn't mean that he had to keep thinking about his haunting memories and torture himself with them. He found that he was becoming happier and was having an easier time working with his colleagues, some of the very people who had brought his first life—his beautiful life—to a devastating end. There was, however, always a possibility of a second chance, of a fresh start, and Allan had found that in Philadelphia. Until the time came when he would be forced to face his past once again and return to his true home and people, Allan was going to savor his new, uncomplicated life and try as hard as he possibly could to set a better future for planet earth.

It was sad to say that he had had a very disturbing dream the previous night about his old friend Marcus, who had been in and out of contact with him for the past two years. Allan dreamt that his friend was arrested by the Philadelphia police force—which was ironic because he was a part of it—and was murdered by the man whom they had all been running from for so long. It had awakened Allan from his slumber, breathless and drenched in sweat. It took quite some time for him to slow his breathing and calm his racing heart. There was no way that man could track them down in Philadelphia, so why had his dream scared him so much? For anyone else, the task of finding them would be impossible, but for that man, maybe it was possible.

Right now, he couldn't worry about his insomnia or his constant fear of discovery and recapture. Pushing his thoughts aside, Allan sipped at his very strong coffee as he made his way back to his office. Lately, he had been drinking nearly four extra-large cups a day to keep himself awake while trying to do his job. Maybe that was why he had so many sleepless nights, but Allan needed to stay awake somehow and ditching the caffeine was not an option.

His office was located on the twelfth floor of City Hall, and it offered a great view of the city. He could see the endless rows of small houses beyond a large reflecting pool located in front of the building. Allan loved to sit in his office chair and just stare out the floor-to-ceiling windows while the sun rose and set, taking in the beauty of the city. The sunrays would reflect off of the surface of the water, and the water sparkled like millions of diamonds.

He still wasn't used to being in a city like Philadelphia, where the air was so full of pollution that it was difficult for him to breathe. In Allan's home city, the air was so clean and fresh, and if there was ever litter or some other form of pollution, someone would immediately be eager to clean it up. The people were not very friendly here either. Whenever something wasn't done exactly right, there would be hell to pay. Where Allan was from, people were kind and considerate to each other. If somebody made a mistake, others waited calmly and gave that person a second chance without unleashing their unmerciful wrath.

Allan had been at a meeting on the fourth floor, discussing the events of the previous night with other important administrators and discussing how to address the public about the matter. A violent bank robbery had occurred, resulting in five deaths and a killer on the loose. Allan had yet to discuss the seriousness of the case with lead officer Lieutenant Graham Odau. Odau was not particularly favored by other department staff, or the mayor for that matter. Allan was expecting a call from him at any moment, which was why he was trying not to get side-tracked by other employees on his floor in his attempt to reach his office. Although he wasn't very social with the others in the building, he seemed to be fairly popular and well-liked. He wasn't sure if it was because he was fairly laid back and soft spoken, or because he always did his best to be kind to everyone. Allan wasn't a member of American society; he may have looked and talked like others, but he was definitely an outsider and couldn't understand the adversarial aspect of superior/inferior relationships. Considering that everyone in his own society was treated equally, Allan preferred not to treat those with a lower status and paycheck as inferior, and he tended to show kindness to just about everyone.

It was nice to know that no one suspected his fraudulent past and people showed him kindness in return; however, it could become rather annoying, especially when he was trying to get to a certain place at a certain time and staffers would stop and try to make small talk. Thankfully, that particular day, he only received passing comments like, "Good afternoon, Mr. Mayor!" or, "How are you today, Mr. Mayor?" and, "You look exhausted, Mr. Mayor!" which could be responded to with simple replies such as, "Good afternoon," or, "Fine, thank you," and, "I imagine I look worse than I feel." When he reached his office, Allan closed the door behind him and locked it so he wouldn't be disturbed. Heaving a loud sigh, he rubbed his weary eyes and groaned when he realized that the day's work was far from over. As he yawned from his exhaustion, he started to walk over to his desk to check if Odau had already called and left a message, but he halted in his tracks when he saw a man sitting behind his desk and reading the daily paper. To Allan's surprise and dread, it turned out that the person sitting at his desk wasn't a man at all.

"Excuse me," Allan started to say angrily before he recognized the person. "Can I help you?" When the girl at his desk lowered the paper so Allan could see her face, Allan's eyes widened in horror and his breath caught in his throat. The coffee slipped from his hand and splattered to the floor, the dark liquid quickly soaking into the light blue carpet. His entire body began to shake, and had there not been a chair directly behind him, he would have fallen to the floor alongside his source of consciousness. Instead, when his knees buckled beneath him, he collapsed into a favorite old chair he had kept in his office. He didn't recall putting it in that exact place, but he had a feeling that the girl had put it there for him, knowing he would be utterly stunned to see her.

The young teen criminal called Hara—although it was still unknown to Allan that she was a criminal—glanced at the spilled coffee completely saturated into the carpet and gave him a disapproving look. "That'll stain, you know," she told him, and then went back to the paper in her hands. "And you know we're not supposed to drink that stuff. It gives us heart palpitations."

He was beginning to feel those heart palpitations. Swallowing hard and taking a deep breath in an attempt to calm himself, Allan demanded in a quavering voice, "What are you doing here?"

Glancing up again, Hara narrowed her eyes. "What, did you think I was dead?"

"Well, no." Allan swallowed again, his mouth and throat beginning to feel very dry. "But you told us that you wouldn't be coming back here."

"Change of plans," the teen muttered. She turned the page of the newspaper and continued reading. Raising her arms slightly so her face was obscured, she held the paper higher so Allan could see the front page. There was a large, smiling photo of himself with the headline: ALLAN BROWN CONTINUES TO REDUCE PHILADELPHIA'S CRIME RATE. "This wasn't exactly what I meant when I said lie low," Hara said flatly, and Allan could detect the irritation radiating from her.

Wincing as he recalled her order to stay under the radar, Allan tried to explain how he felt about his position. "I…I thought maybe this would help. If one city eliminates crime, then maybe it's possible for the whole world to begin to change."

In two quick movements, Hara shut the paper and slammed it down on the desk. Glaring at him angrily as he cowered in his chair across the room, she sucked on her lower lip and a sudden look of pain flashed across her face. She sat back in her chair and looked as if she were holding her breath as she fought through pain that seemed to come out of nowhere.

Allan could feel the room growing hotter as each second passed, and he squirmed in his seat uncomfortably as he watched Hara struggle to get herself under control. He exhaled slowly as he realized just how lucky he was. If that girl didn't have such good self-control, the room could have easily gone up in flames. "I'm sorry," he said softly when he saw just how angry and stressed his choices were making her. "But I thought that maybe I could change some things with this position, and I have…"

"Yes, I see that!" Hara snapped back, waving a hand dismissively at him. For a minute she sat and rubbed her forehead while taking several deep breaths. She really was in serious pain. It made Allan's heart sink because he knew there was nothing he could do for her.

Glancing down at his desk, he saw that the daily newspaper was charred and curling from the amount of heat that was being expelled from her. Allan knew all too well what was happening. "It's happening again, isn't it?" he asked her quietly.

Hara nodded slowly, keeping her eyes closed. "It's getting worse," she murmured. "It's happening faster than before."

Wetting his lips, Allan asked, "So what are you going to do about it?" He knew what would happen once Hara was no longer able to keep herself under control. Allan had been instructed to run whenever one of Hara's abilities was out of control, but once Hara lost control of the heat, Allan wouldn't be able to outrun it no matter how fast or far he ran.

Slowly, Hara raised her head and met Allan's nervous gaze with narrowed eyes. "So you're afraid of me, too?"

Allan stuttered as he fumbled for the right words. "I…uh, I just…" Sighing, he shook his head helplessly and gave her an apologetic look. "I just want to be cautious. You don't look like you're in the most stable state right now, and I just want to be careful around you. You understand, don't you?" He sincerely hoped that she did.

The girl shrugged, as if she couldn't care less. She snickered suddenly. "You're handling this much more calmly than Marcus did."

Startled, Allan asked, "You've spoken to Daniel already?"

Nodding, Hara continued to smirk, but her eyes suddenly looked very tired. She wasn't just losing control; she was getting weaker. With each passing moment, she was losing herself. The internal battle that she had been fighting for so long was finally taking its toll. Still, she was struggling to keep a positive attitude, or at least as much of a positive attitude as she could muster. "He aimed his gun at me," she said, amused. "He looked like he was going to piss himself!"

Allan gazed back at her sadly, but he didn't point out that she was only laughing about Marcus's reaction because she, too, was terrified of what she was becoming. Instead, he asked her, "How long have you been in Philadelphia?"

Hara shrugged again, but then answered the question. "I arrived early on the morning of April first."

"So you just got back," Allan murmured to himself, nodding slowly. "Okay…well, since you've already talked to Daniel, I assume that we're all going to be joining up again soon. Have you talked to Meg yet?"

"No," Hara grumbled, her eyebrows coming together to form a dark scowl on her face. "And Daniel's not going to be joining us."

"What?" Allan said in surprise. "Why not?" Hara didn't reply and she didn't glance up, and Allan began to understand that maybe Hara's presence in Philadelphia meant something far worse than he thought.

"What happened, kid? Why did you come back? I thought you were going to stay behind and look after the refugees?"

"I need your help," Hara replied, and sighed. "But you probably won't want anything to do with me."

Allan couldn't help but laugh. "What are you talking about?"

Hara raised her eyebrows at him. "Well, to start, you're scared to death of my presence."

"You know why that is, kid," Allan told her, raising his eyebrows right back and nodding to the charred newspaper on her desk.

"Yeah," Hara said. "And I don't blame you. My headaches are getting worse, and I can't control this as well as I could before. It keeps slipping away from me slightly, and it's so painful trying to hold it in. Sooner or later—and I'm predicting sooner—I'm going to snap again and this whole city will go up in flames." She sighed again and rubbed her temples. "I can't hold it in much longer..."

"Then let it out," Allan told her, trying to support her as much as he could. As much as Hara scared him, he couldn't bear to see her in such agony. He had seen the pained look in her eyes too often, that horrible expression of physical and emotional torment as well as self-loathing, and seeing it again only made it worse. He had hoped that after being away from her for two years, Hara would have gained back a bit of her sanity and would have started to heal just a little bit, but as he looked at her he knew that she was even more lost. Her eyes, although bright and clear, were tired and held a rage more intense than anything Allan had seen in her before. She was exhausted, but she was also very angry, which seemed like a good thing but definitely was not. If she was tired and beginning to lose her internal battle as well as her battle against the society that was trying to eliminate their kind, then she was going to be even more dangerous. She was going to feel more vulnerable and was going to do whatever she could to protect herself. Allan knew that many people in Philadelphia were in danger. Still, he was going to support the girl who was his only hope at reuniting him with his dead family. "Go somewhere isolated and let it all out."

"If you haven't noticed already, there isn't anywhere isolated on this damn planet," Hara snapped at him. "No matter where I go, there will always be people I could hurt." Sighing yet again, she repeated, "And now Daniel isn't a part of the group anymore."

"Why is that?" Allan demanded, growing angry that his old friend was apparently abandoning his own people. "Did he just grow tired of the fight and quit on us?"

"Not on you, on me," Hara corrected. Upon seeing Allan's bewildered look, Hara groaned and explained. "The cops are all after me. If Daniel can't persuade them, then I need you to convince them to let me be."

More dread built up in Allan's gut. "Dear God, what did you do?"

Hara gestured to the blank TV screen across the room beside the door. With a click, it came to life. Allan had seen her do that before, but it startled him because he hadn't seen it for so long. The channel playing on the television was CNN, and reporters were broadcasting news about the violent bank robbery. Allan was confused at first as to why Hara was showing him that, but then it dawned on him. Horrified, he whipped his head back towards her and his mouth fell open.

"You did this?" he cried in disbelief.

"Is it so surprising?" Hara muttered, rolling her eyes.

Sputtering, Allan barely managed to form sensible words. "You…you killed those men? You murdered them in cold blood?"

Hara nodded, her eyes showing no remorse.

The phone beside Hara on the desk rang suddenly, making them both jump. Before it rang again, Hara picked it up and slammed it back down to disconnect it. She hit it harder than she probably wanted to—or maybe that was her intention—because it shattered into several pieces before she knocked the entire thing to the floor.

Allan had a feeling that it was Odau who called, but he didn't care to talk to him anymore. He was too angry with Hara to care about much else. Shaking his head slowly, he stood up and walked towards Hara and stood beside her while he stared out the window at the grand city. Philadelphia had been his home for some time, but now, it was about to become a battlefield. What she did was just the beginning of something much bigger, and Allan was determined to find out what she had planned before she could hurt any more people. It was clear that she had finally lost it, and Allan wasn't going to let that result in any more casualties.

Hara, of course, was listening to his every thought. "I have not lost it," she snapped.

Glaring out the window without looking to her, Allan murmured, "Then how do you explain this? The sane kid I remember wouldn't ever do something like this, even if those people were criminals!"

"Well, I'm not the same kid anymore!" Hara declared, crossing her arms over her chest.

"Well, that's apparent!" Allan snarled, turning his head and scowling at her.

Hara glared right back.

Taking a deep breath, Allan decided that fighting with her wasn't going to do either of them any good. "You really want me to tell the cops to let you be?" he asked.

Hara nodded. "Less people will get hurt that way, although I really couldn't care less." She shrugged when Allan gaped at her again. "But you may think differently about your new people, so I suppose it's your call."

Allan shook his head once again in disbelief. "Why are you doing this? What have you got planned?"

"Well, for starters, you, Daniel, and Meg are all going back home." Hara continued to glower at him.

A huge amount of relief swept over him. He knew that the jaws of hell would be waiting for him upon his return, but he didn't care. He had wanted to go home for so long. There was only so much of the "normal" world that he could handle at any one time. "We're going home?" he whispered, unable to keep the hopeful smile from his lips.

As soon as the words were out of his mouth, his computer beeped on his desk. Hara turned towards the monitor. Her expression changed and she was now curious rather than angry. "Good, it's done loading."

"What's done loading?" Allan asked, stepping behind her so he could see what was on his computer screen. There was a blueprint of an apartment complex, and as Allan watched, the drawing slowly rotated three hundred and sixty degrees before zooming in to a room that must have been selected by Hara. Dozens of paragraphs in tiny print popped up all across the screen.

"The computers in this society are pathetic," Hara commented as she read. "They move so slowly."

"Where is it?" Allan asked as he struggled to read the tiny words scrawled across the monitor.

"It's the new apartment complex being built over on the west side."

"Right," Allan murmured as he recognized the structure. He wondered how Hara could know about that, considering she had only been in the city for a short period of time. "Why are you looking at this?"

"I figured this would be a good location to take out my next targets," Hara told him bluntly.

Allan's heart sank. "You can't kill any more people, honey."

"I can kill as many people as I want!" Hara snapped. "These are the people who ruined my life, after all!"

"Killing people won't change anything," Allan said softly, reaching out and rubbing her shoulder. He drew his hand back when she flinched away from his touch and glared at him.

"It'll do more good than whatever you've been doing here!" Hara snarled, gesturing to his office. "You haven't changed a damn thing since you left!"

"Murdering innocent people won't help you at all," Allan insisted, trying as hard as he could to reason with her. "You have to stay strong for Dreyson."

"Don't you dare start lecturing me about him!" Hara shouted furiously, her eyes crazed. More papers started curling on the desk.

Allan sighed again. "You haven't gotten him back yet?"

"It's too late for him," Hara whispered, her eyes full of grief. "He's gone. I can't get him back."

"Don't talk like that," Allan scolded soothingly. "We'll find him."

"Maybe you didn't hear me correctly," Hara growled, her voice starting to shake. "He's gone."

The wave of shock that hit Allan next was unbearable. "He's dead?" he whispered in horror. Dreyson, that adorable little toddler? Hara's baby and last living child? Dead? "You saw them kill him?" It was Allan's first thought that Hara had tried to get her three-year-old son back herself and he had been killed as punishment for the attempt, but he started to think that it was something more than that.

With gritted teeth, Hara shook her head and a single tear trickled down her cheek. "I felt him die. His light went out. I felt him go. He's gone."

Allan felt grief for the loss of Dreyson. That tiny child had been the sweetest little thing, and now he was dead. He had been murdered by the same man who killed Allan's family. "I'm so sorry," he told her, and that was true. Dreyson had been all that Hara had left. He was the last living thing that she had been fighting for. Was her son's death the event that had pushed her over the edge? Hara didn't give him the response Allan had been hoping for. "No, you're not," she hissed, her eyes harsh.

Allan's eyes narrowed as well. Hara wasn't going to make things easy for him at all, but he wasn't going to fight her. "How could he have died?" he wondered aloud. "We've been trying to fix everything…"

"You didn't fix it," she informed him sharply. "You messed up somewhere. It's still the same as you left it, if not worse. That's why I came back. The only way to put an end to this is to kill the people who killed us."

"No," Allan said firmly, knowing where she was taking things. "You can't ask me to be a part of this!"

"Allan," Hara said quietly, her eyes expressionless.

"I'm not going to start killing people, even if they're the people who killed us and even if it's our best shot!"

"Allan," Hara said a little bit louder.

"I'll work harder, change my tactics! I'll do anything to set it straight, but I won't resort to murder!"

"Allan!"

"What?!"

"You don't want to help me!" she shouted. "I get it! But if you don't want too many casualties, then tell the cops to stay out of my way!"

"I'll tell them, but they won't listen," Allan told her, familiar with the persistence of Lieutenant Odau.

Hara shrugged. "So be it, then."

"Please, Hara, you've got to stop this!" Allan pleaded desperately. Hara was too stubborn and was beyond listening.

"Try and stop me!" Hara challenged, her voice becoming deadly.

Pursing his lips in frustration, Allan growled, "Watch me. I'm going to help those cops. I'm going to tell them exactly where to find you and how to stop you." Glaring at her threatening body posture, he finished, "Make no mistake; I am going to stop you."

Hara's eyes narrowed even more. Even so, behind her mask of rage, Allan caught the hint of betrayal buried in her soul. "Fine," she said very quietly. "You do that. You can die with the rest of those sons-of-bitches. But just so you know, while you've been sitting on your lazy ass being mayor, I've actually been out there trying to accomplish something!"

For a long minute they both glared at each other, their bodies quivering in their fury over the other's decision. But suddenly, Hara's expression changed. She was in a dreamlike trance, her eyes glazed over for a few seconds before whispering, "They're coming."

"Who?" Allan asked in confusion and concern.

"Cops," Hara murmured. "Lots of them."

"Where are they?" Allan demanded with growing dread. He really didn't want there to be a confrontation in his office.

Hara cocked her head to the side as she listened, her gesture making Allan extremely uncomfortable as he recognized the unforgettable movement. Just like he had predicted and feared would happen before he left for Philadelphia, Hara was slowly becoming more and more like the man who had tortured her and killed their people. That bastard had turned her into him.

"They're coming out of the elevator down the hall."

Allan was completely puzzled. "How do they know you're here? How could they..."

"Daniel," Hara explained gravely.

Looking to his door in anticipation, Allan waited for the two dozen cops that would be coming through his door at any moment. However, Hara had a different plan.

"Get out of the way," she snapped, jumping to her feet and guiding him around his desk before pushing him off towards the wall. "If they decide to shoot, I want them shooting at the person who can't die."

Allan returned to the chair where he had first been seated during their conversation. He cowered against the wall as he watched Hara return to her place behind the desk and stand just inches away from the window, gazing back at the door as she braced herself for the trauma her body would most likely receive once the cops arrived. Even though Hara was clearly furious with him about his decision, she still had some compassion for him. Allan would fulfill his promise to help the police stop her crimes, but she still didn't want him to get hurt. It made Allan feel even more depressed and sick inside.

Moments later, a sharp rap sounded at the door and was followed immediately afterwards by a jiggling of the doorknob. When the person on the other side realized that it had been locked from the inside, the door was knocked down with a single kick and several officers began flooding into the room. At the head of the pack was a breathless and frazzled Lieutenant Odau, and right behind him was Shawn Perry wearing an FBI raid jacket.

His breath catching in his throat suddenly, Allan stared in awe at Perry. A while back, Allan had been acquainted with the man, currently some six or seven years younger than himself. They could have even been considered friends. For a fleeting instant, when the young agent laid his dark eyes upon the mayor, Allan started to smile warmly as a deep sense of relief flooded over him. But, he caught himself, knowing, to his dismay, that Perry wouldn't remember him. He wouldn't yet recognize his old friend.

Allan began to smile at him, but Perry's attention was immediately diverted to the thin form standing at the window.

"Excuse us, sir," Odau was saying. "I have a very urgent matter that I need to speak with you about…" He stopped talking when Perry nudged his arm and nodded to Hara standing at the opposite end of the room.

Odau was the more intimidating figure threatening her freedom, but Hara was concentrating on the presence of Mr. Perry, her face as astonished as Allan's had been. She should have remembered Perry's involvement with law enforcement since she had already spoken to Daniel, but Allan didn't blame her for being startled by the young man's presence. For a few seconds that felt like several minutes, the officers looked on curiously. But soon enough, at least a dozen weapons were aimed at her. Perry was the only one who didn't raise his gun.

"Freeze!"

"Don't move!"

"Hands above your head!"

"Stand still!"

"We will shoot!"

Various threats were shouted at Hara as she stood as still as stone. She didn't look angry as Allan thought she would. Instead, she had a very unnerving sense of calm about her. As they continued shouting threats at her, Hara slowly raised her hands with her palms facing them. A twisted, menacing smile slithered across her face, making her appear as a sly serpent patiently waiting for her time to strike.

Allan sank lower in his chair and stared at her in growing fear, starting to get a bad feeling about what she might do to the officers. Perry was among them, and she wouldn't risk his life to take out a couple cops…would she?

"Alright, now get down on the ground!" Odau commanded, making his way cautiously yet hastily over to where Allan sat, his gun still level with Hara's chest. "Face down, arms and legs spread apart!"

Her eyes diverting to Allan's for one quick second, Hara gave him a little wink before her eyes immediately returned to the lieutenant's. As the corners of her mouth rose slightly in a small, evil smile, she flicked her hands inward a fraction of an inch. An earsplitting bang erupted from the window, and a violent shockwave was sent through the air. Every other person in the room clamped their hands over their ears from the deafening noise and closed their eyes as millions of tiny glass fragments flew towards them. The shockwave knocked the officers off their feet and Allan out of his chair.

Once Allan no longer felt glass shards cutting at his exposed flesh, he opened his eyes a crack to observe what was happening. The cool April air was blowing inside the building from the destroyed window, and it stung his red, weary eyes. Squinting, he saw that Hara had turned her back on the office and was now looking out at the city. Her beautiful brown hair, whipping about her face, was as wild as her spirit. For a moment, she simply stood there, and everyone stared and watched in awe at what she had just done. Hara glanced back long enough to give Allan a stiff nod, and then she stepped off the edge and fell to the pool below.

"No!" was shouted in unison by just about every officer, and Perry and Odau quickly rushed to the shattered window, fearing that their strange young fugitive had plummeted to her death.

Allan made it to the edge before anyone else. He couldn't recollect scrambling to his feet and hurrying to the edge, but he had made it there in the blink of an eye. Confused, he suddenly realized that he had used his own special talent of moving to another place without moving at all. While Hara possessed many, people like him only had one. After two years of not using his ability, Allan found the familiar sensation rather exhilarating. It felt good to remind himself that he wasn't a regular person, even after as long as he spent living among them. He was special, and that fleeting moment in which he used that special part of him was the greatest moment of his lifetime. But, that moment was, indeed, fleeting. As soon as he realized what he had done, the ecstasy he had experienced was quickly wiped clean from his mind. He looked around at the others, his heart beginning to pound with a terror not easily soothed. Had someone seen him? If so, it was the end for him. But no one was paying any attention to him, as he soon saw. They were all gaping in astonishment at the teenage beauty who had leapt from the twelve story window, and in that instant arched her back and gracefully dove headfirst into the pool, barely disturbing the surface.

Once again, no one spoke as they stared at the place where Hara struck the scummy water. They watched, anxiously waiting for the girl to resurface, but she never did. Allan was vaguely aware of Lieutenant Odau grabbing his shoulder urgently and asking if he was okay. Allan wasn't listening to him. He stared solemnly at the place of Hara's submersion, knowing that she was still alive and well, somewhere deep beneath the surface of the pool. And, once she finally did resurface, her awful plan of murder would continue. Even so, Allan prayed that she would be okay, and somewhere—anywhere—she could find someone to turn to.

Sighing heavily, partly from exhaustion and partly from remorse, Allan breathed, "Good luck, kid."

✳ ✳ ✳

Twelve stories below, Hara squinted in the filthy water. The sludge burned her eyes, but she ignored the discomfort. Her body was still in shock from the slap landing she received when she struck the water, and every corner of her—mind and body alike—was screaming in agony. The silence around her allowed her fretful mind a moment to think. Where was she going to go? She couldn't resurface; that was for sure. The Philadelphia police department would be swarming the perimeter of the pool within minutes, and it didn't matter how long she stayed below the surface. Allan would certainly tell them that she had survived the fall and would be able to stay below for at least an hour. There had to be a large overflow pipe somewhere. She just had to swim along the edge of it until she found the opening and she would be free. But where would she go after that? She had nowhere to go. Allan and Daniel were refusing to help, which meant that Meg would most likely deny her as well. As angry and cold as she had been, she felt her heart beginning to sink with the realization that she had lost every last person in her life. She would have cried, but she suppressed her anguish with anger. If her former colleagues chose not to continue the fight, then they were cowards and a disgrace to their kind and she didn't want to work with them. That still left the question of where she would go once she got out of the pool.

Finally willing herself to move, Hara kicked downward so she would stay out of sight. She couldn't see in the slimy water, but she could sense the outermost structure holding in the water. She had been right; there was an opening. It was about four feet in diameter and was plenty big for her to swim through. She hadn't a clue where it would lead, but as long as it got her out she didn't care. The hole was only about twenty feet from and a few feet lower than her current position, so she allowed herself to sink a little lower and swam towards her one exit to freedom.

She jumped when something brushed against her leg. The water was too dirty to hold fish, and if other people went swimming down there then their minds were more warped than Hara's. Spinning herself around as fast as the thick water would let her, Hara scanned the area with her senses. She could only see about a foot in front of her. Nothing was in her line of sight other than litter that had been tossed into the water, but she did sense the presence of another mind somewhere close by. A moment later, something brushed her arm and she jumped again. The dark form of a man was suddenly two feet to her right, and as she watched in confusion and growing unease, he brought his face close to hers so they could look into each other's eyes. Hara squinted even more, and when she finally made out his distinguishable features, her eyes widened in horror.

What?! she very nearly shrieked.

Her first thought was that she was hallucinating, but when he reached out and grabbed her wrist, she knew that he was real. The touch sent her into a fit of panic. Yanking her arm free of his grasp, she pushed him away and kicked towards the surface as hard as she could. She didn't get far before a hand wrapped around her ankle and started to pull her back down. She screamed, for a moment forgetting that she was still under water, and immediately after sealed her lungs in an attempt to save her precious air. She continued to kick at the young man who had such a firm grip on her, but her efforts were useless. Her old friend pulled her back down to his eye level and took hold of her chin in his free hand to get her to look at him. Hara still couldn't believe it was him (after seeing him die, she hadn't expected to ever see him again), but as she gazed back into his dark mahogany eyes, she knew it was really him.

It's okay. He sent the thought in a soothing way, something he was very good at. *Follow me.* His wavy dark hair swirling about his handsome face, he released her, turned, and started swimming off in the same direction that Hara had been going in the first place.

Knowing that it was her only way out, Hara swam after him, kicking as hard as she could to keep up with his fast pace. For a few seconds she thought she had lost him in the murky water, but then he took her hand suddenly and led her onward. They entered the pipe shortly thereafter, but they had to go single file. Hara's heart began to pound in her chest as a familiar feeling of claustrophobia overwhelmed her. Telling herself that it would all be over soon, she pushed herself on, giving her friend's foot a nudge to tell him to move faster. He did, knowing exactly why she wanted to make haste. When they exited the pipe about a minute later, Hara's friend took her hand again and turned to her before pointing up with his finger. They both kicked off the bottom of the wide metal structure they were in and surfaced inside a small compartment at the far end of a large copper-colored chamber. At the end of the pool, there was a giant white filter placed halfway in the water and halfway out, but it didn't look as if it was working. There were patches of black mold covering much of the surface and it looked as if it were several decades old. It took her a moment to realize that the chamber was a filtration system for the pool, but it had obviously been abandoned long ago with the water being as dirty as it was. To Hara's left was a rusted, flimsy metal ladder that would allow one to enter or exit the small pool onto a platform. Once out of the pool, there were two apparent ways to get out of the chamber. One was a narrow, dark passageway that led to several doors, and the other was another ladder, which was taller and looked much safer. It led up to a metal hatch about twelve feet above, which appeared to be access to the outdoors. That was exactly where Hara was planning to go.

She could feel the eyes of her friend on her, but she wanted to avoid him. She couldn't bear being so close to him for another second. Swimming towards the ladder, she pulled herself up and out. Her friend, of course, was right behind her.

"Hara!" he called when she was out of the water and running to the other ladder.

She moved as fast as she could in order to escape his presence. The puddles she ran through would have slipped up most other people, but puddles were no match for her extraordinary sense of balance. In all of her time she had spent running from people, she never thought she would have fled so quickly from someone who cared about her. Still, her fastest wasn't fast enough. She only made it up three rungs before her friend caught her and lifted her clean off the ladder. She was spun around to face him and pressed back against one of the grimy walls. As she had in the pool, she avoided his eyes while she fought him. Aiming hard kicks at his shins and knees, she slapped him in the face twice before she realized that she was hurting him. As afraid as she was, he was still her friend. Perhaps her last. Her struggles ceased, but she continued to refuse to make eye contact.

"Hey," he snapped, repeating his action from underwater and grabbing her chin in his fingers to force her to look him in the face. "Calm down! It's me!"

Hara shook her head hard. "No."

"Yes," her friend insisted, nodding.

"No," Hara repeated in a furious whisper. "I saw you die!"

"No, you saw me get shot." He raised an eyebrow.

"Let go of me," Hara commanded, trying to push him away from her.

"If I let you go, will you calm down and let me talk to you? Please?"

She didn't answer him. All she did was give him a glare that warned him of more dangerous things if he didn't release her.

Very slowly, he let go of her arms and crossed his own arms over his chest. His expression was blank, but he was prepared for the move Hara was about to make. When she lurched forward and gave him a shove backwards, he had her pinned against him in a headlock before she even realized what had happened. He dragged her down the narrow corridor, his grip tight despite her violent thrashing. He took her to the room at the very end, and once inside the doorway he gave her a hard push and entered before closing the door and locking it.

Hara tumbled into a red La-Z-Boy at the far wall of the tiny room, but she was on her feet in a flash to fight her friend again. He had another plan for her.

He whipped something out of his belt and aimed it at her. "Don't," he warned her in an icy voice. He held in his hand a weapon loaded with a very powerful drug that would temporarily paralyze the part of her brain that gave her access to her abilities. She had been shot with a dart from a weapon such as that numerous times in the past, and it had never been a very pleasant experience. The drug made her dizzy, disoriented, and unsteady on her feet, but worst of all, it left her very vulnerable. She could barely stand, let alone use an ability to fight someone off. If her friend shot her with one of those darts, she would be left vulnerable for at least three hours, time she didn't have to waste. He knew she wouldn't risk it. "Sit back down!" he ordered, sharply yet softly.

Damn it, Hara thought to herself, lowering herself back to the soft new chair while eyeing her friend angrily. Everything has to be done the hard way with him!

"Don't think I won't use this." His finger was on the trigger, but that wasn't necessary for Hara to know that he wasn't bluffing.

Deciding to just play it his way, Hara leaned back in the plump chair and crossed her legs casually. Her mind and body were still on alert from the invasion of Allan Brown's office just minutes prior to her abduction. Being held captive in a little room wasn't helping, but she was going to have to control her instincts of fight or flight if she wanted to remain intact to carry out her plans. Trying to move her mind to something other than her claustrophobia, she thought about how gross she felt in her sopping clothes.

Her friend was suspicious of her sudden change of tactics. Keeping his eyes locked on hers and his gun trained on her neck, he pulled a metal chair by the wall towards him with his foot and sat down a few feet in front of her.

Twiddling her thumbs nervously, Hara took in her surroundings. The small room they were in reeked of pond sludge and rusty metal. There were two old cots off to Hara's left with torn sheets, and one had a pillow that had been ripped open with feathers strewn all over. Just to her friend's right, there was a short metal desk from where he had taken the chair. The only light the room had was a single dim light bulb above them.

"So how've you been, kid?" he asked her. His voice had changed. It wasn't stern and forceful as it had been at first. The tone had changed, making his voice the one she remembered. It was soft and gentle, and had an angelic ring that had always dragged her in. Hara had known him as long as she could remember, mainly because their fathers had been close friends, and hearing the voice that had always comforted her in the past left a horrid pang stabbing her heart.

She winced from the pain she felt, but the reminder of her past—the part of her past that she wanted to remember—had already begun to soften her. She was no longer afraid of her best friend, and felt foolish that she even had been. There was a will in her to be with him again, and she was finally able to look him straight in the eye.

It was peculiar to see him after seeing Shawn Perry as an FBI agent who didn't recognize her, but she forced herself to accept the strangeness, knowing that there was much more of that to come. Perry was just as persistent as Hara's friend, and if he was as interested in her as he appeared to be, then Hara knew she would be seeing much more of him, and quite soon. Her best friend looked very much like Perry, possessing the same mahogany eyes, dark hair, tanned skin, and facial features. Hara knew that she would need to keep him hidden from anyone in the outside world, because if he was seen they would start to ask questions about why he looked so similar to Perry. Hara wouldn't be able to answer them. If people knew the truth—the whole truth—it could cause serious problems for the future that was rapidly approaching. Continuing to search his face, Hara saw that he had received several more bruises since the last time they spoke. There was one on his forehead and a particularly large one on his right temple. As Hara's eyes wandered down the rest of his body, she saw that there were also many bruises blackening his biceps. There was also a small round scar where a tube had been inserted in the vein in the crook of his right elbow, kept there to inject him with various painful substances. Hara raised her eyes back to his face and saw the scars on both his temples. Holes had been drilled into his head numerous times as a form of torture when he misbehaved. Hara's gaze softened at the sight of his injuries and the evidence of the torture he had received after his supposed death, but she knew that he was too tough to accept any pity.

His expression was softer than his voice, and he brought back beautiful memories of the time the two of them had spent together. There had been a time in Hara's life when she had been head over heels in love with him, but she had eventually ended up with someone else.

Even so, she would go back to her time with him without a thought if it meant she could escape the sorry excuse of a life she was living now. That time had been wonderful... Besides the thirteen year age difference, Hara's past lover and the man currently working with the police to capture her were almost identical. How they each viewed her was not. Perry had only looked at her with curiosity or hate. Hara's best friend would always look at her with a burning passion in his eyes, no matter what the circumstance might be.

Sighing, Hara shrugged. "Well, let's see. I just jumped out of a twelve story window and landed in the scummiest pond in the world after having over a dozen nine-millimeters aimed at my head, and then my dead friend suddenly appeared to drag me into a reeking metal cage. Yeah, I guess I'm just peachy."

Laughing softly, he set the loaded weapon down on the desk beside him.

Hara shook her head in amazement. "What are you doing here, Jack? I've been trying to move on with my life knowing that you won't be a part of it anymore, and suddenly you're back. What happened to you? You were dead. I felt you die."

"I did die," Jack explained, and he shivered at the memory. "I wished I had stayed that way. They resuscitated me and dealt with my injury."

"They brought you back?" Hara said skeptically. "Why?" After nearly three whole months of being trapped inside the worst laboratory created to study her people, Hara had made a daring escape, but not before she attempted to break out several of her friends. In the very end, only she, Daniel, and Allan had made it out alive. They later found Meg and several others hiding in the mountains, and that had been a good hiding place until it was discovered and almost everyone in the camp was massacred.

Jack swallowed, and Hara saw him attempt not to shudder. "Do I really have to launch into the whole story now?"

Hara's sympathy for her friend was waning. She wanted answers. She didn't care how much pain it caused him to relive it.

Taking the hint from her pitiless expression, Jack nodded slowly. "Well, they saved my life after you left, but they didn't do it out of compassion. They wanted to find out where you had gone, and they wanted to punish me for what I tried to do." This time, he couldn't help but shudder. "For me, the three days following your escape were spent on an operating table while they tortured me to find out where you went." He lifted up his sopping shirt to show her the dozen or more horrific surgical scars that stretched from his neck all the way to his belly button. He pulled his shirt back down a moment later upon seeing no change in Hara's expression. "They finally accepted the fact that I had no idea where you were, even though that was what I kept screaming at them."

Hara nodded, not really understanding why she felt nothing for Jack. "And they left you alone after that?"

Jack shrugged again. "For the most part. I wasn't tortured again after that, thank God."

"How did you get out of there?" Hara asked.

"I don't know if this is true or not, but there was a rumor going around that a fifteen-year-old girl from your refugee camp was captured on a rescue mission and was cut apart until she told our old buddy where you were. She died, of course, but your location was discovered, and he sent something like seventy percent of the security force to go find you. There was an uprising about two weeks ago, and a lot of us escaped."

Hara grew angry at what she was hearing. "That girl told him where I was?"

Jack blinked in surprise. "She was a child. She was tortured to death."

"I was tortured to death almost every day for three months," Hara growled furiously. "She condemned hundreds of people to death when she talked! Hundreds of people died when he found me!"

"I know," Jack whispered sadly. "I know. I saw it. After I escaped, I wandered around for several days in search of you, knowing that you were in danger of capture again. I finally found your little contraption, and I realized what you had done. You came here, so I came here to find you."

"Well, you found me," Hara grumbled, having already felt him probing around in her mind for answers. "Don't try to convince me to stop, Jack. Don't even try. My mind is set."

"I don't want to stop you," Jack told her reassuringly.

Hara tried but failed to mask her surprise. "Excuse me?"

Shaking out his wet hair and hitting her with tiny water droplets, Jack explained, "I saw what he did to your camp. I know why you sent Allan, Daniel, and Meg here. I know. You wanted them to try to steer a healthier path into the future while you took care of the survivors. But you came back when everyone was killed, and I agree with what you're doing. The only way to change things and make the future better for all of us is by killing those kids. That's the only way to even things out. If they die, then the past and the future will be better." Taking a deep breath, Jack whispered, "They killed Mark and my mother, and no one has heard from my father in months. They killed my family too, and I want this fixed just as much as you." Pausing before taking another breath, Jack said, "So I guess what I'm trying to say is…I'm going to help you."

✳ ✳ ✳

Allan must have told three dozen employees that he was fine until he managed to duck into the conference room on the tenth floor to use the computer. He knew that the police had come to question him about his involvement because Daniel had told them about him. He had been expecting to be discovered sooner rather than later, and he was well prepared for that. However, he knew that Hara was up to something deadly and if he wanted to figure out what, he would need five minutes alone on a computer. Agent Perry and the officers were all concerned with trying to pull Hara out of the pool alive, but Allan knew that she would be long gone by the time they got down there. Even so, he was willing to accept any distraction as a good one so long as it bought him enough time to find out what Hara was up to. While they were all in their frantic states, Allan hurried out of his office and attempted to get down a few floors to a vacant room. Unfortunately for him, his popularity got in the way. When he finally brushed everyone out of his way and got into the conference room, he closed the door, locked it, and breathed a sigh of relief. He knew that his meeting with Hara was just the beginning of something far worse.

He sat at the lone computer in the room, impatiently waiting for it to log in to his files. Once it did, he quickly searched for the blueprints that Hara had been looking at before. She had told him why she was going to the apartment complex, but she didn't specify who she was going to kill. Knowing Hara, she couldn't be killing randomly. There were certain people living within firing range of the complex that Hara wanted dead. Allan observed that Hara had somehow hacked in to a secure military website that offered access to the floor plans of houses and other buildings all over the country; it also indicated what family lived in each residence. When Allan realized that, he zoomed out of the complex so he could get a closer look at the houses around it. All he had to do was hover his cursor over the house to see the last name of the family. He moved his mouse around and read each name without seeing any that struck him as familiar. Travers, Webber, Vanko, Lindsay, Morris, Jefferson, and Hayhurst popped up, and Allan was beginning to think that maybe it was all random. Hara was clearly out of her mind, so who was to say that there was any logic to it? But, as Allan moved his cursor farther back on the schematic, he was assured that she wasn't being random. Not at all. The name Riis popped up, and Allan gasped. His heart began to pound, and he suddenly had an epiphany. He knew exactly who Hara was planning to exterminate. Quickly moving his cursor around to scan the remaining houses on the screen, Allan found two of the other three names he was expecting to find. After confirming that the Kessnich, Riis, and Burma homes were within firing range of the complex, Allan searched around for the Odau household. He couldn't find it, but he knew that Jackson Odau would be at the top of that list. Hara would go for the lieutenant's son last after extinguishing the other three children who were threats to their society, but she would most likely kill the boy very slowly in an attempt to show him how much pain he had already caused her. Jackson Odau was just a boy, and even though he didn't know it, he had caused Hara and her people horrible pain and destruction.

"Oh my God," Allan breathed in amazement. "She's really doing it. She's going to try to change the past and change the course of the future at the same time…" He shook his head. "She's going to put the whole world at risk…"

The door suddenly clicked open, and Allan's head snapped towards it in surprise. He stared in confusion at Agent Perry and Lieutenant Odau as they took a step inside and closed the door. He was absolutely positive that he had locked the door upon entry.

Seeing his puzzled expression, Perry smiled. "The janitor saw you come in here." He held up his hand and showed him a ring full of keys. "He let us in." He tossed the keys to Allan.

Allan caught them in one hand and slipped them into his pocket, growing nervous from the prying stares of the two men. Knowing what they had come for, he tried to play it stupid even though it was obvious it wouldn't work. "Can I help you two with something?"

"Is it normal for a man to go back to work after something like that happens?" Odau asked curiously, folding his arms across chest.

Licking his lips, Allan murmured, "Forgive me, but I don't think something like that happens to too many people."

"I suppose you're right," Odau said, not at all amused by Allan's smart comment. "It's not every day that a teenage murderer invades the office of the mayor."

Biting his lip, Allan tried to decide whether or not he should tell the two what Hara was planning to do. Deep down, it would be a relief if Hara removed those children from the world, but he knew that resorting to murder was not the right thing to do. He fought with himself to make up his mind, but Perry saw his hesitance and made the decision for him.

"What are you looking at?" he asked, walking around the long rectangular table to approach him.

In a panic, Allan fumbled to exit out of the program. "Nothing…" he said quickly, but before he could get out, Perry had grabbed his wrist to stop him.

The agent only had to look at the screen for a second to know what Allan was doing was illegal. "Snooping on secure military databases…that's a federal crime. You do know that, don't you?"

"It wasn't me who hacked in," Allan explained, and Perry allowed him to exit out. "It was Hara."

Perry paused, and Allan could feel the weight of his gaze on him. "How do you know her name?" Perry demanded as Lieutenant Odau took a seat across from Allan.

Sighing as he sensed everything was about to come crashing down, Allan muttered, "I'm sure Daniel explained that to you already."

"He sure did," Odau said.

"So you were friends with her father, too?" Perry asked, pulling out a chair beside Allan and taking a seat as well.

His proximity was making Allan uncomfortable. "Once upon a time, yes," he replied.

"Then that must mean that your family was murdered, too, correct?" Odau asked.

Allan glared at him. "Yes, my family is dead. Thanks for reminding me."

"If you tell us how this happened, then maybe we can help." Perry's pressuring stare didn't change.

Allan gazed right back into those mahogany eyes. "You know as well as I do that I won't tell you anything."

His eyes narrowing, Perry demanded, "Why were you on a military database? What purpose did that serve you?"

"I already told you," Allan snapped. "Hara was the one snooping. I was just trying to see what she was up to."

"And I don't suppose you're going to tell us what she's up to?" Odau grumbled, trying to back up Perry.

"Maybe I will," Allan shot back, glaring at him again. "I was actually going to help you out, but since you are clearly more eager to implicate me than find her, then maybe I'll just keep my mouth shut."

"Hey," Perry said as Allan began to rise to his feet. "We're not trying to implicate you. We're just trying to get to the bottom of this." He gestured to his chair. "Please, sit. Any information you have will be helpful to us."

Allan sat back down, and he had a feeling that his already irritated mood was about to get worse. "Before I tell you anything, I want to get a few things straight between us."

"And what's that?" Perry asked.

"I wasn't involved in what happened last night," Allan said firmly. "I didn't even know it was Hara until I found her in my office. Don't go thinking that just because I once knew her, it automatically means that I'm a criminal. It doesn't. I'm not a criminal."

"No," Perry said. "You're just a man who's trying to live your life as normally as possible."

"I guess you really did speak to Daniel Marcus," Allan retorted, once again wanting to just walk out of the room and leave the two men to fumble about in the dark.

"If you were acquainted with Daniel Marcus, then it's clear that your past is just as much of a lie as his," Odau snapped. "Is your entire history a joke? Did you really live the life you claimed to have lived?"

"Of course not," Allan said. "If I told the whole truth to the world, do you really think that I would have become mayor?"

"Is that why you lied?" Odau demanded angrily. "You all lied so you could infiltrate our government?"

"We lied so we could protect the people we left behind!" Allan shouted. "If you listened to anything that Daniel told you, then you know that a lot of people have been murdered! I lied, and yes, I infiltrated your government, but not so I could do you harm! I only did so to try to steer a more promising path into the future. For my future and for yours!"

"Who are you?" Perry asked quietly, the curiosity back in his eyes. "Where did you come from? What really happened to all of you?"

Allan bit his lip again. He couldn't tell the truth. "If I told you the truth, you wouldn't believe me."

"Try me," Perry challenged, staring intently at him.

As Allan gazed back, he realized just how much he missed the Perry he used to know. The Perry he was currently talking to was really beginning to piss him off. "Do you want to know what Hara's going to do, or are you going to continue interrogating me about the horrific past I left behind for a reason?"

Guilt flashed through Perry's eyes before he glanced away. "I'm willing to listen to any information you have about this girl," he said.

"Good." Allan sat upright in his chair. "Now, if you want to catch her, then you have to do exactly as I say. If you don't, you won't stand a chance against her."

"You act as if you know she survived that jump," Odau said suspiciously.

Allan snorted. "Of course I know she did. She's been through worse than that. She's still out there somewhere."

"If you used to work with her father, then why are you going to help us catch her?" Odau demanded.

Before Allan had a chance to tell him to shut his mouth, Perry did it for him. "Just be quiet and listen!" he instructed, looking back to Allan and nodding for him to continue.

Exhaling loudly to express his displeasure to the lieutenant, Allan fought to calm his nerves. "As you've probably already observed, Hara's a little bit…different."

"If I could also get that explanation sometime soon, I would really appreciate it," Perry said, the eagerness and curiosity clearly shown.

"Don't count on it," Allan muttered back. "Because she's a bit different, she has a higher tolerance to many things. As things progress, someone may decide that the only way to stop her is to shoot her, and I can tell you right now that shooting her is a big mistake. It won't stop her. It will only piss her off even more. If she gets shot, you will have a serious crisis on your hands."

"We already have a serious crisis on our hands," Odau reminded him.

"No," Allan replied, shaking his head slowly. "This is nothing compared to the damage she will cause if someone puts a bullet in her. If she gets shot, you'll be dealing with hundreds of dead bodies instead of five."

"How is it that shooting her won't stop her?" Perry asked in confusion. "Is rapidly healing an injury another one of her specialties?"

Allan nodded. "If you want to stop her, shoot her with a very concentrated dose of anesthetic. Horse tranquilizers probably won't even be enough. Here." He took a sheet of paper and a pen out from a drawer under the table and wrote a few words down on it before handing it to Perry. "Request this. It will put her to sleep for a couple of hours, and then I can tell you how to deal with her."

"You're seriously asking us to shoot her with something stronger than horse tranquilizers?" Perry said in disbelief. "I'll shoot her with a regular tranquilizer dart…"

"No," Allan insisted. "Those aren't strong enough. Not even close. A normal dart wouldn't even disorient her. You have to shoot her with something that would put a human—I mean, normal person—in a coma or even kill them. Anything less will give her the opportunity to get away."

"I can't risk that," Perry told him. "If someone were to miss and hit a civilian…" He shook his head. "I can't risk a civilian's life like that."

Allan shrugged. "Then she's going to kill more people, and their deaths will be on your hands."

Perry glared at him. "If you don't give me more information or another option, then their lives will be on you!"

"I can't give you any more information!" Allan cried. "And there are no more options! If you want her, then you're going to have to do as I say!"

"I don't even know where I can find her," Perry said, appearing rather annoyed. "There are millions of people in this city. What's the point of all this if I don't know where to find her?"

"Because I know where you can find her," Allan assured him. "That military database she hacked into? She hacked in so she could find a good location from which to shoot her next four targets. I know exactly where she's going."

"Who are her next targets?" Odau asked, leaning forward in his chair.

"I don't know," Allan replied, a little too quickly.

There was silence. "Don't lie to us," Perry said quietly.

Allan looked him directly in the eye. "I don't know," he repeated, slower and firmer. He didn't want to lie, but he knew that if he told them the targets were kids, they would be evacuated and then they wouldn't stand a chance at catching Hara.

"If you want to help us, then why are you lying to us?" Odau demanded. "And I stand by my question before. If you were working with her father, then why are you helping us catch her?"

"I don't agree with what she's doing," Allan said through his teeth. "Her mind has gone elsewhere, and I want to help her get better. Believe me when I tell you that she used to be a very good person."

"I'd believe it," Perry muttered, looking lost in thought.

"And I'm withholding information because it's for the good of this operation," Allan added. "Trust me. I used to be a good person too. I'd like to think that I still am."

"Where is this place she's going?" Odau asked.

"It's the new apartment complex being built over on the west side."

"That's not far from my house," Odau murmured to himself, looking a little worried.

"I know," Allan muttered. He felt Odau's suspicious gaze on him again, but Perry spoke again before he could inquire as to the meaning of his statement.

"Even so, I don't have access to this sort of thing," Perry said.

"That's not my problem," Allan replied.

"Hey," Odau said suddenly. "I'm friends with Wesley Bennett. He's a doctor at one of the hospitals downtown. I think he could get us the drugs."

Wesley Bennett. Allan knew that name. The name Bennett was an important one in his history, but just like Perry, Bennett wouldn't know him.

"You still need a warrant for that," Perry reminded him.

"I know someone who can get you a warrant," Allan promised them.

Perry sighed. "Is her name Meg Hopper?"

Thanks, Daniel, Allan thought to himself in disapproval. *What didn't you tell them?* "Yes," he said. "Meg will get you your warrant."

"Is her story just like yours and Marcus's?" Perry asked. "She worked with the girl's father but she didn't have anything to do with the bank incident?"

"Hara worked alone on that," Allan said. "None of us had anything to do with it."

Perry sighed again. "Alright. I'll ask her for a warrant, but I want to speak to all three of you together once we get Hara, understood?"

"Perfectly," Allan said.

"When exactly did she say she was going to this complex?" Odau asked.

"She didn't. My gut's telling me that she's going tonight. She arrived on the first and has already made contact with myself and Daniel. I'm guessing that she's looking to get things done quickly. Once you get the drugs from your doctor friend, load them into several weapons and set up snipers in and around the building."

"If we go inside, won't she know we're there?" Perry demanded.

"Yes," Allan said. "But that won't faze her. She'll walk willingly into the trap, and once you shoot her that's it." That really wasn't it. Once Hara was in custody, he was going to have to figure out a way to sneak her out before the FBI sent her off to a laboratory somewhere to be studied. They couldn't be allowed the chance to see her DNA under a microscope.

"This seems a little too easy if you ask me," Perry muttered, not quite going for it.

It was too easy. Allan didn't know how they were going to pull it off. He wanted to stop her before she killed the kids, but he had to accept the possibility that maybe they wouldn't be able to stop her. That wasn't an option for the agent and the lieutenant, which was why Allan wasn't telling them the targets were children. "Trust me," he said through gritted teeth, a pang of guilt striking him in the chest. It took everything he had to force out his lie. "Everything will work out fine."

"I hope you're right," Perry said grimly, eyeing him. "The three of you may not be involved in this, but if this goes sour then you're going to have hell to pay!"

Raising an eyebrow, Allan suggested, "Well, if you don't want this to go sour then I advise that you get moving with your preparations."

Glaring at him again, Perry turned to Odau and handed him the slip of paper Allan had given him. "Speak to this Dr. Bennett and let him know that we're getting a warrant for this particular drug." He glanced sharply at Allan. "You call your D.A. friend and get us that warrant as fast as you possibly can." Slumping down in his chair, he groaned. "In the meantime, I have to call Special Agent Long to request S.W.A.T. backup." His eyes flickered to Allan again. "This isn't going to be pleasant for me. I suppose I have you to thank for that."

Allan smiled at him. "When we catch Hara, you *will* be thanking me."

* * *

When Meg Hopper arrived at City Hall, it took less than five minutes for Allan to get her on his side. It took less than ten for her to get the warrant. It took a little over thirty to get the concentrated dose of anesthetic from the hospital. Everything was moving more quickly than anticipated, and that fooled Allan into believing that they wouldn't run into too many roadblocks. To his dismay, when Odau returned with the drugs he also returned with a very upset Dr. Wesley Bennett. The old doctor then strode straight up to Allan and demanded to know what the hell he was thinking by planning to shoot a teenage girl with such a concentrated dose. Startled by the doctor's assertive questioning, Allan had no idea how to respond. Was he allowed to fill Bennett in on the case? Apparently so, but Allan wasn't the one who did. Since Perry was still busy requesting backup from the Pittsburgh FBI, Odau explained the story to Dr. Bennett.

Allan went back upstairs to his office to hide. The room was freezing because of the cold air blowing through the broken window, but he hardly noticed. He sat in his chair in the center of the room, listening to the constant drone of traffic and urban noise, punctuated by sirens all across the city. Televisions and radios were even audible from adjacent buildings if he listened closely enough. What he yearned most for was silence. Where he once lived, silence was something that could be found anywhere, especially at night. All that could be heard at night was the wind blowing and the trees shifting, natural sounds that were easy to find in his home city, which was five times bigger than Philadelphia. There were no vehicles, no sirens, and no horrid noises to disrupt the peace and quiet. Occasionally, a voice would be heard, but it was always a happy one.

That was something else Allan missed. No one here seemed to be happy. He was currently in a money-driven society, and the only way people could survive was to work themselves to death. Where he originated, people gave to the community what they could. His people used their talents to keep their economy moving and keep their peaceful society flourishing. Everybody was happy and content with that. Allan didn't understand why people in the human world would cause themselves so much pain and suffering and still not be able to achieve happiness.

The door opened suddenly, and Allan's dreams of silence and a happier place left him. He was relieved to see it was Meg. He reached out and pulled another chair closer for her to sit in while she closed the door behind her. After she walked over and sat down beside him, he smiled at her. It was good to see her after so long. The two of them and Daniel had known each other for most of their lives. After being separated for so long and being isolated from their own kind for even longer, it was a relief to see an old friend.

Meg's appearance startled Allan, and then he started to grow worried. Her light hair was pulled back in a pony-tail, which was a rare occurrence for her. Her light brown eyes were red and weary, a strange sight compared to the energetic and enthusiastic young woman Allan remembered. Her warm, friendly face was worn and pale, and Allan had a feeling that she, too, had been having many sleepless nights. Even her body looked exhausted. When she sat, her shoulders were slouched. Meg barely looked like herself anymore. She looked as if she had been working herself to death, just like a human.

Allan was so fixated with Meg's worn-out figure that he didn't have time to say, "It's great to see you," before she spoke.

"I don't understand why she didn't come to me for help," she said quietly, a very sad expression on her wearied face.

Taken aback, Allan asked, "Do you *want* to help her?"

"Of course not. That wasn't what I meant."

"Well, what *did* you mean?"

"We were close!" Meg whispered fiercely, the pain in her eyes becoming unbearable for Allan. "She even called me mom by accident once. I don't understand why she didn't want to come to me for help before she sought out the two of you."

"It's not that she didn't want your help," Allan assured her. "I'm sure that she wanted you to help and I'm sure that she wanted to see you after how long it's been, but Daniel told the police about the two of us and she knew that they would try to arrest her again if they caught her with you."

"Do you really think the threat of arrest would stop her from seeing me?" Meg demanded angrily, and her eyes became harsh. "She could kill them all easily. What was stopping her?"

Shrugging, Allan replied, "She probably just didn't want to waste her time trying to convince another one of us to help her."

"Oh, so consulting me is a waste of time, is it?" Meg snarled.

Allan had never seen such behavior from his friend before. He was surprised by her anger towards him. "That's not what I meant," he said softly.

She snickered. "I know what you meant."

Gaping at her in astonishment, Allan demanded, "What is wrong with you?"

"What's wrong with you?" Meg snapped back, but her voice cracked and that was the end of the act. Her face fell and several tears began to trail down her cheeks. She sniffled once and looked away from Allan's face in shame.

Allan's own anger, which had been increasing with each passing retort, immediately left him. His heart softened for her. "Are you sick?" he asked, beginning to recognize the paleness in her face as illness.

"It's this place," she breathed, struggling to restrain her sobs. "This place is making me sick. This whole planet is a disease! Personally, I'm glad my Hara came back, because I can't take any more of the bullshit this place has to offer me."

"Well, you know what her return means, don't you? It means that we're back in the war."

"I know what it means," Meg snapped. "And I don't care. I'll take the war if it means I can go back to my people." She sighed heavily, and her face appeared even more exhausted. "I loved her," she whispered. "And she loved me. I wish she had come to see me." Her eyes hardened at Allan again. "I can't believe you're actually showing them how to catch her," she accused. "They could hurt her!"

"I would never let that happen," Allan promised. "And you know that."

"They know she's different, Allan!" Meg cried. "What if you can't protect her and they ship her off to another lab to be studied or even dissected? You know she would never survive another round of experiments!"

"I would never let that happen," Allan repeated, keeping his voice level and calm.

Meg continued to frown upon him. "How long do you think it's going to take them all to figure out that we're not normal either?"

Allan had been trying to avoid that question for as long as he could. He didn't know how long it would take for someone to notice. Their talents weren't as noticeable as Hara's, because they each only had one ability. If any of them were to be discovered, it would most likely be Daniel. He would sometimes absentmindedly answer a question that hadn't been verbally asked or would finish someone else's incomplete thought. Now that the investigators knew that there was a girl with non-human capabilities in the world, it wouldn't be hard for them to make the connection if Daniel were to slip up. Allan needed to warn him to be extra careful. He had a feeling that Perry would be the one to make the connection first. Perry was a smart man and seemed to be the most curious one involved. If he did happen to make the connection, there wasn't a doubt in Allan's mind that something very bad would happen. Maybe they would be the ones to be shipped off to a lab to be poked and prodded. One thing was for certain: even Allan wouldn't be able to survive another round of that.

Meg didn't wait for Allan to answer. She didn't want to think of what the consequences would be if anyone discovered their secret. "You do what you have to in order to keep her from killing those little monsters," she told him sharply. "But if anything happens to her because of the information you gave away, I'm holding you personally responsible!"

Allan didn't bother trying to shift part of the blame onto Daniel. Daniel was the one providing information to them.

She leaned closer to him. "Don't you dare let any doctor take a look at her! I loved her like my own daughter, and I won't allow anyone to cause her harm. Even you. I don't care what you do; just make sure she stays safe!"

Nodding, Allan bit his lip as he waited for Meg to calm down. Now that their long argument had apparently come to a close, he wanted the rest of their reunion to be peaceful and pleasant. After a minute, Meg had turned her gaze to the floor and she was breathing heavily to soothe her raging emotions. Allan had a feeling that the fatigue had been a big factor in her extended outburst. Still, he just wanted to have a polite, mature conversation with his old friend. "It's great to see you," he told her softly, and smiled warmly when she looked up. "Really, I've missed you so much."

Meg smiled back, but it was a sad smile. She had missed Allan, but she still couldn't be happy. Allan regretted allowing her to come to Philadelphia with him and Daniel. They hadn't wanted her to go, but she insisted and Hara agreed. This place had really changed her. It had sucked her dry. Her happiness was gone. Even though their home was still a battlefield, Meg had to get back there before she completely lost herself, just like Hara had.

When Meg leaned over and hugged Allan tightly, Allan found himself hugging her back even tighter. He breathed a sigh of relief, finally feeling a small sense of home and comfort after so much time spent in a foreign land. Meg must have felt the same way, because she continued to hold him and breathe in his scent in an attempt to take in the tiny piece of home that was being offered to her. Meg pulled away from him after several minutes, and she had tears in her eyes again. "It's great to see you too," she whispered, reaching out and touching his arm, as if he might spontaneously disappear if they didn't keep in physical contact. Allan was actually able to do it, but he didn't plan on going anywhere. "You have no idea how much I've missed you. When I bumped into Daniel that one time, I almost started crying. I prayed that I would bump into you sometime just so we could talk, even if just for a moment. I guess fate had its own plan."

"It always does," Allan muttered.

They both sat in silence for a few minutes, taking in each other's company. Allan thought about their relationship with Hara. Out of the three of them, he had always had the rockiest friendship with her. The first time they met ended with him snapping at her, and ever since there had been some tension between them. All the same, just like Meg, Allan had always felt a parenting instinct with her. She wasn't a child to either of them, but they had decided to be her surrogate parents after her real parents were murdered. Even when the first signs of madness had begun to show, they vowed to continue their nurturing care and support. And when she started to become resistant to the sound of her true name, the three of them struggled to soothe her and heal the tortured, wounded girl that was driven by her own grief and hatred. Maybe that had been the reason she had sent all three of them to human society. Maybe they had pushed her a little too hard, and she wanted them to just leave her alone. Not one of them was a biological parent to Hara, but they were her family. They loved her and fought a war for her, and now they would continue to love and fight for her even though she was descending into insanity. The poor girl had finally snapped and was lost in her own head, but Allan wouldn't give up on her. He had seen her strength and endurance, and he wouldn't stop believing that there was some way to bring her back.

"Allan?" Meg said in a soft voice, and she squeezed his hand.

"Hmm?" he murmured, glancing at her again.

"What if he comes back?"

Allan's heart stopped beating for a moment. That was another question he had been trying to avoid. He had pondered over it, but each time he had shrugged it off and told himself that it was impossible. Now that Meg had spoken it aloud, he realized just how likely it was. The man Meg was referring to was mentally disturbed, but he was also very intelligent. It didn't take a genius to figure out how their transportation machine worked, and if that man happened to find it he would have no trouble following Hara's trail back to Philadelphia. Allan didn't want to think about what would happen if that man followed her back. Just the simple thought of seeing him again made his insides tie up in knots.

"What if he figures out where she's gone and what she's doing and comes back to stop her?" Meg asked in a squeaky voice. "What if he comes back for her? If he gets his hands on her and does what he did to her before…"

"I won't allow that to happen," Allan said again. "That bastard will never touch her again."

"That's what her father said," Meg whispered, lowering her eyes to the floor.

"Look at me," Allan instructed. "That man will never touch that child again, Megan Hopper. I don't care if I have to offer myself to replace her; that animal is never going to hurt her while I'm still breathing."

"You know that you wouldn't be enough to replace her," Meg told him. "Even considering how rare your ability is, that man will never want anything more than he wants Hara."

"I promise you, Meg," Allan whispered, taking her hand in his. "I will do everything in my power to keep her safe from everyone, and if the time comes when we need to arm ourselves against our old friend, well…we'll deal with it then."

Forcing a smile, Meg sighed and rose from her chair. "I'd better go home and change for tonight. Dr. Perry wants me to be there in case something unexpected happens."

"Don't call him Dr. Perry," Allan warned quickly, lowering his voice as if someone could hear their conversation. "That's not who he is right now. We can't slip up in front of him, because you and I both know that he'll be the one to start asking questions first. He can't know the truth about himself, no matter what. It's too early."

Meg nodded apologetically. "Right. Agent Perry." She headed for the door.

"So…I'll see you soon then?" Allan asked hopefully.

She turned and smiled again as she opened the door, but for the first time it was a real smile. "I sure hope so," she replied, and left.

A warm feeling began in the pit of Allan's stomach. It was so good to see one of his best friends after being alone for so long. He heaved a sigh of deep content and leaned back in his chair. There was a smile on his lips. Most would have found that ironic given the current situation, but Allan didn't care. He hadn't been happy for more than two years, and he wasn't going to let anything spoil the tiny bit of it he was finally feeling. Sadly for him, his swell of happiness was all too fleeting. His door opened again, but it wasn't Meg returning as he had hoped. Allan's smile was wiped clean from his face as Dr. Wesley Bennett entered his office.

Dr. Bennett was an older man. Allan knew that he was at least sixty and must have been approaching retirement. He was African American, and had light brown eyes that were soft even when he was angry. His hair was graying and his brow and the skin under his eyes were wrinkled, making him look older than he really was. Allan was interested to see that Bennett looked almost as tired as himself, and the doctor's fatigue must have been a key factor in his accelerated aging. Bennett was shorter, no taller than five foot eight, but his height was deceiving. Allan was several inches taller than the doctor, but he was much more intimidated by Bennett than Bennett was of him.

"Can I help you?" Allan asked flatly, his rude tone unintentional.

In a quiet voice, Bennett replied, "Maybe you can, Mr. Mayor. Maybe you can explain to me why you're going to inject a teenage girl with a drug so concentrated that it could almost put a blue whale into a coma?"

Allan didn't know why, but the doctor's comment almost sent him into a fit of giggles. It might have been the way he said it, or maybe it was just because he was a doctor and doctors made Allan extremely uncomfortable. Perhaps he just wanted to laugh to make himself feel better. He managed to stifle the laugh, but he couldn't contain his grin. "Didn't the lieutenant explain that already?" he asked, the amusement audible in his voice.

"Do you find this situation funny?" Bennett demanded in a voice even calmer than before. "If so, then the two of us need to have a serious talk."

He just couldn't take the doctor's tranquility seriously. Attempting to get a grip on himself, Allan cleared his throat and apologized, "No, I'm so sorry. There's nothing funny about this at all."

"Good," Bennett replied. "And Graham did try to explain it. Forgive me for not quite understanding it. You seem to be the man with all the answers."

"That would be me, yes," Allan muttered, looking away from the doctor. "But forgive me when I tell you that I'm unable to provide very many."

"What are you hiding?" Bennett demanded, peering at him inquisitively. "Graham was telling me that the girl has a very high tolerance to drugs, and that's why you're planning to inject her with such a concentrated dose. But a dose as powerful as the one you want to give her won't put her to sleep; it will kill her."

"I know how bad this looks," Allan told him. "And I know that you and I are the only ones here who know just how dangerous this drug is. It would kill a bull elephant, but not Hara. It will only knock her out for a few hours."

"I've had patients with high tolerances," Bennett replied smoothly. "I've been a doctor for more than thirty years. I know how high the human drug tolerance can go. You can't look me in the eye and tell me that a mere child could survive an injection like that."

"I've seen it given to her!" Allan insisted. "I know her drug tolerance better than you, Doctor."

"Are you a doctor?" Bennett challenged, raising an eyebrow.

Growing impatient, Allan snapped, "No, but I've known her for a long time. I understand her limits. Trust me."

"I don't," Bennett told him smoothly. "And I'm not going to be any part of this."

"No one's forcing you to stay here," Allan reminded him, praying the doctor would leave. He knew that he wouldn't. "You're free to leave any time."

Chuckling, Bennett said, "Oh, you're not getting rid of me that easily. I'm not letting you out of my sight until you've explained yourself."

Sighing, Allan rolled his eyes. "Alright, then."

Shaking his head in disbelief, Bennett exclaimed, "I can't believe you've got these men convinced that this girl actually has super powers!"

Allan almost laughed again. He hadn't heard the term super powers in quite some time. "Well, I didn't convince them of that," he promised. "They witnessed her power on the security footage of the bank after the attempted robbery."

Bennett took a step forward as Allan rose to his feet. "And how exactly does a teenage girl come to possess abilities seen only in science fiction and fantasy films?"

Holding his ground, Allan wasn't sure if he should be saying what he was about to. "How do you know she wasn't born with them?"

The doctor's eyebrows went up again. "So you do know more than you're letting on? I was beginning to think that you honestly didn't know the truth about this girl."

Unsure of what he meant, Allan's brow furrowed. He had been answering his questions in a more knowledgeable way than Odau would have. "Of course I know the truth about her. Her parents were both friends of mine."

"If you know the truth, then please share."

"I can't."

"Why not?"

"Because the whole truth is not for you to know."

"Why? What's wrong with me?"

Allan laughed. He couldn't help it that time. "There's nothing wrong with you. I'm sure you're a very good person. It's just that no one should know the truth."

"But you know the truth," Bennett said. "What makes you so special?"

Allan didn't answer. He wasn't anything special. His gift was more of a curse than anything. It wasn't his fault that he was born with the fateful gene. He couldn't choose his own genetics. He didn't get to control his own biology! "This isn't my fault," he blurted. "I didn't ask for any of this."

"You say that the girl was born this way," Bennett said. "That means that she's not the only one like this."

Biting his lip, Allan took a deep breath. "She's not the only one. But nobody knows about this. If people found out…"

"Then you would all be at risk," Bennett finished, peering back at him curiously. He smiled reassuringly when Allan's expression became horrified. "You're one of them, aren't you? How else would you know about her when not even the FBI knows?" He continued to smile, knowing that he was speaking to a man who had a power that was scientifically impossible. He was right, of course. Allan was one of them. He was one of the few who had survived. "Don't worry," he said soothingly. "I'm not going to tell anyone. I don't even think anyone would believe it. I barely believe it myself. You have friends hiding in the city, don't you? Friends who are like you. Who are they?"

Allan didn't answer. Bennett couldn't have honestly expected an answer. Allan was exposed enough already, and the doctor could see that. Swallowing hard, he lowered himself back down into his chair. He thought of Meg suddenly, and how she had asked how long it would take to discover them. Not very long at all, my friend, he thought to her, and sighed wearily.

"You don't have to tell me," Bennett told him, taking a seat in what had been Meg's chair. "I didn't think that you would. And that's okay." He was silent for a moment. "What can you do? Can you show me?"

"I can't," Allan whispered, shaking his head. "I've already used it once today by accident, and it makes me sick when I use it too much. I can't risk someone walking in and seeing me."

"I understand," Bennett said softly. "How many of you are there in the world?"

"Just a few now," Allan said. "We're almost extinct."

The doctor was taken aback. "Extinct?" he repeated. "Why? What happened?"

Could Allan trust the man with a secret? Bennett claimed that he wasn't going to tell anyone about his ability, but that didn't mean that he wouldn't betray Allan. Deciding to go with what his gut was telling him, Allan gave the man a bit more of his trust. "Haven't you ever watched the SciFi Channel?" he asked. "People like that are hunted down and killed, or worse, experimented on."

"That's what happened to Hara, isn't it?" Bennett asked. "She was experimented on."

"You catch on very quickly," Allan commented, becoming slightly suspicious.

"I'm smarter than many people give me credit for."

Nodding, Allan explained, "This is what happens when something different arises, something so different that it's terrifying, because no one really understands it. People hunted us down and murdered almost every single one of us. Those who had abilities that were considered rare or unique were saved as lab rats. Hara and I were two of those unique individuals. I can't even begin to describe to you what's been done to me, and it doesn't even compare to what's been done to Hara."

"What exactly is it that you can do?" Bennett asked, still coming up empty handed with that question.

No more talking. That was what Allan was telling himself. He had already put too much trust in a man that hadn't yet proven himself trustworthy. Although, he was a Bennett, so he must have that trustworthy gene in him somewhere. "I...I can't," Allan stammered, and then jumped to his feet. "I've already said far too much. Please, you need to leave."

"Wait, wait!" Bennett cried as Allan went to the door to show him out. The old doctor rose stiffly to his feet and went over to him. "Do you have a card?" he asked hopefully.

"A card?" Allan repeated in confusion.

"Yes, a card. With your name and contact information? If things get out of hand, and I have a strong presumption that they will, then I want to know how to get in touch with you."

"You really don't want to get involved in this," Allan admonished. "It's easy to get into, but it is so hard to get out of. If you want to stay in contact with me, then that means you're trapped in this conspiracy. As you've probably gathered, it isn't at all safe to be a part of this."

"I've made my decision, Mr. Mayor," Bennett told him firmly. "Besides, like you said, I already know too much. And I want to keep in contact with you just to make sure that Hara actually lives through what you're planning to inject into her. Now, how about that card?"

"Right," Allan muttered, trying to remember where they were. Recalling that he had placed them in the storage closet a few weeks back, he went and opened it.

Bennett accompanied him to the closet, and he jumped back as a large box tumbled to the floor from the top shelf. "Whoa!" he cried, bending down to scoop up the contents that had spilled out.

"No, stop!" Allan shouted, dropping to his knees to snatch away the videotape that Bennett had in his hand. He hadn't realized what the contents of the box were until it was too late, and Bennett had already seen the label on the side of the tape.

"What is all this?" Bennett asked as Allan frantically pushed the fallen tapes back into their box. He tried to pick up a stray one again, but Allan took it away quickly.

"It's private is what it is!" Allan snapped at him.

"These tapes were made in 1948," Bennett declared in confusion.

Confused as well, Allan took one from the box and read its label. TRIAL 8: HR 10/26/48. "They weren't," Allan replied quickly. "The date is wrong."

"Oh," Bennett said, still looking confused. He watched in silence while Allan stuffed the overflowing box and then closed the top. As Allan was replacing them carefully on the top shelf, he asked again, "Mr. Mayor, what is on those tapes?" Allan didn't reply. "Allan!"

The sound of his first name caught him off guard. He looked down to him.

"What trial was it referring to?" Bennett asked, his brow furrowed in concern. It was clear that he already suspected what they were.

"Take a wild guess," Allan said sharply, spotting the box with his cards and quickly removing one before slamming the closet door shut. He then leaned over and opened the door that led to the hallway. "You don't want to see what's on those tapes. Now please leave." He handed Bennett the card.

Bennett held the card in his hand for a few silent seconds before he placed it in his pocket. He nodded to Allan, and without another word he left.

With a loud exhale, Allan closed his door and locked it as he had done prior to his close encounter with Hara. He leaned his back against the door and stared wide-eyed at the ceiling, unable to believe what he had just willingly done. He just told a human about the war. He hadn't offered all that much detail, but it was bad enough that Bennett knew what he was. Allan was wrong; it wasn't Perry that would be the first to uncover the truth. At this rate Bennett would soon learn the whole truth about the war and Allan's people. Allan prayed that if he did learn the truth, the walls of the universe wouldn't come crashing down as a result.

✳ ✳ ✳

It was more than two hours before Jack finally let Hara out of the tiny, reeking room. Jack felt the need to keep her hidden until he was sure that it would be difficult for the two of them to be spotted by police. When he finally decided that it was safe to leave, Hara almost knocked him over as she hurried to get out. Her claustrophobia was not something to take lightly.

The tall ladder which she had tried to use earlier to escape did lead to the outside, as she presumed. Jack unlocked the hatch door on the ceiling while Hara practically danced on the ladder a few rungs below him, impatiently waiting for him to get moving. Part of her was beginning to think that he wasn't moving fast on purpose, his way of teasing her. She scolded herself for thinking that her friend would try to torture her like that. He knew what she had been through; he was there to suffer through it with her. Well, most of it anyway. He hadn't endured quite as much as she had. No one had. Once the hatch was open, Hara mentally pushed Jack forward so she could get out. It was a little too hard.

"Ow!" Jack cried as he found himself suddenly lurching upwards. He fell out of the top and sprawled on the grass just outside the hatch.

Hara stumbled out of the top and took several running steps away from it. When she stopped, she threw her head back and took a huge breath of fresh air. Her heart rate steadily began to slow as she breathed, and her instincts of fight or flight were beginning to subside. She found herself smiling as she breathed the fresh, polluted Philadelphia air. Being out in such an open space felt amazing to her.

"That hurt, you know," Jack whined from behind her.

Turning, Hara glared at him where he lay rubbing his forehead. If she had actually been herself and hadn't lost her sense of compassion, she would have felt terrible and apologized. But she wasn't herself anymore. "Maybe next time you'll think before locking me in a tank!" she snarled.

Without waiting for a response, she turned back towards the scum pond to take in the view. She could see police cars and officers on the opposite side at the base of City Hall, where she had jumped. Much of the metropolitan area was on the opposite side of the water, and she was glad for that. The filtration chamber was a large, flat metal surface about fifteen feet wide and twenty-five feet long that was located about thirty-five feet or so from the edge of the pool. She was relieved to see that the area they were in was currently under construction, so nobody was around. It was sometime after six p.m., and work was over for the day. Huge construction equipment, ranging from cranes and excavators to dump trucks and front end loaders, were sitting unattended. There was a medium sized building several stories tall being built off to Hara's left, its skeletal support beams left unclothed. There were a few small islands of grass, one of them surrounding Hara and Jack, but much of the ground had been churned up from the machinery and was a muddy mess. It made Hara sad. Nothing like that would ever be allowed back home. The land was sacred and limited and shouldn't be destroyed in such a way.

"Where are we going, anyway?" Hara demanded of Jack, turning on him again. She disregarded her friend's hurt look from her lack of sympathy. She was extremely agitated from being locked up for so long, and she wasn't going to tolerate any more crap from him.

"Well, first things first," Jack said, hopping to his feet and pointing at her accusingly. "You need to change your attitude. You used to be so much fun, and I just listened to you bitch at me for the past two hours! Whatever happened to your sense of humor?"

All Hara had to do was gaze back at him to answer. She knew Jack didn't want her real answer, because it would come in the form of a third degree burn.

"Yeah...don't answer that," Jack muttered quickly, and then beckoned her. "Come, follow me."

She followed him over to a Bobcat that was parked about twenty feet directly ahead of them. As they walked, Hara noticed that Jack was careful to keep only a few feet of distance between them. His eyes kept darting back to assure himself that she wasn't going to run off like she tried to before, and his thoughts were nervous as he prayed that she wouldn't leave him. He reminded her of her oldest brother Flint, who had always kept an eye on her like a guard dog. Flint was a guard for their father—the leader of their people—so Hara supposed it was just instinctual to protect his younger sister.

As her mind began to wander to her brother, Hara suddenly felt a horrible pang of grief in her chest. She was doing a good job at suppressing her grief so far, but thinking about her brother made her thoughts drift to the rest of her dead family. Images of her mother and father came first, followed by her three brothers and two sisters, and then...

NO, she told herself forcefully. *Don't think about them! Thinking about them will only make you weak!*

Hara desperately wanted to picture their faces, but she ordered herself to push out the thoughts of the family which she had started. Her soul mate and five young children were all dead, just like her parents and siblings, and she knew that if she thought about them the grief would completely consume her. She couldn't allow her mind to be distracted by something that no longer existed. Shrugging off her emotions and hardening herself once more, she pressed on and continued to follow Jack as he led her all the way around the Bobcat to where a brand new red and black motorcycle was parked. "Whoa," she murmured. It wasn't all that big, but she knew this specific bike was built for speed. It appeared to be able to hold the two of them, considering neither of them were particularly heavy, especially after the food depravation they both suffered through for months. "This looks like fun."

Jack laughed. "Yeah, wait until you see how fast it goes."

"Damn," she replied, running her fingertips over the smooth paint. "Where'd you get this?"

"I stole it," Jack told her, and looked at her like she was a fool. "Did you really think I had the money to pay for this baby?"

"How foolish of me," Hara said, and actually grinned. "How fast does this sucker go, anyway?"

"Wicked fast," he whispered. "Want to see?"

"What do you think, dumb ass?"

"Okay, calm down!" Jack said as they both started laughing. "Climb aboard!" He climbed on the single seat and leaned forward so Hara could climb on behind him, and gripped the handlebars tightly so they wouldn't tip over.

"Being a wanted murderer has its fun side," she muttered, lifting her leg over the bike and wrapping her arms around Jack's waist so she wouldn't fall off. As she did, her friend turned his head towards her ever so slightly and she felt the muscles in his abs tense as he caught his breath. Hara then sensed the thought that crossed his mind for a split second. She immediately released him and pulled away, staring incredulously at the back of his head.

"I'm sorry," Jack mumbled quickly, his voice flooded with humiliation.

Hara didn't respond. She felt violated.

When she refused to say anything in reply, Jack turned his head toward her but didn't look her directly in the eye. His expression showed embarrassment and guilt, and for a moment he appeared as if he might apologize in hope of forgiveness. He must have listened to her angry thoughts, because he seemed to understand that he wasn't going to get any. He didn't speak again. Clearing his throat as an awkward silence fell between them, he turned the key in the ignition.

Enraged and disgusted with her friend for thinking such intimate things about her, Hara slowly wrapped her arms around him again, but made sure to grip him around the chest. She monitored Jack's thoughts in case he decided to think something vulgar about her again, in which case she would be forced to punish him, but his thoughts were only of humiliation. Knowing she was going to be upset with him for a while, she held onto him as the bike lurched forward. Once they made it to a paved road, Jack floored it and they accelerated away at high speed. Neither of them spoke for the entire ride.

The thought that crossed Jack's mind and made Hara so upset wasn't exactly a thought. It was a memory. There had been an afternoon the two of them had spent together a time ago, and if asked Hara would have said that it was wonderful. They had both truly loved each other for a time, but they were never meant to be together. After Hara met her soul mate, it was all over between her and Jack. This other man was the father of Hara's five children, and even after all of that Jack was still in love with her. No matter how many times she told him, Hara just couldn't get it through his head that they would never be together again. She didn't love him anymore.

Trying to have a moment to herself that was spared from irritation or anger or vengeance, Hara pushed all her past thoughts from her head. She was going to allow herself a few minutes to be happy and enjoy herself. The bike was very loud, but riding on it felt amazing. The wind was whipping through her hair and causing it to twirl wildly behind her like a flag on a windy day. There was nothing quite like it. She had never ridden on such a vehicle before, and the thrill made her smile and close her eyes. She let go of Jack and leaned away, tilting her head back and just feeling the air around her. Inhaling deeply, she had to do everything in her power to keep herself from laughing. She felt free. It was a feeling she hadn't felt in a very long time. She doubted that any of her people had since the humans had invaded their home and started the war. In that short moment when Hara had the chance to feel free, knowing that no one was tampering with her life in that exact moment, she imagined she was flying. She imagined that she was flying away from the world and all the troubles it had brought upon her in her short life. The ecstatic feeling was so foreign to her but at the same time was so familiar. For a second she even forgot. She forgot the world and about everything that had been done to her. She forgot that she had ever stopped being happy.

Jack whipped around a corner suddenly and Hara was thrown to the left. Her stomach lurched and she snapped out of her little world of pretend just in time to grab Jack by the arm to prevent herself from flying off the side. Panicking for a moment as she felt herself beginning to fall, her heart skipped a beat and she gasped. Luckily for her, Jack had predicted her loss of balance and stuck a hand back to catch her. Hara frantically grabbed his arm and pulled herself back up. Her heart was still pounding, and Jack sent her a calming thought to reassure her that she was okay. Grateful for his help, she clung to him for the rest of the trip. The pace of her heart never slowed.

They arrived at their destination minutes later. For the last few blocks, they had traveled past old, long since abandoned apartment buildings. The buildings were all white and had nine windows across on the second level, eight windows across and a door on the bottom level. Each window was flanked with teal shutters, most of which were detaching from their hinges. The siding on every building was peeling off from the walls, and vines crawled up the sides while weeds infested the grass around them. Concrete sidewalks led to concrete steps before the door, most of which were cracked and broken. The place seemed dead. Silence echoed through the air around the roaring of the bike. An eerie emptiness filled the atmosphere; the neighborhood was a complete ghost town.

A particularly old and trashy looking apartment building lay at the far end of the small neighborhood, and that was where Jack brought the bike to a halt. On the far left side of each building, there was a four-car garage. Jack rolled the bike through the doorway, which was already open, and flipped a switch on the wall. A light above them flickered to life, illuminating the large empty room to expose the other vehicles that Jack obviously stole as well. Just to their right sat a pale blue Lamborghini, a car that was obviously built for speed. Hara knew that Allan would follow up on his promise to warn the cops about her, so if they ever wanted to make a daring escape, that was the car to use. On the other side was a huge black Hummer, which would come in handy if they needed to carry heavy equipment, or if they needed to make a quick escape across rough terrain. Hara didn't comment on the vehicles. She knew perfectly well that Jack had stolen them and she knew what they were to be used for. Even if she hadn't known any of that, she had Jack's thoughts to confirm it all.

Jack took the key out of the ignition and the rumbling of the bike ceased. He allowed Hara to climb off before hopping off himself. Clearing his throat uncomfortably as he had back at the pool, he willed himself to look into her eyes. "Listen, kid, I'm sorry about what you saw in my head. It wasn't intentional..."

"Jack," Hara said firmly. He was her friend, her best friend, but she needed to get a few things straight with him before they proceeded any further. "I don't love you anymore."

That hurt, and the pain was easily seen in his face even though he was trying to hide it. "I know," Jack said weakly, his voice cracking. "But I still love you."

"You need to move on," Hara instructed sharply. She no longer shared his feelings, and she needed him to see that. "This is becoming too much for me."

"There's no one left for me to move on to," Jack muttered, lowering his eyes and walking over to a door in front of them. He walked up the three decaying wooden steps and opened it, not saying a word as he walked through.

Sighing, Hara knew she should feel bad for how roughly she had spoken to him, but she really didn't. What was wrong with her? What type of soulless creature was she becoming? Why couldn't she feel guilty for hurting her best friend? She asked herself these questions, but she didn't have an answer to any of them. Who knew what she was turning into? So much damage had been done to her mind that anything was possible for her now.

She followed Jack into a small hallway. Jack had moved to the end of the left side of the hallway in front of a steel door with his back to her. He was clearly waiting for her, but at the same time he couldn't bear to look at her. As Hara came up behind him, she desperately wanted to smack him in the back of the head and yell at him to grow up and move on with his life, but even with her new personality she couldn't bring herself to do that.

"So...we're hiding in this dump?" she asked him in disappointment, glancing around at the cracked plaster on the walls and ceiling.

"No," Jack replied, still refusing to meet her gaze. Pulling a key from his pocket, he put it into the lock of the steel door. "We're hiding beneath it." He unlocked the door and swung it open with some difficulty. There was nothing but darkness on the other side, but that was no problem for either of them. They both had acute senses and could tell where to step. There was a stairwell a few paces in front of them, and they descended it at a pace they would have used in a stairwell that was brightly lit. At the bottom was another door which Jack opened without the use of a key. As soon as it swung open and they crossed the threshold, a horrendously bright light erupted in front of them and left Hara completely blinded.

She gasped in pain and shielded her eyes, and she heard Jack say, "Oh, sorry about that." A moment later the light was turned off. The room was now lit by fluorescent lights in the ceiling. Hara blinked rapidly, trying to clear the white spots from her vision.

"It's our security system," Jack explained.

"I see," Hara muttered, understanding exactly how it would cripple an intruder. Of course, they would first have to get past the dead bolted steel door at the top of the stairs...

The blinding light had come from a large strobe light positioned at the bottom of the stairs; its switch was attached to a trip wire that was triggered when stepped on. Hara didn't understand why she hadn't foreseen the trip wire or hadn't sensed its presence. She continued with Jack further into the room. Surrounding the door in the shape of a semi-circle were two translucent plastic sheets that stretched from floor to ceiling. Jack brushed one of them aside and stepped to the other side with Hara close behind him. The room was a dull gray color, consisting of gray concrete walls, ceiling, and floor. The room ran all the way from one end of the building to the other. On the end farthest from where they had entered was a flat screen TV supported by a tall metal stand. In front of it was a wooden table and a long white sofa. Hanging from a rod connected to the ceiling beside the left wall was a magenta curtain in case a quick change of clothes was required. In the very center of the room was another rectangular table with eight chairs situated around it. Along the back wall and just to Hara's left was a small kitchen. A few feet down the wall from the kitchen were two metal storage cabinets that were at least six feet tall. Hara gathered from Jack's thoughts that there were numerous weapons inside them.

"If we're hiding here, then why were we just hiding in the asshole of the world?" Hara demanded in annoyance.

"Well, you were inside, so what does that make you?" Jack grinned back at her but then answered. "We were just hiding there to avoid any more confrontations with the cops. It's also there for your use in case you...you know...burst."

"Oh, well, how considerate of you," Hara replied sarcastically. She didn't want to think about the consequences if she burst while she was still in Philadelphia.

Nodding, Jack explained, "We don't have beds, but if we get a chance to sleep we can just use the couch. It's fairly large."

"I highly doubt I'll be sleeping any time soon," Hara muttered. She couldn't recall the last time she had slept, and even if she had been tired she was too nervous and paranoid to fall asleep.

"You'll be able to focus better if you get some rest," the voice of an older man with an English accent said off to her right.

The sound of that particular voice caused Hara to whip around to see if it belonged to the person she hoped. Upon seeing him, her mouth fell open in disbelief.

The man who had spoken was very old. He was approaching the age of eighty, but he was a strong man and didn't look as weak and frail as he should have. He still had a head full of thick white hair and his light blue eyes were still healthy and energetic. His face was wrinkled from age but his expression was calm and confident. Physically, he wasn't all that different from the last time Hara had seen him. But Hara wasn't fooled. She could look into his memories and could see that he had been through an ordeal just as great as that suffered by many of her people. In the time before Hara's race had been destroyed, that man had been a part of Jack's family. He was human, but that didn't matter. He had been exiled by his own people on a false charge of treason and Jack's father had taken pity on him. He had been a part of Jack's family since before Jack was born. When the humans invaded their homeland and wiped out their people, every human living among them was rounded up and was given a choice: they could either return to their place of birth, or they could remain and suffer the same fate as Hara's people. Having been betrayed by the people with whom he had grown up, he chose to remain with those who had shown him mercy despite all the horrible things his kind had done to theirs. He then suffered through unbearable torture just like Hara's people. It had truly changed him. Hara looked into his old, wise, yet troubled mind and saw what he had endured in order to defy the people who had betrayed him. She was horrified at the things she saw and wondered how the old man was still in one piece, but she was also proud of him for his bravery.

"Noah," Hara whispered with a great mixture of emotions. "My God…"

Noah Travis didn't waste time explaining his presence. Instead, he got straight to business in the hidden level of the abandoned apartment complex. "Many, many decades ago, my grandfather built these apartments. It was never his intention for this hidden level to be built under this particular building, but some time ago, my father was visited by a young woman. My father didn't even consider her a human being; he thought of her as a messenger of God sent to warn him. She told him that he needed to build this hidden level because one day in the distant future his only son would require it to fulfill a very important purpose. Sometime before my exile, he explained to me what this young woman told him. He told me that I would need it one day to shelter an angel, a guardian of her people. My father made sure that this level was completed before his death shortly thereafter. Although I didn't understand the story, I still believed in my father because he believed in it with all his heart and soul. And now, all this time later, I finally understand the story. That young woman wasn't a messenger of God, but she did know about the trials our future would face. That angel, that guardian…" he nodded to her, "is you."

"I'm no angel," Hara snapped, disgusted.

Noah's face remained calm. Straightening his back as much as his old body would allow him to, he said firmly, "Yes, you are. You just can't see past the things you've done or the things you're about to do."

Hara gazed back at him, her expression as hard as it had been when confronting any of her old friends. Where had the soft part of her gone? Why couldn't she, just once, feel a tender emotion towards another person? As she gazed upon the old man's face, it hit a nerve inside of her, and she found herself beginning to soften. Sighing wearily, Hara felt her expression crumple. "I'm not a good person anymore, Noah," she said, surprised to hear her voice crack in shame and distress. "I've done terrible things, and I don't want to stop."

"I know," Noah said softly, smiling down at her and making his eyes crinkle in the corners. "I know."

Shaking her head furiously, Hara's tenderness began to fade as quickly as it had sprung. "You don't understand," she whispered fiercely, glowering at him. "The girl you used to know is dead. I'm not the girl you think I am. My name is Hara, and I'm a monster. A cold-blooded killer!" She chose to use Daniel's words, knowing he had been right about her.

Noah continued to smile at her, but an overwhelming sadness lingered behind his gentle gaze. He knew it was true. He could see the change that had occurred deep inside of her and he could see that she was still transforming. That slight moment that she had slipped up and shown her grief, that was the last little bit of the person she once was. Hara, the cold, merciless monster, hadn't taken over fully yet. But she was close to winning the internal battle. It was only a matter of time before Hara would crush the traumatized, terrified girl hiding in the shelter of her arms and take over the mind and body for good. "You're scared," Noah told her quietly, taking a step closer. "You're masking your fear with rage and the thirst for vengeance. You're right; you're not the girl I once knew. But I know she's still in there somewhere. She's not quite dead yet."

"How can you be so sure of that?" Hara demanded.

The smile frozen on his lips, Noah whispered, "Because I just saw her."

Her hardened heart being crushed once more, Hara whimpered hopelessly, "I need help! I can't fight this part of myself for much longer…" Stepping forward to close the space between them, Hara wrapped her arms around Noah and hugged him tightly. Tears spilled out of her eyes, and for the time being she didn't care.

It wasn't all that surprising that Noah was the one who caused Hara's protective shell to crack. She and Jack had played together as young children despite their four year age difference, and Noah, being the one who had always taken care of the house, had looked after them both. Hara had grown up in the sheltered care of Noah Travis. She loved him. And he loved her.

The sympathetic old man held the troubled girl in his arms as he had when she was a child. He had been successful in holding onto the small part of Hara that was good, that was the real her, but his next words brought the harsh, hard Hara back and fully suppressed the emotions that weakened her.

"Maybe fighting that part of you isn't the best choice," he murmured to her.

He was right. Trying to fight the part of her that kept her alive and gave her purpose wasn't what she should be doing. She had a greater enemy to fight. The tears stopped flowing and the anguish immediately subsided. Pulling away from Noah, she looked up into his questioning eyes. He had felt her body tense up and wasn't quite sure what effects his words had created. "You're right," she told him, her tone returning to normal. Or, at least, what had since become normal to her. "I shouldn't fight myself."

Taking a step back after witnessing her personality change, Noah eyed her uneasily. "I didn't mean that you should embrace that part of yourself. I think you need to work with this damaged part of yourself to come to some mutual agreement."

"Oh, we've already come to a mutual agreement," Hara informed him, her eyes narrowing. "We both know that killing these kids is the right thing to do."

Noah stared back into her intense gaze, but he couldn't hold it for long. He looked away moments later and cleared his throat uncomfortably.

She turned to Jack, who was watching her even more nervously than Noah was. "So, how long have you guys been hiding down here anyway?"

Noah answered for the both of them. "A little over a week. What about you?"

"I just got here late the other night," Hara replied. "How did you get here before me?"

Shrugging, Noah muttered, "Miscalculation."

Nodding, Hara addressed Jack once again. "You really want to help me do this? Don't think I'm holding you to it. This isn't exactly a moral thing to do."

Jack snorted. "Hell if I care! I'd kill a hundred kids if it meant I could help bring our people back!"

Shaking his head, Noah stated with a cross expression, "Your fathers would be ashamed of you two."

His comment made Jack lower his eyes in humiliation, but Hara made eye contact with Noah and glared at him. Being Noah, he glared right back, his gaze—this time—never faltering.

This glaring contest went on for some time. Jack was the one who lost his nerve and broke the silence.

Clearing his throat, he asked, "So…once we kill the four of them, how will we know that it worked?"

Still angry about Noah's comment, Hara looked back at Jack. How dare Noah tell her that her father would be ashamed of her! When she was finished with what she was about to carry out, he would praise her for saving their people. "We go back, of course. We go back and see for ourselves."

"And how do you propose we do that?" Noah demanded, crossing his arms over his chest and gazing at her expectantly.

That was the only thing that Hara hadn't thought over: getting back home. Getting back home wasn't the easiest thing to do. But there was somebody who had the power to get them back.

"Yeah...I don't exactly see another machine sitting around for us to use," Jack muttered, growing nervous again.

"No," Hara agreed. "But we have Allan. When this is over we can just rebuild the machine and it can take us home."

"Or," Noah cut in, "we could just wait."

Hara and Jack both looked at him in astonishment. "Wait? Wait! Are you crazy?"

"I didn't mean wait for that long," Noah said defensively. "I just meant wait for... you know...that day, and then we can go back with everyone else."

Hara knew what he was talking about, but that was still far too long. "That's a ten year wait, Noah," she told him. "That's way too long. I don't want to spend any more time in this place than I have to." She peered at him curiously. "Why would you want to wait so long, anyway?"

Noah shrugged. "Well, for starters, it's kind of nice being home. And just look around you! There isn't an endless war being fought in your backyard. Once you go back..."

"When we go back, the war will never have happened," Hara reminded him. "And speaking of the war thing, haven't you noticed how these people are at war with each other? Those men I killed last night? They were going to kill a group of innocents, a group of their own. As long as these people are in a world with us, there will always be war. But when we go home, and we've kicked those people off our land, the war will have never happened."

"You say that, but what if you're wrong?" Noah silenced her objection with a wave of his hand. "What if? What if we go back and it isn't fixed? We'll be walking right back onto the battlefield, and you know who'll be there waiting for you."

Hara shivered at Noah's words. She knew all too well who he was referring to. "I'm going to kill him before we go back," she whispered. "I'm going to find him before he can find me."

"That's just what he wants," Noah told her softly. "That's what he's been waiting for."

"I will fix this," Hara said firmly. "And I will go back. I promised them."

"Well, they're all dead now, and people break promises..."

"Not this one!" Hara snapped.

"Sometimes, you can't help yourself…"

"Okay," Jack said loudly, clapping his hands together. "Before Hara blows us all sky high, can we change the subject?"

Hara hadn't realized how much heat she had been letting out until Jack said something. Her temper was very touchy, and with how close to bursting she was, they would both have to be careful when it came to that topic. "To what exactly?" she demanded in an irritated tone.

Striding over to one of the tall cabinets, Jack thrust the doors open. "To what weapons you're planning to use."

Hara looked in at the contents and her mouth involuntarily dropped open. "Oh, wow," she whispered in amazement.

✳ ✳ ✳

As Dr. Wesley Bennett stepped into Mayor Allan Brown's office, he began to wonder about the logic of his actions. The janitor on that floor hadn't been very intelligent. Bennett told him that he had forgotten his pager in the mayor's office and the janitor unlocked the door to let him in. Of course, he had watched and waited until Brown had left his office in a hurry fifteen minutes after he had kicked him out. Had Bennett been thinking logically, he wouldn't have lied to get inside the mayor's office. But there was something in his office that was out of place, something that Brown wanted to protect. Something that held answers. Closing the door carefully behind him, Bennett walked over to the closet and slowly opened the door. He reached up to pull down the two large boxes of videotapes which were stored on the top shelf. He set them on the floor and then rummaged through them. Each box had at least two dozen tapes in them. The first box had tapes with the label TRIAL and then a number, each with a different date but all in the same year, 1948. But the mayor claimed the date was wrong. He could have been lying, but Bennett couldn't be too sure about that. The second box was the same except the label read MEMORIES.

For a little while, Bennett knelt beside the boxes and simply stared at the tapes, not really sure what he planned to do with them. He never predicted that he would actually get this far. Now that he was here he didn't know if he wanted to carry out his plan. Brown said Bennett wouldn't want to see what was on those tapes, and Bennett knew from the fear in his eyes that he was telling the truth. Brown told him Hara had been tortured, experimented on. Was that what the trial tapes showed? Was Bennett about to watch a young woman being mercilessly tormented to discover what powers she held within her?

He didn't want to start with anything too gruesome, so Bennett picked a tape from the MEMORIES box. It was number 4. Glancing around, Bennett didn't see a VCR anywhere. He hadn't seen a VCR for a few years now. Then he saw that Brown's television on the wall was hooked up to a DVD player with a VCR. Relieved, Bennett slipped the tape into the player and turned on the television. He pulled up one of Brown's chairs and waited for it to start.

For a couple seconds there was nothing but static, but then the tape flickered to life and the screen was filled with color. Bennett knew immediately that Allan Brown had been telling the truth about the date being wrong; the picture was too clear to be from 1948. He blinked at the images he first saw, but then he smiled in adoration. The camera was focused on the sweetest little girl he had ever seen. She looked to be about four years old, with long locks of curly brown hair falling over a cute round face. The little girl was sitting on the floor in what appeared to be a living room. There was a white sofa and long wooden table resting behind her on spotless cream colored carpeting. She was drawing with colored pencils in a large drawing pad. By the way she continued to color, she seemed to have no idea that she was being filmed. She sneezed suddenly, a funny little sound, shaking her head as she did so. Bennett didn't know what Hara was supposed to look like, but he guessed that this little girl was Hara at a younger, more innocent age.

A quiet chuckle sounded, and Bennett guessed that it was the person holding the camera.

"Hey, sweetie," a man said.

Young Hara looked up in surprise, and then a bright, toothy smile lit up her face. "Hi, Daddy!" she cried in a sweet, sing-song voice. Bennett saw that her eyes were a bright, almost glowing green that seemed as remarkable as the finest of emeralds.

"How are you?" the man asked in a delicate voice, the way one would speak to a young child.

"Good," she said, still smiling but returning to her artwork.

"What are you drawing?" her father asked her.

Little Hara held up her picture so he could see. "A rainbow!" she said proudly as she presented her work.

Bennett gaped at what he saw. The drawing was, by far, amazing. The piece of work was too well-done for Bennett, let alone a four-year-old! It was beautiful, perfect in every way. The rainbow was drawn over a cascading waterfall that descended into a small, glimmering pool. The colors, the shapes...it was unbelievable! It was almost as if it were a photograph and not a drawing at all. Bennett leaned forward in his chair.

Her father whistled and laughed, but Bennett could hear the discomfort in his tone as he spoke. "Where'd you learn to do that, kiddo?"

Little Hara thought for a second, but then shrugged.

He laughed again. "I wish I could do that," he said.

The girl looked at him peculiarly. "Can't you?" she asked in confusion.

"No," her father replied with a chuckle.

The girl looked up suddenly past the camera and her face lit up again. "Hi, Mommy!"

"Hey, honey!" a woman said enthusiastically, stepping into view of the camera and kneeling down beside her. Little Hara crawled into her lap and showed her the picture. Hara's mother was a very beautiful woman. She had dark, curly red hair and deep, navy blue eyes.

"Look what I did, Mommy!" Little Hara exclaimed in excitement.

"Oh, wow...that's...very nice!" Her mother was trying to sound supportive, but Bennett could tell that she was just as uneasy as her husband. She looked up and gave Hara's father a worried look.

"Hey, baby," Hara's father called. "Why don't you show Mommy what you showed me this morning?"

Little Hara furrowed her brow and shook her head stubbornly, her shiny locks falling in front of her eyes.

"Please?" he asked. "For Mommy?"

"Why?" Little Hara whined.

"Because I want to see what you can do," the woman told her, looking at the camera in confusion again.

After taking it under consideration, little Hara agreed. "Okay."

"Good," her father said. The camera moved suddenly as he pulled a chair or something over and set the camera on it. He then came into view of the screen, plopping down across from the girl and her mother. Bennett saw that Hara received her good looks from him. She looked exactly like her father. Wavy dark hair with lively green eyes and the same facial features. He picked up one of her colored pencils and held it flat in his palm. "Okay, now show Mommy what you showed me."

Screwing up her sweet, angelic face, little Hara scrunched her eyes together as she concentrated on the pencil. For a few moments nothing happened, and Bennett thought that he had missed it. But then the pencil lifted off of her father's hand and slowly floated over to her. Both her parents stared in amazement as Hara reached out and snatched it out of the air.

"Good job, honey," her mother said quietly, the fear visible in her eyes as she looked up at her husband.

"How come I can draw like this but Daddy can't?" Hara asked her mother, gazing down at her artwork.

"Because you're special," her mother told her, pinching her cheek.

"Yeah," her father agreed, and Bennett heard him sigh. "You're...different." The screen went black.

Bennett stared at the blank screen for a while, trying to register in his mind what he had just seen. He wondered if that video had been a joke, but why would someone make a fake home video like that? The emotions appeared pretty sincere to him. Allan really had told Graham the truth. That little girl, who was now grown up and had become a murderer, had super powers, and there were others in the world like her. Allan Brown was one of them…which meant that the two others aiding him—the detective working with Graham and the new D.A. he had seen in the building before—were also like him. This whole thing, this conspiracy, wasn't a conspiracy at all. It was real. It was happening with every breath he took.

Eager to see more of the girl's capabilities, Bennett quickly ejected the tape and replaced it with another. It was one of the trials, number 8. He wasn't sure he was prepared for what would be on that tape, but at the same time he was too keen on witnessing what that girl could do with her young mind.

The screen remained blank for a moment, as the first one had, but soon the scene was set. It was a completely different setting from the previous tape. This time, instead of being focused on the little girl, the camera was filming an older girl, about eighteen years of age. Bennett knew immediately that the girl was Hara. The tape must have been filmed fairly recently.

The camera zoomed out, and Bennett got a good look at Hara's surroundings. There weren't much really, just blank white walls and the white bench she was cowering on. The poor girl looked nervous and uncomfortable. Terrified would be a better word. She was sitting on the bench, her knees up to her chin and her arms wrapped around her legs. Her green eyes had lost their light. They were duller, even empty. Dead. Something had changed inside of her since that day she drew her amazing picture. Her hair was a tangled mess, falling over her face in matted clumps. She was wearing a light blue outfit that looked like the type worn by inmates of a mental hospital. Had she gone crazy? Had something happened to that adorable child that was so awful, she had completely lost her mind? She had been tortured, and was this where she had ended up?

There was a chuckle from somewhere off camera, just like there had been in the last tape. Only this time, the laugh was mocking. The camera zoomed out again, revealing another character in the room. This person was a man, although Bennett was unable to see his face. He was facing Hara at an angle, so all Bennett was able to see was the back of his head and his right ear. He was dressed in all white. That man was a doctor. He had sandy blonde hair that had grown out somewhat. He was lounging in his chair, his feet resting on a table in front of him with his hands folded neatly in his lap.

Hara flinched at his mockery, which only made him chuckle again. "You're a bit too scared of me, in my opinion," he told her in a taunting voice. He didn't seem concerned at all by her fear. In fact, he seemed to be enjoying it. How he could sit there and just tease her while she sat cowering against a wall...it was disgusting.

The poor girl shivered and wrapped her arms around herself even tighter. "What do you want?" she asked in a shaky voice.

"Oh, I think you know exactly what I want," he informed her, taking his feet off the table and placing his folded hands upon it, leaning forward eagerly. "We're friends, sweetie. Do I need a reason to come visit you?"

Slowly, Hara raised her eyes to gaze back at him. "We've been at this for days. Can't you just leave me alone?"

The man laughed, a cold, merciless sound. It sent a shiver through Bennett as well as Hara. "But I enjoy your company so much! I had a notion that you were beginning to enjoy mine as well. After all, since your precious family is gone, I figured you'd need someone to replace them."

Bennett saw immediately that Hara was upset. Her eyes narrowed for a split second in the man's direction. The muscles in her arms tensed. The man also saw her anger, and his tone suddenly changed from mocking to serious. "Don't even think about it, kid," he warned.

Hara glared at him, but then she looked away. There was a brief pause, but then Hara spoke. "What do you want me to do this time?"

"One more test, and then I'll give you a break for a while," he promised.

"What do you want me to do?" she demanded louder.

Pausing, the man pulled a sharpened pencil out of his breast pocket. Hara raised her eyes again, watching him curiously. The man laid it on the table and gestured to it. When all Hara provided him was a confused expression, he clarified, "Burn it."

Hara stared back at him. "No," she said firmly.

The man cocked his head to one side, a creepy gesture to watch. "Excuse me?"

The girl was playing stubborn, but Bennett could see the fear in her eyes. "I told you," she said. "I don't use that around other people, even psychotic bastards like you."

"Yet you seemed to have no problem using it on the soldiers who captured you."

"That's why I'm not using it again. You saw what was left of them. Nothing. Ask for something else, because that's the one thing you're not going to get."

"See, here is where you get your assumptions wrong," the man told her, his tone threatening. "I am a very patient man, but I didn't ask you to do it. I'm telling you. And I'll tell you again. Burn it."

"And I'm telling you," Hara challenged, putting her feet on the floor and leaning towards him. "Fuck off."

Hara's eyes said that she knew she had made a mistake in saying that, but it was already too late to take it back.

"Maybe I need to use a more…powerful method of persuasion," he told her softly, reaching up a hand and beckoning for someone behind him.

A moment later, loud screams from a very young child erupted off-camera. Another man dressed in black came into view, dragging a young boy by the arm behind him. The second man had a buzz cut of very dark hair and had a muscular build. Maybe he was a guard of some sort? The little boy turned for only a few seconds, but it was enough for Bennett to see his face. He had green eyes and curly brown hair, just like Hara. His facial features were almost an exact match to Hara's from the previous tape. Judging by his height, he couldn't have been much younger than she had been in the previous tape either. He must have been Hara's younger brother, because there were definitely matching genes in both of them. The little boy was wearing the same kind of outfit as Hara, and he was screaming at the top of his lungs. He was struggling to pull away from the man who had a grip on him, but it was useless. Seeing a toddler in that setting made Bennett feel very sick.

Hara stared at the boy in horror. "Dreyson?" she breathed.

The boy stopped struggling and screaming and looked back at the sound of her voice. The two gazed at each other for a moment, but then the toddler yelled, "Mommy!"

Mommy? Bennett blinked in surprise. *Mommy*? That little boy was her son? This terrorist was a mother?

"Oh, God!" Hara cried with a mixture of emotions, jumping to her feet. She started to rush over to him, but in a flash the doctor was on his feet as well, whipping something out of his pocket.

"Ah, ah, ah!" he warned, pointing a gun at the boy.

Hara immediately froze, looking from the boy, to the doctor, and back to the boy again. "You won't," she whispered.

"No," he said, lowering the gun and shoving it back in his pocket. "I won't."

Bennett saw the relief wash across the girl's face, but it was quickly wiped off as the man pulled something else out of his pocket.

"If I killed your son now, nothing would stop you from doing whatever the hell you wanted to. But if we…improvise a little, we may find a way to get through to you." He held up the small object in his hand. A tuning fork.

"What are you doing?" Hara asked, her voice filled with panic.

"Your boy has very sensitive ears, does he not?" the doctor asked smugly, practically waving the fork in her face. "I wonder what you would do for me if I did this…" Hitting the fork on the table, he handed it to the man holding Hara's son. The guard held it down beside the boy's ear.

Bennett heard the soft ping of the vibrations as the fork struck the metal surface, but it was barely audible to him. The boy—Dreyson, as he had been called—appeared to hear it at a much greater intensity. He began screaming again, only it was out of pain rather than fear. He kicked and clawed against the man holding him, but it was, once again, useless.

"Stop it!" Hara shrieked, trying to run to the child again. She stopped when the doctor drew out the gun again, training it on her that time.

If Bennett remembered Lieutenant Odau's story correctly, gunshots couldn't harm her. He wondered what was stopping her from continuing on to her child. He wondered what was stopping her from killing that doctor right where he stood. By what Hara had described, she was certainly capable of it.

"You want me to stop? Do what I tell you! Now!"

Hara hesitated for half a second, staring at her young son with pain in her eyes. "Okay!" she shouted, turning quickly and planting both her palms firmly on the table. The doctor took a step back and the metal surface groaned dangerously. With a loud pop, the pencil burst into flames.

Bennett stared in absolute awe at the girl. What that child could produce with her mind…it was utterly incredible! It was a scientific breakthrough! What people wouldn't do to get their hands on her to discover how she worked, how her genes allowed her to do that. What Bennett wouldn't do to know how her gene sequence gave her that power… Bennett immediately shook off that thought. The kid had grown up knowing she was different from the rest of the world. She had been kidnapped and experimented on for knowledge. He wasn't going to be like that doctor, torturing her and her family for insight. He would just have to deal with never knowing the truth.

"Okay, I did what you wanted, now let him go!" Hara tried to run to her boy again, but the doctor grabbed the front of her uniform and pushed her backwards. She stumbled and fell back onto her bench.

As she attempted to get back on her feet again, the doctor pointed a finger at her and shouted, "Sit down!" He ignored the heartbroken expression on the girl's face and turned back to the guard. "Get him out of here," he ordered, and then the guard left, dragging the screaming boy behind him as he had upon entering.

"No, please!" Hara begged, her eyes overflowing with grief.

The doctor looked down at her and cocked his head in that creepy way again. "I guess it was a good idea to keep your boy alive," he said quietly. "He'll be very useful to me." He snapped his fingers in the direction of the camera. A moment later, the screen went black.

Bennett found himself unable to move. There were too many things running through his mind. The girl—Hara—that poor, broken girl, had changed so much since she drew that amazing landscape in her living room. She had once been a happy, free child who had a regular life like anyone else. She grew older and had a child. And then she was taken and broken. First came the grief. And then came the anger. Bennett had seen the effects of each. He had seen her perform in exchange for relief. That little boy—her son—had been killed after that tape had been made. Maybe not right after, but sometime after. Bennett had seen the emotion on her face. She had already lost the rest of her family. Her son was the only thing that kept her going. And then that doctor had killed him. After the boy was dead, that was when Hara had snapped and chose to kill. But how had she gotten away from that doctor in order to do that? By the way he regarded her, it was extremely unlikely that he had let her go willingly. Had she killed him? She killed that horrible doctor and then went out into the world to seek revenge on those who had caused her pain. It made the most sense to him. That was how Bennett pieced together the puzzle.

One thing that he had been told still puzzled him. Allan Brown stated that what was on the tapes was too disturbing for eyes. What Bennett saw left him disturbed, yes, but not in the way that he had expected. Ejecting the tape and holding it in his hands, the old doctor sat lost in thought for a while. Then he looked down at the boxes of tapes. The MEMORIES box clearly wasn't going to show anything that explained what had happened to that poor girl. But the TRIAL box definitely did. Uncertain if he should continue, Bennett selected the number 1 tape from that box and slipped it into the VCR. For the first minute or so, Bennett was certain the mayor had been bluffing to keep his tapes a secret. But when the screaming began, he finally understood Brown's warning. And he finally understood Hara's fear of that doctor.

4

Calamity

Allan Brown wasn't sure what to do. His first instinct was to pack up his personal belongings and make a run for it, but his face would be all over the media in no time and then he would be arrested. It wasn't such a bad thought. At least he wouldn't have to worry about involving himself in Hara's plot. Worst case scenario, Perry and Odau would force him to cooperate completely. But he told himself that he wasn't going to run. He thought about finding Meg and Daniel and hiding out somewhere in the city until the whole thing blew over, but he knew that Hara would find them and she would not be happy about that. Another thought was to just help her and get the whole thing over with, but then he reminded himself of what she was doing. She was going to kill four innocent kids. Even if they were going to become something awful in the future, the future hadn't arrived yet. They were still innocents. And he would have no part in the killing of innocents.

That still left him to wonder what he was going to do. Perry and Odau were on to him. There was no way he could just act like nothing was happening.

By the time Allan stepped into his apartment, his mind was completely exhausted. Sighing as he dropped his jacket and bag onto the floor, he rubbed the sleep from his eyes, the sleep that was threatening to overwhelm him. He couldn't sleep now, no matter how tired he was. He had to figure out what he was going to do.

He took a seat on his sofa and stared at the opposite wall. So many confused thoughts were buzzing through his mind, so many suggestions, but he didn't know which to listen to and which to ignore. Some were telling him to be a coward and run, some were telling him to just ride it out right where he was, and some were telling him to pick a side. Perry or Hara. Perry or Hara. Perry or Hara. Did he really have to choose? He had promised to stand by Hara no matter what happened, but he had no clue that things were going to end up so bad! Perry had been a colleague of his for years, but Perry had no idea who he was. Who was Allan supposed to choose?

His mind was made up for him when he received a surprising phone call from someone he least expected to hear from.

The ringing phone scared him. He had been lost in the echoing silence of his own mind when it suddenly filled the apartment with its shrillness. Taking a deep breath to calm himself, he reached over to the table beside him and answered. "Hello?"

"Hey, friend," Hara's smug voice said to him on the other end of the line. "Oh, wait, that's right. We're not friends anymore, are we?"

"Hara?" Allan said in pure shock, sitting up straight. "How did you get my number?"

He felt like an idiot as soon as the words were out of his mouth. He groaned as Hara laughed loudly on the other end. "Where did I get your number? Ha! That's really funny, Allan. I don't think I've ever heard you make a joke before."

"I thought you weren't going to have anything to do with me after what went down at our little reunion," Allan muttered, irritated.

"I thought so too," Hara said, still laughing. "But for some reason I've had this nagging feeling that maybe I should give you one more chance to reconsider."

"Well, forget it," Allan replied sharply, finally coming to the conclusion that helping Hara was out of the question. "I'm not going to take any part in killing children."

"Good," Hara said. "Because even if you wanted to, I'm not letting you be a part of this anymore!"

Was she just trying to pick a fight with him? Was that the only reason she called him? "What do you want, kid? Why did you call me?"

"I want you to tell your police buddies something for me," she told him. "I'm coming at exactly 10:30, and I want you to remind them to stay out of my way tonight, or very bad things will happen."

"I've told them that," Allan said impatiently. "And they aren't listening. It doesn't matter how many times I tell them."

"I'm not finished."

"Oh, excuse me."

Hara snickered, clearly enjoying it all. "I also want you to tell them that I'm not in this alone."

"What?" Allan was immediately interested, but also worried.

"So they better watch out," Hara warned.

"Wait, you have help?" Allan couldn't believe it. "Who's helping you? It isn't Meg…" It couldn't be Meg! He just spoke to her!

"No, it's none of you who came back before," Hara stated.

"Then who is it?"

"None of your damn business! I just need you to let your new friends know that they've got more to worry themselves over than just me."

"Hara, is it one of us?"

Hara sighed. "Yes, he's one of us."

"Another survivor." Allan nodded. "Is he a friend of yours?"

"Yes."

"Did he come back with you? Is he dangerous? What can he do?"

"I'm not telling you anything else," Hara snapped. "Leave me alone. I have help, and that's all that matters. If I'm lucky, I'll never see you again. But I haven't been so lucky lately, have I?"

"Hara, wait!" Allan pleaded, but she had already hung up.

Groaning angrily, Allan threw his phone at the floor and it broke into several pieces, but he didn't care. Hara's attitude towards him had finally allowed him to make a decision. If she was going to accuse him of working for the other side, then he was going to show her just how much of a problem he could actually be to her. He was going to that apartment complex, where the FBI, S.W.A.T., and the local police were waiting for her, and he was going to tell them anything that could be used to stop her. Hara might want to be the bad person now, but Allan was going to show her that it was never too late to keep fighting for what they both knew was right.

✳ ✳ ✳

Around 7:30, Perry and Odau were briefing everyone on the situation. They were at the empty apartment complex, trying frantically to get things organized before nightfall. People were to be posted in every room on all three floors, and some around the building as well. Snipers would watch out the windows for the girl's approach and also watch the targeted houses should she change her plan, and in case they missed her—which would be nearly impossible considering they had eyes at every angle—there would be a man watching the door. Due to the amount of rooms in the building and the amount of personnel available, there were to be two to a room. One sniper, one watchdog. Pairs and nothing more. Perry's colleagues had arrived moments before from Pittsburgh, so he would be stationed on the third floor with his partner, Renee Michaels. Andy Martinson and Jaz Hersh would be right next door.

Perry and Odau had decided against warning the parents of the targets. If they did, it would only cause them to panic and if Hara sensed something was wrong there was a good chance they wouldn't catch her that night. They simply warned everyone in the area that there was a drug bust underway and anyone caught within one hundred yards of the building after dark would be arrested.

In less than an hour the sun would be setting, and the two men were frantically moving about to get everyone prepared for what might happen later. What they didn't notice, because they weren't looking for her at that moment, was Hara. She and Jack had pulled up in the blue Lamborghini before any of them had even arrived. Hara had used her abilities to trick them so no one would consciously notice the vehicle sitting there, just yards away from Perry and Odau, and they would also subconsciously avoid it. They didn't know the car was there, but at the same time they did.

Hara watched Agent Perry bounce about, giving and receiving information. She hadn't seen Perry in so long… Ever since the war really picked up the pace, almost everyone in her society had lost track of him. He had been such a good man, and most likely still was. He had been one of the kindest people, especially to her when many people avoided her because of her rare gift. The sad thing was that he wouldn't remember her. Of course he wouldn't! He had aimed a gun at her. The Perry she knew would never have done that. The Perry she was looking at out the windshield was a completely different person from the man she had grown up around. He didn't yet know about the war. He didn't know about anything that had happened. For the time being, she was just going to have to deal with a clueless Perry, no matter how irritated it made her.

"It's weird seeing him here," she muttered.

Jack snickered and turned to her. "And you're telling *me* this?"

He had a point. Hara may have thought it was strange, but it was more of a shock to Jack than anyone. "You look just like him," she said, though he already knew that much. It was bizarre to look at the two men together. They both had the same eyes, same hair, same face, same figure, everything! The only difference was that Perry was taller and older.

Jack nodded. "Yeah."

"Don't get caught," she instructed him. "They'll ask questions. Questions we can't afford to answer."

They both looked to the left as another vehicle whizzed past them, skidding to a halt alongside Perry and the lieutenant. It wasn't any type of law enforcement vehicle, so they both looked on curiously to see who else was coming to help them. A terrible rage swept through Hara when she saw Allan Brown jump out of the car and rush to Perry.

"What…?" Jack said in confusion, leaning forward. "What is he…he's helping them?"

"Apparently," Hara grumbled, trying to contain her fury. She listened in to his mind to hear the conversation.

"Hara contacted me again!" Allan said breathlessly. "She just wanted me to tell you that she's coming at 10:30, and she wanted me to remind you all to stay out of her way."

"Well, the exact time is helpful," Odau said. "But I don't see how reminding us about something we already know is beneficial to us."

What an ass.

"That's not all," Allan said, ignoring the lieutenant's attitude. "She's not in this alone."

"There's someone else helping her?" Odau said in disbelief.

"Who is this person?" Perry demanded. "Is he someone like her?"

"He's someone like Hara," Allan told them. "But I don't know who it is. She wouldn't tell me."

"She trusted you enough to tell you she has a friend but she won't tell you who her friend is?" Odau asked in an irritated voice.

"I really don't know what to tell you anymore," Allan snapped impatiently. "She asked for my help and I denied it, so now she's not telling me anymore. I'm sorry that's an inconvenience for you!"

"Alright, enough!" Perry ordered, pulling out his radio and speaking into it. "This is Agent Perry. Suspects will be arriving at approximately 22:30. There will be two suspects; one is the female, the second is male…"

Perry continued, but Hara and Jack tuned the rest of it out. Hara was too angry to listen. She had told Allan to deliver the message, but the fact that he had turned against her still drove her crazy. "I guess we know now where his loyalties lie," she growled.

"That backstabbing son of a bitch," Jack said angrily.

Hate was pulsing through her body, and in return for Allan's treachery, she sent him a very violent thought. She smiled as Allan's entire body tensed up and he stumbled backwards. He looked around in surprise, sensing her presence but not knowing where she was hiding. At first he appeared determined to go look for her. But a moment later, he shrugged the feeling off, got into his car, and drove away.

Hara chuckled to herself. Her mind games could have an amusing effect on people. As time went on she was finding that playing with people's heads was actually quite entertaining. And Allan had earned the mental torture, so that made it all the more fun.

"You are so cruel," Jack muttered, shaking his head in disapproval.

Hara turned and gave him a dirty look. What did he know? He hadn't gone through half of the things she had gone through! Sure, she had become crueler due to the horrors she had survived, but did Jack need to comment?

Jack wasn't afraid of Hara. Yet. That was why all his mental defenses were down. Narrowing her eyes at him, Hara sent him the same thought she had sent Allan.

He hadn't been looking at her, but he didn't need to be for Hara to do her work. His body went rigid as Allan's had and he gasped from the shock. He turned towards her, intense fear on his face. "Stop it!" he whispered.

She didn't. She didn't want to. She sent him more.

"Hara, please!" he pleaded, his eyes widening as Hara began twisting the already gruesome images.

So she was cruel? Wasn't he about to commit the same crime as her? It wasn't okay for her to do but it was for him?

"You're a hypocrite," Hara hissed at him.

"Please, stop!" Jack gasped, and sent her a desperate thought back. Don't do this to me, too!

That was when Hara paused to take a look at herself. What was she doing? She was torturing her friend. After what she had endured, did she really want to put others through that same thing? Especially if he was her friend? What was wrong with her?

She pulled out of his head and he gasped again, staring at her in confusion. Hara was disgusted with herself for what she had done. She had become so bitter from her experiences that she was treating everyone like an enemy, even the last few people who cared about her, the ones she had held close. She was pushing everyone away. First Daniel, and then Allan, and now Jack! Who would she have left to go home to if she pushed everyone away?

Hara had done it. She had finally gotten to the point where she was willing to torture others for her own satisfaction. She had done it, and she was bound to do it again.

"I'm sorry..." she breathed, and then tried to get out of the car.

"No!" Jack cried, grabbing her arm and pulling her back.

"I'm sorry!" she sobbed. "I'm sorry, I'm sorry, I'm sorry..."

"You can't go out there!" Jack whispered fiercely, taking hold of both her wrists as she attempted to leave again. "If they see you, they'll hurt you!"

Hara looked him in the eye, full of disbelief. "Why are you protecting me?" she demanded as tears poured out of her eyes. "I'm a monster!"

Jack stared at her silently before telling her forcefully, "You're not!"

"I'm not?" she repeated, and couldn't help but laugh. "Look what I've become! Look what I'm about to do!"

Jack pulled her closer so their faces were nearly touching. "You are not a monster!" he told her through his teeth. "That bastard screwed you up! It's not your fault! You never asked for any of this! You're a good person! He altered your judgment; you don't know when you're taking things too far. That's not your fault!"

"I could kill you," Hara whispered, staring him down. "I could kill you, Jack."

He nodded. "I know. I know..."

"Then why are you still helping me?" Hara cried. "You need to stay as far away from me as you can! You're not safe near me! I almost hurt you, and it's bound to happen again!" She stared at him in bewilderment before repeating, "I can feel that you're bothered by what just happened. Why are you still helping me?"

As Jack gazed back at her, he answered her bluntly, "Because I love you."

Shocked, Hara shook her head furiously. "Why? Look what I'm doing! I'm about to kill innocent kids and make you do it with me! I've lost it!" She struggled to get out of the car again, but Jack held her back. "Let go!"

"Look at me!" he commanded. When she wouldn't, he repeated his order louder. "We can't stop now!" he told her when she met his eyes again. "Not after how far we've come! We are so close to fixing everything. We can't give up when we are this close!" Leaning closer, he whispered, "Killing them will fix everything."

Realizing that what he was saying was true, her emotions left her and she hardened again. "Yes," she muttered, nodding. "It will."

Jack stared at her uncertainly but then released her. Hara gazed out the windshield and he watched her for a while. "Can I ask you something?" he asked finally.

Hara shrugged. "Sure," she said.

"All those years ago, when you told me if things didn't work out between you and Bo…"

"Jack," Hara warned, clenching her fists by her sides. She didn't want to think about Bo. Thoughts of him would surely break her down again.

"Just answer me this," he persisted. "When you said we could be together if things didn't work out, did you really mean it? Or did you just say that to give me hope?"

Slowly turning back to him, she assured, "I meant it." She added as his lips began to form a small smile, "At the time. But as you do recall, things did work out."

Jack turned away from her and he bit his lip, his thoughts filled with jealousy.

She didn't want to dwell on the past anymore. "We need to figure out exactly what they're planning to do, so we can work around them." She glanced in his direction. "Can you get inside one of their heads and see their strategy?"

"Yeah," Jack said.

"Use Perry," she instructed, and raised an eyebrow. "He shouldn't be too hard for you."

Jack gave a small smile and took a deep breath. Hara felt him aiming all his concentration on Perry, and she turned to watch him. Slowly, his pupils dilated until they were almost blocking out the entire iris. He was in. It would only take about a minute for him to get everything they needed.

✳ ✳ ✳

By 10:25, everyone was anxiously waiting for Hara's arrival, just minutes away. Mayor Brown had returned to observe the operation.

Agents and officers were checking their watches every couple of seconds, each second feeling to them like much longer. Although they all wanted to keep tabs on everything occurring, every slight movement, everyone was too wary to speak. Nobody could foresee what would happen that night. Many had been assured that it would all end in their favor, but deep down, every single one of them had a terrible feeling that nothing was going to end well. None of them were sure, but deep down they all knew. A calamity was on its way...

✳ ✳ ✳

Thanks to the vulnerable mind of Shawn Perry, Hara and Jack got all the information they needed to kill the kids and escape without a scratch. They knew what everyone's positions would be and exactly how they were operating. There wasn't anything they didn't know.

They now stood pressed up against the side of the building. They had been hiding in the shadows for several minutes. The worst of what they needed to get through was behind them. When they had finally dared to leave the Lamborghini, they both knew that the snipers were on the lookout for her and this new friend they had heard about. Hara had masked the two of them like she had their vehicle so no one would notice them. Once they eased their way inside, there was only the risk of two people at most seeing them at a time instead of ten.

Hara could hear Jack's heart pounding in his chest and could hear the quickening of his breath. Adrenaline was pumping through him. He was scared, although he would never admit that to her. Carefully reaching towards him, she grasped his hand in hers and sent him soothing thoughts. She had felt extremely calm the entire time, so she projected that feeling to him. Before long, she felt most of his tension leave him.

"Thanks," he breathed gratefully.

It was 10:29. "Time to go," she told him. There was a door just inches to her left. Masking the door as well, she motioned with her hand for it to open and it did. Very slowly, it creaked open just enough for them to slip through silently. It was completely dark inside, but that was no problem for Hara. She saw just as well in the dark as she did in the light.

She noticed for the first time that the whole building was completely silent. No one was speaking. No one was moving. No one was even blinking. Deep down, they knew to be afraid of her. Their instincts were correct.

They crept up the stairwell to the third floor. That was when she stopped and turned to Jack. This was the place where neither of them dared speak aloud. *I'm going to block out their radio signals now*, she told her friend. *After I do that, we have to move quickly. They're going to panic when their communications are gone and that will put us at greater risk. Take yours out and then meet me in the room at the opposite end of the floor. And be careful.*

Don't worry about me, Jack said, smiling at her in the dark.

Feeling herself tense up, she frowned at him stubbornly. She didn't want him to feel that she cared too much. *I'm not worried about you. If you die or get caught, then I'm out a colleague.*

Jack rolled his eyes and shook his head but didn't stop smiling. An older, more tender part of Hara most likely cared for Jack's wellbeing, but at the moment she was in predator mode. Nothing and nobody meant more to her than her own wellbeing.

We are experiencing technical difficulties, Hara joked, leaning her head back against the wall and concentrating. Jack kept his mind quiet while she worked. What she was about to perform was not a talent she was particularly good at, and he knew that. She couldn't afford any distractions.

Breathing deeply, she allowed her eyes to flutter shut. Once her eyes were closed, she could see far more than she could when they were open. Her mind was in the deep infinity of space, able to go wherever she wished. But she only wished it to go to one place, a place not very far away but also a place that was very difficult to stay in. Inside her head Hara was capable of seeing, or sensing, everything that is invisible to the naked eye. For example, radio waves. She could sense all the different radio waves pulsating through the air around her, and when she listened hard enough she was able to hear the high pitched buzz they created. Once she found them, she had to sort them out and find the two she was searching for. It could be very difficult, especially around ordinary people. They always had so many different frequencies surrounding them. There were signals from cell phones, satellite televisions, radios, planes in the sky above them, walkie-talkies…

Aha! Hara thought to herself, smiling. *Found one.* Shuffling through the various noises and buzzing in her head, she finally found the second frequency, the frequency connecting all the earpieces. Focusing on the two frequencies, Hara blocked them. The thing she liked about radio waves was that they were like string; they could be cut. Unfortunately, they didn't stay cut. If she didn't concentrate hard enough on them, they could reconnect.

Now that the only forms of communication between the law enforcers were jammed, Hara and Jack could proceed with their mission. Hara heard the men and women in the rooms whispering to each other, their troubled thoughts wondering what had just happened. The whispers only lasted for a few seconds. Within moments the volume of their speech had doubled. They were getting antsy. Hara heard the voice of Allan Brown from down the hall, speaking to two of Lieutenant Odau's detectives, Maggie Finchly and Garrick Aubrey.

"She's here," he announced gravely.

Traitor.

Looking back to Jack, Hara opened her eyes and told him, *Thirty seconds*. That was the longest she felt she could hold the frequencies for. She was already struggling to hold onto them.

Nodding, Jack proceeded to his designated room, the first door on the right. Hara heard an *oof!* and the sounds of a struggle once he was inside, but then it was quiet. Jack had taken control of the room quite easily. Now, it was Hara's turn. She walked to the first door on the left but stopped before crossing the threshold. One S.W.A.T. member was still watching the door while the one who was supposed to be watching the street was fumbling with his radio and earpiece, attempting to make contact with someone, anyone, in the building. A moment later, the S.W.A.T. member guarding the door turned his back on the hallway, directing his attention to the other.

"You have to keep watching for her!" he hissed as his colleague continued futzing with his equipment.

Hara began her silent entrance into the room. She strode inside towards them as they argued. She was so quiet that the second S.W.A.T. member almost didn't see her at all. As he was telling the first man, "Then you figure out what's going on with our coms!" his eyes were drawn to her. The surprised expression froze on his face and he started to yell, "David, behind you!" But before the warning was completely out of his mouth, Hara struck David in the back of the neck and he dropped to the floor. The second man, Jake, took his rifle from its stand at the window and started to turn it on her. Hara knocked it from his hand with barely an effort and then hit him in the throat. He fell to the floor too, but he hadn't been knocked unconscious like David. At first, he lay there with a pained and stunned expression. The coughing and gasping then began. Jake clutched his throat as tears came to his eyes from the blow. His breathing had a raggedy sound to it, and Hara knew she had damaged his windpipe.

She suddenly felt a pang of remorse for hurting him; the reason behind that was unclear to her. Why should she feel remorse for hurting a mere human, after everything his kind had done to hers? He wasn't like her, and he never would be. So why did it hurt her to see him in pain?

Hara stepped to his side and crouched beside him. Jake stared at her in terror as he continued to gasp for breath and tried to push himself away from her. "Don't kill me!" he begged her, his voice raspy and forced. "Please, I have a baby…"

"I'm not going to kill you, Jake," Hara murmured, watching his movements curiously. He, a trained killer, was afraid of her. He didn't even know what she was, but he, a grown man who had been trained to kill, was scared of her.

Jake blinked in surprise at the sound of his name, but shook it off a moment later. Hara had lost her grip on the frequencies and now his walkie-talkie was erupting with the shouts of others in the building. He reached for it at his belt, his earpiece lost in the struggle, but Hara stopped him easily.

"Look at me," she ordered, her voice barely a breath in the air.

Startled, Jake's eyes met hers again. It was a mistake he unknowingly made, but he made it all the same. Once their eyes locked, Hara had complete control over his entire body. She held his mind in hers. She had no intention of letting go. Jake was frozen, unable to move. Hara felt his fear as he realized he was helpless. After giving him a moment to comprehend what she was doing to him, she told him what she wanted him to do. And he did it.

Raising the walkie-talkie to his mouth, he said into it, his voice still raspy and quavering, "She's on the second floor."

✳ ✳ ✳

The fact that Allan Brown had no idea who could be assisting Hara irritated him. Everything else about her plot had been either obvious from the beginning or easily figured out. But no matter how hard he pondered, no matter how many faces ran through his mind, he could not figure out who could possibly be aiding her. All of her friends were dead or were still locked away. Allan knew the conditions of most of those who were close to her. None of them fit the job. She hadn't been lying to him. Hara was proud. If she were alone she would have shouted it to the world. So who could it be? Aside from Daniel and Meg, pretty much everyone else they knew was dead.

"They're all dead," Allan muttered aloud, shaking his head in frustration. "Everyone's dead…"

"Sir?"

Jerking around in surprise, Allan saw that Detective Finchly had overheard him and was staring at him in confusion. Most people would have had trouble seeing her face in the blackness of the room, but he could see her clear as day. It was nearly 10:30, and to keep their presence unknown they kept the rooms dark. "Nothing," he mumbled, shaking his thoughts off as he turned back to the window. He would find out who Hara's friend was soon enough. For the time being he should just focus on identifying the targets.

The room he was in held him, Finchly, and Detective Aubrey. Allan had been asked to assist two detectives in case he could identify Hara's accomplice. Meg was doing the same thing on the opposite side of the hallway. His room had a clear view of the Burma household. As he gazed out at the small, two-story home, he began to question his decision again. He was betraying his mission, his family, by helping Perry and Odau. He had made a promise to his dead family and dying race that he would do whatever it took to set a better course for the future. He had sworn he would stay in the fight until the very end, until his people could be free again, no matter what obstacles he encountered. By helping the humans he was breaking that promise. What was he planning to accomplish by fighting Hara? Although they used different tactics, they both wanted the same thing. They wanted to save their race and go home. Hara's operation would help that happen much quicker than anything he had been doing so far, so why was he fighting her?

Because killing people is the only thing that separates us from them, he reminded himself firmly. His people were the good people, and Allan planned for it to stay that way. He would stop Hara from committing this savage act, and then they would work together to fix the catastrophe some other way.

Suddenly, Finchly's radio began emitting a high-pitched screech that caused Allan's eardrums to rattle. Aubrey was having the same problem. They both pressed their transmit buttons in hope of eliminating the shrill shriek, but had no luck. They both tried to contact their colleagues but received no reply.

"Sir, what's going on?" Finchly demanded, continuing to fiddle with her radio.

"Is Hara causing this?" Aubrey asked nervously.

There was only one thing he knew of that could interrupt a signal like that. Glancing at his watch, he saw that it read 10:30 exactly.

"She's here," he whispered with increasing dread.

✳ ✳ ✳

"Will you please relax, Shawn?"

That was what Perry's partner, Renee Michaels, whispered to him shortly before 10:30. Perry took his eyes off of the street for the first time in a half hour. He looked at his partner standing beside him. She was smiling at him, but he could see that she was nervous too. Her pale blue eyes showed worry just like Perry's. It was so easy for something to go wrong, especially under these unusual circumstances, and they both knew it. But all the same, Renee didn't want the worry they were feeling to turn into panic.

Smiling back at her, Perry said, "That's easier said than done, and you know that."

"Yes, but Hara will be able to sense your tension from the next county if you don't calm down," Renee replied with a shrug, turning back to the window.

Perry watched as she brushed aside a stray strand of her blonde hair that had fallen out of her ponytail. In the dark of the room, with only the faint glow of an orange street lamp lighting up her face, he couldn't help but think how beautiful she was. As he felt that thought beginning to cross his mind, as it had numerous times in the past, he pushed it out of his head. He needed to be focusing on capturing Hara, not the extravagant level of beauty being posed by his partner. Silently scolding himself, he turned back to the window as well. But not before Renee noticed.

"You can stop staring at me like that all the time, you know," she said, peering out at the dark street through her pair of binoculars. They had been instructed to have one of the pair watch the street while the other watched the hallway, but they both knew that someone would see her on the street long before seeing her in the building. That was why they both chose to carefully keep an eye on the street below. "Agent Long already has his suspicions. We don't need anyone here coming to conclusions as well."

"When are we going to talk about this?" Perry asked her, struggling to keep his gaze on the ground and not on her.

"When are we going to talk about what?"

Rolling his eyes, Perry said through his teeth, "You know what."

After a pause, Renee replied, "Not right now."

"We can't avoid the subject forever, you know."

"I know, but now isn't the time."

"I know now isn't the time. I'm just saying that we need to make time."

"Shawn, we have a job to do!"

"Do you two want to keep it down in there?" Andy Martinson's voice said in Perry's earpiece. He and Jaz Hersh were in the next room, and they must have overheard their discussion. The walls in that building must have been really thin. "I understand how irresistible you both are to each other, but do you mind keeping your personal lives in your personal lives?"

Perry started to reach up to his earpiece to snap back, but Renee was already on it.

"Gladly, Andy," she muttered to him. "And while we're at it, why don't you and Jaz do the same?"

"Hey, that's been over for a while," Andy shot back. "And we at least kept our jobs and our personal lives separate."

"We're working on it, Andrew. It would be a lot easier if you would just stay out of it."

"Okay, alright. But can you at least keep it down? We're trying to keep an eye out for a psychotic teenage girl."

"Will you shut up?" Perry snapped at him.

He heard Andy start to reply in his defense, but his voice was abruptly cut off when an unearthly screech erupted from his earpiece. Crying out it pain and surprise, Perry and Renee both pulled their earpieces out of their ears and dropped them to the floor.

"What the hell?" Perry said, taking his radio from his belt and attempting to contact his colleagues with it. But that too was emitting a horrible shriek. "Are you having the same problem?" he asked Renee.

"Everyone's having the same problem!" Renee said, fumbling with her radio as well. She was right. Perry could hear shouts coming from the adjacent rooms, other officers yelling to find out what was wrong. "I thought we had these connections checked before we got ourselves situated?"

Perry glanced down at his watch and pressed the button to make it light up. It read 10:30 exactly. Was it really possible for Hara to jam their transmissions?

"Out the window!" Perry cried, looking through the scope in his rifle and scanning the street below. "She's here! Everyone keep watching for her!" He knew nobody besides Renee could hear him over the screeching sound, but he yelled it anyway. It was a distraction thrown at them by Hara, and while they would all be confused and unable to communicate, she would use that opening to get into the building.

Renee listened to him and looked through her scope as well. "Do you see her? I can't see anything!"

"I don't see her either," Perry replied, but he continued to search. He saw several lights from houses turn on across the street due to the noise their equipment was making. A few curtains were brushed aside as people looked out at the building, and a few even stepped outside onto their porches. But aside from those individuals, he saw no one approaching the building.

A few seconds later, the shrieking stopped and the confused shouts of others in the building could be heard over the radios. Picking his up from the floor where he had dropped it, he said loudly through the jumbled mess, "Does anyone have her in their sight? Stop shouting, God damn it! Somebody answer me! Is she in anybody's sight?"

He listened for a few seconds, but nobody was answering his questions. Nobody could hear him, because everyone was talking into their radios at once, demanding to know what happened. And then, in a very calm and very soft tone, Perry heard an answer.

"She's on the second floor."

Others heard it too, because the next thing Perry heard was the pounding footsteps of everyone on his floor running out of their rooms and down the hall towards the stairwell. Renee had turned and fled the room before he reacted.

"Renee!" he cried, running after her.

115

"Shawn, come on!" he heard her yell back to him. "We can't let her get past us again!"

Perry hung a quick right out the door in an attempt to catch up with her, but he was knocked clean off his feet as someone from the next room slammed into him on their way out.

"Sorry, Perry!" Jaz Hersh apologized as she followed Andy Martinson, Renee, and the rest of the agents on that floor. She apologized, but she didn't stop to help him.

Because of his fall, he was the last one on the floor. It was quiet in a spooky way, the floor below him noisy with life but the air around him completely silent. Groaning in frustration and humiliation, Perry started to leave the hallway to enter the stairwell. He stopped dead in his tracks when he heard the familiar sound of a firearm being cocked. Turning slowly, his eyes landed on the threshold of the first door on the left. The silence he heard following the loud click made him believe at first that he was imagining things. But then he took a moment to observe the doorway of the room from which he had heard it, and he knew something wasn't right. They had all been instructed to keep the doors to their assigned rooms open in the event of a situation, but the door to this room was closed. Perry thought over whether it could have been bumped by someone on their way out, but he decided that didn't seem very likely.

Hesitantly, Perry moved over to the door, being careful to step silently. He still wasn't certain there was actually anyone inside. Still, he wasn't convinced that there wasn't. Placing a hand on the wooden door, he gave it a light push. What he saw inside nearly made him gasp in horror.

In the dim light of the streetlamps, he saw the slim, feminine body of a young woman. She was dressed in all black, her long brown hair flowing down her back. She was at the window, the stand that held the rifle for each sniper now supporting a weapon of hers. It looked like any other rifle, although hers was much larger. She was looking through and adjusting the scope of her weapon.

Perry could only see her back, but he knew who it was immediately. He looked down at the two unconscious men in S.W.A.T. uniforms lying on the floor. How had a girl with no visible physical strength take down two grown, trained men? How had she gotten into the building without being seen? If she was already inside the room and getting her equipment set up, she had to have been there before the announcement that had sent everyone scrambling to the second floor. That meant she had gotten into the building before the electronic malfunction. How had she gotten past without being seen? They had eyes aimed in every direction. It was impossible. But then again, it would seem that numerous things about this girl were impossible.

By the way she slowly turned her head and looked at him over her shoulder, Hara must have already known he was there. Her expression was strangely calm, not the least bit disturbed by the act she was about to carry out. For a few moments the two of them just gazed into each other's eyes. Perry wanted to point his gun at her and demand that she step away from the rifle, but he couldn't. He couldn't look away, and he couldn't move. Something wasn't right about that girl. It wasn't because she was about to engage in something unspeakable; it was because Perry was completely mesmerized by her. Every ounce of instinct in his body was screaming at him to pull the trigger or yell for assistance, but he couldn't even open his mouth. A strange, tingly sense of tranquility was paralyzing him.

It may have simply been a figment of Perry's imagination, but he could swear that Hara's eyes were glowing like a cat's. That was the thought running through his mind when he heard the voice whisper inside his head.

Shh. Be quiet. Don't make a sound. That was what his brain was telling him. At least, he thought it was his brain telling him that. He held still, wanting to move and call for help, but at the same time telling himself to keep quiet.

While Perry stood frozen, Hara turned back to her large weapon and looked into her scope. Perry could see it was aimed at the Burma household. When she broke eye contact with him, Perry suddenly found himself capable of movement again. The numbness overpowering him washed away, and his heart began to pound in realization of what was going to happen if he didn't get over to Hara immediately. As Hara reached up and put her finger on the trigger, Perry lurched forward and screamed, "No!"

He was too late…

The blasting sound of a gunshot filled the air, its force echoing through Perry's entire body. He ran forward, even though he knew he was too late to stop her. Just before he reached her, Hara spun around. Surprised, Perry attempted to skid to a stop and duck out of the way, but Hara had whipped her arm at his head before he could react. Perry's vision turned bright red as her arm collided with his skull. The force of the blow caused him to stumble backwards and lose his grip on his gun. He tripped over one of the unconscious S.W.A.T. members and then crashed to the ground, hearing his weapon clatter to the floor several feet away. Sprawled on his back, Perry gasped at the shocking amount of pain he was in. He had expected the strike to hurt, but nowhere near that intensely. His head was throbbing and spinning uncontrollably. She had really hurt him.

When his eyes managed to focus enough to put pictures with the sounds he was hearing, he saw that Hara had taken apart her weapon and was placing the pieces in her belt. He tried to sit up, but ended up dropping his head back down against the floor again. With a pained groan, he watched Hara as she began to walk to the door. She was going to get away, and there was absolutely nothing he could do to stop her.

But a faint hope was given to him when he suddenly realized that a rifle belonging to one of the S.W.A.T. members was lying just feet from his grasp. If he could just move quickly enough, despite his pain, he could get the weapon and put a dart into her leg before she could make an escape. He had hoped to capture her unharmed, and that was how this was going to end. It was very likely that the child she had fired on had died, and the deaths were going to end with one.

Hara stopped abruptly and froze. She started to turn back to him. Her eyes landed on Perry's, and she glared at him, her face barely visible in the faint orange light.

She knows how you think, Daniel Marcus had told him. He had been telling the truth. But that was a little too abrupt to be a prediction. She had heard him think his plan.

Launching himself to his feet, Perry scrambled for the rifle. But as his hand wrapped around it, her hand wrapped around his wrist. Snapping his head up to meet her eyes once more, she saw them narrowed in ire. Then an emotion struck him that he never expected to feel: fear. Looking into her eyes was like gazing into the eyes of a predator, a predator that was certain to go for the kill.

An agonizing burning sensation flared where Hara's hand was. It was like a fire had been lit and was continuing to burn on his wrist. As Hara's glare became more intense, so did the heat. The feeling was overwhelming, and before he could attempt to stop himself, Perry was screaming from the pain.

"Drop it," Hara growled at him.

Perry did what she said, opening his hand and releasing the rifle. He bit down on his tongue to suppress his cries. His arm felt as if it were in a vat full of acid, and the pain continued to increase with every second she held on.

Suddenly, Hara's grip loosened and her expression changed from anger to confusion. Her eyes widened in shock. "You?" she breathed. She must have recognized him from Allan Brown's office. She had worn a similar expression the first time they had laid eyes on each other. What was so shocking about him? She released his wrist immediately, and Perry fell back down again, gasping and clutching his scorched hand.

Hara stared down at him in alarm. She was horrified by what she just did. There was clearly something about Perry that held meaning to Hara if she didn't want him hurt. Something that Perry didn't know about himself.

Finally finding his voice, Perry sucked in a lungful of air and yelled, "Help!" But Hara pounced on him in an instant. Pinning his good arm down with one hand and covering his mouth with the other, Hara glared at him again. This time, there was some compassion burning in her eyes.

"Quiet, Perry!" she hissed at him, tightening her grip on his arm as he began struggling to get her off of him. His efforts were pointless; he was injured, and somehow Hara seemed to be twice as strong as him. It was odd; she did strike him as a tough, powerful girl, but this was beyond his expectations. Perry could barely move under her, and it wasn't due to her weight. She weighed maybe one hundred thirty at most. She was just so strong! He was completely powerless beneath her, and his fate rested with whatever she decided to do to him next.

Another gunshot sounded from somewhere behind him, causing both him and Hara to flinch. A moment later, there was another shot. He had completely forgotten about her partner in crime. And if they were both good shots as Perry was dreading, there were now three dead children.

Hara sighed and shook her head. "You shouldn't have tried to interfere," she told him softly. "You were too late, anyway."

As Perry had predicted after seeing Hara's discomfort in injuring him, Hara didn't do anything more to him. She just sat on top of him, gazing into his eyes with that look of curiosity. She kept her hand planted firmly over his mouth, and when they heard the sounds of footsteps pounding up the stairwell, she spoke again.

"Sleep now," she said, her gaze unwavering. Without apparent cause, a sudden sense of exhaustion washed over him. His eyelids drooped, and the last thing he saw before he blacked out was Hara's intriguing eyes, which held all the answers to the mystery that was developing more and more with each passing hour.

✳ ✳ ✳

When Hara realized that the man who had confronted her was Shawn Perry, she was absolutely horrified. She had hit him over the head hard enough to cause serious damage, and she knew that if anything happened to him it would result in major problems for everyone. After she saw it was him, she immediately scanned his brain for any signs of trauma. When she was certain that all she had inflicted upon him was a mild concussion, she told his mind to shut down for a while, another talent she had discovered in her youth. Hara knew that sleep would be the best thing for him after a blow like that.

She had left Perry laying there. She wasn't abandoning him; his colleagues were pounding their way up the stairs and would stumble upon his unconscious form within seconds. Her job was to avoid getting caught in the process.

"Jack!" She called to him from across the hall, wanting to get them both out of there rather quickly. They had just killed three children, and they were about to go take out the fourth. Things were about to get very ugly in that neighborhood, and it would be especially bad if they were captured and arrested.

As Jack came out to meet her, Hara placed the last piece of her weapon in her belt. The rifle looked almost identical to the rifles that the snipers in the building were using, because her model was based on those weapons. Hers was actually a prototype, designed and constructed by Daniel Marcus himself. In case a time such as this arose, when they would need to defend themselves with deadly force in order to survive, their society had begun to design deadly weapons. It was against their beliefs to create such terrible things, but when people started dying, they knew something would have to be done to defend themselves. The ammunition used was like nothing the human world had ever seen before, or even thought up. The bullet casing was made from ordinary alloys, but the interior of each slug contained a high concentration of Ballium, a genetically-engineered virus that attacks the cells of the unlucky host. When the bullet made contact with a living organism, such as the child she had just shot, the outer casing would break apart, releasing the deadly disease into the bloodstream. Every cell in the body would then be destroyed by the infection within a matter of seconds, killing the host. As soon as the victim died, the disease would die as well, having no more cells to give it energy. If the child didn't die from the initial gunshot, the Ballium would finish him off. But, because the disease was so terribly dangerous, they had created a failsafe. The body of a human and the body of someone like Hara were not different in appearance, but they were quite different internally. Scientists manipulated the virus to recognize what species it was infecting. If it was inside someone like Hara, it would self-destruct. Therefore, there would be no unwanted fatalities of her kind. But even with that weapon on their side, there were plenty of unwanted fatalities.

They're coming up the stairs! Jack warned her as he rushed out of his room. There was fear in his eyes. They had no time to run, and he thought they were going to be caught.

"Take my hand," she ordered, holding hers out to him.

He obeyed. As soon as his fingers grasped hers, the first FBI agents burst into the hallway, guns drawn. Hara acted quickly. Before the image of the two of them registered in the agents' minds, Hara put a mental shield around herself and Jack. Because the two of them were touching, it was much easier for Hara to do this. All of the agents and officers would come into the hallway, and although they would subconsciously know they were there and be sure to avoid running into them, they would look right past Hara and Jack without so much as a suspicious thought.

"Check every room!" the first agent commanded, running into the room Hara had just left. "Oh God, Perry! I need a medic in here! We have three men down! Three men down!"

The agents and officers kept flooding in. Hara watched every single one of them carefully as they passed, making sure that none of them figured out what she was doing. She had to fight her urge to attack Lieutenant Odau as he passed by, and Jack squeezed her hand when he felt her anger. That man's bastard of a son had been the cause of all the destruction done to her home and her people. Because of that man, her people barely had a chance in the world.

After a few moments, people stopped running past them from the stairwell. Breathing a sigh of relief, Jack pulled at her hand to try to get her to go down the stairwell with him, but Hara refused to move. She stared straight ahead into the darkness of the stairwell, knowing that there were still two more people coming. Two people who, even though she was very cross with them, she still wanted to see one last time. She knew that after they had abandoned their mission—abandoned their race—they wouldn't be coming back with her and Jack once she killed Odau's son. They wouldn't have the courage to face their people again.

Allan Brown and Meg Hopper ascended the final steps slowly, grim expressions on their faces. They knew that all three of the children had been killed, and they now knew that they should have joined up with Hara and Jack when they had the chance. When the two of them escaped, killed Jackson Odau, and were never heard from again, it would be Allan, Daniel, and Meg that would end up being incriminated. They would most likely end up in one of the humans' awful prisons for the rest of their lives. Then again, the whole human world was a prison. They had been trapped in a prison for two years already...

The two of them were also unable to see through Hara's shield, so they started to walk around them and go find a way to help. As they did so, Hara felt a sudden burst of anger at their treachery. Both of them stopped short and inhaled sharply. They turned their heads and stared at her. Neither of them was able to see her, but they knew she was there. For a few moments they all simply stared at each other, and then Allan and Meg nodded to her simultaneously. They had accepted their mistake. They were saying goodbye.

Jack pulled at Hara's hand again. He knew they needed to get out of there quickly.

Her bitterness toward them faded. She wanted them to come with her. Why couldn't they just come with her? It was so much easier...

Come on, Jack murmured to her, and she gave up against his pull. She felt Allan and Meg's eyes on them as they rushed down the stairs. What would happen to them after she left, she didn't know.

When they made it outside and were walking briskly towards their stolen Lamborghini, Jack asked her, "Since we killed the first three, do you think we still need to kill Jackson Odau?"

Hara glanced at him dubiously. "Even if we did do enough to alter things, I'm still going to kill him. Slowly. I owe him that much."

Nodding understandingly, Jack started to jog. "Then we'd better get it over with quickly," he said. "Because I have a strong feeling that Allan is going to tell Odau, and if that happens we're going to have a difficult time carrying this out."

✳ ✳ ✳

"Perry? Perry! Can you hear me? Perry! You have to wake up!"

Blinking rapidly, Perry tried to focus his eyes on the distraught face hovering over him. His head was throbbing, and the room around him felt like it was tilting. A light was being shined in his eyes, and he raised a hand to shield them as he groaned from the pain.

"Perry, are you alright?" Martinson was asking him, patting him on the shoulder. His voice was thick with worry and grief, and Perry knew that whatever had happened after his confrontation with Hara was not good. He attempted to sit up, but several hands pushed him back down.

"Don't try to sit up just yet," an unfamiliar male voice said, and Perry saw the medic leaning over him. "Do you know where you are?" He started shining the light in his eyes again.

"Yeah," Perry mumbled, swatting his hands away. He glanced up at the people anxiously hovering over him. Along with Martinson were Hersh, Renee, Odau, and Detectives Finchly and Aubrey. "What happened? Did you go check the houses that were fired on?"

All six of Perry's colleagues looked away shamefully. With a sigh, Odau told him the terrible truth. "She...killed them," he whispered in anguish. "Three of them. There were only three gunshots, but we have to assume that she's going to find her fourth target and finish the job."

A mixture of emotions was coursing through Perry. He couldn't decide whether he was more angry or more grief-stricken. That girl—no, that murderer—had managed to sneak past all of their defenses completely unnoticed. Nobody had known her exact location until Perry discovered her in this room by accident. She was only a child; how could she evade capture like that? But more importantly, how could she bring herself to commit an act so vile?

"What were you doing in here, anyway?" Renee questioned. "Everyone else had gone downstairs but you came here. What happened?"

Groaning again from the pain in his head, Perry squinted up at her. "Something just didn't feel right to me. The door wasn't open and nothing seemed to make any sense. I came in to check it out and there she was at the window. I tried to stop her, but...I don't know. Something weird happened. Something unexplainable. I couldn't stop her before she pulled the trigger. And then there was somebody else in the room across the hall who fired on two other houses. This girl is going to be much more difficult to capture than we originally thought."

"What exactly happened that's so unexplainable?" Aubrey asked suspiciously.

"Yeah," Hersh piped in. "Could you at least try to describe it?"

Perry felt his face flush red. They were going to call him crazy or give him a look that said exactly the same thing. As he thought over what had happened, he realized just how crazy it sounded. "It was a really strange feeling," he started hesitantly. "I wanted to radio in for help, but she kept staring at me with those eyes. I swear, her eyes were glowing. I couldn't move. No matter how hard I tried, I was completely frozen. And as weird as it sounds, I felt like I was hearing her voice inside my head. She was telling me to be quiet and stay still. It was almost like...it was almost like she was..."

"Like she was controlling you?"

Everyone turned and looked over at Allan Brown standing in the doorway, with Meg Hopper hanging back behind him. They both had expressions of dread, knowing that they had failed to aid them in the capture of Hara and protection of the children. They knew that the blame was going to fall on them. Perry was already feeling his hostility being directed at them.

Scowling at him, Perry replied curtly, "Yes. That was exactly what it was like."

Staring back, Brown nodded. "Do you understand what I meant now? This isn't your average case. She's not your average criminal. Catching her will most likely be the most difficult task you will ever accomplish, should you actually manage it."

"You should have explained to us just how serious this is," Perry growled at him, and glared.

Heaving a sigh, Brown shook his head solemnly. "I tried," he whispered.

"You should have made us believe you!" Perry snapped. "You should have tried harder! We are not prepared for this!"

"I tried to tell you that too," Brown insisted softly.

Odau cut in. "Please, sir," he pleaded. "You're right. We should have listened to you, but we didn't take you completely seriously. I'm sorry. But right now we have a serious crisis on our hands. Hara and her unknown assistant just killed three young children, and she's on her way to kill a fourth. Please. I know you know who the fourth target is. I'm begging you, not as an officer but as a father, tell us who the other child is. I don't know why you want this kid dead, but I can't have another murder on my conscience. Please just tell us the name and we'll figure this mess out later."

At first, Perry was certain that Brown wasn't going to answer him. He held Odau's gaze for several endless seconds before he finally looked away and sighed in defeat. Running a hand through his blonde hair, he muttered in a voice that was nearly inaudible, "It's your son."

No one said anything. Perry's stomach felt as if it had turned inside out, and the looks on the faces of everyone else told him they were all feeling the same thing.

"My...my son?" Odau repeated quietly. "Jackson?"

Avoiding his eyes, Brown nodded very slowly.

"My son...is the fourth target...and you didn't tell me!" With an enraged cry, Odau shoved his way past the mayor and ran down the stairwell, screaming into his radio for every available unit to make its way to his house immediately. Right behind him were Finchly and Aubrey.

Forcing himself to deal with the horrible pain in his head, Perry pushed himself up. The medic immediately began to protest.

"Sir, I must insist that you remain here and wait for the ambulance."

"Look, my injuries aren't life threatening," Perry told him impatiently. "And his son doesn't have time to wait for me."

"Please, sir. You need to take it easy."

"Shawn, you should listen to him," Renee said sharply as Perry rose carefully to his feet.

"I promise you all I will get my head looked at," Perry assured them. "But not right now. We have a boy's life to save." He rushed out the door after Odau and started to run down the stairs. He paused halfway down the first flight, a wave of dizziness nearly causing him to fall. His FBI colleagues followed him and started to ask if he needed to sit down, but he kept going. He probably had a minor concussion, but he would deal with that at a different time. Right now, he had to worry about Odau's son.

The street was crawling with people. Officers, agents, paramedics, and frightened civilians were running around, yelling and calling out to each other. Blue and red lights were flashing everywhere, making Perry's headache worse. Sirens were blaring from numerous directions. It was complete and utter chaos.

When Perry reached the sidewalk, he feared he was too late to catch the lieutenant. But then he saw him, starting up his squad car and squealing down the street with Aubrey and Finchly in the car behind him.

"Lieutenant!" Perry cried, propelling his legs forward.

Odau saw Perry as he ran to his car, and he stopped for a moment to allow Perry to get in the passenger side. Perry hadn't even sat down before Odau was speeding away again.

Hara had slipped through their fingers once again, but Perry knew by the look of determination on Odau's face that she wouldn't slip past them again.

✳ ✳ ✳

The home of Lieutenant Graham Odau was surprisingly cute. It was a small two-story house with porches at both the front and back doors. A large flower garden enveloped the sidewalk on both sides of the house. Inside, Odau's wife, Jane, and his youngest daughter, Caroline, were asleep in their bedrooms on the first floor. On the second floor, his oldest daughter Sarah was chatting on the phone with her friend and Jackson was sleeping soundly. Aside from the soft chatter from Sarah's room, the house was silent. Hara knew all this because she was inside the house.

All along she had been expecting his house to look like something out of a horror movie; an old, decaying fortress filled with cobwebs and dead animals. But it was relatively normal. It was clean and well-maintained, not at all what she expected.

Hara was standing at the top of the stairs facing Jackson's room, which was at the end of the hall. The hall was pitch black and all she could hear was Sarah's soft conversation in her room a few feet down on the left. She could hear her own heart pounding in her chest, the anticipation nearly overwhelming her. This was her moment of redemption, when she killed the last child and set everything straight again. All she had to do was walk down the hall and step through the door... But there was something holding her back, causing her to linger at the stairway. She could sense the evil flowing from the kid's room, the darkness inviting her closer. Hara shuddered as disturbing memories from her past came flooding back to her, memories of the nights she'd lie awake in her cell, wondering when they were coming for her next. Then when they finally did come for her, there was the anxiety of what they'd do to her next. Would they just inject her with various chemicals to make her scream, or just flat out torture her to get her to perform? She was in enemy territory now. She was the one to cross the line this time. She was bringing the battle right back to herself by doing this. The only person she had ever feared would come for her if she didn't get this over with quickly.

Come on. You can do this. You're almost there! Jack sent the thought in a reassuring way, but Hara still couldn't help feeling uneasy. She had been so eager when they had killed the others, but now all she wanted to do was turn and run. Her fear of the man who had experimented on her for so long was what pushed her forward. She had to put an end to this.

I'm done running, she decided firmly, silently walking down the hall to the door. When she reached it, she stood before it, her heart pounding harder. A poem she had once read popped into her head. She couldn't recall the name, but she remembered a few of the words. There was something to do with marching into the jaws of death and hell. That was where she was headed.

Come on, Hara! Jack urged nervously.

Don't pressure me! Hara snapped back, fighting to keep her breathing under control. Jack was waiting just outside the house. She didn't want anyone interfering with what was about to happen, so she had him be the lookout for her, stationing him beside the front door. She didn't want Jack there when she killed Jackson. She wanted to be alone with him. Face to face. Just like she owed him.

What's the matter? he asked her. *You've been waiting to do this for so long.*

He was starting to get on her nerves. *Just be quiet,* she ordered curtly, and then blocked his pestering thoughts from hers. Gazing at the door before her, she raised her hand and made a gesturing motion with her fingers. The door silently swung open, revealing the sleeping child.

Looking upon the boy made her shiver. She could feel the evil flowing throughout the room, felt it pulling her forward. That boy may have been innocent, but that word was not something one could use to describe the man he would become. That boy was the reason her entire race had been wiped out. In this exact moment, the boy was innocent. But Hara couldn't wait around for the day he went sour to wipe him out of history. She had to act now. She had to prevent what was certain to come.

Jackson Odau had sandy-brown hair, just like his father, and even though he was young, she hated him so strongly that she had to restrain herself from marching right up to him and killing him where he slept. She had to do this the right way; take him back with her to show him what happened and then kill him slowly to make him understand the pain he had caused. The boy was lying on his side, his mouth slightly open with the blanket pulled up to his chin. His hair fell over his boyish face, and looking at him brought back memories of her own children...

Don't, she told herself forcefully. *Don't you dare think about them.* But it was already too late. The tears were streaming from her eyes, running down her cheeks and falling to the carpet below. That boy lying quietly before her was the cause of the deaths of her children, the cause of the death of her entire race. He was a child, but it was all his fault.

Violent, angry thoughts erupted from her. They were like bullets being fired from a gun. She couldn't even attempt to contain them. Since her thoughts were broadcasting to everyone within a block of her, Jackson heard her. Stirring, he rolled onto his back and his eyes blinked open. He saw his door wide open and Hara standing inside, and he squinted at her. "Mom?" he mumbled. When Hara didn't answer, he reached towards the table beside his bed to turn on his lamp. When the light flashed on, Jackson blinked to let his eyes adjust and looked up at her. He had been expecting to see his mother, but when he saw who it really was, his eyes widened in shock.

"Hi there," Hara said, smiling down at him.

✳ ✳ ✳

Lieutenant Odau lived a little more than two miles away from the apartment complex, and he and Perry arrived there quickly. It was a good thing it was late, because if there had been any cars on the road there would have been some serious traffic accidents from the many traffic laws Odau violated. He blew through several stop signs and skidded around every corner they encountered. Perry gripped the seat the entire trip and begged Odau to slow down at least five times. But he refused, and Perry couldn't blame him. If it had been his own daughter, Perry would be in the same state of panic. Odau had at least listened to Perry when he told him to turn the siren off. The last thing they wanted was to alert Hara to their arrival.

By the time they reached his house, Odau was in a new state of panic. As they pulled up to his house, they saw the tall male figure standing on the porch beside the front door.

"Shit!" Odau yelled, slamming on the brakes and throwing his car door open.

"Lieutenant, wait!" Perry cried, trying to catch hold of his arm. But he couldn't stop him.

The man standing in front of Odau's house saw them, and in an instant he leapt off the porch and bolted around the house. Odau was moving at full speed towards his front door without paying attention to him. All he wanted in that moment was to make sure his son was alright; he didn't care who got away. So when Perry jumped out of the car to follow him, he decided instead to run after the fleeing man. That man must have been the one Brown claimed would be helping Hara.

The man ran between two houses behind Odau's, and he was a good fifty yards ahead of Perry. The other squad cars were approaching, but by the time they got there it would all be over. Perry was on his own, but he hadn't been the star of the track team just for the title. He could run. The man had crossed the next street parallel to Odau's and was running between the next set of houses. When he reached the back of those two homes, he veered to the left and disappeared from Perry's sight. By then, Perry had closed much of the distance between them and soon after rounded the corner as well. The foot came out of nowhere.

The first kick hit him in the stomach, and the second hit him in the left knee cap. He was knocked to the ground. Gasping for breath, Perry rolled over as another foot came down towards his face. Putting his hands under his chest, he pushed up, swinging his legs around so his foot hit the man in the back of the knee. His knees buckled beneath him and he went down beside Perry. In one quick second Perry jumped to his feet, pulled out his weapon, flipped the safety off, and aimed it at the man's head. "Freeze!" he shouted as the man attempted to get back on his feet. He froze on his hands and knees, his back facing Perry. "Do you have any idea what you and your friend have done?" he snarled, reaching down and taking hold of his arm. Flipping him over, Perry's anger changed to shock. His mouth falling open, he released the man's arm and took an uncertain step back. "What?" he breathed in disbelief.

The man who had been helping Hara, who had helped her kill those kids, had wavy dark hair, a darker skin tone, and in the slight light of the moon Perry could pick out his mahogany eyes.

He was staring at himself.

✳ ✳ ✳

When he burst through the front door, the first thing Odau did was yell to his wife. "Jane, wake up!" he cried, and then he was sprinting up the stairs two at a time. Once he was at the top, he bolted down the hallway to his son's room at the end. He saw that the door was open, which immediately told him something was out of place. His son always slept with his door closed. The light was still off, but he knew something was wrong. Bursting through the door, Odau flipped the light switch, the overhead light flashing on. He drew out his weapon and drew in a sharp breath at what he saw.

Hara was standing in the center of his son's room, her face expressing multiple emotions. She appeared furious, but at the same time she was smirking. She was mocking him. In her right arm she held Jackson, her arm hooked under his arm and around his chest. In her left hand she held a nine-millimeter aimed at his head. Jackson already looked to be in pretty bad shape. His left eye was purple and swollen shut, his lips were cut and bleeding, and bruises and peculiar looking burns were all over his arms. His good eye was drooping, his head leaning back against her shoulder.

Odau couldn't contain his fury. Raising his gun and aiming it at her head, he shouted, "Let him go!" When all she did was narrow her eerie eyes at him, he added, "I swear to God I will kill you!"

Hara snorted. "Yeah, I'll bet," she challenged, keeping her gun level with Jackson's head.

"Dad?"

Furrowing her brow, Hara leaned slightly to the side so she could peer over Odau's shoulder. He didn't even turn to see who it was, for he already knew. Holding his ground and keeping his eyes directly on his son and the murderer holding him hostage, he growled, "Sarah, get back in your room right now."

"Oh my God!" she screamed in horror.

"Go back to your room, Sarah!" he said louder. He heard her whimper, but then her door slammed shut a moment later.

Looking back at him, Hara grinned menacingly. "Well, Lieutenant, it's nice to finally meet you," she said, nodding in mock respect.

"Likewise," Odau replied through his teeth. His heart pounding in fear and anger, he repeated his command from earlier. "Let my son go now!"

"Or what?" Hara snapped, her eyes becoming slits. "You'll shoot me? Ha! You shoot me, I pull this trigger, your son's brains end up all over the wall!"

Fear almost paralyzing his entire body, he whispered in desperation, "What do you want?"

Her stone cold glare burning holes through his skull, she snarled, "Start walking."

When Hara started taking steps forward, Odau started moving back. She pushed him farther and farther down the hall until they reached the stairs. "Down," she said sharply, her eyes never leaving his. Gripping the railing, Odau slowly made his way down the stairs.

"Graham, what's going on…oh my God!"

"Jane, please go to Caroline's room!" Odau begged his wife, still keeping his eyes on the girl's. He had reached the bottom, and he stopped, blocking Hara's path.

"Back off," she ordered, her eyes flashing. Odau, regretfully, did what she commanded. Taking several steps back, he bumped into his wife, who clung to him. He continued to keep his gun level with her head.

"Graham, who is she?" his wife whispered in fear, squeezing his arm.

"Just keep calm," he told her quietly. He realized that he was talking more to himself than his wife. His head was spinning and he had to think of something before Hara could get away with his son and kill him.

Where the hell is Perry? he thought to himself with increasing impatience.

Smirking at the two of them again, Hara stepped off the bottom step and started moving towards the back door. She seemed to know exactly where to go; she was moving backwards without sneaking a glance behind her, and she wasn't bumping into any walls or stumbling around any corners. She somehow knew exactly where the back door was. She must have been watching his house for some time…and now she was going to get away with his son.

His heart pounding, Odau tried to plead with her. "Please, I'll do anything! Just let him go! I'll give you anything you want!"

Leaning towards him, she said coldly, "This is all I want! Now, you're going to let me go out this door, and you're not going to follow me."

"You do realize that you can't escape from this?" Odau growled, although he was having a difficult time believing his own words. "In less than a minute, two dozen of my men will surround the area, and in less than an hour you'll be in a holding cell!"

Hara laughed scornfully. "I don't even need a minute! In less than a minute, I'll be gone, and in less than an hour, I'll be celebrating the death of your boy! Say your goodbyes." Without another word, she turned on her heel and opened the door.

"Stop!" Odau shouted angrily as she stepped outside, his heart falling as he watched her drag his son out with her. When she kept going, he couldn't take it anymore. What had she expected him to do, just stand there and watch? "Damn it, stop!" He did the only thing he could do; he pulled the trigger.

The gunshot echoed through the night, causing him to jump and his wife to cry out. Since Hara was already outside, when she went down she fell out of his line of sight, dragging Jackson with her. Pulling away from his wife, Odau rushed out the door. Hara had managed to hold onto her gun, but she was clutching her left side where the bullet had struck. She had dropped Jackson after she was hit; he lay sprawled awkwardly a few feet from where she was on her hands and knees. He was unconscious, and Odau was glad he wouldn't be awake for what he was about to do next.

Hara was struggling to her feet, still holding her side. Dark red blood was oozing out between her fingers and down onto the wet grass. Once she was on her feet, she turned back towards Jackson, gun in hand.

Quickly raising his gun again, Odau yelled, "No!" He pulled the trigger again, this shot hitting her square in the chest. She doubled over in pain, and Odau was amazed that she could still keep on her feet. But she went down on her knees a moment later, leaning forward and holding her chest where her wound was. Odau wanted to kill her, and he knew that he would get a pass for it after what she had done. He would be doing the world a favor by taking her out of it. But he didn't kill her.

He was finding that it was much more difficult to take a life than he had originally thought, even though that life seemed nothing worth saving.

Jane was screaming inside the kitchen, repeating, "Oh my God! Oh my God!" over and over again. She hadn't seen what had just happened. For all she knew, Jackson had been the one to suffer the wound.

Dodging around Hara, Odau bent down and scooped up Jackson. Cradling his son's unconscious body in his arms, he took several steps away from the girl who was struggling to breathe. Even if he didn't fire the fatal shot, she wouldn't have much longer anyway.

The sound of sirens grew close, and he could see the red and blue lights flashing from the next street over. Odau grinned triumphantly down at Hara, knowing he had won. When his fellow officers arrived, he would have them contact EMS and have them bring two ambulances; one for Jackson and one for Hara. Odau had a slight desire to ensure that Hara lived through the night. If she survived, he was going to make sure she wished she hadn't.

His smirk was wiped clean from his face when Hara slowly raised her head to glare at him. Her face expressed pure hatred as she scowled up at him. But what stunned Odau the most were her eyes. They were no longer the mesmerizing, glowing green. They were now a dark, angry crimson. What made her already terrifying appearance even more frightening was the blood that was slowly dripping out of the corner of her mouth and down her chin. Odau's eyes widened in horror and he took several more steps in reverse.

"Now look at what you did!" she hissed at him, her voice coming out airy and raspy. Odau knew why that was; he had shot her in the lung the second time.

"What are you?" Odau breathed, never before expecting to ask that question to another person.

Letting out a ferocious cry, Hara threw her body upright, spreading out her arms. A violent white light burst forth from her, sending with it a burst of energy that knocked Odau clean off his feet. He was thrown backwards into the doorway, hitting his head on the door frame. Managing to keep his grip on Jackson, he gasped in pain, his vision instantly going white. Blinking to clear his eyes of the blinding light, Odau's last thought was of Perry, wondering if he had managed to stop Hara's colleague from escaping. Then he slumped against the floor, closing his exhausted eyes. He blacked out a few seconds later, not knowing just how lucky he was to have gotten himself and his son out of that situation alive. Had Hara been just a tad bit stronger, she would have fetched her gun from the dark, wet ground and finished what she had come there to do.

While Odau and his son laid unconscious on their kitchen floor, Hara made her way to the blue Lamborghini parked the next street back. She and Jack had just committed the most disturbing crime Philadelphia had seen in years, but what she didn't know—what nobody knew—was that a bigger calamity was on its way, bigger that anything she could cause herself.

And no one—no one—could prepare for it.

5

Genetic Mutation

Everything was falling apart. Nothing was making sense anymore. Hara had slipped past their defenses unnoticed, there was the question of how she could get inside people's heads, and Perry had just arrested a man who looked just like him, the only difference being that he appeared to be several years younger than Perry (probably in his early twenties).

It was one hour after the horrible incident, and things hadn't come close to calming down. Odau's son was being checked over by a medic at the station, the rest of his family in the waiting room down the hall. The lieutenant himself was extremely distressed; he had refused for over twenty minutes to allow a medic to examine him. He had agreed to have his own head looked at after Perry agreed to stay with his son until he was finished.

Perry allowed himself to be checked out when the team first arrived back. A medic told him that he'd suffered a mild concussion—as he had predicted—but was surprised at how quickly it was healing. He said that the burn on his wrist wouldn't heal as fast, though. It was a second degree burn, but what bothered Perry the most was that it was in the shape of a handprint. It had been bandaged, but he couldn't bandage the uneasiness that was steadily growing throughout his entire body. He kept trying to come up with an explanation for how she had burned him, and then rendered him unconscious, but he just couldn't. When he was asked to explain what happened to him, he told the truth. He had no idea. Odau had a very interesting story to share about his encounter with Hara as well. Clearly, there were many things about this girl that they didn't understand. They planned on asking Allan Brown about it after things calmed down a bit.

The thing that was causing Perry big problems at the moment was not the unanswered questions about Hara, but the parents of the dead children. They had too many angry questions that no one could answer, like why Hara wasn't stopped from committing the murders, or why they weren't informed of the gravity of the situation, or why the kids were known targets yet not placed in protective custody. Perry tried to explain to the sobbing, heartbroken parents that the team was attempting to catch her, but they didn't want to hear his excuses.

There was also the matter at hand of the young man who looked just like Perry. He was detained in a high security cell after he was arrested, and no one dared go into the cell to speak with him. Perry himself wasn't entirely certain he wanted to go in there. He had thousands of questions, but he wasn't sure he'd like some of the answers, so he was going to try to put off speaking with him for as long as he could.

For about twenty minutes, Perry had been standing outside one of the holding cells serving as the medics' station. Odau didn't want his son in a hospital while he was required to be at the station; he didn't want his boy out of his sight; so he had the medics set up in a vacant holding cell for the time being. There had been no news on Jackson's condition so far, so Odau had marched in twenty minutes earlier to demand a report. Being polite, Perry waited outside, running over the day's events in his head. When the door finally opened, Perry jumped in surprise and turned to Odau eagerly as he stepped out.

"Well?"

Sighing, the lieutenant shook his head and rubbed his eyes. "They say he's got a mild concussion, and the burns on his arms are third degree."

"Jesus," Perry whispered in amazement, no longer feeling sorry for the pain in his own arm. "Is he going to be alright?"

Shrugging, Odau said, "He's still unconscious due to shock, and the medics want to keep him out for the rest of the night and most of tomorrow as well. But they said he should recover. Physically, anyway."

"Good," Perry nodded, glad that they had at least saved one of the kids. "What about you? Are you okay?" Perry wasn't sure whether the lieutenant could recover from this. He was more worried about Odau than he was Jackson.

He thought for a second. "No, I guess I'm not. But I will be." Turning, he marched down the hall towards the other holding cells.

"Hey," Perry called. "Where are you going?"

"To get some answers," Odau yelled over his shoulder.

Perry followed Odau down the hall. He knew exactly where he was going. As Perry predicted, Odau walked to the very last door, the holding cell containing their suspect. Two S.W.A.T members stood outside the door, and Perry knew there were two cops inside guarding the guy as well. The team wanted extra security, just in case their detainee tried anything.

"Hey, wait a minute!" Perry said, grabbing Odau by the arm as he opened the door.

Rounding on him, Odau demanded, "Why? This boy is our only lead to the girl who tried to kill my son. I want some answers!"

"Well, just take it easy," Perry warned, patting his shoulder. "Don't get too rough with him."

The look Odau gave him wasn't very reassuring.

Walking back a few feet, Perry entered a different door, which led to the observation room. Stepping through, he stopped in surprise. Sitting at the table in the center of the narrow room were Allan Brown, Meg Hopper, and Daniel Marcus. They were talking softly amongst themselves, but when Perry walked in they stopped and looked over at him. Suspicious, he demanded, "What's going on here?"

Pushing out a vacant chair with his foot, Mayor Brown said, "Maybe you should sit down."

Eyeing them all, Perry hesitantly made his way over and sat down beside the mayor. The observation room was a small room, containing several cameras and microphone equipment. There was also the long rectangular table they sat at and about half a dozen chairs. A large one-way glass window separated them from the holding cell. Looking inside, Perry could see Odau shouting things at the boy across a table while the boy sat in a chair and appeared bored. Two cops—Finchly and another Perry didn't recognize—stood on either side of the door, seeming uncomfortable at the lieutenant's state of rage. The microphones weren't on, so thankfully Perry didn't have to listen to what Odau was screaming.

Turning to Allan, Perry asked him, "You do realize that he is going to take you down for this, don't you?"

Sighing, Allan continued to watch Odau yell.

Shaking his head, Perry questioned further, "Why didn't you just tell us who the last target was? Why didn't you tell him it was his own son?" When Allan refused to answer, Perry pressed, "Did you want the boy dead?"

"Yes," Allan replied, turning to him. Gazing into Perry's puzzled eyes, he continued. "I wanted him dead. We all did. But over the past three years, I've had to look too many people in the eye and tell them someone they loved had been killed."

Staring at him in perplexity, Perry demanded, "What are you talking about?"

Leaning forward so they could see each other around Allan, Detective Marcus told him, "You've just entered a very difficult and complicated world, Agent Perry. One that you won't be able to understand for a long time."

Perry snorted. "What world is that? The world of conspiracy and murder? I've been in this world for more than ten years. I'm not a stranger to it."

Marcus and Allan both shook their heads. "It's much, much more than that," Allan promised, turning back to the window.

"If you think you know conspiracy and murder, you're dead wrong, my friend," Marcus said, also turning back. "The world we came from is far worse than anything you'll see over the next day."

Suspicion and curiosity getting the better of Perry, he began to get frustrated. What world were they talking about? What were they all hiding about their past together? Who was Hara and that mysterious boy in the next room? All of those questions were driving him crazy. "And what world is that?" he asked impatiently.

"You'll find out eventually," Allan replied softly, not looking at him.

Still unsatisfied, Perry questioned, "Why would you want that poor boy dead?"

There was a short, awkward pause. Meg Hopper, who hadn't said a single word the whole time, was the one to answer. "Because he was the start of everything."

Rolling his eyes, Perry said, "Let me guess. I'll understand that eventually, too."

All three of them nodded.

Sighing in frustration, Perry rubbed his eyes and looked back to Odau and the suspect. The lieutenant had calmed down some; he was currently sitting in a chair opposite the young man. Perry could tell that he was still very irritated, and no one could blame him.

"So who is he?" Perry studied the boy's oddly familiar face. It made him uncomfortable just looking at the identical features, and if the three of them didn't give him an answer he wanted to hear soon, there was going to be a serious problem.

"His name is Jack," Marcus said to Perry's relief, still not turning away from the window. "He's been a close friend of Hara's since she was quite young. You obviously know that he was the one assisting her."

"Yes, I've gathered that much," Perry muttered in distaste, observing the boy's disrespectful body language. He was lounging in his chair with his head resting back, not listening to a word the lieutenant was saying. Odau wasn't noticing this; he was too upset to notice much of anything. "Why didn't you tell us he would be a potential helper?"

"Because he was supposed to be dead," Meg told him gravely, turning to him. "Two years ago, all three of us watched him get shot right here." She pointed to a spot just above her left breast. "He shouldn't be alive right now. He got lucky somehow." Turning back to the window, Perry heard her mutter, "Or maybe not so lucky."

Staring at Jack and wondering just how they could look so similar, Perry asked quietly, "Why does he look exactly like me?"

There was another uncomfortable pause. "I think that's something he'll have to explain to you himself," Allan replied, chewing on his lower lip.

Perry jumped to his feet eagerly. "Well, I guess I'd better get in there and start asking some questions," he said, turning and walking out the door.

✳ ✳ ✳

As he watched Perry leave, Mayor Allan Brown sighed heavily. "This is becoming far more complicated than I'd feared," he told his colleagues. "What are we going to do about this?" He waved a hand at Jack on the other side of the one-way glass window.

"Nothing," Daniel said.

"Because there's nothing we can do," Meg added, her expression showing exactly what Allan felt: complete hopelessness.

Suddenly feeling angry, Allan demanded, "Why did he have to come back? Of all the people that could have aided her, why him?" Both were rhetorical questions, but he got an answer anyway.

"You know this act wouldn't have lasted for much longer," Meg told him softly. "We can't hide from our past forever. Sooner or later, someone would have become suspicious and asked questions about our fake lives. Our mistakes were going to catch up with us eventually."

"Yes, but Jack should have known better than to come back here," Daniel pointed out. The three of them watched as Agent Perry entered the room and Lieutenant Odau looked up. "With anyone else, we could have made up a cover story without a problem. But with Jack...there's not a lie we could tell that would explain him! Agent Perry's going to ask a ton of questions that we can't give him the answers to, and he's a persistent man. He's not going to let this go without a fight. Jack should have known better than to show his face around here! Why would he do something so stupid and irresponsible?"

"You don't think he'll tell Perry the truth, do you?" Meg asked nervously.

"Never," Allan said immediately, even though he wasn't entirely positive about that. "He would never tell anyone the truth. It's too dangerous! None of them would believe him, anyway, let alone understand him. What would be the point of that?"

"Maybe he wants them all to find out so he can make them feel guilty," Meg suggested. "You know how his attitude has always been towards humans."

"They wouldn't feel guilty because they haven't done anything yet," Daniel reminded. "And don't say 'humans'. People will definitely start looking into us if anyone hears us say that."

Sighing again, Allan grumbled, "Honestly, this is going to be the end of everything. There's no going back now. We'll have to disappear all over again."

Turning to him, Meg pointed out, "If Hara and Jack get their way, we can just go back to our old lives. We don't have to disappear."

Confused, Allan said, "We're not going to let them have their way."

Daniel looked thoughtful. "Why not?" he asked curiously.

Staring at him in shock, Allan said, "Are you serious? You want to just let her march in and kill him?"

"Let me ask you something, Allan," Meg said sharply, "because I'm just a little confused. Why are we defending that boy? No, wait, why are *you* defending that boy? What will protecting him accomplish? You hate him just as much as Hara! What is your motive?"

"Why are you making accusations?" Allan demanded defensively.

"I'm not making accusations. I just want to know what you'll gain from this!"

"I'm not going to gain anything!"

"Then what's the point?" Meg shouted, her eyes angry. "What is your plan, Allan? If we just allow this to happen, we can all go home!"

Unsure of how to respond, Allan shook his head and told her the first thing that came to his head. "I just don't want anyone else to die! I have enough blood on my hands…"

Shaking her head in disgust, Meg told him, "If Hara succeeds, the boy will be the only blood on our hands."

"I don't want to see any more kids getting killed, even if they are evil!" Allan snapped angrily.

"We're in the middle of a war, Allan," Meg reminded him. "Whether you like it or not, it's time you picked a side."

"I have picked my side," Allan told her firmly, skeptical to how she could accuse him of such perfidy.

Meg narrowed her eyes at him. "Maybe you could clarify, because right now it looks like you're siding with them."

Quickly cutting in, Daniel said, "I hate to interrupt our happy reunion, but I think we need to come back to this conversation a little later." He gestured to the door. Seconds later, Odau came barging in, huffing in anger.

"We need to talk," he growled at Allan.

Sighing yet again, Allan muttered, "Yeah, I know."

✳ ✳ ✳

At about that same time, Hara painfully made her way to the place where she and Jack had been reunited. Her entire body was screaming in agony, and her clothes and hands were covered in dark red blood. She had been shot twice; once through her left side and again through her left lung, the bullet just barely missing her heart. She was very badly injured. Blood was running out of her mouth and she was bleeding profusely through both her wounds. Her breathing sounded like short, raggedy rasps, and the pain was nearly unbearable. She knew that she had to get the bullets out soon so she could regenerate or she would be too weak to do so.

What was making her situation worse was that the pain was causing the heat to come out of her. She was going to burst in a matter of minutes. That was why she had gone back to that safe place underground, because it was isolated and she could let the heat out without hurting anyone other than herself.

As she climbed down the rickety metal ladder, Hara felt the heat slipping out. Each rung was hotter than the one before, and she could feel the skin on her palms slowly and painfully sizzling away. It was agonizing, but she had to keep going. Jumping down from the last rung, she cried out and nearly collapsed as a jolt of fiery hot pain shot through her chest. Stumbling, she caught herself on the rock wall beside the ladder. She cried out again and pulled away quickly as her hands made a dangerous hissing sound upon contact.

It's coming out too fast! she thought in fear. *I can't control it!* She moved as rapidly as she could towards the small pool that would lead to the larger scum pond. As she approached it, the water began bubbling and steaming. Feeling a great deal of uncertainty about what she had to do, Hara knew she had no choice. Swaying dangerously, she sucked in a deep breath and allowed herself to fall in face first.

The wave of agony that hit her next was unbearable. Her whole body went rigid, and the boiling water burned away at her skin. Once she was somewhat used to the overwhelming feeling, Hara began kicking furiously downward towards the pipe she knew led to the outside. Forcing her eyes open, she winced but squinted until she spotted it dead ahead. Her limbs feeling like lead weights, Hara pushed herself on through the pipe and out into the pond. When she had reached the pond, she heard the metal pipe behind her creaking from the drastic temperature change. The heat was slipping more and more as the seconds ticked by, but Hara held onto it, still pushing herself further towards the center of the pond. The more water she had around her, the more likely it would absorb her energy.

After a minute more of swimming, Hara knew she had a good three minutes of air left. Deciding that she was far enough, she pushed herself upright, treading water twenty feet below the surface. The water was approaching its boiling point, and the temperature was beginning to fry her skin. Knowing it was about to get a lot hotter, Hara sucked it up and braced herself for the heat wave that was coming next. She thought her pain was bad already, but it was about to get a hell of a lot worse.

Hara was suddenly aware of the large amount of blood flowing out of both her bullet wounds. The warm water was causing her to bleed faster. She had to get help from somebody soon or she was going to bleed out and wouldn't be able to complete what she'd already started.

Sealing her throat so she wouldn't cry out again from the pain, Hara began to slowly let go of the heat. She felt it start to slowly slip out of her, the water gradually increasing in temperature. The headache that had been plaguing her for weeks began to subside, the loss of pressure a foreign sensation to her. But her old pain was soon replaced by a new one. Her skin felt like it was on fire. As she ground her teeth together to fight her urge to scream, Hara made the mistake of forcing the heat out to get it over with faster. She knew that if she pushed it out too quickly there would be a risk of setting surrounding structures on fire, but she ignored that fact and before long she lost control of the ability and she could feel it being ripped away from her.

The temperature of the water caused Hara's body to become rigid once more. A wave of heat exploded from her body, and flames shot from her in every direction. The fire was quickly extinguished by the water around her, but that didn't stop the heat. The heat kept moving away from her at an incredible speed, and Hara sensed that it set the vegetation aflame when it reached the edge of the pool. It didn't stop there, either. She felt the shock wave continuing up past the pool and to the adjacent buildings. The windows in City Hall shattered from the force of the blast, as did every other window within a thousand feet. Fires were starting all the way around the pool, and they were spreading rapidly.

Oh, no, Hara thought in horror. *I have to stop this!*

She couldn't see what was happening on the surface, but she knew she had just caused a devastating amount of damage, and the authorities were going to have a difficult time coming up with an explanation for what had happened. For a split second that felt like eternity, Hara realized that every time she used one of her abilities she was increasing the risk of Agent Perry and Lieutenant Odau discovering the truth about her, and if they uncovered the truth, things in Philadelphia would become very, very complicated.

As the realization of what had happened hit her, she felt a fear that she hadn't felt for a while: the fear of getting caught. What the hell did she think she was doing in this city? She had used her abilities in front of too many people. The authorities were going to start asking questions and pointing fingers, and who was left behind to take the fall for her? Allan, Daniel, and Meg; three people who were her friends whether they were supporting her side or not. How immature and selfish could Hara be to leave her loved ones behind after what she had done? She may be only eighteen, but she had been at the maturity level of an adult since she was twelve years old. It was expected of her where she was from. Making huge messes and then leaving the people she cared about to clean them up was clearly showing just how much she had changed. Her mind was horribly tainted from the catastrophe that destroyed her family, and her life. Now those who remained were about to pay the price.

With that slight push which Hara had given herself, all of the heat left her within a matter of seconds, taking with it most of her energy. Her limbs hung helplessly in the murky water, just acting as extra weight to her. The excruciating headache that had been at its pinnacle the past few days was finally gone, and the stress on her brain was diminishing. Unfortunately for her, the water was still cooking her skin and blood was still flowing from her wounds. One problem had ceased, but another had arisen.

As her chest became tight, Hara tried to kick to the surface, but her legs refused to respond. A panic rising swiftly inside her, she attempted to claw her way up, but she only managed to move her arms a few times before they hung lifelessly in the water as well. Feeling herself slowly beginning to sink, Hara gave up completely. She only had about a minute of oxygen left, and there was no way she could make it to the surface in her state.

Oh, God, help me! she wanted to scream. Of all the hardships she had endured, why did it have to end like this? As her vision started to fade, she thought she saw something moving down through the water towards her. She couldn't make out what it was; all she could see was a large dark object getting closer and closer to her. She thought she was hallucinating from her lack of air, but then a sound met her ears as well. It sounded like the creaking metal pipe she swam through earlier.

As the object gradually came closer, Hara realized what it was. It was the claw of the excavator that was positioned at the edge of the pool. The big metal claw descended down until it was level with her, and then it gently wrapped around her before pulling her up to the surface. It pulled her up until a great whoosh of air struck her face.

She tried to breathe in, but she was too exhausted. Her eyes drooped closed and she slouched over backwards. The air around her was steaming like the water, and Hara hoped that no one had been in the blast radius. If anyone was, they would have burned to death already.

The metallic claw lowered her to the ground, and as it released her she opened her eyes a crack to get a look at the rusting yellow beast that had saved her life. Her first thought was that Jack had come back and used it to pull her out of the water, but it really could have been anyone.

While the claw came to a thundering rest just a few feet from her, Hara was finally able to inhale. She sucked in a deep lungful of air, but the pain in her chest made it difficult. Her eyes fluttered shut again in her exhaustion, but she reopened them when she sensed someone kneel down beside her. It was a man wearing a large black leather overcoat, thick dark pants, gloves, and an oxygen mask covering his entire head. That was the only way a person could have survived the flames: if they had come prepared.

Through the gas mask, Hara could see the concerned blue eyes of her rescuer, a thin layer of sweat forming on his brow beneath his white hair line. It was Noah.

"Hara! Hara!" he was shouting, gently slapping the sides of her face in an effort to keep her conscious. "Wake up! You can't go yet!"

Blinking to peel her eyelids from her eyes, Hara peered up at Noah's worried expression, shocked that he had risked his life to save hers. "Why—did you..." she started, but more blood was leaking into her lung, cutting off some of her air supply. Coughing heavily, blood came running out of her mouth again.

"Don't try to talk," Noah told her, putting a comforting hand on her shoulder and leaning his head over her to examine the wound in her chest. "My God...what have you done to yourself?"

A sudden series of sounds caught Hara's attention. She hadn't noticed it before, but over the roar of the boiling water she could hear several noises that didn't sound particularly good. There were several car alarms sounding through the once calm night, the sound of buildings crumbling to the streets below, screams from people in pain, and even the roaring sound of large fires. Pushing Noah away from her, Hara slowly sat up to see the damage she had done. What she saw made her gasp.

The central city within a thousand feet of the pool was devastated. All the windows were blown out in the surrounding buildings, and huge chunks of concrete and brick were breaking off of them and falling to the ground. Some buildings were smoking, the bright orange flames licking at the midnight sky. Others looked like they were about to collapse at any moment. Everything on the ground appeared to be destroyed as well. Cars were overturned, their horns sounding. Anything in the streets was lying on its side; signs, food stands, benches. Any sort of vegetation was burnt to a crisp. She couldn't see any people, but she could hear the ones inside the burning buildings screaming and calling for help. The area surrounding the pool was in flames, and there were fires burning fairly close to Hara and Noah.

Shocked by the amount of damage she had caused, she whispered, "What have I done? I've destroyed everything..." She wasn't only referring to the city; she was also referring to her plan to dispose of the one thing that had ruined her life. She blacked out then, her body falling back against the hot, singed grass.

✻ ✻ ✻

After Perry left the observation room, he walked up to the door of the holding cell only to be halted by the two S.W.A.T. members.

"The lieutenant requested that he not be disturbed," the one on the left said in a low, droning voice.

"I'm working on this case with him," Perry told him in annoyance. "I don't think he'll mind." He tried to walk through the door, but the agent on the right put a hand on his shoulder to stop him.

"I'm sorry, sir, but he specifically said no one in unless…"

"Look, my authority outranks the lieutenant's," Perry interrupted, growing impatient. "He may be leading this case, but his rules don't apply to me. He asked me to come to Philadelphia to help him, so if I want to go inside, I'll go inside. Understand?" When all the two men did was stare back at him, Perry sighed. "Listen, you've seen the boy, right? He looks exactly like me."

Both men became uncomfortable, shifting their weight from foot to foot.

"I need answers, and I need them now," Perry told them, sensing he was winning the argument. "If something like this happened to you, wouldn't you want to get in there and figure things out?"

An awkward silence lasted for a couple of seconds before the second agent dropped his hand from Perry's shoulder and allowed him to pass. Grateful, Perry pushed the door open and stepped inside.

Jack looked up at Perry's sudden entrance, and Perry saw his brow furrow for a split second before his expression smoothed over again. Then, Jack did something that was unexpected; he sat up in his chair and leaned forward, directing his full attention to Perry.

Odau, who had seated himself in a chair at the table opposite Jack, turned around in a burst of anger. He must have assumed that one of his detectives had entered without an invitation. "What did I say—oh, Agent Perry." Embarrassed, Odau asked with a hint of irritation, "Can I help you?"

"Yes," Perry said, taking an eager step forward. "I've got some questions I'd like to ask our friend here."

As Perry expected, Odau did not approve. "As you can see, I've been asking the boy several questions, but he hasn't said a single word."

"Yes," Perry said again, his impatience with Odau increasing. "I'm well aware. But I have a feeling that he'll talk to me."

"What makes you think he'll talk to you instead?" Odau demanded, taking offense.

Perry gestured with his head to Jack. Odau turned to look at the boy and saw Jack's intense stare aimed at Perry, an obvious change in behavior from before. When Odau looked, Jack's eyes flickered to his for a moment before looking back at Perry. Shocked by the boy's sudden attention, Odau whipped his head back at Perry and glared at him. He obviously did not like the fact that Jack was giving Perry more respect than he was giving to him.

"I think he'll talk to me," Perry said.

Flustered, Odau rose to his feet in anger. Slowly, and in defeat, he made his way around Perry but stopped at the door. "I'm going to wait right here," he replied stubbornly.

Shrugging, Perry muttered, "Suit yourself." He met Jack's intense gaze, and the boy stared unblinking back at him, his expression appearing open and friendly. Nodding to him, Perry stepped up to the table and greeted, "Hello."

Giving him a small smile, Jack responded, "Hi."

Turning, Perry allowed himself the fun and gave Odau a smug grin. The lieutenant's face flushed in anger. When Perry turned back to Jack, Jack was still peering up at him.

"Aren't you going to sit down?" he asked. His voice sounded different from Perry's, as Perry had hoped. It almost sounded as if he was laughing at Perry, but at the same time he sounded jittery, like he was nervous. Nobody could blame him; he was being held against his will in a holding cell and had just been screamed at by an angry cop. If he was guilty of murder like Hara, then he definitely had a reason to be concerned.

Stunned by his politeness, Perry gazed back at him questioningly. Jack simply gestured to the chair opposite him. Unsure of what to think, Perry slowly sat down but kept his eyes carefully trained on the boy. Jack did the same, and Perry could see that his eyes were laughing. Something was clearly funny, and perhaps he was mocking Perry because he knew a secret about the two of them that Perry did not.

Trying to keep himself from growing annoyed, Perry started, "So, Jack...yes, I know your name. I'm Special Agent Shawn Perry. I'm with the FBI."

Jack looked surprised that Perry knew his name, but it didn't faze him for long. Nodding once at Perry's jacket which read FBI in big bold letters, he said, "Yeah, I can see that. It's nice to meet you." He held out his hand.

Hearing Odau shift his weight anxiously at the strange gesture, Perry eyed the hand before cautiously extending his own.

Jack gripped his hand, shook it once, and then released him. Then, just as before, he stared with an odd look of familiarity that Perry couldn't identify.

"So..." Perry muttered uncertainly, the boy's stare making him uncomfortable. "You're a friend of Hara's?" The answer was obvious, but he needed to say something.

Jack nodded without a second's thought. "Yes, I am."

"How long have you know her?"

He shrugged. "Forever. Our fathers were close friends."

Who was your father? Perry wanted to ask, but he would get to those questions later. "You're her partner in crime, then?"

"I was," he replied. "My part in this is complete."

Knowing that meant that Hara's killings weren't over, Perry took a step back. "Did you kill any of those kids tonight? Were you a part of that?"

"Yes," Jack said immediately. "I killed two of the three. Roy Burma and Evan Kessnich. I thought you knew that already?" He glanced uncertainly up at the lieutenant.

"So you admit to that?" Odau growled, walking up to stand beside Perry. When he spoke to Jack, Jack looked up at him, set his jaw and narrowed his eyes. The boy wasn't going to cooperate whatsoever with Odau, but after glancing back at Perry and seeing his expectant expression, Jack answered.

"Well, I did it, so I guess I do admit to it." Blinking curiously at Perry, he asked, "Why would I deny doing something that I did?"

Perry couldn't believe what he was hearing. "Why would you do something like that?" he demanded. "How could you?"

With an expression as blank as a sheet of paper, Jack said, "Would you take four lives to save billions?"

Perry paused, not sure what was being implied, and Odau used the silence to his advantage. "What the hell is wrong with you?" he shouted in rage. "Do you not feel the slightest regret for what you did? You take three lives, and then you go for my son!" He started to advance towards the boy, but Perry jumped to his feet and caught him by the arm.

"You need to leave now," Perry told him, pushing him in the direction of the door. "I can see you're very upset, but injuring our only close connection to the girl will get us nowhere. Go. Take a breather."

Looking furious, Odau obeyed him and left the room as quickly as he could.

Perry hoped the angry officer wouldn't try to seek vengeance on Marcus, the mayor, or Hopper for the near death of his son. Keeping the three of them alive could play a crucial part in bringing Hara to justice.

"For the record, I do feel some regret," Jack said, his comment causing Perry to turn back to him. "But I still know I did the right thing."

Shaking his head solemnly, Perry replied softly, "Murder is never the right thing."

"Yes, well, we come from very different worlds, my friend," Jack murmured.

"You know, you're the second person to say that to me within five minutes," Perry informed him flatly. "And if your world believes that murder is a good thing, then you and I need to have a serious discussion, buddy."

"Wouldn't you sacrifice four lives to save billions of others?" Jack repeated his question from earlier and appeared puzzled. "Or would you let the four live and allow the billions to die?"

Confused, Perry said, "I don't understand what you're talking about. Is this supposed to be going somewhere?"

"Those kids weren't innocent," Jack informed.

"Oh, of course not," Perry replied sarcastically.

Jack ignored him. "You don't need to know why, but they're not. If you had lived my life, you would understand."

"Well, I didn't live your life, so why don't you enlighten me?"

"It's too early for you to understand any of this."

Throwing his hands up in the air, Perry groaned in exasperation. "You know, people keep telling me that, and it's really getting annoying. What, exactly, is so hard for me to understand? I don't need a complex explanation. All I need is a simple answer as to why you felt it was necessary to murder four young children in their sleep."

"I can't answer that," Jack said quickly. Putting his hands on the table, he leaned forward. "But if you have other questions that I'm allowed to answer, I'd be happy to answer them for you."

Having no idea where to begin, Perry began to list the things he wanted to know. "For starters, I'd like to know about you and your family and why you did what you did, and how Hara can do all of that..."

"I'm going to stop you there," Jack cut in. "First of all, as you already know, my name is Jack."

"Last name?" Perry questioned.

"Don't have one," Jack replied, shrugging.

Raising an eyebrow, Perry repeated, "You don't have a last name?"

Jack shook his head.

Growing even more frustrated, Perry closed his eyes. "Alright, I'm going to let that one slide. Carry on." Opening his eyes again, he leaned back in his chair and gestured with his hand to him.

"Uh...I'm twenty-two years old, I've been close friends with Hara for pretty much my whole life, and my whole family is dead."

Perry blinked in surprise. "Dead? What happened?"

"They were murdered," Jack explained, looking away.

"By whom?"

"By the same man who killed Hara's family."

Perry was shocked. Jack did seem uncomfortable talking about it, but he wasn't showing very much emotion over it. "You...you don't seem very upset by this."

Jack thought for a moment. "I guess I've just blocked most of it out. You learn to do that when everyone you love is being torture or killed."

For a moment, Perry wondered if the boy was crazy and making it all up, but Perry had seen crazy and Jack didn't fit into that category. "My God," he whispered in growing horror. "What happened to you?" If that was all true, then it would explain a lot about the murders. Desperate, angry people could do desperate, angry things.

Shrugging off the question, Jack said, "What was your next question? Why I did what I did? I answered that one already..."

"No, you didn't," Perry protested. "You just said that they weren't innocent."

"They weren't," Jack insisted.

"Why?" Perry demanded. "What could they have done that was so horrible that you had to kill them for it? They were children! The one you failed to kill was the lieutenant's son, and from what I hear, he's a fairly well-behaved kid!" When Jack didn't respond, Perry said loudly, "Well?!"

Shaking his head, Jack shrugged and looked down at his hands.

Perry told him angrily, "When kids make mistakes, you don't punish them by killing them! I don't know what you think they did, but one of them was only three years old. He couldn't have done much." He watched as Jack began tracing circles with his finger on the metal table. Leaning forward, he said softly, "I'm sorry about what happened to you and your family, but you can't take out your anger on kids who may have made a few mistakes. We're all human. We all make mistakes."

Jack's finger stopped mid-circle, his eyes flickering up to Perry's. Raising his head and leaning back, he commented, "As a cop, you're not exactly what I expected."

Snorting, Perry told him, "I'm not a cop."

Rolling his eyes, Jack said, "FBI agent, cop, investigator, detective...they're all the same thing to me. You're a law enforcer."

"Why am I not what you expected?" Perry asked curiously.

"My stay here started with being verbally harassed by Lieutenant Odau, and now you come in and start apologizing for something you didn't do. Is this how you people always run the show? Attack the murderer and then show pity for him to try and get something in return?"

Startled, Perry stammered, "I—I just want to know what's going on. Today, I caught a boy who looks just like me, and I want to know why. Today, a girl left a burn in the shape of a handprint on my wrist, and I want to know how." Shaking his head, he explained, "Nothing is making sense with this case. All I want is to know what's going on, and I'm hoping that I can somehow get you to tell me."

Nodding, Jack said, "If you really knew what was going on, then your simple little life would get very complicated very fast, and not in any way would that be good."

Knowing that their conversation was going nowhere, Perry moved to another important topic. "Tell me why we look alike," he commanded.

Scrunching up his face as he thought, Jack started, "Okay, so you wanted to know how Hara could do the things you all have seen her do…"

"No, I want to know why you look like me," Perry told him louder.

Putting his hands up defensively, Jack said, "Have patience, my friend. I'm getting to that. But to answer your first question I must first answer your second. Alright?"

Uncertain of whether or not he was just avoiding the question, Perry gave in and nodded in agreement. "Alright."

Nodding also, Jack asked, "You've obviously noticed that Hara isn't exactly normal, right?"

Perry held up his burned, bandaged wrist.

"Of course, you did. And you must have heard of genetic experiments as well."

Shifting in his chair uncomfortably, the horrible truth started to dawn on him. "Are you about to tell me that she can burn someone with her bare hands because of a genetic experiment?"

Jack nodded again, but then he paused for a second. "Actually, her parents were the results of the genetic experiment. Hara was born that way."

Intrigued, Perry didn't say a word. He was too interested in Jack's impossible story.

Taking the hint that he should continue, Jack started again. "Anyway, her parents were both exposed to a chemical compound that caused their genes to mutate."

"Mutate in what way?" Perry asked curiously, wondering if Jack had specific details to back up his story.

Biting his lip, Jack tried to decide how to explain it. He might have just been trying to make it all up as he went along, but Perry had a feeling it was all true. "They…" Jack seemed to be having real trouble. "They mutated in a way that gave them abilities, like the ones you saw Hara demonstrate."

The details weren't detailed enough for Perry. "What different types of abilities did the parents produce?"

Jack shrugged. "Her mother found out that she had a unique telekinetic ability while her father developed a strong telepathic ability…"

"Okay, that's enough!" Perry shouted, startling himself along with Jack. Breathing hard, Perry struggled to understand why the information Jack was sharing with him bothered him so much. "I don't know why I'm sitting here listening to this nonsense! It's completely ridiculous! Genetic experiments, mutated genes…this is all science fiction! It's stuff found in movies. It isn't real!" Inhaling sharply, Perry looked down at the table and squeezed his eyes shut.

He heard Jack lean forward in his chair again. "If you're saying that none of this is real, then why do you believe it?"

Taking a deep breath, Perry lifted his head so he could look the boy in the eyes. "I don't," he lied, wishing he could believe his own words. He saw what Hara had done to his wrist and he had felt her presence inside his own head. Odau had shared his own experience with the girl at his house with Perry.

Jack nodded yet again. "Yes, you do. I can see it in your eyes."

Rubbing his face with both his hands, Perry sighed heavily. Jack was right; Perry believed everything he had said so far. It was unclear why, but he did. After a brief silence, Perry asked, "So since both her parents became super heroes or whatever, she got the powers genetically, right?"

Jack smiled, glad he was right. "Yes. The mutated genes were passed down to her when she was born, except there was a slight difference between her and her parents. Since she was born this way, she was far more powerful. Far more dangerous."

"What exactly is her ability?" Perry asked, a little confused. "It seems as though you're suggesting that these people only have one ability, but I've seen her do several different things. When I first saw her, she shattered a window with a flick of her hands and then dove out of it and into the pond twelve stories below. She burned my wrist with her bare hands and somehow managed to make me black out, and then there was Odau's encounter with her when she screamed and he was thrown back several feet. He also said that her eyes turned red. What exactly is her ability?"

Jack had a smirk on his face, and it irritated Perry. "What is so funny?" he demanded.

"Nothing," Jack muttered, still smirking. "And you're absolutely right. Each person only possesses one ability, and to tell you the truth, Hara has only one ability. We call people like her Absorbers. She's like a sponge. Her ability allows her to absorb any mutated ability she comes into contact with."

"When you say that, you're implying that there are many others in the world with abilities?" Perry's question was more of a realization. Hara wasn't the only one out there. There were many more people in the world with abilities just as dangerous or even more so. "There were other people exposed to the…what did you call it? The chemical compound? If more people have these abilities, why hasn't anyone heard of them before? Hara has drawn enough attention to herself on her own, and if there were more people like her then we would know."

Pausing, Jack said, "I can't answer that now. Can I please continue?"

Annoyed, Perry nodded.

"As I was saying, she absorbed her parents' abilities as well as abilities from other people. As you have observed, she can change her appearance, she can regenerate her body, which is why she was able to jump from such a height, she can cause matter—such as a body—to shift, she can manipulate the brain, and there are many other things she can do that you were not a witness to. One ability she possesses that is particularly dangerous and difficult to control is the ability to start fires. That brings me to this next detail. There is a problematic side effect to being an Absorber. You see, like a sponge, she has a limit as to how much power she can take in. When a sponge takes in too much water, it starts to leak, and since poor Hara has absorbed a great number of abilities during her short life, she's begun to leak as well."

"Leak?" Perry repeated cautiously. "What do you mean leak?" Leaking abilities didn't sound like a very good thing.

Raising a finger, Jack pointed at Perry's wrist. "You experienced it for yourself. She has so much power and energy building up inside of her that she eventually has to let some of it out. It starts off as a headache, but then it grows into something much worse. The burns on your hand, the burns on the lieutenant's son…those are the results of what happens when she leaks. She's more at risk of leaking if she's under elevated levels of emotional stress, and the more powerful an ability is, the easier it is for her to lose control of it. The ability with the most energy is the fire, and that's why she hurt you."

"She didn't appear to be under any emotional stress when she burned me," Perry muttered flatly.

"You were threatening her," Jack reminded him. "That made her angry, and anger is the worst emotion to have when she's about to burst. Whenever she's angry or upset, that's when she tends to burn people."

Thinking, Perry said, "And she was angry when she burned the boy?"

There was a pause. "She…hates that boy. She was furious when she saw him. He was lucky she didn't disintegrate him in his own bed."

"Why, exactly, does she hate that boy so much?" Perry asked curiously, repeating a still unanswered question from before. "I know you claimed they weren't innocent, but what did he ever do to her to make her hate him so much?"

Dodging the question yet again, Jack finished, "And once the headache gets to be too much for her, she blows altogether. She'll let out a wave of fifteen hundred degree heat, and it usually ends in tragedy."

Realizing that Jack's story was fitting in with current events, Perry asked with a tone of dread, "So you're saying that she bursts after she's been…leaking, correct?"

"That's correct."

"But you just said that she's been leaking," Perry said, the gravity of their situation slapping him in the face.

Jack just watched him, his eyes saying what Perry was thinking.

"Oh, no," Perry whispered in horror. "How long do we have before she…" He made a popping sound with his mouth.

Jack shrugged, as if it was old news to him. "Any time within the next day."

Perry gaped at him. "She's going to blow up half the city and you didn't tell me sooner!" He started to jump to his feet and rush to the door, but Jack stopped him quickly.

"Whoa, whoa!" he said loudly, staring at Perry like he was overreacting. "Relax! I found a place for her to go when she needs to let it all out. It's confined, and the city should be safe from the heat wave."

"Should?" Perry questioned doubtfully, halfway between the door and the table.

"There's a slight chance that she could cause some damage if she lets it out too fast, but she has very good self-control. There's no need to worry yourself." He gestured to Perry's empty chair. "Please sit down."

It wasn't comforting when Jack said that Hara had good self-control, because from what Perry observed, she was completely losing control. At the moment, there was nothing he could do except learn more from Jack, so he decided to sit back down. As he did, he told Jack, "You still haven't answered my question."

"What question is that?" Jack asked, puzzled.

"Why we look the same," Perry reminded him.

"Ah," Jack said. "No, I suppose I haven't yet." Looking thoughtful for a moment, he began to explain. "Well, I'm also the result of a genetic experiment, although not in the same way as Hara. They—the scientists—must have taken DNA from someone in your family—maybe even you—and then created me. I don't know the entire story, but that's what my family hypothesized."

"So you have abilities too?"

"Unless you consider being able to eat an entire fourteen inch pizza in one sitting a super power, then no. I have no abilities."

Perry was surprised that the boy actually made him chuckle. But when he saw Jack's returned smile he straightened his expression and cleared his throat. He had to remain professional. "Who are these scientists? Are they military based or is this something that the government doesn't even know about? How are they taking people's DNA to make test tube babies and creating super humans? Who are these people?"

Jack shrugged, and he looked sad. "I don't know. The chemical compound was a freak accident, and now innocent people are paying the price for it."

Perry asked him, "So if you were made up from a member of my family's DNA, what does that make us?"

Exhaling loudly, Jack scrunched up his face while he thought over the possibilities. "I…I guess we're brothers." He shrugged. It must have not been a big deal to him. "Or some other form of close relation."

"Huh," Perry muttered. Brothers. The word sounded strange and foreign to him. His mother died when he was only four, so he was an only child. No brothers, no sisters. And then, out of the blue, there was Jack, a murderer and probably insane. Out of nowhere this boy came along, claiming that they were siblings. It was a lot to take in at one time, but to his surprise he didn't feel any sort of shock. He honestly didn't feel much of anything. There was some comfort in knowing that he wasn't entirely alone in the world. After his mother died, Perry's father completely broke down. He started drinking and staying out at night, forcing Perry to fend for himself at a very young age. For all those years that passed, he thought he was completely alone, but at least that wouldn't be the case anymore.

Stop this! Perry told himself, scolding the fact that even for a second he was willing to accept Jack as his younger brother. *He's not your brother! He's not your family! He may have some of the same DNA as you, but that doesn't make him a part of you! You never fought in the back seat of your father's car! You never helped him up when he fell down as a child! He's a killer, and probably a psychopath just like the girl! Don't even think for a second that he could ever be a part of your life!*

When he looked up from the table, he saw that Jack was waiting patiently for his response. Smiling hopefully at Perry, Jack appeared as if he wanted to be accepted. His soft, seemingly innocent mahogany eyes were baiting Perry, his gentle expression trying to pull him in. When he smiled, Perry couldn't take it anymore.

Standing up quickly, he cleared his throat. "I—I can't do this now," he said, pushing his chair in and stepping back. Jack looked taken aback, even hurt, but Perry wouldn't allow himself to fall for it. "I just can't deal with something like this right now." Turning, he hurried out the door without looking back.

✳ ✳ ✳

As the flustered FBI agent rushed out, Jack watched his one hope for survival turn his back on him. He hoped the lie about them being brothers would get to him, and it did, but not in the way he planned. Jack needed to get out of there, and fast. The only way he could was through Perry. The part about them being brothers had been an absolute lie, but he thought the man would have felt some sympathy for him. Obviously, Jack had underestimated him.

Feeling the pressure of a stare on him, Jack turned and gazed through the one-way glass. Another lie he told Perry was that he didn't have any

152

abilities. He could communicate telepathically just like Hara, and unlike a regular human he was able to see right through the one-way glass. Unfortunately for him, his ability wouldn't help him get out.

As he looked through the window, he saw a lone man sitting at the table on the other side, someone who was once a dear friend of his father and Hara's. Allan Brown and Meg Hopper had left several minutes ago after Odau stormed over and nearly dragged the two of them out by their hair. Daniel Marcus remained, and he was gazing back at Jack. He shook his head gently, his eyes showing disappointment.

What are you doing, Jack? Daniel asked him.

Jack shrugged in return, and felt a surge of anger towards Daniel. He didn't know what he was doing. Couldn't Daniel just trust that he was able to work his way out of his own mess? All Jack was doing was making things up as he went along. Getting caught was never a part of the plan. He was improvising, and unfortunately, he let his connection to Perry get the better of him. Telling Perry the truth about Hara was a big mistake. He had crossed the line.

Now he knows, Daniel thought gravely, rising to his feet and walking to the door. *And soon, they all will.*

He was right. Perry was bound to tell his colleagues what Jack told him. If that information got into the wrong hands...things would not end well. The last time humans found out about what Hara could do, she had been experimented on and tortured, something no person should ever have to endure. If more people should discover her again, then their situation was bound to get even worse. Jack could sense it. A disaster was approaching, and he could feel it. Marcus could too, and probably the others as well. They could smell the evil slowly and surely descending upon the city, and Jack had a feeling that they wouldn't escape its clutches this time around.

* * *

Pain.

That was the first thing Hara felt when her eyes fluttered open; a fiery burst of agony in her chest that made her eyes water. The pain in her head was gone—hopefully for good—as well as the pain from the gunshot wound in her side. Her skin was no longer raw from the boiling water, but her chest was burning. At first when she woke up, it felt like a little pinch, but within seconds the pain was making her grind her teeth and stop breathing altogether. Her eyes widening, she looked up, wondering where the hell she was. A bright, florescent light was shining down on her, practically burning holes in her retinas. She was raised up on a hard surface; she guessed it was a wooden table by the cool, smooth texture under her fingertips. The air around her reeked of blood and scum water; the putrid stench lingering on her still. A thick, iron-flavored substance clung to the back of her throat, and when she finally allowed herself to inhale it caused her to start coughing hard. More of the thick liquid came up into her throat as she coughed, and she realized that it was her own blood. Then she remembered; the second bullet had penetrated her lung, and now her blood was leaking into it. She could feel that the bullet was still lodged deep inside her chest, not allowing the tissue cells around it to regenerate. That was a problem.

For the first time since she awoke, Hara noticed someone standing beside the table. The person was busying himself with something, and didn't notice that she had regained consciousness. Moments passed while Hara just lay there, unsure of where she was or what she should do. It was when the person above her started pressing down on her wound, which sent another spark of red hot agony through her chest, that she decided she had had enough.

With a loud cry of pain that made her chest hurt even more, Hara jerked her body upright, grabbing the hand of the person pressing down on her wound. She was gasping as she sat there, holding the person's hand away from her and glaring into his eyes. Her breaths were coming out in hoarse rasps, but she ignored it.

It was Noah. In his hand he held a pair of tongs to remove the bullet, and his expression was remarkably calm. After a few long moments he reached out with his free hand and placed it on her shoulder. Gently, so as not to distress her more, Noah pushed her back down.

Her adrenaline was pumping, but Hara allowed him to press her back flat onto the table, trusting that he knew what was best for her. He always did.

"How do you feel?" Noah asked her softly, picking up a small rag and wiping his hands on it. Hara saw that his hands were covered in blood. Her blood.

She tried to laugh scornfully, but the effort only sent her into another fit of scratchy coughs. "Do I have to answer?" she demanded when she could muster up enough strength to speak.

Too many times in the past she had been asked that question. After holes were drilled through her eyes and into her brain, that question came up. When strange, painful substances were injected into various parts of her body, it was always, "How do you feel?" What was the point of people asking her that when they already knew the answer? Horrible! Absolutely horrible! If she had to answer that question ever again, she was going to lose it.

"No," Noah chuckled. "I managed to get the other bullet out while you were still unconscious, but unfortunately you awoke before I could remove this one."

"Perfect," Hara groaned, her stomach churning as she realized she was going to have to endure the extraction while she was conscious.

"Who shot you?" Noah questioned, picking up the tongs again.

"His father," Hara answered, swallowing hard to keep down the blood and vomit that was rising in her throat.

"So you didn't kill the boy?"

"No."

"And the others?" Noah picked up a large wooden spoon from beside her and held it up to her mouth.

"Disposed of," Hara muttered, clamping her teeth down on the spoon. Her heart was pounding as Noah lowered the tongs to her wound.

"Good," Noah said absentmindedly. He looked back at her and saw how tense she was. "Relax."

Yeah, right, Hara thought, rolling her eyes and resting her head back on the table. The procedure was going to hurt much worse than when she had actually been shot.

Pursing his lips, Noah proceeded with the operation. While Hara chomped down on the wooden spoon in anticipation, he sank the pair of blood-soaked tongs into her gunshot wound.

Pain erupted in her chest all over again, making her gasp. She balled her hands into tight fists at her sides and squeezed her eyes shut, but it didn't help. The pain kept growing in intensity, and she desperately wanted to scream. Despite the amount of misery she was in, she kept as still as she could. She knew it would only hurt worse if she moved.

As Hara felt the tongs sinking further and further into her chest, Noah placed his free hand on her shoulder and rubbed it gently. She assumed it was supposed to feel comforting, but it really wasn't. Digging her fingernails into her palms, she fought back the scream that she so desperately wanted to let out.

After several endless, agonizing moments, Noah pulled the tongs out, in them the bloody, deformed bullet. Hara's eyes snapped open and she spit the spoon out from between her teeth. Sucking in a lungful of air, she lifted her head to look down at her injury. Now that the bullet was out, her tissue cells were free to regenerate. The hole where the round had penetrated was slowly growing smaller as her flesh carefully pulled back together. Within seconds, her skin had fully healed, not even a scar remaining. The pain had ceased as well, leaving Hara feeling remarkably well.

"Well, I guess that solves that problem," Noah declared, setting down the tongs and picking up the blood-stained rag again.

With a weak groan that summed up just how exhausted Hara was, she dropped her head back down on the table and passed out again.

✳ ✳ ✳

Lieutenant Odau had literally dragged Allan Brown out of the observation room. He took him by the arm and led him down the hall and into the conference room, the last vacant room before the lobby. Meg Hopper followed close behind, but when Odau shoved him into the conference room he stopped her.

"I need to speak with him alone," he informed curtly, starting to close the door in her face.

"Lieutenant, I really think…" Meg started as she caught the door with her shoulder, but Odau cut her off sharply.

"Miss Hopper, please!" His face was beet red, and his eyes clearly expressed the anger he was feeling.

Allan saw Meg's startled expression, and she stepped away from the door before the lieutenant quickly slammed it shut.

Rounding on him, Odau growled, "You have some serious explaining to do."

Nodding, Allan took a cautious step back. "Yes, I suppose I do," he replied quietly, gazing calmly back at the enraged officer. "But that doesn't mean that I will."

Pointing to a chair at the long wooden conference table, Odau commanded forcefully, "Sit!"

Questioning whether the lieutenant had the authority to order him around like that, Allan realized he was no longer the one in power. After everything that had happened, being mayor meant nothing anymore. Three kids were dead because of him, and if he had just told everyone the truth about Hara they could have prevented their deaths. He should have told Odau that his son was the "unknown" target. He should have told them to move the children to a high security facility and then taken Hara out with a shot to the head when she came for them. It wouldn't have killed her, but it would have immobilized her until the bullet was removed. No matter what he told Odau now, no matter how he tried to justify himself, his position of power was being taken away from him. He was going to jail for a very long time for what he had done. Regretfully, he sat down opposite Odau.

It was easy to see that the lieutenant was struggling to control his rage. His hands were balled into tight fists on the table and he was glaring at Allan, breathing steadily through his nose. When he finally found the words he was looking to say, he hissed through gritted teeth, "Why didn't you just tell me my son was the target?" As he said that, there was something else in his eyes besides anger: devastation. The whole episode with his son had caused the poor man to crack inside. Losing a child was heartbreaking—Allan knew that much—and Odau had almost been a victim to that grief. He hadn't lost his son, but it had been a very close call. He was going to have to live with the fact that he almost let Hara walk out of his house with his boy.

Allan hoped that the pain in his own eyes was visible. Deep down, he really wanted Odau's son to die, but he knew that wasn't the right thing to do. He himself had lost his wife and three children to the catastrophe, and having to watch another poor soul grieve over the child he almost lost was too much for him to bear. "I—I'm…" he stammered, trying to show the remorse he felt. Odau's son was pure evil, but Allan didn't want to make Odau suffer for the kid's own mistakes. Slowly lowering his eyes, Allan looked down at the patterns on the table and his eyes filled with tears.

Don't you cry, you fool! he scolded himself. *You're far too strong for that!*

"You're what, sorry? Yeah, I think it's a little too late for that!" Odau's voice caught in his throat. "I need something more than that."

Allan didn't reply. He couldn't. He had too much guilt to produce words. Staring down at the table, he gritted his teeth to suppress the sob he had been trying to contain for the past two years.

"What did I do to deserve this?" Odau whispered, the agony in his voice crushing Allan's heart.

Looking up at him, Allan saw the depth of the man's pain, but Odau wasn't going to accept any of the answers Allan could provide. "Do you think this is your fault?" Allan asked incredulously. "You did nothing to deserve this! I never wanted to cause you this kind of pain, because I know exactly how it feels."

"You have no idea how this feels," Odau declared, the anger returning to his eyes.

Allan decided he needed to clue the lieutenant in a little on his past. "Did you know that I had a wife and three children?" he demanded, his heart being ripped in half by the tormenting memories.

Odau looked quite stunned, but Allan didn't allow him a chance to answer.

"Of course, you didn't," he answered for him, his voice cracking sharply. "Do you know why you never knew? Because they were all killed a little more than two years ago. I was forced to watch my youngest son slowly die an agonizing death. I'll never forget the look of desperation he gave me just before he died, and there was nothing I could do to save him." Shaking his head in self-loathing, Allan finished, "So don't tell me that I don't know how you feel, because I really do."

Staring at him in shock, the questions began spilling out of Odau. "What the hell happened to you people? Who are you? Why do you keep talking about my son like he was the cause of all of this? Why were your families murdered?"

"Because the five of us come from a very different world," Allan explained, knowing he was repeating himself. "A world that you, Agent

Perry, and many others are going to be slowly sucked into if you pursue this any further."

Odau shook his head in disbelief. "Where are you from? And what happened there?"

Gazing into his bewildered eyes, Allan asked him, "My disturbing past holds all the answers to your questions. Are you sure you're ready to hear them?"

He expected Odau to say yes right away, but instead he backtracked slightly. "Who is Jack? What is Hara?"

Allan's stomach flipped at the last question, but he kept his expression smooth. Turning his head in an effort to act confused, he questioned, "What do you mean, what is Hara?"

Leaning forward in his chair, Odau said quietly, "I think you know exactly what I mean. We both know she is in no way even close to normal, and the same goes for Jack. He looks exactly like Perry, but Perry's parents only had one child and the boy's too old to be his son, so who—and what—are they?"

Allan attempted to come up with a clever lie, but he never got the chance to answer.

Detective Finchly burst through the door and cried, "Lieutenant Odau, sir, your son is awake! He's asking for you."

Appearing rather annoyed by Finchly's poorly timed entrance, Odau glared into Allan's eyes. Slowly rising to his feet, he told him in a deadly voice, "This conversation is far from over." Giving him one last glower, the lieutenant turned and followed his detective out.

Slumping down in his chair, Allan sighed and threw his head back in frustration. His life was officially over. He had started a new life in Philadelphia, but he was completely lost without his family. It didn't matter where he hid or how far he ran; he was never going to escape his past, and he was never going to be safe. The questions would keep coming, and if the authorities found out who and what the group really was, then the same thing that happened before was bound to happen again. No one there could find out about the catastrophe. No one could find out about their pasts. Anyone who knew would only be put in more danger. The demons from his past were too dangerous for the unsuspecting and naïve officers and agents.

Allan knew that he would fight to keep a lid on the situation, but he could sense another problem. He could feel evil drawing closer with every passing second, and a sense of uneasiness was being exchanged throughout their group. Every instinct in their bodies was telling them to leave the city and run as far as they could. They had a pretty good idea of what was coming.

"The Doc found us," he whispered to himself when he recognized the familiar cloud of terror slowly descending upon them. Hara's murders were pure calamity, but the worst was yet to come. Allan prayed he was only being paranoid. If Allan had known just how deadly the next twenty-four hours would be, he would have taken his friends and fled the city in an instant.

He wouldn't have looked back.

✳ ✳ ✳

The relief that flooded through Lieutenant Odau when he saw his conscious son was overwhelming. The medics who had been examining him had set up a stretcher in the center of the empty holding cell surrounded by all of their equipment, and that was where he rested. He lay on his back, an oxygen mask over his nose and mouth, an I.V. in his hand, and his burns dressed in thick bandages. His eyes were barely open, but when he saw his father enter the room they widened and he lifted his head slightly. Rushing to his side, Odau turned to the closest medic and demanded, "How is he?"

"He's shaken up quite a bit, and he's in shock, but he should pull through just fine," the medic said. It was everything they had told him before, and it was everything he wanted to hear.

Sighing in relief, Odau looked down at his son, his heart breaking at the sight of his awful condition. His left eye was still extremely swollen, and large bruises were visible all over his face and arms. The burns were covered, but the bruises were all on display. One was bigger than Odau's whole hand!

"What is this from?" Odau asked in confusion, pointing to the largest bruise on Jackson's arm. He had originally assumed that they were all from the girl striking him repeatedly with her fists, but that particular one was too large to be the result of that.

"He was struck several times," the medic answered simply.

Odau wasn't convinced. Balling his right hand into a fist, he held it above the bruise. It was at least twice as big as his fist, and he doubted that Hara's were even the same size as his. "How do you explain this?" he asked, raising an eyebrow.

"Dad," Jackson mumbled before the medic could answer.

Both men looked down at Jackson in surprise.

"Yes?" Odau said, taking the small wooden stool that the medic offered him and sitting down. Taking his son's little hand in his own, Odau smiled down at him. "What is it?"

"I need to talk to you," Jackson said drearily, his eyes fluttering with the effort to keep them open.

"Okay," Odau agreed, waiting expectantly. Jackson wouldn't say anything; he just kept staring up at his father; but when he glanced up at the medics, Odau took the hint. "Could you give us a minute?" he asked them.

Nodding, the head medic gestured for his colleagues to exit the room. "We'll be just outside if you need anything," he told Odau as he left.

Once they were gone and the door was closed, Odau repeated his question. "What is it?"

"Who was that girl?" Jackson asked shakily, suddenly looking terrified.

His stomach knotted up at the question, knowing his son was going to be traumatized from the experience. "You don't need to worry about her, okay?" Odau told him reassuringly, reaching up and smoothing back his hair. "I'm taking care of her, so there's no need to…"

"What did I do wrong?" Jackson blurted out, his voice cracking with emotion.

Odau was taken aback. "What are you talking about? You didn't do anything wrong!"

"But she told me I'm a horrible person and she was going to punish me for everything I did!" Jackson sobbed, tears streaming down his exhausted face.

Feeling a combination of shock and fury, Odau asked, "What did she say to you?"

"She said I killed millions of people and she said she was going to hurt me the way I hurt her!" Jackson cried in anguish. "But I didn't do that! I swear!"

"Of course, you didn't," Odau told him firmly, leaning closer to him. "I don't want you to pay any attention to her, alright? You didn't do anything wrong, and you most certainly did not kill millions of people. Don't listen to her. She…she's a very sick girl and we're going to catch her soon so she can't hurt any more people, okay?" He prayed that his son couldn't hear the doubt in his voice.

Jackson nodded, but his face was still very scared and confused. "I think she's going to try to hurt me again," he whimpered, his shoulders starting to shake.

"I will never let that happen," Odau promised. "She's never going to touch you again. Ever." *I'll kill her before she comes near you again!* he wanted to say, but he didn't want to scare the child any further.

"She wanted to kill me!" Jackson wailed. "Her eyes were red and she burned me…"

"Don't worry about her anymore," Odau repeated sharply. "She's a bad person, and who deals with all the bad people?"

"You do," Jackson mumbled.

"Exactly," Odau said. "She's going to spend the rest of her life in prison. Once we catch her, then everyone will forget about her just like all the other bad people. Stop worrying yourself over this, okay?"

Jackson nodded again, this time not saying anything more. He rested his head against the stretcher and closed his eyes.

"Get some rest," Odau told him gently, rubbing his hand. Standing up, he turned and headed towards the door. As much as he wanted to stay with his son, he had a job to do. He had to bring in the psychopath who tried to kill Jackson and had killed so many other people already. She was still out there somewhere, and he wanted to be the one to put the handcuffs around her wrists.

"Dad?" Jackson said as Odau reached the door. There was a tentative tone to his voice that caused Odau to pause.

"Yes?" Odau turned back to him.

"Just before you came, she told me that something else was coming, something worse than her. She said that she could feel it. What did she mean?"

Startled, it began to dawn on Odau just how crazy that girl was. "I'm not sure. But don't worry about it. She won't bother you again."

Letting out a small shudder, Jackson nodded again. Sighing, he looked up at the ceiling.

Odau could tell by his son's expression that he was not at all comforted by that statement. Wishing there was something more he could say to calm his troubled thoughts, he told his boy, "I love you, Jackson."

"I love you, too," Jackson replied sleepily, his eyes fluttering shut once more.

His heart breaking again at the sight of his beaten child, Odau regretfully left the room. The anger that blinded his judgment so often was rising up inside him once more, and now that his emotions were controlling his actions, he was about to do something that would result in tragedy for another man. As he left the room, he told the head medic, "Keep a careful eye on him, please."

"Yes, sir," he said, leading his colleagues back inside.

Marching into the lobby, Odau called out to his fellow detectives, "Listen up! As you know, three young children were just murdered." He looked around to the men and women who were all in uniform, knowing that what happened an hour earlier had disturbed most of them greatly. "The boy we have locked up killed two of them, and we already have his confession. The girl known only as Hara killed the other, but they were not working alone. Three people that have been working among us in this city for more than two years now have betrayed us. These three people have been leaking information to our killers, and they must not be allowed to hide among us anymore."

"Who are you talking about?" a younger male detective asked, looking confused.

Odau listed their names without hesitation. "Mayor Allan Brown, District Attorney Meg Hopper, and our very own Detective Daniel Marcus."

Several skeptical glances were exchanged as well as several perplexed whispers. None of them wanted to believe that people of high authority in their government, and also some of their friends, were exchanging information with two murderers.

"Are you sure?" the same detective from before asked. Odau recognized him as one of Marcus's close colleagues.

"Yes," Odau told him regretfully. "And I know that some of you may have been close with Marcus, but he's been feeding information to our killers ever since the incident at the bank yesterday." He didn't hesitate to make stuff up as he went along. "We mustn't allow these people to keep their positions and continue to assist the girl while we're having enough trouble catching her as it is. I want all three of them in separate holding cells ASAP!"

All the detectives paused. "Uh, sir?" Detective Finchly said carefully.

Narrowing his eyes, Odau looked around the room at all the guilty faces. "What's wrong?" he demanded in dread. "What happened?"

"Uh…Detective Marcus left with Meg Hopper not five minutes ago," she told him, flinching at his furious expression.

"And you all just let them go?!" Odau exclaimed in disbelief, his face flushing red.

"We had no reason to hold them here until now," another detective said defensively.

"What about the mayor?" Finchly asked, looking around. "Did anyone see him leave?"

"No one would have let him leave," the male detective, called Aubrey, reminded. "Not after he lied about the girl's plot."

Feeling foolish for not telling his detectives sooner, Odau told them as they began arguing amongst themselves, "He was in the conference room with me a few minutes ago; he should still be there. Finchly and Aubrey, please escort him to a vacant holding cell."

"Yes, sir," they both said, heading towards the conference room.

"I want eyes on Marcus and Hopper now!" he ordered, and everyone began scrambling for their work stations. Looking around in curiosity, he asked, "Where the hell is Agent Perry?"

"Right here," Perry replied, stepping beside him from behind. He appeared rather worried. His usually impassive expression was now thick with anxiety. His brow was furrowed and he was shifting from foot to foot, his eyes darting to the windows and back nervously.

"Where have you been?" Odau demanded, but stopped when he saw Perry's face. "What's wrong?"

Reaching into the breast pocket of his jacket, Perry pulled out a folded piece of paper. "I received this message from Detective Marcus just before he left," he explained, pulling it away from Odau and slipping it back into his pocket when the lieutenant reached for it. "It was requested that only I read this. But I spoke with him, and I think we may have a problem."

"Yes, we have a big problem," Odau reminded him, raising his eyebrows. "As you've noticed, one of the killers is still on the loose, and now two of her conspirators have escaped…"

"You never told me that you shot her," Perry said.

Thinking back, Odau realized that he hadn't told Perry about shooting her. It just hadn't crossed his mind to share that with him. He had shared it with the detectives working on tracking Hara down, but no one else. "No, I guess I didn't."

"It didn't occur to you that that might have been an important piece of information for our investigation?" Perry asked in disbelief. "You shot her, Odau! Twice! Once right through the chest!"

"How did you know about all this?" the lieutenant asked suspiciously.

"Marcus told me."

"I never told him about the encounter."

"Well, he obviously knows!" Perry pointed out. "But that's beside the point. You failed to tell me that you put two bullets through our fugitive! You could have killed her!"

"She's killed nine people in the past two days, and she was about to kill my son!" Odau declared angrily. "So yes, I shot her to protect my son, and it would be comforting to think that she's dying in a street somewhere! And you know what, Agent? This is my investigation! I don't answer to you!"

"As you recall, you called me here to help you!" Perry snapped, his eyes becoming slits. "So yes, you do answer to me!"

Glaring back at him, Odau couldn't come up with a response. Looking down at the floor, he grumbled, "What exactly was Marcus's message?"

Still appearing as if he wanted to persist on the previous subject, Perry told him, "He said we need to take Jack to the FBI field office in Pittsburgh."

Snorting, Odau demanded, "And why should we do that?"

"Marcus said he would be safer further away from 'the center of all of this'," Perry replied.

"And why should we care how safe he is?"

Blinking, Perry continued. "He said a danger was coming that was worse than anything we had seen so far, and he wanted me to go to Pittsburgh with him."

Puzzled, Odau asked, "Why?"

Perry shrugged and sighed. "Apparently, I play an important part in their conspiracy, because he told me I was too valuable to get caught up in this. That's why Hara didn't kill me when she burned me."

Shaking his head in confusion, Odau asked, "What is it with this case that everything has to be unexpected?"

"I'm asking myself the same thing," Perry muttered.

"What value do you hold to them?" Odau questioned. "You're working on trying to stop this! Why would they care about what happens to you?"

Perry shrugged again. "I don't know, and I'm not sure I want to find out, but I really think we need to take Jack to Pittsburgh."

"Why do you care so much about this boy?" Odau asked curiously. "What did he tell you?"

Thinking, Perry promised, "I swear I'll tell you everything, but not now. If you trust me as you've trusted me so far, you'll trust me when I say the best thing for your son and this investigation is to take Jack to Pittsburgh."

Staring at him in disbelief, Odau shook his head, defeated. "You have a lot of explaining to do." Pausing, he sighed in frustration. "Fine. If you say this is best for my son, then I'll go along with it. Take him to Pittsburgh, but I'm coming too, and you're going to explain everything on the way."

"Fair enough," Perry said in relief, nodding graciously. "Oh, and there was one other thing." He suddenly appeared confused. "Marcus told me that you weren't going to go along with the Pittsburgh idea, and he said the only way to convince you that a greater danger is coming is to tell you to look outside."

The lieutenant raised an eyebrow. "Look outside?"

Before either of them could say another word, Odau noticed that several of his detectives were staring open-mouthed out the windows. One of them stammered, "S—sir? I think you should come look at this."

"What's wrong?" Odau asked uneasily, giving Perry a questionable glance. Taking careful steps forward, Odau walked to the window behind one of the gaping detectives with Perry following closely. Leaning his head to one side so he could see out, the lieutenant's mouth fell open in shock at what he saw. As he heard Perry gasp beside him, Odau asked, "My God, what the hell happened?"

"Do you believe Marcus now?" Perry murmured.

"I'm convinced," Odau breathed, staring at the red-orange glow engulfing the night air about a mile away. There was a huge fire downtown, and he didn't need three guesses to find out who had started it. "Pittsburgh it is. But you're still going to explain everything on the way, and then we're both coming back to finish this case."

"I wasn't intending to stay," Perry assured. "This is getting worse as time moves forward, and we need to catch this kid before this 'greater danger' closes in on us. I wasn't going to hide in Pittsburgh like a coward, whether Marcus said it was best for me or not."

"Good," Odau said, thinking about the bigger mess they were going to have to clean up. "You'd better call your FBI and S.W.A.T. friends and let them know what's going on."

"Already on it," Perry told him, whipping out his cell phone and furiously punching in numbers.

✳ ✳ ✳

Ten minutes earlier, while Lieutenant Odau was having his discussion with Allan Brown, Agent Perry left Jack's interrogation room. It was just too much for him to deal with this case and then discover that he had a newfound "brother." Whether Jack really was his brother or not, Perry didn't want to deal with his emotions on the job, so he did the only thing he could think of: he went someplace private to deal with his emotions alone.

He headed towards a men's restroom down the hall. Throwing open the door, he was relieved to find that it was vacant. It was a small bathroom with only two stalls, four urinals, and two sinks. Stumbling over to the closest sink, Perry planted both his hands firmly on the counter in front of it. He took several deep breaths, trying to calm his raging thoughts. *You're being ridiculous!* he told himself. *Get a grip! You're acting like a child!*

He was, in fact, acting like a child. To allow his feelings to distract him from his job…it was utterly humiliating. Taking several more deep breaths, Perry looked up at his worn reflection in the mirror. His dark mahogany eyes were red and exhausted, purple circles forming under them. His normally neat hair was in tousled curls on top of his head. He could see the small welt on his temple that Hara had given him. Now that he thought about it he realized that it was throbbing horribly, but he ignored the pain. He was counting on the medic's word that he would be fine and it would heal quickly.

Knowing he needed to calm down and get back to work, Perry took one last big breath. Bending his neck down, he turned on the faucet and cupped his hands under the water. Splashing the cold water on his face, he flinched as he scraped his welt with his finger, causing it to sting. After splashing his face twice more, Perry wiped his eyes clear and then stood up straight. He started to reach for the paper towel dispenser, but

165

stopped when he glanced into the mirror again. Behind him, standing casually with his hands in his pockets and gazing back at him, was Daniel Marcus.

His shining baby blue eyes looked just as tired as Perry's, and his wavy brown hair was falling across his forehead. When Perry finally saw that he was standing there, Marcus raised his eyebrows and forced a small smile to his face. "Hi."

"When did you come in?" Perry demanded, not recalling hearing anybody enter.

Marcus shrugged. "A moment ago."

"I didn't hear you," Perry said suspiciously, turning to face him.

Taking a small, timid step back, Marcus replied, "No, I'm very quiet." He was telling the truth. The detective had only ever really spoken when spoken to, and when he did it was always in an inferior tone. He waited for Perry to speak.

"Is…is there something I can help you with?" Perry asked carefully, the detective's stare making him uncomfortable. "Or is it a habit for you to sneak up behind people while they're in the bathroom?"

Smiling lightly, Marcus explained, "I needed to speak to you for a moment." When Perry didn't reply, he added, "About Jack."

"Oh," Perry muttered, turning back to the paper towel dispenser so Marcus couldn't see his face. "What about him?"

"You trust him?" Marcus asked. It sounded like more of a statement than a question.

Pulling out a paper towel, Perry turned back to him. When he saw Marcus's cautious gaze, he questioned, "Should I not?"

Marcus shrugged. "You tell me. You talked to him."

"And you're the one who knows him personally, so you tell me," Perry challenged, throwing the wadded up paper towel in the trash can and staring sharply at Marcus. When he didn't respond, Perry sighed. "He was telling the truth for most of the time."

"How do you know?"

"I know when I'm being lied to," Perry assured him, but even he didn't feel so sure of that anymore. "Is Jack really my brother, or is he just a clone or something similar to that?"

"You're the one who knows when you're being lied to," Marcus reminded, his eyes narrowing. "So you tell me."

Becoming rather annoyed with his little game, Perry frowned. "He didn't seem like he knew our relation when he told me," he said. "I thought maybe you would know since you know the boy pretty well."

Marcus shrugged again, his eyes not moving away from Perry's. Perry could tell by his expression that he was hiding something.

"You know what he is," Perry accused angrily. "I can see it in your eyes. You and the mayor and the D.A. know way more about all of this than you're telling us."

For a moment, Marcus just watched him. Then he replied, "Yes, we do know a lot about your case, and we have many answers to questions you haven't even asked yet. Everything that has happened—and will happen—is for a reason. It's just difficult for all of you to see this yet, because you're only looking at it from their point of view."

"Who's point of view?" Perry demanded, confused. Marcus refused to answer once more, so he asked him, "Why can't the three of you just tell us what happened? You said it's complicated, but I'm sure we would eventually understand."

Sighing, Marcus simply shook his head. "I'm going to tell you what we've already been telling you. I know you don't want to hear it, but it is too early for you to know yet. But I can assure you," he added at Perry's irritated look, "that you will learn the truth about everything before tomorrow is through."

"Well, if I'm going to learn everything by tomorrow, then what difference does it make if you tell me the truth right now?" Perry asked in exasperation. Marcus remained silent again, and Perry told him harshly, "You do understand that Odau is going to lock you up for this?"

After a long, awkward pause, Marcus pulled his hands out of his pockets, completely ignoring the question. He held out a folded piece of paper that was crinkled around the edges. "I made this for you, my friend," he said as Perry took it from him, and he stopped Perry when he tried to open it. "Ah, ah! Please don't read it until I've left."

"Why?" Perry demanded, wanting desperately to read whatever was written on the small note. "What is it?"

"It's a little more information about Jack and Hara, but I don't want to be asked any more questions, so wait until I'm gone," Marcus explained. "Also, you cannot show anyone else the information on that paper. Not the lieutenant, not anyone in the FBI, no one. That is a message meant only for you. Do you understand?"

"Sure," Perry muttered, dropping his hand with the note down to his side.

Closing his eyes, Marcus started again. "There's another favor I need to ask of you, and I'm praying that you will do what I ask."

"What?"

Opening his eyes again, Marcus began his explanation. "Something's coming. We—Allan, Meg, Jack, and I—can all feel it. It's worse than anything you've seen so far. It's no longer safe in this city anymore. The favor I'm going to ask of you is that you take Jack to your FBI office in Pittsburgh."

"Why should I take him there?" Perry demanded skeptically.

"Because he's in grave danger in this city, and if you really care about him—and I know you do—then you'll take him there so he'll be safe, where more trouble won't find him."

Still not convinced, Perry said, "You seem so worried about this 'greater danger.' What is it, exactly, that makes your face turn white?" Once again, Marcus chose to remain silent. "I think you're just a paranoid person…"

"Can't you feel it?" Marcus whispered urgently, his voice dropping down until it was barely audible. "Don't even think about it. *Feel.* Aren't your instincts telling you that something really bad is coming?"

Perry decided to humor the detective, and to his surprise, something did feel off to him. His stomach seemed to be knotted up in anticipation, waiting for whatever the world could throw at him next. At first, he thought he was just anticipating another move from Hara, but it felt like something else, something bigger.

"It's not that you're expecting an attack from Hara," Marcus insisted, as if he could read his mind. "What you're sensing is them."

"Them?" Perry repeated.

"Our greater danger," Marcus whispered. "Oh, and when you take Jack to Pittsburgh, you need to stay there with him. Don't come back here. This city is about to become a battlefield, and you can't be allowed to get caught up in it."

"And why not?" Perry demanded. "What's so important about me that I can't fight this battle?"

"You're too valuable to us."

Taken aback, Perry echoed, "Valuable? To you?"

Marcus nodded, but didn't explain what he meant. "You'd better leave soon, too. Take Jack, go to Pittsburgh, and don't come back. That's all I can do for you now. After this, you'll be on your own."

Frustrated with all the mysteries, Perry told him, "Even if I wanted to go back to Pittsburgh with him, Odau would never go for it…"

"He won't be convinced easily. Trust me, I know. To convince him and yourself of the greater danger, just look outside when you get the chance."

Raising an eyebrow suspiciously, Perry repeated, "Look outside?"

Marcus nodded again. "When you get the chance." Turning, he reached for the handle of the door and pulled it open. He started to exit, but Perry stopped him.

"Marcus!" he called, taking a step towards the detective. Marcus looked back at him curiously. Something just didn't seem right about him to Perry, and his story was beginning to bother him. "Who are you?" Perry asked, hoping he'd get an answer.

"A friend," Marcus promised as he stepped out and the door began to close. "In a different lifetime, anyway."

Staring after him, Perry pondered over Marcus's words. A friend in a different lifetime. What the hell did that mean?

Maybe logic won't solve this case, he told himself. Maybe I can't expect the answers to make any sense. It's completely possible that Marcus, Brown, and Hopper are all as crazy as Jack and Hara. They could all be making everything up. The three adults all appeared perfectly sane, but considering what they were saying, labeling them as completely bonkers would be the first thing with this case that actually made sense.

Unfolding the note, he read it intently to see what valuable information it might hold.

Agent Perry,

I know several things have happened over the past few days that haven't made much sense, but all I can say is that it is about to get much worse. Hara is not your enemy in this fight. She's a friend to you, and what she's doing is going to help you greatly. It may be hard to see it now, but as the clock ticks by I fear you may learn the truth of what happened to her and all of us. What you need to know about her is this: she had to watch all thirteen members of her family die, along with several close friends and a vast number of other people. She's traumatized by what happened to her, and very, very angry. That makes her extremely dangerous. She has her mind set on a specific goal: killing Odau's son. And she doesn't intend to stop until she has achieved her goal. Understand this: her parents were the result of a genetic experiment, giving her the abilities she possesses. But her parents weren't the only people affected by this experiment. There were many others, most of whom are now dead. There was a man who discovered all these people with mutated genes, and he set out to exterminate them all, with the exception of a select few. Hara was one of those select few. That man did some sick and twisted things to her and the others, and because of what he did, her mind has become very unstable. It's harder for her to control her abilities, and that's why you've been witness to some of the things she can do. Now that she's made her powers known to your world, the man she finally escaped from is about to find her again. I am leaving with Meg Hopper and Allan Brown, so it is now your job to make sure this man doesn't get his filthy hands on her. We can no longer stay in this threatening environment.

Another important fact you should be aware of is that this man will offer to help you capture Hara. Do not listen to a word he says. He is the man who hurt Hara and destroyed her life, and I cannot tell you enough how much he cannot be trusted. As tempting as his offers may be, don't let him near the girl, Jack, or especially you. Goodbye, Agent Perry. And good luck.

Detective Marcus

P.S.—Double, double toil and trouble.

Blinking, Perry reread the last line. "Macbeth?" he muttered to himself, raising an eyebrow. He had been glad that the letter had offered some decent information and warnings, but the random Shakespeare line added at the end disappointed him. The letter had seemed, for the most part, fairly logical, but the last line just supported Perry's theory that Marcus was crazy as well.

Looking back a bit in the note, Perry picked out several key things. She's a friend to you...her parents weren't the only people affected...most of whom are now dead...a man set out to exterminate them all...he did some sick and twisted things to her...he's about to find her again...this man will offer you help...he can't be trusted...I'm leaving with Meg Hopper and Allan Brown...

"They're leaving?" Perry repeated in surprise. He knew that they were really terrified of what was supposedly coming. They were so scared that they were fleeing their homes to escape it. Either something really was coming or they were all completely nuts, and Perry was beginning to wonder if maybe he should be worried, too, and start preparing for the worst.

The man who had been mentioned repeatedly was beginning to pique Perry's curiosity. Was he the supposed "greater danger"? If that guy was going to offer his help, could he really find Hara, let alone catch her? And if he did catch her, what would he do to her afterwards? Who was the guy, anyway?

Then, there was the subject of Hara's parents. Marcus claimed there were many more people affected, but if such a thing had occurred, why hadn't anyone heard about it? Something that huge could not be kept a secret, unless the evidence itself was destroyed...

Of course! Perry thought in realization. That's entirely possible! This could actually be real!

For the first time, Perry was considering the possibility that there was a logical explanation for Hara's actions. If her family was killed to cover up that accident, then she would definitely be angry, and that would give her a reason to kill. But why the children? Why not go after the people who killed her family? Why take the lives of three innocent children? Where was the justice in killing innocents when she was fighting the injustice of taking the lives of innocents?

There were other questions that Perry had with answers that wouldn't make much sense. Why would Marcus tell him that Hara was a friend when she had severely injured him and could have killed him?

You saw the fear in her eyes when she realized it was you, Perry reminded himself. She was afraid for your life. You're important to her, but why?

So many questions were racing through his mind, but he knew that he was going to have to wait for the answers. At the moment, he needed to pass on his message to Odau.

For some reason, Perry trusted Marcus, even though he knew he shouldn't. For some reason, he believed every word the traitor said, but there was one thing in particular that Marcus said that was bugging Perry. What was so significant about looking outside? What was that going to explain? Marching out of the restroom and back towards the lobby, Perry decided he would find out for himself.

When he and Odau finally did look outside, they were both shocked to see downtown Philadelphia on fire. While Perry contacted his colleagues, Odau demanded to know why no one had made an effort to contact the station about the situation.

"The lines are down, sir!" Detective Finchly explained, holding up one of the office's phones.

"Damn it!" Odau said, looking to Perry as Perry began to explain the situation to his fellow agents. "Someone use their cell phone to contact the fire department! Get them down there as soon as possible!"

✳ ✳ ✳

An hour later, things had calmed down a couple notches. The fire department and EMS had both responded, and Homeland Security and the governor had been notified. Firefighters were working on putting out the fires burning around the pool. Most of the officers in the station had left to go help, and only a few of them remained to help Perry and Odau with their last-minute operation. Three S.W.A.T trucks and five FBI SUVs had also been assigned to assist them.

After Perry briefed everyone on the situation, and as they were getting ready to gather their detainees to move out, Odau approached him with devastating news. "The death toll so far is over fifty, and that's not including the people that are missing and the places we haven't covered yet," he said gravely. "Over five hundred are badly injured…this is horrible! How could we let this happen?"

"You're the one who shot her," Perry reminded as he slipped into his FBI jacket, thinking about what Jack had said about Hara losing control of her ability under elevated levels of stress. He hadn't been so sure if he believed the stuff about her having super powers, but since there was really no other explanation for the burn on his wrist and the mysterious fire, things were starting to fall into place.

The lieutenant looked up at him in surprise, but then his expression turned to anger. "What is that supposed to mean?"

Shrugging, Perry zipped up his jacket and began heading down the main hallway to Jack's interrogation room. Odau had agreed to let Perry escort Jack to the S.W.A.T. vehicle in which all three of them would be riding. There were still a few questions for Jack that Perry needed answered before they got going.

"Hey!" Odau called sharply, catching Perry by the arm.

Perry sighed and turned back to him, waiting for the latest outburst.

The lieutenant looked rather offended. "What is that supposed to mean?" he repeated. "Are you suggesting that this is my fault? Do you know something that you're not telling me?"

"Hara started the fires, Lieutenant!" Perry declared. "You shot her, pissed her off, and now a large portion of the downtown is destroyed!"

"I shot her, Perry!" Odau yelled angrily. "She's likely to be dead in an alley somewhere, and even if she's not, how would she be able to cause that much damage on her own? She doesn't have anyone else left to help her, and she'd be too weak to do much of anything!"

"You don't know her," Perry growled at him, shrugging him off.

"And you do?" the lieutenant said, folding his arms across his chest and glaring back at him.

"I know a hell of a lot more than you do!" Perry informed harshly, turning on his heel and striding down the hall.

"Something tells me that your friend Jack gave you some very valuable information about Hara," Odau called after him. When Perry didn't stop or respond, he shouted at him, "Perry!"

Stopping at the door to Jack's interrogation room, he turned back. Odau's expression was angry and impatient, as it always was. "What?" Perry asked, annoyed.

"What's going on?" Odau demanded, his eyes pleading with him for the first time. "What aren't you telling me?"

Sighing, Perry replied, "As I told you before, I'll explain everything on the way." Yanking the door open, he left the lieutenant sputtering where he stood. The door swung shut as he stepped inside, and he shivered as he gazed upon his doppelganger. Jack was handcuffed in his seat, and Perry assumed that another cop must have done that after Perry left. Jack looked curiously at Perry's worn and frustrated expression, his eyes searching Perry's face for the answers to Perry's emotions.

"What's going on?" he asked as Perry made his way around the table to uncuff him.

"We're going on a road trip," Perry said, taking the boy's arm and pulling him to his feet.

"To where?" Jack questioned in confusion.

"Pittsburgh."

"What the hell is in Pittsburgh?"

The two of them were walking around the table at that point, and when they were nearly to the door, Perry grabbed Jack by the front of the shirt, spun him around, and slammed him against the wall.

"Hey!" Jack cried out, his eyes widening in surprise.

"Listen, kid," Perry growled, his nose nearly touching Jack's. "I don't know who you are or what you are, but I do know that you, Marcus, and your other friends are covering up something huge. Something awful happened and it was covered up by bad people, but that doesn't give you the excuse to take children's lives! Now, I don't know what happened to all of you, and I'm sorry that it was devastating enough to land you here. There's a guy out there who did some serious shit to you, Hara, and many other people, and apparently he's coming back for all of you who escaped this mess. And let me tell you this; we may be blood related, but we sure as hell are not family, so don't go thinking that I'm going to let you off the hook easily just because we look alike. But as much as you make me sick, there's a part of me that wants you safe. Marcus told me that this guy wants to hurt you, and that you'd be safe in a place away from here. Pittsburgh is that place. We're going to the FBI office there, and then Lieutenant Odau and I are going to come back and sort out this mess. When we've dealt with Hara and this other guy, then we'll deal with you, but we're going out of our way to Pittsburgh to keep you safe, so I'd be less smart and more grateful if I were you. Alright?"

"Okay," Jack replied quietly, nodding quickly. His face was white as a ghost's from Perry's sudden outburst, and there was a fear in his eyes that concerned him. As he released him, Jack asked meekly, "Did Marcus really say that...he was coming here?"

"Yes," Perry answered, inhaling deeply. "He said he's almost here."

"Then you can't come back here," Jack declared. "If that man comes back for us then you're in just as much danger as we are!"

"Oh really?" Perry said flatly. "And why is that?"

"Because..." Jack started, but his voice trailed off quickly.

"Oh, wait," Perry realized, and he became sarcastic. "I'm important to you, right?"

Nodding, Jack completely ignored Perry's sarcasm. "Yes, and anyone important to us is a target for him."

"And just why, exactly, am I important to you?" Perry demanded, pushing the door open once more and pulling Jack out with him.

"The same reason I'm important to you," Jack answered. "We're family."

Scowling down at him as he led the boy down the side hall to the back exit, Perry snapped, "We are not family."

"But we will be," Jack said, raising his eyebrows at him.

Rolling his eyes, Perry told him angrily, "You know, I'm really getting sick of all these mysterious little comments. Anything you or your friends say just triggers more questions that only get half answered."

"Welcome to my world," Jack muttered, smiling lightly.

Perry stopped halfway down the hall. Turning to Jack, he demanded, "What world do you people keep talking about, hmm?"

Gazing back up at him, Jack said, "The world of deception, betrayal, confusion, death...a world that you're slowly beginning to enter." Sighing, he added solemnly, "Unfortunately, once you set foot into this world, there's no way out of it."

Leaning closer, Perry whispered, "Well, if throwing myself head first into your world is the only way to figure out the truth, so be it." For several moments he glared into the boy's eyes, letting him know that his talk of death and dangerous secrets didn't scare him. After being in the FBI for as long as he had, it took quite a lot to scare him. Heaving a sigh, Perry took Jack's arm again and led him down the rest of the hall. When they reached the door at the end, Perry opened it and stepped outside, Jack in tow. A series of loud noises met his ears as he stepped out into the cool night air. Off in the distance he could hear the sirens of fire trucks, squad cars, and ambulances. His ears were throbbing from all the commotion, and the sounds of roaring fires and screaming added to the noise. He could see the orange glow of the fires reflecting off the black sky, lighting up the dark night. Feeling a twinge of regret for leaving the city in such a time of desperation, Perry gave Jack's arm a yank as they walked down the three concrete steps onto the ground below.

Out the back exit was a loading dock for supplies, and that was where all his people were waiting for him. Two lines of cars sat just outside the building. The one furthest from him held the squad car that Finchly would be driving, leading the way. Behind it were the first two black SUVs that Perry's colleagues would be driving, and behind them was the first S.W.A.T. truck, and then one more black SUV behind that.

That would be the first line of vehicles to go. In the front of the second line was the S.W.A.T. truck that Jack would be transported in, and following that was the last S.W.A.T. truck, the last two black SUVs, and the squad car that Aubrey would drive, bringing up the rear. There were red and blue lights flashing on the roofs of each vehicle, the colors dancing in the night sky along with the reflection of flames. Very few people were sitting inside their cars; most of them were milling around outside, having small side conversations or just wandering around looking for something to busy themselves with. When they saw Perry leading Jack towards the first S.W.A.T. vehicle, quite a few of the side conversations turned into stares and whispers. Perry didn't blame them. He shivered every time he looked at Jack's face.

Neither of them spoke until they were within feet of the truck. Perry saw that Jack was listening curiously to the sirens in the distance and observing the many colors reflecting off the pitch black sky. "What happened?" he whispered, dread showing in his eyes.

"Your friend burst," Perry told him, walking to the back of the truck and pulling the door open.

"Oh, God," Jack breathed in horror as two S.W.A.T. members came around back to help Perry get him inside. One of them jumped up into the back and reached down for Jack's arm. The other gave the boy a push and they both hoisted him into the back. As the second agent jumped up, Jack turned back to Perry. "Will you bring Allan Brown, too?"

"Why would I do that?" Perry demanded.

"Because he's in danger too," Jack insisted. "And he's only going to get in your way. There's no reason he needs to stay here."

Perry could have given a list of reasons to keep the mayor in Philadelphia, but he didn't want to argue anymore. "I'll think about it," he muttered flatly.

"Stay with me in Pittsburgh," Jack begged as he was pushed onto a bench against the side of the truck.

"Not a chance."

"Please?" Jack pressured, sounding somewhat like a child. He completely ignored the man chaining his cuffs to the floor.

Gazing back at the boy who looked just like him, Perry told him, "I'll see you 'round, kid." Swinging the back door shut, the last thing he saw was Jack's pleading, helpless look.

Debating whether or not he wanted to listen to Jack's advice about taking Allan Brown along as well, Perry sighed in irritation as he gave in. Turning to Finchly, who was a few feet away by her squad car, he asked her, "Would you please go and retrieve the mayor and put him in the back as well? He's going to come with us, too."

Finchly hurried back inside quickly, because even she could feel the evil force that was coming. Perry walked around to the driver's side and climbed up, praying that they could get out of the city in time. What he didn't know was that the danger Marcus had described had already found them all, and it would be difficult for them to escape with their lives.

6

Pursuit

Bright lights were the first things Hara saw when she finally regained consciousness. Blinking, she stared up at the lights and the plain white ceiling. The air around her was hot and smelled of chemicals, a smell that always made her stomach churn. It didn't surprise her that she was back in that room; she'd been expecting to end up there again. She just hated the fact that it was so soon, and she hadn't even finished what she went to Philadelphia to do.

The lights were blinding, and as the terror began to take control of her she struggled to get to her feet and run as fast and as far as she could. But she couldn't get up. Her wrists and ankles were bound by leather straps, and no matter how hard she pulled she couldn't break free.

How did I get here? she wondered in horror. *How did this happen?*

Her heart was pounding and her breathing was becoming quicker and louder. She could feel her sweat pouring down her face and back, and looking around at her surroundings she realized that she was right back where she started. She was right back in the lab, with more experiments about to be performed on her. More torture, more pain, more fear.

As her struggles became more intense, two hands grabbed her to keep her still. One hand was on her wrist, the other on her shoulder. Balling her hands into tight, terrified fists, Hara snapped her head up to look at her abductor. Her breath caught in her throat as she realized who it was. The man above her was dressed in light blue scrubs from head to toe. There was a mask over his nose and mouth and gloves on his hands, like there always was whenever there was a "patient" on the table. Every part of him was covered except for his eyes, but that was all that Hara needed to identify him. She would recognize those cold grays anywhere. They had always reminded her of death.

"No!" she whimpered, her voice barely a squeak. Attempting to shrink back against her bed, she struggled harder in an effort to get away from him.

"*Shhhh*," he whispered in his smooth, silky voice. "It's okay."

"No!" Hara repeated, shaking her head furiously.

The man her was the man who had slaughtered her entire family along with almost everyone else like her. He was the one who had experimented on her for months and had caused her so much pain. She wanted to see him dead so badly; to see him on the table in her place so she could inflict the same pain on him that he had inflicted on her; but there she was again, strapped back on his table in his lab. She doubted that she could make it through another round of his games. Wrenching at the leather straps holding her in place, she started to scream.

"*Shhhhh!*" he hissed again. "Hara, calm down! It's okay!"

"No, no, no!" Hara screamed repeatedly, squeezing her eyes shut and slamming her head back against the table over and over again. Maybe, if she hit her head hard enough, she could knock herself out so she wouldn't have to be conscious for whatever was about to happen.

Hara could feel more people coming to restrain her. Someone put a hand on her forehead and pressed her head down while placing their other hand on her other shoulder. Two more hands grabbed her ankles. That only caused Hara to scream louder and thrash harder. She wanted to use one of her abilities against them all, but she was too scared and too exhausted to concentrate enough. The first man, her worst nightmare, released her shoulder and attempted to pry her left eye open, yelling her name.

"Hara, wake up!" he cried.

"Wake up, baby!" the person to her left said soothingly.

Something wasn't right. For one thing, the person who had last spoken to her was a woman, and none of the doctors assigned to Hara were female. Second, the voice of her worst nightmare had changed. He was currently speaking with a British accent. Hara knew quite well that the man she was so terrified of spoke with the same accent as her, an American accent from what her father had told her. If that man above her wasn't who she thought he was, then who was he? Who the hell were all those people?

Snapping her eyes open, Hara gasped as she realized what was going on. As her vision cleared, her surroundings changed as well. The man above her was Noah, and he wasn't wearing the doctor's scrubs; he was wearing a black suit and tie as he had been earlier that day. No blue pants or jacket, no face mask, and no gloves. It was just plain, old, amazing Noah. Hara had dreamed the entire episode.

There were still six hands trying to hold her down, so she allowed herself to slump back against the table. She was still lying on the wood table where Noah had removed the bullets from her, and she realized that her clothes were soaked in her own blood and sweat. Her hands and arms had been scrubbed clean. Wrinkling her nose at the smell of her filthy clothing, she decided that the first thing she would do when she calmed down was change into something that didn't reek of pond scum. Looking down at the foot of the table, she saw that the person holding her ankles was Daniel Marcus. His wavy hair was falling across his worried baby blue eyes, and even though she was furious at him for betraying her, she was really glad to see him. The third person holding her was stroking her hair, and peering up, Hara's eyes widened at whom she saw.

"Meg?" she whispered in shock, amazed to see Meg's pretty, smiling face gazing down at her.

"Hey, baby," Meg Hopper said, her eyes filled with sadness.

Kicking free of Daniel and pulling away from Noah, Hara pushed herself off the table and grabbed Meg in a tight embrace. She gladly hugged back despite the horrid smell of her clothing.

Hara hated the amount of emotion that she was experiencing with the hug. Over the past several months, she had discovered that living without emotion was easier, but now that she was seeing her past catch up with her again, her emotions were beginning to interfere once more. Hara sensed that Meg was feeling a great deal of pain as well, but it was all for a completely different reason. She hadn't seen Hara in over two years, and now she was able to see what Hara had become. It was killing Meg inside. She hadn't been around for whatever caused Hara to finally dive off the deep end, but she knew that whatever happened had been horrifying enough to completely taint her mind. Feeling Meg's pain just caused Hara more. Meg had been like a mother to her after her own mother was killed, and Hara didn't want to make her feel remorse for leaving. Squeezing her eyes shut, Hara buried her face in Meg's shoulder.

"You just had a nightmare," Hara heard Daniel say, and she could sense his concern for her.

"Yeah," she muttered, gulping down a lungful of air. "Tell me about it."

A few moments passed, but neither Hara nor Meg broke the embrace. She felt Daniel's hand on her shoulder, and he rubbed it in a reassuring manner. As much as he disapproved of her tactics, Hara knew that he still cared for her, and he hated to see her in the state she was in.

Finally pulling away from Meg, Hara hopped off the table and took a few steps away from it so she could turn to face all of them. Shaking off her terror from the nightmare, Hara was faced with reality: she had failed to kill her lead target and now Agent Perry and Lieutenant Odau knew about her abilities, which meant that other people would find out and then find her. Things were not good.

"Are you feeling alright?" Daniel asked her carefully.

Thinking about it, Hara realized that she felt remarkably well. "Surprisingly, I am" she said, nodding.

"Good," he said, giving her a small smile.

"No pain?" Noah questioned, and when she glanced over at him he tapped the side of his head before gesturing to his chest.

For the first time in a long time, Hara felt no physical pain anywhere in her body. "No," she answered, the corners of her mouth turning up at the sudden realization. Lifting up her shirt slightly, she was glad to see that the only marks on her chest were the dried clumps of blood. Not even a scar remained. "No pain. Not even a twinge."

Noah smiled at her, his eyes crinkling at the corners. "Well, I'm glad to say that's something I haven't heard in a long time."

Nodding back, Hara shot a glance at Daniel, who was standing beside the table and peering at her cautiously. When their eyes met, he looked down at the floor, but Hara caught the look of shame before he did so.

"So, are you back in the game or what?" she demanded.

Shrugging, Daniel refused to meet her gaze once more. "I suppose so."

Hara saw that he was in his police uniform, but he had removed all the pins from his jacket and she noticed his badge lying on the floor behind him. He was definitely back in the game. By removing the pins and badge, he was telling the world that he was going to go against the life he had struggled to create to help the person he had struggled to forget.

Cocking her head to the side, Hara told him, "Well, it's good to have you back."

Daniel nodded gratefully, but still refused to meet her eyes.

Turning back to Noah, she asked him hopefully, "Do you have anything else I can wear?" She pointed to her filthy outfit and wrinkled her nose in disgust.

Chuckling, Noah turned to the wall behind him. There was a small wooden chair resting against it, and on it sat a clean pair of jeans and a clean black t-shirt. Noah picked them both up and leaned across the table to hand them to Hara.

Hara took them and looked around for a private place to change. When Meg touched her shoulder and pointed to the opposite wall, Hara saw that there was a curtain a few feet away from the wall that extended all the way from the ceiling to the floor. Walking over, she stepped behind it and stretched it out as far as it would go. Dropping the clean pair of clothes on the cold concrete floor, Hara began to peel her shirt off. As she changed, she noticed that the room was awkwardly silent. No one was speaking, but Hara could hear their thoughts focusing on more delicate matters.

"Everything okay?" she asked carefully, having no desire to discuss what they were thinking about.

"Fine," Meg lied quietly.

Hara pulled the clean-smelling shirt down over her head and smoothed it out. "So, how did you two find us here, anyway?"

"Your distraught, agonized mind isn't very difficult to find," Daniel told her solemnly. "I could hear you screaming from a mile away."

Flinching at the memory of the pool, Hara unbuttoned her jeans and began to peel them off as well. Her mind probably had been making a lot of ruckus because of how much pain and fear she had been experiencing. She was annoyed with herself that Daniel could have heard her from so far away. "Yeah," she muttered. "Right."

"Hara, honey…" Meg started, and Hara could sense her uneasiness. "We need to talk."

"About what?" Hara asked quietly, already knowing.

"About why you came back here," Daniel said softly. "And why you're doing this."

Slipping on the pair of dark blue jeans, Hara was surprised to find that they fit perfectly. Sighing, she hoped that her friends could understand how badly she didn't want to talk about it. "Listen, I really don't want to get onto this subject right now," she told them, her voice cracking with emotion. "Noah saw what happened, so talk to him about it." She was glad they couldn't see her, because her eyes were watering as the horrifying memories of what happened before she left for Philadelphia began plaguing her mind again. It wasn't a topic that she had any desire to look back on, but her friends weren't about to let her go so easily.

"Yes, Noah saw that everyone in the camp was killed, but I think something else happened that was so disturbing that it really messed you up," Daniel said.

Stepping out from behind the curtain, she gave him a very dangerous look. "So trying to stop the people who did this makes me messed up, does it?"

"Honey…" Meg tried to reason with her, but Hara didn't want to hear it. Hara knew she was losing it, but she didn't want to face the truth.

"Don't!" she snapped, pointing a finger at her. "Don't use that tone on me!"

"Hara," Noah said, raising his eyebrows. "Listen to them."

"No!" she shouted, feeling herself becoming angry again. "I'm not going to let you all start coming to conclusions about me based on some theory you've got going!"

"What are you talking about?" Daniel demanded in confusion.

"You're accusing me of being crazy because I've been through a great ordeal!" Hara exclaimed furiously.

"We're not accusing you of anything," Meg told her soothingly, putting her hands up to show that they weren't trying to upset or attack her.

"He's accusing me of being crazy!" Hara yelled.

"You've been killing people, Hara," Daniel reminded. "Something you swore you'd never do. You need to face the facts. You need help."

"Shut up!" Hara snarled. "Maybe I've got a few problems, but I had to watch my entire family suffer from torture or murder or both! I was experimented on for months! I think I've got an excuse!"

"The same thing happened to all of us," Daniel said quietly. "And as you can see, we're perfectly fine."

Taken aback, Hara replied through gritted teeth, "I had it worse than you."

Nodding gently, Daniel whispered, "I know, but you weren't like this before we left you. Something happened after we left."

Shaking her head, Hara took several steps backwards. She couldn't handle remembering it.

Daniel saw her pain and could sense it as well, and he took a couple steps towards her. "Just tell us what happened," he pleaded, sympathy burning in his eyes.

"No!" Hara repeated, turning quickly and striding across the room away from them. She saw the large couch facing the flat screen TV and went to it, sitting down and dropping her head into her hands. Her back was now to them, but she could hear everything that was running through their minds. Meg wanted to just let it go, but Daniel wanted the truth. Noah just wanted Hara to talk to someone about it so she could get help, but he wasn't going to bother her anymore. Tuning out their thoughts, Hara tried to calm herself before she got too worked up. The headache was no longer plaguing her, but if she got too upset, she could accidentally release more of the energy that she could already feel beginning to build up inside her again. After what she had been through that night, she was far too exhausted to control herself if she started to slip. Sighing, she tried to come up with another plan for how she could kill the boy. It was obvious that his father would have put him in protective custody, which meant that Hara would probably have to kill more innocent people to get to him. Deep down, she really didn't want to kill any innocent people, but if that was what she had to do to get to the boy, then so be it. No matter who or what got in her way, she was going to kill that kid.

After several moments of silence from her three friends, she felt one of them take a seat beside her. She didn't have to look up to know it was Daniel. He didn't say anything, but Hara knew that he was going to pester her until she told him what happened. Glancing up at him, her eyes narrowed at the peculiar look on his face.

He was gazing at her with an expression that Hara recognized. His face appeared calm, but she could see his lips pursed in concentration. His brow was furrowed slightly and his nostrils were flaring as he breathed. Hara saw that his pupils were dilated, making his eyes appear almost black. She could tell that he was trying to be sneaky about what he was doing, but, looking down, she saw that his body language was betraying him. His shoulders and hands were tensed up, and the rest of his body was completely rigid.

Getting nervous, Hara tried to scoot away from him. "What are you doing?" she asked, putting her mind on guard in case he decided to use any of his little mind tricks on her to get past her defenses. She suspected that he would.

Reaching up, Daniel put a finger to his lips. "*Shhh*," he whispered.

Becoming extremely uncomfortable from his stare, Hara wanted desperately to get up and run away from him, but she was already feeling a familiar, strange, and powerful sense of calm washing over her. Her voice quavering, she commanded, "Stop it!"

"Daniel," Meg warned, but Daniel ignored her.

As Hara attempted to push him out of her mind, Daniel grabbed her arm to keep a steady grip on her. Telepathy could be a difficult and sometimes dangerous ability to control, and with a powerful mind like Hara's, it took twice the concentration to get inside and keep a firm hold.

"Don't fight me," he told her, his pupils dilating even more with the strain.

The numbness was beginning to paralyze her entire body, and once that happened, Daniel would be able to look into any memory of hers that he chose. Hara wanted to break eye contact with him, but she couldn't. She was in Daniel's trance, unable to move. Before she allowed her mind to be completely immobilized, she gave Daniel's mind a hard push and dove forward, finding her muscles were able to function once more.

He must have been expecting that move, because as soon as she pushed him away he caught her by the hair and pulled her back down. Grabbing her chin with his other hand, he ordered, "Stop this!"

"Let go of me!" Hara cried, struggling to free herself.

Pressing a knee into her stomach, Daniel forced her head back so he could attempt to calm her again. "If you won't give us the information we need, then I'll just have to dig it out of you!"

"Get off!" Hara said, thrashing her arms wildly at him in an effort to get him off of her. "Get off me!" Fear and anger were coursing through her, and for a split second she wanted to use her telekinetic ability to blow him halfway across the room.

"Look into my eyes!" Daniel cried.

Hara made the mistake of making eye contact, and once she did she was again unable to look away or move.

"Easy," Daniel soothed as she struggled against him one last time. His eyes were totally black, and Hara felt the numbness taking over her body much faster than before. As her tensed muscles began to relax, her pounding heart and erratic breathing began to slow. Slumping back, she let out a shaky breath. It was difficult for her to keep her eyes open, but Daniel made sure that she had enough strength for that. Every other muscle in her body was immobilized, and as she gazed into the black holes of Daniel's soul, she knew that she was completely powerless against him. He had taken control of her mind. If he tried that at a time when Hara could actually put up a decent fight, he would have been very, very sorry.

Daniel spoke to her again. "Now, I know this is a disturbing memory to revisit, but I need to see it—stay awake, Hara!" Hara had become drowsy from the pressure of Daniel's mind, and she was having difficulty focusing on his words. "Just relax. All you have to do is think about what happened, and I'll see it. Now take me back to that night, when your camp was massacred. Whatever you see is just a memory; it can't hurt you. Just take me back..."

Her eyelids fluttering, Hara thought, *Oh, what the hell. He's been asking to see this. Let him see it.* Hara let her mind wander back to that night a little over three weeks before, when her refugee camp was ambushed.

✳ ✳ ✳

Everybody was asleep, so by the time the killing started it was too late to escape. There were over three hundred men, women, and children in that camp, all with abilities like her. They had been hiding in the mountains for some time, and they were all caught off guard when the soldiers attacked. When she heard the gunshots and the screaming, Hara awoke to a horrifying sight. People were being gunned down everywhere she looked. The assassins had no mercy on anyone, not even the children.

Terrified by the ongoing bloodbath, she watched helplessly as everyone she had come to know and love over the past few weeks was murdered right in front of her eyes. Gathering up her group of five children she was looking after, she attempted to flee further into the mountains, only to run into an even bigger trap.

The memories became more vivid, until Hara was actually experiencing the events all over again. She was running through the dense forest of pine trees, leaving the screaming and gunshots behind. It was extremely dark, with no moonlight to guide them. In her arms was three-year-old Sophie, whose parents were both killed months earlier. Clutching her free hand was Tyson, a sweet five-year-old whose parents were also long dead. Off to her left were nine-year-old Jaycee and fourteen-year-old Nick, a brother and sister whose parents had become lab experiments. Hara had seen them being tortured and had promised them that she would get their children out of there alive. Finally, to her right side was Jesse, a young boy without any abilities. His parents abandoned him long ago and it was now Hara's duty to protect him, along with the rest of the children.

As they ran on, Hara's chest began to ache along with her legs and arm. She could hear all the kids breathing fast, and she could feel their fear.

Without warning, dozens of armed men jumped out from behind trees and attacked them. Her kids began to scream, but it was too dark to see what happened to them next. Shots were fired, and then little Tyson's hand slipped out of hers. She stopped to go back for him, even though she knew he was already gone, but she was grabbed around the waist by one of the men and dragged away. Kicking and screaming, Hara heard more shots fired and Jesse and Jaycee cried out in pain. Sophie was ripped out of her arms and thrown to the ground, the soldiers allowing their German Shepherds to finish her off. Hara screamed in heartbreak and anger, using her telekinetic ability to throw the people holding her back several feet. The fire was begging her to let it out, so she did. Flames erupted all around her, striking several men in the chest, causing them to burst into flames as well. Anger completely controlling her, she kept the fire outside her body, sending it at any man in black she could see. They screamed in agony, but she didn't stop. She enjoyed the sounds of their screams, and she liked the fact that they were all going to die very, very painfully.

Hara was suddenly hit in the neck by some type of dart, and the fire surrounding her went out immediately. It was an ACD—an Ability Constraining Dart. Gasping in shock from the impact, Hara swayed as her head began to spin. She was tackled to the ground and pinned down, unable to move. Several more men came to help, and Hara began to struggle pointlessly as her vision began to fade.

"Hold her!" a silky voice ordered from in front of her.

Hara knew that voice. Her vision cleared in a few seconds, but she was completely helpless now that she was stripped of her abilities. Gazing up at her worst nightmare, her heart skipped a beat.

"You!" she breathed, glaring at him even though she was deathly afraid of him.

Giving her his sickeningly curious look, he turned as the sound of Nick's screams came closer. Turning as well, Hara saw the boy being dragged up to them. He was fighting as hard as he could, punching and kicking at the men holding him.

Good boy, Hara thought, but dread filled her gut as the boy was dragged right up to them.

Reaching into his pocket, the horrible man pulled out a small vile and held it up to Nick's nose. He pulled the cork out of the top and a thick yellow gas burst forth.

When Nick breathed it in, he began to cough and choke. Falling to the ground, he started to convulse, and Hara could see the blood flowing from his eyes, nose, and mouth. Within seconds, the boy lay still, his glassy eyes still open.

Staring in horror at yet another dead, innocent child, Hara wished she could wake up from her never-ending dream of death and torture. She looked back up at the man who had destroyed her life, and she saw his cold, penetrating gray stare was already boring into her.

She had spent so much time with him that he began to believe they had a mutual understanding. But Hara betrayed him by forcing her way out of the lab and now he was very, very unhappy.

He slinked up to her and crouched down so their noses were almost touching. In the dim light of the fires still burning on the bodies of the dead soldiers, Hara could see his cold gray eyes burning right through her soul.

"Didn't I tell you I would always find you?" he asked icily.

His smooth voice sent shivers through Hara's entire body, and she couldn't prevent the tears from coming. They flowed down her cheeks and onto the cold ground beneath her. More innocent people had just died because of her, and she hadn't done anything to protect them. She was about to be taken back to that place, the source of all her nightmares.

Cocking his head to one side in his familiar way, the sadistic doctor said, "I do recall telling you that if you ever ran away that the punishment would be quite severe."

Flinching away from him, Hara tried to make herself appear as small as possible. She didn't even want to think about what he was going to do to her once they returned.

"Now look what you've done," he told her, gesturing to her dead kids lying on the ground just feet from her. "If you had just been a good girl and stayed with me, then none of this would have happened." His harsh eyes narrowed into slits, making Hara try desperately to pull away from the men holding her. He pulled another item out of his pocket and held it up so that she could see. It was a small metallic cylinder with something that looked like a button on the end. "And now you get to suffer for the foolish choice you've made." His thumb pressed down on the button.

The shock that hit Hara next made her gasp. She felt the horrible sensation of another piece of her being ripped away, gone forever. It was the death of someone in her family, a sensation she had felt far too many times. He was the only member of her family left to die, her youngest son, Dreyson.

While new tears of horror and pain fell from her eyes, Hara got to watch her son's short and sweet life flash before her eyes. She saw his birth about three years earlier, when she had been forced to deliver him while on the run. She saw him as he grew, as he first learned how to talk, then stand up, and then walk. She saw every beautiful moment of his life flash through her mind, every moment up until they were captured and treated like lab rats. After the final memory of him being stripped from Hara's arms as he screamed in terror flashed by, he was just gone. There was no sense of his presence anywhere in the world. It was as if his entire existence had just been wiped off the face of the earth. That sick bastard who had hurt her so badly had just killed her three-year-old son, the last thing in her messed-up life that she had left. That poor, helpless, beautiful child was dead. Gone. Forever.

And it was all her fault…

∗ ∗ ∗

Daniel pulled away from her with a sharp intake of air.

The vivid images faded quickly from Hara's mind, leaving her blinking in confusion. Everything had suddenly changed shape, and it took her a moment to remember where she was. Looking around, Hara saw the flat screen TV in front of her and the three beds with glass dividers between them. She saw the familiar white walls surrounding her, and turning to her left she saw Daniel sitting on the tan sofa beside her, staring at the ground with his eyes widened in shock. He was breathing heavily through his mouth, and as she tuned her mind into his thoughts, Hara found that he deeply regretted butting into her memories. After staring hard at him for some time, she made Daniel uncomfortable and he looked up at her, his eyes shining with tears of guilt and pity.

"I'm sorry," he whispered, and Hara knew that he truly meant it. He had not only seen and heard everything that had happened, but he had also experienced every emotion and sensation that she felt during those horrible moments. The heartbreak and anger, the fear and shock, and worst of all, the guilt and regret.

"What is it?" Noah asked from behind them, his voice expressing concern as well as curiosity.

When Daniel didn't answer, Meg questioned louder, "Daniel, what happened?"

"That was the night…" Daniel started, swallowing hard to keep down the vomit rising in his throat. He had trouble finishing his sentence, so he just said, "Dreyson's dead?"

Hara nodded solemnly, her expression remaining blank as Daniel's began to grow more and more anguished. Her little baby had been killed, just like the rest of her family, but she didn't want to think about him anymore. Picturing his face, knowing that he was still alive, had been the only thing that had kept her fighting. Now that he was dead, she had taken her fight to a whole different level.

"What?" Meg and Noah both whispered, but neither Daniel nor Hara paid any attention.

"And you feel that it was your fault," Daniel breathed. "Because you escaped."

Leaning closer, Hara told him, "Now you know." Angry that Daniel had made her live through that memory a second time, she growled, "Are you happy?"

The pain and regret that showed on Daniel's own face only made Hara angrier. He had no right to invade her privacy like that, and now he was feeling sorry for her? After accusing her of being crazy, how dare he!

Standing up to keep herself from taking a swing at him, she walked around the couch and back towards the table on which she had been laying. When she reached it, she looked down at her blood, which was staining the nice wood finish. She had bled a lot; several pools of it were spread out across the surface. It surprised her that the sight of blood didn't bother her after all she had been through. She didn't flinch at the sight of it, but she did think about all the times she had been strapped to a stretcher while a sick and twisted doctor performed operations on her that made her bleed much worse than that, and she had been awake almost every time.

Shuddering as more disturbing memories filled her head, Hara turned away from the table and looked to the opposite wall, where the cabinet holding their weapons stood. Walking over to it, she opened the doors to look inside again. She could feel everyone's eyes on her as she moved about the room, so she decided to listen in on their thoughts. Each of them felt pain for her, but Daniel felt the worst because he had experienced the whole thing with her. Daniel wanted to discuss the matter further with her, to explain to her that Dreyson's death wasn't her fault. Hara knew that her son's death was her fault, and she would never let anyone convince her otherwise. Everyone like her who had been killed was killed because of her. So, ignoring Daniel's thoughts, she examined the various choices available to her inside the weapon cabinet.

There were several different types of guns, and that pleased her. On the top shelf she could see several nine millimeters along with a few .28 caliber weapons. Boxes of ammunition were stacked in rows in the back half of the cabinet. On the second shelf there were three automatic rifles with a dozen clips lying around them. In the back right corner was a small black net filled with little silver metal balls. Those balls were a very sophisticated weapon called Shine Poppers. They were an advanced piece of equipment created by Hara's people that could be used to get a person out of any situation. When someone was in a hot spot, all they had to do was throw one on the ground. It would let out a loud pop as it struck the ground; it would burst open and emit a harsh white light that would blind everyone. They had been very useful to Hara when she escaped from the lab.

Below the second shelf were several racks holding double barreled and single barreled shotguns. Extra shells were in boxes on the top shelf. The Ballium rifles had originally been stored in the bottom of the cabinet, but she had left them in the trunk of the Lamborghini, which was still parked on the same street corner where she left it before her attack on Jackson Odau. Since those rifles were missing, Hara could finally see what had been behind them, and it sent excitement coursing through her. Pushed towards the back of the cabinet was a shoulder-mounted rocket-propelled grenade. The rockets would cause a massive explosion, and she smiled at the thought of blowing the police station sky high.

After carefully looking over her choices, Hara reached up and pulled a simple nine millimeter off the top shelf along with three boxes of ammunition. She also took one of the automatic rifles, a single barreled shotgun, and five extra clips for the automatic. Debating whether or not she should take it, she pulled out the RPG.

"What are you doing?" Meg asked curiously, the sudden break in silence startling.

"I'm going to finish what I started," Hara answered, carrying her armful of weapons over to the wooden table and setting them all down. She had lost her guns and her pack when she was shot, and she needed to replace them. Glancing around, Hara saw a few extra packs to the side of the cabinet. Selecting one, she picked it up, and hurried back to the table. She was just beginning to put the extra clips and ammunition inside when she heard Daniel stand up and start coming towards her.

"Hara," he said sharply, his tone causing her to turn in surprise. "What happened that night was not your fault. You don't need to do this to redeem yourself. There are other ways that we can fix this."

"Like what?" Hara demanded skeptically. "Like what you've been doing for the past two years? Nothing?"

Stunned, Daniel blinked. "We have not been doing nothing."

"Really?" Hara snapped angrily. "Because that's what it looks like to me! Nothing changed since you left! How is that anything other than nothing?"

Daniel's eyes narrowed, and he looked prepared to fight back, but then he just stopped. The furious look that was on his face vanished and his expression became dreamy. He stared behind Hara at nothing, like he was put in a trance by his own ability. Hara was about to ask what was wrong, but then she felt it too. It was something she hadn't felt in a while, and it wasn't good. Letting out a shaky breath, she slowly turned in the direction where Daniel was staring.

"What is it?" Meg asked, the concern audible in her voice.

When Meg received no reply, Noah demanded, "What's wrong?"

"He's here," Daniel and Hara said simultaneously. The direction in which they were looking was toward the city. What they both felt was a disturbance in the bowels of Philadelphia. Deep in their subconscious, they could feel the minds of every living person in that city. It was easy to ignore, to block out altogether, but when a person had a particularly strong emotion, their thoughts became much louder and more powerful, and sometimes certain thoughts just stood out among others. They could both feel his mind, a mind of evil thoughts and intentions. It was the mind of the man who had destroyed their world. He was there with them. Somewhere in the city, he was plotting something terrible.

"He is here?" Meg repeated, and Hara felt her dread and fear.

"As in Him?" Noah finished, also becoming nervous.

"Yes," Daniel breathed, and Hara heard him shudder behind her.

A sudden realization struck Hara. Someone was missing from her group. At first, she thought it was Allan, but she knew he wasn't going to come back to them, and she wouldn't let him if he tried. He was a traitor. No, someone more important was missing, and she cursed herself for not noticing sooner. Hara turned back to Daniel and asked cautiously, "Where is Jack?"

"Lieutenant Odau and Agent Perry caught him after you were shot," Daniel informed gravely, snapping himself out of his trance. "He told them everything about you. About your powers, your motives, all of it."

Hara didn't care at the moment whether or not Jack spilled his guts. She turned back to face the city again. As long as he didn't tell them the whole truth, she was fine with it for the time being. There were worse things she had to worry about. For example, where Jack was. Concentrating on her friend's buzzing mind, Hara found that he was just outside the police station within feet of Allan, but there was something particularly upsetting about that. It was unfortunate that he had been caught by the man who looked just like him, and especially bad that he had told the officials about her. Jack could talk his way out of almost anything, but he couldn't talk his way out of death. The other mind that stood out against all others, the man who destroyed her world, was getting closer and closer to Jack.

"No, no, no!" Hara said in horror, reaching up with both hands and pulling at her hair. For once, she didn't have to be afraid for herself, but she did have to be afraid for her friend. She no longer cared about what happened to herself. Too many good people had died because of her, and she wasn't about to have her friend be next.

"It's going to be okay," Daniel told her quickly, reaching out and touching her arm to comfort her. "We won't let him hurt you again—"

"He's going for Jack!" Hara cried, ignoring Daniel's concern for her. "He knows where Jack is, and he's going to kill him!"

189

Daniel understood, but he didn't look alarmed. "I told Perry that he needed to take Jack to Pittsburgh so they would both be safe," he assured her. "I think he went for it. Jack will be long gone before our friend can get to him."

Shaking her head slowly, Hara informed Daniel of the seriousness of the situation. "It's far too late for escape now," she breathed. "He's already found Jack. He's setting the trap."

"Oh, God," Hara heard Noah whisper, and Meg gasped in shock.

Daniel looked into Hara's mind, and his eyes widened in comprehension when he saw what she saw.

They were all stunned by how quickly their "friend" had been able to follow Hara back to Philadelphia and find them. The others were all too afraid of the man to be of any use to Jack. Hara, however, knew what she had to do. She had to save Jack.

Running back to the cabinet, she pulled out the bag of Shine Poppers. Stuffing them in to her pack, she zipped up the pack and began loading her collection of weapons. She shoved a nine millimeter and the single barreled shotgun into her belt, and slung the automatic rifle over her shoulder by the strap. Hoisting up the rocket launcher, she slipped her arms through the straps and adjusted it on her shoulder as she buckled it across her chest. Slipping the pack on, she grabbed a couple of extra rockets and headed for the stairs.

"Where are you going?" all three of her friends demanded.

Turning, she answered, "To save Jack."

"You can't!" Meg cried. "You can't throw yourself in the middle of this again!"

"Watch me," Hara challenged.

"You know what he'll do to you if he catches you!" Noah reminded, his eyes pleading with her to give it up.

Fat chance.

"Forget Jack!" Daniel commanded, striding over to her. "It's too late for him now. Come with us, and we'll leave this place while we have a head start!"

Leaning her head closer to Daniel's, Hara snarled, "I'm done running. I'm done hiding. I'm done being afraid, and I'm done watching the people I love die because of me!" Narrowing her eyes, she hissed, "But I'm not done with him!" Turning on her heel, she marched to the foot of the stairs, completely disgusted with the three of them. They were cowards, telling her to run when she still had a chance to save Jack.

"You do realize that this is a trap?" Daniel called after her desperately, trying anything to get her to reconsider her decision. When his question had no effect on her, he cried, "He's baiting you!"

"I'm counting on that," Hara whispered to herself, and she knew that was his plan. But she didn't stop. She didn't even hesitate. Even when her friends kept calling her name, begging her to stop, she didn't. What she said before had been the truth; she was done running and hiding and being afraid, but most of all she was done watching the people she loved die. As the rage began to boil up inside her once again, she promised herself that she wouldn't be done with him until one of them was dead. That man had ruined her life, and now he was about to pay the price.

Hurrying up the stairs, Hara ran to the garage and jumped on the red Harley that Noah had brought back with them, knowing that her never-ending nightmare was about to become even more horrendous.

✳ ✳ ✳

"Super powers?" Lieutenant Odau repeated, raising his eyebrows.

Agent Perry had just finished telling him the story that Jack had told him, and now that he had spoken the words himself, he realized how crazy the story really sounded. "Yeah," he muttered, staring out the windshield of the S.W.A.T. truck. They had been driving for nearly ten minutes, but they were still pretty deep inside the city. Many roads were closed because of the incident downtown, including the one they needed to take to get onto the freeway, so they had to find another way to get out of the city.

"You do realize how you sound right now?" Odau asked. "This is one of the most ridiculous stories I've ever heard."

"Believe me, it sounds just as crazy to me as it does to you. But how else can you explain what she did to the two of us? I have a burn on my wrist in the exact shape of her hand, and you saw what she did to the mayor's window! Not to mention what she did to you and your boy. You may have shot her twice, but I doubt that she's anywhere close to being finished."

"What did you say Jack called her?"

"An Absorber," Perry repeated, glancing at the lieutenant. "She can absorb the abilities of any person she touches. Any person with an ability, that is. I think that's what Jack meant; that after touching another with an ability, Hara could do the same thing that they could."

"Another?" Odau questioned. "Jack said there were more people out there like her?"

"He and Marcus both," Perry answered. "They said that there were many more people out there with abilities, and if that's true then people involved in all of this went through a great deal to cover that up, because I've never heard of anything like this before."

"Well, if people were wandering through the streets with super powers, you'd think someone would have noticed by now," Odau pointed out. "Even if they did try to hide it, people would slip up and someone would have seen them use their ability, especially if they did something as dangerous as starting fires, like you're claiming Hara does. And if she absorbed the power then someone else must have it too."

Perry shook his head. Thinking of the words in Marcus's note, he told Odau, "There was a man who wiped them all out, all except for Hara and a few others."

"Jack told you this?" Odau demanded in surprise.

Shaking his head again, Perry replied, "No, Marcus."

Staring at him in bewilderment, the lieutenant looked as if he was going to suddenly start yelling again, but he didn't. "So this guy killed off everyone like her just to cover it up?"

"Apparently," Perry muttered.

"Well, they did a mighty fine job!"

Startled by his comment, Perry peered over at him curiously. He wasn't quite sure what Odau had meant, and it was hard to tell if he was pleased by that fact or if he was just complimenting how discreet the massacre had been. He ignored the remark and turned his eyes back to the road.

After a short silence, Odau spoke again. "I find it...interesting that one of my detectives is involved in this," he said quietly.

Perry asked, "How so?"

Odau shrugged. "I just...never would have thought that Marcus would be involved with a murderer." He sighed in disappointment, and Perry knew that he was frustrated with himself that he hadn't had any suspicion of Marcus before. "Come to think of it, he always seemed a bit nervous. Paranoid even. But he was always loyal to his job, and I trusted him. I never would have suspected him to be a part of something this nefarious."

"Well," Perry mumbled, "life is full of surprises."

"But our mayor?" Odau persisted skeptically. "And one of our D.A.'s? This isn't just a group of criminal conspirators; these were people of high position in our government! People we all trusted! After the city finds out about all of this...the citizens are going to be very unsettled for a long time."

"Wait a second now," Perry interrupted. "The three of them said that they *were* helping her, not that they are now. We don't know for sure that they had anything to do with this. I'm not even sure that we have much reason to hold the mayor. After all, he was helping us..."

"Yes, he was, but then he lied to us!" Odau declared angrily. "He told us that he didn't know that my son was the last target. He failed to tell us about Hara's...abilities...which caused us to be unprepared and resulted in the deaths of three children! In my opinion, Allan Brown is one of the conspirators!"

Gaping at him in disbelief, Perry exclaimed, "You are blowing this way out of proportion! If he hadn't helped us at all, your son would be dead, and you're acting like he pulled the trigger on those kids! Jack and Hara killed them, not Allan Brown!"

"If he had told people about Hara before these incidents occurred, nobody would have died!" Odau shouted.

"He didn't know she was going to do anything like this!" Perry yelled back.

"Maybe not, but he knew that she was an extremely dangerous person! If he had told the government that people with super powers actually existed, then they could have tracked her down and dealt with her before she could hurt anyone!"

"Have you been listening to a word I've said?" Perry demanded in astonishment. "People did find out about her! They did track her down! In fact—as I mentioned earlier—they wiped out her entire race! People tortured her and performed experiments on her! Don't you understand what happens when something so shocking occurs that it would cause worldwide panic if the rest of the world found out? The government keeps it quiet, and does whatever it can to make the problem go away. That's exactly what happened here!"

"They should have just gotten rid of her when they had the chance," Odau grumbled.

Perry snapped, "You know what? I think that the fact that this girl tried to kill your son has clouded your judgment!"

"And I think the fact that one of these terrorists claims he's your brother has clouded yours!" Odau shot back.

Perry chose to not press his luck on that topic of discussion. "No matter whose judgment is clouded, we can't ignore the fact that someone covered this up, and probably did it in an unpleasant way. Marcus said that this guy is going to come here and cause even more problems for us, and that we should..."

"Marcus said, Marcus said," Odau mocked. "Why are we listening to anything Marcus said? He's probably just fabricating stories to make us think we're going to have more problems. It's what terrorists do; they rile you up and then make you live in fear and paranoia."

Perry grumbled, "You're not going to let this go, are you?"

"No!" the lieutenant declared angrily. "There's no guy coming to get us! It's just a scary story Jack and Marcus told you to make you worry, and you fell for it!"

"How could they both tell me the exact same story?" Perry demanded. "They were never allowed to communicate with each other!"

"Nothing's going to happen!" Odau cried. "We're going to come back from Pittsburgh and find that everything is exactly how we left it; a disaster, but no new criminal masterminds to worry about. And trust me, you're going to feel really stupid when you realize that you fell for their lies."

Agent Perry was about to snap back at Odau's comment, but when the vehicles in front of them suddenly braked sharply, he had to divert his attention to the road. As Perry stomped down on his own brake pedal, both men were thrown forward and then back as the truck screeched to a stop. Looking out his windshield, Perry wasn't able to see what the problem was, but he could see that every vehicle in front of them had been forced to stop in the middle of a large intersection. Perry knew that only something really threatening would be able to stop the escort. Worried, Perry grabbed the radio. "Talk to me!" he ordered to anyone who was listening. "What's going on?"

"I'm not sure," Finchly's tentative voice replied. "There are three cars blocking our path. They're just sitting in the middle of the street without any drivers or passengers!"

"What?" Perry and Odau said in unison, looking at each other in confusion.

The sudden explosion that came next caused them both to nearly jump out of their skins. A ball of fire erupted in front of them, and all four vehicles between them and Detective Finchly were blown up. Their truck rocked and Perry shielded his eyes from the horrendously bright flash.

"Jesus!" he shouted, seeing the destroyed SUVs and S.W.A.T. truck lying in the middle of the intersection. A burst of fear began to swell inside him, but not for himself. His colleagues and friends were in those SUVs, and they could be severely injured or even dead! Renee had been in one of those SUVs...

"What the hell was that?" Odau yelled in alarm.

Without a logical answer coming to mind, Perry turned to his left to peer out of his window as a peculiar sound met his ears. Over the roar of the burning vehicles, he could hear a loud grinding sound that made him cringe in discomfort. It was dark outside, but what he saw steadily approaching the intersection made him question his own eyes. Perry gaped as Odau whispered, "Is that a...tank?"

The huge, black tank was slowly rumbling towards them from their left. Perry recalled that the National Guard had been called in, but why would a tank be shooting at them?

"What...?" Odau breathed in horror.

Perry was startled by numerous people screaming at him on the radio. There was someone from every car behind him trying to get through to him, half of them asking if he was okay and half of them screaming at him to start driving in the opposite direction. Unsure of what he should do, he glanced down at the radio and then back up at the approaching tank. His friends and colleagues were in the overturned SUVs, and he couldn't just leave them while he fled. The tank's next move made him decide that it would be best to just run.

The tank stopped several hundred feet from his vehicle, and it just sat there for a few seconds. Then, the turret made a terrible creaking sound as it slowly turned to aim the gun directly at Perry's truck.

"Oh, Lord," Perry muttered.

"Go!" Odau shouted in panic, grabbing the steering wheel and trying to spin it for Perry. "Go! Drive!"

"Perry, drive!" someone on the radio yelled. "Get out of here now!"

The lights on top of Detective Finchly's squad car were already flashing, but the siren suddenly blared to life as well. Her car spun around and began speeding away from the tank.

His heart skipping a beat, Perry stomped on the gas pedal. Spinning the wheel sharply, he quickly matched Finchly's speed as he followed her.

"Come on, come on, come on!" Perry said through his teeth as both their vehicles gained speed. His heart was pounding in his chest and he held his breath as a horrible feeling of anticipation got the better of him. He was sure that they were all going to die. Any second, the next explosion would come, and their vehicles would be engulfed in flames.

The second explosion occurred just seconds after Perry caught up with Finchly. Thankfully, his truck wasn't directly hit. Perry scrambled to keep control of the wheel as the back end of the truck was thrown into the air from the force of the shell's explosion.

Odau cried out in surprise from the sudden impact, and he grabbed the wheel as well as it slipped out of Perry's sweaty hands. Wrenching it toward himself so they wouldn't spin out of control, he yelled, "Go faster! Get us out of here!"

His entire body shaking, Perry looked in his side view mirror and saw that the S.W.A.T. truck behind them had attempted to follow them, only to take the fatal hit. The remains of the vehicle lay in molten chunks all over the road.

"Dear God," Perry breathed, knowing that all six people in it were dead. Pushing the shock and remorse away from him, he focused on the car in front of him.

A knock behind him made him jump yet again. Relief flooded through him when Odau turned and reached up to open the little window behind their heads.

"What the hell is going on?" one S.W.A.T. member demanded from inside the bay.

"We've got serious trouble!" Odau answered breathlessly. "Just sit tight until…"

"Whoa!" Perry cried, spinning the wheel violently to the left. As he began to pull out into another intersection to follow Finchly deeper into the city, another S.W.A.T truck came roaring into it from the right, cutting Perry off from Finchly completely. He made a hard left turn to avoid T-boning the other truck, and he winced as the back end of his vehicle smashed into the front of the other.

Odau was thrown into his door and Perry heard the S.W.A.T. member in the back swear in surprise and tumble around.

Glancing into the lieutenant's side view mirror, Perry saw that the new S.W.A.T. truck was stopped directly in the center of the street behind them, blocking the path of everyone else who managed to follow them.

With a burst of harsh red light, the S.W.A.T. truck exploded as the other vehicles attempted to sneak past it, sending several of them flying into the buildings over the curb.

"What was that?" Perry wondered aloud in alarm. His initial thought was that the new S.W.A.T. truck had come to assist them, but it was now clear that this wasn't the case. His foot let up on the gas and pressed down slowly on the brake until their truck came to a stop halfway through the next intersection. They had been separated from the rest of the group, and Perry was surprised at how quiet the air around the truck was now that they were alone. Still, something felt terribly wrong.

"What are you doing?" Odau demanded as Perry rolled down his window to peer out and see what was happening behind them. "Don't stop here! You saw what just happened! Whoever these people are, they're all over the place! We need to keep going!"

Ignoring him, Perry pulled his head back in the truck when all he could see were more billowing flames. As he rolled up his window, he turned to Odau. "We have to go back," he told him firmly.

"What?" Odau asked in disbelief.

"We have to go back," Perry repeated, adding more emphasis to his statement. "Those are my colleagues back there, and I have to help them. My partner is back there."

"Are you crazy?" Odau demanded, his eyes wild with fear. "We have to get out of here now! Can't you see that these people are attacking us because of who we have in the back of our truck? They're after this truck! That's why they're shooting at us! That's why they've isolated us!"

"You don't think I've realized that?" Perry snapped at him. He knew they were being attacked because Allan Brown and Jack were in the back. Marcus had warned him about the man who had killed Hara's family and her kind. Perry understood that the man had been the greater danger that Marcus had repeatedly mentioned. Perry understood that the man had killed numerous people and had tortured Hara. Perry also understood that the man would do just about anything to cover it up, including murdering even more people. Perry had made the mistake of getting caught up in these events, and he was about to pay the price. Jack and

Marcus both warned him about what would happen if he involved himself too deeply, and Perry really wished that he had listened to their advice. He had a choice to make. Would he run to Pittsburgh like a coward, or would he stay, fight, and help the people he cared for? The answer to that was obvious to anyone who knew Perry. "I don't care!" he exclaimed. "You went back for your son, and I'm going back for my friends!"

"They'll be fine!" Odau cried desperately, but he appeared to be defeated. "They would have wanted us to keep going! That's why they were..." The lieutenant suddenly stopped mid-sentence, his mouth hanging open and his eyes widening in fear. He was looking past Perry, and his look of horror made Perry's stomach sink like a rock.

A sudden movement out of the corner of his eye caught Perry's attention. Glancing out his window again, his own eyes widened. Coming directly at them from their left, at full speed, was a huge black semi truck. As it rapidly drew closer, Perry could hear the roar of the engine, and Odau started to panic again.

"Go, go, go! Get us out of here now!"

Stomping on the gas again, Perry's stomach leaped into his throat as the semi came dangerously closer. The tires of their truck spun for a moment before it lurched forward, just as the semi came plowing through the intersection. Odau let out a terrified yell, and both men were thrown to the side as the giant truck struck the back end of theirs.

As the two vehicles collided, Perry's head smashed into his window. Crying out in pain, he ground his teeth together as tears came to his eyes and his head began to throb in agony. His truck was spinning wildly and was out of control, but he kept a firm grip on the wheel. As he tried to ignore the steadily increasing pain in his skull, Perry managed to straighten out the truck. He pressed his foot to the floor.

Their S.W.A.T. truck took off again, and Perry glanced in his mirror. The semi managed to make the sharp turn after striking the truck and was now in pursuit. Perry groaned, but it was more from pain than from anything else. He put a hand to his head and winced as it stung from his touch. Looking at his hand, he saw that it was covered in his own blood.

"Are you alright?" Odau asked in concern, leaning forward to try and get a good look.

Perry grunted, forcing himself to focus on the task at hand. "Don't worry about me. Check and make sure everyone in back is alright."

Turning, Odau looked back through the little window. "You guys okay?"

There were various answers, and the lieutenant turned back. "All good," he informed. Looking back out the windshield to see what direction they were headed, he suddenly shouted, "Don't go this way! If you go into the tunnel, that will be the end for us!"

"I know what I'm doing!" Perry insisted, continuing to speed straight ahead. They were heading straight towards the Philadelphia Tunnel. It was about a half mile ahead and Perry could see it as they rapidly approached. The entrance looked like a gate into a black pit of death, the orange lights illuminating the inside. Slightly intimidated by the eerie effect, Perry added, "I'm going to turn sharply to the right at the next intersection, so tell the guys to brace themselves."

"Hold on!" Odau yelled over his shoulder, gripping the arms of his seat tightly as he anticipated the turn.

The semi was closing in on them from behind, and by the time Perry reached his destination, it would be right on his back bumper. Perry would then make the turn as he was halfway through, surprising the driver of the semi. It would be too late for the semi driver to make the turn, and Perry would be able to get out of the city before the huge truck could find them again.

"Please don't kill us," Odau said through gritted teeth as Perry calculated the perfect spot and time to make his move.

"Don't you trust me?" Perry asked him, raising an eyebrow but keeping his eyes on the road.

The lieutenant snorted as they pulled out into the intersection, trying to go along with the humor even though he was anticipating death. He gripped his seat tighter as Perry stomped his foot down on the brake.

Perry could see in his mirror that the semi was nearly touching the back bumper, and when he put his foot down on the brake, the semi made a screeching sound as the two vehicles made contact. He began to spin the wheel, but right before he did, yet another S.W.A.T. truck came roaring through the intersection.

"Shit!" he shouted as the new truck spun so it was parallel to them and collided with their side. Their truck was pushed out into the opposite side of the street, but something on the other side of them was keeping them from spinning out of control again. A shrill grinding noise made Perry and Odau wince, and as Perry glanced out his window he saw that the semi was pulling up alongside him. The rogue S.W.A.T. truck was currently speeding along their right side, and Perry watched as another pulled up behind him. In less than twenty seconds, he would be forced to enter the tunnel.

"They've boxed us in!" Odau exclaimed unnecessarily.

"Thank you for pointing that out," Perry grumbled, trying to suppress his own fear. His head was throbbing from its collision with the window, and he wasn't sure how much longer he could last in his fragile condition.

"I believe you now," Odau told him, his voice expressing his panic. "I believe you, and Jack, and Marcus, and I just want you to know that I'm sorry about everything I've said..."

"I'll get us out of this," Perry muttered gravely as their truck entered the black jaws of the tunnel.

As they roared on through the tunnel, the semi and rogue S.W.A.T. trucks began to pull away from them. There was at least twenty feet between their truck and the semi, but the vehicle behind them was still bumping into their rear, letting them know that they weren't about to get away quite yet.

"What are they doing?" Odau asked, his brow furrowing in confusion.

Peering out of his window, Perry saw that the cab of the semi was right alongside him. The windows of the semi were tinted to a point where he wasn't able to see any facial features inside, but he was able to make out shapes and figures. There was a man in the passenger seat as well as a man at the wheel, and it almost appeared as if the man in the passenger seat was blowing Perry a kiss from inside. As Perry continued to watch in growing horror, the passenger door of the cab swung open and a man leaned out, a nine millimeter held casually in his hand.

The man gripped a bar above his head with his free hand to steady himself as he leaned out. He didn't appear to be at all cautious as he did so, despite the fact that he was hanging out of a fast-moving semi and might be crushed between the vehicles.

To Perry's surprise, the man didn't wear anything to obscure his face, a sign that he intended to kill. If he left any survivors, someone would be able to ID him. Perry really wished he had listened to Jack and Marcus. He didn't see a way out of his predicament.

The man looked to be several years older than Perry, probably in his mid-forties. His sandy-brown hair blew around his face as the air whipped past him. What frightened Perry even more than the weapon were the man's eyes. They were light grey, and had an evil coldness to them that made Perry shiver. His intimidating gaze told Perry to be very afraid. Perry had never seen eyes like that before. They were the epitome of evil.

After taking a long, careful look at Perry's truck, the man made eye contact with Perry. His eyes bore into Perry's, and Perry was mesmerized by the stare that clearly told him that death was coming. When his eyes narrowed harshly, the man raised his weapon and aimed it at Perry's head. He fired several rounds, but his expression showed frustration as the bullets ricocheted off of the glass. He fired a few more rounds but gave up when he realized that Perry was protected behind the safety of bullet-proof glass.

"Is he shooting at you?" Odau asked as Perry ducked down behind the wheel even though it was clear that he wouldn't be struck by any bullets.

"Yep," Perry said, jumping as louder, more rapid shots were fired. Glancing up, he saw that the man with the gray eyes had switched his weapon choice and was now firing with an automatic rifle. His expression grew furious when the new weapon was also ineffective.

"Why?"

"Because I'm the driver! If I die, then everyone else in the truck dies as well!" Perry looked back at the semi again as all shots ceased. The man with the gray eyes had given up on his weapons. Frustrated, he tossed the automatic rifle back inside and pulled a two-way radio out of his belt. He began speaking into it while his eyes remained locked on Perry's. Perry prayed that he wasn't calling for backup.

Suddenly, the man with the gray eyes whipped his head forward and stared open-mouthed at the opposite end of the tunnel.

"Perry!" Odau cried, his voice rising in fright.

Turning back to him, Perry saw that the lieutenant was staring out the front, looking quite alarmed. Perry followed the trail of his eyes and he saw the problem. At the mouth of the tunnel, a slim figure was waiting patiently on a bright red motorcycle. It was too far away for Perry to recognize a face, but he caught the long brown hair whipping behind her, and immediately knew who had decided to join the fight.

"It's her!" Odau exclaimed.

Perry watched her carefully in case she made any sudden movements. Was she there to help Jack? Did she come to stop this man with the gray eyes? If she was there to help, he wasn't about to resist. He and the others were in serious trouble, and with her super powers, Perry doubted that she could lose the fight. He prayed that she was going to help them.

"What is she doing here?" Odau demanded.

Perry ignored his question and continued to stare Hara down. Something was happening to him, and he could not explain it. His pounding heart began to slow, and the pain in his head began to subside. Everything seemed to suddenly pause, like time itself had slowed to a stop. Perry's entire body was tingling, like he was being pricked by a million tiny needles. His hands relaxed on the steering wheel, and his quick breathing returned to normal. A strange feeling of calm was overcoming him, and he had no clue what was causing it. As he pondered over what was happening to him, he heard a voice calling his name.

Perry...Perry...

He swore that he could hear his name being whispered to him in the strange stillness, but he couldn't figure out where it was originating.

What do you want? He said the words in his head, only half expecting to get a reply.

Just listen to me.

Startled that he was actually communicating with Hara with his thoughts, Perry tensed up for a moment, but the feeling was immediately overpowered by the pressure of Hara's mind. Perry thought back to her, *What are you doing to me?*

Don't worry, Hara told him in a soothing manner.

The telepathic communication was making Perry uncomfortable, but the messages he was receiving made him feel reassured.

It's okay, Hara continued. *Now just listen. We don't have a whole lot of time before you and everyone else in that truck is killed.*

Get out of my head! Perry commanded, attempting to take back control of his body. He could feel the presence of Hara's mind; it was like a heavy weight pressing down on his skull. It wasn't painful, but it didn't feel right either. He could feel her mind pressing down on his, but he also found that he was able to push her out if he tried hard enough. He did so, letting her know that she wasn't welcome.

Perry, enough! Hara ordered angrily as a result of the push, and Perry's body relaxed once again. *We don't have time for this! You need to trust me!*

And why the hell would I trust you? Perry demanded.

Because I'm about to save your life, Hara said.

She seemed to be struggling to keep Perry's mind beneath her own, and she instructed him sharply, *Stop fighting me! I'm trying to help! Now, I need you to do exactly what I say exactly when I say it. Keep driving straight, and only when I tell you to, spin your steering wheel to the left as fast and as hard as you can. Do you understand me?*

What are you planning to do? Perry asked her, knowing that when he moved to the left he would most likely crush the man with the gray eyes, who was still leaning out of the semi and gaping at Hara at the end of the tunnel.

Just do as I say, okay?

Perry relented. *Okay, fine.*

Time suddenly returned to its normal pace. Perry knew what he had to do and was prepared to do it. Taking a deep breath as he found that he was able to control his body once again, he tightened his grip on the wheel and pressed his foot down harder on the accelerator. The semi continued to drive right alongside him, and Perry felt the man's cold gray eyes locked on him again. It was almost as if that man knew that Perry and Hara had spoken. Perry ignored his intimidating gaze, maintaining his speed. He kept his eyes locked on Hara, who continued to sit on her motorcycle, motionless.

"What is that thing she's holding?" Odau asked suddenly, leaning forward in his seat to get a better view. "It looks like a…"

Oh, God, Perry thought in dismay. He hadn't noticed it before because of the distance between them, but he realized that there was something large and black strapped to her shoulders. He prayed that Hara knew how to properly operate that weapon.

An orange flash of light erupted from the right side of Hara's head. The rocket shot out of the device and flew straight towards the front of Perry's truck. Smoke and fire were clouding the air behind it, but Perry managed to catch a glimpse of Hara starting her bike and roaring down the tunnel after the rocket.

"Perry, turn!" Odau shouted fearfully, sinking lower in his seat. When Perry maintained his course, the lieutenant's eyes snapped toward him and he reached out and grabbed the wheel. "Perry! Snap out of it!"

Tensing as the rocket grew closer, Perry heard Hara's voice in his head again.

Hold on. Not quite yet.

Are you trying to kill us all? Perry demanded of her, but he listened to her anyway. He figured that even if he tried to turn the wheel, Hara would only stop him.

Odau was screaming at him and tugging at the wheel, but Perry's grip only tightened. He was putting his life and the lives of everyone else in the truck into the hands of a murderer, but at the moment there didn't seem to be any other alternative.

Just as he thought the rocket was too close for them to escape its impact, Hara screamed a single word in his head. *Turn!*

Perry spun the wheel to the left and his truck swerved into the semi cab just as the rocket reached them. It nearly grazed their vehicle, but it made it past and caught the driver behind them by surprise.

Perry could hear the vehicle explode as he collided with the semi. A blazing red-orange light reflected in his mirror. The S.W.A.T. truck on the other side of Odau swerved as well to avoid a collision. As he winced at the sound of the metal grinding between his truck and the semi, Perry saw a flash of red whiz by him in the direction of the flames. Hara was taking a position at the back of the pack. Perry prayed that she had more rockets to deal with the two other problems.

The man with the gray eyes was watching Perry, so when Perry swerved suddenly, he wasn't caught off guard. He quickly ducked back inside the cab to avoid getting crushed. He pressed one hand against his windshield and one on the wall behind him to steady himself as he continued to keep a watchful eye on Perry.

Perry saw the cold gray stare piercing through him for a split second, filling him with a fear that he had never felt before. Looking away, he swerved back into the center of the tunnel and barely managed to make the sharp right turn without flipping the truck over in the process.

"Perry!" Odau shouted again as they veered right.

"Hold on," Perry yelled as he stepped down on the accelerator. The mirror on his side had been taken out by the semi, but he could still see what was happening behind them in Odau's mirror.

The semi driver hadn't been able to brake fast enough to make the turn and continue the pursuit. The huge black messenger of death was forced to drive straight down a different street, and it quickly disappeared from Perry's view.

Perry breathed a sigh of relief, but he had a feeling he would see it again if he didn't get out of the city fast. He eyed the remaining rogue S.W.A.T. truck uncertainly as it gained on them, knowing there wasn't much more he could do to outrun it.

Hara was already on top of that. Although the semi had missed the turn, she had no problem making it. Her bike came flying out of the tunnel and quickly followed after them. More smoke erupted from behind her and the second rocket burst forth from her left shoulder. It struck the back of the rogue S.W.A.T. truck and it too was destroyed in a loud, violent explosion. Staring in disbelief at the flames, Perry saw Hara ride right through the center of the destruction and give him a small, two-fingered salute.

Perry couldn't help but smile to himself as he looked back to the road in front of him. "Well, I suppose that solves one of our many problems," he said to a completely dumbstruck Lieutenant Odau. His attention was diverted once again as a familiar voice came to life from the radio.

"Agent Perry! Lieutenant Odau! Someone answer!"

It was Renee.

More relief flooding through him, Perry groped around his knees until he located the radio and brought it up to his mouth. "Renee, are you alright?" he asked.

"We're fine!" she assured breathlessly. "Well, most of us are, anyway. All of us that took the first shot are okay. I don't know about everyone else. What about you? Where are you?"

"We're fine, but we need backup right away!" Perry told her urgently. "We've been chased through the tunnel and I've taken a blow to the head. I don't know how much longer I can last, and I think we may be seeing a little bit more of these people."

"I'll get assistance to you right away," Renee promised him. "Just tell me where you are."

"We're along the riverfront just east of the Philadelphia Tunnel," Perry said. "We just managed to get out with our lives, but you don't want to go through the tunnel to get to us. We left behind a bit of a mess."

"We'll be there soon…" Renee started to say, but Perry missed the end of her sentence because her voice was drowned out by a loud gunshot.

Perry heard the loud pop and could feel that the back left wheel had been blown out, and as he looked out of his window in surprise he saw that Hara was riding right alongside them with a double barreled shotgun in her hand. She aimed the huge gun at the front wheel.

"What the hell are you doing?" Perry yelled at her as she fired and the front wheel blew out as well. He tried to control the truck as it started to slide across the pavement. The movement caused his stomach to flip and the radio fell out of his hand. To his horror, the wheel slipped out of his hands and then the truck was spinning uncontrollably. He cried out in pain as his head struck his window a second time, and he involuntarily stomped on the brake pedal. The truck skidded and squealed to a stop, and Perry saw Hara whiz past them again.

The second blow to his head took away the throbbing agony, but it didn't comfort him. His vision was going dark at the edges, and the truck was tilting beneath him. Before he understood what was happening, his head fell forward onto the steering wheel and his eyes slowly closed. As he drifted out of consciousness, he heard Renee crying out to him on the radio, her voice sounding as if it were miles away. Her voice was the last thing he heard before he blacked out completely.

✳ ✳ ✳

Praying that Perry was okay, Hara continued to ride down the street as she shoved the rifle back into her belt. She had felt his pain from hitting his head a second time. Then she sensed his consciousness wink out like a light. His head was severely injured, but he was going to have to hold on until Hara took out the semi. She wouldn't be able to help him until she dealt with an old friend of hers.

The semi had missed the turn that Perry had taken once he was out of the tunnel, but the driver took the next right in order to get back in the chase as soon as possible. Hara stopped Perry's truck because she didn't want to have to worry about the big rig still being a threat to them.

Sensing that she was about parallel to the huge truck, Hara eased her hand up on the gas to allow the bike to slow a bit. She could hear that the semi had rounded another corner and was speeding down the street that she was rapidly approaching, where the driver planned to slam into Perry as he traveled through the intersection. Growing angry that he was trying to kill the last few people she had left in the world, Hara braked sharply and leaned to her left, causing the bike to go sliding into the intersection. She halted dead center, facing the truck as it raced down the street towards her.

Reaching back behind her, she wrapped her hand around another rocket poking out of her backpack. She pulled it out and carefully inserted it into the launcher on her right shoulder. Attempting to keep herself steady at the same time, she prepared to fire. The huge truck was still several hundred feet in front of her, but by expanding her senses, she could see straight into the windshield.

At the wheel was a guard she recognized from the lab; he had beaten her son right in front of her several times to get her to perform for the doctors. The very sight of him enraged her to the breaking point, but he could not compare to the man who sat beside him. In the passenger seat sat the man that she so desperately wanted to kill. His cold eyes were all she needed to see to get her entire body to start expelling large amounts of smoke. Those eyes made her soul turn black, and his light smirk made her blood boil in her veins. He was leaning forward eagerly in his seat at the sight of her, and his twisted smile became even broader.

Since Hara had increased the intensity of all her senses, she was able to hear him as he spoke. "There she is," she heard him say with a disgusting tone of pleasure.

At the sight of his smile, rage pummeled any bit of conscience that Hara had left. She glared into the eyes of the man who had ruined her life. She took him in. He was too far away to see her glare, but Hara sent him a thought that let him know how she was feeling at that moment. She wanted him to see that he was going to burn.

"I want to perform an experiment," Hara murmured to herself, repeating words that he had once spoken to her. "Let's run a test and see how many people in this truck will survive after I blow it up." Pressing the trigger, the rocket launched with a loud hiss. She watched as it sailed straight into the grill of the semi. Several screams of surprise and pain were audible as the cab was engulfed in flames. The force of the explosion was so powerful that the truck overturned and slid towards her. After skidding nearly a hundred feet, it came to a halt halfway into the intersection, just feet from the front wheel of Hara's bike. She looked down at it calmly, observing the damage. The front end was completely destroyed, with chunks falling to the pavement. The windows had all been shattered and the remains of the cab were deformed from the explosion.

To Hara's dismay, she could still sense the mind of her old pal somewhere inside the mess. He was unconscious, but he had managed to survive without serious injury. He was the only occupant of the truck still alive, and that was quite unfortunate.

"After my test, I've come to the conclusion that, unfortunately, not everyone will die." Hara stared at the dismembered truck, wanting desperately to go inside and finish him off for good. Sighing in disappointment, she decided that she didn't want to kill him just yet. There was still something she wanted to show him. She was going to kill Jackson Odau right in front of him so he could watch. She wanted to hear him beg. She wanted to see him desperate and helpless, like she had been at his hands so many times before.

Hearing sirens in the distance, Hara quickly turned her bike around and sped back to where she had left Perry's immobilized S.W.A.T. vehicle. She had to make sure that the people she cared for were not hurt. She would just have to deal with him later, at a more convenient time.

Even though she had taken out all of the vehicles in pursuit of Perry's truck, Hara had a feeling that more men were on the way. He wouldn't have used them all in the first run. He would be back with another group of assassins soon.

Cranking up the gas, Hara rode as quickly as she could back to the wrecked S.W.A.T. truck. When she reached it, she cut the engine of her bike and hopped off, rushing to the back doors as fast as she could. They were locked and a special key was required to open them. It was a primitive lock, and she would be able to get it open without much difficulty. Raising both of her hands, she faced her palms towards the doors and began to pull her arms away from each other. The hinges on the doors creaked, but then gave way easily. Both doors snapped apart from each other and were forced outward, the sides of the truck stretching out as well.

Once the doors were open, she dropped her hands back to her sides and the creaking ceased. Taking a deep breath, she gazed inside, praying for the best. She was relieved to see that everyone was still whole. Jack and Allan were both sitting on a bench in the rear with their backs resting against the wall. Their heads were down and Hara saw that they were breathing rather fast, but they were okay. Their thoughts said that they both were certain that they were going to be killed during the chase.

The two S.W.A.T. team members were lying unconscious on the floor. Both of them had been injured from the impacts, but not seriously.

Jack and Allan were lucky; they were handcuffed securely to the floor. They hadn't been thrown around the bay like the S.W.A.T. members.

After Hara stood there and looked in at them for a few moments, Jack slowly raised his head. He was thinking that whoever had opened the doors must be from the semi and had come to kill them, but when he saw who it really was his eyes widened in shock and relief. He elbowed Allan in the side and smiled gratefully at Hara, sending her many thoughts of appreciation for saving them.

When Allan glanced up, he had the same surprised expression that Jack did at first, only his didn't melt into a smile. He simply stared at her with a mixture of confusion and guilt.

It irritated Hara that he didn't feel any gratitude toward her for being saved. He owed her that much. "You guys okay?" she asked, fighting the urge to pick a fight with Allan. They both nodded; Jack quickly but Allan more cautiously. "Good," she said, and then pointed at Jack as she told him, "You owe me one." Looking to Allan, she raised her eyebrows at him expectantly. Jack had already expressed his thanks to her, but Allan still owed her something. "You're welcome."

"Th-thank you," Allan stuttered, his expression unchanging.

Unsatisfied, Hara glanced down at the unconscious S.W.A.T. members, who were beginning to stir. One groaned, and Hara knew she had mere minutes before they would wake up. She would be long gone by that time, hopefully with her friends as well.

She could hear the police sirens growing dangerously close, but she had to be sure of something before she left. "Okay, see you," she told the two of them, marching around to the driver's side. Jack started to call out to her, but she let him know that she would just be a minute.

Opening the driver's door, she saw the blood on the window where Perry's head had struck twice. Wincing, she knew that there was going to be some serious trauma to Perry's head, and she had to do something about that. He had to survive, no matter what. Too many lives depended on him. Stepping up, she reached around Perry and undid his seatbelt. Being careful not injure him any further, Hara pulled him out of the truck. To any normal girl her age, that would have been a difficult task to perform, but she got him out without any trouble. Gently holding his head level with his body, she set him on the ground. There was a large gash on the side of his head that was bleeding pretty badly, and the poor guy looked in terrible shape. She peered down at the pained expression glued on his unconscious face, and she lightly tapped the side of his face with her hand, trying to wake him. His heart was beating; she could hear it, but it was faint.

"Hey," she called softly, snapping her fingers just above his face. Perry didn't respond, so she raised her voice. "Perry! Come on, you crazy bastard! Wake up! I know you're tougher than this!"

Perry didn't even twitch. He continued to lay motionless on the ground.

Sighing at his limp form, Hara whispered, "It's not your time yet. You can't go now. We still need you. *I* still need you."

Knowing that he wasn't going to wake up, she did the only thing she could think of to save him. Placing her hand over the wound on Perry's head, she closed her eyes. She concentrated all of her energy on the injury, and she prayed that she would be able to heal him in time. Feeling everything she could possibly offer flow from her to the FBI agent, she smiled, knowing that, for the time being, he would be okay. He had to be okay.

Before her healing process was completed, Hara felt the nose of a gun being pressed on the back of her head and heard it being cocked. She ignored it, continuing with her work.

"Get away from him right now!" Lieutenant Odau ordered angrily from behind her.

"*Shh*," Hara said, trying to keep herself focused. "Be quiet for a minute, will you?"

"If you don't take your filthy hands off of him this instant, I will kill you!" the cop threatened, pushing the gun harder against her skull.

Growing irritated again, Hara pulled her hand away from Perry's face. The gunshot wouldn't kill her, but it would cause her great pain and would greatly weaken her, which was the last thing she needed now. Plus, if Odau did pull the trigger while Hara was still healing Perry, her reaction could kill Perry while they were that closely connected. Frustrated, she stood up and turned toward the angry lieutenant. He was glaring at her with a familiar look of hate in his eyes. "You are really annoying," she told him, scowling. Not only was he the father of the most evil creature in the history of humanity, he was also threatening her life repeatedly, and that was something Hara didn't take too kindly. "Do you want him to die?" she demanded.

"No," Odau snarled, keeping the gun level with her head. "But what I do want is for you to keep away from him!"

She shook her head. "I don't have time for this. I'm trying to help your friend, so if you'll excuse me…" She started to turn back to Perry, but Odau stopped her by firing a shot just over her head. Freezing for a moment in surprise, she turned back to him with her eyebrows raised. He was dead serious about shooting her again, obviously not learning his lesson the first time around. She decided to remind him about it. "Don't you remember what happened the last time you shot me?" Pulling up her shirt so he could see her fully healed torso, she said, "Yeah, I can heal myself, so shooting me will only piss me off more than I already am."

"Maybe so," Odau muttered as his gun lowered slightly. His expression hardened once again, and he took careful aim at her chest. "But I bet you that it hurts like a bitch."

This guy just wasn't going to let it go.

Her eyes slowly narrowing to intimidate the cop, Hara growled, "Why are you Homo sapiens so stupid? Don't you get it? I don't want to hurt Perry! I want to *help* him!"

"Why would you want to help him?" Odau demanded. "He's one of the people trying to bring you in!"

"He's important," Hara told him matter-of-factly. "And he needs to live."

"What is wrong with you, huh? You think you get to decide who lives and who dies? Well, you don't! You're not God! You're *human!*"

The extra emphasis on the word human just made Hara angrier. In one quick motion, she threw her arm at Odau's wrist, knocking the gun out of his hand. The cop was too surprised to react, and he didn't fight back when Hara grabbed the front of his uniform and lifted him off his feet. She slammed him up against the side of the S.W.A.T. truck, furiously watching Odau's expression as he took in what was happening. He was utterly perplexed by her remarkable strength, and he stared at her in horror as he anticipated her next move.

Leaning closer, Hara snarled, "I am not human!" Taking in a deep breath to try and calm her rage, she ordered, "Don't ever insult me like that again!" She dropped him to the ground and stepped back, glaring at him in contempt.

"What are you?" Odau asked in a whisper, repeating his earlier question. This time, he would receive an answer.

"Your worst nightmare," Hara growled, turning back to Perry. Hearing Odau scrambling to grab his gun once again, she told him firmly, "I really don't like you." She contemplated sending him sailing into one of the windows of the building behind him.

"Well," Odau said curtly, taking aim, "the feeling's mutual!"

"Apart from the man who just tried to kill you all, you are the most pigheaded man I have ever met in my life!" Hara's fists clenched, and she could feel the fire begging to be let out as she grew steadily angrier.

Blinking in surprise, Odau said loudly, "Excuse me?"

"You won't let me help Perry because you're pissed at me for trying to kill your malevolent little boy!" Hara yelled, feeling steam pouring out of her hands. "How selfish is that? You're going to let your colleague die because you're too stubborn to acknowledge the truth about all of this? You're so selfish!"

"Coming from someone who kills people because of some problem that couldn't be fixed in a civilized way?" the lieutenant challenged.

"Don't just assume that you know my motives," Hara hissed. "You humans have lost the right to judge me!"

"Well, someone needs to wake you up!"

"Shut up!" Hara screamed, raising her hand to send her fire towards him. Flames were already erupting from her palms, but the cop seemed prepared for anything she was planning on throwing at him.

He changed his aim and fired at her arm that was expelling the fire, the bullet hitting Hara in the bicep and going straight through, and she heard it clink to the ground several feet behind her.

She didn't want to give the cop the pleasure of listening to her cries of pain, so she didn't make a sound. Biting down on her tongue until it bled, she clutched her arm and hunched over as she inhaled sharply. The pain was overwhelming, but she suppressed it. She had endured worse, and she knew that it would be over in a few seconds. Blood was trickling down her arm and dripping onto the pavement. Opening her fingers so she could observe the wound, Hara watched as it shrank and the sides of it pulled back together. When it was completely healed and all that remained was the blood, she looked back up at the lieutenant, who was staring at her arm in disbelief.

Odau met her eyes again and his own widened even more. Taking a step back, he put his hands up in defense. Hara guessed that her eyes had changed to their frightening crimson color again, as they always did when she was in extreme pain or anger.

Glaring ferociously at him, Hara snarled, "Are you ever going to learn?" Whipping her left arm towards him, the gun flew out of his hand again and clattered to the ground. Then, holding her palm up towards Odau, she let out a burst of energy that threw him into the side of the truck for a second time. She wasn't touching him, but he was dangling several inches above the ground.

Kicking his feet wildly, wondering how he was hanging in mid-air like this, the lieutenant stared at her in horror.

Enjoying the cop's fear, Hara smirked at him and started to bend her fingers inward like she was squeezing an invisible object. Odau began to choke, his eyes bulging as he grabbed at his throat. He kicked harder, but he was doing so in vain. No matter how hard he struggled, he wasn't going to get down and he wasn't going to be able to breathe until Hara decided so. As her fingers tightened, his kicks became harder. He continued to grab at his throat. When Hara saw his face starting to turn blue in the dim street lights, she told him icily, "You know, I could kill you right now so easily, and you wouldn't be able to do a thing about it." Taking a few, menacing steps forward, she narrowed her eyes mercilessly. "All I'd have to do is close my hand, and your windpipe would be crushed." At Odau's terrified expression, Hara's smirk became broader. "But I don't want to kill you just yet. I want to see the look on your face when I kill your boy. I want you to feel so much pain for bringing that wretched monster of yours into the world. But if you ever shoot me again, so help me God I will kill you so, so slowly. Do you understand me, Graham?"

The lieutenant nodded quickly, and Hara let her arm fall to her side. Odau fell to the ground in a heap, coughing heavily and gasping for breath. As she started to walk to Perry's side again, she heard Odau say to her in a raspy voice, "You stay away from my son!"

Turning back to him in disgust, Hara said, "Don't tell me what to do. I don't respond well to orders."

"Why are you doing this?" Odau demanded, supporting himself on his hands and knees as he struggled to breathe normally. "Don't you have any sense of morality inside you?"

"If you knew the truth, then you'd probably want to kill your son as well," Hara told him, going to Perry's side and deciding to ignore anything else the lieutenant chose to say. Before she could crouch down and finish healing Perry's head injury, squad cars and SUVs came flying around the corner at the intersection with the overturned semi. Sirens and lights blaring, the vehicles pulled up to the S.W.A.T. truck, and large numbers of cops and agents jumped out, weapons drawn. A few bright white lights were focused on her from the squad cars to keep her in sight, the unbearable brightness blinding her. Many threats were shouted at her as she stood motionlessly by Perry's side. There were so many voices speaking at once that all the sounds became one jumbled mess.

Hara weighed her options. She could let them arrest her and take her back to the police station, or she could cause even more damage while making an escape. There were so many guns pointed at her that it would be difficult to get away without being shot at least once, something Hara didn't want to go through again. She also had the option of killing them all, but she was tired and she really wasn't in the mood for any more killing at the moment. Besides, her fight wasn't with them. She had bigger things to deal with than the local authorities. She went with the option that would be the easiest for her. Getting arrested couldn't be that bad, because she would be able to get out of the station without a problem whenever she wanted to. Their pathetic little jail couldn't contain her for long. She had easily escaped from more advanced prisons with better security. Also, Perry was still wounded, and he was bound to go back to the station with her once he regained consciousness. If anything should happen to him there, Hara would be in close proximity to help him.

She slowly raised her hands above her head to show them that she wasn't going to resist.

✳ ✳ ✳

"Shawn? Shawn, are you with us? Shawn!"

Groaning as the throbbing ache in his head began to increase in intensity, Agent Perry blinked his eyes open a crack. Wincing at the harsh white lights above him, he shielded his eyes with his hand and peered up at the person hovering above him. He made out bright blue eyes, long blonde hair, and a friendly, concerned expression. "Renee?" he muttered as he recognized his partner, and he tried to push himself upright.

Several pairs of hands pushed him back down, and Renee told him, "Just give yourself a minute. You hit your head pretty hard."

Lying back flat against the ground, Perry groaned again. Reaching up to his throbbing head, he touched the part of his temple that ached worst. He flinched from his touch, and he looked at his fingers covered in his own blood. Looking back up, he saw four other people standing over him. Detectives Aubrey and Finchly were there, as well as two of Perry's fellow agents, Special Agent Andrew Martinson and Special Agent Jazlyn Hersh. The agents had a few cuts and bruises on their faces, but looked surprisingly well considering the circumstances. Above them were bright lights shining down on Perry's face, and above that a black sky full of stars twinkled overhead. Perry was lying on a hard surface which he assumed was the concrete street. Feeling slightly disoriented, he suddenly remembered the events that had occurred.

"I'm still alive?" he asked, closing his eyes again. "How long was I out?"

"Fifteen, twenty minutes maybe," Renee answered, placing a comforting hand on his shoulder.

"Do you feel okay?" Finchly asked in concern.

"Is no a valid answer?" Perry questioned, smiling lightly. The other five of them laughed, and Perry reopened his eyes. A thought crossing his mind, he asked, "Is everyone else in the truck okay?"

"The lieutenant and our captive Jack are perfectly fine," Martinson assured. "The two S.W.A.T. members were scratched up a bit, but they should recover without a problem. But the mayor…" His voice trailed off.

"Oh no," Perry said in horror. "He's dead, isn't he?"

"No…" Hersh started, looking a little puzzled. "He's just…gone."

"Gone?" Perry repeated in confusion. "What do you mean gone?"

"The handcuffs are still fastened, but the doors had been forced open by Hara and the mayor had disappeared by the time we arrived here. The S.W.A.T. members were unconscious at the time of his disappearance and Jack isn't talking, so we don't know how he escaped or where he's gone to."

Perry sighed, disappointed that nothing had gone the way it was supposed to.

"We have a small unit out looking for him," Finchly told him, trying to cheer him up. "So far we haven't picked up a trail, but we'll find him."

"Great," Perry grumbled.

"We do have some good news though," Aubrey offered. "When we arrived, we managed to arrest Hara."

Perry peered up at the detective. "You arrested Hara?"

"Yes, sir," Finchly said, sounding very triumphant. "She went willingly and without a fight. Lieutenant Odau himself accompanied her back to the station."

"Oh, jeez!" Perry moaned, ignoring the pain in his head and pushing himself up. He had a feeling that Odau and Hara in a car together would only end in disaster.

"Shawn, you need to rest!" Renee insisted, trying to push him back down. "Don't strain yourself!"

"I'm fine," Perry lied, struggling to his feet. Finchly and Renee steadied him as he stumbled, but he shrugged them off. "I need to get back to the station." He noticed for the first time that there was a lot going on around him. Red and blue lights were flashing, officers and agents were busying themselves around the area, and Perry saw an ambulance round the corner up ahead of him, its siren howling and making his head feel worse.

"No, you need to go to the hospital," Renee said firmly as Perry's knees began to buckle underneath him, pointing towards the ambulance advancing through the chaos.

"I need to talk to Hara," Perry persisted, walking to the nearest SUV. "It's urgent. I'll be…" He collapsed before he could finish.

"Whoa!" Martinson said, catching him as he fell. "I think you may want to revisit that hospital idea, my friend." He waved his hand at the ambulance, gesturing for it to come to them.

"No, I'll be fine," Perry told him, trying to pull away. Martinson held onto him, holding Perry's arms firmly in his hands. "Hey, let go!" Perry warned.

"Shawn, you're going to the hospital," Renee said sharply. "That's not up for debate."

"Andy, I'm serious," Perry snapped at his friend as the ambulance came to a halt. As the back doors swung open, Perry commanded, "Let go!" Struggling against his friend, he added, "I mean it! If you don't let go you're going to regret it!"

"Perry, knock it off!" Martinson snapped.

Perry stopped, slumping back against his colleague. As medics from the ambulance began unloading a stretcher from the back, he pleaded, "Can I at least go to the station first? I promise I'll go to the hospital as soon as I'm done."

"No," Renee replied stubbornly.

"Please?" he begged, feeling helpless as the stretcher was wheeled over to him. Two medics as well as Renee and Martinson forced him to lie down on it. As he situated himself so he was in a comfortable position, Perry looked to his colleagues desperately. "I need to speak to Hara about something really important! Many people's lives may depend on it!"

"It can wait."

"Are you hearing what I'm saying to you?"

"What makes you think that Hara will want anything to do with you?" Martinson asked curiously, walking beside Perry as he was wheeled back to the ambulance.

"I know she'll want to talk to me," Perry said. "She thinks I'm important for some reason, and that's why she didn't kill me earlier."

"Alright," she finally consented. "But these medics are going with you just to be safe, and then you are going to the hospital!"

Smiling in relief, Perry told her, "Thank you so much."

"You owe me," Renee grumbled, shaking her head. "You are so unbelievably stubborn." Turning to the medic on Perry's right, Renee told him, "Take him to the police station, but if he gets worse you have my permission to divert directly to the E.R."

"Hey!" Perry cried.

"And please take care of him," Renee insisted.

"Yes, ma'am," the medic said, his smirk reaching up to his cold gray eyes.

7

Fatuity

After Hara was taken to the police station and locked in a holding cell, she pretty much lost all track of time. She felt like an animal in a zoo, and she was insulted that the cops thought such a puny, primitive cage could contain her.

There was a single bench in each cell, and Hara was lying on her back across hers, exhausted from the day's activities. Several cops were outside the cells, most actually completing paperwork, but a few were milling around, watching her suspiciously. She sensed primitive, even obscene thoughts from them. When Hara had been trapped in the lab she had been taunted relentlessly by the guards, so it didn't really bother her anymore. Their thoughts were quite easy to tune out of her head. Jack was in the holding cell beside her, sitting on the bench with his back to her. Since he was the only friend that was there with her, and also because neither of them wanted to have to listen to the guards' thoughts, they had resorted to telepathic conversation.

So he's really back, Jack said for at least the fourth time.

Yep, Hara replied regretfully. *He's come back for round two.*

Are you sure that he wasn't killed in the explosion?

He's still out there. I can feel him. Besides, you'll know when he's dead because I'll be doing a dance and singing "Joy to the World."

I'm sorry, Jack said out of the blue.

For what? Hara demanded. *It's not your fault. You can't control this. That monster would have found me eventually, and we all knew that.*

It'll be okay, Jack promised her. *We'll get through this just like we did before. I'll protect you.*

Hara snorted before she could stop herself. *You'll protect me? I can't even protect me! How do you expect to protect me from him when our entire species died trying to protect me? Don't you remember what happened the last time you tried to protect me? Don't you remember what he did to you? Or need I remind you?*

She saw Jack shudder out of the corner of her eye at the disturbing memory of the first time he had been tortured. Feeling guilty, she told him, *I'm sorry.*

It's okay, Jack assured her, but Hara felt his thoughts lingering on that terrible memory. When she and Jack were both in captivity together, Jack felt the need to bring her suffering to an end. He had seen the results of what had been done to her and he didn't want her to have to go through anything like that ever again. One day, when Hara was being retrieved for another test, Jack tried to kill everyone who came for, but his plan was discovered and he ended up being greatly outnumbered. The guards took him away kicking and screaming, and for the following thirty minutes Hara had been forced to listen to Jack's screams of agony as unspeakable things were done to him. Once he was finished with Jack, the man with the gray eyes took Hara and conducted the test anyway. Jack had been traumatized by what had been done to him, and he refused to speak for nearly a month after that. Hara hadn't seen what was done to him, but his thoughts told her everything. After that day, she did her best to keep his mind off of that subject, knowing that it would only upset him and send him into another long spell of silence.

As his mind began to wander back to that horrible memory, Hara pulled him back in her direction. *If and when he comes back for me, I'll take care of him myself. I'm ready for him this time.*

I hope you are, Jack said meekly. *Because I'm not.*

Don't be scared, Jack, she told him, sighing and closing her eyes. *When he comes for me, I'm going to make sure that he doesn't touch you or anyone else ever again. I'm going to make him watch as I kill the boy, and then he can feel every ounce of pain that he's caused us. Once I take care of that, we can go home.*

I hope it's as easy as you make it sound.

Hara did, too. She had made several attempts on that man's life in the past, but he always had some little trick hidden up his sleeve. It was like he could predict every move she made, and he somehow knew how to fight any ability she threw at him. Hopefully, since she had changed a lot over the past few weeks, she would be able to surprise him.

She supposed that it made sense that the man knew how to fight her. He had been studying her kind for years before the extermination began. He could have easily figured out how to fight her abilities by studying others like her, but she still didn't understand how he was so remarkably good at it. Hara was one of the first of a completely new species. She was born the way she was, not changed like her parents were. People born with the altered gene sequence were far more powerful and far more unpredictable, especially the few that were as powerful as Hara. Even after studying her for months, it would be nearly impossible for anyone else to know exactly what she was going to do and when she was going to do it. So how was it that he knew how to? Hara vowed to find out before she killed him.

Do you think everyone will forgive us for what we've done when we go back? Jack asked uncertainly, sounding quite worried.

She wouldn't admit it, but that question had been on her mind as well. What if the two of them finished their mission in Philadelphia, went home, and then found out that they were no longer welcome because of what they had done? Would their people have enough compassion to forgive them for the horrible things they had done? It would be very ungrateful for them not to. After all, the two of them would save their entire species and bring back everyone who had died. *I hope so*, Hara answered uncertainly. *I mean, we're doing this for them. But if they don't, at least everything else will be alright again.*

Jack sighed next to her, and Hara felt guilty again. She shouldn't have accepted his help in the first place. It was her idea and her fight. It was rightfully Jack's fight too, but she shouldn't have pulled him into the mess any deeper than he already was. If things ended badly, he would also be accountable for what happened. She should have told him to get lost the moment they reunited, but she knew that that would have been impossible. Jack loved her too much to let her do this on her own.

So why are you even here? Jack asked her.

What do you mean?

Come on! You're indestructible! Why did you let them arrest you?

Oh, well… Hara flinched, not sure how to break the news to him. She decided it was just best to tell it as it was. *Perry was badly injured during the attack. He suffered a serious blow to the head.*

What?! Jack nearly cried out loud. *How bad is he? Is he going to be okay? Where is he now?*

Hara felt him tense in fear, and she quickly put pressure on his mind to keep him quiet. He was really scared, and Hara needed to reassure him that Perry was going to be okay or he was going to freak. *Shh, shh, shh!* she said, sending the numbing feeling over to him. After a moment she felt Jack's body relax, but his heart was still pounding and his mind was still in panic mode. *He'll be fine. Don't worry. I pulled him out of the truck and managed to heal his injury about halfway before I was interrupted by that damn cop.*

I really don't like that cop, Jack commented when he had calmed down. *He's really been a pain.*

Hara smirked. *Tell me about it. Today, he shot me three times!*

Three times? Jack repeated in disbelief. *Is he crazy?*

Apparently! He shot me twice at his house when I tried to take his son, and once when I was trying to help Perry.

So that's what those shots were, Jack realized. *Why were there two shots?*

He gave me a warning shot.

Oh.

I really want to kill him as well. He's an ass and he keeps hurting me…

You can't do that! Jack insisted. *You know how he's supposed to die. We can't change that. His death is one that is fused in time.*

Frustrated, Hara growled, *The second time he shot me he got me straight in the lung. Noah found me and removed the bullets.*

And even after he found out you weren't dead, he shot you again anyway?

Yep, Hara sighed. *Ever since you opened your fat mouth and told everyone what I am, he's known that I can heal myself, but he shot me anyway because he knows that it causes me pain. I think he's just been enjoying himself.*

I didn't tell them what you are! Jack insisted. *I only told them what you can do!*

Yeah, thanks a lot! Now even more people are after me for what I can do!

There was a short pause, and Jack told her softly, *I'm sorry…I just thought that he had a right to know…*

Hara paused as well, knowing what Perry meant to Jack. *Yes, he does have a right to know, but he's not one of us yet. You can't trust him right now. Did you know that he told the cop everything?*

Oh… Jack muttered, sounding disappointed. He had been so eager to talk to Perry that he hadn't stopped to think that maybe he wasn't entirely trustworthy just yet. The burden of knowing who would be an ally in the future was that they had to wait until that person's time came. Sighing again, Jack asked, *But you're sure he's going to be okay?*

Uh-huh, Hara said. *I mean, he may not be right now, but if that's the case then I'll help him.*

But that still doesn't answer why you're here.

Yes, it does.

No, it doesn't.

Feeling frustrated, Hara snapped, *I let them arrest me so I could keep an eye on Perry! Plus, I really didn't feel like getting shot again.*

Well, how is getting yourself caught supposed to help Perry? Jack demanded.

Because he's coming here!

Why would he come here? If he's hurt he's going to go to the hospital! Why would he go to a police station if he was hurt?

You know him better than I do, Hara reminded him. *He's a very persistent and stubborn man, just like you. He knows what I can do and seems to believe us. He's coming to me with questions, and he thinks that I'm going to give him the answers.*

Are you?

No.

Why not?

It's too early for him to know the truth. He shouldn't even know that we exist, but I guess that we can't change that. No, I'm not going to tell him much of anything. He'll most likely find out what happened before this day is through, but now it's too early.

Is there going to be a problem later if he finds out? Jack asked curiously. *I mean, nobody here should know the truth until it's revealed in the future to the entire world.*

Once Perry finds out, then he'll be fully on our side. It won't matter that he knows the truth.

Well, if you say so, Jack replied, although he still sounded uncertain. *But I'm just worried that…you know, these cops are really getting annoying!*

Hara had been tuning them all out, but she listened again to what they were thinking. *Oh,* she thought. *Just ignore them. That's what I've been doing.*

I should smash every one of their faces into the floor! Jack growled, and Hara felt him tense up again. *Those disgusting, perverted, greedy, foul mouthed…*

They're humans, Jack, Hara reminded him, praying that he wouldn't do anything stupid. *What else do you expect of them? Their lives are pointless, and they're not worth getting angry over. Please don't do anything you'll regret. Seriously, I put up with this at the lab for all those months. It doesn't bother me anymore.*

Well, it bothers me! Jack snapped, shaking with fury. *If you won't do something about this, then I will!*

Alright, alright! Hara sighed, opening her eyes and turning her head so she could see the cops who were looking at her. "You know, you guys can think nasty things about me all you want, but I am never going to move," she told them, raising her eyebrows.

One cop—a big, burly man with graying hair—smirked back at her. "Oh, we don't need you to move, sweetheart. We're getting a good enough view from where you are right now!"

The other cops all howled with laughter that was harsh and cruel, and Hara was surprised that he had actually made her uncomfortable. Her shirt went all the way up to the base of her neck, but it was fairly tight and showed off her figure. Folding her arms across her chest to cover what she assumed they had all been eyeing up, she looked back up at the ceiling, suddenly feeling very small and helpless. Since she had been verbally harassed so much by the guards at the lab, she had learned to ignore it, but the cop who had spoken didn't remind her of a guard. He reminded her of the man who tortured her. The man, just like the cop, had an ever-present smirk on his face, and the body language of both men resembled that of a sly predator, and she wondered when they would strike. Their resemblance made Hara recall a memory that she had struggled for so long to repress. Once, just once, the man had lost his self-control and kissed her, and once he started, he was unable to stop. Had they not been interrupted, he would have raped her. Hara didn't want to think about how lucky she was. Also, there was a certain guard who had repeatedly tortured her with repulsive comments about the shape of her body, and he once attempted to touch her in very inappropriate places. Her captor found out, and that guard was never seen again.

Hara was still young, and very gorgeous. Her wavy, flowing brown hair looked stunning even though she'd been swimming in scum and hadn't had a decent shower in a while. Her iridescent green eyes caused some curious unease among humans. They were quite mesmerizing and lit up her beautiful face. Her tanned skin was flawless, a lucky gift every one of her kind received. Her face was both intelligent and alluring, something that brought second glances and unwanted attention. That was one gift—or curse—of her kind. At least, that was what her father had once said. He said that humans who knew they existed could always identify them just by one physical factor: they were perfect. Perfect faces, perfect bodies, perfect beings. At the moment, Hara really wished that she wasn't so perfect, because it was making the cops difficult to deal with.

"Aww!" another cop said, sneering at her. "Did he make you uncomfortable?" Pressing himself against the bars, he added, "I can fix that."

Hara saw Jack's shoulders shaking in anger out of the corner of her eye, but she ignored her friend as vivid images of the guard and her captor flashed through her mind. Shuddering at the other cop's last comment, she gripped her arms tighter.

"Maybe she's just cold," a third cop snickered. "Hey, babe, if I come in I can warm you up!"

The other cops began to laugh dauntingly again, and Hara just squeezed her eyes shut, wishing she could be anywhere but there. Deciding that she was going to depart sooner than she had originally planned, she exhaled through her nose and tried to tune them out once more. Jack had a bit of a more provocative reaction. Slamming his palms down on the bench on either side of him, he jumped to his feet and faced them, his intense glare frightening even Hara. While the half dozen or so cops looked back at him and stopped laughing in surprise, Jack said in a deadly tone, "If you don't all shut up right now, so help me God you will regret it!"

There was a moment's silence, but then the cops all burst into laughter. Hara knew by his expression and body language that he was close to the breaking point. Everyone thought that Hara was dangerous, but Jack could just as easily cause as much damage.

"Oh, how cute!" the big cop who had first spoken to Hara scoffed as the others continued to chortle. Clearly, none of them knew how to take a hint. "Are you going to defend your little girlfriend?"

"I'm going to rip your throat out!" Jack growled menacingly.

That only made the other cops laugh harder. The big cop narrowed his eyes and started to slowly make his way around the cages toward Jack. "Is that a threat?"

"That's a promise," Jack replied quietly.

Staring in horror as the big cop pulled his weapon out of his holster, Hara sucked in a deep breath and gripped the edge of the bench.

The big cop aimed the gun at Jack's chest and asked him softly, "What exactly is stopping me from pulling this trigger right now and ridding the world of yet another worthless child killer?"

Jack didn't respond. He just continued to stand there glaring at the cop.

"I asked you a question, boy!" the cop snapped, cocking his gun. "What are you going to do, huh? Come on. Kill me! Oh, wait, that's right. I'm the one with the gun!"

Hara was completely nauseated when she realized what was going on. She had seen confrontations like this in the lab when she was around the human guards. The cops had never encountered a female of her kind before, and they were extremely prone to her effects. They were also angry about recent events, making them even more susceptible to Hara's unintentional influence. Being what she was, she unwillingly drew people to her not only with her attractive features but also with a pheromone that was secreted when she was under elevated levels of stress. It was a defense mechanism. The pheromone attracted people to her when she was being threatened. Her attackers would be distracted by her and couldn't concentrate on anything besides fighting over her. Jack wasn't affected by it since he had lived around it his entire life, but it was a completely different story for the cops. Hara felt utterly disgusted by what she was doing to the men, but it wasn't something she could control. The big cop wasn't waving his gun around because of what Hara and Jack had done that night. He was doing it because he was competing with Jack for Hara. He was fighting over her! She could practically smell the testosterone in the air. Soon, the other cops would start fighting as well, and with all the weapons in the room, someone was bound to get hurt. There was only one thing that she could do to prevent them from starting a firefight. She had to make them angry at her so they would stop lusting after her.

Hara slipped her legs off the bench and stood up. Walking over to the bars and pressing herself against them in a seductive manner, she called, "Hey." She pressed her forehead against the bars as well when the cop turned in surprise, the metal feeling cool on her hot skin. Cursing herself for what she was doing, she wrapped her hands around two of the bars and raised her eyebrows at him expectantly.

When the cop first turned to her his expression was annoyed, but when he saw her body posture his mood immediately changed. Looking her up and down, a dopey grin crossed his face.

Hara nearly gagged in repulsion, but she forced herself to simper convincingly. "You know," she said, "I really like a man who demands respect from those inferior to him. Especially if he owns a gun."

Several snickers and giggles were audible from the other cops, and one of them whistled at her.

Jack was skeptical. *What are you doing?* he demanded.

Let me take care of this, she begged, keeping a careful eye on the big cop as he started to move toward her. To her relief, Jack didn't protest.

"Do you now?" the cop asked as he approached her. Stopping just a few inches from her, he folded his arms across his chest and smirked down at her.

Their noses were nearly touching, and Hara could smell the tobacco on his putrid breath. She felt the bile rising in her own throat, but swallowed several times to keep it down. Forcing herself to keep up the act, she fluttered her eyelashes at him. "Oh, yes," she whispered sweetly, making her eyes flash at him. The cop looked surprised at first, but the look was wiped clean off his face as Hara reached out through the bars and ran her hand down his huge, bulky arm. She could sense the eyes of the other cops on her and they watched longingly. Jack was letting her know just how utterly disgusted and infuriated he was, but she ignored everyone else in the room. "They're just so…enticing!" She was sure to add the upward head tilt and the slight contraction of her eyelids at the last word. Knowing that her plan was working from the thoughts that were running through the cop's mind, she grimaced inside as she awaited his reaction.

Keeping his eyes level with hers, the cop lowered his arms and put his gun back in its holster. Then, he reached up with both hands and gently wrapped his fingers around hers while Hara struggled not to shudder. "And I like a girl who knows her guys," he said smoothly, stoking the backs of her hands.

Already feeling completely violated, Hara couldn't take any more of it. She grabbed the front of his police uniform with her right hand. The cop started to lean closer, and Hara gave him a bit more of a surprise than he had expected. Tightening her grip on his jacket, she pulled her head back and wrenched her arm forward as hard as she could. The cop's face smashed into the bars with a sickening crack, and he dropped to the ground like a fly that was just swatted out of the air.

The other cops began to laugh mockingly at their friend as he yelled in pain on the floor, some clapping and cheering for Hara.

As she turned away from the cop in disgust, she saw that Jack was grinning broadly at her. She smiled back, feeling proud of herself.

"You bitch!" the cop shouted nasally as he staggered to his feet. Glowering at her angrily, he held his nose as blood flowed down his face.

The only thing that Hara found herself capable of doing was grinning boldly. It amused her that the cop had fallen for it and finally got what was coming to him, and Hara was glad that she got to be the one to make him look like a fool. Smirking, she shook her head and looked back to Jack, who was trying to keep from laughing.

"You and your boyfriend are trash!" the cop snarled, retreating back to the larger group of his friends.

"Whatever," Hara snickered.

"So says the pedophile," Jack shot back.

The cop glared at him, and Jack scowled in return.

"And he's not my boyfriend," Hara snapped. "So you can stop calling him that. I'm meant for somebody else."

"Oh, so you do have a boyfriend?" another cop asked, jeering at her.

"Sorry boys," Hara apologized sarcastically, giving them all a false smile. "I'm taken." She started to turn back to her bench, but what the big cop said next made he stop in her tracks.

"If you and your real boyfriend ever have kids, are you going to kill them too?"

That big cop had no idea how big a mistake he had just made. Stillness swept the room as everyone watched Hara's reaction.

Jack grew quite uneasy as he realized what the cop had said, knowing that there were going to be unfortunate consequences for that remark. He kept repeating in his head, *Oh, God, he is so dead!* "You seriously should not have said that," he said grimly, taking a few cautious steps away from Hara.

Hara took a moment to let the comment register in her head. Of all the insults he could have thrown at her, why did he have to choose the one that actually struck a nerve? Her mate was dead and they did indeed have children before he died. Several, in fact. Her children were all dead now, and the cop's comment had hurt her in a way that no one could ever understand. How he could even suggest that she would want to hurt her own offspring…it was outrageous! Sure, she had killed those other kids, but they were vile little demons that were going to grow up to kill so many people! Why was it so hard for those damn humans to understand? Turning back to him slowly, she raised her arms above her head in a stretch, bending her fingers into tight fists. As she did that, she made the room shake violently. Plaster chunks fell off the ceiling along with thick clouds of dust. Books fell to the floor from a bookshelf across the room and the metal chairs and wooden desks rattled noisily on the concrete floor. The cops all looked around in confusion, wondering what was causing the sudden quake. Jack shrank away even more to the opposite end of his cell, pressing his back firmly against the metal bars. When Hara lowered her arms back to her side, the quaking stopped.

The big cop stared at her uncertainly.

Hara asked him in a deadly voice, "What did you say?"

Carefully, the cop took a few side steps around to her cell, shooting a glance at Jack's terrified expression. Eyeing her, he said, "Well, since you seem to enjoy slaughtering little kiddies, I just thought maybe you would enjoy murdering your own." He was standing directly in front of her, smirking in at her. He clearly hadn't taken the hint from the shaking room.

Hara didn't know what it was with that man, but he just didn't seem to know when it was the appropriate time to shut his mouth. "Do you have kids, officer?" she questioned softly, peering over at him and taking a daunting step closer. When the cop blinked in surprise, Hara searched his memory to answer her own question. "Yes," she said as she found them pictured in his head, "you do. And a wife?"

The cop's smirk was wiped clean off his face and his eyes became angry and fearful. His fists clenched and his body tensed uneasily. He gritted his teeth and was breathing rapidly. Hara was making him uncomfortable with her questions, but she didn't plan to stop there.

"Yes, a wife," she said, and nodded as she made her eyes flash again. Digging deeper to get more information about his family, she added, "Julie, right? And your kids... fifteen-year-old Kim and eight-year-old Jeff, am I correct?"

The other cops looked to the big one in shock, their eyes wide in amazement. Their reactions alone were enough to confirm that Hara was correct.

Horrified by what she knew, the big cop stuttered, "I-I don't know what you're talking about!"

"You don't?" Hara asked in fake surprise, tapping her chin. Burrowing into his head even farther, she pressed on. "So you don't live out in the suburbs in a little blue house...address 384 Harper Lane?"

"How do you know this?" the cop demanded in a shaky voice, looking both defensive and afraid for his family even though he had just tried to make a pass at Hara and betray his wife.

"The same way that I know your name, Herv," Hara growled, grinning evilly. "Herv the Perv." Catching something else in Herv's sick mind, she asked him, "Oh, does your wife know that you molest your daughter?"

His face flushing, Herv snarled, "That's absurd!"

"Is it?" Hara asked. "Because that's not what you're telling me."

"I haven't told you anything!" Herv insisted in confusion, taking a step back as Hara took a step closer to the bars.

"Yes, you have," Hara told him, raising an eyebrow and nodding slowly. "Everything I know about your family, every sick detail, you just told me."

Herv didn't seem to understand what she meant. He was staring at her with a mixture of horror and confusion.

Hara tapped her forehead and then pointed at his head. It seemed like it was beginning to dawn on him what she was implying, but he didn't believe it was possible. He kept repeating in his head, *That's impossible!* so Hara decided to let him know that it was possible. "I hate to break it to you Herv, but it's not impossible," she said quietly, gazing back at him.

Backing up until he bumped into the wall, Herv stared at her in pure terror. "How are you doing that?" he cried. His breathing was in shallow gasps, and when his colleagues asked what was wrong, he told them, "She can hear what I'm thinking!"

"Yes, I can," Hara declared silkily, walking up to about a foot from the bars. "I can uncover any dirty little secret about you that I want. Any question I need an answer for, I can get from your head." Cocking her head slightly, she said, "Do you love your wife? Because after that move you just made on me that's hard to believe. I think that once I get out of here I'll have to stop by your house and let her know just how great of a husband—and father—you really are."

Springing forward from the wall, Herv whipped out his gun and aimed it right at her face, the nose less than a foot from her right eye. Hara had seen in his head that he was going to do that, so she wasn't at all startled by his reaction. She could hear his heart pounding and his chest was huffing up and down in the effort to keep himself from pulling the trigger. "You stay away from my family, do you hear?" he ordered furiously, his gun hand shaking. "You stay away from them, you wicked little child-slayer! Stay away from them or I will kill you!"

Glaring back at him, Hara took three careful steps back. That cop didn't know when to shut his mouth, and now he was going to pay. As the rage built up inside of her, time seemed to slow down. Glancing over at Jack, she saw his eyes go wide as he felt how angry she was. He gave her a small shake of the head, telling her that Herv wasn't worth the trouble. His head only moved a fraction of an inch, but she saw it. Her friend had originally wanted to hurt the cops for thinking those dirty thoughts about her, but now that she was pissed off, he knew that what she was about to do would not be good. Turning back to Herv, she told him quietly, "You should be more careful about what you say, Herv."

The sound of a door opening made Hara turn. She was glad to see that Lieutenant Odau and Agent Perry had entered, just in time to see just how dangerous she could be.

Taking in the scene, both men stared wide-eyed in surprise at Herv, who was still glowering at her and keeping his weapon level with her head. Perry met Hara's eyes and his brow furrowed in confusion. He appeared to be fine, but looked a little unsteady on his feet. His eyes were cloudy and exhausted, and his face was a sickly gray color. Dried blood caked the left side of his head where the initial cut had been, but the wound had been healed completely. Hara felt that he was not entirely whole, and she prayed that he would be able to hold on until he received help.

Turning away from the FBI agent, Hara looked back to Herv, who hadn't taken any notice of them. She glanced down at the gun for a

225

moment before looking back into Herv's eyes and gave him a single wink.

With a series of deafening bangs, Herv's firearm exploded. Bullets erupted from it and ricocheted off the ceiling and walls, causing everyone in the room to duck. Gunpowder flew out onto Herv's arm and chest, and it caught fire immediately. He dropped the remains of the gun and stumbled backwards, gripping his arm in terror.

"No!" Odau shouted, rushing to his side. Hara didn't know what the lieutenant was planning to do, but moments later Perry came running with the fire extinguisher. Pulling out the pin, he squeezed the handle and hosed Herv down. White clouds filled the air and as the flames winked out, and Herv fell to the floor.

Hara snickered and tried not to burst into laughter from Herv's ridiculous appearance. He had white foam covering most of his body, and his wild expression only made it better. Turning to see Jack's reaction, she saw that he was grinning too, but mainly out of relief. Because of how angry she had been, Jack had expected her to do much worse than that. He chuckled to himself as the cop shook in fear on the floor and held his burned arm in pain.

"What the hell are you?" he cried, peering up at her in fear. Still grasping his arm, he scrambled to his feet and rushed to the door. Throwing it open, he ran out without looking back.

Smirking after him, Hara listened as Odau laid out his orders. "Everybody out now! More help is needed downtown. I suggest that you all get down there and make yourselves useful!"

There were several mutters of, "Yes, sir," and then the cops all hurried after Herv.

Hara turned back to Perry and Odau as silence filled the room, only to find that they were both staring at her curiously. After what she had been through in the past with her captor, it made her extremely uncomfortable when people stared at her with that particular look on their faces.

"You know, trying to kill the people holding you captive isn't going to get you anywhere except a padded cell," Odau told her disapprovingly.

"And showing your face in the same room as me isn't going to get you anywhere except a hole in the ground," Hara replied with a counterfeit smile. "As much as I appreciate the visit, I'm not in the mood to be pestered anymore by a bunch of perverted cops. And Daddy here has lost all his privileges to talk to me." Turning, she walked back to her bench and sat down.

"Actually," Perry said as he set the fire extinguisher down, "I was the one who wanted to talk to you."

"And what makes you think that I want to talk to you?" Hara demanded, putting on a bored expression.

"There has to be a reason for why you saved my life," Perry replied. "And because you talked to me first."

Blinking in surprise, Hara peered across the room at him. Perry's expression remained blank, but his eyes said a thousand words. Smiling warmly at him for the first time since they had met, she nodded in respect. "You're quite right," she said. "Well, if you insist. What do you want to talk about?"

Lieutenant Odau stared incredulously at her, stunned at how much more polite she was to Perry. He didn't understand why his life meant nothing to her while Perry's meant a great deal.

"Everything," Perry answered. "Who you are, what you are, why you're doing this, what happened to you and your people...I can keep going if you want."

Hara put up her hand to signal that she had heard enough. Planting both hands on her knees, she told him, "Quite a few subjects are not topics for discussion, but if you come in here, and you ask the right questions, you may be able to walk away with a few helpful answers."

"No one is going in there with you!" Odau informed, taking a defensive step forward so he was in between Hara and Perry.

Her eyes flickering to his, Hara leaned forward even more. "Lieutenant, once again you are failing to let me help this man. I do not wish to speak with you anymore, so please don't speak to me."

His face turning bright red, Odau looked at the floor and stepped back again.

"What are the right questions?" Perry asked, half curious and half frustrated.

Glancing back at him, Hara raised a hand and beckoned for him to come join her. With a click, the padlock around the chains on her gate clicked open and they fell to the floor with a loud clank. The gate creaked open about six inches, and both men stepped back in surprise. "You'll know they're the right questions when I give you a decent answer." She leaned her back against the bars behind her. Perry's eyes traveled to the door that was standing open and then back to hers. He was still uncertain of her, and Hara didn't blame him. "Perry, if I wanted to hurt you, I would have done so when I had you pinned to the floor in that apartment room," she reminded, raising an eyebrow. "Or when I was trying to heal your head injury as you lay helpless on the street." She shot Odau an unappreciative look.

Looking confused, Perry chose not to question that. Eyeing her carefully, he walked around to the gate, pushed it open a little farther, and stepped inside. Odau was watching intently from outside, keeping his hand on his gun in case he needed to use it. "If you can break out of here whenever you want, why are you even here?" Perry asked her, puzzled.

"Because I needed to keep an eye on you and make sure you didn't keel over dead."

"How did you know..." Perry started, staring at her in shock. "How did you know that I was going to come here?"

"I just did," Hara told him quietly. "That's all that matters."

Perry took a few hesitant stops closer to her. He still looked unsteady on his feet, and Hara watched nervously as he began to sway slightly. Looking to his left temple where he had struck the window of his S.W.A.T. truck repeatedly, she feared that the injury was going to begin affecting him sooner than she had hoped. There wasn't even a bruise underneath the dried blood, but Hara couldn't be deceived by that. Inside him was a jumbled mess, and she prayed that he would allow her to help him when the time came for that. His eyes were dull and drooping, and whenever he took a step his legs shook noticeably.

"Maybe you ought to sit down," Hara suggested with concern. Perry's thoughts told her that he still didn't want to get too close to her, so she scooted to her left towards the far end of the bench and gestured for him to take a seat at the opposite end. "Seriously, I won't bite."

Pausing, Perry slowly made his way to the vacant end of the bench and sat on the very edge of it, as far from her as he could possibly get. He watched her carefully as she studied him, trying to decide whether or not she was a threat.

To let him know that she wasn't, she leaned back against the bars again and crossed her legs casually. "So, how's the head?"

Perry's eyelids contracted slightly. "It hurts," he said, and Hara could hear the pain receptors in his head screaming at his brain. His expression betrayed his pain as well. The muscles in his face were tensed as were his shoulders, and his eyes were moist as his tear ducts overworked themselves.

Nodding, Hara replied, "After you were knocked out, I pulled you out and started to heal your injury—which is why you have no external wound—but I was rudely interrupted halfway through." Glancing in the direction of Odau, she saw by the look on his face that he finally realized that she had been telling the truth when she said she was only trying to help Perry. "I still think there's some internal damage, however, which is why it hurts so badly."

"You can heal other people besides yourself?" Perry asked curiously. He appeared to be quite keen on learning more about her abilities.

"Yes, I can," Hara answered, nodding again. "I tried to help you, but your friend shot me. Again."

"Give him a break," Perry said sternly. "He was just doing his job. Besides, blowing out our tires didn't exactly make it look like you were trying to help me."

"I only did that so you wouldn't get into any more trouble," Hara explained.

Sighing, Perry let it go. "The medics say that I have a concussion and probably some internal bleeding. Can you heal something like that?"

"Do you want me to?" Hara asked, lifting a hand towards him.

"No, I was just wondering if you could," Perry clarified quickly, eyeing her hand warily as she dropped it back into her lap. "Why did you try to help me? What use am I to you?"

Staring at him, Hara chuckled. "I'm sure Jack here has already told you that." Shooting a quick glance at her friend, who was still pressed up against the bars at the far end of his cage, she raised an eyebrow. He shrugged uncomfortably and looked at the floor in return.

"All he told me was that I'm important," Perry explained impatiently. "But he didn't tell me why."

"Well, I can't tell you why either," she said apologetically. "But if things play out like I think they will, then you'll most likely find out the truth by the end of the day. I just ask that you be patient."

"If I'm going to find out by the end of today anyway, then what difference does it made if you tell me now?" Perry demanded.

"Not enough has happened yet," Hara informed him. "Everything that you want to know about me is information that cannot be told. It has to be seen, experienced for yourself. By the end of the day, it's likely that you will have witnessed enough to be told the truth or even figure it out yourself."

Looking very frustrated, Perry pursed his lips and scowled down at the concrete floor. Hara felt guilty. Perry was a good man and deserved the truth, but she knew that the truth would be too much for him to handle just yet. She could feel more dilemmas heading their way, and once they were all over Perry would have seen enough to be able to comprehend her reality. Cocking her head slightly to one side, she said, "But I'm sure that there are some smaller, less complicated questions you have that wouldn't be too much of a problem to answer."

Perry nodded and gazed back up at her. "Actually, I do."

"Fire away."

"What's your real name?" Perry asked intently. "And don't tell me it's Hara, because I know that's just an alias."

Gazing back at him, Hara thought of how she should respond without making him angry. "My real name doesn't matter anymore," she whispered regretfully. "I've changed so much because of what was done to me that I'm not the same person anymore. I'm a completely new person. I am now—and will forever be—Hara. Hara the psycho

229

murderer." She turned her head away in shame, and could feel Odau smirking at her.

The great deal of sympathy that was flowing from Perry was surprising. Hara hadn't expected him to feel sorry for her after what she had done. "You know, you say that, but you're wrong," he told her softly. "I don't know what it is, but there's something more to this—more to you—than just the killing. I think you really were a good person. Something terrible happened to you, and I know it has to do with the man who just tried to kill me and your friends. I don't know the whole story, but whatever happened, it really messed you up and it wasn't your fault." When Hara looked up at him in a mixture of confusion and sorrow, he gazed back at her with compassion burning in his eyes. "I know there's more to you that this. I can see a different person hiding behind your eyes, and I think it's the person you once were, terrified to come back out. I can't see what it is, but I think there is a logical reason you're killing these kids, and I swear to you that if you tell me everything about what went down with you that I will personally help you figure this mess out in a more peaceful, civilized way. Trust me, you're not as bad as you think you are."

"I am worse than you can imagine," Hara growled, narrowing her eyes at him.

Perry shook his head. "No, you're not."

"How can you say that after what I've done?" Hara demanded skeptically.

A small smile coming to his lips, Perry whispered, "Because you saved my life."

That shocked Hara. She may have saved his life, but that did not make her a good person. She killed children and other people that didn't deserve to die in such horrible ways, so how could Perry think that she was good for sparing one life while sacrificing so many others? It was nice to know that somebody in the human world didn't hate her for what she did, but at the same time she wanted to slap Perry in the face to wake him up.

For seemingly unprovoked reasons, Hara was once again becoming angry. She didn't want him, or anyone, to pity her. Perry didn't even know the whole story, so he couldn't come to conclusions so soon.

"You're not a bad person," Perry repeated softly, the growing amount of pity on his face making Hara start to cringe.

"You'd better stop saying that," Hara warned him. "Because I am a bad person, and that's not going to change any time soon."

"You're not all bad!" Perry insisted, staring hard at her as if she would be able to see that fact in his eyes.

"Really?" Hara said, and laughed sarcastically. "Because even though I know what I've been doing is wrong, I don't want to stop! I want to finish everything that I've started!" Leaning closer, she hissed, "I need to finish it! Are you going to keep telling me that I'm not a bad person?"

Perry continued to stare at her with that pathetically sad look on his face. He wanted to pretend that he knew what she'd been through, but he had absolutely no idea.

"Don't," she growled in disgust, shaking her head angrily at him. "Don't you look at me like that. Don't feel sorry for me. If you knew half of what I've done, you'd hate me more than he does!" She waved her hand dismissively at Odau.

"What do you mean?" Perry asked quietly.

"Do you want to know a secret?" Hara asked him, unable to keep her tone from being eerie. All Perry did was watch her without changing his expression, so Hara continued. "Did you hear about all the other people like me that were killed, those unimaginable numbers of innocent people? They all died horrifying, gruesome deaths at the hand of someone even worse than me, but do you know something? Everyone who died, died because of me! It was all my fault!" Tears spontaneously began to spill down her cheeks, and she looked back to the floor.

"No, it wasn't!" Jack told her firmly, speaking for the first time since Perry and Odau's entrance. Walking forward to the bars dividing their cells, he knelt down on his bench and peered in at her. Hara and Perry both turned to look curiously back at him. "It was not your fault! Don't even tell yourself that for a second! You didn't ask for any of that to happen!"

"Maybe not, but if it wasn't for me then everyone would still be alive," Hara whimpered through gritted teeth.

"You couldn't have prevented what happened, no matter what you say..."

"Why are you defending me, Jack?" Hara demanded dubiously. "Your family died trying to protect me!"

Pain flashed across Jack's face for half a second before he straightened out his expression again, but Hara had seen it and that was enough for her. Jack's mother and little brother had both died during the year-long massacre of her kind, while attempting to keep Hara safe from the vile doctor who wanted to get his filthy hands on her. Unfortunately, they had done so in vain. Jack missed his family and was sorry that they were gone, but he still would never blame Hara for any of that. He loved her too much to do that.

It made Hara so angry. "Don't you see?" she hissed at her friend, wanting him to face the facts. "We did what my father told us to, but it all went down anyway! We resisted The Doc's offer, we fought him, all to keep him from getting to me! But everyone was killed in the process, and he found me anyway! He still did everything to me that he promised he would, and now look at the results! If my father hadn't been so

231

stubborn and had just handed me over in the first place, then no one would have died! Don't you see?" she repeated urgently, trying to get Jack to understand that she was and always would be the one to blame. "Everyone died defending me!"

"Do you really think that just handing you over would have kept The Doc from killing people?" Jack asked her, a peculiar looking half-smirk on his face. "That would have only proven that we were weak, and the humans would have wiped us out much faster. At least we went down with a hell of a fight! I would have gladly died for you!"

Gazing back at her friend with a great amount of gratitude for trying to make her feel better, Hara smiled weakly.

"This was always bigger than just you," Jack explained. "There was more to this than what was said. The Doc had something personal against all of us, and you were just the excuse he used to kill peaceful people."

"Wait—The Doc?" Perry questioned. "Who's that?"

"The man who started all of this," Hara answered. "The man who just tried to kill you and Jack."

Perry nodded, glad that he could place a name with the face. "He was the one who experimented on you?" It was more of a statement than a question. Hara and Jack's conversation had been enough to explain that. "And he was trying to kill me to kill Jack and Allan Brown."

Hara nodded. "He knew that if he shot the driver while the truck was at such a high speed, the truck would most definitely flip. There was no way that any of you could have survived that. It wasn't like The Doc held a grudge against you, at least not yet, anyway." She ignored Perry's startled glance at her. "So try not to take it too personally."

"What is Allan Brown's part in all of this?" Perry asked, folding his hands on his knee and leaning forward eagerly now that he was a bit more comfortable around Hara. "Or is that not a 'right question'?"

The corner of Hara's mouth turned up into a half smile, and she regretted that she would be forced to lie to answer his question and keep her friend safe. "He's just a friend," she told him. "Nothing more, nothing less."

"He abandoned us," Jack reminded.

"He abandoned me," Hara corrected. Speaking to Perry again, she explained truthfully, "He, Daniel, and Meg were all close friends of my father's before everything went down, and after our people were all killed, they escaped and went undercover here to hide from The Doc and everyone else who aided him." Looking away, guilt began to cloud her eyes. "Once I got away, I came back to find them, expecting to see them working hard to bring this all to an end. I expected that they would all be eager to get back in the fight." Closing her eyes, she swallowed hard as a great deal of emotion overwhelmed her. "But instead, I found that all they really wanted was to forget anything had ever happened, and to just live the rest of their lives as normally as they could." She sighed. "Their families were all slaughtered along with everyone else, and by coming back I forced their memories back upon them. By coming back I brought the war back to their doorsteps. By coming back I ruined the simple lives they were trying to rebuild."

Jack reached through the bars separating them and placed a comforting hand on her shoulder. "They want the war to come to an end just as much as you do," he told her softly.

"So…the three of them were just friends to your father?" Perry questioned. When Hara looked up at him in confusion, he added, "I mean, that's all they were to him?"

Unsure of what he was getting at, Hara listened in on his thoughts to fully understand his question. When she realized what he meant by that, her stomach knotted up. "I'm not sure what you mean," she muttered, shrugging off Jack's hand and throwing him a sharp glance. *He knows!* she sent to him in fear.

Jack's eyes widened and he looked over at Perry.

"Well, I mean…" Perry's voice trailed off as he searched Hara's eyes for his answers. Leaning closer to her so Odau couldn't hear, he whispered, "I guess what I'm trying to say is…are they…like you, too?"

Hearing Jack's breath catch in his throat, Hara gazed back into Perry's awaiting eyes. For a moment she actually considered telling him the truth. Had Odau not been in the room she may have blurted it out without thinking it through first. But although the man was still uncertain as to whose side he should take, he still hadn't proven his trustworthiness. A thought that had crossed his mind earlier had caught Hara's attention, and it immediately told her that Perry was not going to respond to the truth in her favor. "No," she lied quietly yet firmly. "They were just regular people who wanted to try and help struggling people like my family. Look at what that got them."

Perry nodded, but he didn't look convinced. His thoughts said that he had decided to just deal with the answer he had received.

No one spoke for a moment, and Hara waited uncomfortably for someone to say something, but when the silence continued to drag out she tilted her head toward Perry. "Any more questions?"

"Yes, a few actually," Perry said. "Can you tell me what made your people like this?"

"What, you mean you want to know what gave us the abilities?"

"Yes."

Looking at Jack, she threw her arms up in exasperation. "I thought you said that you told him everything!"

"I understand," Perry started, putting up his hands in Jack's defense, "that they were caused by a genetic experiment. It was from a chemical compound, correct? But I don't understand how a chemical compound can make everyone who inhaled it into a super-human. How could that work?"

"Oh, jeez!" she groaned, making a face. "You're going to make me explain that?" Scratching her head, she really didn't want to launch into the complicated explanation. "Well, I don't know how much you know about biology, so I'll just dumb it down for you. The reaction of the chemical in our bodies caused our DNA to change when it replicated. In DNA, there are certain orders that the bases have to be in or else there will be mutations. The order was completely rearranged after the chemical was ingested, therefore resulting in remarkable mutations. These mutations flipped a switch in our brains and allowed us to have more access to it. That was how the abilities were created. Each person had a different mutation, therefore everyone had a slightly different ability. It's still confusing to human scientists and even our own scientists, but that's the basic gist of it."

"I'm sorry!" Odau interrupted as he laughed suddenly. "This is just ridiculous. What you're saying is physically impossible!"

"Yeah, well, so am I!" Hara snapped back. "Everything you thought you knew is wrong. Nothing's impossible anymore." Pausing and staring at him skeptically, she demanded, "And what the hell would you know about DNA? You're a cop! How would you know if it's impossible or not?"

"I originally majored in forensics," Odau explained flatly. "I took biology in college. Studying DNA was required."

"Huh," Hara said thoughtfully. "Well, once you step into my world you'll learn that anything is possible."

"A DNA sequence can't be altered after it's already been determined," Odau insisted stubbornly. "And even if it could be, it would be very painful and would most likely result in death."

"Why is it so impossible for that to happen?" Perry asked, confused, looking to both of them. "I mean, if the DNA sequence was tampered with enough, couldn't they somehow make it work?"

Staring at him, Hara wondered what the hell people were being taught in school these days. Obviously, not enough. "Perry, as the lieutenant said, a DNA sequence cannot be altered after it's already been determined. One little glitch in the gene sequence alone will lead to a genetic disorder or worse. Imagine what the results should have been after every DNA strand in the body was completely altered to a point where it completely changed the genetic makeup of a person!"

"What are you saying?" Perry asked, the truth dawning on him.

"Anyone who was affected by the strain should have died," Hara finished, shaking her head. "No one should have survived that change."

"Wow," Perry whistled. "How did they then?"

"Because it never happened," Odau muttered.

"Lieutenant," Hara said flatly. "I appreciated your earlier input, but now I think it's about time you shut your mouth again."

Glaring at her, Odau turned and walked back to one of the desks to sit down. He didn't appreciate that he was being repeatedly humiliated by a teenage girl.

"The scientists who created the compound aren't even certain how the people survived," Hara explained to Perry. "The first people who inhaled a full dose of it died immediately after exposure, but others—like both my parents—survived the gene alteration, and as I said before, it was the altered gene sequence that gave them the abilities. As more generations came and went, it was discovered that abilities were a new type of trait. Every child born to an affected parent possessed an ability of some sort. There was no way for the parents to keep the trait from being passed down. Since both parents had the mutation, there was no way for them to give birth to a 'normal' child." She was sure to put air quotations around the word "normal."

"What were your parents' abilities?" Perry asked her.

"My mother had telekinesis, and my father had very powerful telepathic abilities."

"You're called an Absorber, right?" Perry said.

Hara was impressed. "Very good," she congratulated, giving him a praising smile. She almost felt like she was speaking to one of her children. "Yes, I am called an Absorber, and Absorbers are actually quite rare. There are only about two or three of us every generation. My father's cousin was also an Absorber, but she died right after the initial outbreak..." Her voice trailed off as she realized that she was babbling. What did Perry care about her father's dead cousin? Clearing her throat, she moved back on topic. "Do you know what it means now that our DNA sequence is completely changed?"

"What?" Perry asked uncertainly.

"It means that we're not even human anymore," Hara answered, her eyes flickering to Odau, who gazed back at her with a loathsome glint in his eyes. "We cannot interbreed with humans, so there is no way to breed the gene out. We're a completely new species."

It was obviously shocking information for Perry to take in. Hara could hear his mind working hard to process all of the facts. "How could an entire new species of humans suddenly be created without anyone finding out?" he asked skeptically. "How could anyone—no matter how rich or powerful—cover up something that huge?" When Hara just stared back at him without answering, he rolled his eyes in frustration. "Let me guess. I'll find out by the end of the day."

Forcing a smile to her face to let him know that he was right once again, Hara asked him yet again, "Anything else?"

"Yeah," Perry muttered, jabbing a thumb towards Jack. "What's up with him?"

"Excuse me?" Jack said in confusion.

"What is his part in all of this?" Perry continued, ignoring him. "Is he a clone? One of you? A test tube baby? What is he?"

"Hey, I already told you..." Jack started angrily.

"Well?" Perry demanded, still ignoring Jack's protests. His outrageously distinguishable mahogany eyes were half angry, half desperate. He knew that he was being lied to by Jack, and he didn't appreciate the half-ass answers he was receiving. He desperately wanted to know what Jack was to him. He was telling himself that he needed to know.

Uncertain of what she should tell the poor man, Hara suddenly remembered that Lieutenant Odau was sitting at the desk across the room. He was studying some papers inside of a large manila folder, but Hara could hear his thoughts buzzing as he listened intently. The man had something major against Jack as well as Hara, and Hara knew that she couldn't tell Perry the truth for fear of what Odau would do to Jack. Without another choice, she continued to lie.

"He's none of those things. He has no powers. He's not like me. He's just..."

"What?" Perry asked urgently, frantic to know the truth.

Without knowing what else to say, Hara blurted out the first thing that came to her tongue. "An accident!"

Gee, thanks, Jack grumbled, rolling his eyes in her direction.

I'm trying to protect you! Hara reminded him as she watched Perry drop his head into his hands. At first, she thought that he was doing it out of frustration, but when he started to gently massage the area where his head was injured, Hara started to grow nervous. His hands were shaking and his breathing was becoming erratic, and she asked him carefully, "Are you okay?"

"I'm fine," Perry mumbled, his voice cracking with the effort.

Hara didn't believe him. "Maybe you should go lie down for a bit," she advised. Peering at his face in concern, she added, "You're as white as a ghost."

Leaning closer to her so it would be difficult for anyone else to hear, Perry whispered, "Is Jack really my brother?"

Startled by the sudden question, she shot another glance at Jack. *You told him you were brothers?*

What was I supposed to say? he snapped back.

Realizing that her friend had been right to lie to Perry, Hara continued to stare into Perry's exhausted, pained eyes. What else was there to tell him? Certainly not the truth. She decided that it was for the best that Perry remained fixated on what Jack had told him. "He's whatever you need him to be," she said, and that was indeed the truth.

Sighing, Perry gave up. He winced suddenly and let out a soft gasp of pain, clutching his head with widened eyes. Hara began to grow more worried, so she listened in on Perry's thoughts to find out just how bad his pain was. It was very bad. The injury was beginning to look more serious, and Hara knew that he needed to get help right away.

"You're not fine, Perry," she told him, reaching out to him.

Standing up quickly before she could touch him, Perry teetered dangerously on his feet. "I think maybe I should go lie down," he murmured, his speech slurring. He took a few hesitant steps forward before his knees buckled and he started to go down.

Hara was immediately on her feet, rushing forward to aid him. "Whoa!" she cried, catching him before he collapsed. Holding him under his arms until he managed to regain his balance, she added with concern, "I think maybe you should let someone drive you to the hospital instead."

"Yeah," he said, looking a little disoriented as Hara helped him over to the gate. "I'll do that."

Lieutenant Odau had hurried over to the gate after Perry had lost his balance, and he stood there waiting for Hara to bring him over, worry evident on his face.

"You know," Hara whispered in Perry's ear just before they reached Odau, "I can heal you fully if you want."

"No, thanks," Perry replied, turning to smile kindly at her. It made Hara happy to see true gratitude in his eyes. "I'll let a real doctor help me."

"Suit yourself," Hara muttered as they reached the gate. She held out Perry's arm for Odau to take and stepped back. Once Perry had stumbled out, Odau pulled the gate closed and locked the door. "Are you going to make it?"

"I think so," Perry answered uncertainly, allowing Odau to lead him to the door.

"Oh, and Special Agent?" Hara called after him. When he looked back, she warned, "Please watch out for him."

"For who?"

"The Doc," Hara explained, raising her eyebrows to let him know how serious she was. "He's going to come crawling to you claiming he can help, but don't trust him. He'll just use you to get to me, and then dispose of you afterwards. No matter what he tells you, don't listen to him."

Perry nodded, and Hara heard him think to himself that he would be sure to watch out for the man. He then allowed himself to be led to the door.

Hara watched him attentively as Odau opened the door and guided him out. It worried her that his head injury was making him stumble about, and she prayed that the doctors at the hospital would be able to treat him. She wanted desperately to heal him herself because she would do the job effectively and efficiently without leaving a sign that anything had ever happened, but she respected him enough to let him make his own decisions.

As Perry stepped through the door, Hara realized that sometimes his own decisions wouldn't be right for him. She gasped as she heard and felt something in Perry's brain snap, and she grabbed two of the bars in her hands as she yelled, "Odau, bring him back to me!"

Perry hadn't even made it to the door before his legs gave way and he collapsed in a heap on the floor, clutching his head and crying out in pain.

Odau knelt beside him and screamed for a medic, but Hara knew it would be too late by the time a medic reached him.

"Odau!" Hara repeated louder.

"Medic!" Odau continued to shout, ignoring her.

Hara could hear Jack panicking in his head, repeating over and over in his head, *Oh no, oh no, oh no...!* Sending him a mental thought of reassurance, she told him that it wasn't time to freak out yet. "Bring him here!" she yelled.

"I'm not bringing him anywhere near you!" the lieutenant snarled harshly, shooting her a sharp glare of contempt. "Medic! Man down! Get in here immediately!"

Perry was rolling around on the floor, clutching his head and screaming in agony. Hara could hear his mind screaming, and her heart began to pound when she figured out what was wrong with him. She could not only hear what was going on inside Perry's head, but under certain circumstances she could also see what was going on. Focusing on Perry's left temple—where he had been hit—she saw through the outer layer and into the area surrounding his brain. There was a massive amount of swelling due to the severe concussion he had received, and because of that a blood vessel had been blocked and it was rapidly clotting. He was having a stroke. If Hara didn't do something right away, he was going to die within a few minutes.

"Lieutenant, I can help him!" she cried fearfully, watching in horror as Perry began to seize uncontrollably.

"No!" Odau snapped, trying to hold Perry's shoulders down.

Hara, do something, please! Jack pleaded desperately. *He's going to die! He can't die!*

Thinking quickly, she gripped two of the bars tightly and pulled them away from each other as hard as she could. Her face scrunched up with the effort, and for a few seconds nothing happened, but then the supports of the cage began to creak and groan with the strain, and she felt the bars start to give in. The lieutenant looked up in surprise at the peculiar sound of bending metal, and his eyes widened when he saw what Hara was doing. As she continued to pull at the bars, they began to bend outward, providing a space just large enough for her to squeeze through. When she couldn't move them anymore, she let go and gasped in pain as her muscles screamed in protest.

"What are you doing?" Odau demanded, holding Perry in his arms. Perry was still holding his head, but only a few soft whimpers were escaping his throat.

Hara knew it was critical that she get to Perry as fast as possible. Reaching up with both hands, she grabbed the bars at a higher point and pulled herself up off the floor. Lifting up her legs, she slipped them through the enlarged gap and hopped out of the cell. As soon as she was on the ground, she rushed over to Perry. Lieutenant Odau, who had been watching her perform the entire stunt in amazement, stood up and started to draw out his weapon again. Hara didn't know what it was with humans, but some of them just didn't know when enough was enough.

When Hara reached the lieutenant, Odau attempted to raise his gun, but Hara took him out easily with a punch to the face. She didn't show him any mercy, either. He had shot her three times, and now it was her turn to cause him pain. She hit him just above his left eye, so she didn't break anything, even with the excessive force she applied. To her relief, however, he was knocked out instantly, and she felt him lose consciousness before he even hit the floor. Looking at his body lying spread eagle on the floor beside Perry, she shook her head in disbelief. The man was impossible, and he was really beginning to strike a nerve.

Jumping as shouts came from in front of her, Hara glanced up to see several cops and medics running down the hallway towards the door. Waving her hand at the door, it slammed shut and the locks slid into place. It would take them a while to get through that. Turning back to Perry, she crouched down beside him. She heard pounding and shouting at the door, but she ignored the noise, already too focused on the task at hand.

Perry's arms had fallen back to his sides, and he was now in a terrible state. His eyes were wide and bloodshot, and he was staring up at the ceiling with a mortified expression. He knew what was happening to him, and there was nothing he could do to stop it. The stroke had already paralyzed him, and his body lay rigid and trembling. Inside his head, Hara could hear him screaming in agony and terror. He seemed to take notice that she had come to his side, because he started yelling to her, *Please help me! God, make it stop!*

Shh! Calm down! she ordered, placing both hands on either side of his head. *Screaming isn't going to help you at all!*

That's easy for you to say! Perry shouted, but he obeyed her. He calmed down a little, but he was still in too much pain to completely stop. *What are you doing?* he demanded as he felt the vibrations of energy begin to flow into him.

I'm saving your life! she told him, focusing on the swelling around the clogged blood vessel in his brain. She ordered every white blood cell in his body to attack the injury, but it wasn't enough. There was too much damage happening too quickly for them to save him. *Damn it*, she thought to herself.

What? Perry asked in alarm.

Just relax, Hara said, and gave his mind a push to keep him calm. If he panicked, then her job would become extremely difficult. *This will probably hurt. A lot.* Doing the only thing she could, she sent a large amount of energy to Perry's white blood cells. With the push that she had originally given them, they wouldn't be able to fix the problem in time, so she gave them an extra shove. She gave them enough to heal the stroke and any other problem with his body.

Aaaarrrrhhh! Perry cried, trying to force her mind out of his as the process began.

Don't fight me! Hara snapped, pushing his consciousness under. Since he was then nearly asleep, his screams and cries had stopped, leaving her head ringing with the silence. For another minute or so, Hara forced Perry's body to work briskly, ridding his head of anything that was even remotely out of place. First, the swelling subsided, returning the tissue around his brain to the correct size. Then, the clogged blood vessel was unblocked and the blood flow was allowed to continue at its regular pace. Finally, everything was returned to normal and Hara sighed with relief. The cells left Perry's head—their work complete—but they were still buzzing with Hara's energy. For the next several days, possibly weeks, the cells would rapidly repair any wound that was inflicted on him. They were all on alert and ready to attack any injury or foreign invader that entered the body. He wouldn't even be able to catch a cold for a while.

Pulling away from Perry, she slowly let up the pressure she was putting on his mind. Doing it quickly could result in unwanted side effects. As his consciousness began to return, Perry blinked up at her, looking like he had no idea where he was. Then, his legs started to move and he winced, groaning with the effort. The paralysis had left him, but it was going to take him several hours to recover. It was going to take up a lot of his energy to move and speak, and he was going to be extremely tired.

A sudden look crossed his face and his skin became snow white. His body became rigid again, and Hara realized what was coming next. Grabbing him by the hair, she gently but hastily turned his head to the side opposite her. Then, his entire body convulsing once, Perry threw up all over the floor.

Wrinkling her nose at the wretched smell, Hara rose to her feet and stepped back, giving him some space. When he was finally done vomiting, Perry turned his head back to the ceiling. His eyes fluttered closed and he let out a heavy sigh. He would be fine once he got some rest.

"Hara!"

The sudden shout snapped her back to reality. It was Jack calling out to her, and he did so in a warning tone. She stumbled forward as she was suddenly struck in the back of the head. Whipping around in surprise, she saw that Lieutenant Odau had hit her. He, too, had regained consciousness, and now he looked pissed. A bruise was forming where Hara had punched him, already a nasty purple. Once again, his gun was level with her head, a look of fury clouding over his gray eyes.

Before he could pull the trigger, Hara put her hand up and let forth a burst of energy, sending the cop flying across the room. As he sprawled over on his back, Hara marched up to him, her anger coming forward once more. "I've had to deal with your fatuity for too damn long!" she yelled in a rage, kicking him in the gut when he attempted to climb to his feet. "How long is it going to take you to see the truth?"

Glancing up at her quickly, Odau aimed a sharp kick at her knee, but she dodged it and kicked him hard in the groin. He cried out and rolled onto his side in pain.

"I just saved one of your colleagues, and this is the thanks I get?" Hara demanded angrily, standing over him.

"Why can't you just leave and stay away from all of us?" Odau groaned, scowling up at her. "No one wants you here! You're too dangerous to be around normal people!"

Stunned by his harsh comment, Hara stepped back. She didn't know why it hurt her so much. She was told that numerous times before, even by her own people. Perry's injury was her fault, and if she hadn't come back to Philadelphia, then he wouldn't have been hurt. She knew that it would be best to stay away from everyone for their own protection. As much as his comment hurt, Odau was right. No matter what she did, she would always be a threat to those she loved and everyone else around her.

"Hara!" Jack shouted urgently. "They're coming through the door! You need to go!"

Hearing that the cops and medics were nearly through the door, she rushed over to Jack, who was still locked inside his cell. Knowing that they only had seconds, she grabbed the lock and started to force it open, but Jack stopped her.

"You need to go!" he said, grabbing her hands in his.

"I'm not going without you!" Hara told him, swatting his hands away.

"Forget me!" he ordered, squeezing her wrists firmly to prevent her from breaking in. "Get out while you still have time!"

"I won't leave you behind again!" she informed sharply.

"I have to watch out for Perry!" he hissed. "And you have to watch out for The Doc! He's close...I can feel him..."

Gazing up at him, tormented by what he was asking her to do, she tried to plead with her eyes. His brilliant, mahogany eyes were only saying one word back: *run*. Snapping her head back toward the door as the wood began to splinter, she turned back and told him forcefully, "I'll come back for you. I promise."

A glimpse of longing in his eyes, Jack reached out through the bars and pulled her towards him, and before she could protest, he was kissing her. It only lasted about three seconds, but that was all it took to leave Hara shocked out of her wits. For a moment, she just stood there staring back at Jack in astonishment, and Jack actually had to push her in the direction of the other door before she snapped out of it. Hurrying to the door leading to the interrogation rooms, she threw it open and stopped. Looking back, she gazed upon Perry's unconscious body, and then at her best friend who was sacrificing his freedom for her once again. Nodding to her, Jack gave her an encouraging smile. She tried to return it, but the corners of her mouth just refused to turn up. Giving him a helpless look, Hara turned and fled the room, mere seconds before the cops broke down the door and rushed in with their weapons drawn.

✳ ✳ ✳

About ten minutes later, as they were wheeling Perry out to an ambulance on a stretcher, Allan Brown stood watching from a distance. His greatest fears were coming true; everything was about to come crashing down again. Hara and The Doc had both returned, bringing with them the war that Allan had tried so desperately to forget. Anybody could see just by looking at either of them that Hara and The Doc left only terror and destruction in their wake. Allan was already a wanted fugitive, he was on the brink of being discovered, and now Perry was being taken to the hospital for a serious blow to the head. Everything was going to hell. Again.

"Mr. Brown?"

Allan jumped at the sudden voice behind him. Turning, he said in surprise, "Dr. Bennett?"

"What are you doing out here?" Dr. Wesley Bennett asked, stepping up beside him and putting his hands in his pockets. He looked over at the scene in front of the police station. The ambulance loading Perry was parked near the main entrance with its lights flashing while cops and medics scurried about. "What happened? Who's hurt?"

"Agent Perry," Allen answered solemnly, turning to watch again.

"Is he alright?" Bennett asked in concern.

"I hope so," Allan murmured.

For a moment neither of them spoke, but then Dr. Bennett glanced over at him. "So, I heard about what happened with the three kids."

"It's terrible," Allan replied softly, not really hearing the good doctor.

"Yeah," Bennett said, nodding. "I tried to get a hold of you several times, but everyone said you were unreachable."

"Uh-huh. I've been busy."

"So it would seem. I also heard that you were in police custody, and that you're now a wanted fugitive."

Snapping his head towards Dr. Bennett, Allan stared at him with a mixture of shock and fear.

"Don't worry," Bennett reassured, seeing his expression. "I'm not going to turn you in."

"Oh," Allan said in confusion. "You're not?"

"Nope," Bennett told him, gazing back upon the scene.

Feeling a little uncertain, Allan asked him carefully, "Why not?"

"I watched the tapes," Bennett informed, without turning back to him.

It took a moment for Allan to understand what Bennett meant. When it dawned on him that the doctor had indeed watched the tapes stored in his office, Allan's eyes widened in horror. "You watched the tapes in my office?"

Bennett raised his eyebrows in reply.

"What ones did you watch?" Allan questioned, dread growing in his gut at what the man may have seen.

Staring at him with a scrutinizing glint in his eyes, Bennett sighed. "All of them."

His stomach lurching several times, Allan stepped away from him. "All of them?" he repeated, feeling bile rising in his throat. "As in *all of them?*"

"Yes," Bennett said, eyeing him. "Now I know everything about you, about Hara, about The Doc, and about your people. I know exactly what's going on. I understand why Hara killed those kids, and I understand why she needs to kill Odau's son. I know everything. It took me a long time to fully grasp it all, but all the pieces came logically together from watching those films. Everything makes sense now." He looked out at some distant object across the street.

When the doctor had nothing left to say, Allan asked him uncertainly, "So…what now?"

"Well," Bennett sighed, "now that I know, I suppose I have to help you."

✳ ✳ ✳

Running through the halls of the police station reminded Hara of being trapped in the lab. It was like a maze. There were so many different hallways leading into so many more hallways, and it seemed like she would never be able to get out.

The cops had followed her out of the holding cells after Odau told them where she went, so she had been forced to turn down the first hallway and keep turning as many times as possible, getting herself completely lost. At one point, she ducked into an empty office to hide until the cops passed. All the halls in the back were empty because of the situation downtown, so she would have no problem sneaking around. After waiting in the room for several minutes, she went across the hall and crawled out a window. She was on the left side of the building, and she slowly inched herself away from it, making sure that no one could see her. There were many buildings across the four-lane street, so all she had to do was make a break for them without being seen and she was free. Watching the front of the building to make sure that no cops were coming from around the corner, she stopped when she saw flashing red lights. There was an ambulance in front of the building—probably for Perry—and most of the cops who had been chasing her were currently hurrying about, trying to help the medics load Perry into the back. She guessed that they would most likely be too preoccupied to notice her if she darted across the street, so she quickly started to take off. After she got across the street, she planned on getting in one of the alleys between two of the buildings and figure out how to get back to her hideout, but she only managed to get halfway across before her body went rigid and she stopped dead in her tracks.

Her eyes widening in horror, she stumbled back a step. As she had been running, she was listening in on the thoughts of everyone in front of the station just in case one of them saw her, and one mind in particular caught her attention. It was the mind of a man who had, in fact, seen her. It was the mind of a man that was only able to be heard by Hara, but instead of calling out to the others to announce her escape, he was carefully watching her every move. Having the man see her wasn't what caused her heart to start pounding even faster and her breathing to be shaky and shallow. She knew the man and recognized his shrewd thoughts, and unfortunately, she wasn't particularly fond of him.

There was an egotistical sneer to the man's thoughts, like he was satisfied with something that he had done. He wasn't thinking directly about what it was, so Hara couldn't figure out the meaning of the implication, but she could hear him laughing at her inside his own head.

Slowly turning back towards the source of the thoughts, Hara saw The Doc leaning against one of the open back doors of the ambulance, gazing back at her with that look that he had always given her.

Hara looked him up and down to try to figure out what he was doing there. He was wearing a dark blue EMS uniform, which was unusual for Hara to see considering she had rarely ever seen him out of his white doctor's lab coat. A stethoscope was dangling around his neck, and there was a pair of gloves in one of his hands. His curious, penetrating gray eyes were boring holes into hers, and after a moment of them gazing at each other, he smiled. It wasn't harsh; it was gentle, almost as if he was trying to reassure her, but that only made Hara feel even more disturbed. Shuddering, she took a hesitant step back still eyeing The Doc cautiously. Knowing him, she was terrified that he might have set a trap for her anywhere she stepped to try to capture her again. For some reason, The Doc didn't appear as if he was trying to catch her just yet.

He turned his head slightly as Perry was lifted into the ambulance, but then looked back to her, a light smirk playing at his lips. His right arm was resting up against a bar on the door, and he raised two of his fingers to give her a small wave.

Oh no, Hara thought in horror, realizing what The Doc was doing at the ambulance. He was disguised as a medic—and he had more than enough medical skills to pull off the act—and he was going to be in the back of the ambulance with an unconscious Perry. He would be able to do unspeakable things to the agent if he wasn't stopped. None of the cops knew what he really was, so they would have no reason to stop him. The only person who would be able to stop him was Hara, but now that she had come face to face once again with her nemesis, she didn't feel ready to confront him so soon.

The Doc turned away from her and jumped into the back. Two cops closed the doors and then everyone who remained outside either ran back into the building or got into squad cars to escort it to the hospital. Sirens blared and several vehicles drove off, but Hara was only focused on the ambulance at the back of the pack, containing a very vital member of Hara's future and also the man who had set out to destroy her future.

Taking off after it, Hara started screaming. "No! Stop! You can't take him!" After about a block, she decided to just give up and stopped in the center of the road. The escort was already long gone. Watching the ambulance disappear around a corner several blocks ahead of her, tears began streaming out of her eyes. "Perry!" she cried, falling to her knees as a helpless sob escaped her throat. Grabbing her hair in both her hands, she pulled it as hard as she could, letting out a wail of rage and defeat. If The Doc hurt Perry—or worse, killed him—all would be lost.

"Let him go, Hara," a familiar voice called from behind her.

Jumping to her feet, Hara whipped around and was immediately on guard, but she soon saw that there was no need to be. "Allan?"

"The Doc won't do anything to him yet," Allan promised as he walked up to her, stopping about three feet away. He put his hands in the pockets of his black pants, and Hara saw how different he looked from the first time they had reunited. His brilliant blue eyes were exhausted and looked half dead, the lively glow that was normally in the eyes of their kind gone. His wavy blonde hair was tossed about his face, and he appeared as if he was already giving up the fight.

"I didn't expect to see you back on our side again so soon," Hara said curtly, narrowing her eyes suspiciously.

"I never left it," Allan reminded her, his eyes ever so sad.

Before Hara could make a smart remark, she saw that another man was accompanying him. He was older than Allan by at least fifteen years; probably in his late fifties or early sixties. He had very dark skin and looked strangely familiar to her. His face looked tired and confused, but he seemed eager to see her. It was like he knew who she was, and he wasn't afraid of her either. It was almost as if...

She gaped at Allan as she caught what the other man was thinking. "You're working with them entirely now?" she demanded angrily, backing away from the two of them.

Looking confused, Allan asked her, "What are you talking about?"

"You told him everything!" she accused, pointing at the human. "He knows everything!"

"He didn't tell me anything," the human said, taking a few steps toward her. "I saw the tapes..."

Allan threw out his arm to stop the human from advancing any further. Hara already felt vulnerable enough with the stranger knowing the truth about her, and Allan knew that she would feel extremely threatened if the human came any closer. She would be willing to defend herself using any means necessary.

After retreating several steps, Hara glared furiously at both of them. "You weren't supposed to be helping humans in the first place, Allan! You were supposed to be helping us! Why would you tell him everything?"

"Please listen to me!" Allan begged her, taking a tentative step towards her. When she jumped back, so did he. Putting his hands up to show that neither of them was a threat to her, he explained, "He's not going to be a problem, alright! He's a friend!"

"No human will ever be a friend to me!" Hara snarled. "They can't be trusted!"

"Hara, look at him!" Allan commanded, stepping aside so she could get a clear view of him. "You know him!"

"No!" Hara shouted, feeling heat radiating from her.

"Kid, please!" Allan pleaded desperately, reaching out a hand to her.

"Stay away from me, you traitor!" Hara hissed, turning on her heel and taking off down the center of the street.

"Hara, no!" Allan cried, and Hara heard him start to come after her. "Please, stop!"

Tears blinding her, she kept running long after Allan's calls died away. She ran for miles, until she collapsed in exhaustion in the middle of an empty side street, sobbing herself to sleep.

8

Desperate Measures

When Perry finally awoke, he had no idea where he was. Above him were bright white lights and a white tiled ceiling, which all faded in and out of focus. Blinking a few times, he groaned and turned his head to the side. Squinting, he looked around at the peculiar surroundings. He was in a large room filled with strange looking equipment. Looking down, he saw that he was in a large bed with shining white sheets. There were two plastic rails on either side of him, and glancing down he saw an IV inserted into his right arm. On the left side of his bed he saw a bedside table with a lamp on it, and in front of that there was a plastic tray resting on a stand with syringes, a stethoscope, and a small light. Off to his right was a large window with its green curtains drawn, but he could see bright sunlight filtering in through the light fabric. Under the window were two cushioned chairs resting against the wall with another wooden table in between them. A lamp was also on that table, as well as several magazines whose titles Perry couldn't make out. In front of him close to the ceiling was a television attached to the wall. There was also a curtain that was bunched up at the foot of his bed that could be pulled all the way around on either side. Directly to his left was a large wooden door, and he wondered where in the world he could possibly be.

Am I in the hospital? he asked himself in confusion. His mind felt fuzzy and none of his surroundings made any sense to him, but a sudden throbbing in his head told him that it was unlikely that he was anywhere else. His left temple was pulsating painfully, and he reached up with his IV-free arm to gingerly finger it. Pulling his hand away as his head screamed in agony, he winced and groaned. He was quite certain that he had been taken to the hospital, but he couldn't remember why or how he had gotten there. Struggling to recall any recent events in his hazy memory, he suddenly remembered what happened. There was the high speed chase with a man who was shooting at him, and then his head struck the window of his truck repeatedly as Hara came to his rescue. He blacked out in the end, and he realized that he must have hit his head very hard to have ended up in the hospital. He couldn't remember anything that happened after the chase, so he must have been out all night.

Off to his left, the door suddenly opened, startling Perry. Glancing over, he saw a man in a white lab coat step inside the room and close the door behind him. The doctor was holding a clipboard full of papers and was flipping through them, so at first he didn't see that Perry was awake and watching him. There were white gloves on his hands and a stethoscope around his neck, so Perry assumed he was the doctor in charge of his recovery. The doctor had medium-length sandy brown hair, and when he looked up, Perry saw that he had cold gray eyes that seemed to puncture holes straight through his soul. The doctor appeared strangely familiar. The man looked to be in his mid to late forties, and his inviting, slightly mischievous face reminded him of someone he had just recently seen, but no matter how hard he thought, Perry just couldn't place him.

Looking a little surprised to see that Perry had regained consciousness, the doctor smiled warmly at him. "Oh, good," he said, walking over to him. "You're awake."

Flinching as he tried to raise himself up on his elbows, Perry groaned and fell back down against his pillows.

"Yeah, you're going to want to take it easy for a while," the doctor told him earnestly, setting the clipboard down on the bedside table. "How's the head?"

"Well," Perry started uncertainly. The question—just like the doctor's face—also felt familiar to him. Glancing up at the doctor's curious face, Perry muttered, "It feels like my brain imploded."

A smile playing at his lips, the doctor picked up the light and put his index finger in front of Perry's face. "Look here," he instructed, shining the light in Perry's eyes.

Trying not to blink as the light made his head feel even worse, Perry stared at the doctor's finger until his eyes watered. "How bad is it?" he asked after the doctor pulled the light away, trying to see through the bright spots embedded into his retinas.

"Well," the doctor started, picking up the clipboard to read whatever was on it. "Considering that you had a concussion so severe that it caused you to have a stroke, you're doing remarkably well."

"I had a stroke?" Perry repeated in shock.

The doctor blinked. "You don't remember?"

"Remember what?" Perry demanded, perplexed.

"Do you remember anything at all about being at the police station?" the doctor asked, his brow furrowing in concern.

"What are you...?" Perry started, utterly bewildered. All the images came flooding back to him, and he nodded. He remembered convincing his colleagues to let him go to the police station so he could speak to Hara, and there had been an explosion of pain in his head partway through their conversation. "Oh, yes," he murmured as the recent events were stirred in his memory. "I was having a stroke?"

"Yes," the doctor told him, looking back down to the chart in his hands. "There was massive swelling in your brain tissue, which caused a blood vessel to clot." Setting the chart back down, he smiled reassuringly. "But you're perfectly fine now. There's no sign that anything ever happened. You should be a dead man, so if I were you I'd consider myself lucky. You'd better thank your friend the next time you see her."

"Who, Hara?" Perry asked, and shuddered at the memory of Hara healing his head injury. It had probably been the worst pain he had ever endured. He didn't know what happened to Hara after he blacked out, but he prayed that she didn't get away. Knowing how persistent Odau was, Perry had a feeling that it would have been difficult for her.

"Oh, is that what she's calling herself?" the doctor asked with a tone that suggested he was amused by something. Smirking to himself, he took the stethoscope from around his neck and stuck the buds into his ears.

"Yeah, it is," Perry replied, watching the doctor's smug expression curiously as he listened to Perry's heart.

"What exactly did she do to you?" the doctor asked him, taking the stethoscope out of his ears and replacing it around his neck. "You should have died from the damage inflicted on you, but somehow she managed to save your life."

Shrugging, Perry wondered how he was supposed to keep that a secret. "I don't know," he answered truthfully. "All I know is that it hurt."

His expression becoming serious, the doctor said, "There are rumors going around that this...Hara... has super powers. Is that true?" The man looked like he actually believed it, but Perry didn't want the truth to get out about the situation so soon.

"Super powers?" Perry repeated quickly, and then forced out a dry laugh that caused his head to throb. "That's ridiculous! No, the kid doesn't have super powers. She's just a little...different."

"Different how?" the doctor asked, the curious look on his face making Perry extremely uncomfortable.

It bothered Perry that he still couldn't place the doctor's face, and he peered up at him for a while in an effort to recognize him. He was certain that he had met him or seen him somewhere before. "I'm not entirely sure," Perry replied finally, staring into the man's peculiar gray eyes. "Hey, do I know you from somewhere?"

Chuckling, the doctor said, "Possibly, but not likely. You were saying?"

"Oh, um..." Perry realized that the doctor wasn't going to let the subject drift too far from Hara, and he tried to come up with something to shield the truth. "She's just a different type of criminal."

"How so?"

"Uh..." Perry bit his lip nervously. "Forgive me; I just really can't speak about this to you. It's a security thing."

"Oh, come on," the doctor coaxed, smiling at Perry in an intimidating way. "I won't tell anyone."

Eyeing him uncertainly, Perry mumbled, "She's just...she's just not quite what I expected her to be. Although she's done some terrible things over the past few days, I don't think she's quite as bad as everyone's made her out to be." Perry shut his mouth, knowing that he had already said too much.

"Well, it's nice that you can see the good in someone when others can't," the doctor complimented.

Nodding, Perry looked away from his searching gaze. "But she's a very complicated person," he added. He tried to stop himself from speaking, but for some reason he could feel himself beginning to open up to the doctor. "She's not like any criminal I've ever dealt with before. Deep down, I don't think she wants to do what she's doing, but at the same time I can't help but feel that she's trying to cause trouble."

"Double, double toil and trouble," the doctor said suddenly.

Looking up in surprise, Perry said, "Excuse me?" The P.S. from Marcus's note flashed into his mind, and he began to grow suspicious of the doctor.

"What?" the doctor asked, confused by Perry's dumbfounded expression.

Why had the doctor been so interested in Hara in the first place? He repeated the same Macbeth quote that had been in Marcus's warning, so what did that mean? "Why did you say that?" Perry demanded, his voice harsher than he intended it to be.

The doctor shrugged and didn't look even the least bit offended by Perry's tone, but he was still perplexed by Perry's distrustful gaze. "It's from Macbeth. The witches said that repeatedly because they were working hard to cause trouble for others. I only said that because it seemed suitable for what you were saying."

"Huh," Perry muttered, nodding slowly but keeping his eyes locked on the doctor's. The doctor's gray eyes were making him extremely uneasy. His face was familiar, he had a strong interest in Hara, and he had quoted Marcus's note. That had to be a coincidence. As Perry stared hard at the doctor, he started to remember. There was a man with cold gray eyes who tried to kill him in the tunnel, the same man that was standing beside Perry's bed. If he wasn't mistaken, this man was called The Doc, and he had a feeling that he was in serious trouble. "You?" he whispered in horror.

The doctor seemed to understand what Perry had realized, but he only continued to stare back at Perry. He didn't ask what Perry was talking about, nor did he try to defend himself.

"You were the one on the semi!" Perry clarified, pushing himself up on his elbows despite the pain. "You're the one who's after Hara!"

Raising an eyebrow, the doctor continued to gaze back into Perry's anxious eyes. He wasn't denying the accusation, so obviously Perry was correct. If he was the one who tried to kill Perry and they were currently in a locked room together, then what was he planning to do to him?

Eyeing him cautiously, Perry pushed himself further back in his bed, shooting a hopeful glance at the door. He knew that there was no way he could make it out the door in his condition. Looking back at the doctor, Perry saw that the man hadn't moved. He was still staring at Perry with that creepy glint in his eyes, like he was daring Perry to make a break for it. Not knowing what else to do, Perry suddenly thought of the call button that was always attached to hospital beds. He shot a quick glance down at his call button beside his left arm, resting between him and the doctor. If only he would be able to press it before the doctor could do anything … A quick glance back to him showed Perry that the doctor had raised both eyebrows warningly, telling him to not even bother, but Perry was a persistent man. His life may depend on pressing that button. Trying to be as quick as possible, Perry snapped his hand towards his button to press it.

Perry's quickest wasn't quick enough. The doctor had predicted the move, and in an instant his hand was around Perry's wrist, pulling his hand away from the call light.

"Help!" Perry started to shout, but the doctor's other hand was over his mouth before he could make any more noise. His cry muffled, Perry tried to wrench his head out from under the doctor's hand.

The doctor was wrestling Perry back, trying to keep him down on the bed and from making any sounds that would cause someone else to enter the room. "Shh!" the doctor ordered, holding him down as Perry's struggles became more intense. "Shh!" he repeated as Perry grabbed at the hand over his mouth. "Fighting isn't going to get either of us anywhere! I'm not going to hurt you!" His voice sounded urgent, as if it was critical for Perry to keep quiet. To Perry's surprise, the doctor's voice also sounded soothing.

Perry didn't believe him. He kicked at the doctor, but he was in the wrong position to actually hit him. He tugged harder at the hand muffling his cries for help, but it was in vain. The doctor was surprisingly strong, and Perry was no match for him under the circumstances.

"I'm not going to hurt you," the doctor repeated, but it was in a softer voice than before.

Perry looked back up at him, surprised by the sudden change in his tone. The doctor's eyes were saying that he was telling the truth; he wasn't going to hurt Perry. But what else could he want? Still unsure about everything, Perry stopped struggling and stared back at the doctor, anxiously awaiting his fate.

"Are you done?" the doctor asked.

Perry nodded quickly.

"Are you going to keep quiet?"

Again, Perry nodded.

Releasing Perry, the doctor stepped back to give him some space.

Pushing himself back into a sitting position, Perry quickly patted where his pockets should have been, searching frantically for his nine millimeter. "You tried to kill me!" he hissed, lifting up the sheet draped over his body. He realized something that he hadn't noticed before; he was wearing a hospital gown, and his gun was nowhere to be seen. He was defenseless. Looking around desperately for his clothes, Perry saw the doctor reach into one of his many pockets. He watched as the doctor pulled out his firearm and held it up for him to see.

"Is this what you're looking for?" the doctor asked smugly, smirking again. As Perry grabbed for the gun, the doctor pulled it out of his reach. "Ah, ah, ah!" he said, slipping the gun back into his pocket. "I think I'll hang onto this until we get to know each other a little better, and then you can decide if you still want to shoot me."

"I already know enough about you," Perry growled, glaring at him. "You were the guy who tried to kill me during the chase downtown!"

Putting his hands up in his own defense, the doctor told him, "Hey, no hard feelings. I have nothing against you; I was just trying to get rid of the miscreants in the back of your truck."

"Are they miscreants, or were they just a threat to you and you failed to dispose of them the first time around?" Perry demanded harshly.

The doctor said quietly, "Don't go assuming too much just yet. You only know a small part of the story."

At first, Perry was tempted to argue further, but the doctor was right. Perry didn't know the whole story—only bits and pieces of it—so he clenched his jaw to keep his mouth shut. After a moment of the two men carefully eyeing each other, Perry asked him, "So you're The Doc, huh? The guy that everyone seems to be afraid of."

"If by everyone you mean your five fugitives, then yes," The Doc answered, nodding. "I am indeed The Doc."

"What's your real name?" Perry asked suspiciously.

Turning his head slightly, The Doc said with another smirk, "Do you really think I'll tell you that?"

Glaring at him again, Perry let it go and looked around the room. "So you work here?" he asked dubiously.

The Doc laughed. "No, I don't, but I am a doctor."

"Really?" Perry said distrustfully. "Does your job description include killing and torturing people, or is that just a side hobby?"

The Doc's expression froze. "I'm sorry?" he said. His face showed that he knew exactly what Perry was talking about, but he was surprised that Perry knew about it.

"How could you practically wipe out an entire species but keep a few as lab rats for your sick experiments?" Perry demanded.

"Now where did you hear a thing like that?" The Doc asked, but Perry could see the smirk coming back to his face.

"Do you find this funny?" Perry snapped in disgust.

Shaking his head, The Doc replied, "No, what I find funny is that you're judging me when you know nothing about me or anything that has happened." His eyes were cold as he spoke.

"I know enough," Perry told him through gritted teeth.

"No," The Doc said again. "You don't. You've only heard one side of the story."

Angry that the man was indeed correct, Perry replied, "Well, maybe I can hear your side, just so I'm clear on things."

"Maybe a little later," The Doc told him, his fake smile beginning to irritate Perry.

Thoroughly annoyed, Perry asked the man, "What do you want from me?"

"I just want to discuss your case and your little criminal whom you folks call Hara," The Doc explained, folding his arms across his chest and gazing back at him with his intimidating look.

"That information is confidential," Perry told him flatly, "Why, are you trying to find her and torture her again?"

"That information is confidential," The Doc replied with a sneer. "If you want to find out my secrets, then you're going to have to share some of yours first."

Shaking his head in disgust, Perry turned away from him. "Forget it," he grumbled. Wrapping his left hand around the IV in his arm, he winced as he started to pull it out.

"What are you doing?" The Doc demanded quickly.

"Leaving," Perry answered bluntly, pressing his index finger against the vein on his arm as it began to bleed heavily. "I've had enough of this crap." Slipping his feet off the side of the bed and ignoring the terrible throbbing in his head, he started to get up, but he stopped when The Doc picked up a loaded syringe and held it inches from Perry's face.

"I don't think so," The Doc disagreed quietly, his expression austere. Starting to move the needle closer to Perry's face, he added, "We're not finished here."

"Okay," Perry said, putting his hands up in surrender and sitting back down on the bed as the needle hovered dangerously close to his right eye. His heart was pounding, and he didn't like the fact that he was now powerless against The Doc, as he was quite certain Hara and many others had been in the past.

"Lie back," The Doc instructed sharply, moving the syringe closer still. "Although Hara may have healed your head, you're in no state to be walking around."

"Okay, I get it! Just please put that thing down!"

The Doc pulled the syringe away from him and set it back on the tray.

"You know, I could arrest you for holding a federal agent hostage," Perry warned. "Along with several other charges."

Snickering, The Doc said, "You're not going to arrest me, Shawn Perry."

His stomach churning at the sound of his name, Perry demanded, "And why wouldn't I?"

"Because I'm going to help you catch Hara."

Shocked, Perry blinked. "Why?"

The Doc blinked back at him. "I'm the only one who can."

"I think you ought to know that several colleagues of mine managed to capture her after you tried to kill me."

Snorting, The Doc asked smugly, "And how did that work out for you?" Chuckling as Perry glowered back at him, he explained, "She went willingly. If she had put up a fight, most of your friends would be dead, and as I do recall, as soon as she was finished saving your life, she escaped without a problem."

Looking down, Perry's spirits fell. Hara had escaped after all. "We'll catch her," he insisted, although he felt doubtful. "We don't need your help."

Out of the corner of his eye, Perry saw The Doc cock his head. "With all due respect—and I don't say that to many people—I really think you should stop being so proud and learn to accept free help when it is offered to you."

"Right," Perry muttered flatly, nodding slowly at him. "I'm sure the help is free."

"Why wouldn't it be?" The Doc's smirk was back.

"There's always a catch! What's in it for you?"

Raising an eyebrow, The Doc said, "I catch her for you, and you just..." He shrugged. "Give her to me."

"No," Perry answered immediately. "I'm not just going to hand her over like she's a piece of merchandise!"

"I'm afraid that's not up for debate," The Doc told him quietly. "I'm going to catch her whether you accept my help or not."

255

"If catching her is so easy, then why haven't you done so yet?" Perry demanded.

Waggling a finger at him, The Doc stated, "The first step in catching her is finding her. You have resources I require to find her."

"What are you talking about?" Perry asked, although he didn't need an answer. He already knew who The Doc was referring to.

Smirking some more, The Doc listed off the names. "Allan Brown, Daniel Marcus, Meg Hopper..." Cocking his head yet again, The Doc peered down at him. "Jack."

"You stay away from him!" Perry warned with a snarl.

"Why?"

"Because I said so! Let's remember who owns the gun in here!"

"And let's remember who *has* the gun. What does Jack matter to you?"

"He has no meaning to me!" Perry snapped. "He's just another criminal who happens to look like me."

"You care for him, don't you?" The Doc asked. When Perry pursed his lips in response, he nodded. "That's very interesting."

Perry shuddered at his inquisitive gaze. What was so interesting about him that The Doc kept staring at him like that? Yes, it was true that he cared for Jack, but why did that matter so much to The Doc? It was none of his business how Perry felt about anyone! "So what if I do?"

"Why is that, I wonder?" The Doc pressured.

"Why does it matter?"

"I'm a very curious man."

That was apparent. "I don't know," Perry grumbled, looking away from him.

"Hmm," The Doc said thoughtfully, still searching Perry's face. "I see."

"He claims he's my brother, but I don't think he's telling me everything. I think he's scared to talk to me because of what you did to him." Perry thought back to how scared Jack was when talking about The Doc and believing that he was coming for him.

"What exactly do you believe I did to him, hmm?" When Perry refused to respond, The Doc said coldly, "Stop pretending that you know everything, because there is so much that you don't understand."

The two men glared at each other for some time before Perry spoke again. "So you want us to let you talk to Jack so you can find out where Hara is, and once you catch her you'll just take her away from here? Forever?"

"That's the plan, yes," The Doc told him, nodding once.

"What exactly do you plan on doing to her once you've caught her?" Perry asked. When The Doc didn't reply, Perry said, "See, that's one of my many objections to accepting your help. You refuse to tell me what you're going to do to her."

"What does it matter what I'm going to do to her?" The Doc demanded quietly. "Isn't she just another criminal like Jack? Don't you want her off the streets?"

"She's not just a criminal," Perry said angrily. "She's a better person than what she's been made out to be. The good part of her has been driven out, and all she is now is a damaged, angry girl who doesn't know how to deal with her rage. Maybe you can tell me why that is?" The Doc gave him a dangerous look, but he didn't stop. "I want her off the streets, yes, but I don't just want to hand her over to you without asking any questions first. Who knows what you might do to her? As you said before, I know nothing about you, but it seems like you've done enough damage already."

"Why is the well-being of this child so important to you?" The Doc asked curiously. "All she's been doing is causing trouble for you and this city. Why does it bother you so much that she may be poked by a few needles? Why do you care so much?"

"Because no one else does! You obviously don't! You only want to use her as your human guinea pig. Don't tell me I'm wrong, because I can see it in your eyes! I can hear it in your voice when you talk about it, too. You're fascinated by her, but only because of what she can do, and it makes me sick. I'm not going to stand by and watch you cart her off to be an entertaining experiment, because she's not just an animal. She's a person."

Sighing, The Doc shook his head in disappointment. "You just don't get it do you?"

"Get what?" Perry snapped.

"You just don't understand the importance of her capture," The Doc said softly. "Or the importance that she holds to the world. She could help so many people, save so many lives. Don't you think the well-being of one girl is worth sacrificing if it benefits the rest of the world?"

Remembering Jack's remark about sacrificing four lives to save millions, Perry's expression hardened once more. "You know, that's the second time today I've been asked a question like that, and I'm thinking that the answer's no. The lives and well-being of a few individuals are not worth sacrificing for the advancements of technology or whatever other crap you've been using her for."

"It's not just for technological advancements," The Doc explained with a sigh. "She can do so much more for us than that."

"Like what?" Perry demanded. "I can't see any benefit she can offer that's worth more than her sanity, unless she can spontaneously cure cancer or something like that."

The Doc stared at him for several long moments without speaking. Perry thought at first that he was at a loss for words, but then it dawned on him.

"Oh, come on!" Perry said in disbelief.

Raising an eyebrow, the corner of The Doc's mouth turned up in a smile.

"You are kidding me!" Perry declared. "Hara can cure cancer?"

Shrugging, The Doc reminded, "She fixed your stroke, didn't she?"

"Well..." Perry started, trying to argue the point. "Yes, but cancer is different. How can she cure a disease that is incurable?"

"Hara has never been sick in her life," The Doc explained. "Her blood will not allow a disease to enter her body. Her blood fights off any invader and heals any injury. She managed to fix the clot in your brain, and with enough manipulation, she'll be able to destroy tumor cells as well. Not only could she cure any type of cancer, she could also cure autism, Huntington's disease, diabetes, Alzheimer's, and any other illness that people believe to be incurable. Her blood provides the perfect antidote for anything. Now don't you think that's worth all of this?"

Pausing, uncertain of how to answer, Perry looked down at his hands in his lap. It was a difficult decision to make. Hara was just a kid, traumatized by what The Doc had done to her and afraid that the rest of the world would treat her in the same way—as an experiment. However, that didn't give her the excuse to do what she did. She murdered all the men who robbed the bank, and regardless of what they did, they didn't deserve justice in that form. She killed three children and attempted to kill a fourth, and then destroyed a great deal of the central city after letting out some of her energy. Then, she participated in the destruction of several government vehicles and insisted that she did it for the well-being of everyone else. The kid may have had a disturbing past, but that was no excuse for everything she had done. Maybe it would be in everyone's best interest if The Doc did take Hara away. It would benefit the world if she wasn't around to destroy it, and if she really could cure all those diseases, wouldn't it be worth it? Hara may have saved Perry's life twice, but she had taken the lives of many others. Was protecting Hara worth the consequences he had experienced so far, or was her sacrifice worth the rewards? It was tough for him to decide.

"Hmm?" The Doc asked, peering down at him as he pulled Perry out of his thoughts.

"I..." Perry couldn't decide. He knew that there was something more to this, something big that he couldn't see yet. Was accepting The Doc's help without knowing the truth first going to come back to bite him in the ass later?

"Let's look at this from your perspective for a moment," The Doc offered. Taking a step forward, he unfolded his arms. "You let me speak to your friend Jack for a few minutes, just a few short minutes, and he'll tell me exactly where Hara is. I have the appropriate equipment required for capturing her, and once I do, you and Lieutenant Odau get all the credit for ridding the city of another dangerous criminal. The two of you make up some story about how she was killed and her body was disposed of, while I take her away from here. You'll never have to worry or even think about her again. She'll never be able to cause you any more problems. Everyone, including you, can just forget that she ever existed and you can move on with your boring little lives."

"Yes," Perry realized, nodding. "But will I be able to sleep at night knowing that she's still out there somewhere, and at your mercy? I think I've already discovered too much to just go back to my regular life. I've stepped in too deep, and I don't think I can just forget what I've seen over the past two days."

"That's your decision," The Doc told him quietly. "But what you decide next is for the good of more than just yourself. Are you willing to do what I've asked in order to protect the lives of countless others, because you and I both know she's not going to stop killing until somebody stops her."

Pondering over what would be the best for everyone, Perry realized that neither decision benefited everyone. Someone was going to get hurt one way or the other, but he had to make the choice that would hurt fewer people. So far, it seemed as if the best choice was what The Doc was offering. "Alright," he muttered, feeling a terrible sense of self-loathing. It was going to be difficult for him to forgive himself for what he was about to do. "You can have her, so long as you catch her first."

Out of the corner of his eye, Perry saw The Doc's face light up into a broad grin. "Wonderful," he said eagerly. "I'm glad that we finally understand each other."

"But I'll have to discuss this with my colleagues first," Perry added, glancing up. "They're going to want to know why the man who tried to kill me is now assisting us."

Nodding, The Doc's grin didn't leave his face. "That's fine," he replied. "Oh, and just so we're clear, I'm sure that you and your fellow agents are quite upset with everything I put you through with that little scene downtown late last night, so I assure you that once I'm finished here, I'll disappear forever along with Hara."

"You'll never show your face anywhere again?" Perry questioned suspiciously. "Because saying that we're upset with you is a bit of an understatement. I don't care if you start curing cancer with Hara's blood or whatever it is that you do. I don't want to ever see or hear about you again."

"Understood," The Doc said, still smiling at him.

A thought suddenly crossed Perry's mind, something he hadn't considered before. "What about the others?" he asked. "Allan Brown, Detective Marcus, Meg Hopper, Jack…what happens to them?"

The Doc shrugged. "They hold no further value to me once I have Hara. If you want, I can get rid of them too."

"Hara is the only one you're getting," Perry told him firmly. "We will deal with the other four in our own way."

"Fair enough," The Doc replied. "They shouldn't be too much trouble for you. You've already got one of them. Meg Hopper and Allan Brown shouldn't be much of a problem. I'd say that Marcus will be the most difficult to catch. He's got some tricks up his sleeve, that one."

Without asking him to elaborate, Perry slipped his feet off the side of the bed again and stood up carefully, unsure of how steady his balance was. It seemed to be fine even though his head still had a nagging ache to it.

"What are you doing?" The Doc demanded again, immediately going on guard.

"Relax," Perry said, looking around for his clothes once more. "If you're going to catch Hara, then I need to explain to my colleagues so they know what's going on." Looking up at The Doc when he didn't see his clothing anywhere, he asked, "Can I have my clothes back, or must I go parading around with half my ass hanging out of this gown?"

"Sure, I'll go get them." He started to turn, but Perry stopped him.

"Can I have my gun back too?" he asked hopefully, knowing he would feel safer around The Doc if he had a weapon. When The Doc gave him a look that clearly said, *Are you serious?* Perry begged, "I promise I'll behave myself."

Shaking his head, The Doc pulled the firearm out of his pocket and held it out to him. "I suppose we'll just have to trust each other, won't we?"

Snatching it out of The Doc's hand, Perry checked to make sure his gun was still fully loaded. It was, and setting it by his side, he looked back up at The Doc, who was eyeing him carefully and making sure that he wasn't going to open fire the moment his back was turned. Nodding stiffly once, The Doc turned away and left the room.

Exhaling in relief, Perry sat back down on the bed. His encounter with The Doc had agitated him, but now that the man was gone, he felt remarkably at ease. Now would come the hard part: convincing his colleagues that what they were planning to do was for the best. Some would be willing to accept The Doc's help, but others would need a little more assurance. They would have to be certain that accepting The Doc's help after what he did would be for the best, and Perry knew that it would be his job to make them understand.

* * *

Jerking awake from another nightmare, Hara blinked and chomped down on her tongue to keep herself from crying out. She tasted blood as it poured into her mouth, and she swallowed several times. Shivering as the images from her dream lingered in her mind, she squeezed her eyes tightly shut and pulled her knees up to her chest. Tears began to fall from her eyes as she began to cry all over again. Too much had happened to her recently, and she could feel the last bit of her control slipping away. She was trying desperately to just forget everything that had happened to her, but how was she supposed to do that when she relived her past every time she slept? The only way she could be at peace with herself was to kill that wretched little boy, but could she do it before she was captured or lost what little bit of sanity she still possessed?

As she cried, she suddenly became aware of her surroundings. She remembered collapsing somewhere in Philadelphia in the center of a street, but that wasn't where she was now. Through her eyelids she could see dim light shining down from above her, and the air around her was no longer cold and wet. A soft, cushiony surface was beneath her instead of the hard, scratchy concrete. Running a hand over the smooth texture under her, she breathed in the smell of new furniture. It was a homey smell, and it made her feel at ease. As she lay there feeling a small sense of security, she became aware of another being's presence. There was someone else with her, but she was too empty inside to give much thought to it. Opening her eyes a crack, she peered through her tears at the person sitting in front of her wearing a dark blue uniform. Her eyes trailed upwards and she realized that it was a cop's uniform. Her eyes flickered to the cop's face. Daniel was gazing back at her with a terrible sadness in his eyes. Out of the corners of her eyes she could see the familiar blank concrete walls, and behind Daniel was the long wooden coffee table. She was back in the only place of asylum she had left.

A few moments after Hara made eye contact with Daniel, he smiled weakly down at her, pain visible in his eyes. "Hey," he said gently.

Hara could hear in his thoughts that she had been crying out in her sleep, and he had stayed beside her until she woke.

Wanting to crawl into a corner and hide from the rest of the world, Hara buried her face in her arm. She didn't want to feel or see Daniel's pity for her. All she really wanted was to be left alone, but she knew that Daniel wasn't going to let things go so easily.

"Do you dream about these things often?" he asked her softly, and for a split second he sounded exactly like her father.

"Every time I close my eyes," Hara whispered, shuddering as the memories of the most horrifying experiment with The Doc filled her head.

"Did he really do that to you?" Daniel breathed, his voice quavering in rage and grief for her.

"Yes," Hara answered feebly, trying not to picture it.

Hara heard Daniel sigh and felt his emotion for her. A moment later she felt him place a comforting hand on her shoulder. She flinched away from his touch and whimpered softly, but Daniel shushed her and gently rubbed her arm. Her entire body began to shake, and Hara suppressed her sobs by sucking in her lower lip. Tears blinded her once more and a single sob escaped her throat.

"*Shh,*" Daniel hushed, stroking her tangled hair. "Everything's going to be okay."

"No," Hara whimpered. "Nothing's going to be okay anymore."

As Daniel continued to stroke her hair with his hand, Hara heard his mind running over various thoughts. Finally, he asked, "What's happening to you? You're beginning to slip away. Is it because of that thing he did to you, or was it just a combination of everything?"

"He took Perry!" Hara sobbed, pulling herself into a tight ball.

There was a pause before Daniel spoke again. "Yes, I know, but The Doc won't do anything to him yet. He needs Perry. It'll be fine, don't worry."

"Nothing's fine anymore," Hara cried again, pulling away as Daniel put his hand under her chin and tried to make her look at him.

"Sweetheart, you don't need to blame yourself for this," Daniel told her. "It wasn't your fault, and Perry's going to be fine!"

"It's not just that!" Hara said through her teeth, turning her head slightly so she could see Daniel's sympathetic face. "I feel like the only way I can come to terms with what happened is to kill that boy, and so far I've been everything but successful! People keep getting in my way, and now with these nightmares it's so difficult to keep myself going. All I want to do is save everyone, and my plan has been failing. Sometimes, it seems like the easiest thing to do would be to just give myself to him, but then I remember what he did to me and I keep fighting. The nightmares are getting worse, and they're taking away whatever bit of a soul I still possess."

Daniel leaned his head closer to her. "Don't ever for one second think that handing yourself over is the right way to go," he whispered. "We need to keep fighting for our right to survive. We are so, so close to changing the course of everything, and despite everything you've done I still think you've done a good job." He smiled down at her and rubbed her arm again. "You were willing to go to extreme lengths to protect our past and our future, and I think that proves what a terrific leader you are.

After all you've been through, you still got up and threw yourself back into the fight. Once we finish this, and I theorize it will only be a short time before that happens, we'll go back and we'll find you some help. We have good medical staff that will be more than capable of…"

"Are you crazy, Daniel?" Hara demanded, shrugging him off and pushing herself up into a sitting position. "No one can help me, not after what I've done. I'm beyond help. Nothing can save my mind from this. By the time this is over, I'll be completely gone."

"No, you won't," Daniel promised her, but his reassurance wasn't working.

"Stop acting like you know how everything ends!" Hara snapped, jumping to her feet as he reached for her again. "You don't!"

"Your fate is still undecided," a familiar voice said from behind the couch.

Whipping around, Hara glared at Allan. "What are you doing here?" she snarled.

Without looking offended, Allan explained, "You were unconscious in the middle of the road. I brought you back here so no one would find you."

"How dare you show your face here!" Hara shouted angrily. "After betraying us the way you did, you're lucky I don't burn you alive!"

"What's going on?" Meg asked in concern, coming around a corner. Following close behind her was Noah.

"Did you bring your little human friend along with you?" Hara demanded harshly, ignoring Meg and looking around the room in search of Allan's human.

"Hara, do you know who that man was?" Allan asked her quietly, his expression remaining calm.

"I don't care who he was!" Hara snapped. "Enough of those humans have already gotten involved! Why are you bringing more of them into this? You know firsthand that none of them can be trusted!"

His eyes flashing angrily, Allan pursed his lips. "That's the biggest load of crap I've ever heard from you," he scolded her. "You trust some of them yourself."

"I would never put my trust into the filthy hands of one of those miserable, backstabbing, pointless excuses for a living creature!" she shouted, but she stopped screaming when she realized that Allan was right. She did trust some of them, but once one of them proved trustworthy, she always saw them as one of her kind. Sometimes she completely forgot that they weren't the same as her. Regretting her words as soon as they were out of her mouth, she gazed apologetically across the room at Noah.

The look Noah gave her in return was heartbreaking. His expression remained blank, but his eyes said it all. Noah was a human, and what

Hara said had deeply offended him, even though he knew how horrible his own race could be. He had always been a loyal friend to her, and now in return racist insults were being flung at him. Although he knew that what his kind had done to hers was wrong, Hara's comment still hurt.

"What about Noah?" Allan asked, raising his eyebrows. "You trust him, don't you? The last time I checked, he was still a human."

Remorse melting her heart, Hara turned away from Noah's penetrating stare and sat back down on the couch. Dropping her head in her hands, she pulled at her hair and cursed herself for speaking before thinking.

"How about Shawn Perry?" Allan added, making Hara feel even worse. "Don't you trust him too? What about your human family? Peter, Ellyn, Charlie…"

"Enough!" Hara pleaded, squeezing her skull in her hands. It was true, she did trust a select few humans, but humans who lived among her kind weren't really human. They were something more, something better.

Allan said no more. Hara sensed him walk around the couch to stand in front of her. For a while he just stood before her, and Hara heard his mind pondering over what should be said next. Finally, he told her, "For two years, I've lived among humans in a political position. I've learned a thing or two about them. One is that you can always tell the trustworthy from the untrustworthy just by their eyes. Their eyes will betray them every time. That man you saw? He saw all the tapes hidden in my storage closet, and that's how he knows. When he told me that he wanted to help us, well, his eyes told me that he was telling the truth."

"Who cares what his eyes told you?" Hara snapped, lowering her hands and lifting her head to glare into his insistent, hopeful face. Dropping her voice to barely a whisper so Noah couldn't hear, she hissed, "You don't trust any of them here, no matter how convincing they may be! The only reason we can trust humans like Noah is because they were exiled just like us! We can trust those who were forced to live among us. But when one comes crawling to us claiming he wants to help, that's when we know to turn our backs. Don't you remember how things began with The Doc? He told us that he only wanted to help, and look at what he did!"

"Yes, but no one trusted The Doc in the first place," Allan reminded her, lowering his voice as well.

"Exactly!" Hara declared, trying to get her point across. "And our first response to his claim should have been to kill him! Don't you see? They say that they want to help us, and then they crush us!"

"There's another thing I learned while living with humans," Allan said, and Hara sensed that his next words were going to be difficult for him to say. "They're not all the same, just like us. There are select individuals who are bad, but most of them are basically good people."

"Select individuals?" Hara repeated, gaping at him in astonishment. "Allan, they wiped out our entire species in a matter of months! Millions of people! They needed more than just select individuals to perform that operation. We're talking about genocide. They were all involved in this!"

Watching sadness fill Allan's eyes, Hara felt his desperation to make her understand. "None of the people here even understand what we are! They can't all be involved if they don't have a clue about what's going on!"

"You still can't trust them!" Hara insisted, knowing that she wasn't going to change his mind. Dropping her head back down, she heaved a frustrated sigh.

An awkward silence filled the air. Everyone seemed to be waiting for someone else to speak. Hara heard the others shifting their weight uncomfortably until finally someone spoke up.

"Hara," Daniel started slowly. "The man you saw with Allan…his name is Dr. Wesley Bennett."

Her heart literally skipping a beat, Hara turned to stare at Daniel. His expression was gravely serious, and his thoughts also told her that he wasn't lying. "Bennett?" she said carefully, still not believing it herself. When he nodded in response, she knew it was the truth.

"Will you trust me now?" Allan pleaded quietly.

Looking back to him in wide-eyed amazement, Hara studied Allan's blank expression. He had been angry that she had fought him on the subject, but was immediately ready to forgive her. It was beginning to bother her that they were all so willing to forgive her every time she screwed up. One day soon, she was going to mess up big time and they would need to learn that sometimes a person cannot forgive another for everything, no matter how compassionate that person might be or how close to that person they were.

"Yes," Hara murmured. "But can you trust me?"

Blinking in surprise, Allan questioned, "What do you mean?"

"I mean, can you trust me?" Hara repeated, raising her eyebrows at him. "After everything I've put you through?" Turning, she looked around at everyone's faces. "After what I've done to all of you?"

"What are you talking about?" Allan demanded in confusion, reaching out to put a hand on her arm.

Pulling away from his touch, Hara jumped to her feet.

Unsure of how she was going to react, Allan also stood up and took a step backwards, eyeing her carefully. Just in case anything went wrong, Daniel—who hadn't moved from his chair in front of the couch—rose to his feet as well and took a step closer to her.

Glaring first at Allan and then at Daniel, Hara growled, "You know exactly what I mean! As soon as I showed up in this city I ruined the perfect, simple little lives you all had built for yourselves. I dragged you all right back into the middle of this thing, and all I've been doing so far is hurting you. I can see it in your eyes; you're all devastated by your lost families, and their deaths were all my fault. Don't even try to deny it. When you came back you were hoping to start over, and you did, but then I came back and brought the war with me, one you know you have to fight. Look at me now! I'm a complete disaster! My mind is unstable, and a fat load of good that does us when you need me to be fit to fight. I'm asking you, can you trust me after I've screwed your lives over twice?"

Both men stared at her skeptically.

"Of course we can!" Allan said. "We needed a wake-up call anyway. We couldn't just build a new life for ourselves and forget about our families and our people! You came back and reminded us why we were here in the first place! Of course we trust you!"

On the other side of Hara, Daniel nodded twice, and when Hara looked over at him he smiled compassionately at her. Both men's eyes showed loyalty to her, and it made her angry.

Turning back to Allan, she hissed, "Wrong answer."

"Hara, sweetie," Meg started softly as Allan and Daniel watched her with puzzled looks. "Although you may have made a few mistakes, we all still trust you."

"Why?" Hara demanded. "All I've been doing is hurting people!"

"That's not your fault!" Meg declared forcefully. "That girl is the dark, damaged part of you. The real you is someone far greater, and we all know that."

"Listen, Hara," Allan ordered firmly, grabbing her by the arm and pulling her towards him.

"Don't touch me!" she snapped, trying to wrench her arm away.

Allan refused to release her, a glint of stubbornness clouding his eyes.

"Listen to him, kid!" Daniel commanded from behind her, telling her telepathically to stop fighting them and pay attention to what they had to say.

Allan continued without her consent. "All those years ago, when your father was chosen as the president of our people, it wasn't because he impressed them all with fine speeches and slogans, but because he proved himself worthy. He saved our species when we were just starting out, and because of that everyone trusted him. They elected him to be their leader, and they would do anything to protect him." Leaning his face closer to hers, he told her quietly, "Your father's spirit still lives in you, and everyone can see it. Ever since you found your soul mate, everyone knew you were your father's daughter. Bo wasn't one of us, but we knew that you would be a peace keeper because of how much you loved him, despite his differences. You began to slowly gain the people's trust, whether you knew it or not. That was why everyone died for you. We will die for our leaders, no matter how painful our death may be. When your father was done serving his time and was ready to step down, he was going to give his position to you. Not to Flint or Katherine or Malcolm, but you. The people trusted you, and our leaders are built by trust. They sacrificed themselves to protect our future." Nodding to her, he breathed, "You."

Hara turned her head to look at Daniel to see if he agreed with what Allan said. He did, and his kind smile surprised her even more. "You were next in line," he said. "Our future leader."

"That's why your father gave you that International Peace Ambassador position," Meg added, walking around the couch to stand beside Allan. "He wanted you to be prepared for when your time came."

Utterly dumbfounded, Hara looked down at the floor. What they were telling her was beyond any expectations that she ever had. Her people's government hadn't been a monarchy, but everyone trusted her family and they wanted her family to stay in power for as long as possible. She had assumed that her oldest brother Flint would have taken after her father, and if not him then her sister Katherine or brother Malcolm. All of them had already received high government positions, and the people trusted them. Hara was the fourth child. Was it really supposed to be her the entire time? Hara's soul mate, Bo, was not one of her kind, and because he was a different species her people disliked him. To keep him and their small family safe, Hara left her home to go into even deeper hiding. Not too long after however, her father requested that she and Bo consider taking positions in his Cabinet. Among that small group had been Allan, Daniel, and Meg. Hara's father had asked the three of them—since they were the three people he trusted most—to look after her if anything ever happened to him. When he was killed, his three friends did their best to keep her safe, until they were captured. Now it was Hara's chance to return the favor. If she was next in line, it made her responsible for everyone who was left. Her father, the leader of her people, was now dead, so that made Hara president. She would do everything in her power to keep those who were left safe.

"You're our leader now," Allan told her sincerely. "You are the one we all trust, and we believe that you'll be the one to save what's left of us." Still gazing into her eyes, he slowly got down on both knees. Nodding to her, he glanced up at Daniel, who copied his movement. After a moment, Meg was on her knees as well. They were showing her the most formal sign of respect they could give. Her people were a proud race; they knelt before one person and one person only. Kneeling

267

before her indicated that they truly did believe in her as their one and only leader.

Hara didn't feel confident. Turning, she looked at Noah, who hadn't moved the entire time. After what she had said about him, she doubted that she could ever consider herself as a leader. Leaders were supposed to accept everyone, just like her father had, and just like she had before the catastrophe. Like all of her kind, she disliked the humans for exiling them, but had forgiven them because she understood that they had done so out of fear. After the killing began, she developed a burning hatred towards them. All she wanted was for them to burn. Then she remembered the humans like Noah and the Bennetts. Daniel was right; they weren't all bad.

Noah shook his head and gazed back at her in disappointment. "I may be human," he started, "but I'm fighting for the same thing you are." Reaching into the breast pocket of his jacket, he pulled something out and handed it to her. It was a wrinkled piece of paper with torn edges.

Taking it from his hand, Hara turned it over and realized that it was a photograph. Gasping at the image she saw, she clamped a hand over her mouth to keep in the sob that was threatening to escape her. It was an image she had been praying to see for a long time, something so beautiful that it caused tears to come streaming down her face. It was a picture of her and her small family.

In the center of the photo was her and her soul mate Bo. She was wearing a dress that Bo had bought for her when they first started seeing each other. It was orange with white polka dots and flower designs. Bo had told her that she looked amazing in it, so she chose to wear it especially for that photo. Her wavy brown hair was blowing about her face in the slight breeze, almost obscuring her brilliant green eyes. The image of herself startled her. She actually looked very happy, and she knew that she really was once. It felt like a lifetime ago, but there had once been a time that her life was exactly the way she wanted it to be. Her radiant smile struck a nerve in her heart. For the first time in months she felt the person she really was resurfacing. Looking at Bo, she saw his head resting against hers. His dazzling smile also softened her, and his dark brown eyes brought back wonderful feelings of love and acceptance. His black hair was also blowing in the wind, but instead of being hidden, his face was being revealed. He looked very happy, and Hara prayed that she could finish her mission for just one more chance to hold him in her arms. Bronze and glowing, his skin glimmered in the bright sunlight beaming down upon them. He was wearing dark blue jeans and a plain red t-shirt that showed off his strong arms, which happened to be around their oldest daughter, Grace.

Before she was killed, Grace was a sweet, shy five-year-old. She had blonde hair that appeared iridescent in the picture. She also had a huge grin on her face as she hugged her father back. Although she had taken most of her father's traits, including his brown eyes, she had gotten her blonde hair from Hara's side of the family. She was wearing her favorite pink shirt that said "Princess" across it and her favorite jean skirt that was ripped at one of the seams.

Behind her and hanging on Bo's back was Hara's second daughter, Katie. Her wild brown hair was completely covering her dark brown eyes and bright, gleaming teeth. Because she was on her father's back, only Katie's arms and head were visible. It was difficult to see her, but it was good enough for Hara. In front and sitting in the grass were Hara's first son Colin and her baby daughter Lizzie. Colin had just turned four, still possessing a baby face with round, red cheeks. His short cropped blonde hair was barely visible, and his brown eyes expressed clear joy. He was wearing a simple pair of black shorts and a black long-sleeved shirt that said "I make this look good." In his lap was Lizzie, Hara's youngest child who had been about ten months old when she was killed. She was wearing a dark pink dress with white flowers and wore little white baby booties on her feet. Lizzie's personality was more like her father's—stubborn—but she looked just like Hara. Their baby pictures were almost identical, both of them having wispy brown hair and a happy face. Lizzie too had Bo's brown eyes, and that was the only thing that was different from Hara. She looked absolutely delighted to be in her older brother's lap. Her hands were clapping together and she was laughing conspicuously. It was a sight Hara loved to see.

What she failed to notice before was the little two-year-old boy in her arms. Her youngest son Dreyson was embracing her tightly, and Hara was holding him close as well. He was beaming at the camera and his dazzling green eyes showed immense happiness. Dreyson had been the only child to receive Hara's green eyes because he was the fourth born. Only the fourth born in her family would have the green eyes. Nobody knew why, but no one questioned it. His dark, wavy hair was blowing across his beautiful face as well, and Hara ran her fingers over his image. Dreyson had been the last member of her family still alive when she had been captured by The Doc. Unfortunately, she had been unable to protect him after that. The Doc had also experimented on him, and before Hara could save her baby he too was murdered. Dreyson had been the one thing remaining that had given her hope. After he was killed she had completely lost it. Once she had avenged him and the rest of her family, she would finally be at peace.

Smiling at the memories of her family, Hara looked back up at Noah as several tears fell from her face and to the floor. She could feel herself beginning to change, to transform into something better. She hoped that the evil inside of her could be destroyed as easily as it had been created.

While she was basking in the warm feeling she received from gazing upon the photo of her dead family, Noah had also kneeled in front of her. The corner of his mouth turning up, he finished what he had started to say before. "I'm fighting for our families."

Feeling as light as air, Hara smiled back at him, and her true self returned for an instant. Noah had started to heal her soul. Turning back to gaze down at her friends, she nodded to them, possessing a new sense of redemption. They were all looking to her for leadership, and now she was going to prove herself worthy. She was going to finish what she had started, and she was going to finish it by the end of the day.

"What do we do now?" Daniel asked her, awaiting orders.

Unsure of how to answer, Hara just stared at him.

"Hara, honey, you're the one in charge now," Meg told her, a hint of pressure audible in her voice.

"Tell us what we need to do to help you," Allan added, waiting eagerly.

Looking down at the photo of her family once more, taking in their faces one last time, Hara sighed. "Nothing," she said, slipping the picture into her pocket and turning away from them. Walking around the couch and across the room towards the weapons cabinet, she knew exactly what she needed to do.

"What?" Daniel said in surprise, and Hara heard all four of her friends stand up and begin to follow her. "What do you mean, nothing?"

"As in, you're not going to do anything," Hara responded smartly. Once she reached the cabinet, she opened it and gazed inside.

"Honey, what are you talking about?" Meg asked her gently as she followed. When she reached Hara, she put her hand on her shoulder.

Turning back to her after pulling out an automatic rifle, Hara explained, "You're not going to do anything. I'll take care of The Doc and Odau's son myself. I got us all into this mess, and now I'm going to get us out of it."

"You can't take on The Doc yourself and you know that!" Noah declared. "Let them help you!"

"You may think you'll be able to, but you can't beat him on your own!" Allan told her firmly, his voice also sounding desperate. "He's not any ordinary human, and you know it's true. He always manages to be one step ahead of you. Every time you've had an encounter with him, he's won the fight."

"Not every time," Hara corrected, remembering one time that she and The Doc had met a long time before. He had wanted Hara's father to hand her over to him, but when he refused and people began to die, Hara had tried to turn herself in. The Doc refused to take her and let her go for no apparent reason. "He wants me to put up a fight, because he enjoys struggles. What if I didn't put up a fight this time?"

"What are you suggesting?" Daniel demanded. "What are you planning to do?"

"He won't try to capture me unless I put up a fight first," Hara told him. "If I refuse to give him a fight, he won't know what to do or what to think. Besides, I don't want to kill him just yet. I want to make him watch while I kill Jackson Odau. I need to talk to him first though, so I can strike some fear into his heart."

"I think he's a bit smarter than that," Allan said. "He'll figure out what you're doing. You've seen how manipulative he can be."

Groaning in frustration, Hara shouted, "Will you please get it through your heads what I'm trying to say to you? I'm doing this myself because I don't want to put anyone else in harm's way! You trust me as your leader, so trust me when I say that I can do this myself!"

"We won't let you go to him alone," Allan told her sharply, folding his arms over his chest.

Glaring at him, Hara growled, "I need to do this! You can help me by staying here away from me so I can't hurt you. Besides, I'm too dangerous to be around normal people." Taking the rifle with her, she pushed past her friends and headed towards the stairs. She had used Lieutenant Odau's words without realizing it, but the cop was correct when he said that to her.

"Normal?" Meg repeated in disbelief, sounding deeply offended. "Hey!" she shouted as Hara continued to make her way to the exit without turning back. When Hara did turn back, she saw that Meg had a furious expression, one of the few times that she would ever see her angry. Keeping her eyes locked on Hara's, Meg reached out and placed a hand on the door of the weapons cabinet. After a moment her pupils began to slowly dilate, and flower buds began to sprout from the metal of the door. Soon, thick green vines were crawling up and down the door and small white flowers grew off of those. It was a magnificent gift Meg had, to give life to objects that had none.

"None of us are normal," Daniel informed her as Meg dropped her arm back to her side.

Sighing, Hara shook her head.

"I understand that you want to kill him for everything he's done, but please allow us to help you," Allan begged.

"I don't want any of you to be injured or captured by mistake," Hara said softly, trying to get them to understand. "I just want you all to be safe."

A small pause filled the room as Meg, Allan, and Noah turned and looked at Daniel. Looking grim, Daniel told her, "If you'd be willing to listen, I think I have an idea. One that should keep all of us safe and allow you a chance to speak to that monster alone."

"Do tell," Hara requested eagerly, ready to consider anything.

✳ ✳ ✳

"Noah, I need to talk to you."

Daniel spoke those words after everyone else had left the lower level. Noah was sitting on the sofa and was about to turn on the television, but he paused at Daniel's words. The tone of his voice was scared. It caused Noah to peer at him with concern. "Is something wrong?" he asked cautiously.

Attempting to keep calm so Noah wouldn't worry, Daniel whispered, "I...I don't have much time."

"What are you talking about?" Noah asked, rising stiffly. "What's wrong? Did you see something?"

Daniel lowered his eyes to the floor and shook his head. "I...think that I'm going to die."

"Why?" Noah demanded, walking over to him briskly and putting a firm hand on his shoulder.

"I just..." He didn't know how to explain it. "I just have a feeling. You know? I just have a feeling that my time is coming."

"You can't die," Noah whispered, shaking his head. "We need you. Hara needs you. You can't leave us now."

"It's not like I have a desire to go," Daniel said. "And I don't even know it's for sure. I'm just saying that I have that feeling."

"Why are you telling me this?" Noah asked him. "Why are you telling me and no one else?"

"I don't want to worry them," Daniel replied.

"They're your friends!" Noah exclaimed. "They have a right to know!"

"I just wanted to tell one person!" Daniel said. "To get it off my chest. And so that at least one person will know I'm gone."

Noah sighed and shook his head. "If it is your time...I can't tell you how much you will be missed, by everyone."

"Let's just pray that it's only a feeling," Daniel muttered.

Noah sighed again. "Will staying behind prevent this from happening?"

"I can't stay behind," Daniel said. "Besides, it's my fate. I have to accept that I'll go when it's my time."

"You just wanted to tell me so someone would know? You think you'll die alone?"

"I think so, yes. I wanted one person to know so they could tell the others when they wondered what happened."

"What are you going to do about your body?" Noah asked him. "You know what they'll do with it if the wrong people get their hands on it. They'll dissect you!"

"I have a good friend who's another detective in the police department," Daniel explained. "His name's Garrick. Garrick Aubrey. I think if I give him a little push, he'll help get my body to the right place."

"The right place," Noah said. "You're talking about...?"

Daniel nodded.

"Well, thanks for telling me," Noah said, forcing a smile to his face. "You have no idea how much this hurts, but I'm grateful that you decided to let me know."

"There's one other thing," Daniel said, running a hand through his hair nervously. "Jack has been putting too much trust into Agent Perry."

"Agent Perry," Noah repeated. "As in Agent Shawn Perry?"

"Yes, the one and only," Daniel replied. "Anyway, I think Jack is going to send him here when he thinks he's ready to start learning the truth about us and where we came from. So don't be surprised if he comes walking through that door."

"What do you want me to tell him?" Noah asked uncertainly.

"The basics," Daniel said. "Answer some of his questions, but don't go in depth about where we're from. He's not ready for that yet. None of them are."

"Are we actually going to tell them in the end?"

"I don't know. Maybe. If they're ready to know the truth, I think we may have to."

"Alright," Noah said. "I'll give him a little bit of insight. I'll be sure to stay off of the dangerous topics."

"And one more thing," Daniel said, lowering his voice even though there wasn't anyone around to listen in to their conversation. "Hara healed Perry's head injury. Now, I know she's not one of the first generation, but I think the energy exchange between the two of them caused his trigger to go off."

"You think he's already changing?" Noah asked in shock.

"I think so," Daniel said gravely. "I don't know for sure, but I think Shawn Perry was just triggered ten years early."

"What are we supposed to do about this?" Noah asked.

"I think you may have to tell him," Daniel answered, not really liking that idea.

"Do you think he's going to handle that well?" Noah wondered grimly.

"He'll handle it better hearing it before seeing it," Daniel replied. "I think the best option is to just tell him so he can mentally prepare himself for when it happens the first time. You know how some of the first generation reacted when they suddenly began moving objects without touching them, or spontaneously started fires. If I were in his place, I would want to know ahead of time. It would be easier. So, please."

Nodding his head, Noah agreed. "Okay. I'll tell him, but I doubt he'll like it."

"Well, I think you know how to handle him better than any of us," Daniel said.

"I suppose you're right," Noah murmured, forcing another smile. "Well, I suppose I'll be seeing you. Or…maybe I won't be."

"In the Afterlife," Daniel promised him. "Until then…" He stepped forward and wrapped Noah in one last hug, struggling to prevent the tears from leaving his eyes.

"Goodbye," he whispered.

✳ ✳ ✳

After Perry's encounter with The Doc, he asked the hospital staff to set aside one of their conference rooms for them to use. The Doc told him to call only a few people who he thought would be trustworthy. Agent Long, being his commanding officer and also a very experienced agent, was called first. He then contacted Renee, his partner, and also Martinson and Hersh. Knowing that Lieutenant Odau would want to see the case through, Perry called him as well. Perry agreed to allow his two detectives, Aubrey and Finchly, to join them. Those seven people were the only ones he trusted to understand and help him while keeping the whole situation under the radar. Now they were all seated around a rectangular table, with Perry at the head and Agent Long at the opposite end. It was ultimately Agent Long's decision whether or not they were going to accept The Doc's help. None of them had met The Doc yet. Perry thought it would be better if he explained the situation first before introducing him, so The Doc was waiting outside the room.

"You'd better have a damn good reason for calling this meeting, Perry," Special Agent Rhett Long said flatly. Agent Long wasn't pleased with being dragged out to Philadelphia in the first place, and now with the catastrophe downtown he was in an even worse mood. But despite his negativity, he was very good at his job. "There's a huge mess we have to deal with downtown, and as I do recall, you should be in one of the hospital beds yourself."

"Yes, sir," Perry told him, looking around the table at his colleagues. They were all gazing back at him expectantly. "I called this meeting for a very important reason, and believe me, it took me a while to agree to go this far. Earlier this morning I was informed that Hara escaped police custody as I was being transported to the hospital. I have some valuable information about her that I would like to share. I feel it's crucial that you be made aware of just how complicated this case really is, and just how difficult it's going to be to catch this girl."

He saw Lieutenant Odau squirm uncomfortably in his chair beside him, understanding that Perry was going to start talking about her abilities.

"Then by all means, share," Agent Long replied, looking slightly bored. "Any information about the girl is valuable if it helps us catch her and actually keep her in custody."

Shooting a glance at Odau, Perry saw that he was staring down at the table with his arms folded tensely across his chest. The lieutenant still didn't want to believe the truth about Hara, even after witnessing it firsthand. "Hara isn't exactly...normal, so to speak. There are certain...strange and impossible things she is capable of. I doubt any of you were witness to the calamity she can create, but..."

"Are you referring to the fires downtown?" Aubrey interrupted, leaning forward eagerly.

When everyone turned to him in surprise, Finchly added, "Others at the station have been saying that Hara caused all the damage downtown with some sort of unique weapon she possesses. Is that what you're getting at?"

"Yes, it is," Perry answered, feeling both relief and fear that the others had begun to notice Hara's strange capabilities. It wouldn't take much to get them to believe it all, but that meant that it was possible for people on the outside to notice as well. If people knew, they would start to ask questions, questions no one could answer. And that would only lead to panic. How was anyone supposed to explain to the public that an entire species was created and destroyed without the world knowing? How was anyone supposed to explain that Hara wasn't even biologically a human? For the time being, Perry was going to save that information for himself and his colleagues. "Hara possesses a weapon that can create any kind of disaster you can think of. She was the one who started the fires downtown. But this weapon of hers isn't anything any of us have seen before. It's not something we can simply take away or destroy. This weapon is inside of her. She started the fires, blocked our radio transmissions, and even burned my wrist with her bare hand. All this she did with just her mind." He held up his injured wrist. "I have the burn in the shape of her handprint as proof of her power."

"So what are you suggesting?" Agent Long questioned, his expression still bored. "That this child is some sort of super-human?"

"Not exactly a super-human," Perry said slowly, knowing how unbelievable his next words were going to sound. "More like a member of a new species that has branched off from the human race."

There was a short silence before Renee, Martinson, and Hersh started snorting and laughing at what Perry had said. The three officers remained silent, the lieutenant already having been witness to her capabilities. The two detectives were ready to believe it, having heard stories from the other officers about Hara's demonstration of her destructive forces in the holding cells. Agent Long kept quiet as well, his brow furrowed as he lost himself in his thoughts. Perry would have thought him to be the one least likely to buy into it, but he actually seemed to be considering it. He then shot the three amused agents a dirty look and they immediately cleared their throats and put serious expressions back on their faces.

Agent Long's expression was no longer bored. He looked deeply interested now.

Perry rubbed his exhausted eyes, trying to find an explanation for the information that was rattling around in his head. "I'm not exactly sure how to explain this myself, because I only received a brief explanation from Hara before I was taken in to the hospital. Some time ago, an unknown number of people were exposed to a chemical that altered their DNA sequence. It switched around some genes and caused them to develop these abilities that Hara was so kind to demonstrate for us. An entirely new species has been created because of that." Taking a breath, Perry told them the part that he knew would disturb his colleagues the most. "Hara isn't one who was exposed, however. She's the offspring of two of the affected members."

Agent Long raised a hand to silence the uproar that sounded after Perry's last comment. His expression showed anger, something that Perry hadn't expected. "Is this some kind of joke you created to amuse yourself?"

"I assure you, this is no joke," Perry promised.

"If she's the second generation, then why hasn't anybody heard about the first generation?" Renee demanded in confusion.

"How could an entire species be created and go undiscovered until now?" Martinson asked. "If this is for real and this girl really does possess these abilities, someone would have noticed a long time ago. You've seen how dangerous she is. She couldn't have hidden from the rest of the world for so long."

"Somebody covered it up and kept it a secret," Perry explained, an image of The Doc crossing his mind. "The people affected also went into hiding to keep their existence a secret as well."

"If there are more people like her out there, we would have definitely heard about them by now," Finchly said. "If there are people out there who can create destructive forces similar to those that Hara created, then it would be impossible for these people to keep their existence under the radar. Things like this just don't go by unnoticed."

"That's another part of the story you all should know," Perry said gravely. "Nearly every single one of them was wiped out. All that remain are Hara and a few other survivors. That's why Hara has exposed herself. She's angry for her family's death and the death of the rest of her race, so she's come to carry out revenge on those responsible."

"And who exactly are the people who caused it?" Hersh questioned curiously.

"Us," Perry replied. "Humans."

"She's killing children because of something a select group of people did?" Aubrey asked dubiously.

"Hara hasn't explained her motives for that," Perry told him. "So I'm still not sure why she did it. She might just be angry at our race for what was done to her and now she's trying to get back at us in any way she can. She might just be trying to get attention focused on her people and those who murdered them. Who knows? Until she gives us the full story, we can only make assumptions."

"How do you know that she hasn't already given you the whole story?" Agent Long asked him quietly.

Perry raised an eyebrow. "She told me that the kids were evil and were the reason for what was done to her. Correct me if I'm wrong, but that doesn't sound at all like a logical explanation."

"Maybe she was telling the truth," Agent Long said. "Did you ever consider that?"

"What are you saying?" Odau demanded, speaking up for the first time. "Remember, one of those four kids was my son. He didn't do anything that could have caused the death of these people! Perry's right. We have yet to have a real reason for the murder of those three boys."

"I'm just trying to figure out these facts," Agent Long defended. "And we have to consider every possibility with something as complicated as this. It's entirely possible that what the girl claimed is the truth."

Odau started to snap back in defense of his son again, but Perry spoke up first. "Do you know something about this that we don't?" he asked curiously, not really understanding why his commanding officer was defending their fugitive.

Agent Long stared blankly back at him. "Of course I don't. I'm just trying to take into consideration that maybe Hara isn't as guilty as everyone thinks. You should too."

Everyone was quiet for a minute, which was surprising to Perry. He would have thought that the lieutenant of all people would have had something to say about that. What Agent Long said was true. Hara really did seem like the crazy one in this investigation, but what if she wasn't? What if it was him and his people that were the ones missing the big picture? How did Perry know that he wasn't seeing the answers because they were hidden right in front of him?

Agent Long seemed to read his mind. "How do you know that all the answers aren't right in front of you, and you're just overlooking them?"

Once again, no one had any reply for that. After a bit, Martinson cleared his throat and asked, "But why would anyone want to wipe out an entire group of people, even if they were a different species from us? They obviously didn't do anything to us, otherwise we would have heard about it. Why would anyone want to harm a peaceful race?"

"Why not?" Perry asked him. "We've seen it before. Hitler and the Jews, the Hutus and the Tutsis, the Khmer Rouge in Cambodia...it's happening right now in Africa, but many people don't even know about it. When people don't understand another group of people, or are afraid of that group of people, or think that they are superior to that group of people, they try to wipe them out. Imagine if you had just discovered that an entire species was created overnight and are now living among us. Wouldn't you be afraid?"

"I already am," Martinson replied uneasily. "But what you've been saying is impossible. As some of us have already pointed out, someone would have found out about this, no matter who tried to cover it up. We're in the FBI and we would have been notified about incidents caused by these people."

"Well, I'm not saying this makes sense," Perry said, growing frustrated. "But it's the truth. These people existed for an unknown length of time and were all murdered with barely anyone in the outside world knowing about it. This is what happened, and we just have to deal with that fact."

"So what exactly are we dealing with here?" Hersh asked uncertainly.

"An angry girl with unlimited capabilities and a vengeance," Perry told her. "Basically, a living time bomb with its timer counting down to zero."

"And what do you propose we do about this living time bomb?" Agent Long asked, his bored expression back.

"We could just kill her," Odau muttered thoughtfully.

Seven pairs of eyes landed on him.

"Are you out of your mind?" Perry asked him in astonishment. "No, we are not going to kill her. We're going to catch her again."

"And how do you propose we do that?" Odau demanded. "The last time we caught her, she went willingly and then she escaped with barely an effort. With these abilities of hers...it's going to be damn near impossible!"

Glad that they were all finally getting down to business, Perry said, "That's the main reason why I called you all here. Someone is going to help us, someone who knows how to catch her."

"And who exactly is this person?" Agent Long asked curiously.

Perry pointed his thumb at the door. "He's just outside. Can I bring him in?"

Agent Long nodded, and the others all looked towards the door eagerly.

Perry stood up and went to the door. He looked out and spotted The Doc a few yards away. He was standing with his back turned, speaking in a low voice to two men in front of him. Both men were dressed in black t-shirts and cargo pants, were very muscular, had short buzz cuts and had very blank expressions.

"Hey," Perry called, and The Doc turned around. "We're ready for you."

The Doc started to walk into the room, but Perry stopped him when the two large men began to follow. "Who are they?" he asked suspiciously.

"Just a few friends," The Doc said, smiling pleasantly at him. "You don't mind if they come in, do you?"

Perry stared at The Doc's smug expression. "No, not at all," Perry said curtly. He followed the three men into the room and quickly closed the door behind him. The three remained by the door, but Perry returned to his chair and gestured to The Doc. "This is The Doc and…two of his friends."

The Doc smiled politely at everyone sitting at the table, but received nothing in return.

"Doctor what?" Agent Long asked through gritted teeth. Perry couldn't tell if he was annoyed or upset or what.

"It's just 'The Doc.'"

Raising an eyebrow, Detective Aubrey said, "People call you 'The Doc?'"

Nodding, The Doc continued to smile down at everyone. "Yes, they do."

Nodding as well, Agent Long watched their guest uneasily. "Okay," he said. "So how is it that you know Hara when the FBI knows nothing about her or her kind?"

"Well," The Doc started, taking a step closer to the table. "We were old friends a while back. I lost track of her a few weeks ago and I've been looking for her. I finally found her and the mess she made."

"And how did you come to know her?" Agent Long questioned.

"In the same way that everyone else knows her," The Doc replied. "I knew her father. But that's not what you need to be worrying yourself over right now. You need to know that you're dealing with a very destructive force far more powerful than any kind of weapon you've ever witnessed. This weapon has a mind and emotions, and will release her powers with barely a warning…"

"Yes, thank you," Agent Long said impatiently. "I've already gotten this lecture. What makes you think we need or even want your help?"

Raising his eyebrows at the agent's rudeness, The Doc said, "Because she's not going to stop killing until someone brings her down."

"And I take it that someone is you?"

"Right you are."

"What does it matter to you whether or not we stop her?"

"Do you have children, Agent Long?"

Perry and his FBI colleagues cringed. Agent Long had never told them himself, but everyone knew the story of his family.

Pursing his lips and glaring at him harshly, Agent Long growled, "I would have many years ago. But my wife and unborn daughter were taken away from me by someone sick and malevolent. Someone like you."

The Doc cocked his head to the side and smirked at him. "And what makes you think there's anything wrong with me?"

"Why else would you be trying to catch Hara?" Agent Long demanded. "Why else would you know about her? You're the one who was experimenting on her. You're the one who caused her to do all this."

"I didn't force her to do this," The Doc stated, his eyes narrowing. "This was her own conscious decision. Believe me, I want her to stop more than you do."

"You make your living off of the sufferings of innocent people," Agent Long said plainly. "Why would you give a damn about a couple of kids getting killed?"

The Doc snickered. "You'd be surprised."

"So what exactly was the point of reminding me about my dead family?" Agent Long, irritated.

"Everyone in this city with a child is scared to death at the thought of someone slaughtering them like the other three last night. Anyone in this room with a child wants her out of this equation. You want your children safe, I want my girl back. It's a win-win situation."

"Not for Hara, it's not," Agent Long said quietly.

The Doc peered at him. "And you care about her why?"

Agent Long dodged the question. "Once we've caught her, then what? You help us catch her but what do you get in return?"

The Doc raised an eyebrow. "I think you've already figured that part out, Agent Long."

"Absolutely not," Agent Long said firmly. "After what you've done to her, there's no way I would ever allow her to be alone with you again!"

"I'm afraid this is non-negotiable," The Doc told him. "As I was telling Agent Perry, I'm going to catch her with or without your help.

But I'm afraid if we don't help each other, I'm going to have no choice but to cause more damage to this city than I already have."

Everyone around the table exchanged confused looks, and then Perry realized that he was going to be the one who would have to explain who The Doc really was.

Clearing his throat, he told them all, "He was the one who led the attack last night on our caravan."

An immediate clamor of shocked and angry shouts sounded from around the table. Martinson was the first on his feet. "I'm placing you under arrest for…"

He barely got out half his sentence. He and everyone else in the room froze at the sound of weapons being cocked. Turning in surprise, Perry saw that both of The Doc's companions had pulled out handguns and were aiming them at Martinson's head.

The Doc simply smiled at him. "Sit down," he said softly.

Martinson didn't need to be told twice.

"I'm about to offer you the easy way out of this situation," The Doc told them all. "I suggest you shut up and listen to what I have to say before going around making arrests."

Agent Long chuckled. "You just held a federal agent at gunpoint. What makes you think we're going to listen to anything else you have to say?"

"Yes," Renee agreed coldly. "You killed more than a dozen men last night! Men we all knew and cared for!"

"Someone I knew since childhood was in one of those vehicles you demolished," Hersh hissed at him.

"And you experimented on a teenage girl and drove her over the edge," Aubrey added.

Finchly nodded. "So basically, you're the cause of *all* of this."

"Why the hell should we listen to you anymore?" Agent Long piped in harshly.

The Doc didn't answer. He didn't need to. Somebody was already on his side, and he was going to provide the answers for him.

"I think we should give him a chance," Odau said. "Or at least hear him out. He may have killed our men and caused significant damage, but now he's offering to make up for it. He's offering to help us catch the most dangerous criminal we've encountered in our careers. Now I know the concept of working with a murderer seems immoral, but if he's been experimenting on her then he knows these people! He knows what he's dealing with, and that's what we need right now. We were brought into this completely unprepared. None of us knew what we were getting ourselves into until it was far too late. But now that he's here, we actually have a decent chance of catching her which means we have a better chance of getting rid of her! My son's life is on the line! And many more lives are probably at stake! If he has the ability to stop her, and we all know he does, then the least we can do is listen to what he has to say. We've already proven we can't do this ourselves. Now is not the time to be picky about who is helping us."

The Doc was very pleased by that speech. He beamed down at the lieutenant, but Odau was avoiding eye contact with him. He may have wanted Hara to be caught, but it didn't mean that he wasn't going to be uncomfortable working with the man who had killed several of his officers.

No one spoke after the lieutenant. Everyone was thinking it over. He was right after all. Cooperating with a murderer to help them went against everything the bureau stood for, but many lives would be on the line if they didn't accept the offer.

The Doc looked around at everyone curiously. "May I continue?"

Seven pairs of eyes turned to Agent Long, who was the one to make the call. Sighing, he muttered, "Go ahead."

"Thank you," The Doc said, still beaming. "Agent Perry has already questioned me on why I haven't captured Hara myself already. It is because she is very difficult to find. Unless she comes to you first or you happen to be in the same place at the same time by coincidence, it is nearly impossible to track her down. Her people preferred living undisturbed, with others having no idea they existed, so she's very good at hiding. I have absolutely no idea where she is, but there are a few people who do. You have one of the people who knows where she's hiding in your custody."

"Jack," Odau said thoughtfully.

"Are you asking us if we'll allow you to interrogate one of our prime suspects?" Agent Long demanded in disbelief. "Because the answer is most definitely no."

"It won't exactly be an interrogation," The Doc explained. "All I need is ninety seconds or less with him, and that's it. I'll get the information we need and then I'll go get our little friend."

"And what do you plan to do to get the information you need?" Martinson asked, finally finding his voice again after the surprise from The Doc's companions. "Beat the boy until he talks?"

Shrugging, The Doc replied, "I was just planning on asking him where she was."

"And you're expecting an answer just like that?" Renee said in disbelief. "What makes you think he'll give you an answer just because you asked him? We've already tried that and we haven't gotten anything."

"I'm fairly certain that Jack will give me what I want when I ask for it," The Doc assured her.

"And once you talk to Jack and capture Hara, what happens then?" Odau asked him.

The Doc shrugged again. "I speak to Jack, I catch Hara, and then I take her away from here and you never hear about either of us again."

"So neither of you will take responsibility for what you've done?" Finchly asked. "You'll catch her and then waltz away like nothing ever happened?"

Again, The Doc shrugged. "I catch Hara and take her far out of reach from the rest of the world, and that's one of your problems solved. If I go away too, then that's two of your problems solved. Both people causing you trouble will have left your little world for good. Don't you think that's a bonus?"

"Hara has to take responsibility for what she's done!" Aubrey declared. "What are we supposed to tell the families of the people she murdered?"

"Tell them she was killed," The Doc told him. "I think they'll appreciate that."

"And what are we supposed to tell the families of the people you killed?" Renee demanded angrily.

The Doc smiled at her. "You can tell them the same thing if you like. I couldn't really care less what you tell them."

Perry wanted everyone to be clear on what The Doc was planning to do to the girl once he took her away. Agent Long seemed to understand it fairly well, but Perry needed everyone to be aware of the crime they would all be committing by letting the poor girl become a helpless lab rat again. "What exactly do you plan to do to Hara one you've caught her?"

His eyes flickering to Perry's, The Doc told what was clearly a lie, or at least an understatement. "My group of scientists and I will contain her and her abilities so she cannot escape or hurt anyone else." Perry wanted to pressure him into giving all the dirty details, but The Doc started speaking again. "I've laid out the terms for you nice and clear. You let me speak to Jack and anyone else who may have information about Hara's whereabouts. Then, I will capture her and contain her. You and your people then make up some story about how she was killed in the struggle, and if anyone asks you can say her body wasn't found or was destroyed. I take her away from this place and we both disappear forever. You all get to take credit for ridding the city of her. After this whole mess comes to an end, you never have to think or worry about either of us again. You could just forget we even existed. You'll be able to spend as much time as you need on reconstructing the city. The parents of the dead children and the families of everyone else who died in the past few days will be more at peace believing that the person who killed their loved ones is dead. Their nightmare will be over, and so will yours. Doesn't that sound like a fair solution for everyone?" Leaning forward and folding his hands upon the table, he asked, "But are you prepared to make the choice that will benefit everyone, even if it means accepting the help of a man who broke a few rules?"

The Doc's terms and argument were outrageous, but as Perry continued to think them over, he realized just how tempted he was to go along with it. Odau really had been right; none of them were prepared for what Hara had brought to their doorstep, and The Doc clearly knew what he was doing. The Doc was their best chance to get Hara with as few casualties as possible. They simply let him speak to Jack, he catches the girl, and then they'll disappear forever. They all say Hara's dead, and forget any of it ever happened. Case closed.

Could it really be that simple?

Gazing around at everyone as they thought it over carefully, The Doc leaned back in his chair. "It's your choice. But I advise you make it carefully."

Another minute passed. Nobody was looking at anybody else. Everyone's eyes were aimed down at the table. They were all pondering over the difficult choice. Should they follow protocol and let more people die? Or should they bend the rules and save innocent lives?

"Agent Perry," Agent Long said suddenly, rising to his feet. "A word with you outside, please. Now."

Perry rose as well and followed his boss to the door, but they were both stopped by The Doc's companions. They stood in the way and refused to move, staring down at them without emotion. Perry looked back at The Doc, who was eyeing them both suspiciously. "If you don't mind?"

The Doc gestured to his guards to back off. They obeyed immediately, stepping in opposite directions at the exact same time, as if they were androids powered by a remote control. It made Perry shudder. He wasn't planning to ask, but he knew that there was something wrong with those two. The way they moved and the unchanging expressions they wore were not human. Maybe they really were androids.

Both Perry and Agent Long left the room, and when the door was tightly sealed, Agent Long whispered to Perry, "Do you have any idea what you're doing?"

"Sir?" Perry asked uncertainly.

"I'm just asking if you know what you're getting yourself into," Agent Long explained, his voice dropping in volume. "What you're getting us all into. You were the one who introduced The Doc to us. I'm just curious if you understand what the consequences will be if this goes sour?"

Perry lowered his eyes to the floor. He knew exactly what the consequences would be. They would all be incriminated for taking part in a conspiracy and would most likely spend time behind bars. And even worse, the truth about Hara could be revealed to the rest of the world and people would go looking for her kind. Her people—or what was left of them—would be hunted down again and either killed or used for science experiments, just like they had been when only a few humans knew about her.

"He killed a lot of good people today, Perry," Agent Long reminded him softly. "He nearly killed Renee."

Startled, Perry looked up. "Yes, and he almost killed Andy and Jaz too."

Agent Long said, "From what I've heard, it would seem as if he's hurt a lot of good people in the past as well. Hara's people? If he used her as his pet, then it's only safe to assume that he's hurt a lot of people like her. What say you?"

"I don't want to think about what that nut's done," Perry answered truthfully. "If I think about it, it only makes me angry and I have to put my personal feelings aside at the moment. I'm afraid I'm siding with Odau on this one. The Doc may be what he is, but he's our best shot at finding this kid and getting her out of here. I think we should just go with it and let him do his work."

"This man held your friend at gunpoint a minute ago," Agent Long said, raising an eyebrow. "And he's expecting to be let free when this is over. Are you really going to let him go after he killed some of your colleagues?"

"I think we should just catch Hara first and then go from there," Perry said. "I'm not saying we should play this whole game by The Doc's rules. We could cheat a little bit, if you know what I'm saying. Let him think he's in control for a while." He shrugged. "But it's up to you. I'm game for whatever you decide."

Agent Long shook his head solemnly. "No. This is your decision. This time, it's on you."

Perry was surprised that he was getting to make the call. "I...uh...I say we do what I said. Start playing by The Doc's rules and then make up our own once we've caught the girl."

"I don't trust him," Agent Long stated bluntly. "I don't think anyone in that room does either. Do you trust him?"

No, Perry wanted to say. He didn't trust The Doc, not one bit. But accepting his offer was the best course of action. They were in a desperate time, and desperate times sometimes called for desperate measures. "I trust that he can get Hara," he replied.

Sighing, Agent Long nodded. "Okay," he said, the regret visible in his eyes. "But we're going to run this operation under my orders, understand?"

"Yes, sir."

"And if we get busted for this, I'm coming after you." Agent Long turned and opened the door so they could fill the others in on the decision.

When Perry sat down, he could feel The Doc's piercing stare, but he made an effort to avoid eye contact with him. He simply watched Agent Long and waited for him to speak.

Taking a deep breath, Agent Long announced to everyone, "I spoke with Agent Perry, and we are in agreement that we will indeed accept The Doc's offer. But with some restrictions," he added sharply. "He can speak to Jack, but under our supervision. He'll be accompanied by one of us wherever he chooses to go, and once he captures Hara we will personally escort him out of the city. We'll be watching you very closely, Doc. Is that clear?"

"Perfectly," The Doc replied. "Are there any more questions before we get started?"

"Yeah, I've got one," Renee snapped, her eyes resentful. "Who exactly are you?"

The Doc smiled at her, trying to deflect the question. "I'm a scientist."

"Care to elaborate?"

"I have degrees in biology, genetics, chemistry, anatomy, and surgery. Although I prefer researching and performing experiments in a lab, I am also a qualified and licensed doctor." Glancing over at Perry, he gave him a smug look that was returned with a scowl. "For the past twenty years or so I've been studying peculiar genetic mutations, mainly the mutation that occurred in the people affected by the Colician strain. That's the name of the chemical compound that created Hara's race," he explained when he received multiple confused looks. "I studied that mutation for a very long time, along with the Caiten strain, which is quite similar in nature to the Colician strain. I am one of the only people who knows practically everything there is to know about the mutation. I understand how it affects people and how it makes their abilities work. That's how I created the technology designed to capture, contain, and control them." Leaning toward Renee, he asked her, "Is that enough for you, or shall I continue?"

Renee glared back at him, but before she could respond, Hersh spoke up. "When you said you studied the mutation, that meant you studied people, right? You studied Hara?"

Finally, somebody else was asking that question. Perry leaned forward eagerly, watching The Doc's smooth expression. Maybe pressure from people other than just Perry would actually get the man to admit some of his crimes.

There was a moment's silence. The Doc appeared to be debating whether or not to answer. "Yes," he said finally.

Everyone was holding their breath as they waited for him to continue, but when he didn't, Finchly asked, "How exactly did you study them?"

The room was awkwardly silent, and Perry waited intently for The Doc to answer her. Again, the man paused. But then he shrugged and told them all rather slowly, as if he were trying to make his answer more friendly, "I analyzed their blood, DNA, and various parts of the brain to better understand how the strain affected them and functioned as a part of them."

It was Perry's turn to ask a question. "So you experimented on them?"

After staring back at Perry for quite some time, The Doc answered, "Yes."

Trying to fight back his own smirk, Perry asked, "And you tortured them?"

The Doc's expression was no longer friendly. His eyes were almost glaring, something Perry hadn't really seen from him yet. He didn't want to answer Perry, and he didn't look like he was going to. He didn't have to either. Everyone could tell by his face that he had done some terrible things. Perry would never know if The Doc was going to answer, because one of Odau's detectives suddenly stepped inside.

The detective, a middle aged man, appeared flustered, as if he had just seen something completely unbelievable, and when Perry heard his next words he understood why. "There are two men...there are two men here to see you," he stammered to Perry, breathing heavily.

"What do they want?" Odau asked.

"They came to give Agent Perry a message," the detective said breathlessly. "And they also came to turn themselves in to you, Lieutenant."

"What?" Perry said, puzzled.

"Who are they?" Odau demanded.

Perry already knew.

"It's the mayor and Detective Marcus!"

The Doc was leaning forward in his chair, eagerly awaiting the visit.

"Wait, they're here?" Odau said. "They're turning themselves in?"

The detective nodded quickly. "But first they wanted to talk to Agent Perry. They said it was very important."

All eyes turned to Perry. He nodded to the detective. "Alright," he said. "Let's see them."

The detective leaned out the door and beckoned for the two to enter. A moment later, Daniel Marcus stepped inside with Allan Brown in tow. They both looked different. For one thing, they looked even more tired than they had when Perry first met them, but that wasn't it. They seemed a little more sure of themselves, like they knew everything would work out fine, yet their eyes were still flickering warily over them all. Their eyes landed on The Doc and that was where they stayed. Perry could easily see their fear.

"Well?" Perry said, trying to break their gazes away from The Doc, even if it was for just a second. "You're the ones who came to me, so let's hear it."

Marcus slowly shifted his eyes away from The Doc and made eye contact with Perry. "Hara asked me to tell you something," he said, his voice quavering with each word. He glanced in The Doc's direction again.

Perry nodded, waiting for him to continue.

Swallowing, Marcus told him, "She told me to tell you this: you've been warned, you've seen us both, now choose your side."

"Thank you," Perry said flatly. "But I've already picked my side."

Allan Brown piped in. "She also said to choose wisely." His gaze also flickered back to The Doc. "She wants you to be sure you're siding with what you feel is right."

"I am," Perry told him sternly. "I'm not going to let her hurt any more people."

The two men looked like they wanted to argue with him more, try to make him see it Hara's way, but neither of them spoke.

"That's it then?" Odau asked, standing up and pulling out a pair of cuffs.

"Not quite," Brown said, staring at The Doc. "She also has something she wanted to tell you."

"Oh?" The Doc said, cocking his head to the side.

"She says, 'double, double toil and trouble.'"

The Doc's eyebrows raised and he sneered. "Does she now?"

"Yes," Brown replied, starting to get nervous from The Doc's intimidating stare. "She also wanted me to tell you that she wants to talk to you. Nine-thirty a.m., first interrogation room at the station, just you and her without any weapons."

Others around the table began murmuring to each other about the strange request. Hara wanted to walk willingly into a room to talk with The Doc? There was no way that was all she wanted to do.

The Doc nodded. "Huh." He pulled something out of his jacket pocket, and Perry saw that it was a small firearm. It looked almost identical to a nine-millimeter, although it was smaller and had a needle protruding out of the barrel. The Doc was going to hit her with a tranquilizer dart, something that had been tried already and had ended in calamity.

"You're going to shoot her?" Perry muttered disapprovingly.

"Have you ever seen something like this before?" The Doc asked him, holding up the weapon for all to see. Without waiting for an answer, he continued. "Of course you haven't. This is one of the various pieces of technology I have created by studying Hara and others of her kind. It's probably the best defense one could have against them. Shooting Hara with a regular tranquilizer will barely make her head fog up. This is something special. Inside is a drug that, when injected into Hara or anyone with an ability, will paralyze the part of the brain that controls the abilities."

"Wouldn't that kill them?" Perry asked, taken aback.

"No, not at all," The Doc reassured quickly. "They become slightly confused and disoriented, but it doesn't hurt them."

"Right," Renee said sarcastically. "Because shutting off a part of a person's brain wouldn't hurt them at all!"

The Doc explained, "The Colician strain caused a part of the brain that isn't normally active to come to life, which is what allows a person to control their abilities. It's not a part we need functioning to survive. Shutting it off only makes them incapable of using their abilities, which makes them much more vulnerable. Once I inject her with this, she'll be defenseless. I can shoot her from three feet away or three hundred feet away." He slipped the gun into his belt so it would be more accessible. "And now, since the two of us will be locked in a small room together..."

"Um..." Brown cleared his throat. "You really don't want to do that."

"And why not?"

"I already told you. She said no weapons."

The Doc laughed crudely. "Considering she's a walking weapon, I think I have a right to keep this with me."

Marcus snorted. "She said you'd say that. She also said that if you bring one of those things with you, she'll kill his son." He nodded to Odau.

The lieutenant became outraged. "You tell her to stay away from him, do you hear me? Do you hear me?! Tell her to stay away..."

"I don't take orders from you anymore," Marcus snapped, scowling across the room at him. "I was done as soon as Hara found me."

Shocked by his sudden change of attitude, Odau stared at him with his mouth half open. But he said no more.

The Doc was staring Marcus down, but he looked like he was thinking his options over. What would The Doc care about Odau's son, anyway? Jackson wasn't important to him. Was he? "You had to throw in the boy," he muttered.

Shrugging, Marcus said, "Those were her conditions. If you don't want to meet them then you're out of luck."

Heaving a sigh, The Doc said, "Okay. I'll go to Hara's little meeting unarmed, if that's what she wishes. What exactly does she want to talk about?"

His eyes narrowing ever so slightly, Marcus whispered, "Everything."

"Doc," Martinson called from a few seats away. "What does 'double, double toil and trouble' mean?"

"Oh, it's just a little phrase the two of us used to share with each other," The Doc explained. "It just means she's coming for me."

"Should we be worried?" Aubrey asked uneasily.

"Not you," The Doc replied, glancing over to Perry. "So, Mister, it looks as if the rest of these folks are going to take part in this. What about you? Are you still in?"

Confused, Perry stated, "I never said that I wasn't. And it's not like I have much of a choice anyway."

Giving him a little sneer, The Doc said, "Great. Glad to have you." Glancing down at his wristwatch, he informed them, "Well, it's getting close to nine, so I guess we'd better get over to the station and get ready for our little visit."

Everyone began to slowly rise to their feet. Agent Long called to them, "Not a word of this to anyone! We'll discuss what to tell the public once Hara's gone." There were a few mumbled replies, and then everyone flocked to the door.

"Please escort the two of them back to the station," Odau was telling Finchly and Aubrey, referring to Brown and Marcus. "Put them in holding."

"Yes, sir," they both said, giving each other a mutual look of regret. Marcus was still their friend. They didn't want to put him through any more.

Perry passed them and headed for the door. Right before he reached the exit, Agent Long patted him on the back and whispered, "Watch your back," before exiting.

Puzzled, he paused to let Finchly, Aubrey, Brown, and Marcus out the door. Once they were gone, The Doc caught his arm, and Perry knew what Agent Long had been referring to.

"Hi there, kiddo," The Doc said merrily, pulling him back inside and shoving him against the wall. "I want to talk to you."

"Don't push me around," Perry warned, glaring at him.

Laughing, The Doc stared mockingly but coldly back at him. "Let us remember who almost killed whom."

"And let us also be aware of who's pointing a gun at who," Perry told him, pulling out his gun and pressing it into The Doc's stomach.

The Doc didn't look scared at all. He just kept grinning and chuckling at him. "You don't have it in you to kill me. I can look into a man's eyes and know if he's willing to pull the trigger." He shook his head slowly. "I'm looking into your eyes, and I just don't see it."

"You'd be surprised," Perry replied.

"I know what you were trying to do back there," The Doc said. "Did you really think I wouldn't catch on to your stunt to corner me? Well, let me clue you in on something. Even if we had gotten onto the subject of torturing Hara, I'm a smooth talker. I can get myself out of just about anything."

"So you're admitting to torturing her?" Perry asked, smirking back.

"Nice try," The Doc said quietly. "But I'm going to suggest that you shut your mouth. You already know far more than you should, and I'd hate to use any unnecessary force to keep you quiet."

His eyebrows raising in surprise, Perry demanded, "Are you threatening me?"

"Not just yet," The Doc replied, still staring into Perry's eyes. "But I'm watching you."

The Doc was not going to push him around. Pressing the gun harder into his stomach to get him to back up, Perry snarled, "Stay away from me!"

The Doc raised his hands in defense and took a couple of steps back.

"Okay?" Perry snapped, wanting him to understand that he was deadly serious.

Nodding slowly, The Doc gestured to the door. "Okay," he said softly. "Okay."

Quickly, still fearing that The Doc would shoot him when his back was turned, Perry strode out of the room and followed the others down the busy hallway. Most of them were heading towards the elevator to make their way out the main entrance, but Lieutenant Odau had fallen behind. He stopped to speak with a shorter, African American man dressed like a doctor. Perry recognized the doctor from Mayor Brown's office the afternoon before. His name was Barrett, or Bonsett, one of the two. Bennett, maybe? He couldn't quite recall, but by the way they were speaking and by what Perry remembered, Odau and the doctor seemed to be pretty well acquainted. He thought they were friends. Perry didn't know for sure, and he didn't care much about it either. Spotting Perry out of the corner of his eye, the lieutenant smiled and shook the doctor's hand goodbye. He turned and started walking alongside Perry, matching his brisk pace. There was some relief in the man's eyes.

"What's going on?" Perry asked, glancing back at the doctor as they rounded a corner. He caught the doctor watching him suspiciously as they left.

"That's Dr. Wesley Bennett," Odau told him. "He was the one who gave us the tranquilizer for Hara, the drug that we never used. I just asked him if he could post extra security around my son's room. I'm not going to be here to protect him this time, and with Hara's most recent threat, I'm not sure what's enough."

Nodding understandingly, Perry questioned, "So what are we going to do about The Doc?"

"What do you mean?"

"I mean, how are we going to get him to the station? Are you going to drive him?"

"Me? Why would I drive him?"

"You're already getting a bit chummy with him. You gave him your full support back there."

Shrugging, Odau gave him a sly grin. "No, I just assumed you were going to drive him."

"Ha!" Perry laughed, but shook his head immediately. "No way."

"Well," Odau started, his grin getting broader. He clearly had no interest in transporting The Doc, and he seemed to be enjoying Perry's hesitance. "You are the one who brought him into this whole mess. I think it's only fair that you deal with him." He stepped into the elevator that held a few members of their group and also a few civilians. Moving over slightly, he gestured to the empty space between them. "Are you going to get on?" he asked.

Scowling at him, Perry snapped, "I think I'll catch the next one."

As the doors closed between them, Odau smirked at him. It was funny. With that look on his face, Perry could have sworn he looked just like The Doc.

Perry turned when he felt the presence of another person behind him. He almost jumped when he realized The Doc had snuck up on him.

Taking a step back to honor Perry's request that he stay away, The Doc nodded at him. "You don't have to worry yourself about driving me anywhere. I have my own form of transportation." When another door opened into a second elevator, he gestured to it. "After you."

How had he heard that conversation? He hadn't been close enough to hear it. Had he? Eyeing him uncertainly, Perry stepped inside the elevator and pressed the button labeled G. He moved to the corner, waiting for The Doc to step inside with his two pals.

The Doc gave him another smile. "I'll catch the next one," he said quietly.

Relieved, Perry relaxed a little bit and tried to overhear what one of The Doc's friends was muttering in his ear. He missed it, but he heard The Doc's reply.

"Yes, he's going to be the most trouble to us. He already feels like he knows them."

Until The Doc turned toward him, Perry didn't understand who he had been talking about. Perry's brow furrowed in confusion, and he held The Doc's strong gaze until the doors closed and separated them.

9

Confrontation

The ride to the police station was deadly silent. Perry rode with Renee and Hersh, with Martinson as their driver, and the only time anyone spoke was when Renee asked Perry if he was sure he was well enough to go back to work so soon. After he said he was, not another person spoke for ten minutes. By the time they were pulling around the corner beside the station, everyone was shifting awkwardly in their seats. As their SUV pulled into the station parking lot, Martinson finally burst. "Perry, do you even trust that guy?"

"Nope," Perry answered immediately. What was he expected to say?

"Then why are we letting him in on this?" Martinson demanded as he pulled into a vacant parking stall. "You were a witness to what he's done! He very nearly killed you!"

"Actually, that was Hara's fault," Perry reminded him.

"Who cares whose fault it was?" Martinson snapped, cutting the engine and swiveling in his seat to glare at him. "He pointed a gun at my head, for crying out loud! He stole a tank! A tank! He killed at least twelve people, and with what I've seen I wouldn't be surprised if he's killed a number of others!"

Perry flinched, realizing that he hadn't told anyone about his confrontation in the hospital room with The Doc. If the time came when he needed to share the incident with the others, then so be it. But for the time being, he didn't want to add any more tension to the situation.

"What?" Martinson asked upon seeing his pained expression.

"Nothing," Perry mumbled, looking down at the gray carpet on the floor of the truck.

"There's something else about him too," Renee said, almost as if she were speaking to herself. When Perry glanced up at her he saw that she was staring fixatedly at the back of Martinson's seat. "He makes me uncomfortable, and it's not because of what we've seen him do. It's something else, something more. He feels so familiar to me, like I've seen him before. And I know I haven't, because I would remember someone like him." She blinked and looked from face to face. "I can't be the only one feeling this. Haven't we seen him somewhere before?"

"Yeah, actually," Perry muttered, certain that he had seen those eyes before.

"Yeah," Martinson piped in.

"I agree with you, Renee," Hersh said, turning to her. "I look at him and I feel the same thing every time. It's those eyes. I swear I've seen them before."

"And that's not the only thing that bothers me," Renee added. "He admitted to experimenting on those poor people. He didn't answer your question, Shawn, but I know that he tortured them. I could see it in his face. He played with them, had fun with them, and then he probably killed them, too. I look at Hara's face from the security footage and I can see the pain in her. He did it to her. He hurt her, and now we're paying for it. I hate to say it, and I could be wrong, but honestly..." She shook her head. "I don't think she's the bad person here. I don't think she's the one we should be focusing on."

The SUV was silent for a few moments. Perry knew why that was. The same thought had crossed each of their minds after meeting The Doc. Compared to The Doc, Hara was not that bad. Maybe she wasn't a bad person at all. Maybe there really was a logical reason for her actions.

Martinson sighed. "I think that you're right, but what can we do about it right now? This guy seems like our only hope to successfully catch Hara, and although she may not be the one that we should be focusing on, you can't deny that she's a problem right now. Once he catches her, I think we should start thinking about what to do with him."

"So you're going to agree with me when I say that we can't just let him leave with her?" Perry inquired hopefully.

Giving him a dubious look, Martinson said, "When you hit your head, did you lose your common sense? After that bastard pointed a gun at me, I knew he wasn't getting a free pass. But there's no problem in letting him think that for a little while, now is there?"

Smiling gratefully, Perry nodded to him. "It's nice to know I'll have someone on my side when the time comes for us to take action against him."

"Hey," Hersh cut in sharply. "I'll be there too, buddy. I'm not going to stand by and watch you two have all the fun hauling his ass to prison."

"And I'll be there too," Renee said quietly.

"Well," Martinson said with a sigh. "It's nice to see that we're all going to bat for the same team, but I think for now it'll be best if we get out there and see how this next hour or so plays out." He nodded out the back window.

The other three turned to see. The entire caravan had parked in the lot, The Doc's semi coming to a halt right alongside the building. Perry had no idea where the man had gotten another one, and he figured it was best if it stayed that way.

Martinson and Hersh both climbed out quickly and hurried over to join the group assembling at the center of the lot. Perry found himself wanting to just sit there for a second before joining them. He was tired, and his head was still aching. Plus, Renee hadn't gotten out either. Maybe they could have a minute to just talk.

"Are you going to get out?" Renee asked him quietly, her eyes on the back of the driver's seat.

Perry shrugged. "In a minute. You?"

"In a minute," Renee whispered.

Something was bothering her, and Perry knew what it was. "Are you going to be okay working with this guy, knowing what he's done?"

"Shawn," Renee said, turning her head to meet his awaiting gaze. "I don't know what he's done. That's what bothers me."

Nodding, Perry repeated his question. "So…are you going to be okay?"

With an irritated sigh, Renee shrugged. "I guess I'm going to have to be. I'm not in charge. If I don't like something, I just have to deal with it. I never thought that following orders would ever be this hard."

"Well, just think," Perry told her, trying to cheer her up. "All we have to do is put up with him until he can catch Hara. After that, he's done. He goes to prison, and we don't have to worry about him hurting anyone else ever again." Perry thought over what he just said, realizing that he had once said that exact same thing regarding Hara. It was amazing how fast things could change course.

"Right," Renee muttered, still gazing back at him. "It's just…I'm going to have a difficult time putting up with him for that long, knowing that he nearly killed you."

Finally, Perry thought in relief. It had taken so long for her to come out of her shell and express her feelings for him.

"I don't want to let that girl anywhere near him," Renee continued. "When you collapsed in the station this morning, I thought you were going to die. I really did. At the very least, I was certain that you would have brain damage. But then she helped you." She shook her head in amazement. "There's not even a mark left. An extraordinary gift that girl has, to heal the injured." Reaching up, Renee gently touched his left temple. There had been a decent sized cut there, but now not even a scar remained. "Does it even hurt?" she asked in a whisper, awestruck.

"I've a bit of a headache," he replied quietly, inhaling sharply from her touch. "But it could be worse." How he wished he could tell her everything he was feeling in that moment. When she touched him, he felt as if he were flying, like nothing could bring him out of that moment. When he touched her, he was drawn out of the world around him and he became aware of only her. Her warm, caring eyes, her waves of blonde hair rippling over her shoulders and down her back, her beautiful face. Her hand on his face. With his own hand, he reached up and wrapped it around hers.

Renee's eyes widened for a split second in a mixture of surprise and fear, but then they softened. Gazing back at him, she murmured, "Shawn, we can't do this now."

"Why not?" Perry whispered, holding her hand against the side of his face. He wanted nothing more than to just live in that moment, and he could see the longing in Renee's eyes as well. But for some reason it was making her uncomfortable. He could feel her uneasiness. Why was it so hard to just say how she felt?

There came a sudden rap at Perry's window that caused them both to jump and drop their hands. Annoyed, Perry turned and glowered at Lieutenant Odau, who asked, "Are you two coming?"

"Yeah," Perry said, scowling at him. "We are."

Renee was already getting out the other side. When Perry protested, she glanced back at him. "Because we have a job to do."

Their job. It was always their damn job. When was their job not going to get in the way?

In frustration, Perry kicked his door open, shoving Odau out of the way. Without apologizing, Perry marched after Renee towards everyone. Gathered in one group stood Agent Long, chatting with Martinson and Hersh. In another group were Finchly and Aubrey, standing awkwardly alongside Marcus and Brown. Off to the side was The Doc with his guards, but there weren't just two anymore. There were half a dozen standing around him. Each guard was over six feet tall with large muscles—tight t-shirts to show off those muscles—broad shoulders, expressions blank but indicating they could cause a great deal of damage. Who were these men? Perry had an urge to catch one of them when they were alone and question him about their business with The Doc, but he didn't think that any of them would want to talk. Besides, with their build, each one of them looked like they could kill him with one punch. He would keep his distance, and everybody else seemed to be doing the same.

The Doc was staring off into space. *What was he thinking about?* Perry wondered, knowing it couldn't be anything good. Perry looked in the direction of where he was looking and saw that he wasn't staring off into space; he was eyeing up Allan Brown and Daniel Marcus. The Doc gestured for two of his guards to come closer, and when they did he pointed at the two men who were currently talking softly with the two detectives. The guards nodded and started towards them.

Perry's pace quickened as the guards approached Brown and Marcus. He hadn't heard what The Doc told them to do, but he knew. And he wasn't going to allow it.

The group of four looked up in surprise as the guards reached them, each taking one of Brown's arms. They then started pulling him in the direction of the semi, not stopping despite the protests of the others. For a split second, the mayor and Perry made eye contact, and Perry saw the terrible fear in his eyes.

"Hey!" Perry shouted, his brisk walk turning into a run.

The other agents looked around at the sudden commotion. They immediately objected.

"What the hell do you think you're doing?" Martinson demanded, stepping in front of the guards and putting his arms out to stop them.

"Where the hell do you think you're taking him?" Agent Long snapped, glaring at The Doc viciously. "You can't just drag a man away like this!"

"Actually, I can," The Doc replied smugly. "I'd like to speak with this man for a few moments before Hara arrives. I believe that was part of our agreement."

"Our agreement was that you could speak to Jack!" Perry reminded furiously, marching over to Marcus and shoving him behind him in case they tried to take him too. "For ninety seconds while being supervised! This has nothing to do with Allan Brown!"

"This has everything to do with Allan Brown," The Doc said quietly. "And our agreement was that I could speak to any sources you may possess. That includes Allan Brown, Daniel Marcus, and Meg Hopper should you catch her. Those were the terms!" he snapped as Perry started to protest again. "You all agreed to those terms, so keep your mouths shut and deal with it. I'm going to speak to this man alone, and you're going to let me do so without any more of this nonsense. And you," he growled, jabbing his finger at Martinson. "You can stand aside now."

Martinson refused to move. He didn't take orders from The Doc. He looked to Agent Long.

Agent Long nodded his consent.

Martinson was shocked, but he stepped aside.

Perry was utterly horrified. "You're letting him go?" he said.

"We made a deal, Perry," Agent Long muttered, the regret raging in his eyes.

As Perry shot a baffled look at The Doc's smug face, he felt Marcus grab the back of his jacket and tug on it quickly. "Perry," he whispered fearfully. "You can't let them take him!"

Turning in surprise, Perry said, "Excuse me?"

Marcus's expression was mortified. "Don't let them take him!" he pleaded. "Please! The Doc will do more than just talk to him!"

Feeling the detective's fear, Perry looked back at the mayor. Brown turned his head and exchanged a terrified look with Marcus, struggling as hard as he could to pull away from his captors.

"I want him back in my custody before Hara arrives!" Odau was yelling at The Doc. Perry didn't hear the response. Marcus was begging in his ear again.

"Please! Stop them! You have no idea what's going to happen in that truck! I've seen it! You have to do something!"

"There's nothing I can do!" Perry apologized helplessly, watching as the two guards continued to drag Brown to The Doc's trailer. He knew that once Agent Long had made a decision, he would have to obey orders. He turned back to Marcus to explain how sorry he was, but he was startled to see that his expression had changed drastically. Marcus's eyes were still scared, but his lips were pursed and his face was now serious, even angry.

"I want you to know that I truly am very sorry for this," Marcus told him quietly, his voice quavering.

Confused, Perry asked, "What are you talking about?"

Giving him an apologetic look, Marcus grabbed him by the front of the jacket and kneed him in the groin as hard as he could. As Perry collapsed to the ground, he felt Marcus grab his gun from his holster. Gritting his teeth to keep from crying out, Perry curled up in agony. Hearing shouts from his colleagues, he looked up to see what was going on.

Marcus aimed the gun at the backs of the guards holding Brown, and before anyone could react he fired three times. Perry saw both guards go down hard, and then saw Brown take off running away from the station.

"Don't shoot him! Don't shoot him!" The Doc was shouting. Perry wasn't sure who he was defending; Brown or Marcus.

As soon as the guards were down, Marcus dropped Perry's gun and took off as well. He was running in the opposite direction as Brown. Perry knew he wasn't going to get very far.

"Stop!" everyone was yelling at him, a few people drawing out their weapons. "Marcus, freeze!"

Marcus didn't stop. Perry glanced away from him and caught The Doc pulling a small firearm out of his jacket pocket. It looked like the same one he had shown them back at the hospital. Taking careful aim, The Doc fired at Marcus.

Whatever was in that gun took effect immediately. Marcus dropped like a stone. Falling sideways onto the hood of a parked squad car, he rolled off and hit the ground hard. He started to convulse violently where he laid, his limbs twitching. After a while, the seizing began to lessen, and he stopped moving altogether.

"What the hell were you thinking?" Odau screamed at The Doc, rushing to Marcus's side. Perry's other colleagues hurried over as well, all except for Renee, who went to help him.

"Are you okay?" she asked. Kneeling beside him, she peered down at him.

Groaning in pain, Perry pushed himself onto his knees. Holding his groin, he stood up carefully and used Odau's squad car for support. Taking a deep breath, he straightened himself up, his cheeks red with embarrassment.

"Are you alright?" Renee repeated, taking his arm.

"Fine," he grumbled, forcing himself to walk in Marcus's direction. When he reached him, he gazed down at the detective. "How is he?"

Marcus did not appear well at all. His face was paler than a ghost's, and his lips were a deep purple. Lieutenant Odau and Detective Finchly were kneeling on either side of him and calling his name, but his eyes were staring dully up at the sky. Odau even tried slapping his face a few times, but he was unresponsive. He wasn't moving, except for an occasional twitch of his leg.

Rounding on The Doc, who had come up behind them and was peering down at Marcus curiously, Perry demanded, "What the hell did you shoot him with?"

Slipping the weapon back into his jacket, The Doc continued to watch Marcus. "A special tranquilizer mixed with a neurotoxin and a shock of about ten thousand volts," he told him. "A little something I cooked up. Like a tazer and tranquilizer in one. It comes in very handy."

"Why would you shoot him with something like that?" Odau asked furiously, still staying beside his detective. "He had no weapon and his back was turned to you!"

"Yes, but he also killed two of my men," The Doc said coldly, looking back to the bodies of his two companions. "And he helped his friend escape."

Perry realized that was true. In the confusion, nobody went after Brown. He was gone.

"So you shot him?" Finchly snapped angrily.

"I'm going to call an ambulance," Aubrey declared, whipping out his cell phone.

"Don't bother," The Doc replied, taking a few steps closer to Marcus. "He'll be fine in a few seconds. He's tough."

As he finished speaking, Marcus's entire body jerked upward. Falling back against the concrete, he began to cough heavily. There was a throaty sound to his breathing, like his airways were constricted. He began to move his legs slowly, and made an attempt to lift his arms before they fell back against him.

"Take it easy, man," Aubrey told him as Odau undid his handcuffs. Glancing around at everyone, he added, "We should get him into one of the holding cells as quickly as possible so he can rest."

"Good idea," Odau said, slipping the cuffs into one of his pockets and helping Aubrey pull Marcus to his feet. Each man put one of Marcus's arms over their shoulder as Marcus tried to steady himself, and then began to slowly walk forward. Marcus was trying to walk with them, but his legs looked like they were made of rubber. Neither one was moving properly, and he ended up being carried inside.

Finchly, Hersh, and Martinson accompanied the three of them into the station, leaving Perry, Renee, and Agent Long to deal with The Doc. The three of them turned around to face him, and The Doc took a careful step back at their infuriated expressions.

"Where do you get off thinking you can go around shooting people whenever you like?" Agent Long snarled.

"I was only helping you," The Doc declared, holding his ground as Agent Long got right up in his face. "He was a criminal, wasn't he? Did you want him to escape? I stopped him from getting away."

"Shooting him wasn't the answer!" Agent Long shouted.

"He killed two of my men," The Doc told him quietly, his eyes narrowing.

"If you do anything like this again, I'll kill you myself!" Agent Long growled.

Both men stared at each other for a long moment before Agent Long turned away and stalked angrily into the police station.

Perry and Renee both stared at The Doc for a while. Perry then took her by the arm and led her inside. He could feel The Doc's cold eyes burning holes into the back of his skull.

* * *

When Allan Brown felt solid ground beneath his feet once more, he stumbled as his knees buckled beneath him. Reaching out in a panic, his hand latched onto something hard and sturdy. Blinking as he tried to clear his vision, he looked around, disoriented. Everything around him was white. As his vision became more distinct and the objects around him came into focus, he tensed in fear as he saw where he was. Beside every bed was a tray filled with various types of medical equipment. Allan had grabbed onto the foot of one of the beds, and he let go as the dizziness left him.

The room had a sterile smell to it, making him cringe in panic. At first he thought he had accidentally ended up back in the lab, but then he realized what it really was. It was just an ordinary hospital room.

Sighing in relief, Allan cried out and clutched at his head as a fiery pain shot through it. It was excruciating, and he held his breath hoping that it would soon pass. When it didn't, he reached out to support himself on the bed again.

Oh God, he thought in horror as the pain grew steadily worse. *I've used my ability too many times! It's killing me!* His vision was now going red, and he groaned from the terrible throbbing.

After several long, agonizing moments, he heard a door open in front of him and someone stepped inside. It scared Allan that he couldn't see who was there with him, or that he wouldn't be able to teleport away in self-defense if he was attacked. He prayed that whoever was with him was a friend.

Allan heard the person shuffling around in the room, but then all of a sudden the sound stopped. He heard what sounded like papers falling to the floor, and then the uncertain whisper of, "Mr. Mayor?"

Relief flooded through him as Allan realized who the voice belonged to. "Dr. Bennett," he choked out, reaching out his free hand. He still couldn't see, but he knew that Dr. Bennett was in front of him.

"Dear God," Bennett said in horror, and Allan heard him rush over. "Your nose is bleeding and you're as white as the walls! What the hell happened?"

"The Doc has Daniel," Allan tried to tell him, but his words were slurring. "Had to use my ability to escape…"

"How many times have you used your ability in the past twenty-four hours?" Bennett asked him, taking Allan's free hand with his own and putting the other on his forehead.

"Too many," Allan breathed, falling to his knees.

"Allan!" Bennett called, catching him as he started to fall backwards. But his voice was becoming hazier and hazier as Allan's consciousness began to slip. "Allan! Talk to me!"

The last thought Allan had was of Daniel. What was going to happen to him? Would The Doc kill him for what he did? Allan blacked out before Bennett could set him gently on the floor.

* * *

Ten minutes had passed since Marcus had been brought inside, and things had pretty much settled down. Marcus was sleeping in his holding cell, Agents Long, Hersh, and Martinson were discussing what to do if Hara managed to escape again, and Lieutenant Odau, and Detectives Finchly and Aubrey were setting up their interrogation room for Hara's arrival. The last anyone heard, The Doc and his men were disposing of the dead bodies outside.

Other than the soft voices of Perry's colleagues, the station was pretty much silent. All of the other officers were still helping with the mess downtown, so they were the only people in the building.

There had been a short discussion regarding what to do about Allan Brown, but everyone decided to just let him go for a while. They already had enough to deal with: Marcus, Hara, The Doc. Allan Brown seemed like a very minor problem at the moment.

Since Perry didn't have much to do and he was feeling rather anxious just sitting around and waiting, he decided to go look for Renee to try to talk to her. Finchly said she saw her in the conference room a few minutes before, so Perry decided he would check there first. He had noticed that Renee had looked upset after Marcus was shot.

About three years earlier, there was a terrorist group in Philadelphia that was planning to smuggle explosives to different parts of the country. A group of agents were sent to a warehouse where the operation was unfolding. Renee and her older brother Josh were both on the team. There was a struggle, and in the firefight they lost four agents. One of them was Josh. The death of her brother was very hard on her, and ever since it was difficult for her to fire her weapon at anyone or watch another person be shot. Marcus was going to be okay, but it was still bothering Renee.

Once he reached the conference room, he paused just outside the door and took a deep breath. He wasn't sure how to speak to her after their awkward moment, and he wasn't sure if he would be able to comfort her. Turning the knob, he pushed open the door and stepped inside. Sure enough, Renee was sitting at the table with stacks of papers surrounding her. Her briefcase was open, and more papers were stacked inside. She was reading intently, her brow furrowed in concentration. Perry hadn't a clue what she was doing, but he figured it was something to distract her. He closed the door behind him, and Renee's head snapped up in surprise.

"Oh," she said when she saw him. "Hey, Shawn." She gave him a small smile, but Perry could see she was faking it.

"Hey," he said back, walking around the table to her. "You okay?"

"Yeah," she lied, glancing down at her papers. Gesturing to them all, she added, "Yeah, I'm great. I'm just…going over my notes."

"Are you sure?" Perry asked, peering down at her.

Appearing irritated, she sighed. "Yes, I'm sure. I'm just trying to make sense of this whole damn thing."

Perry told her quietly, "You know, you don't need to lie to me."

Pursing her lips angrily, Renee said, "Shawn, I was fine until you came in here and started pestering me. So how about you take your sympathy and go throw it at someone else!"

"Renee," Perry started sternly. "We've been partners for nearly five years, friends for even longer than that. I think we can have a talk when you're upset about something."

"I am not upset!" Renee shouted, slamming her palm down on the table and standing up quickly. Her breathing was fast and heavy, and she was glaring at him with a sense of indignation.

In a soft voice, Perry asked her, "Then why are you yelling at me?"

"Because…" Renee couldn't say what she was thinking. She let out a frustrated cry. "You treat me like a child! Ever since Josh died, you've been hovering over me like you're my father! Every time we deal with an incident where someone ends up getting shot in front of me, you're always there, trying to get me to talk about my feelings! It drives me crazy! You drive me crazy!"

"It's only because I care about you," Perry explained, taking a step towards her.

Renee yelled, "Have you ever thought that maybe I don't need—let alone want—you to care about me? Did it ever occur to you that maybe there was a reason I came in here alone? I knew you would do this, and here's a news flash for you: I don't want to talk to anyone! If I have an issue with something, I'll deal with it myself!"

"Renee, stop it!" Perry said, coming towards her again.

"No, you stop it!" Renee snapped back, balling her hand into a fist and punching him in the chest. She was very angry; her eyes showed that and her punch had actually been meant to cause pain. And it had. "You're always so nosy and stubborn! Why can't you give me my own space?" She hit him again.

"That's enough!" Perry said, grabbing her wrist after she struck him.

"Let go of me!" she cried, trying to pull away. Tears were beginning to stream down her face, and when Perry refused to let go she cried even harder. "Get away from me!"

Grabbing her other arm as she tried to hit him again, Perry pulled her towards him and wrapped his arms around her. It pained him to see her in this state, and he wanted to do everything in his power to comfort her.

"Let go!" Renee sobbed, clawing at his arms as he held her.

"*Shh,*" Perry hushed gently. As Renee continued to cry on his shoulder, Perry continued to hold her and comfort her. She had stopped fighting him and now just gripped him tightly as she sobbed. "Everything's going to be okay."

"I just can't get the image of Marcus's face out of my head!" she whispered, and Perry felt her shudder against him. "That confused, helpless look on his face… It was the same look Josh had on his face before he died! It was horrible!"

"*Shh, shh,*" Perry said again, turning his head slightly so he could speak into her ear. "I know how hard it's been for you since Josh died. I've seen it in your eyes every day. I know it was difficult for you to watch Marcus get shot, even though he's going to be fine. Every time you draw your weapon, I see the same question in your eyes. Can I really pull this trigger? I need you to know that I understand how you feel. I've lost family too. And I need you to know that I'm here for you. I'll always be here for you." Closing his eyes, he sighed. He wanted to tell her how sorry he was, but there was no way to. He wanted to tell her how much he loved her, but there was no easy way to say that either. There were many things he wanted to say to her in that moment. He kept his mouth shut.

"Well, I guess that just about says everything," Renee choked out suddenly.

Puzzled, Perry asked, "What do you mean?"

"I've been trying so hard to tell myself to forget about you, that I can't be with you," she explained, hugging him tighter. "We shouldn't be together. It's dangerous as partners. If we get distracted by one another… I kept telling myself to ignore you whenever you gave me that look, that it was all just my imagination. But it wasn't. It never was. And trust me, it was so hard to try and pull away from you every time you started to talk to me. I didn't want my personal feelings to get in the way of my job. But I guess it's a little too late for that." Pulling away from him, she looked up at him. "I know you'll always be there for me, and that's what bothers me. When you came in here, I knew you did because you cared about what happened and you wanted to help me. You were really the only one who was always there for me after Josh died, and it made me angry because I knew you could see right through me. That scared me. I didn't think anyone could ever know me that well."

Reaching up, Perry wiped the tears from her face. "There's got to be at least one person," he told her quietly.

Renee smiled weakly.

Giving her a small smile in return, Perry bent his head down and kissed her. He had no idea how long the kiss lasted. It could have been a few seconds, or it could have been several minutes. He wasn't really sure of anything anymore.

When they finally pulled apart, Perry felt a surprising amount of relief. He had needed her to see what he had been trying to show her: the love he felt for her. He felt that that kiss expressed a lot of what was to come. Gazing back into Renee's soft eyes, he forgot all his problems. The remarkable feeling didn't last long. Renee's eyes focused beyond Perry for a split second, and then she stepped back quickly and turned away with a horrified look on her face. Turning in surprise, Perry saw that The Doc was standing in the doorway. Leaning against the door frame with his hands in his pockets, he stared back at them with that same odd look of curiosity.

Feeling his cheeks become hot with anger, Perry stepped in front of Renee as The Doc's eyes locked onto her. "How long have you been standing there?" he demanded sharply.

"Long enough," The Doc answered with a smirk.

Striding up to him, Perry growled, "Is there something you want, or do you just enjoy spying on people?"

His expression unchanging, The Doc paused before saying, "The others were wondering if the two of you wouldn't mind joining the group at the interrogation room. Hara will be here in about ten minutes."

"And so instead of just delivering the message like you were supposed to, you decided to stand there and watch us?" Perry snapped.

Cocking his head to one side, The Doc leaned in and whispered, "It's not like I didn't already know you two had a thing for each other. It was obvious from the first moment I saw you two together."

Grabbing The Doc by the front of his jacket, Perry pulled him closer so they were less than an inch apart. As Perry glared furiously into his eyes, he just grinned mockingly back. He wasn't taking a hint.

"What are you going to do, huh?" he asked, his eyes challenging. "Are you going to hit me? Hmm? Go ahead. I dare you." He waited, but Perry gave him no response. "I know your little secret, so hit me."

It was tempting. After everything that man had put him through, it took a lot of self-control to keep from knocking all his teeth out. Perry gripped the man's jacket tightly in his fists and fought to get his breathing under control.

"No?" The Doc said, raising his eyebrows.

Continuing to glare at him, Perry shoved The Doc backwards. He stumbled, but the smirk never left him. Once he regained his balance, he snickered and told him, "No, you're intelligent enough to know that that wouldn't end well."

"Get out of my face!" Perry snarled, stepping through the door and shoving past him. Fuming, he started to march down the hall in the direction of the interrogation room. But then he stopped when he realized he had left Renee behind. Alone. With The Doc. Turning back around, he hurried back to the conference room.

The Doc was still standing in the doorway and looking at Renee. While Perry was approaching, he started to take a step into the room. Before he got more than a few feet inside, Perry's hand snapped out and caught him around the arm. The Doc turned his head in surprise, but his smirk was still present.

"Stay away from her," Perry warned in a deadly voice. "Or I'll kill you."

Raising his eyebrows again, The Doc nodded and pulled his arm free before leaving.

Scowling after him, Perry peered into the room at Renee. She was gazing back at him with a worried expression on her face, but once they both made eye contact she looked down and began scooping up her papers. Perry shook his head and followed The Doc, praying that the man would actually listen to him and stay away from her.

✳ ✳ ✳

By the time Marcus awoke in the holding cell, the side effects of the Corkscrew dart had worn off. His muscles still tingled, but other than that he felt perfectly fine. Physically, anyway. He knew while he was doing it that the move he made had been very unwise, but he couldn't let The Doc take Allan. After everything The Doc had done to Allan in the past, Marcus knew better when he said that he only wanted to question him. So Marcus had stolen Perry's gun, shot two of The Doc's guards dead, and then allowed Allan to escape unscathed. His little stunt would cost him his life. He knew that much. He was going to die.

Since his own telepathic abilities were of no interest to The Doc, his life wasn't worth anything to him. That's why he only tried to take Allan. Allan's ability to teleport was always a marvel to The Doc. He wanted to study Allan more and more so he could learn as much about it as possible. Allowing Allan to escape made The Doc quite angry, and being of little significance to him, Marcus was going to pay a steep price. It was amazing he had lasted so long. He prepared himself for it, nevertheless. For some time he was certain he was going to suffer at the hands of The Doc. He was never locked up in a lab, but he always knew that in the end it would be The Doc who would take his life.

A story had been told to him a few years before—more of a prophecy, really—that hinted at his fate. He was told that he would die at the hands of a soul-less being, someone who had lost all his humanity. It was said that he would die because he would do a valiant thing, a selfless act that most others would not have done. After he saved Allan, the prophecy came back to his mind. Helping save the life of his friend while putting his own life on the line was a very valiant act. The Doc could definitely be compared to the devil and had proven that he didn't have much humanity left in him. Now that the connection was made, Marcus knew that his time was coming.

The worst part about it was just sitting there waiting.

He wasn't awake for more than twenty minutes before the door to the containment unit slowly creaked open. Marcus was sitting on his bench in his cage with his hands clasped together and his eyes on the ground. He knew that The Doc would come for him while he was alone and vulnerable like he was, but he was doing his best not to think about his approaching death. He was trying to think about all the things in his life that made him happy. He remembered being in the care of Dr. Perry, a kind man named Patrick Lemoore, and Hara's mother after the start of the outbreak. He recalled being taken to their new permanent home and taken in by Hara's mother and father until they could find foster parents to care for him. He remembered the beach where he always went when he needed cheering up. The festival that was held every year to celebrate their Independence Day, swimming with the orcas in the ocean, his pet red panda named Stitch, preventing crime with Hara's father, falling in love under the full moon...

More recently, he met the love of his life, or his "soul mate" as his kind called it. Her name was Anna, and she was amazing. She was the best thing that had ever happened to him. They had a daughter together, whom they named Cara, and his little girl had been just one more joy added to his life. But then The Doc came into their world and took his soul mate from him after killing Cara.

It had been the most awful experience he ever endured. After he fought his part in the war and Hara sent him and the other two back to Philadelphia, he did his best to just forget them. Their memories brought too much pain, so he thought that forgetting they ever existed would bring his sorrow to an end. Now that he was thinking of them, he wished he had spent more time remembering them. All the amazing moments they cherished together, all the fun times they shared. It seemed like a lifetime ago that he last thought of his family, and he realized just how much he missed them. But he was surprised to find that thinking of his deceased family actually comforted him. Thinking of them, for some strange reason, made him feel at peace. So when The Doc finally entered the room, Marcus sucked in a deep breath and continued to think of their beautiful faces.

He was ready.

Since he was keeping his eyes on the floor, Marcus could only see The Doc out of the corner of his eye. When he stepped inside, Marcus saw him stop for a few seconds before he slowly walked over to the wall beside the desk. He was going for the keys to the cage. He didn't speak, and that made the discomfort in the room even worse. Unable to take it anymore, Marcus looked up at him. As he did so, two of The Doc's body guards stepped into the room as well, closing it quietly behind them. Their emotionless expression made Marcus shudder. Glancing over at The Doc, he saw him take the keys off of the hook on the wall. Tossing them up in the air, he then caught them in the palm of his hand and looked up at Marcus.

"Hi, Daniel," he said softly, walking around the cage until he reached the gate.

His stomach started churning, so Marcus closed his eyes and lowered his head. Just think about Anna and Cara, he kept telling himself. Don't think about him. The pace of his heart was beginning to quicken, but he was going to keep calm, no matter what.

"Surprised to see me?" The Doc asked him snidely, and Marcus heard the door swing open.

"Actually, I've been waiting for you," Marcus replied as The Doc came closer, impressed by the smoothness to his voice. He felt The Doc take a seat beside him, just inches away. It was difficult not to cringe.

"Really?" The Doc said thoughtfully. For a while he didn't say anything else, like he was waiting for Marcus to speak. But Marcus had no reply. "That was a very noble thing you did, saving Allan. But it was also quite stupid. You do know that, right?"

Sighing, Marcus nodded. It was stupid, but he would never regret it.

"Then you also know why I have to do this?"

Slowly, Marcus raised his head to face The Doc. His heart was thumping, but he wasn't scared. Not anymore. "And you know what Hara will do about it?"

The Doc's expression was solemn, cold. At first, Marcus thought there was a bit of an apologetic tone to his voice, but he could see that he was mistaken. He had no remorse. "Oh, yes," he said, his cold eyes bitter. "I'm hoping this will give me the reaction I need from her right now."

Marcus couldn't believe the words he just heard. Incredulously, he whispered, "So that's what this is all about? You're going to kill me just to make her angry?"

Leaning closer, The Doc told him, "It's much more than that." Searching Marcus's face, he explained, "You let Allan get away. And you killed two of my guards."

"So?" Marcus muttered, forcing himself to hold eye contact. "You killed my entire race."

The Doc snickered. "You really hate me, don't you? But killing your race isn't the reason you hate me. No, you hate me because I killed your daughter. Right in front of you. That's it, isn't it?"

Pain and anger stabbing at his chest, Marcus looked down.

"Isn't it?" The Doc whispered, leaning forward to attempt to make eye contact again. "Your sweet little girl. Your only child. What was her name? Kara?"

"Cara," Marcus corrected harshly, his voice cracking as he spoke her name. Squeezing his eyes shut, he felt a single tear fall from his eye to the floor.

"Right," The Doc murmured, and Marcus sensed him nod. "Watching your daughter die right in front of you must have been an awful experience. But feeling her go must have been even worse. Am I right?"

Nodding again, more tears spilled from Marcus's eyes. Feeling his daughter die, her soul disconnecting from his, had been one of the most horrendous pains he had ever suffered. He was too full of grief to speak, but The Doc was handling the silence easily. That man always had a knack for inflicting pain—physical and emotional—on others.

"Yeah, you've probably missed her a great deal," he went on, knowing how much agony he was causing Marcus. He was enjoying every moment of it. "And your soul mate. Anna, right? It must have been difficult coming here, starting a new life without them, pretending as if they never were." There was a pause. "Tell me, what did it feel like when your family died?"

"Are you going to get on with it, or are you just going to keep torturing me like this?" Marcus demanded, looking up and giving him a pleading gaze. "Yes, I hate you with every ounce of my heart and soul for what you did. Yes, I miss my family. You don't even know. Yes, it was very hard to come here and act like nothing ever happened." He took a deep breath. "Feeling my family die was worse than any physical pain I have ever endured."

"But what did it feel like?" The Doc persisted, leaning forward again. He was really enjoying himself.

"I know you take pride in causing people pain, but I've had enough!" Marcus cried. "I've suffered for nearly three years. I don't need your help to make me feel any worse."

"Tell me," The Doc ordered slowly, "what it felt like."

Marcus opened his mouth to respond angrily, but then he stopped and took a good long look at The Doc. He wasn't mocking him with that repeated question. He really wanted to know. There was an eagerness, a desperation so deep inside him. Something had happened to him—whether it was a long time ago or recently, Marcus did not know—an event powerful enough for the answer to that question to hold meaning to him. Had he lost someone close? Had he lost someone without feeling them go? Did he wish that he could feel that same pain that Marcus felt? It was impossible. Nobody could ever love that monster. The Doc just wanted more answers to his never-ending inquiries. Marcus wasn't going to indulge him. He wasn't going to put himself through any more pain to satisfy that man. His voice barely a whisper, Marcus said, "Just kill me."

Blinking, The Doc peered at him curiously. "Aren't you scared?"

Had he not caught himself, Marcus would have blurted out a yes without even pausing to think about it. His heart was pounding and his stomach was doing so many flip-flops it hurt. But he didn't fear death. After his suffering, the end was a relief. Death was the easy way out. The pain that might come with death gave him fear, but death itself was not frightening. Gazing back into The Doc's pitiless eyes, Marcus answered, "No."

The Doc had obviously not been expecting that answer, because his eyebrows came together and a look of befuddlement crossed him. "No?" he repeated.

Shaking his head, Marcus said, "I'm not afraid. I've come to terms with it. I think that I did a long time ago, probably when my family died. What else have I got left here? I live in a shitty apartment in this dying, depressing world. I work for the father of Jackson Odau. How shameful is that? My family has moved on to the Afterlife, and as long as I can be with them I don't care where I go. In killing me, you'll be doing me a huge favor."

"Huh," The Doc said, nodding absentmindedly. "For some reason, I thought I would be trying to calm you down by now."

"I don't fear death," Marcus stated. "Now, life…that is something I fear."

"So, how did it feel?" The Doc asked the familiar question, but this time he was mocking him. "How did it feel, knowing exactly how you were going to die?"

Startled, by the question, Marcus stared back at him. He hadn't said anything about the prophecy. "What are you talking about?"

"Oh, you know exactly what I'm talking about," The Doc insisted, his eyes narrowing to slits.

Stammering, Marcus finally felt afraid. "How…how did you know? I never said anything about it…"

"I know you didn't," The Doc said softly. "But all the same, I'd like an answer."

"But…" Marcus was so confused. "How? How could you know? That information was only told to me."

His expression blank, The Doc whispered, "You're not the only one who's hiding something, Daniel."

It came to mind that maybe he didn't want to know how The Doc knew. The Doc had ways of getting information out of people. Had he found Clyde Stetzer, the man who made the prophecy? "I don't know how," Marcus said, and he was thankful for that. "I just had a hint as to when." A sudden memory crossed his mind, one that was also beginning to come into perspective. "Come to think of it, I think I was also told about how you would die."

This knowledge deeply interested The Doc. "Please share," he requested, his eyes intent on learning about his death. Marcus knew why. He wanted to prevent his death. But there was no way to prevent something that was already set in stone. Whatever Clyde Stetzer saw in a prophecy, no matter how disturbing or absurd, it always came true.

"Why should I?" Marcus asked quietly. Even if he did share, The Doc would kill him anyway. If he didn't, he would only buy himself a few minutes while The Doc tried to persuade him to talk, but in the end he would still die. It didn't really make much of a difference if he shared or not; each decision would buy him a few extra minutes. But, sharing the information might put some fear into The Doc. That would be a comforting thought to die with, knowing that he had scared The Doc. Sighing, he repeated Clyde Stetzer's prophecy. "'In the same time that you will die, the time of war and pain and death, two demons shall fall. One will suffer a fate worse than death; the other will be judged for his wrongdoings. His fate from then until death is unknown, but one thing is certain: he will be killed by one of those whom he scarred, and sentenced to an eternity of hell.'"

It was working. The Doc was trying to play it cool, but Marcus saw the glint of uncertainty in his eyes. "Would you mind explaining what that's supposed to mean?"

"What do you think it means?" Marcus asked.

Now The Doc was getting irritated. His eyes cold, The Doc demanded, "And what is this eternity of hell supposed to be?"

Shrugging, Marcus told him, "I guess you'll just have to wait and find out."

The Doc sighed in frustration. He was getting nowhere. "Who is supposed to be the other demon?"

Astonished, Marcus snarled, "How about the girl whose life you ruined, the girl who you're still torturing! Know her?"

"And she's supposed to suffer something worse than death?" The Doc asked, his expression serious.

Marcus whispered sadly, "She already has."

A small grin began to creep onto The Doc's face. "You're a little dramatic."

Completely disgusted, Marcus made a face. "Am I? After everything you did to her, I'm surprised she hasn't tried to kill herself!"

"Oh, she has," The Doc corrected him, his expression turning to a harsh glare. "But she can't die, remember?"

"You disgust me," Marcus replied with a scowl. "You're using me to torture that poor child to suit your own diabolical needs! You're a vile, twisted person, and I hope that Hara is the one to lead you to your eternity of hell!"

For a moment, the two men just glared at each other. Marcus was so infuriated that he completely forgot why The Doc was there in the first place. It made him so angry that The Doc was about to commit this heinous act just to make Hara snap. That man was a selfish, cruel excuse of a human being, but at least he would eventually pay for everything he'd done. And after he was gone, Marcus prayed that Hara would unleash everything she'd been holding back and destroy every last remnant of The Doc.

Without much of a warning, The Doc whipped his arm at Marcus and struck him square in the chest. Marcus started to cry out as pain erupted around his heart, but his breath had left him. Looking down, he saw that The Doc had just jabbed him with a large syringe. There was a murky brown liquid inside, and Marcus knew all too well what it was. He had seen it before.

With the needle piercing through his chest, it was quite difficult for Marcus to breath. He tried sucking in a lungful of air, only to be rewarded with a fiery pain every time he inhaled. When The Doc began injecting him with the liquid, the agony became much worse. If he had been able to he would have yelled. His hand automatically shot out in an attempt to pull the syringe out, but The Doc caught his wrist and held it away. Marcus was in too much pain to fight back

"*Shh*," The Doc whispered as Marcus groaned. As the last bit of liquid was drained into him, The Doc leaned closer so he could speak into Marcus's ear. "Thanks for your input, but telling me how I'm supposed to die wouldn't have kept me from doing this." Pulling the syringe out, he caught Marcus by the shoulder as he started to fall forward. As The Doc pushed him back against the bars of the cell, Marcus's eyes wandered to the ceiling. His arm was released, and he clutched at his chest as it began to burn. Gasping for breath, his eyes fluttered as his vision got significantly darker. He managed to make out the figure of The Doc as he was walking back to the gate, and he forced himself to speak. He had one last thing to say.

"The rest of my kind will come for you," Marcus promised in a dull whisper, the light around him winking out. He had gone blind. Thankfully, there was no more pain. Exhaustion was all that remained. He could feel his heart beating slower and slower, until it was barely working at all. "And when they do, you'd better beg for mercy. It'll be amazing if they offer you any at all."

Marcus closed his eyes, but he knew that The Doc was still standing there, staring at him. "Rest well, Daniel," he said softly after a moment. The gate clicked closed, and there were footsteps moving away.

"I feel sorry for you," Marcus mumbled, and that was all that he had energy left for. His head lolled to the side, banging painfully against the iron bars. Had he been able to see, he might have seen The Doc turn back one last time with pain burning in his eyes.

After a few more seconds, Daniel heard the door close and was forced to listen to the slowing pace of his heart. Now that the pain was gone, he realized that dying wasn't so bad. It was easy. With the pain, his terrified thoughts had also left him. For the first time in nearly three years, he finally felt a sense of ease. The only thing that was left to bother him was the lingering question of what Hara was going to do once she discovered his body. Would she snap and finally kill The Doc? Would she destroy the entire city in her anger, or would her emotions simply get the best of her? Would she break down and allow herself to be captured? The Doc had played them. Again. He refused to take her without a fight; that was just how he was. Hara knew that as a fact, which was why she had agreed to the calm, face to face encounter with him. But The Doc must have figured out right away what they were doing. He wouldn't let it end without a fight. The fault in Daniel's plan was that he hadn't paused to think through what would happen after he was taken into custody. He didn't pause to think what would happen if he died. And now he had to ask himself the question: what next?

No one could answer that.

But as Daniel Marcus took his final, shaky breath, he didn't think about The Doc or Hara or anything else to do with the war. He didn't worry about what was to happen in the future. No, his dying thoughts were of his family, of the wonderful, beautiful years they had spent together. His last moments were spent remembering the best moments, hoping that wherever he went next, he would find his girls again.

✳ ✳ ✳

By 9:27 a.m., everyone was in position. It had taken a few minutes to locate The Doc, who was eventually found lurking in one of the back hallways (as Perry had phrased it). The Doc quickly situated himself in the interrogation room, with Lieutenant Odau accompanying him for the time being. Everyone else was in the small observation room overlooking them, planning on intently watching Hara's confrontation with The Doc.

"So when did you first discover Hara's kind?" Odau asked after a minute or so of awkward silence. The Doc had requested that he stay just inside the door until Hara arrived, and he had agreed to do so. He wasn't sure why, but he agreed anyway. By capturing Hara, The Doc was saving his son's life. The lieutenant decided that honoring that simple request could be a small gesture of gratitude.

The Doc took a seat at the table in the chair facing the door, so he and Odau were facing each other. For some time The Doc had been examining the designs of the rusted, flaking paint on the surface of the table, but when Odau spoke he glanced up. "Why are you so interested?"

Odau shrugged and looked back at the floor. Every time The Doc looked at him, every time they made eye contact, the lieutenant couldn't help but feel a strange sense of familiarity. Everything about The Doc, from his eyes and hair color, to his facial expressions, to his body posture, and even to the way he spoke, reminded him of someone. It made him uneasy. It was like his presence there shouldn't be possible. He was a friend, but at the same time he was not wanted. And no matter how hard he tried, he just could not place him. He felt like he should be able to fairly easily, but he couldn't put a name to the face.

"I've known about them for a long time," The Doc answered suddenly.

Odau looked up in surprise, having not expected an answer. The Doc was gazing back with a peculiar look of fascination. That expression was also familiar, yet it caused some discomfort in the pit of his stomach.

What bothered him the most were the eyes. He had seen The Doc's eyes before, several times in fact. Still, there was no placing them.

"Since their beginning, actually," The Doc continued conversationally, glancing up at the one-way mirror. Neither of them could see into the next room, but Odau was certain that everyone there was listening intently. "I didn't learn about Hara until just a few years back though. She was sort of a breakthrough in my studies, really. A very fascinating child, she is. If you were a scientist like me, you would understand."

Nodding uncertainly, Odau stared back at him and struggled to place his face. But once again, he was unsuccessful. He decided to ask about it, because it was entirely possible that The Doc recognized him. "Have we met before? You seem so familiar to me."

A strange look crossed The Doc's face. He actually looked scared. Even sick. "I think we may have crossed paths once or twice before, yes," he said, nodding slowly.

Feeling relieved that he wasn't just imagining things, Odau pressed on eagerly, "Do you know where? I'm certain that we've seen each other before, but I just can't place you."

The look didn't leave The Doc's face. "No," he said through his teeth. "I don't know where." He looked down.

Odau was certain that The Doc really did know where they had met before, but he decided not to pursue it. The topic of conversation clearly bothered The Doc. Odau didn't know why he cared about that, but he did. So he changed the subject. "What do you think she wants to talk to you about?"

"Oh, I'm sure she just wants to try to kill me," The Doc responded, not seeming worried by that at all.

Confused, Odau waited for him to say more, but when the room was met with only silence the lieutenant asked, "And that doesn't bother you?"

Glancing back up, The Doc smirked. "I'm a smooth talker," he told him slyly. "There have been many times when Hara was going to kill me, but didn't because I managed to talk my way out of it. It's not that difficult. You just need to know the right things to say. Her emotions control her, and I control her emotions. By the time our meeting is over, I'll have her under my control again."

"What do you want us to do when she comes?"

Shrugging, The Doc replied, "Stay out of her way. Let her come in on her own. Listen quietly. Don't do anything that will threaten her. We're standing on very thin ice with her as it is, and I don't want her to hurt anyone else because you startled her. Make her feel welcome. Do you get what I'm saying?"

If Odau was being truthful, he would have answered no. Why should he make Hara feel welcome after what she did? She put his ten-year-old son in intensive care with burns and bruises all over his body, killed three innocent children, destroyed part of the downtown, and left hundreds of people dead and thousands more terrified. And now The Doc was asking him to make her feel welcome? He wanted to ask if putting a bullet in the back of her head was considered welcoming, but instead he just nodded. "Sure."

Cocking his head to one side, The Doc told him, "You don't look so sure."

With a shrug, Odau lowered his eyes again.

"You really don't like her, do you?" The Doc pointed out.

"You're kidding me," Odau said, dumbfounded. "You've seen what she's done! All that destruction! Hundreds of people are dead! Of course I don't like her!" He had been planning to leave his son out of the discussion, but he knew immediately that The Doc was going to bring him up.

"What about your son?" he asked, his brow furrowed in perplexity. "She tried to kill him too, didn't she? Didn't that upset you?"

Taken aback, Odau declared, "Of course it did! He's my son, for crying out loud! I just…don't want it to seem like my personal feelings are interfering with the investigation." He had been thinking a lot about what Perry said to him before the road chase, and he realized that his emotions really were getting the best of him. At The Doc's curious expression, Odau insisted, "But I love my son. I'd do anything for him. When Hara went into my house and I watched her try to take him away from me…it was the hardest thing I've ever had to deal with in my life."

The pain that crossed into The Doc's eyes was only visible for a moment, but it was long enough for Odau to see. Startled, he blinked. But then he understood. "You have children too?"

His expression hardened. "Not anymore."

Shocked, Odau stared at him in a mixture of surprise and pain. Not anymore… Was that supposed to mean they were dead? Had Hara killed them? The questions kept coming to him, but he didn't dare speak one aloud. How much pain The Doc must be feeling for the loss of his children. Odau almost lost a child, but The Doc actually had. It was difficult enough trying to recover after watching his son get abducted, but he didn't know what it was like to completely lose a child. If The Doc had lost one, Odau didn't want to make him feel any worse by asking him questions about it.

"So she tried to murder your son, blew up a large portion of the city, and killed countless numbers of people," The Doc muttered thoughtfully. "I can understand how that would make you dislike her."

Gritting his teeth, Odau wanted to tell him it was more like he loathed her. But again, he kept his mouth shut.

"She really is a good person though," The Doc told him quietly. At Odau's astonished look, he added, "At least she used to be."

"I don't understand how someone like her could have ever been good," Odau said stubbornly.

His eyes narrowing slightly, The Doc replied, "I used to be a good person."

Odau didn't respond.

"But we've both changed," The Doc continued casually. "It's apparent that she's changed a lot since the last time I saw her. She didn't used to be anything like this."

"Why is she doing this?" Odau demanded, hoping he would finally get a straight answer.

"Because she's angry," The Doc answered. "I hurt her, and now she's trying to get even."

"And how is she getting her revenge by bringing havoc upon Philadelphia?" Odau asked, annoyed yet puzzled.

Shaking his head, The Doc apologized, "I know this isn't the answer you want to hear, but the truth is that you really wouldn't understand."

Biting his tongue so he wouldn't have another outburst, Odau sighed in frustration and looked back down at the floor. Perry was right; there were too many mysteries building upon each other, and none of them were getting answered clearly. What was so complicated about everything that no one would explain what was going on? Did they all think that he and his unit were idiots?

"I suppose this is just a way for her to tell me that I can't always control her," The Doc informed. "And she wants to show me how much damage and chaos she can cause, just like I've shown her how much I can cause."

Suspiciously, Odau questioned, "What exactly happened between the two of you?"

Slowly, The Doc turned his head to his right and looked out at the one-way glass. He knew that Perry and the others were watching and listening to their conversation, and it seemed as if he wanted to tell the lieutenant but wouldn't in front of the others. It made Odau wonder what was so special about him.

Turning also, Odau looked at his reflection in the glass. His face was exhausted, with his eyes sunken and purple circles around them. He hadn't slept in well over twenty-four hours, and was certain he wouldn't get any rest for quite some time.

The Doc glanced back to him, his expression very serious. "You need to leave now."

"Excuse me?" Odau said in surprise.

"You need to go," The Doc repeated insistently, his tone becoming impatient.

"Why?" Odau demanded, looking down at his watch. It read 9:30 exactly. Realizing why The Doc wanted him out, he looked back up.

Carefully, The Doc gestured with his head behind him.

Puzzled, Odau glanced behind The Doc, but didn't see anything or anyone there. Then he remembered Hara's capabilities, and he stared at The Doc in alarm. "Is she here?" he whispered.

Nodding, The Doc raised an eyebrow. "I really think you should leave now."

Shooting one more prudent look over The Doc's shoulder, Odau nodded once and turned towards the door.

"And Lieutenant, no matter what happens, don't let anyone through that door."

Unsure of how to respond, Odau left the room, a grim feeling sweeping over him.

✳ ✳ ✳

Anger. Uncontrollable rage. That was all Hara could feel when she saw The Doc again. There was no fear. Only fury. Her entire body was shaking as she attempted to keep herself rooted where she was. If she moved too quickly, her camouflage would be ruined. It was difficult, but she managed.

When Lieutenant Odau finally left the room, it took all of her self-control to not immediately pounce on The Doc. She was going to kill him, but first she needed to say some things that had needed saying for a very long time. So she held her ground, forcing herself to wait.

For several moments the room was completely silent, until The Doc turned his head slightly to the side. "I know you're there, kiddo," he told her, his voice soft. "You don't have to hide from me."

Hara slowly walked around the table to stand on the side opposite him. Her camouflage was gone now, and she heard the surprised thoughts of everyone on the other side of the one-way glass. But she wasn't focusing on them. She was busy trying to contain her abilities that were begging to be set free.

Once she was facing The Doc, she was sure to keep her eyes lowered. If she so much as looked at his face, she would snap. Sucking in a deep breath, she urged herself to keep calm and to deal with the situation maturely, which meant no yelling, screaming, hitting, or burning.

As she stood there, she heard The Doc sigh. She also heard his ecstatic thoughts of finally seeing her again. It disgusted her, but she didn't meet his gaze.

"Hello, Hara," he greeted quietly, his voice taking on the soothing tone it always did when she was upset. It only made her angrier. "It's nice to finally see you again after all this time." When she didn't reply, he continued. "I hear that in your anger, you caused a lot of damage to this city. I was also told that you killed three innocent kids."

When The Doc said the word innocent, something burst inside of Hara that made her lash out at him. He knew damn well that they weren't innocent. So when he spoke that word, Hara swung her fist as hard as she could at his face. She struck him just above the left eye, and she was surprised she didn't break a finger. The punch left The Doc stunned for a few moments, and Hara made the mistake of looking at him. He didn't look any different from the last time they saw each other. He still had the longer, dirty-blonde hair that always fell over his cold gray eyes, which could intimidate a lion. His face was still the same, smug yet curious. But at this moment he looked a little surprised. A bruise was already forming above his eye, and after a moment he winced slightly. Seeing his pain made Hara feel a wonderful sense of pride.

"Oh, I'm sorry," she apologized sarcastically, her voice quavering. "Did that hurt?" It suddenly occurred to her that the room was rapidly heating up, and she realized that in her anger she had begun to slip again. Her heart pounding, she placed her hands down on the table and directed all the energy to it. It was very painful, but she fought through it so she wouldn't set the entire room on fire.

The Doc finally snapped out of his trance and gazed back at her in amazement. Hara was glaring back at him, but when he saw the pain in her eyes he immediately became concerned. It drove Hara nuts; he could cause so much pain, but when he didn't know where the pain was coming from he would get so worried. He was a strange man, and she never intended to figure out how his sick mind worked.

As the table absorbed the heat flowing from her body, the metal creaked and groaned. The Doc had his hands upon it, and Hara heard a hiss before he pulled them away quickly. He watched her carefully as she closed her eyes and continued to let the heat out. After several silent seconds he whispered, "You're in pain."

"It's your fault," she accused, muttering at him through her teeth. She pulled her hands away and began to teeter as a wave of dizziness swept over her.

The Doc started to rise to his feet. "Let me help you," he begged.

"Sit down!" she ordered, opening her eyes and glowering at him.

Her expression evidently startled him, because The Doc sat back down and peered across the table at her with a mixture of confusion and worry. "What's wrong?"

"Oh, I don't know!" she snapped, her entire body shaking. "Why don't your ask yourself? Your experiments screwed me up!"

His eyes soft, The Doc invited, "Well, at least sit down."

"I'll be giving the orders, thank you," Hara growled, resting her hands on the table once more to support herself. Her hands started to burn and blister from the scorching metal, but she ignored the pain. Glaring back at him, she swallowed hard.

"Hara," The Doc murmured, almost to himself. "I'm surprised you chose that name to go by."

"Why?" Hara asked. "You gave it to me."

Watching her, The Doc said, "Well, you're the one who called me here. Would you like to explain why?"

"Yeah," Hara replied. "I'm going to kill you. But first I'd like to know if you have anything to say for yourself."

The corner of his mouth turning up in a half-smile, The Doc chuckled. "I do, actually."

Raising an eyebrow, Hara smirked. "Really? Let's hear it."

Still smiling at her, The Doc sighed. "Everything I did, I did to help you."

"Shut up!" Hara shouted furiously, the entire room shaking from her anger. "You didn't do this for me! You did this for yourself!"

"No," The Doc promised her, shaking his head. "It was all for you."

"You tortured me!" Hara screamed in a rage, pounding her fists on the table. "You drilled holes into my head! You strapped me to a table and cut me open! You made me hallucinate and watch my family die over and over again! You killed my entire species! I had to listen to you torture my friends! Don't tell me that it was all for me!"

"You still don't understand, do you?"

"Understand what?"

"That everyone else had it coming."

Shocked, Hara took a step back. "How could you say such a thing?" she demanded, her voice cracking with emotion.

"Because it's the truth," The Doc told her quietly, gazing gently back at her. At her horrified look, he asked, "Didn't they cast you out after you had your first child?"

"No!" Hara declared quickly, but then she thought over what had happened after Grace was born. "Well…they didn't cast me out, they just…"

"Avoided you?" The Doc finished, raising an eyebrow.

"Yes," Hara muttered, looking away.

She saw The Doc nod out of the corner of her eye. "They were afraid of you because your soul mate wasn't one of them. It's human nature. Anything that's different is dangerous."

"We're not human!" Hara hissed.

"No, you're not," The Doc agreed. "But you used to be. If you stopped to think about it, you'd see that our species are quite alike. Apart from your abilities we're not that different."

"Yes, we are," Hara growled, scowling at him.

The Doc shook his head. "Don't you remember? The human race exiled you all for being different, and your species avoided you because your soul mate and children were different. Weren't they all afraid of you at first too, because you're an Absorber?"

"What are you getting at?" Hara demanded, growing even more upset. "I don't see how that makes them bad people. So what if they were afraid of me? That doesn't mean they deserved to die!"

"They were foolish. You have so much potential, yet they cast you out because you were a little different."

"So that means they deserved to die? Does that mean all of you humans deserved to die for casting us out?" When The Doc didn't immediately reply, Hara told him, "And you know what? I was the one who decided to live an isolated life after my children were born! No one exiled me! I chose to live the way I did because I wanted to keep my family safe! Nobody deserves to die because they're afraid of someone else! You want to know something else? After you put Flint in the hospital, I left my home to go see him. My father confronted me then and asked if I would take a new Cabinet position. How else do you think I got that job? He said that the people were willing to accept me and my family and our differences since they all knew what it was like to be outcasts. He said they were all inviting me back into the city and were begging me to take my seat at the table! They weren't like you humans! They learned to accept me and my family for what we were! They changed! As the scientists all said, we evolved from humans!" Glowering at The Doc's bored expression, she continued angrily, "Do you want to know something else I found out today? I was told that after my father was ready to step down, the people wanted me to take his place. They wanted me as president. Don't tell me we're exactly like you, because we're not. And don't tell me that my people deserved to die, because you cannot logically make that argument!"

"Hara," The Doc started, raising his eyebrows. "No matter what they decided to do, it doesn't change what they did before. They made you leave your home."

"No one made me do anything!" Hara yelled at him. "I left for my own reasons!"

"You left because you felt like a freak," The Doc informed her sternly. "After they found out about your children and soul mate, no one ever looked at you the same way again. Your parents, your siblings, your friends…they all made you feel like you didn't belong. That's why you left."

"Don't act like you know how I felt!" Hara commanded, but he was absolutely right. "You don't know me that well!"

"I know you well enough, sweetheart," The Doc told her quietly.

Hara hated it when he called her that. "I left for my own reasons," she repeated, taking a step away from the table and concentrating on the one-way glass until she could see through it. She could see who had gathered to watch them from the next room. There were ten men and women, some she knew and some she didn't. On the far left were two of The Doc's guards whom she unfortunately recognized. They were leaning against the wall with blank expressions and their arms folded across their chests, looking so tough yet so pathetic. Next to them were two younger cops, one a man with curly black hair and brown eyes, and a woman with dark skin, hair and eyes. Sitting at a long wooden table in the center of the room were Lieutenant Odau and Agent Perry, both watching her with expressions of curiosity, fascination, and hesitation. Beside Perry was a blonde FBI agent whom Hara was pretty sure was Perry's partner, and on the other side of her was an older FBI agent with black skin. Standing to the side on the far right was a male FBI agent with brown hair and green eyes and a female agent with blonde hair and brown eyes. Everyone except for Perry, Odau, and the two guards was staring at her with a mixture of confusion, horror, and wonder. They had all witnessed her use two of her abilities so far, and by the bewildered thoughts running through their heads, they were having a hard time processing it all.

Her eyes locking on Perry's, Hara sent him a thought. *I warned you, Allan warned you, Jack warned you, and Daniel warned you. Do you wish you had listened?*

Perry's eyebrows came together in surprise, but then his face hardened. *He offered his help. I accepted. As far as I can tell, you're still the bad guy. I wonder whose side is better to take.*

You're an idiot! she told him angrily. Speaking of Allan and Daniel, where were they? She had lost contact with them a while ago, and it was beginning to worry her. Had The Doc done something to them?

"It's the same way with most species," The Doc was saying. "Any individual who's different is pushed away. The same thing happened to me."

"Don't you dare try to compare yourself to me!" Hara snarled, taking another step back.

Cocking his head, The Doc asked, "Why not?"

Glaring at him, Hara snapped, "Just don't!" Folding her arms tightly, she waited for The Doc to come up with some smart remark, but when he had nothing to say she demanded, "How would killing my species help me, huh? You never answered that the first time."

"They were holding you back," he explained, and at Hara's puzzled look, he smiled. "Since they were all afraid of you, you couldn't be who you really were. You weren't able to demonstrate how powerful you really are. You were the most powerful of them all, and by getting rid of them all you could finally be yourself. Once you let your emotions take over, the person you truly are comes forth."

Staring at him in shock, she yelled, "I didn't want to demonstrate how powerful I was! I'm too dangerous! Yeah, I let my emotions take over, and now look what I've become!"

"You should never be afraid of who or what you are, honey," The Doc whispered.

"You did this to me!" Hara shouted. "This is your fault! Look what I've become!"

"I helped you!" The Doc told her. "I set you free! Yes, there were some unwanted side effects, but we can handle them. Together."

"Screw you!" Hara cried, backing up even more. "You're crazy! This wasn't to help me; this was so you could figure out my kind! You just wanted knowledge and power and control, and you used me! If you had really been doing this for me, you wouldn't have tortured me!"

"It wasn't torture," The Doc promised.

"Like hell it wasn't! What do you call everything you did to me? We have tapes of every little 'session' we had together. Why don't we let your friends in the next room watch them and see what they call it!" She pointed at the one-way glass and snapped her head in their direction. Some of them looked surprised that Hara knew they were there, but others—Perry and the agent with black skin—were eyeing The Doc suspiciously. Lieutenant Odau was glaring at Hara, and Hara heard him thinking that he didn't even care what had been done to her.

"I was trying to understand your abilities better so I could..." The Doc began defensively.

"So you could use them for your own purposes!" Hara interrupted.

"So I could help you learn to control them all once you discovered how many you actually possess," The Doc finished patiently.

"What are you talking about?" Hara asked in confusion.

"Do you have any idea how many abilities you actually have?"

"Too many!"

"You have an unlimited number!" The Doc declared. "You can do anything! Whether you know it or not, you have any power you could possibly think of."

"Why me?" Hara whispered, shaking her head. "Of all the people you could have chosen to 'help,' why me?"

Cocking his head again, he told her softly, "Because you were just like me."

Pursing her lips furiously, Hara growled, "I am nothing like you!"

The Doc nodded slowly. "You may not want to accept it, but you are."

"No!" Hara yelled, stomping back to the table. Placing her hands back on it, she leaned forward and stared menacingly into his eyes. "I'm not like you! You're insane! You kill people to serve your own purposes..." She stopped when she realized what was coming out of her mouth. Gazing back at The Doc with her jaw half open, she said quietly, "Oh, no."

Raising his eyebrows, The Doc leaned forward as well. "And what exactly is it that you've been doing?" he asked. "Aren't you killing people to serve yourself, too?" When Hara lowered her eyes, he added, "Last I heard, everyone thought you were the crazy one."

"I'm not crazy," Hara muttered, trying more to convince herself than convince him. Now that they were discussing it, she realized that she and The Doc really did have a lot in common. She didn't want to believe it was true, but unfortunately it was.

"Are you sure about that?"

That was the question Hara really had to ask herself. Was she sure she wasn't crazy? Did she believe she was completely sane? Misery sweeping over her, she stepped back again. Sensing there was a chair behind her, she sank down into it. She rested her elbow on the table and put her head in her hand.

"I admit that I hurt you, and I'm sorry," The Doc told her. "Truly, I am. I didn't want to hurt you, I only wanted to help you. I'm sorry." He said that louder, causing Hara to look up at him. His eyes sympathetic, he continued, "But that's no excuse for what you've been doing."

Her eyes becoming slits, Hara demanded, "And what's your excuse? Oh, wait, you don't have one!"

"I already told you," The Doc reminded.

"That's no excuse!" Hara snapped. "Killing everyone wasn't going to help me at all! Don't try to make that excuse!"

For a while, The Doc didn't say anything. He just gazed across the table at her, and then asked, "Why did you come here, kid?"

Her heart skipping a beat, Hara inhaled sharply. "You know why."

"Maybe so," The Doc said, shrugging. Leaning back in his chair, he gestured to the people sitting in the next room. "But they don't, and I'm sure they'd like to know."

Hara glanced at everyone, and they were all gazing back at her with hopeful expressions. But, looking back to The Doc, her face hardened. "I came back here so I could save everyone."

"They're all dead," The Doc informed impatiently. "How are you supposed to save them if they're already dead?"

"I can bring them back," Hara insisted. "All of them. All I have to do is get rid of that damn boy!" Looking again to the group in the other room, Hara locked eyes with Lieutenant Odau. His expression became furious, and she glared ferociously in return. "You want to know why I'm trying to kill your kid, Odau? Because when I do, my family and everyone else who was killed will all be saved! You sacrifice him, my entire species will come back! And I assure you, I will never stop until his blood spills. No matter what you do, or what you throw at me, I'll keep coming for him!"

The lieutenant's entire body tensed and his face became even angrier, but he didn't try to tell her to stay away. His thoughts were threatening enough. He had images of himself putting a bullet through her brain; images of killing her if she got away from The Doc.

Oh, I'll get away from him, alright, she thought to herself.

"You can't save them, Hara," The Doc told her.

"Yes, I can!" Hara exclaimed.

"No, you can't!" The Doc said louder, standing up quickly. Planting his hands on the now cooled tabletop, he leaned forward with his eyebrows pressed together and shouted, "They're dead! Gone! It's too late to save them now!"

"I can bring them back!" Hara yelled insistently. "I know I can!"

"If it were possible, I would have brought my family back a long time ago!" The Doc cried, and for the first time since Hara had met him, she saw a flash of intense pain cross his face.

This was startling news to Hara. Stepping back in surprise, she stared at him. "What did you say?"

His eyes filled with emotion, The Doc looked down in shame. "If there were a way to save your race, I would have figured out a way and brought back my wife and daughter a long time ago. I tried to find a way to bring them back, but there is no way. They're gone. Forever."

Hara had never seen sadness in The Doc before. She never even knew he had a heart. She couldn't believe that anyone could ever love such a monster in return. He had always been such a smug, arrogant know-it-all who showed no mercy unless it served him, and Hara had never imagined he could be capable of having emotional pain. But she saw now that he was hurting, and for a moment, she felt a surge of pity. "You had a family?"

The Doc nodded, his eyes still lowered.

Pausing, Hara asked carefully, "What happened to them?"

His eyes flickering up to hers, The Doc sent her mental images so he wouldn't have to explain verbally.

The first picture Hara saw was of a young woman. She had light brown hair and eyes, looked to be about thirty, and had a beautiful smile. Hara then saw a younger image of The Doc beside her. He was clean and tidied up. He looked happy. They both appeared to be very happy together. As Hara dug deeper she discovered that the woman's name was

Marisa. She and The Doc had been married for two years before they had their daughter, Ariana. The child had been as gorgeous as her mother, but with her father's cold gray eyes. For four years the family lived happy, normal lives, but then disaster struck. Marisa suddenly collapsed dead one day, and after an autopsy was performed it was discovered that she had died of a brain aneurysm. It was also discovered that the aneurysm was genetic. The Doc had his daughter examined, and a horrible truth was revealed: Ariana was also prone to the fatal brain aneurysm. Desperate and grief-stricken, The Doc then devoted the rest of his life to find a way to correct his daughter's defect. He began studying Hara's kind in hopes of finding a cure. There had been rumors that the blood of a few of them could heal any type of illness or injury, so he spoke to Hara's father through a messenger. He asked him for a few blood samples of a Healer—that was all he asked for—so he could try to find some way to save his daughter. Hara's father had refused, believing that if he agreed, The Doc would start demanding more things at a greater cost. The Doc continued to plead with him, but he couldn't persuade him in time. Ariana was fifteen when her aneurysm ruptured; she died instantly.

His life in ruins, The Doc was completely devastated. He blamed Hara's father for not helping him, and ever since then he held a grudge against Hara's kind. That was the real reason, Hara realized, that The Doc had wiped out her entire species. He hated them for not helping save his daughter, and he wanted revenge against them all. But then he discovered Hara, and he felt that he knew her in a way. Once he began to study Hara's kind, his own people began to avoid him because of everything he was doing and learning. He felt exiled from the normal world, apart from his small group of guards and fellow scientists. When he found out about Hara's ability to heal others as well as herself, he set out to find her and use her to help anyone else with a fatal illness. It was his way of coming to terms with being unable to save his daughter. But after he realized how Hara had been living—isolated from her people— he had a change of heart. He felt as if she were just like him: abandoned by her own people. So while he helped his own people he decided to help her as well, in a manner of speaking.

Blinking in shock and understanding, Hara whispered, "You spoke to my father about saving your daughter?" When The Doc nodded, her mouth fell open. "You told him what was going to happen to her, yet he refused to help you?"

Shaking his head, The Doc muttered, "I pleaded with him for years to help me. I begged him for just a blood sample from a Healer. I needed something that would help fix the aneurysm. I told him about Ariana and her mother, but he wouldn't give in. No matter what I said or promised, he wouldn't even give me a blood sample. He wouldn't help a desperate father save his dying daughter."

Disbelief overwhelming her, Hara covered her mouth with her hand. Her own father had refused to save a dying girl when he had the means to do so. He could have given him some of Hara's blood. But he hadn't. And what was even worse, he never told Hara about any of this. Not when they first met The Doc in person, and not when The Doc began killing millions of their people. If her father had helped him, the war might have never happened in the first place.

Dropping her hand back down to her side, Hara told him shakily, "I don't believe that. I can't believe it! Why wouldn't he help you?"

"Because he was prejudiced," The Doc informed her flatly. His face was no longer pained; it was once again hard. "He wouldn't help a dying child because the human race exiled him."

Hara stared at him in confusion. "So you killed them all? You killed countless people just because one man didn't give you what you wanted? My father did this to you. Why didn't you work it out with him and spare all those innocent people?"

"We've been trying to exchange information with your people for decades," The Doc said. "If they hadn't all been so selfish, then I might have been able to save my wife too."

"Let's not forget that your people exiled us first!" Hara snapped angrily. "Damn right we weren't going to share our abilities with you!"

"Is it so hard to forgive?" The Doc demanded.

"Your people experimented on us!" Hara shouted. "Tortured us! Murdered us! Banished us to an isolated place where we had to fend for ourselves and start over! We had no shelter, no food, no spare clothing, nothing! It's a miracle we all survived! What's even worse; when my father went to make peace with your leaders, he was almost assassinated! You're asking if we can forgive? Maybe your people should give us a reason to forgive you!"

"Our governments banished you!" The Doc exclaimed defensively. "Our governments tried to assassinate your father! Not the people! But he decided to let us all die when he could have helped us!"

"Listen to yourself! You're accusing my people of abandoning you, but your people did it to us first! You're blaming us about leaving you all behind to die but then you come and destroy us! Your people may have been innocent, but so were mine! You committed genocide because your poor wife and baby died! You were upset because of the loss of your family, but then you went and took away everyone else's! I don't see how you can only blame my people when you and yours are just as guilty! You're the cruel and selfish one here!"

"You don't know what you're saying!" The Doc growled. "You're too young to fully understand…"

"To fully understand what?" Hara demanded in exasperation. "What it's like to know love? Betrayal? Loss? Grief? Hatred? I know all of those things! I am so sick of everyone underestimating me because of my age! Don't tell me that I don't understand what you went through, because I do! But that doesn't mean you can get away with mass murder!"

"But you do?" The Doc challenged, raising an eyebrow.

"At least I've got a decent reason!" Hara snarled. "I'm trying to save my kind! You were just out for revenge!"

"Does that makes it any better?" The Doc growled.

"Yes," Hara hissed, glaring at him.

Several long moments passed before The Doc spoke again. He was glaring back at Hara, anger burning in his eyes. "Let me ask you something, kid," he said, stepping around the table. "How does loss feel to you?"

Suspicious of his intentions, Hara eyed him and stepped backwards cautiously. "What do you mean, 'how does it feel?'"

"I mean, does it make you sad?" The Doc questioned, the sickeningly curious look back on his face. "Depressed? Angry? It's different with every person. How does losing someone you care about make you feel?"

"You've seen what it does to me," Hara growled, her body shaking with rage. "You know exactly how it makes me feel."

"I saw how it made you feel before," The Doc pointed out, sitting on the edge of the table. "You're very different now."

"Gee, whose fault is that?" Hara demanded.

Cocking his head again, The Doc looked like he was hiding something. "I'm only guessing, but it seems to me that, nowadays, it would make you very angry if someone you loved were killed. Don't you think so?"

"Are you enjoying yourself?" Hara snapped. "Do you want me to hit you again?"

The Doc just shrugged. "I'm just curious is all. Would it make you angry?"

"Wouldn't you like to find out," Hara growled.

"I would, actually," The Doc declared, smiling at her. "Maybe we can find out together."

Beginning to understand what he was hinting at, Hara threatened, "If you come near any of my friends, I'll..."

"You'll what?" The Doc asked, peering at her from across the room. "Hit me again? Burn me? Give it your best shot, kiddo."

In a state of uncontrollable fury, Hara used an ability that she rarely ever used—even when it came to protecting herself. Taking a single step forward, her entire body dissipated into trillions of atoms and then reorganized into the proper shape directly in front of The Doc. Teleporting was a dangerous ability to possess; one couldn't use it too often and survive. It could only be used for the most urgent of circumstances.

After she teleported over to The Doc, she grabbed him by the front of his jacket and teleported again. Only this time, she teleported them both. At first, Hara wasn't sure where they ended up, but then she saw that they were about four feet from where they had just been; right beside the wall opposite the one-way glass. Lifting The Doc clean off his feet, she slammed him against the wall and held him there. Her breaths coming out fast and heavy, and she commanded, "Stay away from them!"

He was grinning broadly. "Yes," he said, keeping his eyes on hers. "I see you've still got some fight left in you."

The door to the interrogation room suddenly burst open, and Hara and The Doc both looked over. Lieutenant Odau and the agent with black skin stood in the doorway with their weapons drawn and aimed at Hara's head. Odau's expression was furious, but the agent—whose name she discovered from his mind to be Rhett Long—looked more worried than angry. His eyes were timid and he hung back hesitantly, watching her as she held The Doc a foot off the ground.

"Hey," The Doc called, waggling a finger at Odau as he cocked his gun and stepped forward. "I told you not to come back in here!"

Blinking in surprise, Odau sputtered, "But...she's..."

"Out!" The Doc ordered, pointing at the door. "I've got this under control."

"You'd better listen to him, Lieutenant," Hara growled in a deadly voice, glaring at him. Her body was still quivering with rage, and she was in no mood to deal with Odau. His disturbance had angered her enough, and if he came any closer she would most likely end up killing him.

Eyeing her, Odau's grip tightened on his weapon. Gritting his teeth, he held his ground.

"Lieutenant," The Doc said firmly. "Go."

Giving Hara one last wary look, Odau slowly backed out of the doorway, Agent Long moving with him. Once he closed the door, Hara made sure no one else could get back inside. Lifting a hand, she pointed a finger at the crack between the door and the frame and slowly lowered her hand. The metal on the edge of the door turned bright orange as it melted into the door frame. When the door was sealed, she turned back to The Doc with a terrifying expression on her face.

The Doc was still finding the situation amusing; his grin was even bigger than before. It was disgusting how he enjoyed seeing Hara angry. It was all just a game to him.

"If you go anywhere near any of them, you will regret the very day of your birth!" Hara shouted, tightening her grip on his jacket. It was taking all of her self-restraint to keep from breaking his neck right there. "On second thought, you're not even going to have a chance to go near them."

"You may not want to do that just yet," The Doc told her as she raised her hand. His grin had morphed to a smirk, but there was something to his expression that fazed Hara. He was too calm, which meant he was hiding something that he was about to use against her.

"And why not?" Hara demanded, growing impatient. "Give me a reason why I shouldn't roast your face right here and right now!"

"If you kill me, then one of my men will destroy the car that Meg Hopper is in outside the hospital," The Doc explained smugly.

Hara's eyes widened and her jaw fell open in horror and astonishment. "What?" she whispered in disbelief. How did he know?

"I knew when Daniel threatened the boy that someone would have to be watching over him," The Doc said casually. "It wasn't too difficult to narrow it down to Meg. A few of my guards stayed behind and searched around, and guess who they found?"

At first, Hara wanted to threaten him again, but she knew that that would get her nowhere. "Please," she begged, her voice still thick with anger. "Please don't hurt her."

"Oh, I won't," The Doc promised softly, and Hara knew that he meant it. "Just so long as you don't hurt me."

"Why are you doing this?" Hara demanded helplessly, not understanding why he hadn't already killed Meg. Letting him drop to the floor, she released him and stepped away.

"Because I'm not finished with you yet," he told her, smoothing out his jacket. "And as you know I can't have you finishing what you came here to do. So the more you cooperate, the fewer people will be hurt."

Retreating several feet as The Doc stepped away from the wall, Hara didn't know what else to do. Feeling defeated, she lowered her eyes and muttered, "I'll do whatever you want. Just stay away from Meg and the others."

Snickering, The Doc said, "I'm afraid it's a little too late for that." At Hara's puzzled expression, he cocked his head again. "I assumed you would have figured out something was wrong before now. The mental bonds you share with the people you care about are so powerful."

Making the connection, Hara's expression once again became furious. She knew Meg was fine because Meg's mind was still conscious and unsuspecting, and Hara could sense Jack's mind in another interrogation room down the hall from her. But she had noticed before that Allan and Daniel's minds were both missing, and now she understood what The Doc was implying. "What did you do to them?" she yelled, striding forward and grabbing him again.

"Who?" he asked, smirking down at her.

"Allan and Daniel!" Hara shouted, shoving him backwards. She miscalculated how much force she applied, and The Doc fell back against the wall. Coming closer, she grabbed him by the throat as he struggled to regain his balance and slammed his head against the wall. "What did you do to them?"

His expression was dazed for a moment, but then he grinned again. "Can't you read my mind?"

She very well could, but she was too angry to focus on his racing thoughts. Swinging around, she threw him down to the floor. He slid several feet and started to get up as she came back toward him, but Hara kicked him in the stomach before he was completely upright. Again, she applied too much force and The Doc was thrown into the one-way glass. He then fell to the ground and didn't attempt to get up again. Rolling over, he put his arm in front of his face in self-defense. He was still smirking and had also started laughing. Hara knew that The Doc wanted to make her angry and was doing everything on purpose, but she was too upset to stop.

"What have you done to them?" she screamed, making herself pause.

"You know, the two of them had been getting on my nerves for some time," The Doc sneered, his eyes mocking.

Kicking him again, she demanded louder, "Where are they?"

The Doc coughed from the force of the blow, but then chuckled again. Pushing himself upright and against the wall, he shielded his face again. "They kept interfering with my attempts to find you, even before your father was killed."

Smacking his arm out of the way, Hara slammed her fist down on The Doc's head. "Answer me!" she commanded furiously.

Falling back down to the floor, The Doc peered up at her, still smiling. "I am," he insisted, continuing. "Not too long ago this morning, Daniel helped Allan escape custody by killing two of my guards. I wasn't too pleased by that."

Fear taking control, Hara grabbed The Doc by the jacket again and pulled him closer to her so their faces were fairly close. She was about to slam his face into the concrete floor again, but he quickly stopped her.

"Allan's fine," The Doc told her, gripping her wrists tightly as Hara held him off the ground. He wasn't terrified of her enraged state, but Hara could hear him thinking that he really didn't want to be struck or kicked again. Glancing over to the door as people began pounding their fists on the other side of it and loud shouts erupted, he looked back to Hara and explained, "He got away. I don't know where he is, but he escaped and I swear I did nothing to him."

"And Daniel?" Hara asked, her heart pounding.

Pausing, The Doc said, "Not so lucky."

Dread weighing her down, she stared at him in horror. "Oh, God," she whispered. "What did you do?"

"Why don't you go see for yourself?" The Doc offered cruelly. "He's in a holding cell. But be warned; you may not like what you see."

Hara managed to catch the thought that floated through The Doc's mind for a split second, and gasped at what she saw. It was an image of Daniel in his holding cell, but something wasn't right. He was sitting on his bench while leaning back against the bars, his head tilted at an awkward angle. His body appeared relaxed—too relaxed—and slouched over. But the worst part was that there were no evident signs of life.

"NO!" Hara cried in dismay, dropping The Doc to the floor and stumbling backwards. She stared back into his cold, merciless eyes with a mix of disbelief and terror swirling in her gut. The Doc still found everything amusing. Hara couldn't believe she had been so stupid. She had agreed to Daniel's plan to allow him and Allan to pass the messages on to Perry and The Doc and then infiltrate their defenses, discover their plots, and then pass the information back to her. It had seemed like a good plan at the time, but now it just seemed plain dumb. She should have realized before that the risk would be very high for Allan and Daniel. It was easy to see now that there was a very slim chance that The Doc wouldn't harm them. And now Daniel was...

She couldn't believe it was true unless she saw it with her own eyes. The Doc was very good at playing mind games with her, so she could never assume what he was thinking was the truth. She would need proof before she could believe such a horrible thing.

The door and its frame suddenly came crashing down into the room. Hara watched as The Doc's two guards stepped inside, each carrying a loaded weapon. These weapons were like none Hara had ever seen before; a little larger than a nine-millimeter with a greenish tint to them, and a long spike sticking out of the back of each. The sound that came from them was like the soft purring of an engine. They didn't appear very threatening, but Hara knew that anything she hadn't already seen was bound to be more advanced and therefore more of a threat.

"Oh," she said in surprise. "That's new."

Both guards fired simultaneously, and a long metal spike burst forth from each weapon. Being in the anger-induced state she was in, Hara's reflexes were three times as quick. As soon as she saw the spikes move towards her, she threw her body to the ground. The spikes whizzed over her, and when they struck the one-way glass she heard a series of loud noises that sounded like electrical charges. Glancing up, she saw that each spike was lodged into the glass and white sparks were falling to the floor. The Doc had invented a new type of tazer, and by the looks and sounds of it, it contained well over twenty thousand volts. It was enough to knock her out cold for several hours and leave her with a splitting headache for days.

Before they could make an attempt to take another shot at her, Hara whipped her arm at the guards. The energy she unleashed knocked them clean off their feet and sent them sailing across the hallway into the wall. Part of the wall behind them blew out as well. In an explosion of plaster and concrete, it crumbled to the ground in a deafening roar. A cloud of dust rose up and was so thick that she couldn't see through it. Holding her breath, Hara ran straight into it. To her surprise, The Doc let her go without any objection. As she leaped over the pile of rubble now covering the floor, the guards began to pull themselves to their feet. Once she cleared the dust cloud, Hara looked around in an attempt to remember which way led to the holding cells. Catching the panicked thoughts of one of the cops still inside the observation room, Hara searched their memories until she found the information she needed.

At the moment, she needed to take a right to get into the office area. There was a door in her way, and as she ran towards it she waved her hand at it. It flew open and she dove through it. Behind her, she heard the door to the observation room slam open and everyone start barreling out. Threats were shouted at her, but she ignored them and kept running. Dodging desks and chairs, she rushed to the door at the far side that led to the holding cells. Without any effort, she slammed her entire body into the door and it splintered into a thousand chunks of wood. Looking around in growing dread, her eyes locked onto Daniel in the nearest cell. Letting out a wail that would terrify even the most frightening of beasts, she stumbled forward in blind fury and despair. Daniel looked exactly as he had in the image in The Doc's head. His head was turned at an awkward angle, his back rested against the bars, his body slouched in an uncomfortable position, and his mind was silent. He was dead.

"Why?" Hara howled, kicking in the gate to the cell. It clattered to the floor noisily, and she stepped over it without really noticing. Sobs escaping her throat, she fell to her knees in front of her dead friend. Tears streaming down her face, she cried in misery, "Daniel!"

Part of her hoped that Daniel would suddenly open his eyes and ask her what was wrong, but she knew he wouldn't. He was gone.

"Why?" she sobbed again, dropping her head and pulling her hair.

After a moment, Hara heard Perry's group of people come barging inside as well, but she didn't even acknowledge their presence. Someone gasped behind her, a woman's voice whispered, "Oh my God!"

"Marcus!" Hara heard Odau say in shock, and then she heard him start stepping over the broken gate towards her. Many more gasps were audible from the doorway before Odau suddenly demanded, "What did you do?"

Infuriated, Hara turned her head and gave him a disgusted look. He was standing a few feet behind her, staring at her in contempt. She was about to protest his accusation angrily, but forgot about him when she saw The Doc entering the room.

When she met his eye and glared at him with rage, The Doc smirked at her and then waved his hand at Marcus's body. "See what happens when you involve your friends?" he snickered, enjoying her pain. "People get hurt."

"You did this?"

Agent Perry was standing inside the room in between the female cop and blonde FBI agent, and he was staring at The Doc, pure astonishment present on his face. Hara was glad that at least someone in the group would eventually change over to her side. And she was glad that person was Perry.

As she looked at the faces of everyone in the room, Hara realized that maybe more people than she originally anticipated were going to switch sides. Both of the younger cops were horrified by Marcus's death, and when they saw Hara's reaction they rounded on The Doc.

She was aware of several pairs of eyes on her, but the only thing she could focus on was The Doc and his smirk. Climbing shakily to her feet, she screamed at him, "You killed him!"

Cocking his head, The Doc's grin widened. "Oh, now why would you think something like that?"

Shrieking in rage, Hara ran forward. She was moving so fast that she was just a blur, and The Doc didn't have enough time to react before she threw herself at him. Tackling him back into the office area, she landed hard on top of him. Still howling wildly, Hara started hitting him wherever she could: his face, his arms, his stomach, anything that wasn't protected. And she showed him no mercy.

"You killed him! You killed him! You killed him!" She repeated the cry, pounding her fists down on him.

Hara had caught The Doc by surprise, and had knocked the wind out of him. At first, he just laid in a daze underneath her while she hit him, but then he blinked and raised his arms in defense. He was no longer smiling. His eyes were wide in shock and his expression looked pained. It made Hara feel triumphant that she was hurting him, so she hit him harder.

"Get her off of him!" Odau shouted from behind her.

"Why?" someone else asked.

"She's going to kill him!" Odau exclaimed, and then Hara felt two firm hands on either arm.

Wrenching her arms free from the lieutenant's grasp, she turned and swung her fist at his face. Catching him right in the nose, she wanted to laugh at his surprised expression as he fell over backwards, but she had more to deal with at the moment than just him. She turned back to The Doc and was caught off guard as one of his fists collided with her chin, causing her to bite down on her tongue. The force of the blow knocked her off of him, and she fell to the floor. Tasting blood, she attempted to get back up, but The Doc was on top of her in an instant. His hands wrapped around her throat and tightened, and his expression was no longer amused. Hara's eyes widened as she felt her air supply cut off, and she stared up in terror at The Doc's soulless eyes.

"That's enough," he growled, his grip becoming tighter.

Grabbing at his arms, Hara struggled underneath him. His eyes bore holes through hers and he didn't loosen his grip. He had caught Hara by surprise, and it was taking her time to think straight again. As her lungs screamed for oxygen, she tried to slow her racing heart. Once her mind was functioning correctly, she wrapped her hands around The Doc's wrists. Forcing herself to focus on her hands, she let forth a burst of heat. She felt his skin begin to cook beneath her hands, and before long he was screaming in agony.

Releasing her throat, The Doc quickly pulled his arms away from Hara. His expression showed intense pain as he clutched at his burned wrists, which were now a dark red color and looked to be already blistering.

Sucking in a lungful of air, Hara coughed heavily. Using the few seconds she had to spare, she punched The Doc in the face as hard as she could. He lost his balance and flipped over backwards. Still gasping for breath, she stumbled to her feet and ran blindly from him.

"Stop!" she heard Perry, Odau, and several others shout. They were coming after her. She could hear them drawing their weapons, and she knew she had to come up with something fast.

Her mind was still scrambling from the lack of oxygen, but she could think clearly enough to propel herself toward the door she had originally come from. Ignoring everything that was being shouted at her, she made it through the door before she quickly stopped herself. The Doc's two guards had followed the group and were now mere feet in front of her. She stumbled backwards as they drew their new weapons again. As they raised their arms, Hara threw up hers in defense. She felt a sudden burst of pain in her head that made her cry out, and she thought she had been struck by one of the spikes from the guns. But as she felt the pain, her surroundings also went deadly silent.

Blinking in confusion, she dropped her arms and glanced around. Her vision was going white and the images in front of her were swimming. It was impossible for her to see where she was or what was around her, but she could sense another mind in the room with her. To her surprise, the other mind seemed to know her. He recognized her, but he was puzzled by her presence. Hara sensed that he was directly in front of her, so she stepped backwards in alarm. Raising her hands in defense once more, she tried to get her eyes to focus on the figure looming before her.

"Hara?" the low, gravelly voice of a man said in amazement.

Startled by the voice she heard, Hara muttered, "You?"

"What are you doing here?" Dr. Wesley Bennett asked. Hara could only see the outline of his body, but she could see that he was coming towards her.

"Stay away from me!" she ordered, stumbling backwards. Her head was now throbbing, and as she moved away from Bennett she tripped over something hard and lost her balance. When she hit the floor, her head struck a hard metal object. Crying out in pain, she clutched at her head. She felt blood trickling through her fingers and streaming into her hair, and letting out a last, helpless groan, she blacked out.

✳ ✳ ✳

The moment Hara fell to the floor, Dr. Bennett rushed to her aid. Kneeling beside her, he gently touched her arm. She wasn't moving, and he was afraid that if he startled her she would do something to further harm one of them. But she didn't respond to his touch, and appeared to have lost consciousness completely. Her hands were still clutching her head, and Bennett carefully set them back down by her sides. He saw that there was blood covering one hand, and a small pool of it was forming beside her head. Her eyes were closed and her expression still had a hint of pain to it.

It had shocked Bennett when Hara had suddenly appeared right in front of his eyes, and he realized that she had absorbed Allan Brown's ability to teleport. Why she had teleported to the exact spot Allan Brown had thirty minutes earlier, he did not know. After Allan had teleported into the vacant hospital room, he had almost immediately lost consciousness and hadn't awakened since. If anyone knew he was there, The Doc would somehow find out and most likely kill him. So Bennett kept his presence a secret, hiding him in the very room he arrived in. Bennett was also treating him in secret. From the videos he had seen in Brown's office, he discovered a way to treat someone when they overused their ability. To keep the mayor from dying, he formulated a drug to allow the brain to recover. He was now resting comfortably in one of the beds, and now that Hara was there too, he realized that he would have to treat her in the same discreet way. Could Bennett save two lives in secret? Teleportation evidently damaged brain cells and could very easily kill the possessor, and even Hara couldn't escape the effects.

Sighing, Bennett gazed down on Hara's unconscious body, knowing that once she awoke, she was not going to be happy.

10

The Other Plan

T hings had gone very slowly since Hara disappeared right in front of Perry's eyes. The entire building was so silent that a person could hear the beating of a butterfly's wings. After everything that had happened in the past half hour—everything Hara and The Doc said, everything they saw Hara do, and the discovery of Marcus's body—no one wanted to speak with anyone else or be anywhere near The Doc.

Once Hara vanished, everyone was in a state of confusion. They had witnessed many of her extraordinary capabilities, but nothing as impossible as teleportation. For a few moments after she left, everyone stood staring at the place she had just been. They thought at first that maybe she was just playing a mind game on them and expected her to suddenly reappear in a different location. But when she didn't, The Doc stood up and said that she was gone. The response he received was less than what Perry had expected.

Agent Long was furious. He demanded an explanation from The Doc for why the girl wasn't in custody. When his rant was finished, Lieutenant Odau started yelling as well. He too wanted to know why Hara had been allowed to escape, and then went on about how he and the girl had caused significant damage to the station. Later, he and everybody else began shouting about Marcus's dead body. The Doc denied that it was he who killed Marcus, even though no one believed him. Aubrey became so angry that he stormed out. He was quickly followed by Finchly and Renee. Martinson and Hersh left soon after that, leaving Perry, Agent Long, and Odau to deal with The Doc. Perry told him that he knew who killed Marcus and that no matter what he said he couldn't turn them away from the obvious facts. The Doc just smirked and said, "What are you going to do to prove it?"

Glaring, Perry walked away, knowing that he couldn't prove it. As he departed, the others who were left continued to shout at The Doc. Before he managed to get out of earshot, Perry heard The Doc actually offer to "remove the body from the building." Everyone shouted, "No!" in unison, and Perry wrinkled his nose in disgust. It befuddled him how The Doc operated. He would make a huge mess and cause problems for many people, and he seemed to enjoy the chaos he brought upon the world. But then he would offer to clean it up when he was done. That was the part that was confusing Perry. Why would he make a mess of things and make it clear that he was enjoying himself, and then go clean it up? Perry understood that there were many things about The Doc that he didn't understand, and he hoped that he would begin to understand his strange ways. He was counting on Hara's promise that he would learn the whole story about all the mysteries that were building up, and hoped that included why The Doc was the way he was.

Perry returned to the conference room, in hopes of finding Renee there again. But to his disappointment the room was empty. He decided to remain there anyway. It was very likely that Renee wanted to be alone like she did before their last confrontation, and Perry had no desire to upset her any more. After watching Marcus get shot right in front of her and then coming across his body later, she would obviously be upset.

Perry stayed in the conference room, seating himself in one of the chairs. A few minutes later, Martinson came into the room and sat across from him. He explained that Renee and Hersh both left together to get away from the group for a while, and that Aubrey and Finchly disappeared as well. Agent Long and Lieutenant Odau apparently decided to keep Marcus's death quiet for the time being, and were planning to keep the body where it was until they had time to complete a proper investigation. They still had to focus on finding Hara. Perry, of course, had been furious by this news, and so had Martinson, but Martinson explained that there was nothing they could do about it. Agent Long had his mind set. No matter how much they disagreed with Agent Long's decision to continue working with The Doc, they would just have to deal with it.

When Perry asked about him, Martinson told him that The Doc was out in his semi. He had been asked to leave the building for the time being, and was waiting with his guards and a few guards assigned by Agent Long to be called back inside. Odau and Agent Long both needed to figure out how they were going to deal with the huge mess inside, and said that if they even heard The Doc speaking they would most likely shoot him. All the other cops were also becoming very curious as to why they weren't being allowed back into the station, and were demanding an explanation for the huge semi and group of armed men outside. Odau was running out of excuses, and he knew as well as everyone else that they were already in too deep. If it was revealed that they were working with the man who killed over a dozen men the night before—and were still working with him even after what he had done to Marcus—they would all be incriminated as accessories to murder. Marcus's death would have to be revealed eventually, but they needed more time to come up with a viable explanation for everything they had done. Working with a murderer and then letting him get away with it was not acceptable. None of them looked forward to lying to their colleagues, but at the moment it needed to be done.

Martinson said that Odau told the officers who were requesting entry that they would need to relocate to another station for the time being. It would only be a matter of time before the other officers became overly suspicious and entered the building regardless of orders. It would be damn near impossible to keep them out for too much longer. So Odau and Agent Long were scrambling to clean up the mess before anyone could figure out what was going on or who they were working with.

For a few, painfully long minutes, Perry and Martinson sat in silence, thinking about the huge mistake they were all making. Then Martinson sighed and stood up, saying he was going to go help clean up. "I'm not going to prison for that mad scientist," he muttered before walking out the door.

Left alone with only the ringing silence and his clamorous thought to accompany him, Perry laid his head down on the table and closed his eyes. He had gotten barely any sleep over the past two days, and with the head injury he was utterly exhausted. Sighing, he allowed his mind to run over the events that had occurred in the last twenty-four hours.

He must have drifted off without realizing it, because he awoke some time later to confused and angry shouts just outside the door. Shaking off the last bit of sleep that was clouding his senses, Perry climbed to his feet and hurried to the door to see what the fuss was about. It was clear that he had been asleep for a while, because Renee, Hersh, Aubrey, and Finchly were back. All seven of Perry's colleagues were in the hallway, and they were all shouting.

"What's going on?" Perry asked in confusion.

"Have you seen The Doc at all recently?" Agent Long demanded urgently, his voice thick with agitation.

"No," Perry answered, dread weighing him down as he wondered what could have possibly happened now. "Why?"

"Marcus's body is gone," Renee explained.

"What do you mean, gone?" Perry said in disbelief.

"I mean, he's gone!" Renee snapped impatiently. "As in, he's no longer there!"

"How can he be gone?" Perry muttered to himself, taking off down the hall towards the holding cells. Throwing the door aside, he gazed inside and gasped. Renee was right. Marcus's body was gone.

"Shawn!" Renee cried, running in after him.

Infuriated, Perry knew that it had to be The Doc. He was the one who had originally offered to dispose of the body, so he must have been the one to take him. His heart pounding in rage, Perry ignored Renee and strode back out the way he came. If The Doc thought he could just march in and do whatever the hell he wanted, then Perry was going to be the one to personally let him know how wrong he was.

"Shawn!" Renee repeated angrily, following him as he cut back through the offices and to the hallway again. "Shawn, where are you going?"

"To find out what the hell he did with Marcus," Perry declared, pushing his way around Martinson and Agent Long as they reached out to stop him.

"Perry, don't get yourself involved with him any more than you already have," Agent Long commanded, quickly following him. "Let me deal with him."

He ignored them all. He entered the lobby and started for the front entrance, planning to find out exactly what The Doc had done with Marcus.

To Perry's surprise, The Doc was coming to him. He entered the lobby from the outside with three of his guards just as Perry entered from the hallway. For once, he didn't have a smirk on his face, and his expression was actually concerned. When he and Perry made eye contact, his eyebrows came together and he asked carefully, "Is everything alright? I thought I heard shouting."

"Oh, really?" Perry said in false surprise. He grabbed the front of The Doc's jacket and pulled him forward. "Well, the shouting is about to get a lot louder!"

Looking quite confused, The Doc peered at Perry cautiously. He waved a hand at his guards as they started to raise their weapons. "I'm not sure what you mean," he told Perry quietly, his eyes saying that he didn't want to upset anyone any more.

"You know damn well what I mean!" Perry snapped, giving him a rough shake.

"Well…" The Doc started, still bewildered. "Why don't you refresh my memory? I'm having difficulty recalling what exactly it is I did."

"Don't you give me that crap!" Perry snapped, shoving him backwards. "We know you were the one who took the body!"

"I'm sorry?" The Doc said, looking even more puzzled.

"Marcus's body!" Perry shouted. "Where is it?"

"You're saying it's gone?" The Doc whispered.

"Yes, of course it's gone…!" Perry began, but he stopped. "You really don't know, do you?"

Shaking his head slowly, The Doc turned to the others. "How long has he been missing?"

"I just discovered he was gone not five minutes ago," Finchly explained. "But no one knows how long ago he was taken."

"Somebody here must have taken him," Agent Long declared. "Nobody else could have gotten in or out of the building without our knowledge."

"It could have been anyone!" Renee said. "Nearly everyone was alone, and several of us left the building over the past two hours."

Perry was still convinced it was The Doc. "It must have been you," he growled, eyeing him suspiciously.

"How do we know it wasn't *you* who took the body?" The Doc demanded taking a step forward.

Turning his head, Perry took in The Doc's suspicious expression. "Excuse me?"

"How do we know it wasn't you who took the body?" The Doc repeated, his eyes narrowing. "You're so quick to make accusations, but can you provide an alibi for the past two hours?"

"Yeah, actually," Perry snapped. Looking to Martinson, he ordered, "Tell them. You were with me."

"I was only with you for fifteen minutes, Perry," Martinson muttered, his eyes slowly lowering.

"Yes, but I was in that room until you all discovered the body was gone," Perry insisted, amazed that he actually had to defend himself. "You all saw me come out. I hadn't left until then."

"You were against The Doc right from the start," Martinson added, appearing flustered. "It was almost like you didn't want Hara caught."

"Enough!" The Doc said. "It wasn't Perry. Someone else did it."

"How do you know?" Odau demanded.

"Because I know when I'm talking to a guilty man," The Doc told him. "I can look into his eyes and tell you he's innocent. But somebody here is not." He took a step forward and in turn gave everyone a long, lasting stare. "All the proof is sitting right in front of us. You just need to know what to look for." His eyes locked onto one face in particular, and he said pleasantly, "Detective Aubrey, you've been rather quiet lately."

Confused, Perry looked to Aubrey. And sure enough, the detective was the only one staring down at the floor. He hadn't spoken during the entire conversation with The Doc, and his expression was—to say the least—worthy of guilt. When The Doc spoke to him, he didn't respond in any way. But when he felt ten pairs of eyes on him, he slowly looked up. Perry had been wrong before, but Aubrey was definitely hiding something.

"Would you mind telling us where you've been for the past two hours?" The Doc asked him softly.

"Out," Aubrey replied simply, his expression unchanging.

"Out where?" The Doc questioned, taking a few steps closer to him.

"That's none of your business," Aubrey snapped, lowering his eyes once more.

"It is now," Odau growled.

"Where did you take the body?" Agent Long demanded, his face stunned. Aubrey was the last person any one of them would expect to pull a stunt like that.

"I think the question we should be asking him right now is why," The Doc murmured. His words now directed at Aubrey, he asked, "Did someone tell you to move it to a different location? Did someone make you do this?" He paused, giving Aubrey a chance to answer. He didn't. "Or are you a double agent?"

"Jesus, Aubrey!" Odau said angrily. "What the hell have you gotten yourself into?"

"Look at me," The Doc ordered suddenly.

Perry turned to see who he was talking to, and saw that he was still looking at Aubrey. But The Doc's expression was different. It seemed like he understood why Aubrey did what he did.

When Aubrey refused to meet his gaze, The Doc repeated louder, "Hey! Look at me!"

"No," Aubrey mumbled, his voice beginning to sound afraid.

"Why not?" The Doc asked him quietly, cocking his head to one side. He started to come towards Aubrey. "Is it because you're afraid I'll find out who made you do this?" When The Doc reached Aubrey, he grabbed the detective by his head with both hands and pulled him forward. Aubrey started struggling immediately, attempting to push away. But The Doc kept a firm grip on his head and ordered, "Stop fighting me! I'm trying to help you."

"Hey!" Odau warned, his hand on his weapon.

"Let him go!" Perry commanded.

"Relax!" The Doc told them, speaking to everyone in the room, including Aubrey. "I'm not going to hurt him. Hold still!" He had Aubrey's jaw gripped tightly in his left hand and was trying to pry his eyes open with the other, but Aubrey was still putting up a fight. The detective was clawing at The Doc's arms, but it was useless. "Relax!" The Doc said again, and managed to get Aubrey's eye open.

"What are you doing?" Perry demanded.

"Come and see for yourself," The Doc invited, gazing into Aubrey's eye.

At first, Perry didn't see what the big deal was, but then he saw why The Doc had peeled back Aubrey's eyelid. The colored part of Aubrey's eye was completely black, as if his pupil had expanded to cover the entire diameter of the iris. "What the hell?"

"That son of a bitch," The Doc muttered, releasing Aubrey.

Stumbling backwards, Aubrey glared ferociously at him. Now that Perry knew what he was looking for, he could see it. Both of Aubrey's pupils were completely dilated, and he seemed angrier, and more dangerous. His posture wasn't the same. As he scowled at The Doc,

Perry could see the arch to Aubrey's spine, and saw that his knees were slightly bent as well. He looked like an animal prepared to attack.

The Doc's last comment confused Perry, however. "Who?"

"Marcus," The Doc replied, watching Aubrey's unusual movements carefully. "Marcus made him move his body."

"May I remind you that Marcus is dead?" Odau said, his voice bored.

"Oh, come now, Lieutenant!" The Doc exclaimed, looking to him with his smirk. "After working with Marcus for so long, didn't you notice that there was something off about him? Something different?"

"Daniel had abilities too?" Finchly breathed.

"Of course," The Doc told her. "You don't think Hara would have put her trust in ordinary humans, do you?"

"So that means…" Perry thought out loud. "Meg Hopper and Allan Brown have abilities too."

"Very good," The Doc praised, grinning over at him.

"And Jack?" Perry added, his stomach sinking.

Shrugging, The Doc started to reply, but was cut off by Agent Long.

"How many of Hara's kind are involved in this?" he demanded. "It seems as if they've infiltrated all levels of our government. One of our cops, a District Attorney, and our own mayor! How many more of them are here, and in positions of power?"

"Just Marcus, Hopper, and Brown," The Doc assured. "Those were the only ones in your government. Jack and Hara just arrived."

"But they've been here for years!" Agent Long declared, shaking his head. "They've had these positions for such a long time! There are profiles about their lives all over the internet! Records of past jobs and positions…"

"It's all fake," The Doc informed, his face apologetic. "They made it all up so they'd have a cover story if anyone started asking questions. After all, they came out of nowhere. They needed background stories to keep from getting caught."

"Have they been penetrating our defenses?" Odau asked grimly. "Have they been passing information or planning an attack on us?"

"No, of course not!" The Doc promised, sounding as if it was a crime to accuse them of such treachery. "They would never do anything like that."

"Why this city?" Finchly wondered aloud. "What's so special about Philadelphia that they chose to come here to cause problems?"

Again, Perry saw uncertainty in The Doc's eyes. He knew the answer to that, but he wasn't going to share. Sighing, Perry asked him, "What could Marcus do, exactly? How could he possibly make Aubrey move his body after he died?"

"He had low levels of telepathic abilities," The Doc explained, looking once again to Aubrey. "He could hear people's thoughts, put his own thoughts into their heads, and manipulate them."

"Mind control," Perry concluded. "But Marcus is dead! How could he control Aubrey's thoughts if he wasn't alive?"

"Why don't we ask him?" The Doc suggested, nodding to Aubrey.

Glancing at the detective, Perry saw that he had shrunk back even further from the group. His eyes were still black, and he was still crouched in a defensive position. When The Doc began to take a few cautious steps closer, Aubrey stepped away, trying to keep his distance.

Slowly raising his hands to show he wasn't a threat, The Doc asked Aubrey, "You were the one who drove Marcus to the station, weren't you? You and Detective Finchly?" Turning to Finchly, he questioned, "Were the two of them ever alone in the car together? Even for just a moment? Did Marcus ever touch him?"

Shaking her head and shrugging quickly, Finchly stepped back with a desperate, confused expression on her face. "No...I don't know!"

"*Shh*," The Doc said in a calming manner. "We're not trying to pressure you. We're just asking that you think. Do you remember them ever being alone together between the time we left the hospital and the time of his death?"

"Uh..." Finchly thought, still confused and upset. "No, he was always with me..." She stopped suddenly and her eyes widened. "Oh, God," she whispered. "Right when we arrived back here, I got out of the car first, but Daniel grabbed Garrick's shoulder before he could get out. He said something to him just before I closed my door, but..." Her voice trailed off.

"What?" The Doc asked eagerly.

"I...I don't remember."

"What did he say?" he asked louder, taking a step in her direction. "You heard him say it, now think!"

"Uh...he said..." Perry could see that Finchly was thinking frantically, and she kept shooting nervous glances at Aubrey. He hadn't seen it before, but Perry realized that Finchly was very concerned for Aubrey's well-being. She knew that Marcus did something to him, and it was scaring her. Aubrey was a close friend. She didn't want him hurt because of what Marcus had done. "I think he said, 'Do one thing for me.'"

Nodding once, The Doc opened his mouth to speak but was cut off by Aubrey.

"He asked one favor of me, just in case something should happen," he growled, eyeing The Doc. "In case you should do something that would cost someone their life."

"So you did kill Marcus?" Perry asked The Doc, trying to get a confession.

Shushing him with a wave of his hand, The Doc's eyes narrowed at Aubrey's words. "He asked you to take his body to a certain place if he should die, didn't he?"

Aubrey nodded. "If any of them should die, I was to take their body away from you."

"Why away from me?" The Doc asked. "What good would that serve?"

"I don't know. Why don't you tell me? You should know."

"Where did you take the body?"

"Why would I tell you that?" Aubrey demanded. "Considering everything you've done."

"You don't know half of what I've done," The Doc told him in a deadly voice.

"I know all of what you've done!" Aubrey declared, sneering. "Marcus showed me what you did to his people. He explained why he and the others were forced to come here, and why Odau's child must die. I understand everything now. And I will never tell you where I took the body!"

"That's a shame," The Doc sighed. "If you've seen everything that I've done, then you must have seen that I have very powerful methods of persuasion. I will get you to talk, son. That's a promise." Turning back to the others, he explained, "Using his telepathic abilities, Marcus told Aubrey what to do if any of them should die. Marcus saw his death coming. He apparently wanted to make sure that his body ended up in a specific place for a specific reason. That's the beauty of telepathy. It can cause a reaction even after the possessor is dead."

"So Daniel really made him do this?" Finchly questioned, her voice desperate. "I mean, this isn't Garrick's fault that he's like this?"

"Have you seen his eyes?" The Doc asked her, pointing. "That's the result of having your mind meddled with. This was not his fault."

"How do we know he wasn't just drugged?" Renee demanded, peering uneasily into Aubrey's black eyes.

The Doc gave her an annoyed look, and directed his attention back to Finchly as she began to speak once more.

"Is there something we can do to help him?"

"Nothing we can do except wait until the effects wear off, I'm afraid. Keep him comfortable, and make sure he can't do anything to harm himself or others. I would advise locking him in a secure room, just to be on the safe side. Take his weapon and anything that could be a danger to him. I'll warn you now that there have been cases of suicide or self-mutilation as a result of mind manipulation. You may want to tie him down somewhere. Sedating him would probably be the best thing."

Odau, Finchly, and Agent Long started to move carefully in Aubrey's direction, but Aubrey didn't like that. He stepped back quickly and eyed each and every one of them distrustfully, looking as if he would attack the first person who decided to come any closer. The Doc saw what was happening and took a slow step forward, gesturing for everyone else to back off. "Hey," he called. "Relax. We don't want to hurt you. We're only trying to help you."

"You don't want to help me!" Aubrey snarled, baring his teeth. "You filthy humans always use us to help yourselves! You only give a shit about yourselves! And you're the worst one!" He pointed his finger accusingly at The Doc. "You slaughtered us all!"

"Did he just call us humans?" Perry heard Odau ask from behind him. Perry, too, had been wondering about that. Did Marcus really convince Aubrey that he was one of them?

"You're not one of them, Aubrey," The Doc told him, looking worried.

"Yes, I am!" Aubrey exclaimed furiously.

"This is a paranoid delusion you're experiencing," The Doc explained, his voice soothing. Taking another step closer, he continued. "It's not uncommon in a situation such as this, but you can fight it. You're not one of them."

"Yes, I am!" Aubrey repeated, his voice rising. "Stay away from me!"

The Doc backed off as he saw Aubrey's anger, and he kept his hands raised. "You're not," he said firmly. "You're human."

"You're human, you bastard!" Aubrey snapped. "I'm Colician!"

The Doc dropped his hands in frustration.

"Garrick, please!" Finchly begged, walking up to him and placing a hand on his shoulder. "Let us help you. You're not well."

In one quick movement, Aubrey had smacked Finchly's hand away and given her a hard shove backwards. He gave her the same fearsome look he had given The Doc, and a strange hissing noise began to slip through his teeth.

Aubrey was her friend, her partner, and Finchly could see the truth along with everyone else; Aubrey was completely gone. Something had taken over Aubrey's mind and was now speaking through him. Was it a small trace of Marcus that lingered behind to take control of the detective? Or was it something else? Something worse?

"This isn't you, man," Perry told him, and Aubrey snapped his head in the direction of his voice. "We're trying to capture Hara, remember? She's murdered people and you're helping us find her. Can you remember? Hara's the bad guy, not us."

"Hara's not the one we need to be worried about right now," Aubrey muttered. "We need to worry about the humans threatening our lives!"

347

"We?" Odau said in confusion, glancing curiously at Perry. "What is he talking about?"

"Aubrey," Perry called, trying to get the detective to snap out of it before he did something regrettable. "Garrick Aubrey. That's your name. You're a detective working with the Philadelphia Police Department, and you're working on the Hara case under the direction of Lieutenant Graham Odau. Your partner is Maggie Finchly, the woman you just pushed away from you. These other agents around you are all your friends, and they don't want to hurt you. Daniel Marcus was your friend too, but he's hurting you right now. He made you think that you're a...Colician, but you need to remember who you really are. You're Garrick Aubrey, and you're a human being. You're just as human as I am."

"Are you crazy, Perry?" Aubrey demanded in confusion. "You're not human either!"

Taken aback, Perry stared at him. He could feel every eye in the room on him, and after a moment Odau muttered, "What?"

Anger coming back to his face, Aubrey shouted, "They've all got you brainwashed! That's what they do! They take everything that you are and destroy any trace of it!"

"Detective, calm down!" Agent Long ordered.

"Shut up!" Aubrey snapped, and spoke to Perry once more. "These people are our enemies, Perry! And we need to get rid of them before they kill us just like they killed everyone else!" He whipped out his firearm and aimed it at The Doc.

"Take a look at everything you've done!" Aubrey screamed at The Doc, cocking his weapon and squeezing the trigger.

The gunshot caused Perry's ears to ring. He turned in horror towards The Doc, expecting to see a bullet hole in his forehead. But apart from his wide eyes and stunned expression, he was completely fine. No bullet wounds, no blood staining his clothing, nothing. Turning back around, Perry saw that Lieutenant Odau had the exact same look on his face as The Doc. The only difference was that he had his arm raised, with his weapon in his hand. And it was aimed at Aubrey.

Hearing a clatter, Perry looked at the detective and gasped. Aubrey's gun had fallen to the floor, and his face showed confusion. He glanced down at his chest to see blood pouring out of a wound centered dead over his heart. Letting out a choking sound, he fell over backwards to the floor.

Perry turned to Odau as everyone else rushed to Aubrey's side. Reaching out, he placed his hand on the lieutenant's. Odau's hands were shaking terribly as Perry made him lower them. His face was horrified at what he had done, and he released his weapon and let it fall to the floor.

"He…he was going to kill him," he stammered, staring at Aubrey's limp form. "I had no choice."

"I know," Perry told him quietly. "It's okay."

Raising his eyes to meet Perry's gaze, Odau's face showed great pain. He knew it wasn't okay. He had shot one of his officers in an attempt to protect a man responsible for murder, torture, and many other terrible things. "Oh, my God," he whispered, realizing that he had sacrificed the life of one of his own for the life of a terrorist. "What have I done?"

"It's okay," Perry repeated, patting him gently on the shoulder. Leaving the lieutenant where he was, Perry hurried over to the group crowding around Aubrey.

"Will you back off?" The Doc was asking Finchly. "I'm a doctor. I know what I'm doing!"

"Yeah, you knew enough to get him killed!" Finchly cried, tears streaming down her grief-stricken face.

"Enough!" Perry commanded as The Doc opened his mouth to argue back. Taking Finchly's arm, Perry pulled her away from the group. "Let him help," he told her, seeing the agony on her face. "This was his fault, now let him do something to help."

Grief clouding her face, she wrenched her arm free of Perry's grip and ran off in the direction of the offices. Perry could see it was going to be difficult for her to cope with this incident. But he had Aubrey to worry about at the moment. Pushing Martinson aside, he knelt beside Aubrey's body. To his relief, Perry saw that the detective wasn't dead, just unconscious. The Doc's hands were covered in Aubrey's blood as he pressed down on the wound, and Perry could see Aubrey's chest rising and falling slowly.

"Go and get my medical bag!" The Doc shouted back at his guards, and they ran out of the building immediately. Studying Aubrey's face carefully, The Doc called, "Aubrey, wake up! Come on, kid. Give me a sign." He slapped the side of his face three times, leaving a streak of blood on his cheek. "Wake up, Aubrey!"

With a sudden jerk, Aubrey's eyes shot open and he gasped for breath. His breathing was fast and heavy, and Perry saw pain cross onto his face. For a moment he just looked up at everyone around him, until his eyes locked on The Doc's. Letting out a roar of anger, he threw both his arms at The Doc's head. The Doc caught both his wrists in his own hands and pushed them back down to his sides.

"Good boy," he said as Aubrey went limp again. Pressing down on the wound once more, he glanced around at the half dozen others surrounding them. "How about everybody take a few steps back and give the two of us some room?"

The group obeyed and moved back several feet. Perry started to climb back to his feet, but he stopped when Aubrey reached up and

349

grabbed his arm. Dropping back to his knees, Perry lowered his head down closer to Aubrey. "Just…try to take it easy, okay?" he told him, resting a hand on his shoulder.

"You're—one of us," Aubrey choked out, every word sounding like an effort.

"No, I'm not," Perry murmured.

"Yes," Aubrey whispered, his eyelids drooping dangerously. "And he will kill you, just like he killed the rest of us."

Glancing up at The Doc, Perry saw that he was staring back with that curious expression again. Perry began to wonder if what Aubrey was saying was the truth. The Doc had obviously killed Marcus, so would he be next? Hara had saved his life twice. Jack had seemed fairly interested in him right from the start, and it wasn't just because they looked alike. The Doc had also taken a strange interest in him. Marcus had originally attempted to warn Perry about The Doc's intentions, and now Aubrey— who happened to be affected by Marcus's mind—was doing the same thing. Something about Perry that he himself could not see had caught the attention of these Colicians. Was he somehow connected to everything that was occurring? Was he really "one of them?"

"Poor Hallie Reifert," Aubrey muttered, more to himself than anyone else. His voice was becoming distant, and his expression was becoming dazed.

"How did you know that name?" The Doc demanded shakily, his voice actually showing fear.

Ignoring The Doc's uneasiness, Perry asked, "Who's Hallie Reifert?"

"Save her," Aubrey told him, nodding. "She'll be lost without your help."

"But who is she?" Perry repeated urgently, wondering if she was another child Hara was targeting.

"How did you know that name?" The Doc asked again, his tone even more disquieted.

Shushing him quickly, Perry shook Aubrey's shoulder. "Tell me who Hallie Reifert is so I can help her! Please!"

Disregarding him, Aubrey turned his head to look The Doc in the eye once more. "I saw everything," he said. "That's how I know. Marcus showed me everything. Everything that happened…everything that's going to happen. I saw everything you did to those poor people. What you did to us. And it makes me sick. But do you want to know a secret?" Aubrey had begun to grin up at The Doc. "That boy who you're still experimenting on? Yeah, he's going to be the end of you."

"How did you know about him?" The Doc demanded, and Perry looked up to see him wide-eyed in confusion and fear.

"You're going to burn in hell," Aubrey told him, and he started to cough heavily.

"How did you know?" The Doc repeated louder, grabbing Aubrey's chin in his hand to make him look at him again.

"I was supposed to be one of them," Aubrey said suddenly, and a flash of sadness swept across his face. "And now look at me."

"It's going to be okay," Perry promised him, taking his hand and squeezing it reassuringly. "You're going to be okay." Glancing up at The Doc, he asked, "He is going to be okay, right?"

His face still flustered, The Doc raised his eyes to meet Perry's. Shaking his head solemnly, he answered, "No, he's not."

Perry's heart sank. Looking back down at Aubrey's sad face, he realized that the end was coming quickly for him. The detective's eyes were closed and his breathing was becoming uneven. The Doc was still pressing down on the wound, but a great amount of blood was seeping out from under his hand. Aubrey's face was as pale as the white walls around them, and his lips were losing their color as well.

"Save her," Aubrey mumbled again, sighing wearily. Blinking his eyes at Perry, he repeated, "Save her!"

"Okay," Perry said softly, nodding. "I will."

"And the boy," Aubrey added, his words barely audible.

"Who?" Perry asked in confusion.

"Save her boy, too," Aubrey breathed, his eyes closing again.

"Aubrey, what boy?" Perry demanded, shaking his shoulder. When he didn't move, Perry shook him again. "Aubrey, answer me!"

The Doc put two fingers to Aubrey's neck to feel for a pulse, and then grabbed Perry's wrist and pulled his hand away from the detective. When Perry looked to him, The Doc explained, "He's gone."

Feeling a deep amount of regret for the loss of yet another officer—and friend—Perry gazed down at Aubrey's lifeless body. Considering how angry and violent he had been just minutes earlier, Aubrey now looked quite peaceful. It was almost as if he had never put up a fight to begin with.

✳ ✳ ✳

"Who's Hallie Reifert?"

That was the first question Perry had for The Doc when the two of them were alone in one of the offices. Twenty minutes had passed since Detective Aubrey had breathed his last words, and Perry wanted to make sure he didn't die for nothing. It was time that The Doc shared everything he knew.

There were so many things Aubrey said that didn't make any sense, but The Doc seemed to understand it all. Some of what was said seemed to make him uncomfortable, and even frightened him. But who was Hallie Reifert, and why was she so significant? What boy had Aubrey been talking about? The boy The Doc evidently was holding somewhere? And if The Doc really did have a boy locked up, what was the reason? Was the boy one of these Colicians? What did Aubrey mean when he said, "I was supposed to be one of them,"? One of whom? One of the Colicians? Was The Doc really going to kill Perry like Aubrey said? And why did everyone keep saying that Perry was "one of them"? The questions were endless, and Perry wanted them answered as soon as possible.

"It doesn't matter," The Doc muttered after a moment's silence, staring down at his hands. Perry confronted him while he was sitting alone at one of the desks. Ever since he came in The Doc hadn't once met his gaze. He was deep in thought about something.

Standing on the other side of the desk, Perry planted his hands on the wood surface and declared, "It does matter! Maybe not to you, but it does to me! So are you going to answer me or not?"

Finally, The Doc lifted his head to look into Perry's frustrated eyes. His own eyes appeared mystified and perturbed as he gazed back at him, and he asked curiously, "Why does it matter to you so much?"

Growing agitated, Perry explained, "Because I promised a dying man that I would save a girl called Hallie Reifert. I haven't a clue who she is, but I made a promise and I intend to keep it."

"Why would you promise to save someone if you don't even know who she is?" The Doc questioned, leaning back in his chair and peering up at Perry suspiciously.

"Too many people have died today!" Perry told him angrily. "And if this girl—whoever she is—is in trouble, then I'm going to help her. So who is she? Is she another child Hara's targeting?"

Shrugging, The Doc looked back down again, his expression becoming distant.

Perry decided to try a new method of persuasion. "Doc, how many people have died because of you in the past three years?"

His eyebrows coming together, The Doc looked back up in surprise. "Excuse me?"

"In the past three years, how many people have you killed?" Perry repeated, making an attempt to keep the irritation out of his voice. "By your hand or as part of a conspiracy."

At first, The Doc appeared offended, but then he whispered, "Too many."

"How many?"

"Too many to count!"

"Do you feel any guilt or remorse at all?"

An unidentifiable emotion flashing across his face, The Doc answered, "Some."

"Then don't you want to redeem yourself?" Perry demanded. "At least somewhat? If you tell me who she is, then her blood won't be on your hands if she's killed. I can save the girl and you won't be responsible for yet another death."

The Doc's eyes narrowed by a fraction at Perry's harsh words, but he didn't give a straight answer. All he said was, "You already know her."

"Damn it!" Perry shouted, slamming his palms down on the table. At The Doc's startled expression, he glared. "I'm sick of these riddles! Can't anyone just answer me properly?"

"You know who she is," The Doc repeated calmly. "You just need to put the pieces together first."

"Just tell me who she is!" Perry ordered.

"You tell me," The Doc replied, raising an eyebrow.

Fuming, Perry resisted the urge to swing a fist at The Doc's smug face. "I don't have time for this!" he snapped, pulling his radio out of his belt. Pressing down the talk button, he called into it, "Andy! Andy, are you there?"

"Yes, Perry?" Martinson's voice crackled.

"Will you do a search for anyone in the area with the name Hallie Reifert?" Perry requested.

"I already am," Martinson replied.

"And?" Perry said eagerly.

"I'll let you know if I find anything," Martinson promised.

Disappointed, Perry set his radio down on the desk and sat down in a spare chair behind him. Glimpsing The Doc watching him, Perry demanded, "What?"

"You could have figured out who she was all on your own," The Doc told him sternly.

"I don't know anyone named Hallie Reifert!" Perry yelled.

Sighing, The Doc shook his head slowly and looked back down at the desktop.

"Why must you always speak to me in riddles?" Perry asked him. "Can't you ever just give me the answer I need instead of just telling me I'll figure it out eventually?"

"But you will figure it all out eventually," The Doc said.

"Exactly!" Perry cried. "If I'm going to eventually figure it out, why can't you tell me now?"

"Because you need to figure it out on your own," The Doc explained.

"Maybe I don't have the time to sit and figure it out on my own!" Perry snapped. "People's lives are on the line here! I can't sit around putting a puzzle together while people are out there dying! You know who this girl Hallie is, yet you refuse to tell me. Her life could be in serious danger, and you're not going to help me find her because you're waiting for me to take the time to figure it out!"

"Maybe if you stopped and thought for three minutes, you might figure it out," The Doc shot back.

"A great load of good three minutes is going to do me," Perry muttered, more to himself than The Doc.

"You know," The Doc started thoughtfully. "You and everyone else in your little posse think Lieutenant Odau is stubborn, but you're as stubborn as they come."

"What?"

"You're so determined to have all the answers, yet you won't set aside a few minutes to just stop and think about it!"

"I have thought about it!"

Snorting, The Doc smirked at him. "Not hard enough, apparently! The answers to everything you're looking for are right under your nose. But first you need to open your eyes and look."

Scowling at him, Perry looked down at the floor. The answers were not right in front of him.

"Any more pointless questions? Or can we start focusing on the really troubling news?"

"Oh, boy," Perry muttered sarcastically. "What could possibly be more troubling than an endangered child who no one wants to save?"

"Don't get smart with me now, boy," The Doc warned, giving him a sharp look of disapproval.

"And enough with this 'boy' and 'son' and 'kid' crap!" Perry snapped in annoyance. "I'm not a child!"

"How about you grow up a bit and then maybe people won't make that mistake again?" The Doc suggested, raising an eyebrow and smirking.

Deciding to ignore The Doc's provocative comment, Perry demanded, "So what exactly is this troubling news you speak of?"

"Aubrey," The Doc replied. "He knew stuff that he shouldn't have known."

"Didn't you say his mind was possessed by Marcus's? He said Marcus told him everything that happened, and if Marcus could get into Aubrey's mind couldn't it be possible for Aubrey to see into Marcus's mind as well?"

"Yes, that's exactly how it works," The Doc said absentmindedly, lost in thought about something. "Marcus showed him everything, so Aubrey saw everything in his mind. But there were some things Aubrey spoke of that Marcus couldn't have possible known about. Things that barely anyone knows about."

"Are we back to the Hallie Reifert thing again?"

"No," The Doc said firmly, his eyes saying that he most definitely did not want to go back to that subject. "Marcus knew the name, so Aubrey must have picked it up from him. I'm referring to what he said about the boy."

"Oh." Perry nodded in realization, growing wary once more. "You don't seriously have a boy locked up somewhere, do you?"

"That's beside the point. We need to figure out how Aubrey knew about that, because there's no way that Marcus could have known."

"You have a boy locked up somewhere?" Perry asked again.

"Perry, focus!" The Doc pleaded.

"I thought you said that Marcus had telepathic abilities?" Perry said, not happy about the change of subject. "He could have read your mind and discovered all your secrets."

"Marcus couldn't get inside my head," The Doc explained, and Perry thought he heard a hint of self-importance in his tone. "No one can."

"And what the hell makes you so special?"

Seeing the disgust on Perry's face, The Doc quickly stated, "It's not that I'm special, it's that I've got this…shield, I suppose…around my mind, so Colicians can't get inside my head. Except for Hara. Now, she is special. She somehow broke through the barriers."

"So what are you suggesting about Aubrey?" Perry asked, not understanding why it was so important. "He figured you out somehow, that's all."

"'I was supposed to be one of them,'" The Doc murmured, nodding thoughtfully. "Those were some of his last words."

"Does that hold some special meaning to you? Because it doesn't make any sense to me."

"What was his blood type?" The Doc asked out of the blue, turning back to Perry.

Bewildered, Perry stared at him. "Why?"

"Will you please just answer the question?" The Doc requested rather impatiently.

"I've been working with the man for one day!" Perry declared. "How should I know? Why does it matter, anyway?"

"It may not seem relevant to you, but I can assure you that it could have a huge contribution to all of this." Leaning back in his chair again, The Doc gazed up at the ceiling. He was lost in thought yet again, leaving Perry more confused than ever.

"How does…" he began.

"Shh!" The Doc ordered sharply, keeping his eyes up. "Let me think."

Perry could practically hear the gears grinding in The Doc's head. He was struggling to figure out whatever was troubling him, and Perry hoped that he would explain everything shortly.

"I think…" The Doc began uncertainly, looking worried. "I think that maybe when Marcus invaded Aubrey's mind, he may have caused

Aubrey to…" He swallowed hard. "May have caused him to somehow gain an ability of his own."

Completely astounded, Perry raised his eyebrows and asked, "You think Marcus somehow gave Aubrey an ability?"

"It's rare, but it's not unheard of," The Doc said thoughtfully, rubbing his chin as he spoke.

"How?" Perry demanded. "I thought the abilities were created by a chemical compound? How could Aubrey have gotten an ability if he was never exposed?"

"Because Marcus was exposed!" The Doc explained coldly, irritated that Perry didn't understand everything. "The bond he created between himself and Aubrey might have been enough to expose Aubrey to the compound as well!" Sighing, he looked down at the floor. "Aubrey knew too much for it to be Marcus's effect. He was talking about things that were to come…"

"So you think Marcus somehow exposed Aubrey to the compound with his mind and gave him the ability to see the future? Do you have any idea how you sound right now?"

"It's only a theory. The only way we would know for sure is if we knew Aubrey's blood type."

"If this is going to get any more complicated you should let me know now," Perry told him. "I'm not sure how much more of this I can take."

"This is going to get much more complicated very shortly," The Doc replied to Perry's dismay. "If you think it's complicated now, then you've got a huge surprise heading your way."

"Great," Perry said sarcastically. "That makes me feel so much better. I am completely reassured now."

"He said the boy was going to be the end of me," The Doc said to himself.

"Oh, yeah," Perry said. "You still have yet to tell me about the boy."

"He's one of them," The Doc explained in annoyance. "One of the last."

"So you decided to lock him up like an animal?" Perry demanded furiously.

"They're all animals!" The Doc snapped, pure hatred in his eyes.

"You know what? I'm betting that Hara and her kind would say the same thing about the human race right now!" Perry was enraged by what The Doc was saying. "It's a child, for Christ's sake!"

"Children grow up, Perry!" The Doc reminded. "Eventually, he'll go bad just like the rest of them."

"Listen to yourself!" Perry cried. "You're judging an entire race by the actions of a few! Did you know every one of them personally? Did you even know *one* of them personally?"

"I knew them well enough," The Doc hissed, his eyes slits.

"What exactly did they do that was so horrible that you decided to kill all of them?" Perry asked.

The Doc refused to answer. He just stared back at Perry, half in contempt and half in despair. Suddenly, Perry understood. He saw it in The Doc's cold eyes. He finally saw the reason. And it wasn't because the Colicians had been a threat to the humans, or because they had the strange capabilities. It wasn't because they had committed violent acts against the humans, or any other logical reason Perry could think of. No, it was personal.

"So it really was because of your family?" Perry whispered, remembering everything Hara had spoken about during the confrontation earlier. "You killed them all because one man refused to help you save your kid?"

"Do you have any idea what it's like?" The Doc asked him. "Do you know what it feels like to lose everything?"

"I know what it feels like to lose family," Perry said. "My mother died when I was a child. I killed my father in self-defense. My only child lives about a thousand miles away and I never get to see her. But this isn't about me. You killed those people—that entire race of people—out of revenge."

"I prefer the word justice," The Doc muttered.

"You sick fucker!" Perry whispered, jumping to his feet. "That isn't justice! You did it because one man didn't help you! And you experimented on the ones who were interesting to you! You...you tortured Hara! And who knows how many others? No wonder Hara is the way she is!"

"Are we going to have a problem here?" The Doc asked him, his eyes and voice both threatening.

"Yeah, we are!" Perry immediately answered angrily, glaring down at him. "Because if Hara doesn't end up killing you, I will!"

The Doc was silent for a moment, gazing up at Perry with an amused expression on his face. He seemed to find Perry's threat funny. Rising to his feet slowly, he walked around the desk to where Perry stood.

He meant what he said about killing The Doc, but he was still intimidated by him, and most likely would be until they got rid of him. Watching anxiously as The Doc walked up to him, Perry swallowed and stared back into the man's daunting eyes.

"You?" The Doc asked, raising his eyebrows. "Kill me?" He laughed scornfully, but then his expression became very serious. Leaning forward, he growled, "I'd like to see you try."

Perry took a fearless step closer to The Doc. They were already pretty close together, but Perry closed the gap and glared fiercely into his eyes. Standing up as tall as he could, he stated, "The others may be willing to let you get out of this, but not me. Once this is over, it will be over for you too."

"Let me ask you something, boy," The Doc said. "Why exactly are you going to kill me? Is it because you're 'one of them?' You need to clarify for me whose side you're really on, because right now it is very difficult for me to tell. So whose side are you on, Agent Perry? The girl who killed hundreds of people and destroyed half the city? Or me, who has been helping you find her? You need to choose now. Who's it going to be? Me or her?"

Perry lowered his eyes to the floor and ran over his options one last time. He chose the one that would benefit more people in the future rather than the past. "You," he muttered, too ashamed at himself to look The Doc in the eye.

He could almost feel the pride flowing in waves from The Doc. "Very good," The Doc praised, patting him on the shoulder. Giving him some room, The Doc backed up a few steps and waited for him to meet his gaze. "Now that that's settled, I think we ought to move onto other matters."

"Like what?" Perry grumbled.

"Hara," The Doc replied. "That's the reason I'm here, after all. I've been thinking of ways to find her, and I think I've found one."

"Great," Perry said very unenthusiastically. "Let's hear it."

"You may not like it," The Doc warned.

"Just tell me!" Perry snapped.

"I need to talk to Jack," The Doc said.

"Over my dead body," Perry immediately responded.

"Well, that can be arranged," The Doc replied, grinning.

"I think you've tortured enough people for one day," Perry stated. "Figure out a different way to find her."

"You know," The Doc sighed after a pause. "That kid is not your family."

"Yes, he is!" Perry said.

"No, he's not," The Doc told him firmly. "There may be a biological relation between the two of you, but that doesn't make him family. You just met the boy! You don't know his favorite foods, his favorite things, what he's like, what he does for fun. You don't know anything about him. Being related to someone doesn't make them your family."

Realizing he was right, Perry sighed and ran a hand through his hair. But after what The Doc had done, Perry didn't want to let him anywhere near Jack. He didn't want to let him near anyone. It may be true that he didn't know anything about Jack, but he was the only thing close to a family that Perry had. And he didn't want The Doc in close proximity to the boy.

The Doc seemed to understand what was going through Perry's head, because he began to reassure him. "I only need two minutes with him. Possibly less. Two minutes in that room with him, and I'll have my answer and we'll have a location on our girl. Two minutes. I promise. As soon as he answers my question I'll leave, if that's what you wish. Two minutes."

"How do I know you won't hurt him to get your answer?" Perry demanded suspiciously.

"I don't need to," The Doc said, raising his eyebrows. "I'm not going to hurt him, Perry. You can even go in with me if you like. I have nothing to hide."

"And why should I believe you?" Perry asked him. "I'm having trouble telling when you're lying and when you're not."

"Trust me."

"Trust you?" Perry repeated, snorting. "You never had my trust to begin with! Why should I trust you now?"

"I'm offering you a place in the interrogation room," The Doc reminded. "Do you really think that I would try anything with you in the room, especially when you clearly would not tolerate it?"

He did have a point. Watching his expression carefully, Perry made his own request. "Let me talk to him first. Let me ask him about Hara, and if he doesn't answer..." His voice trailed off.

"Haven't you already questioned him on the matter?" The Doc asked. "Did he give you any answers? What makes you think he'll talk to you?"

"Because he talked to me before! Not necessarily about Hara's location, but he gave me some answers before. Maybe he'll talk to me now."

The Doc didn't reply. He just stared at Perry.

Perry told him, "Just give me ten minutes to talk to him, and if he won't talk to me, then...then you can have your two minutes."

The Doc shrugged. "Okay. I suppose we can try that first. But it's everyone's time you'll be wasting."

Relieved that he was finally giving in, Perry nodded and leaned back in his chair. There was still something that was bothering him, so he decided to ask The Doc about it before he committed himself to something that he would regret. "What makes you think that Jack will talk to you, anyway?"

His eyes flickering to Perry's, he replied, "I can be very intimidating. When he sees that I'm here, he'll tell me what I want to know. Even if he's betraying his best friend."

"And why exactly are you intimidating to him? Is it because you did something to him too? Was he one that interested you?"

"As I was trying to tell you earlier, Agent Perry, Jack does not have an ability."

Perry thought about what The Doc said earlier. "But you said before that Hara wouldn't trust an ordinary human!"

"Jack isn't an ordinary human," The Doc reminded him. "Surely you've noticed?"

"If he doesn't have an ability, and he's not an ordinary human, then what is he?"

Shrugging, The Doc answered, "I don't know. A mistake? That's what I've been trying to figure out."

"So you did experiment on him?"

The Doc groaned. "Are you going to go talk to Jack, or are we just going to keep wasting time?"

Perry shrugged. "Fine. Let's go. The sooner we get rid of you and the girl, the better. I do need to talk to a few people first, though." Standing up, Perry started to walk to the door. The Doc stood up as well and began to lead the way, but there was one more thing Perry needed to know. "Why did you kill Marcus?"

The Doc refused to reply.

"Don't tell me you didn't," Perry commanded. "Because everyone knows it was you. I just need to fully understand why you did it, so please—for once—give me the truth."

"Alright then," he muttered. "I killed Marcus for two reasons. Number one: he let Allan Brown escape. And I wanted him. I wanted him badly."

"Why?"

"Because his ability fascinates me. You don't find many people with an ability like his. He's almost as rare as Hara. Technically speaking, he has the ability to separate every atom in his body from the others, move them all to another position, and then rejoin them all in the proper form."

Perry pondered that statement for a moment. "He's a teleporter."

"Yes," The Doc replied, nodding.

"So you killed a man because you couldn't experiment on another man who can teleport?" Perry concluded. "Talk about a temper tantrum."

Snickering, The Doc smirked back at Perry's disgusted face. "You could call it that if you want, but I still had some important research to perform on Allan, and I was sick of Marcus getting in my way. That wasn't the first time he interfered with me."

"What, so you just kill anyone who fights back?" Perry demanded angrily.

"Isn't that how it always works?" The Doc asked him.

"Then why haven't you killed me yet? You said you dispose of anyone who fights back against you, which I'm guessing included all of Hara's people. I've been fighting you since the beginning, yet I'm still here. And I'm apparently important to Hara in some way, so wouldn't that be another reason to get rid of me?"

Cocking his head to one side, The Doc asked him, "Are you not grateful that I'm letting you live? This may surprise you, but I am capable of compassion. I'm a man of second chances. Have you stopped to consider that maybe you're important to me as well?"

Startled, Perry furrowed his brow in confusion. How could he be important to both sides of the fight? If he was important to Hara and the others, wouldn't that make him a threat to The Doc? If he was important to The Doc, then why did he try to kill him during the road chase? There was so much he didn't understand. Perry cleared his throat. "Well…that was reason number one. Let's hear reason number two."

"I needed to make Hara upset," The Doc said.

"You…you killed Marcus to make the girl upset?" Perry sputtered. "What the hell is wrong with you?"

Shrugging, The Doc acted like it wasn't a big deal. "I needed to get a strong emotional reaction from her, and Marcus was already on thin ice with me. It worked out perfectly. As you may or may not have noticed, Hara is extremely difficult to catch. There are two ways she can be caught. One way is to take her by force using advanced technology designed especially for her. It takes less time, but there's a high risk of losing valuable men from your side. Another way is to just wear her down, make her not care if she's captured. This process takes a little more time, but fewer people get hurt."

"Well, two men are already dead!" Perry snapped. "How many more is it going to take to satisfy you?"

"Her mind was weak to begin with," The Doc continued, ignoring Perry's rage. "As soon as she arrived in this city, her mind was unstable. She was devastated from the losses she had endured, so it shouldn't take much to get her to snap. Marcus's death may have done the job already. Once Jack tells me where she's hiding, we can surprise her and she won't be able to fight back much in her fragile state."

Perry shook his head, unable to believe what he was hearing. "I don't…I don't understand."

"Understand what?" The Doc wondered.

"You!" Perry declared. "The things you've done…the things you're still doing! How can you live with yourself, knowing that you've hurt so many people?"

It surprised Perry that The Doc actually stopped to think over the question. After a few moments, The Doc said, "Let's go talk to Jack."

Turning back to the door, he walked out and went in the direction of the interrogation rooms.

Left behind to ponder over everything The Doc had said, Perry sank down into the nearest chair. "Dear God," he whispered, running his hand through his already messy hair. He and his colleagues were accepting assistance from a complete psychopath. If The Doc killed anyone who got in his way, then how many more people were going to die before Hara was caught?

"Are you coming?"

Startled by the sudden voice that broke the silence, Perry looked up to see The Doc standing in the doorway. He appeared puzzled by the pained expression on Perry's face, and Perry knew The Doc did not understand the moral implications of his actions.

"Yeah," Perry muttered regretfully, standing up once more and heading towards the door.

Perry led the way out of the hall and towards the interrogation rooms. The door had been ripped off two of its hinges when Hara plowed through it, so all he had to do was give it a light push to open it. There was a clamor of voices as he stepped through the door, and he was pleased to see that nearly everyone was present. Detective Finchly was missing as well as Martinson, who was still doing the research on the Reifert girl. All the others were milling around arguing about something. Perry suddenly realized that they were glaring past him. Aubrey's death had struck a nerve in them all, because now even Agent Long and Lieutenant Odau were furious with The Doc.

Deciding to leave The Doc at the mercy of the others, Perry met Agent Long's gaze and gestured with his head toward a side hallway. He wanted to speak with him alone about their plan to talk to Jack first, so he would understand that it was their only remaining option.

Nodding back understandingly, Agent Long walked away from the group with Perry and they went several feet down the adjacent hall so they couldn't be overheard.

"So what did he tell you?" Agent Long demanded eagerly.

Shrugging, Perry sighed. "Not much that was important, really."

"You were with him for quite some time," Agent Long pointed out. "He must have told you something of importance!"

"Well," Perry started hopefully. "He confessed to killing Marcus."

Agent Long grumbled a bit. "It was obvious from the start. Who else would have done it? It obviously wasn't Hara. You saw how devastated she was when she found his body."

Gaping at him, Perry said, "You said before that we needed proof! You were defending him, yet now you're saying we don't need to prove it? What's going on? What are you doing?"

"The reason I defended him was because I knew he was the only one who could catch Hara," Agent Long explained, lowering his eyes. "We all knew we couldn't do this alone, and after seeing the technology he possessed it was clear that he had encountered her before and knew what he was doing. It was obvious that The Doc murdered Marcus, but we couldn't make an arrest when Hara was still out there. Remember what she said before? She isn't going to stop until she kills the lieutenant's son. Enough people have died in the past two days. I understand that you and everyone else do not want to work with The Doc anymore, but we need him. Hara's the enemy, remember?"

"I'm beginning to doubt that," Perry said, understanding the tough decision Agent Long had earlier faced.

"What do you mean?" Agent Long asked curiously, surprised by Perry's change of mind.

"The bank incident and killing the children made her our enemy. Everyone says she's doing it because she went mad after what was done to her, but I think she has a more valid reason for taking all these lives. I don't know what it is, but Hara evidently thinks it's justifiable. She also said before that killing Odau's son would save her species, and it's clear that she believes it will."

"And how is it that doesn't make her a threat?" Agent Long demanded.

"Well, consider what she's done for me," Perry explained. "She's saved my life more than once, even from The Doc's actions. If you look at it from a different perspective, you can see that we're fighting the wrong person right now. We're not disposing of the enemy who's actually among us now, the enemy who wiped out an entire species."

"Are you saying we should just forget about Hara and let her kill more people?" Agent Long asked. "Because that's what we'll be doing if we arrest The Doc now. You'd rather get the guy who's helping us than the girl who's murdering innocent people?"

"No," Perry sighed, trying to think of the proper way to say what he was thinking. "But I'm saying that we're fighting someone who has gone out of her way to do the right thing, while we work with the guy who killed several officers and committed genocide. The first time I saw The Doc he was trying to kill me and everyone else in my truck. Hara stopped him and saved us. Sparing lives means that Hara is indeed capable of compassion. I don't think we should just allow her to get away with everything she's done, but after she saved my life I don't think I can return the favor by handing her over to that psychopath. I won't let The Doc just take her. Hara killed innocent children and many more people, but she saved my life. I owe her enough to make sure she never has to go through one of The Doc's torturous experiments ever again."

"So what are you suggesting?"

"I suggest that we go along with The Doc's plan until Hara is in custody, and then we arrest him and charge him for all the chaos he's caused. We can figure out how his weapons and technology work and then we'll be able to keep Hara in custody without his help."

"You want us to steal his technology from him?" Agent Long repeated in a slightly amused voice.

Thinking about it, Perry felt that it only seemed fitting. "Sure, why not?"

"Sounds good to me," Agent Long said, grinning broadly.

"The Doc needs to answer to the things he's done," Perry murmured, nodding as he spoke. "I won't just let him walk away with that girl. I'll make sure he goes to prison for the rest of his life, and then he can explain to the world what he did to Hara and her race, and how he covered up their very existence."

"What do you plan to do with Hara once she's caught?" Agent Long asked. "Are we going to lock her up as well and let our own scientists figure out what she is?"

"Never," Perry declared forcefully. "She's already been hurt enough. We're going to get her help. Her life has been turned inside out and her mind is extremely fragile. Once she's better, we'll decide where to go from there."

"You're actually willing to give this girl a second chance after everything she's done, when I bet you almost everyone else in this group wants to see her dead? No wonder she likes you."

Perry shrugged again. "As I said, I owe her my life."

"Maybe she saved your life for a reason," Agent Long wondered, peering at him.

"Well, she obviously had some reason," Perry mused. "She wouldn't have gone through all that trouble for nothing."

"No, but maybe she knew you would show her mercy," Agent Long suggested. "Maybe she somehow foresaw that you would help her."

"Maybe," Perry half-considered. "But you do agree with me, right? We can't allow Hara to be experimented on any more. As soon as The Doc catches her, we arrest him and then find a way to help Hara."

"Yes, I agree with all of it," Agent Long said. "I don't trust The Doc and I don't want him or Hara loose on the streets. Once Hara's in custody, The Doc will be put away as well."

"Good," Perry breathed in relief, glad his idea met approval.

"So what else did you and The Doc talk about?" Agent Long asked curiously.

"The Doc killed Marcus so he could...oh, how did he put it? Oh, yeah, so he could get 'a strong emotional reaction from her.'"

His eyes widening, Agent Long repeated, "A strong emotional reaction?"

Nodding, Perry wished it wasn't true.

"He killed the detective to upset Hara?"

"Yeah," Perry muttered. "He did."

"Why on earth would he do that?"

"Because he's nuts!" Perry said, getting angry all over again. "He's trying his hardest to destroy this kid's life and make her miserable, and he does it by killing everyone she loves and cares about!"

"But why? What's the point? What's his motive?"

Thinking it over, Perry suddenly recalled something from the earlier conversation between The Doc and Hara. "Because he wants her to be like him," Perry said. "He's trying to bring her down to his level. Hara lived a life similar to The Doc's. She lived isolated from most of her people, and The Doc lived mainly among other scientists. Maybe The Doc felt like Hara was his parallel or something. A counterpart to him. But then his family died, and he wanted Hara to experience every ounce of grief he had. Killing everyone she ever knew or loved was his way of doing it. He wanted her to understand the way he felt, and I really think he made her understand. His grief drove him mad, and now Hara's grief has driven her mad as well. Now they really are parallels, but I don't think the Doc is going to stop until he's killed everyone close to Hara. Which means Jack, Meg Hopper, and Allan Brown. I think he may try to kill all of them."

"I recently had Lieutenant Odau radio a few of his team to go search for Meg Hopper at the hospital," Agent Long told him. "As I said, I don't want anyone else to die. Maybe we can get our hands on her before The Doc does."

"What about Allan Brown?" Perry asked. "Do we have any leads on him yet?"

Agent Long shook his head regretfully. "We don't even know where to start looking! After Marcus helped him escape, it was almost like he disappeared into thin air. I went outside to see where he might have gone, and guess what I found?" Reaching into one of his jacket pockets, he pulled out a locked pair of handcuffs. "I found these lying on the ground near the edge of the parking lot, in the direction that the mayor ran."

"Were they locked when you found them?" Perry asked in surprise, taking the cuffs and examining them.

"Yes. He must have somehow gotten them off when he started running. I don't understand how, though. Lieutenant Odau tightened them as much as possible without injuring him after his stunt in the S.W.A.T. truck." Agent Long scratched his head. "But he's one of them, right? The Doc said he had abilities too. He must have used his to get out of the cuffs and escape."

Thinking back to his conversation with The Doc, Perry told him, "The Doc told me what ability the mayor has, and it definitely explains the cuffs. He's a teleporter."

"A teleporter?" Agent Long repeated in disbelief. He seemed to be lost in thought for a moment, but then he said, "That must be how Hara could teleport as well. She must have gotten her ability from Allan Brown."

Nodding in agreement, Perry said, "If Allan Brown can teleport, then I doubt we'll be seeing him again. He could be anywhere! He most likely went somewhere far away, where no one would ever find him. He probably teleported to Bali or Tahiti or somewhere nice like that."

"I don't think so," Agent Long muttered. "His friends are still here in this city, which makes him still a part of this fight."

"So what are we going to do with him and Meg Hopper when we find them?" Perry asked.

"When we find them, I'll make sure they stay locked in a maximum security area where they can't escape and The Doc can't get to them."

There was something else on Perry's mind, something he felt Agent Long should know. "Hara has the ability to communicate mentally with other people, and she has with me a few times. Each time she came into my mind to converse with me, I saw and felt things that I believe came from her thoughts."

"Such as?" Agent Long asked, looking deeply interested.

"Well, it's hard to explain," Perry told him, trying to find words for the thought he had experienced. "The images I saw didn't really make sense. They were mainly of destroyed cities and burning buildings, but some were of different people."

"Do you know who any of them were?"

"No, but there were several children and several adults. I couldn't make out any of their faces, but I could tell that they were important to her."

"How?"

"Because she felt intense emotion for them all. I think they were her friends and family who were lost. Her thoughts seemed to linger on them, and whenever she did think of them directly she felt a large amount of pain. But the pain is overpowered by her anger. Anger was always the dominant emotion she felt, and her anger is what's currently driving her. The need to avenge her family is what keeps her fighting, but I also felt that her anger was suppressing another emotion: fear. Once you get past the anger, all she feels is fear. She's afraid of us humans because of what The Doc and his people did to her. It was what made me start to wonder if she was the enemy to begin with. She's a scared, desperate child, and desperate people do desperate things."

"Did you see why she's doing this?" Agent Long asked him.

"No," Perry answered. "But she believes the children caused the deaths of her family, friends, and entire species."

"How could children have anything to do with what The Doc did?" Agent Long demanded. "How could she believe such a thing?"

"I have yet to figure that out," Perry muttered, deciding it would be best to now explain the plan to him. "There was one thing I discussed with The Doc that I think you should know about."

"Let's hear it then."

"Since we failed to capture Hara the first time around, The Doc believes that he has another strategy to find her," Perry explained, regretting that he was actually agreeing to the idea. "He wants to talk to Jack to find out where she's hiding."

"No," Agent Long immediately said. "We've already seen what happens to the people he wants to talk to. Two men are dead because of him, and I won't allow anyone else to succumb for the same purposes."

"Speaking of which," Perry began curiously, "whatever did you do with Aubrey's body? Where did you hide it?"

"We didn't hide it anywhere. We called a unit away from downtown to come pick it up and take it to the morgue. I'm done hiding bodies here."

"What are you going to tell them?" Perry asked tentatively.

Agent Long shrugged. "The truth. He tried to open fire on a colleague and was gunned down in the process."

"Are you going to tell them why he opened fire?"

"Not now. When The Doc and Hara are in our custody and I fill out a report then I'll tell them everything that happened."

Nodding, Perry changed the subject back to the matters at hand. "Back to Jack."

"There's no way he's going in there with that boy," Agent Long said firmly. "You don't need to worry about it, Perry."

"No, I think maybe it's a good idea," Perry told him, hardly able to believe the words that were coming out of his mouth.

"What?"

"Just hear me out. I agreed with The Doc that he should be allowed to interrogate Jack on one condition: I speak to him first."

Agent Long considered it. "But what if he won't talk to you?"

"Then...we'll send in The Doc," Perry said, cringing at his own words. "He claims he can get the information in two minutes or less."

"And you're actually willing to send him in there?"

"He assured me that I could go in with him, so I'm guessing he was telling the truth when he said he wasn't going to hurt Jack."

"I still don't know," Agent Long muttered uncertainly. "Something could go wrong."

"It's the only option we have left," Perry told him. "Jack's our last connection to Hara. Besides, if he talks to me, we won't even have to send in The Doc."

"I wouldn't get your hopes too high," Agent Long warned, his expression serious. "The two of you may have some connection that you can't explain, but I'm quite certain that he's loyal to Hara before you."

"What do you mean?" Perry asked in confusion.

"When you were having your stroke and Hara was escaping, Lieutenant Odau saw Jack kiss her before she left," Agent Long explained. "And it was a real, passionate kiss. I'm guessing he's in love with her."

"What about her? Does she share the same feelings?"

"Well, considering the extremely surprised look on her face, I don't think she remotely shares the same feelings. But Jack certainly feels something for her, and I don't think he's going to betray the girl he loves."

Sighing, Perry grumbled, "Well, that definitely complicates things."

"Yeah," Agent Long agreed. "Do you still think he'll talk to you?"

Perry shrugged helplessly. "I don't know. But I have to try. And if it doesn't work...well, we have that other option."

Agent Long's thoughtful expression said that he was about to go along with it. He didn't mind Perry going in to interrogate Jack, but he was worried that he wasn't going to succeed. "I'm going to have to agree with you on this."

"Thank you, sir," Perry replied gratefully, accompanying Agent Long back to the main hallway.

"I think everyone should be present," Agent Long told him. "We'll all watch in the observation room while you do what you need to do."

"Fine by me."

"And Lieutenant Odau will most likely demand to be a part of the interrogation. Please just deal with him and bear with me on this."

Grimacing, Perry said, "With all due respect, I don't think the lieutenant should be present during the interrogation. As you may or may not have observed, Jack, Hara, and the others have no respect for him. I highly doubt that Jack will say a word to me as long as Odau is present. It would be best if I went alone."

"Just do whatever you need to do to get the boy to talk," Agent Long grumbled as they rounded the corner. "I can't guarantee that Odau will listen when you tell him to stay out of it. You have my word I will strap him to a chair if I need to."

Martinson and Finchly were still absent, and everyone else continued to wait in the hallway. They glanced up absentmindedly as Perry and Agent Long approached, but no words were exchanged. The Doc was no longer present; he must have been unable to endure the wrathful glares of the others and decided to leave.

"So here's what's happening," Agent Long said, addressing the entire group. "Agent Perry is going to speak to Jack about the location of Hara. Jack's the only lead to Hara we have, so we're going to take advantage of him. The rest of us are going to be spectators in the observation room, and we are not to interfere with Perry's work whatsoever. If his methods fail to get us the information we need, then The Doc will interrogate him. Any questions?"

"Do you really think it's wise sending that man in there with him?" Renee demanded.

"Two men are dead from his interrogations," Hersh pointed out. "Good men who lost their lives because of his irresponsibility."

Perry explained, "If The Doc ends up going in there, I'll keep him on a three foot leash. Any sign of a threat and he'll be out of there before he realizes it." At Renee's and Hersh's hesitant expressions, Perry assured, "Don't worry. I don't want him to go in there any more than you do, and I wouldn't send him in there if I wasn't absolutely certain I could keep him under control."

"Anything else?" Agent Long asked, looking to each of them. "Well, now that we all agree, we'd better get started! Where's Martinson?"

"Right here, sir," Martinson answered as he stepped through the door into the hall.

"Agent Hersh, please fill him in on the plan," Agent Long told her, and then looked around again. "What about Finchly? Where is she?"

"I think she's in the conference room," Martinson replied.

"I'll get her," Perry offered, heading back to the door. He approached Martinson on his way out, and hoped he had gotten some helpful information about the mysterious Hallie Reifert.

"Did you find anything?" Perry asked him eagerly.

Martinson sighed in frustration. "I started searching for girls with that name within the city, but when I didn't find anything I expanded my search to the whole country. Perry, there isn't a single girl in this country with the name Hallie Reifert."

"Not one?" Perry said in disbelief.

Shaking his head, Martinson said, "There are a few Hallies in the area, and also a family of Reiferts, but no Hallie Reifert."

"What about name changes?" Perry asked.

"I checked for that," Martinson told him. "This Hallie Reifert doesn't exist."

"She must, though!" Perry said.

"Let's remember the name was spoken by a dying man," Martinson said. "He was probably just talking nonsense."

Feeling very frustrated and confused, Perry told his friend, "Well, when we have the time I think we should go talk to the Reifert family living in the city, just to see if they know of anyone with that name."

Martinson shrugged and mumbled, "Sure, whatever you think we should do."

"Are you okay?" Perry asked. Martinson's voice was tired and depressed, and his eyes were dull.

"Fine," he muttered. Brushing past, he walked away to join the others.

Deciding to let it go and deal with Martinson later, Perry continued on his way to find Finchly. He had just made it through the door when Odau called his name. Turning, Perry saw the lieutenant hurrying over to him.

"I want to go in with you," he said insistently.

"No," Perry automatically replied and kept walking.

"No?" Odau repeated, following. "What do you mean, no?"

"Listen, Lieutenant," Perry started in annoyance, rounding on him. "If you've noticed, Jack has no interest in talking to you, so if you'd just kindly watch with everyone else I would be very grateful."

"We're trying to get him to give us the location of the girl trying to kill my son!" Odau declared angrily. "I want to make sure he gives it to us!"

"Yes, and I'm very capable of getting it myself, thank you," Perry snapped back. "I'm sorry, but if we have a shot at getting the information we need, then I have to go in alone." The lieutenant started to object again, but Perry quickly shot him down. "You're not going in with me, and that's final! If The Doc ends up going in, then you can come in with us, but for now you're just going to have to watch with the others. Please just deal with it!" Turning on his heel, Perry left Odau sputtering where he stood.

When he reached the conference room, the door was closed. Knocking twice, he pushed it open and stepped inside just in time to catch Finchly attempting to quickly wipe the tears from her eyes. Her face was red and her eyes were swollen and wet. She looked completely distraught, and for the first time Perry saw how much pain Aubrey's death must have caused her.

"Are you alright?" Perry asked as she turned away in shame.

"Yeah, I'm fine," she sniffed, and tried to wipe away her tears once more. "Does the lieutenant need me for something?"

Walking over to her, Perry placed a comforting hand on her shoulder. "You're not fine," he told her softly.

Sniffing again, Finchly continued to rub her eyes and avoid Perry's gaze. "I'll be alright," she mumbled, sucking in a deep breath.

"Aubrey was a really good friend of yours, wasn't he?" Perry said, thinking back and remembering them being together most of the time throughout the investigation. "You weren't just partners. Do you want to talk about it?"

"I've known him since elementary school," Finchly whispered, and her shoulders began to shake. "We trained together. I...I can't believe he's gone!" She let out a sob and then burst into tears.

Perry wrapped his arms around her and pulled her in for a tight embrace. Finchly sobbed harder and hugged him back, gripping the shoulders of his jacket tight in her hands. Her entire body was quivering in Perry's arms.

"It's going to be okay," Perry told her quietly, and his words may have actually had an effect on her if he had believed them himself. "We're going to get through this."

"I'm sorry," Finchly hiccupped, pulling away from him and lowering her eyes to the floor in embarrassment.

"Don't be," Perry said, placing his hand on her shoulder again. "He was your friend, and I understand how hard it is to lose someone you care about."

"It just seems to me like no one else even cares that he was killed!" Finchly whispered. "Everyone just went about their business like nothing happened! Even Lieutenant Odau didn't give it much thought!" Pain flashed across her face again and she ran a hand through her long black hair.

"Yeah, I noticed," Perry agreed, remembering how dismissive Odau was after Aubrey's sudden, unexpected death.

"I'm really, really sorry about this," Finchly apologized again, taking a deep breath and wiping the remaining tears from her eyes. "This is really embarrassing. I told myself I wasn't going to do this..."

"Don't worry about it," Perry reassured. "Are you going to be okay to go back to work now? We need you."

"Yeah," she replied. "For now, anyway." Sighing, she forced a weak smile and asked, "So what is it you need me for?"

"We're about to interrogate Jack again, and everyone was hoping you would join us."

"Who's interrogating him?"

"Me, and if I'm not successful then...we're sending in The Doc."

Finchly stared at him in shock. "You're sending *him* in?"

"It wasn't my first choice."

"We can't trust him," Finchly said. "He's a liar and a manipulator and a murderer and I don't understand why none of you see that!"

"We all see it," Perry promised, and lowering his voice he added, "And if you just play along with this for a little while longer, I can assure you that Agent Long and I will make sure The Doc is taken care of."

"What do you mean?" Finchly asked, puzzled.

"We all know that The Doc can't be allowed to just walk free after everything he's done. Once Hara is in our custody and we are able to contain her, we're going to arrest The Doc. He's going to pay the price for what he's done."

Nodding in agreement, Finchly told him, "Good, I can deal with that. So long as The Doc is put away in the end, I'll do anything you ask."

"Good," Perry said, nodding also.

"Shall we head back then?" Finchly asked.

"If you're ready. You're sure you'll be alright?"

"You just assured me that the man responsible for my best friend's death is going to be locked up for the rest of his life." The eager look crossed her face again. "I've never been better."

When they reached the observation room, Agent Long asked Perry, "Ready?"

Shooting a glance at The Doc's piercing gaze, Perry replied, "Absolutely."

"Detective," Odau called. "Over here, please."

"Yes, sir," Finchly muttered, and Perry caught the angry gleam in her eyes. He began to feel bad for Finchly all over again, but was sidetracked from her as The Doc approached him.

"You're sure you want to do this?" he questioned, his eyes searching Perry's tired face.

"All I'm sure of is that I don't want you anywhere near my brother."

The Doc blinked in surprise, but then he smirked. "Let's see your stuff then, Agent Perry." He gestured to the door that led to Jack.

Glaring, Perry growled sarcastically, "Wish me luck."

Cocking his head, The Doc replied, "You're well aware how much I want to go in there."

"Well, then let's hope to God I'm successful," Perry muttered, brushing past him and marching into the interrogation room, praying for Jack's sake that he would cooperate.

11

Interrogation

Hara had long since grown used to waking up in strange places, but she would never get used to the disorientation that came with it. The first thought that came to mind when she finally awoke was wondering where the hell she was. Blinking furiously, she stared up at the white tiled ceiling and tried to remember what had happened to her before she blacked out. She started to sit up, but cried out in pain as her head began to throb. Falling back, she groaned and reached her hands up to rub her forehead. Her right arm was being held down by something, and ignoring the horrible pain, she forced herself to raise her head to see what it was.

A white Velcro strap was wrapped around her arm, and Hara saw that she was lying on a large white bed. The strap was attached to the bed, and she could only lift her arm up a few inches. It was peculiar that only her right arm was strapped down and not her left, but then she saw the thick IV jutting out of her vein and realized that the strap was only to hold her steady. But why did she have an IV in her arm?

Disturbing memories came flooding back to her and made her shudder, but it didn't feel like a threatening place to her. Dropping her head back down, she took a deep breath and tried to calm her frantic mind. She still couldn't remember how she got here, but she didn't want to wait around to find out. The room around her had the familiar smell of a hospital, and being locked in a hospital for several months and tortured relentlessly didn't leave her fond of medical institutions. The urge to escape was overpowering, and all she wanted was to get out of there before some doctor walked in the room. It wasn't a good thing that she was in this place; it meant that somebody knew about her.

Reaching her left hand across her body, Hara fumbled with the strap until she was able to peel the Velcro apart, letting loose a loud stripping sound. She flinched, anticipating that a doctor would come running in, but when no one did, she undid the strap the rest of the way and slipped her arm out. Gritting her teeth, she wrapped her hand around the IV and gave it a sharp tug. The IV slid out easily, and she set it aside as the small cut in her arm healed over. Closing her eyes once more, she fought to recall what had happened. Her head ached too much for her to stand up just yet, so she lay on her back and cleared her head to find the one memory she was searching for. It took several moments, and she was becoming quite frustrated until a sudden image flashed into her head.

The Doc.

He's back, she thought with dread. *He found me, just like he said he would. But how did I end up here? Did he capture me again? Is he going to do to me what he did before?*

Her fear subsided as another memory returned to her which told her she wasn't anywhere near him. She teleported away from The Doc and must have ended up in the hospital before blacking out from so many hops. And then that Bennett man had been there, so he must have been the one to put her in the bed.

One more memory came back; one that caused a sob to escape her. "Daniel!" she whispered in grief, choking back the tears that threatened to leave her. "Why?"

How could The Doc do this to her? After everything he had put her through, after every horrible thing he had done to her, why would he take away the last rays of hope that kept her going? Because that's the way he is, Hara reminded herself solemnly. He takes the best people and destroys everything they've ever loved, until they have nothing left worth fighting for. But that's not going to happen with me, she vowed. Allan, Jack, Noah, and Meg are going to live, because if they don't I won't be able to finish what I started.

A single tear trickled down her cheek, and forcing herself to put Daniel out of her mind, she rolled over onto her side. Gasping in surprise, her eyes widened at what she saw off to her right. As she had suspected, she was in a hospital room. There were a few other beds in the room, but only one other was occupied.

In the next bed was Allan. He was out cold, and he was hooked up to an IV as well. Glancing up, Hara saw that a light blue liquid was being injected into his arm, and it was the same substance that was in her IV. Hara recognized it; it was injected into her once before, but she didn't understand how the two of them could be getting that specific treatment in the place they were now. Nobody in the outside world knew about them until just a few days ago, so how could Bennett know what treatments they needed? Unless The Doc really did capture them… She didn't know what happened to Allan after Daniel sacrificed himself to help Allan escape, so maybe The Doc had found him and then found her after she blacked out.

Or maybe Bennett's just a smart son of a bitch and figured out the solution to our overdose, Hara thought, remembering how smart the Bennetts had always been. *It would be nice to again find a doctor I can trust.*

Allan didn't look very good. Unlike Hara, he didn't possess the ability to heal injuries, which was probably why he was still unconscious and he was at the mercy of the treatment. He looked like he really overdid it this time. Fighting her splitting headache, Hara scanned his mind for any activity, but found nothing. Allan most likely would be brain dead if whoever was holding them hadn't hooked him up as soon as they did.

"I guess we're both in the same boat," Hara murmured, sliding her legs off the side of the bed and steadying herself on her feet. The headache was worse than when she had burst before. Very carefully, Hara reached out her hands and slowly stepped towards Allan's bed. She felt like a child attempting to take her first steps, and she unwillingly and unwarily thought back to the time her youngest son Dreyson took his first steps. Dreyson had always been a stubborn child; whenever he saw his older brother and sisters doing something that he couldn't do, he wouldn't stop until he could do it too. He grew frustrated seeing that everyone else in the house could walk except for him, so he tried every day to get himself upright and take those first few steps. At first, he could only pull himself to his feet before falling back down onto his bottom, but before long he could take several steps while holding on to some object in front of him. And not too long after that he took his first actual steps. Hara remembered he had called for her to watch, and when she turned her head he let go of his toy shopping cart and took three, tentative steps forward. She had been so proud of her baby boy; he had begun to walk and talk at just five months, long before any of her other children. Of course, he had fallen over on his face after the third step, but it didn't matter to either of them. She remembered her son had burst into tears when he fell, and she had scooped him up in her arms and sung the lullaby she sang to each of her kids before they went to sleep at night. Dreyson's cries stopped soon after, and he said "Mommy." Just that one word softened her heart—the gentle voice of her baby calling her what she really was: a mommy.

How she now wished for one more moment to hold her son, to hold all of her children, and just hear them whisper, "Mommy." How she wished she could let them all know she loved them, and would never stop. How she wished she could turn back time...

I will turn back time, Hara promised her son. *I'll do it for you, baby. I won't stop until I can hold you in my arms again, until I can hold the others too.*

Grief rolled through her once more, but she quickly shook it off as she caught her balance at the side of Allan's bed. Looking down at her friend's still form, Hara sighed. Allan looked so peaceful, and it was the most peaceful she had seen him since before the war began. When the treatment fulfilled its purpose, he would wake up feeling refreshed and rejuvenated. For a few moments he would sit up and completely forget about everything. He would look around, wonder where he was and how he got there. But then he would remember that the war was still raging around them, and that The Doc had found them yet again. He would shudder, and pray that they could fix what happened before The Doc came into their lives. There was one more thing he would think about, something that would cause him great pain.

"I'm sorry, Allan," Hara whispered, placing a hand gently on his forehead. She couldn't stick around until he woke up; she had work to do. But Allan had the right to know that Daniel, one of his oldest, closest friends, was now dead because their original plan had been thwarted. She would push her memories into his head so that when he awoke, he could see everything she had seen. His mind was in a delicate state, so she would have to be careful as to how much and how hard she inserted the images. He could very well go into shock after seeing the horrifying things Hara had witnessed, but he deserved to know.

"I'm really sorry, my friend," she apologized again, and she was sincere. "I'm sorry I wasn't there to save him. But I'm going to make this right. This is the final straw." Hardening herself, she let her anger take control of her mind once more. "The Doc has pushed me too far this time. I only have four people left to keep me fighting, and I'm going to make sure I use that. The Doc and his crew are going down. Today. I don't care if I die trying, but I'm going to make sure he suffers for what he's done to us. And then I'm going to finish off the boy and his father, and everything will be back the way it was before. I promise." She reached out and touched his shoulder. "Daniel was right. Everything will be okay."

If only she could have believed her own words. She was going to kill The Doc and the Odaus for the destruction of her kind; that was a promise she would keep. But after the hours that had already rolled by, she began to wonder if everything really would be alright. She was positive that her world would be restored once again, and that her family would come back to her, but what would happen to her when this was over? What about Allan, Jack, Daniel, Meg, and Noah? They had all broken the law by coming back to the human world, so what would happen to all of them when they were finally able to go home? Would they be forgiven, or would Hara be exiled again for the murders of those children? But the destruction they would cause later in their lives would be devastating. Did that really give her the excuse to decide whether they got to live or die? Hara thought back to Odau's words, how she wasn't God. She may not be God, but if she knew a terrible catastrophe was on its way, didn't the responsibility for protecting the future fall on her? Hara's father had been their leader before the war, and still would be when it was over, but would he be able to forgive her for what she had done? In the end, everything may go back to the way it was, but Hara doubted that everything would really be okay. She could hope and pray, but her gut told her that nothing was going to ever be quite the same again. Everyone had changed from the trauma of the war, so her world was going to be different, possibly unrecognizable, when she finally went back to it.

Hara was startled when a door suddenly opened in front of her, and she realized that she had been careless. The time she spent talking to her unconscious friend should have been used to figure out where she was, how she could escape, or where she could hide. She once again became aware of her surroundings very quickly. There were six beds in the room; hers, Allan's, and four others that were in a straight line across the room towards the large wooden door that stood about fifteen feet directly in front of her. There was a large window behind her and slightly to her right, and she sensed that there were four floors in between her and the ground; it would be a nasty fall if she decided to jump. There was a tray beside every bed filled with empty syringes and other medical equipment, and along the wall adjacent to the door there was a large wooden bureau. A single white curtain hung bunched up and draping along the floor at the head of each bed. There was a single window beside the door, but it had its blinds drawn so she was unable to see out of the room. She hadn't noticed how silent the area was; there was always a constant noise in her head so she never really noticed when it was quiet around her. It seemed strange for a hospital to be this quiet, especially after the damage she had caused the night before. She assumed the place would be flooded with patients who had survived her wave of fire. Unless of course she wasn't in a Philadelphia hospital... But she knew she was. She could hear the doctors rushing around frantically to help patients on every other floor of the hospital except for the one she was on.

Her eyes darting nervously to the opening door, Hara braced her arms on the side of Allan's bed, preparing herself in case she needed to flee. Adrenaline racing through her veins, she watched an old man enter the room. He had dark, chocolate colored skin, graying hair and mustache, and he was wearing a white lab coat. His face looked tired and sad, and when he eventually glanced up she saw that his eyes seemed to draw people in, like he had a secret that nobody understood, yet everyone wanted to learn. He had his shoulders hunched up, but he held himself strongly with a type of authority that no one wanted to disobey. His walk was stiff, most likely from his old age, and when he stepped forward his right leg dragged behind him with a slight limp. Hara sensed that the man was in a great deal of pain, and doing a quick analysis she realized that cartilage in his right hip was deteriorating very slowly and had been for more than twenty years. She remembered this disease as arthritis, and although none of her people could ever have it, she understood that it could be very painful. After her long year of suffering, Hara forgot that everyone else, even humans, felt pain. It made her feel less vengeful to know that she wasn't the only one in agony.

The man seemed so familiar to her, and it took her a few seconds of hard thinking to realize that it was Bennett, just as she had suspected it would be. He really was the genius who had figured out the treatment. The Bennetts had always been there to help her and her kind, and she supposed they always would be.

Bennett had been looking down at some papers on a clipboard when he entered, so he didn't realize Hara was standing there until he glanced up several feet into the room. "Oh!" he said in surprise when he saw her leaning over Allan and staring up at him. She was breathing hard and every muscle in her body was tensed. Her eyes were red from lack of sleep—all in all a terrifying, unexpected sight. Bennett's eyes widened, but not for the reason Hara would have assumed. He was concerned for her well-being, a sympathy she didn't normally get from humans. "Hello," he called uncertainly, not sure if she was able to hear him or not. Taking a hesitant step forward, he set the clipboard on one of the empty beds and started to come toward her.

At first, he didn't realize his mistake. But as Hara stumbled backwards at his sudden movement, he understood what he had done and stopped immediately in his tracks. "Whoa!" he said, raising his arms and retreating a few steps to give her some space. "It's okay, I won't hurt you."

Hara knew he was telling the truth, but still had difficulty trusting him. She continued to move away from him, bumping into her own bed as she did so. Catching her balance quickly, she turned and started to move for the window. Her head was still pounding and she was weak from exhaustion, definitely not in a suitable condition to jump. But when she was high on adrenaline she could do just about anything.

"Hara, stop!" Bennett yelled urgently, almost pleadingly. "Please!"

She did stop. At the window, she turned and gazed back at him. It was clear this man wanted to help her, so why not let him? For once, she decided to let go of her pride and allow the help that was being offered.

"Read my mind!" Bennett begged, pointing to his head. His eyes were frantic, and for a moment Hara saw her father looking back at her. "Please! I know you can. I don't want to hurt you."

Hara didn't read his mind. Her head hurt too much, and she saw the truth just by looking into his eyes. Bennett meant her no harm.

Relief flooding the man's face, Bennett smiled weakly at her. "Please," he said again. "You're very ill. Let me help you."

Hara nodded gently. "Okay," she whispered.

✳ ✳ ✳

The door to the interrogation cell slammed closed behind him, and Perry stared at Jack sitting at the table in the center of the room. He felt like he was being pinned down, like a huge weight had just been dropped on his shoulders. He felt like he was being forced into this, and he was. If he wouldn't interrogate Jack himself then The Doc surely would, and he couldn't risk that. Sighing wearily, Perry made his way towards the table and studied Jack's curious expression. The sight of the boy and how strangely similar his face was to his own made him shudder.

"Finally!" Jack said in exasperation, sighing in relief and leaning back in his chair. When Perry had first entered and Jack looked up, Jack seemed alarmed, but he looked comfortable now that he saw it was Perry. "I was beginning to wonder if you were going to keep me alone in this room all day!"

"Sorry," Perry apologized, seating himself across from Jack. "We've been… preoccupied with a few matters. But not to worry; we haven't forgotten about you." He said his last sentence with a sort of sarcasm that made the corners of Jack's mouth turn up slightly.

"Well, now that you're here, my friend, would you mind telling me what the hell has been going on?" Jack raised his eyebrows, indicating he was impatient for an answer.

"What do you mean?" The question was pointless; Perry knew exactly what he was talking about.

"I've been hearing crashes, shouting, and gun shots over the past several hours!" Jack declared. "Not to mention the entire building shook at one point. What the hell happened?"

Wondering if the information about Hara might allow Jack to open up to the coming questions, Perry decided to just fill him in on everything that happened.

"Well," Perry began, "after I was taken to the hospital, I was paid a little visit."

"By whom?" Jack asked curiously.

Deciding to leave The Doc's involvement a secret for the time being, Perry shrugged off the question. "No one important. But he said he wanted to help us out, so we came back here to discuss the recent incidents, and then Hara decided to drop by and say hello."

"Oh," Jack nodded in realization, his expression grim. "So how did that turn out?"

"Just wait until you see the hallway," Perry muttered, visualizing the pile of rubble outside the first interrogation room. "An officer is dead, and we're running out of options to find this girl."

Jack nodded slowly, taking in what Perry was hinting at. There was an awkward pause as both of them stared silently at each other, but then Perry cleared his throat uncomfortably. "I guess what I'm trying to say is…"

"You want me to help you find her?" Jack finished for him, crossing his arms over his chest. "Sorry man. Even if I knew where she was I wouldn't tell you. I don't know about your lot, but my people and I never betray our friends. Especially the ones we..." His voice cut off quickly and he lowered his eyes to the surface of the table.

"The ones you love?" Perry asked, raising an eyebrow.

Without looking up, Jack unfolded his arms and rested them on the table. He began to draw little patterns on the metal surface with his index finger, and still he did not answer.

"I heard about your little moment with Hara before she escaped the cells," Perry explained, trying to see if Jack would talk to him about how he felt. Maybe then he would open up about what he knew.

"Shut up!" Jack grumbled, keeping his eyes down. His brow was furrowed in anger, and Perry's tactics were obviously not going to work. He would have to come up with another strategy if he wanted the information. Clearing his throat, Perry was about to pressure him further, but Jack looked up again and spoke before he even opened his mouth. "I know you're planning to ask me a bunch of questions, but before I answer any I have a question of my own that I'd like answered."

Seeing it was only fair, Perry nodded. "Alright. Just so long as you promise to answer all of mine. Truthfully."

"No guarantees," Jack replied, gazing evenly back at him.

Irritated, Perry snapped, "What's your question?"

"Who's watching?" Jack pointed to the one-way glass separating them from Perry's colleagues in the next room.

"What do you mean?" Perry asked, trying to act confused.

"I know that the lieutenant and a bunch of your friends are watching our conversation, but there's something else in there with them." Perry saw Jack shiver in his chair, and he wondered what could be bothering the kid. Inhaling deeply, Jack began again. "I can't...I can't tell what it is, but it's something bad."

"What are you talking about?" Perry looked at his reflection in the one-way glass, and wondered if Jack could tell that The Doc was in the next room.

"As I told you, Perry, I have no ability," Jack said, and it seemed like he was about to repeat Perry's thought. "But living with people with abilities has heightened my own senses and awareness. There is someone else in that room with your friends who does not belong. Now, I'm assuming that it's the person who contacted you and is now helping you. All I can tell you is that he is not a good person. I can feel that this person can't be trusted and is plotting behind your back."

That sounded like The Doc, but how could Jack possibly sense his presence? He's lived with heightened senses his whole life, Perry reminded himself. He's been evolving as well.

"It feels like..." Jack's voice trailed off. He stared down at the table again, his eyes showing that his mind was elsewhere. "This feeling makes me think of someone in particular, but that's impossible. It can't be him…"

He knows, Perry realized. He really knows! But he doesn't know that we know about The Doc yet, so he won't talk about him. "Who do you think it is?" Perry asked.

Without answering the question, Jack looked back up and asked again. "So who is he? The man you brought here with you. What's his name?"

Perry also did not answer. He was too busy thinking over what he was doing. Now that he saw how uneasy Jack had become just by sensing The Doc's presence nearby, it was like a light had been turned on inside his head. It hadn't occurred to him how threatening The Doc was to these people, even when he and Hara had their confrontation down the hall. Hara hadn't shown any fear of The Doc. If there had been any fear to begin with it was completely covered up by her anger. Now he could see that just the very thought of The Doc made them uncomfortable, so what was he supposed to do? It was very unlikely that Jack was going to tell him anything about Hara's whereabouts, which meant Perry would have to hold up his end of the deal and let The Doc in to interrogate him. He reminded himself that he would be inside the room to make sure nothing happened, but what if that didn't stop The Doc from doing something to Jack? Or what if Jack, out of fear, reacted in a panic and did something stupid that would end up hurting himself or someone else? What then? These questions ran through Perry's mind several times, but at the same time he wanted to keep The Doc's involvement out of the discussion. If and when Perry had to give up his role as interrogator, the shock of seeing The Doc might be enough to cause Jack to break down and share everything he knows.

For the first time in Perry's ten-year career, he felt torn between doing what was logical—letting The Doc interrogate Jack to find out where Hara was so they could stop her from causing any more damage—and doing what was ethical—helping the people torn apart by death. This boy he had only just met was changing who he was. Never before had Perry cared about what was in the best interest for the criminal in the investigation. But now that the criminal claimed to be his brother—a part of his own genealogy—he felt different. Perry found himself thinking about Hara, the supposed young mother who had lost her children and family, and was now seeking revenge against other children and a man whose true identity remained unknown. Perry knew the word "psychopath" was running through the minds of each and every one of his colleagues. Was Hara really a nut job, or was she just a mother grieving for the loss of her children and loved ones?

"Perry!" Jack said urgently, leaning forward. His eyes were wide, and Perry saw the terror growing inside them. "What have you done? What did you bring here?"

Hara's face leaving Perry's thoughts, Perry focused now on the face of Jack. The face of his brother. It was filled with fear and apprehension, and Perry realized that his previous blank stare must have seemed quite ominous. Jack's unexpected arrival had indeed changed Perry's perspective on certain things, but for now he just had to do what was best for everyone. Hardening himself and refusing to give in to the urge to protect Jack, he continued with the original plan. He couldn't afford to get emotional at a time like this. "It's no one important," Perry lied, shrugging. "No one you need to worry yourself over."

"You're lying to me," Jack accused.

Perry hated himself for what he said next. "Trust me."

The surprise on Jack's face that changed to guilt made Perry curse himself even more. He wished Jack wouldn't trust him, because he couldn't trust himself anymore. He was being completely untrustworthy by lying to this boy, and what made it worse was that he could see Jack wanted to trust him. Why he could possibly want to trust someone holding him prisoner, Perry didn't know. Nodding slowly, Jack looked down again. "So what exactly happened when Hara came here?" he asked quietly. "Why would she come in the first place?"

More lies, Perry thought to himself. "She...uh..." How he could leave The Doc out of the explanation, he was not sure. "I think she just came in anger."

"There would have to be a better reason for her to risk herself like that," Jack said, his dark eyes prying. "She would have come for a specific reason."

Again, Perry was experiencing something for the first time in his career: he could not think of a decent lie to tell Jack for what had happened earlier. In any other situation, he could come up with lies to tell on the spot, but again he found himself looking at this interrogation from a different perspective. He thought Jack deserved to hear the truth. But reminding himself what side he was on, Perry thought of something that was partially true that he could use as his cover up. "I think she just wanted us to get it through our heads that she's not going to stop until she kills Lieutenant Odau's son. She made a pretty big deal out of it."

A strange look crossed Jack's face, and for a moment he just stared back at Perry. His eyes looked like they were trying to bore holes through Perry's and Jack's expression appeared strained, like he was concentrating so hard on discovering the real answer that his head ached. Finally, his words slurred, he accused, "You were always a terrible liar, did you know that? Always!"

Taken aback, Perry repeated in confusion, "Always?"

Jack let out a whoosh of air and dropped his chin down to his chest. Reaching up, he gingerly massaged his temples, something Perry had seen Hara do once or twice. After about twenty seconds of breathing deeply and rubbing his head, he looked back up. His eyes suddenly appeared exhausted, and he seemed about ready to give up on fighting Perry. "Something's wrong," he mumbled, his shoulders sagging as he slumped down further into his seat.

"Something's really wrong here," Jack stated. "And you won't tell me what it is. I have a feeling no matter how hard I try I still won't get the answer, so I'm done asking. Normally, I'd be able to figure it out on my own, but for some reason I just can't. I don't understand..." He glanced warily towards the one-way glass again, but then lowered his eyes to the table's surface again.

Perry didn't know what he should say. Jack seemed defeated and depressed. Should he try to comfort him or just start asking questions? His question was answered when Jack snapped his head up angrily, "Are you going to just sit there?" he demanded. "Ask your damn questions and get out!"

Shocked by Jack's sudden anger, Perry shot a glance at the one-way glass himself. He didn't need to see through to know that The Doc was watching him carefully. Perry could feel the intensity of his cold gray eyes. He forced himself to turn away and ignore the uncomfortable feeling he had so he could focus on Jack. "Would you tell us where she is?" he asked as politely as he could.

"As I told you before," Jack said flatly, "I have no idea where she is. And, as I also made quite clear, I wouldn't tell you if I did."

"You're basically the only friend she's got here," Perry reminded, already frustrated. "How do you not know where she is?"

"Because I don't!" Jack snapped. "There was a place we were all hiding before, but she's not back there now and I doubt she ever will go back!"

"You all?"

Jack stopped for a second and seemed to think over whether he should answer. Perry was afraid he was going to shut down completely and refuse to talk anymore, but then he spoke up. "All of us. Me. Hara. Daniel. Allan. Meg. After the lieutenant issued warrants for them all, they took shelter in the place where Hara and I were hiding. But that place doesn't matter anymore," he added as he saw the eagerness in Perry's eyes. "None of us are going back there anymore."

"Well, can you tell me where it is anyway?" Perry asked.

"Will you get it through your head that I'm not going to talk!" Jack cried, his eyes incredulous. "And if you really think that asking me nicely is going to change my mind, you're dead wrong, man!"

His face flushing red, Perry chewed on his lower lip and this time he was the one to lower his eyes. He was beginning to lose hope in himself, and for a moment he thought of just walking out and shoving The Doc in instead. But when his eyes flickered to the one-way glass and felt The Doc's piercing stare once more, he told himself to try harder. Despite Jack's sudden harshness, Perry still cared for him. But to spare him from dealing with The Doc, he would have to become a little rougher with the boy. Putting on the stern face he did with most other suspects he interrogated, he acted like he was growing very frustrated. He didn't really have to act all that much. "Tell us where your damn hideout is!"

Jack raised his eyebrows.

"I don't care whether or not anyone is currently hiding there!" Perry snapped, finding that the anger wasn't too hard to fake. "I'm sick and tired of protecting you when all I get in return is a few half-ass answers and a bratty attitude! Enough is enough! Now you're going to start talking to me or I'm going to do something that both of us are going to regret!"

"What are you going to do?" Jack challenged, holding Perry's furious gaze. "Are you going to hit me? No offense, but you don't seem like you've got enough balls to take a swing at me."

Pursing his lips, Perry growled, "I'm not going to hit you, but I'm going to bring someone else in here to talk to you and trust me, you're not going to want to talk to this guy."

"Why?" Jack demanded. "What makes him so special?"

"He can be very persuasive," Perry said, quoting The Doc. "You'll talk to him."

"So if I don't tell you what you want to hear you're going to leave and send a big boy in to scare me," Jack concluded, and he laughed scornfully. "Do you have any idea how much of a pansy that makes you?"

Without really thinking, Perry leapt to his feet, grabbed the table in both hands, and shoved it full force towards the wall. Before Jack could react, Perry had traveled the three feet between them and had his hand wrapped around the boy's throat. Jack's eyes were wide in shock, but Perry ignored it and glared back at him. He was no longer the kind, merciful agent. Now, as he stood with his hand around Jack's windpipe, his fingers the only thing between the boy and his source of life, he was the intimidating, angry investigator who was sick of games and eager to solve a mystery and save lives. He was done being pushed around.

"Ever since you were brought here, I've defended you," Perry said in a low voice so no one except Jack could hear. "When the lieutenant went in to talk to you the first time, I made sure he didn't do anything to hurt you in his anger. When Marcus said that taking you to Pittsburgh was in your best interest, I went along with it. When our van was under attack, I nearly died trying to keep you alive. Even now, I'm interrogating you so you don't have to deal with the asshole that's waiting just outside the door. He's a nut case, and I'm getting really sick of him, and the only way any of us are going to get rid of him is if you start behaving and tell us where Hara is! This guy scares the hell out of everyone, and believe me when I tell you that you do not want him to walk in this room. So how about you do us all a favor, return a bit of the courtesy I've shown you and start shaping up!"

A switch seemed to go off in Jack's head; maybe it was what Perry had said or maybe it was the fact that he could see the muscles in Perry's arm prepared to flex around his throat and cut off his air supply, but it was evident he was going to stop mouthing off. Shifting uncomfortably in his chair so he could pull slightly away from Perry's threatening stature, Jack cleared his throat nervously. He was avoiding Perry's leveled gaze, and as he opened his mouth and spoke his voice shook. "I was telling the truth when I told you I didn't know where she was. I don't know. She doesn't stay in one spot for very long and hasn't for many years. She'll never go back to the hideout, and unless you're experienced with people like us—like her, then you'll never be able to track her down. You'll have to get her to come to you instead, and believe me when I tell you there are not many things that will get her to do that willingly." Pain flashed across his face. It was just for a second and then it was gone, but it was long enough to notice. When he spoke next his voice cracked with emotion. "She didn't even try to bust me out of here when she came back. There's no way you're going to catch her."

Stunned by the dejection Jack felt for being left behind by the girl he deeply cared for, Perry released him and stepped back. Jack kept his head down and stared at the floor with a depressed look on his face. He had finally cracked from everything that had happened, and it was beginning to show through. He thought that Hara just left him there to save herself the effort to help him escape, but he didn't understand why she hadn't helped him. Why she couldn't have helped him. Hara was the only thing he had in the human world, and now it seemed to him that she didn't find him valuable enough to risk her life for anymore.

Perry stepped back and sat back down in his chair. Feeling a small spark of pity for Jack, he decided that he deserved to know his friend hadn't abandoned him intentionally. "You know, even if she tried, I doubt she would have been able to break you out."

Jack glanced up. "Why not?"

Perry still wasn't going to break the news about The Doc just yet, so he forced himself to lie yet again. "She was shot several times and also didn't seem to be in the best physical or mental condition to coordinate a breakout. So don't take it personally. I'm sure she would have helped if she could."

"And what about Allan?" Jack asked, his spirits seeming to brighten a bit. "You haven't found him yet, have you?"

"No, we haven't found him yet," Perry informed, realizing that Jack hadn't heard any news since Hara's escape. Which meant that he didn't know about Marcus's death yet. "He came back to confront us as well but ended up escaping again."

Nodding, Jack asked, "And what about Daniel and Meg? Still hiding as well?"

Pausing, Perry tried to think of a gentle way to break the news to him. In the end, it wasn't as gentle as he would have hoped for, but at least it was better than the way The Doc had told Hara. "I—I don't think we're going to need to worry about finding Marcus anymore," he said quietly.

"Why?" Jack's expression changed. It was obvious he knew something had gone terribly wrong. Now his eyes were filled with apprehension at Perry's ominous statement. "Oh my God," he whispered when Perry didn't immediately answer. "What happened?"

Running a hand awkwardly through his hair, Perry told him, "Marcus is dead, son. We found his body about two hours ago."

Another flash of pain was visible in Jack's eyes. Dropping his head in his hands, he shook his head in disbelief. He sat like this for a while, and Perry didn't dare bother him. If Perry had been in Jack's position he would have wanted a little bit of time for the news to sink in. When Jack finally looked up, his eyes were moist and he appeared inches away from tears. "How?" he barely breathed. "How did he die?"

More lies. "We don't know yet," Perry replied. "It's still being investigated, but," he decided one shred of truth wouldn't hurt, "we think he was murdered."

"Why?" Jack muttered, shaking his head again.

Perry faintly recalled Hara's same, simple question when she first discovered Marcus's body, and Perry found himself asking it as well. Why would someone murder that man? The Doc may have explained it to him, but he still didn't understand. He wished he was able to tell Jack the truth about how his friend died, but for the time being he was going to have to keep lying.

"So did you like, find him in a street somewhere or something?" Jack asked, his voice quavering.

"Yeah," Perry lied, reaching up and scratching the back of his neck in an attempt to hide his shame.

"Can I see him?"

The question broke Perry's heart. Anyone else would have been easy to say no to, but again, Jack was not anyone. "No," he told him softly, gently shaking his head in apology.

386

Jack did not like Perry's answer. "I've seen him once in the past two years," he said through gritted teeth. His eyes were angry and for a split second, Perry felt fear. "We fought in a freaking war together! I've known him practically all my life! He's almost family! And you're not going to let me see his body? What the hell happened to my rights? Isn't America supposed to be the land of the free?"

"No place is entirely free," Perry said, realizing this for the first time himself.

"My home was free," Jack mumbled at him. "I want to see him!"

"No," Perry repeated.

"Please!" Jack begged, balling his hands into fists on his knees and leaning forward.

"I'm sorry," Perry apologized, and he really was. "But let's remember why you're in this room. You killed children. You're not leaving this room until you give us Hara."

Jack's expression changed again. He was about to start pleading. "Please," he whispered. "His death was partially my fault. I need to..." His voice cracked again. "I need to apologize. And I need to say goodbye."

That was it. Perry couldn't take it anymore. He was sick of all the lying. Ever since Hara came into the equation, he'd been lying to his colleagues, to his friends, to the parents of the dead children, and worst of all, he'd been lying to himself. Where was the honest man he had once been? Where had he gone? How could one case change him in the way this one had changed him over the past forty-eight hours? Too many of his questions would go unanswered by the time it was all over—he knew that much—but he couldn't let himself be corrupted by a madman just because the going was getting tough. He was going to stop the lying and go back to the standards he had lived and worked by for over ten years, and he was going to start right then.

"I'm sorry," Perry repeated, "but I can't let you see the body because we have no idea where it is."

"What?" Jack cried.

Perry knew that his colleagues and The Doc would not be pleased with him sharing the information with Jack, but he didn't care anymore. Leaning closer to Jack, Perry whispered urgently, "One of the cops working on the case was possessed by Marcus after he died, and he took the body somewhere. We have no idea where, and I guess we never will."

"What happened to the cop?" Jack asked, seeming to understand the situation fully now that Perry was telling the truth.

"He's dead too."

"No," Jack mumbled, screwing up his face as he lost himself in thought. After several seconds of silence, he stared back at Perry. "He wanted his body taken to a specific place!"

Perry had heard this statement before from The Doc, and maybe this time he could get a straight answer. "Where?" he asked hopefully. "Why?"

"I don't have a clue where," Jack replied, thinking hard again. "But that would be the only reason Marcus would dare mess with a human's mind. See, there are laws in our society that clearly state we are not allowed to mess with the humans' society, unless of course they strike first."

"We?"

"I meant they."

"But why would Marcus want his body taken away somewhere?" Perry asked again, still confused and not seeing a logical answer. "I mean, he's dead, so what good would moving his body do him?"

Jack was speechless, and Perry immediately saw the boy had another answer which he did not want to share. Before either of them could speak again, a sharp rap at the door caused them both to jump and look around. Someone obviously didn't want Perry sharing too much information with Jack. Glancing back to meet Jack's wary eyes, he said, "I'll be right back." He stood up but didn't take two steps before Jack stopped him.

"Who is the man you're working with?" he demanded suspiciously, and Perry turned. Upon seeing the uncertainty and hesitance in his eyes, Jack drew in a breath. "And why are you so afraid of him?"

"You'll find out soon enough," Perry mumbled, continuing to the door.

✳ ✳ ✳

It took five minutes before Dr. Bennett convinced Hara to lie back down. It took five more minutes before Hara allowed him anywhere near her. It took another ten for her to let him put the IV back in her arm. Thirty minutes after Bennett had entered the room, Hara was lying on her hospital bed with her hands resting lightly on her stomach. She stared up at the ceiling and traced the many patterns on the fiberglass tiles, trying any way she could to make herself relax. Hospitals held too many unpleasant reminders of her past. She knew that she was in no danger as long as Bennett was there with her, but she couldn't help worrying herself that someone was going to walk into the room, discover her there, and call the police. If that happened, The Doc would know where to find her, and she was still far too weak to fight him. Bennett assured her she was safe; he said that the level they were on was under construction and that no one except for him would be on that floor, yet she was still worried. To her, nowhere was safe. There was always somebody to be wary of, and she would never be able to let herself fully relax again.

But she continued to try. She breathed deeply, and she thought the words "in and out, in and out" repeatedly to make sure she breathed at a slow and steady pace. When that didn't help, she tried to focus on her hands resting on her stomach, slowly lifting up and down with each breath. It began to work, but there was a loud, startling thud from the floor above and her heart began to pound in her chest. In a vain attempt to calm herself again, she listened to the raspy, uneven breathing of Allan in the bed beside her. He was still unconscious, and Bennett said he would be out for a long time. The drug was beginning to take effect, but there was still some time required for the scarring around his brain to heal.

"And the same goes for you," Bennett had scolded, just before Hara had laid back down.

The ache in Hara's head had lessened to a dull throb, and she estimated she would be able to take the IV out and walk around again within the next forty minutes. But for the time being, she tried to tune everything out—Allan's uneven breathing, the noises above and below her, the air vents in the ceiling, and the uncertain, confused thoughts of Dr. Bennett. He had taken a seat in a chair a few feet away from her once he managed to get the IV back in her arm. Ever since then his mind had been racing with questions. Most were about the anatomy of her people and how the abilities worked, but there were others that lingered on the subject of the war. Bennett was like any of the other humans who had found out about her and her species; he was curious. He wanted to learn more about what had happened. Although he understood why she was in Philadelphia, he wanted more details about her people's history.

Unlike most of the doctors who had discovered the secret of the Colicians, Bennett wasn't greedy. True, he was eager to understand them, but Hara heard him telling himself to forget about it and to leave her alone. He had a trait Hara hadn't seen in most humans: respect for her feelings. He actually thought of her as a living thing, and he cared for her as he cared for any of his other patients. The tapes he had watched had shown him what horrible things had been done to her, and he knew that if he asked any of the questions he wanted to, it would greatly upset her. And the nice thing was he actually cared that they would upset her, unlike The Doc, whose goal was to find any way possible to upset her.

Hara could feel the emotion Bennett felt about her, and she felt her heart warm when she realized how much he truly, honestly cared for her. When she first understood, fear gripped her and she thought of The

Doc. He said he cared for her even after what he did to her, and Hara always sensed that the man felt something for her. Bennett cared for her too, and he was already becoming dangerously curious about her species. The Doc had started off as just a curious man, but then Hara thought of what he had become and couldn't help wondering if Bennett would end up like him, torturing and killing innocent people to satisfy his own curiosity.

He won't, Hara assured herself. *He's a Bennett. They don't go bad.* She grew more convinced when she caught a gritty thought running through his mind. He desperately wanted to ask her questions about her life and her species and the war, but then he began to scold himself for even thinking of asking her.

You know what she's been through! he was thinking. *You know what's been done to her! How dare you even consider making her recollect the horror she experienced! How much more selfish can you get?*

"You have a restless mind," Hara commented softly, continuing to trace the patterns on the ceiling with her eyes. She had needed an excuse to break the tense silence, and she wanted to start a conversation with him, to become better acquainted with the first of the Bennetts.

She felt Bennett jump in surprise from her sudden voice. "I'm sorry," he apologized quietly, and Hara felt his embarrassment. His voice was low and deep, but it had a kind of gentleness to it that soothed Hara and made her feel safer. It was fatherly, and Hara found herself thinking of her own father again.

"It's fine," she told him reassuringly. "A restless mind is better than a dull mind."

"There's just so much..." Bennett stopped. Hara knew he had planned on finishing the sentence with, "that I want to ask you," but he bit down on his tongue to keep himself from doing so. After a pause, he mumbled, "...about you that I find fascinating."

"You sound like The Doc," Hara said.

Again, she felt Bennett's guilt. He knew who The Doc was from the tapes, so he very well knew that was not a compliment. "I'm sorry," he repeated, this time with pure shame. "I didn't mean to."

There was silence once more. Hara was forced to listen to the disturbed thoughts of Bennett's mind again. He was completely horrified at himself for what he said; he felt as if he had upset her already. Questions began to run through his head again, and Hara could hear them ricocheting off the sides of his skull. One question in particular caught Hara's attention, so she decided to see if she could answer it for him.

"You have something you'd like to ask me," she pointed out, turning her head to the side to look at him.

His dark eyes looked as guilty as he felt. "There are many things I'd like to ask you," he told her quietly.

"Go ahead then."

"I don't want to upset you."

Forcing a smile to her face, she said, "You saved my life, Dr. Bennett. Answering your questions is the least I could do." And it was true. How could she possibly repay him for helping her the way he did? The man was helping a wanted murderer without thinking twice, so why not repay his kindness by answering a few harmless questions? She had not received this much kindness from a human besides Noah for so long, and she wanted to express her gratitude to Bennett in any way she could.

"I don't know where to start," Bennett whispered, lowering his eyes when he met her light yet intense gaze.

"Ask the one you wanted to ask about my family," she instructed, feeling her heart seize up at the mention of her family.

He cursed himself over and over for even thinking the thought. He continued to avoid her eyes, and after debating over what he should say, he ended up stuttering again, "I-I don't want to upset you."

Gritting her teeth, she growled, "I'm already upset. Ask the question!" It was no longer a suggestion; it was an order.

Slowly looking up, Bennett did something no human had ever done: sent an apology to her mentally. *I'm sorry,* he thought to her. Then he whispered, "Did you...did you really... feel when your family was murdered?"

Hara didn't feel as much pain as she thought she would when she heard the question aloud. She felt a slight nagging at her heart, but nothing more. It was finally happening, the thing she had feared the most. She was becoming empty. "Yes," she answered, and looked back up at the ceiling. "I felt when every one of them died, when their minds went out like a light."

There was a wave of sorrow that billowed off of Bennett, like an ocean of emotion. Hara heard him wonder to himself how horrible and traumatizing it would be to know when each person he loved passed. He wondered what it would be like to feel the light of their minds go out, and to know that those lights would never return. Those lights in his own mind would have meant so much to him, signaling his loved ones were alive and well. The thought of physically and mentally sensing the death of his family made him cringe and wonder how Hara could stand it, but then his thoughts changed. As he began to look at it from a different angle, Hara turned her head again and locked her eyes on his. "I can hear everything you're thinking," she told him. "And you really don't want to be able to feel when the people you love pass. It's not as pleasant or beneficial as you may think."

Sadness filled Bennett's old, intelligent eyes. Something about this subject was bothering him, and Hara saw a sudden image pop into his head. It was of a woman; young, beautiful, brown hair and blue eyes. Bennett felt extreme love for this woman, but he also felt extreme loss. Hara made the connection between the woman and Bennett's desire, and she felt pity for the man.

"Your wife?" she asked him.

He nodded solemnly.

"She died?"

He nodded again.

"How long ago did this happen?" Hara began to feel that this man—this mere human—could actually understand and relate to her.

"Twenty-one years," he whispered. "Two months. Three weeks. Six days."

"And you loved her," Hara said, trying to express her sorrow for him through her eyes.

Bennett blinked at her from his chair. "I didn't feel a thing when she died," he told her, his voice cracking. His face looked crushed, and his eyes began to water up. "Nothing felt different. I always thought I would know when someone I loved died or was hurt, but I was wrong. You don't feel a thing. Not us, I mean."

"Sometimes I think you humans are lucky," Hara said, propping herself up on one elbow. She was careful to put her IV arm on her side, and she noticed for the first time that her headache was almost gone.

"Why?" Bennett snorted, brushing the tears away. "What's so special about us?"

"What's so special about us?" Hara asked him, raising an eyebrow. When Bennett's face showed utter confusion, she explained, "Sometimes it's better to not know when our loved ones are in danger. You may wish you could feel them in your mind, but it's more painful that way. With my people, our families are physically part of us, so when they die..." She took a deep breath. "It's almost like part of your soul is being ripped from you."

"I think that would be better than not feeling anything at all," Bennett muttered, though he didn't really seem like he believed it.

"I'm not going to tell you what you do or don't want," Hara told him, lying back down, "but just know it would have been harder to deal with your wife's death if you had actually felt her go." Sighing, her insides churned with her own internal agony. "I know because it was very difficult for me."

Hara heard Bennett's mind fill with jumbled questions once more, and the question he decided to ask made her heart throb. "What was your husband's name?"

"Bo," she answered, and was surprised to find herself smiling at the sound of his name. "It was short for Bobby, which was short for Robert. And he wasn't my husband. We don't have matrimonial ceremonies anymore. Weddings are a very primitive way of uniting two people."

"So what exactly was he to you then?" Bennett asked.

Hara could see that this man was not going to stop with the questions now that he had started, but for some reason she felt better now that she could talk openly about her past with someone. Maybe, as Daniel had earlier pointed out, it really would be better for her to talk about what happened with someone. "I guess you could call him my soul mate. That's what we've always called them."

"Soul mate?" Bennett repeated, and he seemed to find this interesting.

Deciding to fill this kind man's thirst for knowledge, Hara explained. "Our scientists called it 'The Bonding Effect.' In our short existence, our own scientists haven't been able to fully explain how our minds work, but they've developed hypotheses about certain things. The Bonding Effect is one of those things difficult to understand. But for some reason or another, each person of my species has a parallel; a counterpart to themselves, another person whose mind matches up with theirs. They're like puzzle pieces, and when the two pieces meet each other, they connect and after that it's like fire. It's completely unstoppable. The two parallels always fall in love, and nothing can come between them. Nothing except death, of course."

"So you never choose who you'll end up with?" Bennett said, not seeming to like that idea. "You just get randomly matched up with some other person?"

Hara turned to him again. "It's not like we're forced to love our parallel. Imagine it as this: in high school, teens fall in love, but it doesn't always last. Later in life they fall in love again, but if it doesn't last then they were never meant to be together. Sometimes humans run into their parallel and they get married, because the universe wanted them to be together and a part of each other. You may have loved other women in your life, but your wife was your soul mate. You were always supposed to be together. Bo was who I was always meant to be with, so our minds made the connection and we eventually ended up falling madly in love with each other."

"But you can never experience love until you find your soul mate?" Bennett was making the whole thing sound like a cruel and unusual punishment. "You never had another boy you found cute or fell in love with until Bo?"

"Actually, to be completely honest, I was in love with someone else when Bo and I went through The Bonding Effect," Hara admitted, remembering how difficult it was to let what she thought was her true love go. "I was so sure he was the one, but then Bo came along."

"What was his name?" Bennett asked. "The other boy, I mean?"

"Jack."

"You mean…"

"Yes, the Jack who is still trapped in the police station."

"You loved him, but Bo was your soul mate?" Bennett was trying to understand. "Has Jack found his soul mate yet?"

"No. He's still in love with me."

"What did Bo think about that?"

Biting her lip, Hara thought back to all the problems she and Bo had encountered over the years with Jack. "He understood that Jack was upset and apologized to him several times for stealing me, but no matter what he said Jack never forgave him or let me go."

"If you and Bo are not the same species, then how did the two of you end up being soul mates?"

Hara was surprised that he knew about that. "I don't know," Hara admitted, shrugging and then wincing as the IV in her arm tugged at her skin from the shoulder movement. "How did you and your wife fall in love when you're black and she was white?" At Bennett's startled expression, she explained, "When it comes to love you don't have to be the same race, whether it be black or white, Colician or Caiten.

"Caiten?"

"That's what Bo's species is called."

The dreaded silence came upon them again. For once, Bennett's mind wasn't racing with questions, so Hara finally had a chance to think. When the silence became too much for her, she decided to ask one of her own questions. "What was your wife's name?"

"Amanda," Bennett told her, and he smiled just as Hara did when she spoke Bo's name.

"That's a pretty name," Hara commented.

"I know."

"She was very beautiful."

"Yes, she was."

"Where did you meet?"

"In college. We bumped into each other in the hallway and I knocked her over, so I offered to make it up to her by buying her lunch. We were inseparable after that day." He smiled again.

Hara smiled too. "See? Even humans can find their soul mate."

"I suppose you could call it that," Bennett murmured.

"When did the two of you get married?"

"July 4th, 1978. It was the nicest day of the year, almost like someone made it that way for us." Bennett peered at her and asked, "Why do you keep asking me all these questions if you could just read my mind to get them yourself?"

Thinking the question over, Hara wondered why she didn't just read his mind. But she already knew why. "Your voice is soothing," she told him softly, and she realized how true it was. She was no longer frightened or paranoid, and she mentally thanked him for that. "I don't remember the last time I've felt this relaxed. Just talking to you makes me feel safer. And besides," she shifted her position as she began to grow uncomfortable, "I hate silence. The Doc used to torture me by locking me in a completely silent room for hours at a time. Too much silence can drive a person mad."

"I see," Bennett said, and Hara heard him wondering to himself if the silence was what caused her to snap.

"It's also nice to have a real conversation once in a while," Hara added, feeling her face flush red in humiliation. Even Bennett, who was treating her with unbounded kindness, thought she had completely lost it. And he was right. They were all right. "Just because we have different forms of communication doesn't mean we don't like to talk."

"Hmm." Bennett gave a small indication of acknowledgement and then didn't speak again. It was almost as if he didn't hear anything she said, or he didn't understand what she was implying.

"So... will you keep talking to me?" Hara asked hopefully.

"Yes. What do you want to talk about?"

"Anything. I just can't take the silence."

Bennett thought for a moment, and then asked, "What's your real name?"

Hara bit her lip. "Anything but that."

"Is there something wrong with your name?" Bennett watched her carefully to try and figure it out himself.

"No."

"Then why don't you want to tell me?"

"Because I'm not that person anymore," Hara replied. "She died with the rest of my family."

It was clear that Bennett understood her. He didn't press the matter any further. "Alright. You don't have to tell me if you don't want to. Do you still want to talk about something else?"

"Yes."

"Okay. You and Bo had children, right?"

"Yes, five."

"What were their names?"

"Grace was the oldest," Hara said, enjoying the subject of her children. "She was five. Katie and Colin were both four. Dreyson was two, and Lizzie was about nine months old when she... when she was killed." Each and every day it was becoming easier to think about her family. It was upsetting her that she could talk about her dead children and hardly feel anything anymore.

"So you were what—twelve... thirteen when you had your first child?"

"Twelve."

"You were so young."

"Most of my people have children at a young age," Hara explained. "What about you? You have children as well?"

"Just two," Bennett said, and then snickered to himself. He found it funny that an eighteen-year-old could have more children than a fifty-four-year-old. Hara found it kind of funny too; the man didn't understand that her people didn't reproduce through sexual intercourse.

"Names?" she asked, smiling to herself.

"Abby and Jordan. They each have three children of their own. Abby has Tanyon, RJ, and Rose, and Jordan has Sophie, Brandon, and Danny. They're all under six years, so they're a bit of a handful. But they're good kids..." Bennett went on about his grandchildren for a while, but Hara didn't hear him. She was too busy thinking about the names Bennett had just listed off. RJ... Rose... Brandon... and the name she recognized most—Danny. All of those names were so familiar to her, and she was honored to meet the man who would start them on their path to protecting the future. Hara's future. Bennett could never fully understand how important his grandchildren would be to the Colician race.

The air was silent once more, and Hara turned her head toward Bennett in surprise. He was staring at her with a sort of concern in his eyes, and he said, "You didn't hear a word I just said, did you?"

"I heard half of it," she told him apologetically. "I'm sorry."

"What's on your mind?" he asked, crossing his legs and folding his hands on his knee.

Hara gazed back at him, gazed into those intelligent, innocent human eyes. How could she possibly explain to him that four of his six grandchildren were going to become enemies of their own species? *He won't understand,* she told herself. *And even if he could, you can't tell him the fate of his grandchildren.*

He deserves to know, she decided firmly. Sucking in a deep breath, she began to explain what could never be explained. "Can I tell you something, Dr. Bennett?"

Shrugging, he said, "Sure. It's not like I'm going anywhere."

She bit her lip. "This isn't some little fact about me or my species. What I'm about to tell you... it will affect you in ways you can't imagine. It may upset you, and I need you to know this before I continue. Do you understand?"

"Yes," he answered, his brow furrowed in confusion. "Go on."

"If I told you something that would seem impossible, would you believe me?" she asked hopefully.

Bennett snorted. "Your very presence in this room is impossible, child! No, your very existence is impossible! I've learned to accept that nothing we could think up is impossible anymore. Whatever you want to tell me, whether it be impossible or not, I'll know it's true. After all, what reason would you have to lie to me?"

Hara felt guilty. She hadn't yet, but she would most likely end up lying to him just as she lied to everyone else. Sighing, she turned her head back to the ceiling and shut her eyes in exhaustion. "The only reason I let you help me, the only reason I trust you the way I do, is because of your name."

Bennett was surprised. "What's so special about my name?"

"It's Bennett," she told him, hoping he would catch on.

"I don't understand," he whispered.

See! He's not going to be able to take it. Hara continued anyways. "I trust you because I trust your grandchildren."

"Why would you trust my..." he started, and Hara heard the click as he realized what she was suggesting. "Wait...that's—impossible!"

"Nothing's impossible," she reminded him. "In our future, your grandchildren are going to be friends to my species. They're going to help us, and help us to move past our hate for the humans. Danny will actually live among us. Those kids are very important to both of our futures."

"But how..." Hara could feel him staring at her. "My grandchildren are human! Why would you trust them? Are you sure this will actually happen?"

Hara turned back again and raised an eyebrow at him. "You saw those tapes. You know I know what's coming. They may only be children, but I know what they will become. Just like I know what Jackson Odau is going to become."

"Is that little boy seriously going to grow up to be a monster?" Bennett asked, hoping it wasn't true.

"Adolf Hitler and Josef Stalin were both children at one point too," Hara told him. "All children grow up, Bennett. Just not always into the best people."

Nodding regretfully, Bennett said, "But my grandchildren will be good people?"

"You have my word on that," Hara promised.

"What about me?" he asked. "What happens to me when that day comes?"

"Do you really want to know your future, Dr. Bennett?" Hara knew Bennett wouldn't be able to handle what she knew about his future.

He thought for a long time about how he could answer. Finally, he muttered, "No. I suppose... knowing their fate could drive a person mad."

"Yes, it very well could," Hara said, and neither of them spoke for a while. Noticing that her headache was completely gone, she asked, "How long do I have to keep this IV in my arm?"

"How do you feel?"

That damn question again. "Fine," she grumbled.

"What about your head?" he asked, "Does it still hurt?"

"No. For once I feel normal. No pain anywhere."

"I suppose that's good then," he replied, and he made Hara jump when he suddenly appeared by her side. She hadn't heard him get up, and he startled her with how silent his footsteps were. He smiled down reassuringly at her when he saw her alarm, and his eyes crinkled up in the corners. Hara thought of Noah, and how his eyes always crinkled up when he smiled. What was it with Bennett reminding her of everyone she knew? "I guess it should be okay to take this out now," he said, and he gently pulled the IV out of her arm.

Flinching as it slid out, Hara carefully pushed herself up into a sitting position and glanced up at Bennett, who had just set the IV tube down on the tray beside her bed. He was staring at her arm where the IV had been inserted. At first, Hara didn't understand what he was looking at, but then she realized that he was watching her regeneration process heal the small cut in her arm from the needle. "Does it bother you?" she asked him.

"N-no," he stammered, wide-eyed. "It's just..."

"What?"

"Different," he said, and he seemed afraid of her now. As he should be. "I've never seen anything like that before, that's all." He lowered his eyes and pretended to study the items on the bedside tray.

Hara stared at him, trying to make him uncomfortable, but after a minute with no reaction from him she decided to just let it go. She had more questions she needed to ask. "How did you know how to help us, anyway?"

"Some of the tapes in Brown's office were from hospitals in your society," Bennett explained, finally building up enough courage to look her in the eyes again. "They were records of medications for rare cases or problems. One tape showed the formula required when a Hopper overused his ability. We didn't have quite the same drugs here, but the antidote I developed based on the original seems to be doing the trick."

"What about Allan?" Hara asked in concern, glancing over at her friend who was still unconscious in the bed beside her. "How much longer until he's better?"

"It'll be several hours yet," Bennett said, and attempted to explain why. "He overdid his ability to a greater extent than you. He hopped less than you, but you're able to withstand more of it than he is. Your body wants to heal itself, so that is why you recovered so quickly. Not to mention you were most likely on an adrenaline high when you hopped. Allan isn't able to take as much strain as you, so he'll need to spend a lot of time recovering after using his ability as much as he did. He'll most likely need to sleep for a while afterwards as well. If I were you, I wouldn't expect him to be up and moving around until tomorrow."

"We don't have until tomorrow," Hara muttered.

"What?"

"Nothing." Growing antsy, Hara slid her legs off the side of the bed. "How long until I can start moving around?"

"Whenever you feel up to it."

Hara felt a sudden energy, an energy she could feel when an enemy was near. Her body stiffened in anticipation and she let her mind leave the room, searching for the source of the energy. When she discovered it on the fourth floor, she balled her hands into fists and curled up into a ball. The thing that had brought her back to this city, this opposing force, was so close that she would have no difficulty ridding the world of its depravity without anyone noticing.

"Hey!"

Snapping out of her trance, Hara attempted to focus her eyes on Bennett's concerned face swimming just inches in front of her. He was cupping her face in both his hands and was looking into her eyes, evidently searching to find out where she had gone for those few seconds.

"Are you alright?" he demanded, looking very worried. He hadn't moved since she brought her mind back to her own body, and when she didn't answer he seemed to grow even more concerned.

Gasping from coming back so quickly, Hara supported herself by placing both hands firmly on the bed on either side of her as her head spun like mad. Blinking rapidly to clear her jumbled vision, she tried to lower her head to get the blood flowing back to it.

"Hey, look at me!" Bennett ordered, forcing her to stare straight ahead at him. "What happened? What's wrong? Is your head hurting again?"

"He's here," Hara whispered.

"Who?"

"The boy," Hara said, regaining focus in her eyes. She jumped off the bed. "Jackson Odau. He's here. On the fourth floor."

"Oh, yes," Bennett muttered, nodding when he realized what she meant. "The lieutenant admitted him after the injuries you caused him. He's been here since the attempted escape to Pittsburgh."

"Why didn't you tell me?" Hara demanded angrily, staring him down.

"I didn't want to upset you right away. Are you going to go kill him?" He almost looked hopeful.

Hara stared at the door with a terrible longing in her heart. He was a source of pure evil. She should kill him, to spare the countless lives that would be lost because of him. It was her responsibility to protect the future since she knew what was going to happen. The boy was the whole reason she had come back in the first place. Now he was only being protected by three cops and a wooden door, so why not just do it right then and get it over with? But there was something she really wanted to do first, so she told Bennett, "No. Not yet."

Lowering his eyes to the floor again, he turned away and walked back to his chair. His behavior seemed rather peculiar to Hara, and when she heard the negative turn his thoughts took her mouth fell open in astonishment.

"You want me to kill him!" she said in shock.

Sitting down stiffly, Bennett looked evenly at her. "I know as well as you what that boy is going to become. I saw the tapes. Didn't you come here to kill him?"

"Yes, I did," she answered, eyeing him suspiciously. "But you're human, remember? You're supposed to be protecting him."

Raising an eyebrow, Bennett told her, "I may be a human, but that doesn't necessarily mean I have to be on their side." He glanced out the window and his eyes seemed lost. "After everything we did to you—and everything we're going to do—I can't see myself fighting on my species' side. The Doc is fighting on the human side, and both of us know the horrible things he's done and the things he's got planned, and I don't want to be a part of it. I don't care what species I am. I'm fighting for the side I think deserves my help. And I think it's about time you stop discriminating against all the humans and start recognizing who your friends are, because I'll bet you if everyone knew the truth there would be a lot of people on your side."

"Really?" Hara stared at him, at first expecting it to be a trick. But then she reminded herself, *He's a Bennett. The grandchildren must get their love for our people from him.* Snickering, she folded her arms. "Aren't you the doctor who's supposed to be taking care of the kid?"

"Yes." Bennett nodded.

"Then why didn't you kill him while you were looking after him?" Hara demanded, narrowing her eyes. "You had plenty of chances to do so. I'm sure you were alone with him more than once. You could have given him an overdose of anesthetic and claimed his heart failed from all the stress he had been put through, or you could have smothered him with his pillow and no one would ever know what happened. If you want the kid dead so badly, then why didn't you take any action?"

Bennett muttered, "I thought you'd want to be the one to do it. After all, that is what you came all this way to do."

"Ha!" Hara cried, and then started laughing. The noise she was making sounded strange to her. She hadn't laughed in so long that it was almost foreign to her. Bennett acted puzzled as well, staring at her like there was something seriously wrong with her. When she finally managed to stop, she gasped for air. "Haven't you figured out that you can't lie to me? I can hear everything you're thinking, and your reason for not killing him had nothing to do with leaving it to me. You didn't kill him because you didn't have the guts to do it!"

Sighing, Bennett glared over her shoulder, and she could hear him yelling at himself for being a coward. It surprised her, because she didn't mean for him to feel like one.

"Hey," she said mildly. "There's not a problem with that. I'm actually glad you didn't do it, and not because I want to do it myself. Enough people have been turned into murderers because of this damn war, and we need someone who won't kill at first glance. I only said what I said because you thought you could actually lie to me. I don't think you should be a killer just because you're on my side."

Bennett looked up at her again. "I may not be a killer, but you seem to be fully capable, so why aren't you going to go kill him now?"

"I have to do something first," she told him gravely.

"What's that?"

Hara sighed. She didn't like to talk about the experiments The Doc had performed on her, but she knew she would have to eventually. "You saw all of the tapes, right? All the ones with The Doc's experiments and tests with me?"

"Yes. Why?"

"So you know how he treated me, and how he caused me pain? You saw him drill holes through my eyes to get to my brain, and impregnate me with all his little 'painless' injections? You saw him drown me over and over again to see how my body responded?" She swallowed hard to keep the bile from rising in her throat. "You saw him cut my heart out of my chest while I was still conscious?"

Bennett nodded. "All of that, and many more things."

"I'm not going to kill the boy now because I want The Doc to watch," Hara explained. "After all the pain he's caused me, I think it's only fair that he gets to watch me rip the heart out of the one thing in this world that he actually cares about." She felt like a sadist, but she didn't care. She wanted to watch them both suffer. "And what a magnificent end to the war this will be. I'll get to kill the boy and The Doc in the end."

A flicker of sadness crossed Bennett's eyes, and Hara heard him wish that she hadn't ended up this way. He wondered then what she must have been like before the war. Pictures of her playing and running through grassy fields with her children flashed through his head, and Hara had to turn away to hide her smile. Bennett was the only human she had encountered in the past few days who actually knew she hadn't always been a bad person. Everyone assumed she had always been this way; a crazy, messed up teen with a messed up past. They thought her entire life had been filled with murder and bloodshed, but it hadn't. Just the last year of her life—when The Doc finally came into it—had been ruined by death and anger and revenge. Before then she had a mostly peaceful life. Apart from the problems with her and Bo's families that had gone on for a few years, her life had been as normal as anyone could imagine. She lived calmly with Bo and their five children, and despite their youngest son's medical problems they never really worried about much of anything. She and her family lived in the hills near a large cliff on the edge of the ocean, and they grew their own food with the help of three humans who lived close by. She and Bo raised their children well, and they lived isolated in the countryside until almost a year earlier, when she had gone to the Colician capital city to see her oldest brother, Flint, who had been hospitalized after The Doc's first attack. That had been the first time The Doc had ever come to her world, and she hadn't know it at that time, but that attack on their Defense Building had been the beginning of the end.

Her father found out about her secret visit to the hospital and cornered her there before she could flee. The reason Hara left in the first place was because of Bo being what he was. He was not a Colician, but a Caiten, another group of people affected by a similar chemical that created the Colician people. Every Colician had a different ability, but the Caitens all had the same ability. Each of them had very powerful telepathic abilities and they were all connected in a strong mental bond that was very similar to the bonds Hara's people had with the people they loved. Since each species was prejudiced against anyone different from themselves, everybody knew from the start that there were going to be problems if the two societies lived together. So they lived separate from each other, until Hara's father, the president of the Colicians, and Bo's father, the president of the Caitens, attempted to make reconciliations. They were signing peace treaties together, and that was how Hara met Bo.

In the beginning, they hated each other and they didn't want anything to do with each other. Hara knew he was her soul mate and it disgusted her, but when their species found out about their strange connection it began to cause problems for both of them. Bo tried at first to keep Hara on his side, but his own brother wanted to kill her, so they ended up moving back to Hara's side of the border. Again, they faced the same problem as before: people on Hara's side did not like Bo or the fact that their rapidly arriving children possessed abilities from Colicians and Caitens. After receiving several threats and enduring a heartbreaking fight with one of her brothers, Hara and Bo took the children and moved them to the hills where they then lived for two years. Once they moved, they finally accepted they were soul mates.

Her father was one of the few Colicians who didn't care about her bonding with Bo. She was his child, and he loved her no matter what she did or who her soul mate turned out to be. He immediately rushed to the hospital when he heard his daughter was there, and apologized for everything that had happened two years earlier. He pleaded with her to bring the rest of the family to the city and stay for at least a few days. After all, he barely knew her family and hadn't even met Dreyson or Lizzie. Hara had obliged and after she moved her family into the city, her father then asked her and Bo to join his Cabinet. They reluctantly agreed, and the Cabinet was where Hara had first met Meg, Allan, and Daniel. The three of them were Cabinet members as well. Soon after she and Bo joined, however, The Doc began his attacks against her people. Hara had managed to live a mostly normal life until she was seventeen years old; then the devil decided to move hell to her doorstep.

But Bennett's pictures of what she must have been like before were fairly accurate. She had played with her children in the hills, and she had been a loving mother. There were so many things she had been before that no one could picture now, but that was because of what the war had turned her into—a monster, so desperate for revenge and salvation that she would kill little kids to fix the calamity at hand. Little kids that were harsh reminders of her kids and what had been done to them. The Doc was right; she was like him. She killed people to serve herself.

She was such a hypocrite. She thought she could go around crying to everyone that her family and species had been murdered and her homeland destroyed, and then she went to Philadelphia and did the same thing. What had she become? Hara hated it as much as Bennett did. She missed the person she once was, the person she was afraid would never return. But she wanted desperately to be able to do something generous, to prove there was some decency left inside her blackened heart.

Her eyes landed on the tray that was beside her bed. On it was a large syringe that looked like it could penetrate all the way to a person's heart. An idea came to her, and she picked it up and stared at it. She hated needles. Too many had been stuck into her and just the sight of one made her shiver. But she didn't feel as terrified of the one she held in her hand, because she knew she could do some good with it. Bennett had done a very brave and risky thing for her, so now she was going to return the favor. Taking a seat on the edge of her bed, she held her arm out in front of her and flexed her bicep. She lifted the needle and held it above her arm, gulping in a lungful of air to prepare and calm herself.

"What are you doing?" Bennett asked, getting up and walking to her side again. His voice changing to a tone of worry, he added, "Please put that down."

"You did me a huge favor," Hara told him, jabbing the needle into the vein in the inside of her elbow. It pinched but she didn't flinch and she began to fill the syringe with her blood. "I'm going to give you a gift in return to try and express my sincere gratitude."

"How is torturing yourself in front of me a gift?" Bennett demanded, frowning down at her in an attempt to make her stop.

Startled, Hara looked up into his disapproving eyes. The man really understood what made her uncomfortable and unhappy. It was kind of scary, since he didn't even know her personally. Those damn tapes must have made it pretty obvious what bothered her.

When the syringe was loaded with her dark, thick blood, she pulled it out of her arm and held it out to him. "Here, take it. It's yours." When all Bennett did was stare back at her with puzzled eyes she smiled at him. "My gift to you."

"What are you talking about?" Bennett eyed the vile of blood in disgust. "How is this a gift? Are you playing some sick joke on me?"

Snorting, Hara said, "You put yourself at great risk by involving yourself in this. This is a very dangerous situation to be in, and if The Doc finds out you're helping me he will surely kill you. I'm very grateful that you did this for me and Allan, and I would feel terrible if you were murdered because you did a kind thing. So I'm giving you my blood as a gift, in case anything should happen to you."

Seeming to understand, Bennett reached out and took the syringe. Hara caught his hands in her fingers, and when he looked up in surprise she explained how it worked. "If you are injured in a way that could kill you, inject yourself with this. My blood will heal any injury and save your life."

"What if I'm killed quickly or I'm too hurt to inject myself with it?"

"If you know you are in physical danger, inject yourself with it. My blood will stay in your system for several hours, so you'll be fully prepared should anything happen. And not to worry." She released Bennett's hand and smiled encouragingly at him. "I'm a universal donor. My blood won't hurt you."

Smiling in return, Bennett looked down and studied her blood in his hand. "Thank you," he said gratefully. "I suppose this could come in handy."

"Consider us almost even," Hara replied. "Now if you'll excuse me. I don't mean to be rude, but I've taken advantage of your hospitality for far too long and I really think I should get going."

"You're leaving?" Bennett's face fell and he had a look of despondency in his eyes.

"Thank you very much again for helping me, but I can't stay here any longer," she apologized, walking towards the door. "I hope you'll understand. It's difficult for me to stay in one place very long and besides, I have more work to do. Jack is still stuck in that police station with The Doc and Odau, and I have to get him out of there. Please take care of Allan until he's better."

"Please don't leave," Bennett begged, following her. "You may be a living flame thrower, but you're still a kid and you're not safe out there alone. Especially with The Doc and all those cops looking for you." He put a hand on her shoulder when she turned to face him and his expression was pleading with her. "What happens if you use more of your abilities and the strain on your brain causes you to collapse again? I won't be there to help you if that happens."

"Don't worry about me," she told him reassuringly." I can take care of myself. It's yourself you should be worrying about."

Their conversation was interrupted as they heard a low groan from across the room. Both of them looked over in surprise, and Hara gasped as she saw Allan's feet move underneath his sheets.

"Allan?" she whispered, and walked over to his bed. Looking down at him, she saw that his eyes were moving beneath his eyelids, representing brain activity. Then he groaned again, and his head turned to one side.

"Mr. Mayor?" Bennett called hesitantly, following Hara and pulling back one of Allan's eyelids. For a few moments nothing happened, but then Bennett and Hara both jumped as Allan's eye rolled and focused on Bennett's confused face.

✳ ✳ ✳

As Perry suspected, when he opened the door there was a stern-faced lieutenant Odau standing on the other side.

"Can I help you?" Perry asked, already annoyed.

"What are you doing?" Odau demanded.

"I was trying to get some answers," Perry replied, trying to express in words just how unappreciative of the interruption he was.

"Why are you telling him about Marcus? He has no right to know!"

"He has every right to know!" Perry declared, stepping through the door and closing it behind him. "They were friends! Wouldn't you want to know if someone you cared about was killed? Like your son?"

Anger flashed through Odau's gray eyes. "This is different," he growled through his teeth.

"How?" Perry demanded, crossing his arms and glaring at him stubbornly. He was suddenly aware of several pairs of eyes watching their argument. Odau was saying nothing in response to his one word question, just holding Perry's glare with his own. Agent Long then stepped away from the group and put a hand on Perry's shoulder.

"Son," he started softly. "I understand that this boy means something to you—"

"Don't even start!" Perry snapped angrily.

"But I don't think that gives you the right to endanger our operation," Agent Long finished, ignoring his protests.

"How is telling him his friend is dead a threat to our operation?" Perry demanded.

Agent Long started to answer, but The Doc cut him off from across the room. "I think telling the boy may have actually been helpful," he said as he leaned casually against the wall in the corner. "He could have told us where your cop took the body—"

"I don't believe I was talking to you," Agent Long replied curtly, shooting him an annoyed glance.

The Doc stared blankly back, but Perry saw the smirk slowly creeping to his lips.

"What I think we're trying to say, Perry, is that the conversation you were having was going nowhere," Odau explained a little more calmly. "It wasn't getting us any answers and it almost seemed like the two of you were just chatting. We need someone in there who will actually get the job done." He lightly cocked his head in The Doc's direction.

Perry glared at him, but he was right. His chat with Jack had been going nowhere. But as he looked over at The Doc and saw that "Ha, I won!" look in his eyes, Perry knew he couldn't give up just yet. And besides, his ten minutes were not quite up.

"Give me two more minutes," Perry requested, yet to him it sounded more like a demand.

"Perry," The Doc said sternly, "let it go."

"You said you'd give me ten minutes with him," Perry snapped back, pointing at the clock hanging on the far wall. "So far, it's been eight. I still get two minutes. That was the deal!" he reminded as The Doc started to open his mouth in protest. "Just two more minutes, and then you get your two."

For a moment, The Doc just stared back at him, but then he shook his head and waved his hand, gesturing for him to get back inside and hurry it up. Perry looked back to Agent Long. "Two minutes," he promised.

"You'd better get some results this time," Agent Long grumbled.

Glancing at Odau, Perry saw that he wasn't pleased. His expression made Perry want to laugh at him, but he was more mature than that and he knew that would not be very professional on his part. So he just shrugged, pushed the door back open, and stepped inside.

"So I guess I don't have any rights after all," Jack muttered when the door closed and Perry walked back towards him.

"I'm sorry about that," Perry apologized, and he could almost see Odau rolling his eyes in the next room. It made him want to smile, but he held it in.

"What did they want, anyway?" Jack asked, leaning back in his chair.

"Just for me to hurry things up." Perry grabbed the table that was parked beside the wall and moved it back to its proper place between himself and Jack. "You need to talk to me, and I mean right now." Walking around the table and behind Jack, he pulled a pair of handcuffs from his pocket and grabbed Jack's arm.

"Hey!" he cried in protest, trying to pull away. "What are you doing?"

"I need you to understand how serious I am, and how serious this situation is," Perry explained, fastening the cuff around Jack's right wrist and then grabbing his left arm to do the same with his other wrist.

"Is this really necessary?" Jack demanded, struggling against the cuffs.

"Yes, it is." Standing up, Perry put a hand on Jack's shoulder to keep him in his place as he tried to get up.

"Why?" Giving up against the cuffs, Jack slumped down in his chair and looked up helplessly as Perry walked around the table to his chair and sat down. "Do you really need the cuffs? Can't you talk to me without them?"

"I have less than two minutes to get the answers I need from you," Perry told him, folding his hands on the tabletop. "So I need to get down to business and make sure you realize how crucial this is."

"And just how crucial is it?" Jack asked, looking annoyed.

"If you don't tell me where Hara is right now, I'm completely serious when I say I will bring someone in here who will make you talk. And trust me, you will not like this guy."

"What is he going to do? Beat me?" Jack snorted and grinned in amusement. "I've taken enough beatings in my time to assure you that punching me will not get me to say a word."

"Focus, Jack!" Perry ordered, reaching across the table and slapping him in the face. "Your time for fun is over! Now tell me where she is, and don't give me any more crap!"

Shocked by the unanticipated smack, Jack stared back at him for several seconds before muttering, "I told you before, I don't know where she is, and even if I did I wouldn't tell you."

"Don't give me that!" Perry snapped, slapping him again. "You're her friend! Of course you know where she is!"

His nostrils flaring in anger, Jack snarled furiously, "If you hit me again I swear to God—"

"What?" Perry demanded smacking him again. He had no idea what had come over him, but he couldn't stop himself now. "What are you going to do, huh?"

"I don't know where the fuck she is!" Jacks shouted at him, pulling against his cuffs in a blind rage. "Why can't you assholes just believe me and leave me alone?!"

"Don't you dare talk to me like that, boy!" Perry growled.

"I'll talk to you however I fucking feel!" Jack yelled, his face red with anger and his eyes flashing. Perry could have sworn he'd seen that flashing somewhere before. "That's the only way you damn humans have ever talked to me! You think you're all better than us; beating us, torturing us, spitting on us, and murdering us like animals! And then you lock me up here and once again act like you're all superior to me and that you have more rights than me, and now you're telling me I have to respect you like you're some fucking king or something! Who the hell do you think you are, huh? Just because you have me strapped to this chair doesn't mean I have to bow down to you like you're Walter Reifert or someone!"

"What did you just say?" Perry asked in surprise. Walter *Reifert?*

"Well, you know what? I'm done!" Jack stomped his feet angrily on the floor, ignoring Perry's question. "I'm done dealing with your selfish, arrogant, stinking race! I'm sick of your bullshit and your lies and your attitude! And just to make my conscience feel slightly better, I'm going to allow you a sliver of the truth, to let you know that my species isn't filled with lies like yours! You know how before I told you I wasn't one of them? Well, I lied! I'm one of them! A Colician, a freak, whatever you want to call me! And yes, as you have realized, I am in love with Hara, and I have been ever since she was four years old. So if you seriously think I'm going to tell you sick shit holes where she is, well, sorry!"

Perry stared at him. He assumed almost everyone in the next room was too. Jack had just told him a secret that could possibly cost him his life, and he didn't seem to care. As Perry had come to suspect, Jack really was one of them. And now that everyone knew, what were they going to do about it? People would want to study him, to figure out what makes a Colician a Colician, but Perry couldn't allow that. If Jack really was what he said, and everything he said before was true, then he would have gone through almost everything Hara did. "You're really one of them?" he asked quietly, going for the calm approach this time.

"Yes," Jack sighed, his eyes showing the regret at what he had just admitted.

"Why didn't you just tell me before?" Perry whispered, hurt. "You didn't have to lie."

"Yes I did," Jack murmured, lowering his eyes in shame.

"Why?"

"Because, at the time, you didn't understand the seriousness of the situation." He glanced up. "But now you do, so I figured it was time for you to know. And I do know how serious you are about this, Agent Perry, but I have no idea where she is. I'm proud to say I would never tell you where she was if I did know."

"Jack," Perry started, glad that the boy was finally beginning to tell some of the truth. "I need you to at least give me a hint. This isn't going to end well if you don't cooperate."

"I've seen the way you look at your partner," Jack told him softly.

"Excuse me?" Perry said in surprise.

"The blonde woman?" Jack repeated. "She's your partner, isn't she?"

"Yes," Perry answered slowly, feeling his face flush. "But—"

"I've seen the way you look at her," Jack said insistently. "And I know the way you feel about her. You love her, don't you?"

"I don't see what this has to do with anything," Perry began, completely flustered. He could feel Renee's eyes on him.

"Imagine yourself in my place," Jack instructed, "and her in Hara's place. If your partner was wanted for mass murder and various other crimes and you knew where she was, would you tell someone? Even if it meant you would lose your freedom if you didn't?"

Perry didn't answer.

"Would you?" Jack demanded louder. "Could you?"

"I...I'd like to think I would," Perry whispered, looking down, "But...I don't think I could bring myself to do it."

Sighing, relieved that he and Perry were finally seeing eye to eye, Jack said, "Now you understand why—if I really did know—I couldn't tell you where she was. I have no hints for you. I'm sorry. I hope you can realize how hard it would be to choose between righteousness and love." Sitting back in his chair, he sighed again. "I have nothing left to say to you."

Perry waited, praying Jack would change his mind and give him something—anything—but it was no use. Sighing as well, he told him, "I'm going to have to bring my guy in here now. My two minutes are up."

"You do that," Jack muttered, not seeming the least bit concerned.

Rising to his feet, Perry regretfully trudged to the door. He felt ashamed of himself when he realized that he was giving up.

"Hey," Jack called as Perry pulled open the door.

"What?" Perry grumbled, pausing with his back to Jack.

"Your partner, what's her name?"

"That's none of your business," Perry said and stepped through the door.

"Is it Renee Michaels?!" Jack yelled at him.

Catching the door before it could swing shut behind him, Perry stared into Jack's peculiarly worried eyes. He didn't reply, because he didn't understand how Jack knew that name. Or why it mattered so much to him.

He must have seen the answer to his question in Perry's eyes, because Jack's face fell suddenly. Looking back down at the table, he squeezed his eyes shut and shook his head. Perry thought he saw him mouthing the word "no" over and over again. He started to ask what was wrong with Renee as he felt himself become alarmed, but he was startled out of his thought as someone shoved him back into the room.

"Get back inside!" Odau ordered impatiently when Perry dug his heels into the floor to halt himself.

Surprised, Perry obeyed and walked back in a few feet as Odau closed the door behind them. Then, striding back to the table where Jack sat with his head bowed, Odau pulled out a chair and seated himself. Perry watched with curious fascination as the lieutenant folded his hands neatly upon the table and gazed across at Jack's hunched form. He had no idea what Odau was doing or why he was sitting at that table, but he supposed it was better than having The Doc there instead.

"So, Jack," Odau said pleasantly, leaning forward and staring hard at the boy. Jack didn't respond; he just continued to sit there with his head bowed, still upset over the whole Renee matter. His hands were still in cuffs behind his back, so his position seemed awkward and uncomfortable. But he didn't move to make himself more comfortable or to make any acknowledging gesture to Odau. The lieutenant ignored his lack of respect. "We've all grown tired of your lack of cooperation, but I'm going to give you one last chance to tell us about your friend." When Jack refused to acknowledge his presence once again, Odau shouted, "Look at me, damn it!"

Jack jumped at his sudden burst of anger, looking up in surprise. Perry shivered as he gazed upon the boy's face again. Looking at Jack was like looking into a mirror, only he was seeing himself thirteen years earlier. Jack even had Perry's dark mahogany eyes, a feature many people had commented on over the years. "Yes, sir?" Jack muttered. Odau now had his full attention, but the boy still possessed the bored tone he had expressed in their earlier conversations.

Glaring into the young man's eyes, Odau growled, "You and your little friend tried to murder my son, and you murdered three other innocent children. Either you tell us where she's hiding, or we'll bring in someone who will make you tell us."

"Ooooo," Jack said in mock fear, scrunching up his shoulders. "I'm scared now. Who could possibly be scarier than you, Daddy?" He spoke his last sentence with a child's voice, pretending to shake in his chair.

Perry was shocked at how Jack's attitude could change so abruptly, and for a moment he had a feeling that Odau was going to lose it. But the lieutenant took a deep, steady breath before turning back to Perry and saying, "Alright, bring him in."

Perry stepped back to the door and opened it. Almost immediately, The Doc stepped inside, but remained at the doorway beside Perry. Perry shot him a suspicious look; The Doc returned it with a smirk of his own.

Jack was staring back down into his lap again, this time with a grin on his face. Perry could only wonder how fast that grin would be wiped off his face when he saw it was The Doc who had come to join the conversation. "Who is it?" he asked. "The scary interrogator who's going to beat me up if I don't talk?"

"More like the scary doctor who's going to shoot you up with some nasty things if you don't talk," The Doc answered, entering the room.

Snapping his head up at the sound of his voice, Jack widened his eyes in disbelief when they landed on The Doc. His mouth slowly fell open and his shock began to change to horror. "What?" he whispered.

"Hi, Jack," The Doc said, almost as pleasantly as Odau had. His smirk changed to a grin and it grew broader with each passing second.

Perry was growing steadily more uneasy, not just because of Jack's expression, but because of what The Doc had said. Shoot him up with some nasty things? He didn't even want to know what The Doc meant by that. It made him angry to think that The Doc would actually make that kind of threat. But if he could get Jack to talk, then Perry just had to deal with it.

"How did you find us here?" Jack demanded, his voice shaking uncontrollably. His breathing had also changed; he was inhaling sharply while his shoulders jerked with every intake of air. He began to sink lower and lower into his chair and his eyes remained locked on The Doc's.

Odau had turned to watch The Doc to wait for the results he had promised, but Perry paid no attention to either of them. His eyes were focused on Jack's mortified expression. He was trying to figure out how Jack, a young murderer, could be so terrified of this guy. At first glance, The Doc seemed harmless enough. Maybe a little creepy, but he didn't look dangerous. But anyone who saw the look on Jacks' face would automatically know that there was something about The Doc that was not right. In all of Perry's time as an FBI agent, he had never seen so much fear for one man! Perry had received brief explanations from Jack, Allan Brown, and Daniel Marcus, but he had never gotten the full details of what occurred during their war. It must have been terrible, because Jack was utterly horrified just by having The Doc in the same room.

"You children do a terrible job of cleaning up after yourselves," The Doc answered softly, raising his eyebrows at him. "It wasn't too difficult to follow you back here once I found your contraption."

Quickly, Jack looked from Perry, to Odau, to Perry again. The amount of fear on his face began to increase. "What have you done?" he whispered.

What *had* he done? *I should have arrested him while I had the chance,* Perry told himself.

Odau didn't seem to be having any second thoughts about The Doc; he was too intently focused on catching the girl. So when The Doc began to slowly approach the table, the lieutenant had no objections.

"These two gentlemen have been telling me that you haven't been answering their questions about...Hara, correct?" The Doc said, slowly making his way around the table towards Jack. His eyes were on the floor, but he continued to have a terrorizing effect on the boy. "They say you haven't been cooperating with them, but I knew that couldn't be true, so I decided to stop by myself and pay you a visit. And guess what?"

"Stay away from me," Jack warned, trying to sound tough. But his attempt failed as his voice continued to quaver.

The Doc ignored the order. "It seems that you really haven't been cooperating, which I found funny since you seemed to have no problems cooperating with me."

"Stay away!" Jack said louder, tugging at the cuffs binding him to his chair.

"Your friends in the next room filled me in on what's been happening over the past few days, and they say that you've killed people, Jack."

"Go!" Jack cried, sinking even lower in his seat.

"Apparently, Hara's been a bad girl and now the police are after her, too."

Get away! Get away! The thought was being screamed repeatedly over and over inside Perry's head, although it didn't really feel like his own thought. It felt to him like someone else was screaming the words, but there was no sound, and he had no clue where it was coming from. Perry's uneasiness continued to rise, until it felt to him as if he was experiencing fear himself. He didn't understand why he was feeling fear at first, but then it occurred to him: he was protective of Jack because they were brothers, so the fear he was feeling was for Jack. The Doc was a threat to him, and if that was so then he was a definite threat to Perry as well. He would have felt a similar protective and fearful feeling if his daughter, Jillian, had been in Jack's place. When his family was threatened, so was he. Trying to shake the fatherly instincts from his subconscious, he gritted his teeth and forced himself to focus on the matter at hand.

"When I saw that you really weren't cooperating with them, I knew something had to be done about that," The Doc was saying. He had reached Jack's chair, and he stopped and stood there for a few moments. "I mean, you're killing people, Jack, and Hara's still out there devising her little plots to save the world." Placing a hand on the table and the other on the back of Jack's chair, he leaned closer so their heads were only inches apart. "So I thought to myself, maybe you'd be more willing to talk to me about Hara?"

Get away from me! GET AWAY!

Get away from *me?*

The thoughts continued to be screamed inside Perry's head, but now it was clear that they didn't belong to him. Watching Jack's expression become more fearful, Perry felt the intensity of the thought grow stronger. Then he remembered what Jack had said before, about being a Colician. If he was like Hara, why hadn't he revealed his ability yet? Why hadn't he tried to use it to escape? Perry realized that he had just discovered Jack's ability. It was clear the boy had telepathic abilities, and if he was scared then it would make sense that he was screaming things inside his own head, and maybe even projecting thoughts and feeling into other people's minds without realizing it. It all made sense.

"Where is she?" The Doc asked softly, leaning closer to him.

Breathing rapidly through his nose, Jack tried to lean away from The Doc, but the cuffs kept him from moving more than a few inches. Now that Perry knew what Jack's ability was, he was waiting for any other emotions that Jack might accidentally send to him.

When he refused to answer, The Doc shook the back of the chair, causing it to rattle against the floor loudly. "Where is she?" he shouted.

"I don't know!" Jack cried in fear, yanking harder at the cuffs. His face was desperate.

His voice dropping into a deadly tone, The Doc growled, "You do remember what happens when you don't tell me what I want to know, right Jack? Or need I remind you?" Giving Jack the creepy head cock, he leaned closer still.

"I don't know where she is!" Jack shrieked, his body trembling uncontrollably. "I swear to God I don't know! And I'm so glad I don't because if I did I would tell you!" He cowered beneath The Doc's hovering form like a dog that had just disobeyed his master. His heart was pounding in his chest, and it took Perry a moment to comprehend that that was what he was hearing.

The Doc paused at that remark. "Yes," he said. "You would, wouldn't you?" Taking a few steps away from the table, he seemed to lose himself in thought.

Odau was not at all pleased with that answer. "That's it?!" he demanded. "You can't stop now! You were getting through to him! Where's the answers you promised us?"

"Patience is not one of your virtues, is it?" The Doc asked him, still lost in the depths of his own thoughts.

"You said he would tell you where she is!" Odau cried angrily. "I can't accept the answer 'I don't know!'"

"I said he would tell me where she was if he knew!" The Doc reminded him in annoyance. Gesturing to Jack, he commanded, "Look at him, Lieutenant! Have you ever seen this amount of fear on a person's face? This is pure terror, and terror implies that if he did know Hara's location, he would tell me. Now if you wouldn't mind shutting up for a few minutes, I can get your answers another way."

"What are you talking about?" Odau demanded, irritated.

"Just because we aren't going to get the answers you wanted to hear, it doesn't mean we aren't going to get any at all."

"What?"

"He may not know where the girl is, but he knows where someone is that might actually know," The Doc explained, eyeing Jack again. "Do you know where Allan is, Jack?"

"No," Jack whispered, cringing at the name.

"Are you sure?" The Doc asked warningly.

"I'm sure," Jack breathed.

"Okay. That's fine. I can live with that. But I know you know where your other friend is, and you're going to tell me."

"What other friend?" Jack asked in confusion.

"Your other friend who came back here with you."

"Oh great," Odau grumbled. "There's another one of them out there?"

Nobody in the room acknowledged his comment. Perry was too intently focused on the conversation at hand. The Doc was studying Jack's expression carefully, and Jack was staring at The Doc, his eyes showing that he knew he had just been caught.

"You and Hara were not the only ones who came back recently were you?" The Doc asked him softly. "There's a third person like you hiding out there, am I right?"

His eyebrows slowly coming together, Jack muttered, "I have no idea what you're talking about."

Odau threw Perry a confused glance, but Perry just kept watching the conversation, growing worried with each passing second that The Doc would try to harm Jack to get his answers.

Snorting, The Doc smirked down at him and said, "Now we both know that's a lie. So which one of your buddies is it, huh? David? Greg? Adrial? Oh, wait, that's right. I killed Adrial, didn't I?"

A wave of anger was radiating from Jack, and Perry felt a jolt of anger himself for The Doc. So he had murdered one of Jack's friends and now he was bragging about it to the boy like it was some kind of magnificent achievement? Could the man be any sicker? Perry could sense that Jack wanted to hurt him, but considering he was cuffed to a chair it would be difficult to do so. Despite his temptation to lunge at the man and rip his throat out, Jack just set his jaw and turned his head away. His move did not gain The Doc's appreciation.

"Don't turn your head away from me when I'm talking to you," he snapped. "Look at me, and tell me who and where the third one is."

Pursing his lips, Jack muttered something inaudible.

"I'm sorry?" The Doc said in a deadly voice. "I didn't catch that."

Slowly, Jack turned his head back towards him. Glaring furiously, he growled, "Fuck you."

For a moment The Doc remained where he was, staring into Jack's mahogany eyes. But without warning, he grabbed a handful of Jack's hair and snapped his head back.

"Whoa!" Perry said in surprise, taking a defensive step forward.

"Hey," Odau warned, standing up to step in between Perry and The Doc. "Don't interfere with him."

"That's enough," Perry growled, ignoring the lieutenant. He took another step forward, but The Doc hadn't taken notice of either of them.

He was snarling something into Jack's ear that neither Perry nor Odau could hear, but whatever it was seemed to have an effect on him. Jack's mortified expression was back, but now he was struggling against his cuffs with every ounce of strength he possessed. Placing his other hand on the boy's shoulder to keep him in his seat, The Doc hissed, "You know what comes next, Jack. Now tell me what I want to hear, because I know you know the consequences."

Having seen enough, Perry strode forward angrily. Odau started to step in his path, but Perry just shoved right past him. "I said, that's enough!" he yelled, grabbing The Doc by the arm and yanking him away from Jack.

Stumbling backwards, The Doc shot Perry a surprised look when he regained his balance. "Excuse me?" he said, taking a few steps forward again.

"Get out!" Perry snarled.

"I'm sorry?"

"I said get out!" Perry's shout startled himself. He had just stepped between the only link to Hara and the one man who could extract the information they needed. The Doc was staring at him with his mouth half open, and Perry could feel Odau's eyes on him as well, but Perry didn't really care. He was done with The Doc.

Jack began sputtering out words, trying to get out a specific sentence. "P-Perry," he spat, his voice shaking. "I'll t-tell you anything you w-want to hear! J-just get him out of here! P-please...please..." Squeezing his eyes shut, he started begging quietly under his breath.

"Do you have any idea what you're doing?" The Doc asked him quietly, his eyes narrowing.

"Get out," Perry repeated, his voice beginning to quiver with rage.

"I think you're making a huge mistake here—"

"Your two minutes are up!" Perry snapped.

"Perry, I think you really need to listen to him," Odau started, advancing a step.

"Get out!" Perry turned to Odau. "Both of you."

Perry had had enough, and they seemed to see that in his eyes. Giving him a disapproving glance, The Doc walked to the door. Odau's confused eyes remained on Perry's until they heard the door click shut, and then he asked in a whisper, "What are you doing?"

"Just go," Perry ordered.

"He was going to give us another lead!" Odau said, his eyes pleading. "We might be able to actually find her!"

Sternly, Perry pointed at the door. The lieutenant obeyed this time, and Perry followed him with his eyes as he moved towards the door. Odau took the handle in his hand and pulled it open, but he turned back to Perry to plead with him one more time.

"I need to find this girl," he whispered, his eyes and voice desperate. When all Perry did was stare blankly back at him without responding, he turned hopelessly and left the room.

Exhaling in relief, Perry turned, grabbed the empty chair, and pulled it around to the opposite side of the table so he could sit directly beside Jack. When he was seated, he reached out and placed a comforting hand on Jack's shoulder. "Jack," he said, praying the boy would at least speak to him now. "You need to talk to me!"

Jack flinched away from his touch and he squeezed his eyes shut. His body continued to tremble and he refused to reply.

"If you meant what you said before and we really are brothers, then you need to trust me and speak to me!" Perry was growing frustrated very quickly, and when Jack shook his head furiously and continued to keep his mouth shut, he asked, "Who is The Doc?"

To Perry's surprise, Jack looked up. His eyes were overflowing with tears, and the way he gazed at Perry made Perry hate himself for putting the boy through that. "I'm sorry," he apologized sincerely, hoping he could make Jack understand his regret. "I'm sorry for bringing him in here. I know he did some horrible things to Hara, and when you told me you have abilities too I should have taken into consideration that he may have done things to you as well." He waited for a reply from Jack, but he got none. "Did he do things to you too?" Still no response. "What did he—"

"So he's the guy who's been helping you?" Jack blurted, his voice weak.

"Yes," Perry answered.

"Do you have any idea how big a mistake you've made in trusting him?" Jack demanded frantically, his voice shaking. "Do you have any idea how screwed we all are now?"

Perry was confused. "We...?"

"Me, you, Hara, Allan Brown, Meg Hopper...anyone with a connection to us! Do you realize how dead we all are now?"

"I don't understand," Perry said softly, growing worried. "Why would we all be dead?"

"Have you not yet figured out who this guy is?" Jack's voice dropped down so no one on the other side of the glass could hear. "Haven't you realized what he is?"

"I think I've got an idea," Perry replied flatly.

"He's the Adolf Hitler of the twenty-first century!" Jack declared, ignoring him. "Didn't you hear a word I said to you when we first met? He not only killed my family and Hara's family, but he ordered the massacre of millions of people! Millions! And if he found someone with a unique ability—like Hara—then he saved them for his little torture sessions! Don't you see? I warned you, and Daniel warned you, and Hara warned you, yet you still fell for The Doc's cunning lies!"

"What are you saying?" Perry asked, dread filtering into his nearly calm tone. Jack, Hara, and Marcus had indeed warned him, yet he still accepted The Doc's help!

Jack's voice was barely a murmur. "All he wants is Hara. You don't even want to think about the sick, twisted things he's got planned for her. What he's already done to her! Hara may have killed those people and is going to kill Odau's boy, but you can't let that psychopath son of bitch get his hands on her!" The fear in Jack's eyes told Perry he was telling the truth. "Don't you see why he came to you in the first place? He didn't come to help you, he came so you could help him! He's only using you and the lieutenant to get to her, and once he's done using you he'll just stab you in the back and kill every one of us who's left!" Staring back at him insistently, he clarified, "If you don't do something about him now, he's going to kill you, Perry! And if you die, our future will die with you!"

"You seem to know an awful lot about the future," Perry said suspiciously.

"I come from a society where people can tell the future," Jack reminded. "We all know what's coming, and you are very important as time goes on. I don't need to see the future to tell you that."

"But why would The Doc want to kill me if I'm helping him?" Perry demanded, puzzled.

"Because you're one of us," Jack whispered.

For about a minute, all they did was stare into each other's eyes. The only sound was Jack's breathing, which refused to come under control. Perry was busy trying to comprehend Jack's comment, but he couldn't make sense of it. He was one of them? One of who? A Colician? He had no ability, so that couldn't be possible.

"What do you mean, I'm one of you?" Perry demanded.

He wasn't exactly given an answer, but for the first time throughout the interrogation Jack finally gave him a shred of something. "I'm going to give you an address," Jack said in a low voice. "It is very important that you not tell anyone else. If The Doc finds this place, someone I deeply care about will be in extreme danger. Can I trust you not to tell anyone?"

"Yes," Perry answered. "Absolutely."

"Good. Do you know the abandoned apartment blocks along the riverfront?"

"Yes."

"Good. I want you to go there, and find number 786. Go inside and take the stairs down to the lower level. There's someone there I think you should talk to."

"Is it Hara?" Perry asked, hopeful.

"No, but I think talking to him will do you some good. He may be able to fill you in on a few details that I haven't been able to. Don't worry," he reassured upon seeing Perry's wary look. "He's unarmed. He wouldn't hurt a fly. So please show him the same consideration. He's a very good man, and he's the only family I've got left."

"Why are you telling me this?"

"Because I trust you."

"You hardly know me," Perry reminded, snorting skeptically.

"I know you better than you think," Jack told him, raising an eyebrow. "Watch your back out there, okay?"

"Should I warn Lieutenant Odau about him?"

Jack shook his head. "Don't bother with him. If you haven't noticed by now, he's not too keen on listening."

"But I think I should still let him know—"

"Perry, trust me. I'm quite sure he has a better chance of getting out of this alive than you do."

"Why do you think that?" Perry asked.

"Because he's one of them." Jack growled the words.

Perry squinted at him. "Are you implying something here?"

Jack looked away from him. "I think you should leave now."

Startled, Perry remained in his seat, expecting Jack to begin talking again. There were so many questions that had gone unanswered, especially if he was implying that Odau was somehow aiding The Doc. But when Jack didn't add anything more, Perry took the hint. He wasn't going to answer any more questions, but maybe this man he was sending him to would. Slowly, he stood up and headed to the door. One question in particular had been nagging at him, so he stopped and turned with his hand on the handle. "How many of you are left?" he asked softly

Gazing blankly back at him, Jack murmured, "There can't be more than a few hundred left alive."

Nodding, Perry wondered how a powerful civilization of millions could drop to a number in the hundreds in just a few years. But then he thought back to World War II, when Adolf Hitler murdered over ten million people in less than a decade. And he remembered the Mayans, a very powerful society that eventually disappeared over time. When you have someone with great power, or if the civilization is destroying itself from within, then it won't take much to cause the civilization to fall. If The Doc had power and the Colicians were having internal issues, then it would make sense that The Doc managed to wipe most of them out.

Sneaking a glance at the one-way glass window, Jack hissed at Perry, "You need to go!"

Realizing that he had been standing frozen at the door, Perry blinked in surprise and nodded again. As he pulled the door open and stepped out, Jack whispered a reminder, "786!"

Everyone was eagerly awaiting his return as Perry entered the observation room. None of them had been able to hear their soft conversation, and they all appeared as if they expected Perry to have all the answers they needed. Odau was standing right beside the door, shifting his weight anxiously from foot to foot. He jumped when Perry stepped out, and immediately demanded an explanation.

"Well?"

Agent Long stood up when Perry's eyes met his, his expression hopeful. "What did he tell you, Perry?" he asked eagerly.

The others were anxious for Perry's explanation as well, but Perry was eyeing The Doc, who was leaning against the far wall. Before the interrogation, Perry had been wary of The Doc, but after seeing Jack's fear and hearing the things they both had to say, he knew that he had to keep The Doc from hurting anyone else.

The Doc was gazing evenly back at him with curious eyes, their evil glint making Perry shudder. Perry felt that he had pissed him off for kicking him out. Now Perry knew something that he didn't, and Perry began to grow worried that The Doc would try to extract the information from him. But Perry had already decided that he was done with The Doc. He was no longer going to help him with anything. After he was done speaking to the man Jack wanted him to see, he was going to track down Hara on his own and deal with her himself. Giving The Doc a harsh glare to let him know he was no longer an ally, Perry turned and started to move towards the door.

"Perry!" Odau said impatiently. "What did he tell you?"

Pausing, Perry turned back and lied, "Nothing." Then he left the room and headed down the hall. He was going to go to the conference room, grab his bag, and hope no one tried to interfere with him. But of course, nothing could be that easy.

On his walk to the conference room, he heard Odau following him, but to his surprise the lieutenant didn't say a word to him the entire time. But when they both entered he brought the hammer down.

"What do you mean, nothing?" Odau demanded, the familiar tone of frustration back in his voice. "You had an entire conversation with him! He must have said something of importance to you!"

"Look, Lieutenant, I think there's something the two of us need to get straight here," Perry growled, turning on him. "When I say I have nothing to share with you, then I have nothing to share with you. Now if you'll excuse me…" Grabbing his jacket and shoulder bag, he started to push past Odau, but the strap on his bag snapped, and all the contents came tumbling out onto the floor. "You can't be serious," he muttered, stooping to scoop everything up.

Odau was becoming angrier. "Are you telling me you're going to hide valuable information from me?"

"Look pal," Perry snapped, shooting him a scowl as he continued to pick up his things. "I know you're eager to find the girl who tried to murder your son, but once again your attitude is starting to get in the way of our jobs here."

Stunned by his remark, Odau stammered before finally spitting out what he was trying to say. "Where are you going?"

"I have to make a quick run," Perry mumbled.

"How long are you going to be gone?"

Perry thought about that. "An hour," he replied uncertainly. "Possibly longer. I'm not really sure…"

The lieutenant peered down at him peculiarly, as if he suddenly understood something. "What?" Perry asked warily.

"He told you where she is, didn't he?" Odau seemed certain of this, and the eagerness in his eyes was increasing in intensity.

"Jack doesn't know where she is," Perry reminded him, turning back to his things once more.

"Well, he obviously told you something valuable to this investigation," Odau pointed out, his voice remaining calm for once. "You wouldn't leave us like this for any old errand."

Perry closed his eyes, praying the man would go away. But he knew he wouldn't, so he then began to pray that the lieutenant could be trusted with a secret. "I need to go talk to someone who may or may not know the locations of our fugitives."

"You mean the third person The Doc was talking about?"

"Yes."

"Why didn't you just tell me in the first place?"

"Because I don't know who I should trust anymore," Perry told him, sitting down in a chair at the long table.

Odau closed the door and leaned against it, listening intently. "What do you mean?" he asked softly.

There was that question again, the one Perry had been asking repeatedly ever since he discovered Hara. Only this time, he wasn't the one asking it. It was now his turn to make clarifications. Rubbing his face with both hands, he realized how exhausted he was, and wondered how long he would sleep once they dealt with Hara and The Doc. "I think you know what I mean," he muttered, raising an eyebrow.

The lieutenant seemed to understand who he was referring to. He tilted his head slightly in a way that strangely resembled The Doc. "You don't trust him?"

"Do you?" Perry asked, already knowing what the answer would be.

Shrugging, Odau answered, "Yeah, sure. I suppose. Well, I trust that he can get Hara. He's made it quite clear that he knows how to deal with people like her."

People like her. Every time he heard that phrase, the word "prejudice" flashed through his mind. "That's what scares me," Perry replied. "He knows too much about her people, and you heard about what he did to the rest of them."

Odau shrugged again. "Just because Jack and Hara said it doesn't make it true. I'm not saying it didn't happen, but how come we've never heard about any of this genetic experimentation? If it did really happen, then I guess it's a good thing there aren't many of these people left. I mean, just look at what one of them did to this city!"

Perry gaped at him. "How can you say something like that?" he demanded incredulously. "These are millions of lives we're talking about here! Innocent children and people who were brutally tortured and murdered!"

"Again, look at what Hara did," Odau said. "Imagine the damage millions of them would do! Imagine the destruction they would cause! It's a miracle that the planet hasn't been blown to bits already!"

"This man we're working with savagely murdered millions of people!"

"And what would have happened if they had attacked us first?"

"Do you even care that these people were killed?"

421

"If they all act like Hara and go around killing innocent children, then no, not really. But this doesn't explain why you don't trust The Doc to get Hara."

"I never said I don't trust him to get her. I know he can get her. If he's fast enough, that is. I just don't trust him. Didn't you see the terror on Jack's face just from hearing The Doc's voice?"

"Yes."

"And that didn't bother you?"

Odau watched Perry's expression carefully, hoping he wouldn't get angry over his answer again. "Not particularly."

Groaning, Perry rubbed his eyes and shook his head. *Please, God, help me make this man understand!* he silently prayed. But then he remembered what Jack had said about Odau being one of them. The lieutenant seemed to be siding with The Doc and not really caring about what happened to Hara and her people, so maybe Jack was right. Odau wasn't going to listen if Perry warned him about The Doc. Sighing, Perry mumbled, "There's just something about this guy that seems so familiar to me, and it's freaking me out. There's something about him that just doesn't feel right...can't you feel it?"

"Like I said before, it doesn't really bother me that he killed that particular group of people, but the fact that he's got the manpower to kill millions does bother me, and that's what's bothering you."

"No, I'm not talking about anything to do with that," Perry said in irritation. "Let's set all that aside, pretend we don't know he killed all those people, and look at just him. There's a creepy familiarity I get when I look at him, like I know him or something, but I've never met him before today. Do you get the same feeling?"

Shrugging, Odau replied, "I suppose. Yeah, I do actually. But it's probably just paranoia we're feeling."

"Paranoia?" Perry repeated skeptically. "Have you not seen how even murderers cringe at the very mention of this man's name? That's definitely worthy of scaring me."

As Perry got up to leave, Odau tried again. "Well...wherever you're going, I'm going with you."

"No!" Perry said forcefully. "I promised Jack I'd keep his friend safe, so I've got to go alone. I need to figure this out for myself first."

"What if it's a trap? What if the guy ends up being really dangerous and attacks you? Who's going to be there to back you up if you go alone?"

"Jack said he's harmless, so I'm going with his word."

"You're trusting his word?" Odau asked in disbelief.

"I trust his word a lot more than The Doc's," Perry told him. "I'm important to Jack, remember? What could he gain by harming me now?"

Odau considered this. "I'll give you that one."

"I need you to cover for me," Perry said, knowing that he really needed to get going. "Don't tell the others what I'm doing."

"What do you want me to say?"

"Anything. Make something up. Tell them I'm going grocery shopping for all I care."

"But will you at least tell me where you're going?"

"No."

"Well, for God's sake, be careful!" Throwing the door back open, Odau stormed out of the room.

Thankful to finally be rid of him, Perry gathered his belongings and turned towards the door. He ran right into The Doc.

"Jesus!" he cried, stumbling backwards in surprise.

"Oh, I'm sorry," The Doc apologized in a dull monotone. "Did I scare you?" The sickeningly curious expression on his face was making Perry's blood run cold.

Perry tried to sneak past him, but he was standing directly in the doorway. "Sure," he replied, taking a step backwards again when he realized he was being cornered.

The Doc followed his movement, taking a step closer to keep the distance between them the same. He didn't say anything else; he just kept staring at him with that creepy glint in his eyes.

Clearing his throat awkwardly, Perry asked him, "Is there...uh...something I can help you with?"

"Yes," The Doc said, keeping his eyes locked on him. "I believe there is."

Perry waited for him to add to that, but he didn't. "Well?"

"I think you know what I want," The Doc told him, taking another step forward.

Perry retreated another step as his stomach began to roll over. It was obvious what The Doc wanted, but Perry had no intention of giving it to him. For now, it was best to play stupid. "Actually, I don't, so why don't you enlighten me?"

The Doc snickered. "Do I strike you as stupid, Agent Perry?"

"What?"

"Why don't you take a seat?" The Doc invited, nodding to the chair behind him.

Perry saw that The Doc had finally given him enough room to sneak past him. "Look, Doc, if you're not going to tell me what it is you want, then go talk to Lieutenant Odau. I'm sure he'd be more than happy to play guessing games with you. But I don't have time right now, so if you'll excuse me, I need to be on my way." He started to walk around The Doc, but he didn't get far.

His hand shooting out and catching Perry by the arm, The Doc said softly, "I said sit down." He gave Perry a hard shove backwards.

Falling back down into a chair, Perry dropped his jacket and bag and started to jump to his feet. But The Doc was already upon him, and before he could react to help himself The Doc had one hand around his throat and the other around his right wrist, pinning Perry's arm to the table.

"Get off me—" Perry started to say, but The Doc's hand tightened around his windpipe, cutting off his oxygen supply.

"*Shh!*" The Doc hissed at him, his evil gray eyes taunting him as Perry's free hand clawed at the one around his throat. "Now, I want you to listen to me very closely, boy. No one else is coming down here for you, so if I wanted to I could kill you right here and now. But you have some information I need, so I'm not going to kill you, although that still leaves you at the mercy of my hand here."

Perry struggled violently against The Doc's strong grip. When he understood that he wasn't going to be able to pry the man's fingers from his neck, he tried clawing at his face. But The Doc just leaned his head back so he couldn't reach him. Perry then tried to grab for his gun on his right hip, but when The Doc saw what he was doing he lifted Perry's head off the table and then slammed it back down.

"Don't try anything," The Doc growled in his ear. "I know that Jack let you in on a little secret of his, and you're not leaving here unless you tell me what it is!"

He was out of air. His vision was going dark at the edges, and he grabbed at The Doc's arm in one last feeble attempt to get his hand off of his throat. Perry marveled at how strong The Doc was; he had to be at least ten years older than Perry, yet he was managing to strangle a well-trained FBI agent.

For a few terrifying moments, Perry thought that The Doc really was going to kill him, but then it all stopped. The pain in his head from the lack of oxygen was suddenly gone as he was able to inhale again, and the pressure around his neck and wrist was gone as well. Sucking in deep gulps of air and beginning to cough heavily, Perry saw that The Doc had released him of his own accord and was currently standing a few feet in front of him, the mocking smirk back on his face.

Clutching his throat as he coughed and gasped for air, Perry leaned forward and squeezed his eyes shut. His throat felt narrow and dry, and it hurt when he breathed in deeply. He felt a hand on his shoulder, and then he was pushed back upright into his chair.

"Keep your head up," The Doc instructed, crossing his arms over his chest and gazing down at him when he was sitting back again. "You'll be able to breathe easier."

Glaring at him, Perry did what he said. It helped a lot. He was able to take in more air with less pain.

"I'm sorry about this," The Doc was saying. "But I needed to get my point across."

"What point?" Perry croaked, wincing at a flash of pain in his neck.

Placing his hands on his knees, The Doc leaned down. His eyes glinting, he told him, "My point is that when I want answers to something, I will do just about anything to get them. And that includes physically assaulting an FBI agent."

"What the hell do you want from me?" Perry demanded, his voice raspy.

"I want you to tell me everything Jack told you," The Doc replied, still boring holes into Perry's eyes with his own. "And as you've seen, I have very powerful methods of persuasion, so why don't you just tell me without giving me any trouble?"

Still gasping for air, Perry fought back the fear that was steadily rising inside him. "He didn't tell me anything!" he lied, bracing his hands on the arm of his chair in case The Doc tried anything else.

He just sighed. "This is going to be a lot easier for the both of us if you just cooperate."

"Screw you!" Perry snarled, finally regaining his breath. Feeling strong enough to stand up, he did, only to be pushed right back down again. "Let me out of here!"

"I don't think so, son," The Doc said solemnly. "You're staying right here until I get my answers."

"You can't do this to me!" Perry's voice was barely a whisper, and he felt exhausted and vulnerable. He couldn't fight The Doc off, and he didn't have enough strength to call for help. "My colleagues are going to fry your ass when they find out what you did!"

"Relax, Agent Perry," The Doc told him, standing up straight and grinning down at him. "I'm not going to hurt you. That wouldn't do me any good. But what about your partner? The cute little blonde. Would you talk to me if I hurt her?"

"You touch her and I'll kill you," Perry growled, feeling the rage pulsing through his veins. The Doc could strangle Perry all he wanted, but he was not laying a hand on Renee.

"Will you?" The Doc asked, still grinning. "So why don't you talk to me and then no one has to get hurt."

Springing to his feet, Perry gave The Doc a hard shove backwards. "If you hurt anyone else, I won't save you for Hara! I'll kill you myself!"

The Doc was laughing, evidently enjoying himself. "Where's his friend?" he asked between laughs.

"What?"

"Jack's other friend that came back with him. I know he told you where he is."

"I don't know where his damn friend is, and frankly, I don't care!" Perry snapped. "Now, I need to be somewhere."

"What's 786?"

"Agent Long is going to arrest you for assaulting a federal agent!" Perry warned, avoiding the question. "You're going to be locked up for a very long time, and not just for this…"

"You're not answering my question," The Doc said, ignoring Perry's threats.

"You never answer any of mine!"

"Is it an address?"

"It's none of your business what the number is! It's my business! Jack gave it to me, not you! He trusted me with it, and I'm not planning on betraying that trust."

"You know," The Doc started, sighing. "I thought you understood the general concept for bringing this girl in. I can see in your eyes that you want her caught almost as much as I do, but you and I," he shook his head, "I don't think we're on the same side."

"I don't side with murderers," Perry said, narrowing his eyes.

"I don't like working with liars," The Doc challenged, raising an eyebrow.

"Well, you're a little hypocritical, don't you think?" Perry asked him.

The Doc blinked. "I've been as honest as I can be."

"Jack's not one of them, huh? Right. So who was the one screaming inside my head, hmm? Was it you?"

Gazing back with half a smirk, The Doc muttered, "So I suppose you do have a connection to him, huh?"

"Why didn't you just tell me right off the bat that Jack wasn't normal?"

"What's your definition of normal?"

"Definitely not telepathic abilities!"

Laughing, The Doc told him, "I was waiting to see how long it would take you to figure it out. And besides, I couldn't risk you sending him to some facility to be studied."

"Why, so you could save him for yourself?" Perry demanded. "Tell me, how can you get such a kick out of messing with people's heads? Are you trying to make everyone have as messed up a mind as you?"

All he did was snicker.

Sick and tired of his mind games, Perry said, "Maybe your family dying was an act of karma!"

That wiped the smirk clean off The Doc's face. Staring back at Perry with a deadly look in his eyes, he whispered, "What did you just say?"

Glad that he could finally hit a nerve after everything the man had done, Perry smirked at him to see how he would like it. "If you destroy families and ruin the lives of others, then it was bound to happen to you eventually. Have you ever stopped to consider that maybe it was karma that killed your wife and daughter?"

Perry could almost feel the rage radiating off of The Doc. Although his expression was calm, Perry saw the hate in his eyes. Wondering if what he said was a mistake, if he had gone a little too far with his comment, he took a cautious step back.

To Perry's surprise, all The Doc did was shake his head. "You have no idea what you've said, have you?" he asked, his calm face intimidating.

Unsure of The Doc's intentions, Perry watched him carefully. But once again, his next response was just as calm as his last. Taking a step to his left, The Doc gestured at the door behind him with his head. "Go," he said.

It took Perry a moment to comprehend that The Doc really was letting him go. He wondered why, after all he had done to keep him there to get his answers, but then Perry understood that The Doc really was upset about what he had said. The Doc wasn't showing his emotions, but Perry could sense them. Carefully, he picked up his things and stepped around him, keeping his eyes on him the entire time. Once he was past, he hurried out the door and down the hall towards the side exit. Perry prayed that he would not have any more confrontations with The Doc. But he knew he would most likely have many more. Hopefully, this new source would know where Hara was and Perry could then arrest The Doc without any more incidents.

He made it to the exit door and was starting to leave when he was stopped.

"Shawn," The Doc called down the hall.

Turning in surprise, Perry stared at him. The only person who ever called him by his first name was Renee. His friends even called him Perry.

Giving him that sickeningly curious look again, The Doc asked, "How old are you?"

"Why?" Perry asked, wondering why that mattered.

The Doc shrugged casually, but Perry saw that there was something else in the question. For reasons unknown to Perry, there was a significance in his age. "Just curious."

Perry shifted his weight awkwardly at the pressure from his stare. "Thirty-five," he answered uncertainly.

Nodding, The Doc muttered, "Huh."

Waiting for him to say more, Perry slid his jacket on and gazed back at him expectantly. But The Doc didn't say anything else. All he did was stand in the doorway while leaning against the frame, staring at him with that weird look on his face. Perry waited a moment longer, but when the silence became unbearably uncomfortable he pointed to the door. "Um…I'm going to leave now."

Nodding again, The Doc continued to watch him silently.

Feeling a peculiar sensation in the pit of his stomach, like he had curdled milk inside of his body, Perry nodded as well and turned towards the door. Not quite sure what had just happened, he forced himself to not look back as he felt The Doc's stone-cold gaze burning holes into the back of his head. He decided that he was never going to figure out The Doc's strange personality. Ever.

12

History of Violence

On the twenty minute drive to the abandoned area along the riverfront, Perry had some time to think over everything that had happened in the past 24 hours. He thought about how the investigation started, with only an angry teenage girl as their problem. After that, everything became a jumbled mess. Perry hoped that whoever he was going to see would explain everything about…everything! Hara kept telling him that he would learn the truth by the end of the day, but he was too impatient for that. He needed the answers now.

Once he found the abandoned apartment blocks, it took him another ten minutes to find the one labeled 786. He parked his car and locked the doors just in case. He approached the door with caution, his hand resting on his gun. He stood on the front step for a few moments, wondering what new mysteries were waiting for him on the other side of the door. Shaking his head, he turned the rusty brass knob and stepped inside.

There was no electricity because the buildings were no longer habitable, so it took his eyes a moment to adjust to the dim light in the front entryway. Blinking rapidly so he wouldn't stumble over his own feet, Perry let his hand trail against the wall as he slowly walked forwards. His heart was pounding in anticipation and his hands were sweating, expecting someone to jump out and grab him at any moment.

A strange smell met his nose, and it bothered him that he couldn't identify it. It was like rust combined with raw sewage, but in the darkness he couldn't find the source, so he couldn't be sure. Continuing slowly into the quickly fading light, Perry felt the wall end as a hall connected to the foyer. Sliding his hand around the corner, he gazed down the hallway into a pitch blackness that looked like it would swallow him if he dared go further. He rounded the corner and moved slower than he had before. For a while he traveled like this, careful to step lightly to avoid making any noise.

Jack had told him to take the stairs down to the lower level, and that was what Perry was trying to do. Now that he was a good ways down the hall, he couldn't see a thing, but he stopped short when he felt his hand go around another corner. Hoping this new hall would lead to the hidden stairwell, Perry rounded the corner and slowly took a step forward. It was still pitch black, but Perry took another step forward.

And another. And another. On his next step, there was no more floor beneath his feet.

Crying out in surprise, he lost his balance and fell forward. He tumbled down a flight of stairs, his shoulders and head banging up against the walls on either side of him. When he finally reached the bottom, his head made a loud *thwack!* sound as it smacked into a door. Muttering the word shit a few times, he groped around in the dark for something he could grab onto so he could stand up. His hand wrapped around a door knob and he braced one hand against the wall and pushed himself up.

"I guess I found the stairs," he mumbled to himself. Wincing as he felt several bruises begin to form, he gritted his teeth and waited for himself to regain his balance. When he felt ready to continue, he sucked in a deep breath, lowered his hand back to his weapon, and turned the knob.

He flinched as the door creaked open, but no one came lunging through the doorway at him, so he relaxed. As the door opened wider, Perry's eyes were greeted by a dim light coming from a small bulb on the ceiling just inside the door. He looked around and saw thick, translucent tarps stretching from the floor to the ceiling surrounding him in a semi-circular shape. Seeing that there were more lights on the other side of them, Perry stepped forward from the doorway. The last thing he was aware of before he was blinded was the hard concrete floor beneath his feet, his shoes scuffing across it. Then a harsh white light erupted from behind the tarp directly in front of him, completely blinding him. Throwing up his hand to shield his face from anything that might come at him, he closed his eyes tightly and stumbled back towards the door. He kept his eyes shielded, but what seemed like permanent spots were burned into his retinas. And just like that, the light turned off again.

"Sorry about the security system," a voice with a British accent called.

Breathing fast, Perry turned his head towards the sound of the voice. He heard the tarp crinkle as someone moved it aside and he immediately became alarmed. Pushing himself along the wall again, he moved in the opposite direction of the sounds.

"It's there in case an enemy of ours should find us," the voice explained, sounding only a few feet away. Perry noticed that the voice seemed tired and worn-out, like it belonged to an elderly man, but he was still uneasy about how close the man's voice was. "It may take you a while to regain your sight," he added. "Here. Take my hand."

"Don't come near me!" Perry warned as he lost his balance and fell over backwards. He heard his gun fall out of his belt and he felt around for it, but he couldn't find it. Blinking up at the sound of the man's voice, he managed to see the outline of his figure leaning over him through the white ocean his eyes were seeing. "I mean it!"

He heard the man chuckle. "If I wanted to hurt you, old friend, I would have done so already. Take my hand."

Perry hesitated. He couldn't see who the man was and therefore didn't trust him, but when he heard the words "old friend," he had second thoughts. The man sounded like Jack in a way, and Perry for the most part trusted Jack. If Perry was important to Jack, then he must be important to Jack's friend as well.

"You can trust me, Shawn Perry," the man told him, a smile in his voice. "I won't bite."

Hoping that he was telling the truth, Perry slowly stretched out his hand. He still couldn't see, but the man took his hand and helped him climb to his feet. Swaying as he caught his balance, Perry reached out in front of him and gripped the man's shoulder in an attempt to stay upright. "Who are you?" he asked.

"Noah," the man answered. "Noah Travis."

"You're Jack's friend?"

Noah paused. "I'm more like his nanny," he replied, and Perry detected the grin on his face.

Furrowing his eyebrows in curiosity, Perry glanced up in the direction of Noah's face. "What, you mean like a babysitter?"

He felt Noah shrug. "I suppose you could call it that."

Assuming he was joking, Perry nodded slowly. "Right," he said. "Okay."

There was a small pause before Noah released his hand and took his arm. "Come," he invited, pulling Perry along. "We'll get you seated."

Perry let Noah guide him past the tarps and across the floor. When they stopped, Perry heard a chair being pulled out in front of him.

"Sit," Noah said.

Perry did. His vision was slowly beginning to return, and he could just make out the shape of the table in front of him. Placing his hands upon it, he jerked his head away as he felt something brush against his neck.

"What happened to you?" Noah asked in concern, catching Perry's chin in one hand and lightly grazing his fingers along the sides of his neck.

"What do you mean?" Perry asked, trying to pull away.

"Hold still," Noah ordered. "There are bruises all over your throat, on either side of your neck."

"Oh," Perry said. "I...uh...had a slight encounter with...um..."

"The Doc?" Noah questioned, releasing him. Perry heard him step away for a moment, but he returned a moment later. "Here," he said, pressing something ice cold against Perry's neck. Perry jumped at first, but then he took the cold object—most likely a bag of frozen peas or corn—from him and held it against the side of his neck. He hadn't noticed until now, but his throat actually did hurt. Feeling Noah sit down in a chair beside him, he turned towards him and waited for him to speak again. Noah obviously knew The Doc well enough to know that it was him who had given Perry the bruises, so maybe he could provide some more information. "I could make you some tea for your throat, if you'd like," Noah offered.

"No thanks," Perry replied. "I'm not really a tea drinker."

Noah seemed to pause at this. "Really?"

Perry shrugged, unsure of why that was such a surprise.

"You know," Noah began with a sigh." You really should not be working with that man. In fact, you shouldn't ever be anywhere near him."

"So I've heard," Perry replied.

"I would say you should know better, but I suppose you wouldn't, would you?"

Raising an eyebrow questioningly, Perry waited for him to add to his comment. But to his dismay, Noah changed the subject.

"So, my friend, what brings you here?" he asked.

"Jack sent me," Perry explained.

"But what brings you here?" Noah repeated. "He didn't force you to come here, so why did you choose to come here?"

Perry thought for a moment. "I was hoping you could tell me."

Noah chuckled again. "Daniel said you would come when Jack thought you were ready to hear the truth. Is that why you came?"

"No, but the truth would be nice," Perry admitted.

"So what did you really come here for?"

"Why does it matter?"

"I want to hear you say it."

Sighing, Perry told him, "I came here so I could find Hara before The Doc does."

"That's what I thought," Noah said softly. "But I can't tell you where Hara is. I haven't any more of a clue than you."

Perry rubbed at his eyes, hoping he would be able to see clearly soon. Shapes were still coming into focus, but he couldn't make out any important features of his surroundings.

"I must say though, sir," Noah added. "It's a pleasure to see you again after so much time."

"Again?" Perry repeated, turning back to him. He could just make out Noah's snow white hair and his bright blue eyes. "What do you mean, again? I've never met you before!"

He received no answer. Noah sighed and turned his head away, but he didn't speak again.

"Why does everyone act like I'm a friend of theirs?" Perry demanded. "They all act like they've known me forever, but we only just met! What is going on?"

"Everyone treats you like a friend because you are a friend," Noah told him. "I don't expect you to understand why, or even how, but you just are."

"You offered me the truth, Mr. Travis!" Perry declared angrily. "It would be mighty helpful to get it now."

"Some things can only be explained by certain people," Noah said.

Throwing his head up, Perry groaned again.

"But I can tell you this," Noah added, taking no notice to Perry's frustration. "All of Hara's people know you, and you know them."

"What?" Perry said, startled. "How?"

"You were a close friend of Hara's father before he was murdered by The Doc," Noah explained.

"What?" Perry repeated in confusion. "I've never had a close friend who was murdered, and I haven't met The Doc before today."

Noah looked back at him. "Yes, you have."

Perry demanded, "If I've met these people before, then how come I don't remember it?"

"I suppose that's one of the mysteries you'll have to wait to solve," Noah replied.

Wanting to know how he could have possibly known these people and not recall their meetings, a thought suddenly came to him. A terrible, agonizing thought. "Did he—" he started, choking on his words. "Did The Doc mess with my mind? Did he make me forget?"

"I assure you, sir, that no one made you forget anything."

"Well, then how…"

"Maybe we should move on to a different subject," Noah suggested.

Biting his lip, Perry tried to just go with it. "Alright. Why don't you tell me how your species started?"

"My species?" Noah repeated, and then laughed. "Shawn, I'm as human as all your other friends back at the station."

"You're human?" Perry said in surprise. "But…I thought humans were enemies of Hara's kind! Doesn't she hate humans?"

"Yes," Noah answered. "The Colician race hates humans, but quite a few of us were accused of treachery and were exiled to live among them. When I was exiled many years ago, I was taken in by Jack and his family and have lived with them ever since. See, when a human is exiled and forced to live with the Colicians, they usually accept us because we have no way to go back to our old lives and have nowhere else to go."

"You were exiled?" Perry said, puzzled. "How could you be accused of treachery when nobody except The Doc and his people knew about them?"

"Oh, people knew," Noah promised, nodding solemnly.

"How?" Perry asked. "How did you know when the FBI didn't?"

Sighing, Noah looked away again. "So," he said. "You wanted to know how the species began?"

Growing irritated with the sudden subject changes, Perry also sighed. "Sure, since you won't tell me anything else I want to know."

"Didn't Jack already explain this to you?" Noah asked.

"He gave me a brief description," Perry answered. "Which is all any of your other friends seem to be doing."

"Fair enough," Noah replied. "So you know about the chemical compound that started everything?"

"I was told about it," Perry said. "But I don't understand how that could give people superhuman capabilities."

"The Colicians still don't understand it completely either," Noah admitted. "All they know is that it rewrote their DNA and set off a switch in their brain that allowed them to develop abilities. Have you ever heard the saying that we only use ten percent of our brains? Well, scientists think that the chemical triggered the other ninety percent."

"So the other ninety percent gives you abilities?" Perry repeated, trying to explain it to himself.

"They believe so, yes."

"But where did the chemical come from, anyway?" Perry asked. "How did scientists come up with that?"

"It was originally constructed as a biological weapon," Noah explained. "Built to target select individuals with certain genetic traits. In this case, blood type."

"They were targeting people with a certain blood type? Why?"

"It was for future use in case we entered another war as terrible as World War I or II. If the United States entered a war and needed to exterminate a specific group of people, they wanted to be ready."

"We designed that so we could kill people?" Perry said in disbelief. "This was the military's plan?"

"It was the government's plan."

"I'm part of the government," Perry reminded. "I haven't heard a thing about this."

"Not all parts of the government knew," Noah told him.

Perry couldn't believe what Noah was telling him. "We made it so we could kill people? We actually created a biological weapon and planned to use it?"

"Yes," Noah said, nodding regretfully. "The scientists wanted to eventually narrow the target list to a small group of people, such as people with blue eyes or black hair or a certain genetic trait, but they decided to begin testing on blood types."

"They only made it for the blood types?" Perry asked hopefully. "I mean, they stopped after making the chemical for the blood types?"

"Yes."

"And they actually tested it on people?"

"No, of course not," Noah chortled. "They were testing it on blood. They made it so when people with the matching blood type were exposed to it, all of their red blood cells would die. And red blood cells carry oxygen around the body, so if they all die, then the person basically suffocates."

"How were people exposed to it then?"

"There was a spill, and once exposed to room temperature it became a gas. It escaped to the surrounding areas, and scientists feared that everyone with the matching blood type would die. There was panic, but they soon realized that they had made a mistake. Nobody died from it. Nobody on the outside even knew about it until the side effects of exposure began to show. By the time the scientists realized the terrible mistake they had made, it was too late to reverse it. No one was killed from exposure, but something else began to happen to the people affected."

"They began to develop abilities," Perry finished, nodding.

"Yes. Some people began showing later than others, but soon everyone with that blood type within a mile's radius of the facility was showing some sort of advanced capability."

"And Hara's parents were inside this radius, weren't they?"

"That's correct."

"Where was this facility located, anyway?"

Pausing, Noah said, "The lab was just outside Philadelphia, in a small town called Hatfield."

"What?" Perry snorted. "It couldn't have been!"

"I assure you it was."

"How?" Perry demanded. "I've been in the state of Pennsylvania for the past ten years! If something that big happened, I would have heard about it!"

"Not necessarily," Noah replied.

"Which blood type was affected?"

Noah paused again. "O negative."

"O negative?" Perry repeated quietly, staring at his blurred face. "O negative?"

"Yes, O negative," Noah said.

"I have O negative blood," Perry said. "I would have been affected."

"No, you wouldn't have," Noah promised.

"I have O negative blood!" Perry reminded, his voice rising.

"You wouldn't have been affected, Shawn," Noah repeated.

"Why the hell not?"

"You wouldn't have been affected because this happened thirty years ago," Noah explained.

Perry raised his eyebrows. "Thirty years ago? That long?"

"Didn't Jack tell you that Hara was born this way?" Noah asked.

That was a good point. Jack had said that Hara was born that way, and he most likely was as well. Perry supposed it must have had to have been a long time ago, but something just didn't feel right about that.

"How could our scientists have come up with technology that advanced thirty years ago?" he asked. "That was about 1978. Computers were very primitive then."

Shrugging, Noah said, "You'd be surprised how intelligent people can be."

Eager for more knowledge, Perry told him, "Please, continue. What happened after the exposure?"

"The scientists and military went about containing the affected area," Noah said. "But exposed people had left the area before they realized they were affected, and before the government managed to quarantine the area the contamination was spreading. If an unaffected O negative came into close proximity with an affected O negative, then they would become affected as well."

"How far did it spread?"

Noah shrugged again. "Everywhere. The whole world."

"Everywhere?" Perry said in astonishment. "Why wasn't everyone in the world with O negative affected? Why wasn't I affected?"

"You obviously never came into contact with anyone who was contanimated," Noah explained. "The government moved quickly when they realized the mutation was spreading, and soon they had traced the original carriers and tracked down everyone who had come into contact with them."

"How many were affected by the time the government contained the mutation?" Perry asked, dread weighing down on him.

"Far too many," Noah answered solemnly.

"Millions, right?"

"Yes."

"So millions of people across the globe developed super powers?" Perry repeated, just making sure he was taking all the information in correctly.

"Yes," Noah said again.

"How could millions of people develop super powers without anyone knowing about it?" Perry realized he was asking that question a lot. "There is no way anyone could possibly cover that up."

"That's because no one did," Noah replied.

"What did you say?" Perry demanded. "No one covered it up? How can that be possible? If millions of people developed super powers and then went missing because they were being quarantined, the entire world would know about it!"

"It's hard to explain," Noah said. "Hara's going to have to explain that one to you when the time comes."

Perry shook his head in confusion, hoping the time would come quickly. Something else was bugging him, and he needed it clarified. "My blood type is the reason Jack and Hara trust me, isn't it? They trust me because if I was exposed, I would become one of them."

Smiling lightly back at him, Noah told him, "Shawn, my friend, you already have been exposed."

Feeling his heart stop for a moment, Perry stared incredulously at Noah's calm face which had come a little more into focus. "Come again?" he said, feeling the horror slowly creeping over him.

"Only someone who was directly exposed can pass the mutation on to an unaffected O negative, but Hara did heal the wound inside your head, did she not?"

"What?" Perry was beginning to panic.

"A Healer heals by sending energy to the victim's body," Noah explained, his voice completely calm. "That means that energy from her body was transferred to yours. Once the energy came into your body, that was when you began to turn. You're changing, Shawn."

Shaking his head in denial, Perry sputtered, "I...I can't be turning into one of them!"

"How's your head?" Noah asked softly.

"What?" But then Perry remembered the slight ache in his head that was steadily getting worse.

Noah seemed to be reading his mind. "The ache signifies the increase in brain activity. It will become progressively worse for the next week or so."

"So I'm just going to randomly develop an ability?" Perry demanded. "I'm going to end up as one of The Doc's science experiments? How am I supposed to explain this to the Bureau?"

"I wouldn't do that if I were you," Noah cautioned. "If they find out what you can do, your freedom is gone, my friend."

"It's going to be a little difficult to explain when I begin to start fires or start blowing things up!" Perry cried, jumping to his feet and stumbling backwards.

"Whoa!" Noah said, and Perry felt him grab his arm. "Relax! You won't ever be one of The Doc's experiments! Don't worry about being discovered. It's very doubtful that anyone will ever know about you."

"And why is that?"

"Because your ability is not very noticeable."

"What?" Perry said again, growing more confused. "How the hell do you know what ability I'll develop?"

"Don't ask how I know," Noah told him. "Just know that I do. Now will you please calm down and sit?"

"Calm down?!" Perry cried. "I will not calm down! I'm going to have to live in hiding for the rest of my life because some psychotic teenager turned me into a...a...a freak!" Gripping the back of his chair, he lowered his head to his hands and took a deep breath. Noah was right. He needed to calm down. But he wasn't going to be able to; he was too scared. If Noah was right and he really was changing, then his life was about to take a terrifying downhill spiral.

"She's not psychotic," Noah said quietly. "She's just desperate and confused. And you won't need to live in hiding. Life isn't as bad as you'd expect while living with an ability. Trust me, I've lived among people with them for decades."

"This can't be happening," Perry whispered, shaking his head. He felt slightly more under control, but his heart was still thumping in his chest. "This is crazy! This can't be happening to me!"

"Well, it is," Noah told him softly, releasing Perry's arm now that he was sure he wasn't going to completely break down. "The sooner you face the truth the better off you will be."

Shaking his head again, Perry choked on his own words when he asked, "So what's my ability going to be? What am I going to start doing?"

"I think it will be best if you discover that on your own," Noah replied, leaning back in his chair.

Turning to stare at him, Perry's voice began to rise dangerously as he spoke. "The reason I asked was so I could watch myself to make sure I don't hurt anyone!"

"You can't hurt anyone with it," Noah assured. "It's a self-serving ability; it will only affect—I mean benefit—you. And besides, your ability is a part of you. That's something you have to discover for yourself."

Perry looked back down and shook his head for a third time. "So when is it going to start showing?"

"They usually come into effect under high levels of emotion. Mainly fear or stress."

"Does now count?" Perry asked sarcastically.

Noah chuckled. "You'll have to have a bit more emotion than this, Shawn."

"Why do you keep calling me Shawn?" Perry questioned curiously. "I know you know me somehow, but no one ever calls me Shawn anymore. Everyone just calls me Perry."

Leaning towards him, Noah said, "I call you Shawn because you asked me to."

"What?" Perry said in surprise. "When did I—no I didn't—!" He was completely lost, but then he saw Noah's raised eyebrow and rolled his eyes in annoyance. "Oh, right. Let me guess, I don't remember this either?"

All Noah did was shrug once.

Perry muttered, "This is getting extremely frustrating."

"I'm sorry," Noah apologized sincerely. "But it's going to get much worse."

"Great."

"You can see now?" It was less of a question and more of a statement.

Glancing up to his face, Perry realized that he, in fact, could see. And now that he could see, he managed to finally get a good look at Noah. He was quite old; he looked to be at least seventy-five. His face looked tired and the skin beneath and around his eyes was creased. His blue eyes seemed to glimmer with knowledge, and Perry knew he held answers to many secrets. Noah was wearing a black suit and tie. Remembering what he had said about being Jack's "nanny," Perry wondered if Noah had been a butler for Jack's family. He wasn't about to ask, but it made him wonder.

Perry finally got to take the first good look around him as well. He was sitting in a small wooden chair next to a wooden table. There were a few more chairs spread around the table, but other than that everything in front of him seemed rather plain. Nothing was on the table other than Perry's firearm. Deciding that there was no reason that he needed to take it back just yet, Perry looked around some more.

They were in a large concrete room; concrete walls, concrete floor, and concrete ceiling. It seemed just as plain as the table and chairs. The area was surprisingly clean. It didn't look like there was a speck of dust anywhere.

"Yeah, I guess I can see now," Perry replied. "What is this place?"

"My grandfather built this hidden level for me when he was constructing the blocks. He told me I would need it one day, and what do you know?"

"How did he know you would need it?" Perry asked curiously, taking in the peculiar sight on the other side of him. The next wall he saw was at least fifty feet away, and in the intervening space there were three fairly large beds covered in plain white sheets, each separated from the others by tall, translucent glass dividers. Assuming they were only for Noah, Jack, and Hara, Perry's eyes traveled around again to see what else there was. Near the beds was a large tan-colored sofa facing away from him, and between the beds and the sofa there was a small coffee table. Hanging from the ceiling over the table was a large flat screen television. Against the walls on either side of the couch were tall file cabinets that nearly brushed the ceiling.

A short distance away from the cabinets and closer to the far wall was a long red curtain which hung from a runner on the ceiling and dangled all the way to the floor. They swayed slightly as cool air flowed into the room from a vent directly above it. He noticed that besides the curtain, there really wasn't any color. The walls were simply painted white, and the floor and ceiling were a dull gray; the color of concrete. It made him feel depressed, but it made sense to him. People with negative feelings often projected their negativity into their surroundings. Hara had some very negative feelings, and Jack did too. Perry wasn't sure about how Noah was feeling, but he figured that Hara's anguish was enough to make the place seem so depressing. He could almost feel her angered presence in the room, burnt into the dull white walls and bouncing off the crumbling floor and ceiling.

Finally, Perry's eyes landed on the final item in the room: a large wooden table similar to the one he sat at, but taller. There was a tray lying on it, and on that were several tools that almost looked like surgical instruments. He couldn't see it very well, but he could swear there was a dark red stain on the surface of the table. And to him it looked very much like blood. Slowly, he rose to his feet and walked over to investigate.

"Honestly, I haven't a clue how he possibly could have known," Noah admitted as Perry made his way over. "He just used to always tell me that I would play a very important role in the life of a very important person, and that this secret place would be a place of asylum for this person. This angel, as he used to call her."

"Angel?" Perry repeated absentmindedly when he stood in front of the table. He only half heard what Noah had just said to him, for he was busy observing the dark red blood splotches that were staining the top of the table. He had been right. The stains really were blood. But whose blood was it? "Hara," he said softly while brushing his hand lightly over the blood stains. As his fingers touched the tabletop, a sort of shock jolted through his body. Taking in a sharp breath, Perry's entire body stiffened from the force of the shock. An image suddenly flashed into his mind, one of Hara lying helpless on the table while she bled out onto it from the two gunshot wounds she had received. Noah was standing over her, and she was screaming in agony from something he was doing to her. Was he hurting her? No, he was helping her. He was removing the bullets from her side and chest. Hara had no pain relief, no drugs to keep her from feeling everything. How could she endure something that painful? Perry could mentally sense her agony and in the image could see her pained face. How could someone go through that torture? To avoid seeing any more, Perry pulled his hand away with a jerk and stepped back, staring in confusion at the stains on the table.

"Yes," Noah replied, and Perry heard him stand as well. "Hara. My grandfather somehow foresaw what has occurred over the past few days, and what will happen over the next few hours. I have no clue as to how, but he did, and he built this place for me." Noah stepped beside him and peered up at him curiously. "Are you alright?"

"Uh..." Perry wasn't entirely sure. "Yeah, I think so. Yes, I'm fine."

"I tried everything I could, but the stains just refuse to come out," Noah muttered, brushing his own hand across the surface.

"How is Hara an angel?" Perry asked softly, still staring at the table. "I can see in the faces of her people that she's something special, something amazing...something beautiful. She was once something that you and her people all loved, but I can't see what it was they found so remarkable. All I see is an angry child out for revenge, not caring who she kills or who she hurts. I don't see anything special."

"You've been in the Bureau for some time now, correct?" Noah questioned quietly, keeping his eyes down as well.

"Yes," Perry answered.

"And all this time you've caught criminals who commit heinous acts to get money or something else of value. They all wanted basically the same thing. But now you've come across someone who has done terrible things for something you don't fully understand. If you knew the truth, then you would see the things I see in her." Noah glanced up at him. "You haven't discovered the full truth yet. You've always understood the mind of every criminal you've come up against, so now that you've met one you don't understand it bothers you. I can see it in your eyes. You want to be able to understand your criminal, but you know you can't."

Turning his head to meet Noah's blazing blue eyes, Perry said, "I want to see what you see in her."

For a moment, Noah stared back at him, and then he sighed. "You won't be able to see what I see in her, but I can tell you what I see in her." Stepping away from the table, he started limping back to his chair across the room.

It was the first time Perry had seen Noah walk, and for some reason he hadn't expected to see him limp. "If you've been living with people who can heal and cure, couldn't you...I mean...wouldn't they help you fix your...you know...limp?"

Chuckling, Noah sat back in his chair when he reached it. "You can't cure old age, my friend," he said, smiling. "They could have fixed my leg, but I told them not to bother. It would end up going back to the way it was, and I didn't want them trying to delay my death. I've lived a full life, and a good one despite the past year's events. Hara's been trying to convince me to get help from our doctors, but I don't want a life extension. I'm ready to go whenever my time comes."

441

Nodding, Perry started to head back to his seat as well. "It seems like she really cares for you."

"Yes, she does," Noah replied as Perry sat back down. "And you asked what I see in her that is so good; well, it's that. It's her love."

"I'm not exactly sure how love makes her such a great person," Perry said quietly.

Noah sighed again. "Alright, let me rephrase that then. Her ability to love is what I see in her."

"I've met criminals before who love another person," Perry told him, raising an eyebrow.

"This is different, Shawn," Noah replied sharply. "Your criminals say they did what they did for their families, but I can tell you that they aren't necessarily telling the truth. Most of them did what they did to help themselves. Now look at Hara. It may seem like she's doing all this out of revenge, but she isn't. Sure, she's vengeful, but these aren't acts to get even with The Doc. She's doing this to save the lives of her family and the rest of her people. She wants to reverse everything."

"Her people are all but extinct," Perry reminded. "How is terrorizing a city going to help bring them back?"

"It's the boy," Noah explained solemnly. "It's always been the boy."

"Jackson Odau?" Perry asked, feeling himself growing angry. "I don't suppose you could tell me how killing that little boy is going to save anyone?"

There was a short pause before Noah answered. "He was the cause of all of this. He was the reason her species was killed. He…he killed her people."

"He's a child!" Perry exclaimed. "He didn't kill anyone! It wasn't his fault!"

"Yes, it was," Noah said softly. "It was and will always be his fault."

"How?" Perry demanded. "How could a little boy wipe out an entire species?"

Noah paused. He looked like he was trying to make something up. "What if I told you that the boy is going to grow up to be a very bad and powerful person?"

"How could you possibly know that?"

"We all know what's coming," Noah answered in a mysterious way.

"We?" Perry repeated, beginning to understand. "You mean Hara?"

"She and her people all know what is to come, and I've seen what is coming as well. All I can say is that the future is not good."

"And how exactly does something that is supposed to happen in the future cause something that happened in the past?"

Sighing, Noah looked down at the ground. He appeared frustrated, and Perry could see that he was struggling to find words for the answer that was running through his head. But it seemed as if he wasn't going to be able to reply.

Suddenly grasping an idea, Perry started in shock, "Wait...you wanted the boy dead when you saw what he would eventually bring, whatever that may be. But the humans—I mean we—stopped you and killed most of Hara's people in the process. That's right, isn't it?"

Noah sighed again. "The war didn't start for that reason."

Perry was so confused. "Alright, now you've just lost me."

"Shawn," Noah started, leaning forward. "The boy has to die."

"He's a child!" Perry declared. "Are you really going to take the life of a child?"

"He's evil," Noah replied. "And he's going to kill millions of people if he grows up. Shawn, you need to understand the severity of this boy's future, and why the entire world will be better off with him dead. Hara's going to kill him."

"I won't let that happen," Perry whispered sincerely.

"You can't stop her," Noah assured him. "And if you saw what was coming, you wouldn't try."

Eyeing him angrily, Perry asked, "This is never going to make sense, is it? I am never going to figure this out."

"Oh, you will," Noah promised. "You're one of us now; you'll need to know the truth."

"I will never be one of you!" Perry said harshly. "I don't care if I'm going to be like Hara, but I will never be a part of this!"

Sighing, Noah told him, "You may say that now, but we've seen your future too."

Shocked, Perry sat back in his chair. "What?"

Noah nodded slowly. "We've seen what the boy will become, but we've also seen what you will become."

Staring at him in disbelief, Perry shook his head. He finally felt that he understood why he was so important to Hara and her people, but he couldn't believe it.

"Hara may have changed you now, but nothing has happened to you that wouldn't have happened in ten years anyway." Noah looked certain, and Perry felt nervous.

"What happens in ten years?" Perry asked uneasily.

Raising an eyebrow, Noah waited for him to finish the puzzle.

"I was supposed to change in ten years anyway," Perry concluded. "But why in ten years? What so special about 2018?"

"That's the year that it all begins," Noah said, rising slowly to his feet and walking towards the sofa.

Puzzled, Perry stood up and followed him. "When what all begins?" he demanded. When Noah didn't answer, Perry caught his arm. "Hey! What begins in 2018?"

443

Gazing back at Perry with an intense air of gravity in his eyes, Noah told him, "I suppose you could call it the beginning of the end of life as you know it."

Taken aback, Perry hesitated on his next question. "The end of the world?"

Noah shrugged. "Not necessarily," he replied, continuing on his way to the couch. Going around and taking a seat against the far right arm, he finished, "Just the end of the modern age. For the human race, anyway."

Perry continued to follow him, but instead of sitting down beside him he stood in front of him. The truth about what was supposed to happen in 2018 was beginning to dawn on him, and he realized why Noah said it would not be good. Keeping his eyes on Noah's face so he could watch his expression, Perry asked, "There's going to be a big outbreak, isn't there?"

Again, Noah just raised an eyebrow and stared back at him.

"Dear God!" Perry whispered, sitting down at the other end of the couch. He was in a bit of a state of shock. The answer to his question was a definite yes from the look on Noah's face, and Perry couldn't believe it. In just ten years' time, who knew how many people were going to end up with abilities! Perry was affected already, but he knew so many people with O negative blood that could be potential victims. His five-year-old daughter Jillian had O negative blood, and he was quite certain that Renee did as well. He had many more friends with his blood type as well, and he knew there were hundreds of millions more out there who also were O negative. What would happen to all those people when they suddenly developed these abilities? What would happen to Renee and Jillian? What would the world do to them? Perry realized that nothing would happen that hadn't already happened in the past. The world killed, tortured, and exiled the ones who were already affected, and the same would happen in the future. It was the way humans always did things. "How many will be affected by the outbreak?"

Clearing his throat uncomfortably, Noah told him regretfully, "I shouldn't tell you the future."

"Noah," Perry began with a dangerous tone. "My child and the woman I love are O negative. I need to know."

"You're not ready to know."

"Ha!" Perry laughed. "Over the past twenty-four hours, I discovered that a species branched off of the human race and has been in existence for thirty years without half of our government system knowing about it. I've also discovered that I'm turning into one of them, and that in ten years there's going to be an outbreak of this mutation. I doubt there's anything that could be more shocking than that. I think I'm plenty ready to know. How many will be affected?"

Gazing back at him uncertainly, Noah sighed and finally said, "All of them."

Perry's mouth fell open. "All of them?" he repeated.

"Every single one," Noah replied gravely.

"No, no, no…" Perry whispered, dropping his head in his hands in horror. "This can't happen…"

"I'm sorry," Noah said. "But it will."

"It's going to be a blood bath," Perry breathed. "The humans are going to kill us all!"

"You said 'us,'" Noah said, a small smile coming to his face.

"Did you hear what I just said?" he demanded. "The only family I have left is going to be butchered by the people they used to know and care about! Not to mention the millions of other people that are all going to die! This is terrible! How many hundreds of millions of people are going to be murdered because of this?"

"It won't be nearly as bad as you're thinking," Noah told him, the smile lingering on his lips. "There will be many casualties, yes, but most of the newly developed species will survive. Like you."

"What happens to us?" Perry asked as his stomach began to churn. "Those who make it?"

Noah shrugged. "I'm not going to tell you your future. If I do, it will probably drive you mad. I've already said too much."

Now that Perry knew a prophecy that foretold the end of days, was it his responsibility to prepare the world for the fall of the modern age? Would anyone even believe him? He remembered when he was in Washington and he saw a small group of homeless men with cardboard signs that said things such as "Repent: The End is Near," and he realized that they were all right. Everything was going to come to an end, but no one believed the warnings.

Suddenly, a thought came to his mind about something he hadn't understood at first, but now made perfect sense. Thinking back to Detective Aubrey's death, he recalled how strangely Aubrey had acted. The officer had shouted about how the humans were cruel and evil and how they were selfish by only caring for themselves instead of for the Colicians as well. No one had understood what he was talking about or how his view had suddenly changed, but now Perry realized why. Marcus must have shown him the future and what was going to happen, because Aubrey had also told Perry that he was, quote, "One of us." Marcus must have known what Perry was becoming after Hara healed him, and either he told Aubrey about it after taking control of him or Aubrey somehow managed to see back into Marcus's mind as Marcus could see into Aubrey's. The whole incident fell into place right then.

"'I was supposed to be one of them…'" Perry murmured to himself, remembering Aubrey's dying words.

"I'm sorry?" Noah said in confusion.

Perry glanced up. "A colleague of mine was killed earlier today because your pal Marcus took control of his mind," he explained. "Now that I know a lot more about Hara's—our—species, and about the future, the things he said before he died make a lot more sense." For the next few minutes, Perry described what Aubrey had shouted about before the lieutenant had shot him. Noah was fascinated by it, but when Perry got to the part about Hallie Reifert he froze up. When Perry asked him why the name was so significant he just said it didn't matter, and Perry decided with regret to let the questions about her slide. "And the last thing he said to me before he died was that he was supposed to be 'one of them,' which I assume now meant that he somehow saw what was going to happen and knew he was going to change." Remembering something else, he added, "The Doc did ask what Aubrey's blood type was." He paused. "So The Doc knows about the future as well?"

"Of course he does," Noah replied. "That's why he's here trying to stop Hara."

"He wants the boy to live?" Perry asked in surprise, but then again, The Doc was evil too. "Oh, I suppose he would."

"It's not that he wants the child to live so he can bring the horror that is to come," Noah explained. "It's because the boy's survival is very crucial to The Doc's."

"Why?"

"It's complicated. All I can say is that Jackson Odau is very important to him."

"Why exactly is Jackson going to be so bad?" Perry asked, wanting to understand. "What is he going to do?"

Noah's expression was haunted. But as ominous as it was, Perry still waited to receive the full details. "Imagine the worst possible thing a human being could do to someone else," Noah instructed. "Now imagine that thing being done to millions and millions of people, and imagine that boy being the one who carries it all out."

"Oh, my God," Perry whispered in horror. "He's going to grow up to be just like The Doc, isn't he?"

Noah shrugged awkwardly, like there was more he wanted to say.

"That's it, isn't it?" Perry asked, praying he was guessing right again. "He's going to murder millions of people—our people—just like The Doc did! That's why The Doc wants him to live, so he can finish what The Doc already started!" When Noah didn't answer, Perry grew worried and confused. "That is right, isn't it?"

"You've got most of it," Noah told him. "But you are right about the boy. He is going to kill millions of Colicians in the future."

"What am I not getting?" Perry didn't understand what more there could be to it. The boy was going to grow up to become a murderer. What else was there to it?

"It doesn't matter right now," Noah replied, avoiding Perry's gaze.

"Noah, my future—our future—depends on this!" Perry begged. "I need to know more if I'm going to prepare everyone for what's going to happen!"

"You're not going to prepare anyone," Noah told him, his voice surprisingly sharp.

"What do you mean?" Perry said, taken aback.

"There's no way you can prepare the world for what's to come!" Noah told him angrily, scowling. "Do you really think that anyone would believe you if you tried?"

"I believe it," Perry said.

"Because you've seen it! You're a part of it now! No one will ever believe it until they are finally a part of it."

"But…"

"You can't warn people about this, Perry!" Noah said firmly, using Perry's last name for the first time. "You need to accept that fact. The human race is ignorant; they won't believe hell is coming until it is knocking at their door."

"But I'm gaining an ability," Perry reminded, finally admitting it to himself. "I could show them, and then they would believe…"

"No!" Noah exclaimed. "You can't show anyone! They'll lock you in a cage and feed you through a tube in your arm! We can't risk losing you, Shawn. The future is set. You can't risk changing the outcome."

"Then why does Hara think she can change it?" Perry demanded. "The Doc said she can't change it, and you seem to be agreeing with him, so why does Hara think she can make an exception for this?"

Sighing, Noah answered, "We need to have some hope of making things right again for us. The world—not to mention the future—would be a much better place if that boy were gone."

There was a silence that erupted over that and it lasted for several minutes. Perry was busy pondering over what had been said. Maybe Noah was right; if Odau's son was going to grow up to be a parallel to The Doc, maybe it would be best to just let Hara kill him. But he knew he couldn't allow himself to just stand by and watch her kill that boy. He took the job as an agent so he could help fight people like her. Then again, wouldn't that mean he should protect the millions of people that were going to be murdered by Jackson by letting him die? Jack had said, "Four lives to save millions." Perry was beginning to think he was right.

That was another part of the investigation that hadn't quite fallen into place yet. Perry asked, "If Hara wants to kill Jackson because of what he's going to become, then why did she kill those other kids?"

"Jackson will learn from those children," Noah explained. "They grow to become geneticists who study the Colician Strain. They will be his inspiration, his source of knowledge. Hara thought it would be best to kill the source as well, in case someone else ended up taking Jackson's place."

"I see," Perry murmured.

There was more silence. Perry was now trying to come up with a gentle way to break the news to Odau. His son was going to be a mass murderer, and Perry had to tell him. Odau had been desperate to know why his son was being targeted. Now that Perry knew he felt that the right thing to do was to tell the lieutenant. It would be rough on him to know that his only son was going to be evil like The Doc, but at least he would understand why this was happening.

"So," Noah started, interrupting the lasting silence. "Daniel is dead."

Looking up, Perry realized that he hadn't told Noah about Marcus's death. How did he know? He's lived with these people for years, he reminded himself. I'm sure he's picked up on some stuff, or maybe he was lying about being human just like Jack did. He did say "we" whenever talking about the Colician race. It was definitely a possibility that he was lying, but Perry felt that he was telling the truth. Unlike Jack, Noah didn't have any reason to lie.

"Yes," Perry answered. "How did you know?"

"He told me the last time I saw him that he felt his time was coming soon," Noah explained. "And not to mention that you told me he would be dead before 9:30 today."

"I did what now?" Perry said, but then decided not to pursue it. Maybe Noah was a liar, maybe Perry had an alternate personality, or maybe Noah could communicate with the future Shawn Perry, but whatever it was, he wasn't going to understand.

Chuckling to himself, Noah grinned at Perry's confusion. "I'm very sorry about Detective Aubrey as well. Daniel never intended for him to get hurt."

"Well, he did. A good cop was killed because one of you decided to mess with his mind!"

"I'm sorry," Noah said again, his voice still calm. "Daniel would have never purposely put Mr. Aubrey in harm's way. He said they were good friends and claimed Aubrey would help him get his body to where it needed to be should anything happen to him."

"Wait...so you know where Aubrey took the body?" Perry said, and then turned to look around at the large cabinets.

Noah found this hysterical. Laughing hard, he reassured, "I promise you we did not shove his body in there. They're storage cabinets for our weapons."

"Then where did he take it?"

"To a safe place."

"And that would be where?" Perry demanded, again annoyed with the half-answers.

"Why do you want to know so badly?" Noah asked him. "What is a dead body to you?"

"Well, for starters, it's part of our murder investigation," Perry told him stubbornly, and then flinched when he realized he was calling Marcus an It. "And it would also be nice to know why my colleague was possessed so he would move the body. "So I'd really like to know where he was taken."

Noah leaned forward in his chair. "If it really is important, do you honestly think I'm going to tell you where he is?"

"No, and I suppose that's why you won't tell me anything about what's going on, because it's important."

"Actually, it's because you would consider the truth to be impossible."

Meeting Noah's eyes again, Perry said, "Everything that I've learned is impossible. What makes the big picture any different?"

"The big picture is a tad more impossible than people with super powers," Noah said.

"The Doc killed Marcus, right?" Perry blurted, needing to know for sure.

"Of course," Noah replied. "Who else would have?"

Perry shrugged. "I just needed to be certain."

"Well, yes, The Doc did kill him. The Doc was always going to kill him."

Confused, Perry asked, "What do you mean?"

"Never mind."

"Why did he kill Marcus in the first place? He said he did it to piss off Hara, but I thought he wanted to keep the Colicians for science experiments and torture and other wonderful stuff?"

"You misinterpreted The Doc, my friend," Noah told him. "When The Doc first started studying Colicians, he was a somewhat sane individual. He studied the genetics of the species and actually used his findings for a good cause. He found cures for diseases and illnesses that no one would have thought possible, and when doing tests on Colicians he attempted to make the procedures as painless as he could. He was a good person, and actually cared what the person strapped to the table was feeling. But when his daughter died, that was when he completely lost it. You see, after his family was gone, he no longer cared what anyone else felt. That was when he decided that he just wanted everybody to die. He invaded their homes and killed almost everyone, except for the select few that had an ability he found fascinating. Hara and Allan are examples of people with unique abilities. People like them he kept for his science experiments and other things he liked to do."

Perry wrinkled his nose in disgust. "That's sick."

Nodding, Noah added, "If he had managed to capture Meg Hopper, she would have been in the same boat. She would have been kept for The Doc's entertainment along with Allan and Hara."

"What can she do?" Perry asked curiously.

"She gives life to objects that have none," Noah said, smiling fondly.

Trying to comprehend what that meant, Perry asked for clarification, "She's like the opposite of Hara? She heals others instead of herself?"

Noah shrugged again. "She can, but she best works with plants. She can give life back to a dead flower, and can even make a flower grow from anything, like glass or wood or metal. It's an ability that is very puzzling and The Doc has been eyeing her ever since he discovered what she could do."

"But...why would The Doc want to kill Marcus?" Perry asked again, still confused. "Telepathic abilities would certainly fascinate me."

"So many Colicians have telepathic abilities, though," Noah said. "A good thirty-five to forty-five percent of Colicians have some sort of telepathic ability. The Doc goes for the ones who have a rare ability or one that he doesn't fully understand. The reason he went for Hara is that her ability is the rarest of all. Jack may or may not have told you, but there are only one or two Colicians every generation born with an absorbing ability. Of the few that were alive, Hara was the most powerful and the most unstable because of her young age. That made him eager to get his hands on her."

"Why would The Doc want to use her for science experiments if she was unstable? Wouldn't that make her dangerous?"

"Oh, yes. Very dangerous. That's the way The Doc likes it. He enjoys a challenge, and Hara was the toughest lab rat he's ever had to deal with."

"But if he upset her, couldn't she hurt people?"

"That was the point," Noah told him. "He hurt her and angered her to the point of bursting, and when she couldn't keep her destructive forces inside any longer he used her against her own kind. She wiped out an entire city on her own because The Doc tormented her to the breaking point."

"That's horrible."

"You may think that's bad, but sometimes he would test the effects of her ability on a captured Colician. The Doc sometimes forced abilities out of her with drugs or electric shocks and directed the power at someone else."

"That's quite enough information, thank you!" Perry cried, choking on the bile that was rising in his throat.

Noah finally saw that his descriptions were having a negative effect on Perry. "I'm sorry," he apologized. "I didn't realize this bothered you so much."

"Of course it bothers me!" Perry exclaimed. Taking a deep breath to calm his racing mind, Perry asked, "So if The Doc had caught Marcus before, he would have just killed him? Anyone with a boring ability to him was just a piece of trash?"

"That about sums it up," Noah said. "Marcus angered him and wasn't of any use to the man, so he had no escape from death."

"But why don't telepathic abilities fascinate him?" Perry asked. "I know a lot of people had them, but why wouldn't he want to study them?"

"Because The Doc already figured out how they work," Noah explained. "Once he learns how the brain controls the ability, the ability doesn't matter anymore."

Sighing, Perry nodded sluggishly. "But he never figured out Hara's ability, or Allan's."

"No," Noah answered. "He didn't. The Colicians don't even understand how Absorbers and Hoppers work."

"Absorbers and what?"

"Hoppers," Noah repeated. "It's what we...they...call teleporters. Hoppers."

"Oh." For a while Perry sat in his chair without speaking, taking in all his newfound information. The Doc really was crazy. The loss of his family had caused him to completely lose his mind. Then Perry realized something: The Doc was exactly like Hara. Both of them had been driven over the edge by the loss of their families and had done terrible things because of that. Hara may believe that she was doing good by hurting people, but the murders just proved Perry right even more. The Doc and Hara both wanted to avenge their families by killing, even though they both knew perfectly well that it wouldn't bring anyone back. Hara would most likely kill Perry for thinking that, but The Doc was right. They were very much alike in many ways. They were parallels of each other.

"You look perplexed," Noah said when Perry didn't speak again.

"No," Perry replied, jumping as he came out of his own thoughts. "I'm just thinking."

"About what?"

"Everything."

"You have another question?"

Shrugging, Perry asked, "If Hara can regenerate, then why doesn't she regenerate the injuries on her face?" That was something that had puzzled Perry. Why had Hara never healed the burns and scars on her face?

"Because she can't," Noah replied.

"Why not? I thought she could heal anything."

"Only if she sustains the injury while she has the ability to heal. If her abilities are taken away from her and an injury is inflicted on her, then she can't regenerate."

"What do you mean when you say taken away from her?" Perry asked. "How can her abilities be taken away from her?"

"Humans developed a drug that when injected will block the part of the brain that controls the power. Basically, it strips her of every ability she possesses."

"And what happens after that? Wouldn't that hurt or kill her?"

"From what I've observed, the drug causes disorientation, confusion, and other minor symptoms. I haven't seen it harm anyone, but The Doc found it interesting to see what would happen while she was on the drug."

"So you're saying that The Doc gave those injuries to her intentionally while Hara was on the drug?"

With a slight pause, Noah nodded. "Yes, he did. He did several disturbing things to people while experimenting."

Timidly, Perry asked, "What exactly did The Doc do to Hara during his experiments? I don't want full details, I just want to know what drove her off the edge of the cliff."

"You really want to know?" Noah asked him, raising an eyebrow warningly.

Thinking it over quickly, Perry nodded. "Yes, I want to know."

Nodding slowly, Noah rose stiffly to his feet once more and limped into the kitchen. He went to a cupboard just to the left of the refrigerator and opened it, reaching in and pulling out a large cardboard box. The way he carried it made it appear heavy, and as he walked back towards Perry something bumped against the side of the box with every step he took. When he reached Perry, he gestured with his head to the center of the room. "Come with me," he said and continued.

"Sit," Noah ordered when they reached the sofa.

Obeying, Perry sat and stared at the box still in Noah's arms.

Setting the box down on the coffee table in front of Perry, Noah reached inside and fished out a rectangular object in another box. It was a videotape, with the words Trial: HR scrawled on it in black marker.

"This will show you some of the things The Doc did to Hara," Noah told him, his expression grave. "I warn you, some images may be disturbing, but they will show you some of the horror Hara was put through, and what caused her to snap. Are you sure you want to proceed?"

Swallowing hard, Perry nodded again. "Let's see it," he said.

Reaching down, Noah put the tape in the cassette player and turned on the screen.

Watching intently, Perry couldn't begin to comprehend just how horrifying the images would be.

* * *

Ever since The Doc left the holding cell about forty minutes earlier, all Jack could think about was how vulnerable and helpless he was. He was handcuffed to a chair and now that The Doc could block his ability without drugs, there was no way Jack was going to be able to defend himself should The Doc decide to pay him another visit. Alone. All the cops and FBI agents were preoccupied with other matters, and no one would know if The Doc silently took him out. Perry wasn't around to protect him, and neither was Hara. If The Doc got any violent ideas, Jack was screwed.

His mind was screaming with the thoughts of hundreds of people in close proximity to him. Normally, he would only be able to hear the minds of a few others that were nearest to him, but now that he had adrenaline pumping through him, he was able to hear much more. Although he could hear the thoughts of everyone within a mile radius, he wasn't listening to any of them. He was only trying to focus on the thoughts of one person in particular. While searching for him, he heard the blonde woman—whom Perry was in love with—working with the two other Special Agents on something on their computer screen a few rooms down. He also found the lead FBI agent pacing back and forth in the men's restroom while speaking urgently to someone on the phone. Detective Finchly was back in the conference room, sitting in a chair and staring off into space, wondering what she could have done to save someone called Garrick. Jack could hear all these people, but the person he was trying to find wasn't there. Well, in a manner of speaking he really was there somewhere, but Jack couldn't find his mind anywhere in the shuffle of pained, angry, and confused thoughts. He could feel The Doc's presence in the building, but his mind was just a blank, vast emptiness. How could a mind so full of knowledge be so extensively empty? It was a paradox, so full but so vacant at the same time. And with that vacancy came the inability to find his location.

The thought that The Doc could be anywhere scared Jack. His inability to track the man made him feel weak and feeble, and all he wanted to do was find out how close he was to death. But there was nothing. No thoughts coming from his mind, and no clue as to where he was. So when The Doc finally did pull open the door, Jack jumped in surprise. But when he saw who it was he immediately began to panic. Tugging as hard as he could at his cuffs, he felt the skin on his wrists beginning to tear with the effort. He was trapped. "Help! Help!" he started to shout.

Putting a finger to his lips, The Doc pushed the door closed behind him and said, "*Shhh.*"

"Somebody help me!" Jack yelled, but he knew it was useless.

"Nobody can hear you, boy," The Doc told him softly, starting to come towards him. He was carrying a small, silver, rectangular case in one hand, and Jack could only shiver at the thought of what could be in it.

"No, no, no!" Jack said, giving up against the cuffs. As his fear began to intensify, he used his adrenaline rush to his advantage. Since The Doc's mind was blank, Jack wouldn't be able to get inside and tell him to leave. But there was one thing he could still do: call for help.

Hara, hear me! Find me! Help me! he cried, hoping she could hear him, wherever she was. Hara may not love Jack the way she had so many years ago, but she still cared for him and thought of him as her best friend, so if she heard his distress call she would come running to his aid as fast as she could.

"Don't bother," The Doc said, taking out a small black disk which was emitting a high pitched frequency from his pocket. "Your pathetic cry for help won't get further than the next room."

Letting out a whimper of defeat, Jack slumped down in his chair, allowing his fear to take over. There was nothing left for him to do. He couldn't fight his way out of this, and no one was coming for him. He was going to die right there in that chair, and no one would know or even care.

"You're alone now," The Doc said harshly, completing Jack's thought. Coming up to the table, he set his case down on it and clicked it open. Then, he pulled out a long syringe that made Jack's stomach leap to his throat.

"You've been blocking my thoughts this whole time?" Jack cried, his voice squeaking in terror. He had been wondering why he was unable to figure out that The Doc was in the building until they were in the same room.

"I couldn't have you figure out I was close by, now could I?" The Doc replied, taking out a vile of murky brown liquid and sticking the needle into the top of it. "I had to let you keep believing everything was fine and dandy."

"You're so twisted!" Jack snarled, shaking his head in disgust. His heart was pounding in his chest, but he kept trying to act tough. "But if you kill me now, Hara's going to rip your eyes out and shove them down your throat!"

The Doc gave him an amused look. "You know, I keep getting these threats about what Hara's going to do to me if I kill this person or that person, but then I kill them and nothing happens. Marcus told me Hara was going to murder me if I killed him, but I did anyway and look at me! I'm still here!"

Jack's stomach churned some more. "So you're the one who killed Marcus!"

Raising an eyebrow, The Doc snorted. "Of course I did," he said. "Who else would?"

"Why?" Jack demanded.

"He killed two of my men and helped Allan Brown escape," The Doc growled.

"Oh, one more poor soul you don't get to experiment on."

Glaring back, The Doc finished loading the syringe and set the empty vile back in the case. Then he came around the table towards Jack.

Panicking, he cried, "Please! Don't do this to me!"

"Are you scared?" The Doc asked quietly, staring down emotionlessly at him while waiting for an answer.

What did he expect him to say? Of course he was scared!

Jack nodded slowly, a tear sliding down his cheek.

A smirk came to his lips for half a second, but then The Doc's expression became serious. "You don't have to be," he told him, his voice taking a gentler note. "Marcus certainly wasn't when I killed him."

"I'm not Daniel Marcus," Jack whispered, lowering his eyes in shame. He felt pathetic, begging for his life, but he wasn't ready for it to be over just yet.

"No, I suppose you're not," The Doc replied, coming closer still.

"I don't want to die!" Jack whimpered, clenching his fists as the tears came pouring out of his eyes.

Pausing, The Doc cocked his head to one side, something that had always freaked Jack out. "Your family is dead," he reminded him. "Let me rephrase that. Your entire species is dead. What else do you have?"

"I have Hara," Jack immediately responded, knowing he would always have her.

The Doc snickered. "She doesn't love you. She hasn't since Bo came into the picture. She'll never love you." He leaned forward. "You have nothing left to live for."

He may have been right, but Jack still felt like there was something out there worth fighting for. There would always be something worth living for. Hara may not ever feel for him what he felt for her, but she needed him so she could keep living. And Jack would always be there for her no matter what. If Hara did in fact set everything straight and reverse the catastrophe, then there would definitely be something worth living for.

Sighing in remorse, Jack allowed his head to drop forward, his chin practically touching his chest. No matter what he said to The Doc, he was still going to die, so he just tried to accept his fate and deal with it like Marcus had. There was no way out, and no one left to save him.

But was giving up really the best option?

The Doc's syringe was loaded, and he was standing over Jack with an air of triumph about him. He knew that he had won and Jack was beginning to accept his defeat, but he didn't move closer. He didn't make his strike to kill or even say a word. Maybe he sensed the question that Jack so desperately needed answered and he was just waiting for it to be asked. Maybe he was just toying with Jack.

"Do you have anything else to say to me before I kill you?" The Doc asked him bluntly.

"Why are you doing this to her?" Jack whispered, shaking his head in grief for his friend. Hara had already lost Marcus, so how was she going to take losing her best friend in the same day? The poor kid was already screwed up enough because of what that asshole did to her, and he was still trying to destroy everything in her life that kept her fighting. Why was he doing that to her? What could possibly motivate him to completely kill her from the inside out? It was so sick and wrong, and before Jack died he wanted to understand why The Doc had gone through all the trouble just to ruin Hara's life. He needed to understand.

"Because I need her to understand," The Doc said, his voice heavy and firm.

"Understand what?" Jack demanded.

"What it's like to lose everything," The Doc replied.

Gaping at him, Jack exclaimed, "I think she understands that perfectly! You've already taken away everything she could ever care about!"

Shaking his head, The Doc murmured, "Not quite everything." He grabbed Jack by the hair and lowered the needle towards his heart.

Flinching in anticipation, Jack squeezed his eyes shut and clenched his fists behind his back. This was the end.

He felt The Doc's grip on him slacken suddenly, and he blinked his eyes open in confusion. Jumping as he heard a loud bang from overhead, he looked around in surprise. He was still alive, and he was very lucky.

The Doc was still standing over him. Glancing down, Jack saw that the needle was hovering just inches above his chest. Unsure of what had just happened, he looked up to see The Doc staring up at the tiled ceiling apprehensively, as if waiting for something to come crashing down. Then a rumbling sound started. Both Jack and The Doc eyed the ceiling suspiciously. Was it a broken pipe? Had someone just used the bathroom and the flush had sent some not-so-pleasant contents rumbling through the building? They discovered that it was not a pipe or an oversized bowel movement, for with the next bang came a crash that caused the wall on Jack's left to explode.

Turning his head away so no dust would get into his eyes, Jack's breath caught in his throat as he anticipated something terrible coming through the wall. The Doc released him and took a step back, and for the first time Jack felt some emotion coming from the man. It was shock. The voice Jack heard next sent a wave of shock through his own body.

"Oh, excuse me," a young man said, with an amused tone like The Doc often used. He had a British accent, and Jack could recognize that voice anywhere. "I'm sorry to barge in like this, but I wondered if you wouldn't mind letting me borrow Jacky-boy for a while?"

Jack's jaw dropped open. Behind him, looking rather happy considering the circumstances, was a young man the same age as him. He had very light, sandy colored hair and extremely pale skin, making his bright green eyes seem like emeralds in snow. His hair had grown longer since Jack had last seen him, falling over his forehead in clumps. He was wearing a black t-shirt and baggy khaki pants, pretty nice clothes for someone who was fighting a war that was nearly lost. He was thinner and looked weak, but no matter what his appearance he would always be the same person he had always been to Jack: his best friend.

"Davey?" Jack whispered incredulously.

"Hi, Jacky!" Davey replied, a bold grin shining on his face. Looking back to The Doc, he asked again, "You don't mind, do you?"

The Doc just cocked his head, his expression a mixture of confusion and uncertainty. He looked like he wanted to say something, but was too dumbfounded to speak.

"What are you…how…?" Jack sputtered in skepticism, unable to believe that his best friend was really there in front of him. It was impossible! How could he have found him? And more importantly, why did he look like he was stoned? His hands were sweating and shaking, beads of perspiration being flicked off of him and onto the floor. His pupils were dilated and the muscles in his face were randomly twitching here and there. He kept grinning the dopey grin, making his teeth chatter uncontrollably. "What the hell happened to you?" Jack finally demanded.

"Yes," The Doc agreed. "I think both of us would like the answer to that."

Rubbing his hands together, Davey's grin became even broader. "Wouldn't you like to know!" he said in his shaky, hyper voice.

Eyeing him for a moment, The Doc quickly snapped his hand down to his pocket, whipped out an AD weapon, and fired it at Davey. Not even Hara could have reacted in time to evade the dart, but Davey had vanished in the blink of an eye and reappeared six feet or so behind him. The dart struck the concrete wall where Davey had been standing, and realizing what had happened, The Doc spun around, prepared to fire again. But Davey seemed to be prepared for just about anything, so while The Doc was turning Davey teleported directly in front of him and punched him full out in the face.

The force of the blow should have only knocked The Doc off balance slightly, but Davey must have somehow added extra energy to the punch, for there was a shockwave that sent The Doc hurtling backwards into the wall. As he sprawled face first on the floor, Davey turned back to Jack, giggling like a little girl.

Staring back at his best friend with his mouth hanging open, Jack cried, "What the hell have you done to yourself?"

Still giggling, Davey walked right up to Jack and said, "I think we should get out of here. Somebody probably heard that!" With a squeal of delight, Davey put a hand on Jack's shoulder.

Jack felt everything whizzing past him at tremendous speed and heard the air whistling past his ears as he was teleported from the room with Davey, leaving The Doc behind to stare in confusion at the spot where the two of them had disappeared.

✳ ✳ ✳

Perry had been doing well, but to his and Noah's dismay he ended up puking before the video ended. It had been too much for him.

He had managed to make it to the sink in the kitchen before the contents of his stomach—which wasn't much—were emptied out the wrong end. Once he was finished, he gripped the counter in an attempt to keep himself on his feet. His knees were shaking and were threatening to collapse beneath him. As stinging tears of horror and despair developed in the corners of his eyes, Perry gasped for breath and tried to keep down whatever else was trying to escape his stomach.

"Are you alright?" Noah asked in concern as he approached Perry, putting a comforting hand on his shoulder.

"That was disgusting," Perry replied shakily. Turning around carefully, he rested his lower back against the counter and slowly slid down to the floor. As he let out an airy breath, he allowed his eyes to close and his head to rest back.

"Here," Noah said, and Perry heard the refrigerator door open. There were sounds of rummaging around before the door closed again. "Drink this."

Blinking down at the water bottle that was hovering in front of his face, Perry absentmindedly reached out and took it, unscrewing the cap and taking a long drink from it. Now that he was beginning to calm down some, Perry could try to process everything he had seen on the video and try to come to terms with it. He shivered as the gory images reinserted themselves into his memory. What he had seen had been so disturbing, and the fact that it had actually been done to someone he knew only made it worse.

"If I had known you were going to react this way, I wouldn't have shown that to you," Noah apologized as he pulled up a chair to sit across from Perry.

"It's fine," Perry assured, waving his hand dismissively. "I needed to see it."

"Perhaps I should have started off with one of the less disturbing ones and worked my way up," Noah murmured to himself, lowering his eyes to the floor.

"Don't worry about it," Perry told him, taking another drink. Then he sighed, praying that someday he would be able to get the memory of The Doc cutting Hara open out of his head. Even from the beginning, Perry knew The Doc had a history of violence, but he never anticipated something this brutal and sadistic. He now knew that some of The Doc's actions weren't for scientific purposes. They were to satisfy his own diabolical thirst. "The Doc really did that to Hara?" he asked.

"I'm afraid so," Noah said softly.

Shaking his head in disgust, Perry whispered, "He actually cut the heart out of that poor girl's chest? And while she was still conscious?"

Noah nodded. "Yes."

"How did she survive that?"

"She grew a new one."

"Why on earth would The Doc ever do that?" Perry demanded. "What possible benefit could that serve?"

"Hara is an Absorber," Noah said. "She has just about any ability you could possibly think of. That includes—as you've seen already—the ability to heal. The Doc wanted to cut out her heart to see if she could produce a new one. He wanted to see if her body would regenerate the organ that was pumping her full of the regenerative blood. So he cut out her heart, and he got his answer. She could."

"That's awful. Why did he do it while she was still conscious? How could he? She was screaming the whole time! Couldn't he at least put her to sleep? What the hell is wrong with him?"

"He is a very disturbed man," Noah said.

Perry snorted. "That's apparent! I cannot believe I actually collaborated with that sick, twisted son of a bitch! I knew all along that he was a monster, but I never imagined anyone could possibly be capable of such torture!"

"Shawn, you need to understand that there are people in this world you will never fully understand," Noah told him calmly.

"I understand him perfectly!" Perry snapped.

"No, you don't," Noah replied. "The man is driven by grief, though it may not quite seem like it. Just like Hara, he is being propelled by two of the most powerful emotions there are: grief and rage. They're the emotions that make them dangerous and push them to do terrible things."

"Losing their families doesn't give either of them the right to do what they're doing!" Perry growled.

"No, it doesn't," Noah agreed. "And I'm not saying it does. I'm just trying to explain to you what caused The Doc to go around the bend."

"I never even had a proper family!" Perry protested. "My mother died when I was a boy and my father neglected me until the day I was forced to kill him! I think I've suffered just as much as he has, but you don't see me going around cutting out internal organs from people's bodies!"

"You never had a chance to fall in love with your family!" Noah challenged. "So when your father died it wasn't much of a loss."

"How is my situation any different than The Doc's?" Perry demanded.

"Because The Doc loved his family, Shawn! And he lost every single one of them! When he was twenty years old, he killed his father after discovering he was helping the Colicians. His mother and two sisters were all exiled when they became contaminated. Most of his friends were either killed or taken away from him after the initial outbreak. His wife dropped dead of a brain aneurysm, and a few years later his only child suffered the same fate. You ask me how your situations are different? They're different because he lost every single person he ever loved, but you only lost the people you didn't love or didn't have the chance to love. The people who you love and are your true family are still with you now. Your daughter, Jillian, whom you will need to protect in the years to come. Your partner, Renee Michaels, the love of your life. And Jack."

"I don't love Jack," Perry said, feeling offended by the assumption.

"You will," Noah promised. "But do you see now how your situations are very much different? You still have people left to love. The only person in the world he feels he has left is Hara. Everyone else he has lost, and that is what pushed him over the top."

"I swear to God," Perry warned, "if you say that The Doc loves Hara, I *will* hit you."

"He loves her in a way even I will never understand," Noah said, completely ignoring Perry's threat. "He believes that he is Hara's parallel, her likeness or counterpart, and in a way he is. Now he is trying to make their lives identical, so he really can be her parallel. He took away nearly everyone she's ever loved, and now she's slowly being forced into insanity just like him."

"But why would he do that?" Perry asked. "I just don't understand why he would want someone else to go through what he went through."

"Don't you see? He wants her to go through everything he did. Because he wants her to understand what he's been through," Noah told him softly. He sighed heavily at Perry's gawking expression. "He needed somebody to understand him, and he chose Hara to be that somebody."

"So he killed millions of people just to make one person understand what his life was like?" Perry demanded in disgust.

"The Doc would have wiped out the Colicians one way or another," Noah explained. "Their time was up. But The Doc kept the few he wanted to research further, and that included Hara. Ever since he began the invasion, he knew he was going to take her life away from her. She was his target from the very beginning. You see, he didn't kill them all just to make her crazy. His plan was always the same, he just chose the most fascinating one to keep as his own."

The information starting to finally sink in, Perry started, "He kept her so that when everything came crashing down on him…"

"He would have someone to crawl back to," Noah finished, nodding. "Someone who endured the same things; someone who would feel his pain and feel sympathy for him."

"His plan wasn't to take over and remain in charge forever, was it?" Perry asked quietly, standing up and turning his back on Noah. Gripping the edge of the counter tightly in his hands as he had before, he exhaled loudly. "It was never his original intention to be a leader. He wasn't another Adolf Hitler."

Noah sighed again. "No, it wasn't. But he was willing to do anything to annihilate the Colicians."

"Does he care about anything?" Perry asked.

Shrugging, Noah considered it. "He cared about his family, and I think he cares about getting his revenge."

"But he knows that he won't stay in power forever, right? He knows he will have his downfall?"

"Of course he does," Noah said. "Despite his developing insanity, he is a genius."

"You admire him, now?" Perry demanded, scowling to himself.

"He knows how it has gone with every major dictator in history," Noah continued. "Adolf Hitler, Josef Stalin, Saddam Hussein…in the end, they always fall. The Doc understands that somehow he will be taken down, and he doesn't care. That's because his position in power is not important to him. It never was. It just made it easier for him to wipe everyone out."

"He always intended for himself to be taken down," Perry realized, shocked. "He only wanted his job to be finished before that time came."

"That's correct," Noah replied. "Once he has killed every last Colician in existence, then he will stop and step down. But, technically speaking, when he is taken down he won't really be gone."

461

"What do you mean?" Perry asked in puzzlement, turning to him.

"Hara," Noah said. "The Doc may be locked up or dead, but what he was will remain in this world forever. The angry, vengeful, grief-stricken person he is will be passed on to Hara, and despite the goodness she once possessed, I doubt she will ever be able to heal from what has happened to her."

"Her family was murdered," Perry snapped. "Of course she won't be able to heal."

"You don't realize how this war will end, Shawn," Noah told him gravely.

"Now what are you saying?"

"I've been told how this all ends, Shawn, and it is going to end well."

"How could this possibly end well?" Perry stared at him in disbelief. "There is no way this will end well!"

"You'll find out," Noah muttered.

"Yeah, I'm sure," Perry grumbled. There was silence until he asked, "If the Colicians are so powerful and have such powerful and dangerous abilities, how exactly did they fall in the first place?"

"That's a great question," Noah commented. "At first, Hara's father, who was the president, didn't want to retaliate after The Doc's first attack on them. It wasn't a major attack. The Doc and his men stole the files that showed every Colician's ability and how to defend against them, in case one of them were to go bad and would need to be stopped. The rest of the society's defenses were then exposed, so when The Doc finally launched the invasion they were unable to stop him. The humans knew how to fight every single one of them, and their weapons had become far more sophisticated since the strain first became a threat.

"Her father did attempt to strike back, however. He and some powerful Colicians caused some nasty things to happen around the world, to send a warning saying that they could cause more damage than the humans. But The Doc called his bluff and took out the heart of Colician society before anyone could make another stab at your world. Hara's father was never a violent man, and all he ever wanted was for their world and your world to be at peace with one another. That was a weakness in The Doc's eyes, and The Doc used his hesitance to his advantage. The Colicians were unprepared for the humans' onslaught. Had Hara's father reacted sooner, he might have been able to stop the calamity."

"Being peaceful is not a weakness," Perry whispered. "It is a strength."

"I know," Noah said softly. "Her father was a great man, and his peaceful state of mind is something I wish more of our world leaders possessed."

"I bet he was great," Perry mumbled to himself, trying to imagine what Hara's father must have been like as a leader. It was difficult for Perry to picture a man not wanting to fight against a people who first experimented on them, then banished them, then threatened them, and then attacked them. It was even more difficult to picture Hara coming from that man. "What was his name?"

There was a slight pause. "It...doesn't matter," Noah said dismissively.

"Of course it does! Listen, I want to remember the guy who tried to prevent global chaos, that's all."

"He doesn't need to be remembered," Noah told him. "Not yet, anyway."

Perry groaned in frustration. Why did everything need to be a secret?

"To finish my story, The Doc started off in a lower position and led his first few attacks on his own with a small group who followed him. The Doc had tried to convince world leaders to go to war with the Colicians, claiming that they needed to be wiped out because they were a danger to mankind, but everyone thought he was nuts and no one wanted to listen to him. So he started off by provoking the leader of the Colicians to the point where he had to strike back."

"The Doc wanted him to strike back?" Perry asked in surprise.

Noah nodded quickly. "Yes, because if the Colicians attacked the humans, then the humans wouldn't have a choice but to strike back. The Doc purposely antagonized Hara's father to the point of heartbreak, knowing there would be an attack on U.S. cities in return.

"What did The Doc do?" Perry asked.

Noah explained solemnly, "The second attack killed his soul mate, Shauna. The third killed his eldest son, Flint. Love can be an amazing thing. But it can also be the ultimate weapon."

"If they made their attack on American soil, then how come we didn't know about it?" Perry asked in confusion.

"You wouldn't have noticed anything too unusual," Noah said. "The attacks were in the form of natural disasters. It was a very effective warning to the humans that they could and most definitely would use any force necessary back against them. And once they did, everybody knew it was about time to get rid of the Colicians for good."

"How many of them are left now?"

"Very few. Only a couple thousand are still living free. Dozens are still being used as lab experiments."

"Daniel Marcus, Allan Brown, and Meg Hopper were of those few thousand," Perry said, mainly to himself. "They escaped from The Doc's massacre and came here to hide."

"That's right. When Hara escaped the labs with Allan, they met up with Meg and Daniel and the three of them came here to try and meddle with things slightly."

"How so?"

"Just to see how much the humans knew, and also to try and steer a steady and promising course for their future. Two months or so ago, Hara was still somewhat sane, and she asked the three of them to come here to try and make things better for the whole world."

"Wait just one second," Perry said, deeply puzzled. "They've been in this city with jobs for over two years now."

"Yes, I'm well aware of that," Noah replied, seemingly unaware of the paradox.

"You said they escaped two months ago," Perry reminded.

The expression that popped to Noah's face showed that he had said too much about something that shouldn't be discussed.

Staring at Noah's petrified face, Perry remembered something else that didn't quite add up. "You know what else I just realized? You and your friends keep saying that the actual war began about a year ago, yet Marcus, Brown, and Hopper have been here for two years." He narrowed his eyes at Noah. "If they've been here for two years, then the war couldn't have begun last year. We would have noticed if they were missing because of genetic experiments."

Slowly, Noah raised his eyes to meet Perry's. When he didn't reply, Perry grew irritated.

"Noah, what's going on?" He had asked that question so many times, but never so urgently. To his dismay, his phone started vibrating in his pocket before his question could be answered. "Damn it," he muttered, pulling it out. "Special Agent Perry."

"Perry, where the hell are you?" It was Agent Long, and he sounded angry.

"I'm…uh…interviewing a witness," Perry said, flustered as he was caught off guard.

"Bullshit!" Agent Long snarled. "Get back here right now!"

"What's going on?" Perry demanded.

"Jack's gone! That's what's going on!" Agent Long yelled.

"Gone?" Perry cried. "How can he be gone?"

"Jesus, Perry, maybe if you had been here doing your God damn job, we might know!" Agent Long shouted.

Staring at his phone in shock, Perry filled Noah in on the situation. "Jack's missing, and my boss needs me back right away."

Nodding, Noah started for the door at the stairs. "Alright then. Let's go."

"What?"

"Well, I'm going with you."

"Why?" Perry demanded. "They'll lock you up for working with Hara!"

"I'll have you to protect me, right?"

"Of course," Perry said after a second's hesitation.

Noah nodded again. "I have something I would like to tell The Doc myself."

Perry was still uncertain. "Alright, but I don't know if that's such a good idea. If Jack's missing, then The Doc must have something to do with it..."

"The Doc won't hurt me," Noah promised. "I'm certain. Now, shall we head out before you're fired?"

Perry grinned. "Okay."

✳ ✳ ✳

As soon as Jack's feet landed on solid ground, he clutched his head and gasped for breath. His surroundings were spinning around him and before he realized what was happening he fell flat on his face. He put his hands out to catch himself, but there was nothing below his chest. Groaning, he blinked until his vision stopped spinning. When he could finally see again, he gazed down to see why there was no ground beneath half his body. He screamed like a little girl. He was hanging halfway off the top of a building a good thirty stories high, staring down at a highway with cars roaring by. Quickly pushing himself back up onto the rooftop, he stumbled to his feet and backed away from the edge.

Davey was cackling behind him. "You should see your face!" he cried.

Turning towards his friend, Jack demanded, "Where are we?"

Trying to suppress his giggles by covering his mouth with a hand, Davey shrugged. "I don't know, man! How should I know?"

"How did you teleport so many times without keeling over?" Jack asked, knowing Hoppers could only use their ability once or twice in one sitting. Davey must have teleported at least half a dozen times in the past minute. He should be dead.

Unable to contain himself any longer, Davey burst into a fit of loud, obnoxious laughter. Clutching his stomach, he doubled over as several guffaws erupted from him.

Gawking at his friend, Jack shook his head and whispered, "My God, Davey, you've gone completely mad!" Jack hadn't seen Davey in several months, not since he was captured by The Doc. Davey managed to escape via teleportation, but he left Jack behind in the clutches of the Beast. Something obviously happened to Davey after that, causing him to end up in this crazed state. Jack assumed his friend had been killed in the dozens of attacks that occurred after his capture, but now that he knew Davey was alive, Jack had something he needed to give him.

"No, it's not that!" Davey cried between laughs. His eyes were watering and he was gasping for breath, but he continued to laugh in hysteria. "It's...it's just so funny!"

"What?" Jack demanded, having no idea what Davey was talking about. "What is so funny?"

"Everything!" Davey shouted, stumbling backwards as he lost his balance. His foot slipped off the edge of the roof.

"No!" Jack screamed, lunging forward. But it was too late. His friend had fallen off the rooftop, but Jack arrived at the edge just in time to see Davey disappear into thin air. When he heard cackling start up again behind him, Jack whipped around and stared in shock at his friend doubling over in front of him. "Davey, are you stoned?" Jack asked. The uncontrollable laughter, the constant teleportation, the dilated pupils...it would all make perfect sense if Davey was completely hopped up.

"Yeah!" Davey giggled, his laughs beginning to die down some.

"Is that why you can hop so many times?" Jack questioned, trying not to smirk at Davey's blunt honesty.

Davey nodded while covering his mouth again.

"How did you figure that out?"

"He told me to take it just before he sent me back here!" Davey said while gasping for air. "He said it would let me hop as many times as I wanted for twenty-four hours!"

"Who told you to take what?" Jack asked, confused.

"He told me to take the drug," Davey explained.

"What drug?"

"He didn't say what it was!" Davey said urgently, giggling again. "He just said it would help."

"Who said?" Jack cried impatiently.

"Your dad!" Davey said, and then burst into laughter all over again.

Taken aback, Jack's breath caught in his throat. "My...my dad?"

"Yeah!" Davey laughed, jumping up and down. "He gave me this drug and now everything is so funny! I could die of laughter if I look at you for too long!" And with that, he collapsed and began rolling around.

"My dad's still alive?" Jack whispered in disbelief. He was so certain his father had been killed almost six months earlier. "How?"

"Your dad can't die, you plunker!" Davey said, jumping to his feet with a bold grin on his face. "You're his baby boy; I thought you would have known that!"

"Where the hell has he been?" Jack demanded.

Davey shrugged. "Around."

"Around where?" Jack snarled.

Davey shrugged again. "In some underground lab. Haven't you heard?"

"Haven't I heard what?" Jack snapped, having no patience for Davey's games.

"He's building something," Davey said, lowering his voice as if someone else might hear. "A big weapon that will stop the humans and save everybody. But *shh!*" He put a finger to his lips. "It's a secret! Don't tell anyone!"

Jack stared at him. "He's making a weapon?"

"Yeah! He's been finding all the refugees and bringing them to this huge underground laboratory. Once the weapon is fully operational and he turns it on, that's when the resistance is going to attack and we're going to blow the humans back onto this dirt hole they crawled out of!" Davey looked around and wrinkled his nose. "Seriously, bro, have you seen how disgusting this place is? Can you taste that crap they're pumping into the air?"

"What kind of weapon is it?" Jack asked.

"He never said," Davey replied. "All he told us was it would give us a huge advantage. Enough of one to crush the humans."

Jack sighed. "So my dad gave you this drug so you could teleport all you want?"

"Actually, he gave it to me so I could teleport enough times to get you out of there," Davey giggled. "And now that it's in my system, I can hop! hop! hop! all I want!" Each time he said "hop," he teleported to a different area on the rooftop. His final hop landed him directly in front of Jack. "It's so incredibly amazing!"

Unable to contain his fury any longer, Jack let Davey have it and punched him as hard as he could in the mouth.

Startled, Davey's grin was finally wiped off his face and he stumbled backwards. Clutching his bleeding lip, Davey stared back at Jack in confusion. "What the bloody hell was that for?" he asked quietly, his eyes hurt.

"You abandoned me, you asshole!" Jack shouted furiously, not letting himself fall for Davey's puppy-dog eyes. "You abandoned all of us! How dare you leave us behind like that and think we could still be friends!"

Pleadingly, Davey whispered, "But…we are still friends."

"No," Jack snarled. "Friends don't leave their friends behind to die!"

Deep sorrow coming to his eyes at the painful memory, Davey started to open his mouth again.

"Don't!" Jack yelled. "Don't even think for one second that apologizing will make anything better!"

Lowering his eyes in shame, Davey looked like he was going to start crying.

"Did you really think that abandoning your friends was the best way out?" Jack demanded harshly. "Do you know what they did to us when you fled? Adrial's dead now, you son of a bitch! They shot him right in the face! Do you know why? Because his ability wasn't 'interesting enough!' He was murdered because all he could do was play any musical instrument he touched! He's dead because you're a stupid fucking coward!"

Davey raised his eyes slightly, but when he saw Jack's enraged expression he lowered them again. He understood what he had done, and by the look on his face he deeply regretted it. But Jack wasn't about to let him off the hook that easily. No, he was going to let Davey have it bad. He was going to make him suffer like he and Greg suffered.

"I don't even know what happened to Greg after we were taken to that place!" Jack continued angrily. "They probably tortured him like they did me! Do you have any idea what those monsters did to me in that place? Do you even want to know? I have no clue why The Doc wanted to keep me so badly, and maybe he didn't either, because it seemed to me that whenever he got bored he would just strap me to a bed and drill holes into my skull! That's all he ever did! No experiments, no tests; just holes through my head if I pissed him off! Do you know how much that hurts? Do you know how traumatized I was? Do you even care?"

Gaining enough courage to gaze back into Jack's furious eyes, Davey raised his head. His eyes were welling with tears and when he blinked they spilled out over his cheeks. His lower lip began to tremble and he whispered as his voice cracked, "I'm sorry!"

"Oh, you're sorry!" Jack mocked, growing even angrier. "Are you really?"

"I'm so, so sorry!" Davey cried, sniffling as more tears streamed down his face. "You will never know how…"

"Save it!" Jack snapped, turning his back on his friend. "I don't want to listen to your crap!"

There was a pause before Davey tried again. "I…I was just so scared!"

"I was scared too," Jack growled. "We were all scared!"

"I know it's just an excuse, but I let my fear take over and I took the only way out that I could think of! I teleported out of there as soon as I saw we were surrounded," he explained. "I panicked! I didn't know what else to do! But as I hopped I realized the terrible mistake I'd made. I had left behind the three people who would always be my best mates." He waited for an emotional response from Jack, but when he got none he let out a pained sob. "I'm sorry I didn't take you with me! I should have grabbed the three of you before hopping! Believe me when I tell you I tried to go back! I really tried, but you know how pathetic I was! I could never hop more than once at a time. I tried as hard as I could, but I blacked out before I could get back to you! When I finally awoke, I went back to the place I left you, but you were already gone. I know you didn't do well there, Jack. I saw Adrial's body. There's nothing I've ever done that I wish I could take back more than that."

"And it's a damn good thing nobody found you!" Jack snapped. "The Doc has a thing for Hoppers. You don't even want to hear about what Allan Brown went through. His experience was almost as bad as Hara's. So I guess your cowardice paid off! Your friends were tortured and killed, but it's all fine since you didn't get any of it!"

Davey was sobbing. Shaking his head in remorse, he said repeatedly, "I'm sorry, I'm sorry, I'm sorry…"

"Yeah, you said that!" Jack shouted. "And I don't care! Even if I panicked, I wouldn't have teleported away!"

"I didn't mean to leave you!" Davey sobbed. "I never wanted anything to happen to you! I love you guys!" And with that, he lurched forward and grabbed Jack in a tight hug. Using Jack's shoulder as a tissue, Davey cried waterfalls, spilling out all his mistakes and regrets.

Jack couldn't take the torture anymore either. Davey had clearly been through a great ordeal himself, and Jack saw that he really did regret abandoning them. How much more torture could he inflict on his friend? Jack knew how terrible it was to see someone he cared about in pain for a mistake they had made; that was the only thing he had seen in Hara ever since her family was killed. He couldn't bear to watch his friend in agony over his mistake. He hugged him back, tears flowing out of his own eyes.

"I'm so sorry!" Davey cried softly, his body shaking in Jack's arms. "You'll never know!"

"I know," Jack promised, attempting to keep his own emotion out of his voice. "I'm sorry, too."

"I should die for what I did!" Davey whispered.

"No!" Jack said, pulling away and looking his friend full in the face. "Don't you ever say that! Ever! You made a mistake! You were scared! It happens!"

"Adrial and Greg are dead because of me!" Davey sobbed, a new batch of tears coming forth.

"Greg is dead?" Jack whispered, feeling the familiar sensation of grief wash over him. "You know for sure?"

Davey nodded regretfully. "We found his body half eaten by dogs in one of the abandoned labs along the bay," he explained, his eyes haunted by what he had seen there. "There were so many bodies…I found at least twenty people I knew."

"That sick son of a bitch," Jack said, wishing he had something to punch. There was Davey, but Jack needed to give him a break. "It was along the bay, you said?"

"Yes, in what used to be the National Intelligence Building."

Jack felt his throat choke up at the memory of that specific lab. "Did...did you find my mother there?"

Pausing, uncertain of whether he should answer, Davey whispered, "Yes."

Swallowing hard, Jack asked, "And Mark?"

Davey didn't reply.

"Did you find my little brother, David?" Jack demanded loudly.

"Yes, he was there too."

Shaking his head, Jack dropped to his knees and let out a wail that was probably heard for miles. He had known that his mother and twelve-year-old brother were both dead, but it was difficult for him now that he had confirmation.

"I'm sorry, Jack," Davey said for what seemed like the trillionth time, and Jack felt him come closer.

"Don't touch me!" Jack growled the warning, sitting back on his heels and glaring up at him. "How the hell did you know where to find me?"

Shocked by his harshness, Davey took a step back. "I...I didn't," he stammered. "Your dad told me where to find you. He said you needed my help at exactly the time I picked you up. He said it was urgent that I get you out of there because you were in trouble and you needed help. So I took the drug and came to help you, hoping I could somehow redeem myself for my past actions..." His voice trailed off and he lowered his eyes shamefully.

"My dad knew when and where to help me?" Jack muttered, dumbfounded. "Is that the only reason he sent you back?"

Davey paused again. "No," he said slowly and uncertainly. "Not the only reason..."

"Why else are you here, then?"

"I...uh...I'm supposed to find Hara!"

"What? Why?"

"She's the final piece of the weapon!" Davey cried. "He needs her to finish it and set it off! We can't set it off without her! We can't win the war without her!"

"What are you talking about, Davey?"

"She's the fucking trigger!"

"Davey," Jack started quietly, putting his hands on Davey's shoulders. "How did you know she's calling herself Hara?"

"What do you mean?" Davey asked in confusion.

"I mean, I never told you that was her alias," Jack said through gritted teeth. "And no one in our world does, so how do you know?"

Still confused, Davey shrugged.

"How did you know?" Jack shouted, snapping his hand to Davey's throat.

His eyes bugging out, Davey pulled at Jack's hand. "Your dad said that was what her new name was! An alias or something like that! It was your dad!"

"My dad," Jack repeated, releasing Davey. He then did something he didn't think he'd do for a very long time. He laughed. He laughed hard.

"What's so funny?" Davey asked, taking a cautious step back.

"What's so funny?" Jack said, looking back to Davey and putting on a serious face. "My dad is what's so funny! Haven't you noticed how he knows everything?"

"Huh?" Davey was very confused, and he was looking at Jack like he had lost his mind.

"He knew Hara's cover-up, and he knew the exact time and place to help me! Now he's building this weapon to crush the humans? It's like he already knew what was coming! Oh my God! We messed with things, so he always knew what was going to happen!"

"What?"

"Think of where we are!"

"Wait, what is today?" Davey asked, beginning to understand.

"April 4, 2008," Jack told him, crossing his arms.

"Holy shit!" Davey cried. "I can't believe it! He bloody knew!"

"And you know what makes this even better?" Jack asked, growing furious all over again. "He never said a word about it!"

"He could have prevented our world from coming to an end," Davey whispered.

"But he never said anything," Jack muttered.

"He could have altered the course of the future!"

"Yet he never said a word."

"That wanker!" Davey cried. "Oh, sorry."

"No, you're right," Jack agreed. "If I ever get the pleasure of seeing my father again, I'm going to hit him so hard he won't even remember why."

"I can't believe he knew all this time and never said anything," Davey breathed. "But at least he's going to fix everything. He said he knew it would work."

"That doesn't matter, since nearly everyone is dead now," Jack growled. "This is all his fault! He killed them all!"

"Not all of them," Davey said.

"How many are left?"

Davey shrugged. "About six or seven thousand spread out across the continent," he informed. "That's not including the rest who are still in captivity."

"Six or seven thousand?" Jack repeated, amazed by the number. "Wow. But still a small fraction of the more than two billion we began with."

Davey lowered his eyes again. "He'll fix it…"

"He's already destroyed it! There's no way to fix it!" Jack paced around the small length of the rooftop, anxiety getting the better of him. "He's a murderer, and I'm going to make sure he pays for what he's done!" Looking back to his friend's despaired face, he asked, "But this machine, do you really think it will work?"

"If he believes it, then I do," Davey said proudly. "After all, he's already seen it."

"And he needs Hara to complete it?"

"Yes, do you know where she is?"

"Not a clue," Jack answered, but then suddenly he had an idea. "But I think I may know someone who might."

"Then we'd better find this person quick," Davey said. "Remember, it's April 4th. This is the day it all goes down." Gazing out at the city around them, he asked, "Where did we end up, anyway?"

Taking a look himself, Jack saw in the distance a tall building that looked familiar from a book he once looked at with his father, its top obscured by the clouds. "Well, there's the Empire State Building," he told Davey, pointing to it. "We must be in New York."

Davey nodded in approval. "Wow. I'm impressed. You know Earth's geography well. Did they teach that in school while I wasn't paying attention?"

"No, my dad taught me a lot about the United States because that was where he was from."

"Huh," Davey muttered. "Well, we better get back to Philadelphia and find this person you're talking about. Who is it, anyway?"

"His name's Wesley Bennett," Jack replied.

Davey's mouth fell open.

"I don't know for sure that he's helping Hara, but if anyone would be then it would be him."

"Let's go then," Davey said, holding out his arm. "Grab on."

Hesitating, Jack looked out again at New York. He had always wanted to see what it was like, with all the gray, boring buildings and other things that weren't in his world. It was beautiful yet horrifying, because it was an entirely new place, but this world was tearing itself apart. There was no green here. It was all concrete and chemicals and lifelessness. And when the big year came, the year of 2018, it would only be worse. Much, much worse. No wonder the humans had, at one point, wanted to share the Colicians' world. Their world was dying.

Jack really had no desire to teleport again, but he really had no choice. Taking a deep breath, he took Davey's arm.

✳ ✳ ✳

The ride back to the police station was completely silent, and Perry felt a repetitive familiarity to it. It seemed that every drive to the station resulted in an awkward silence due to one issue or another. Neither Perry nor Noah spoke a word to each other. Maybe it was the earlier discussion that left them silent, allowing them both to ponder over the revealed truths. Maybe it was the dawning sensation that things were about to get much worse. Maybe it was because they were just tired and didn't feel like talking. Perry certainly didn't feel like talking. He allowed Noah to sit and quietly stare out the window while his mind raced over endless thoughts and questions. But it wasn't about the earlier conversation with Noah. No, his mind hardly wandered over to that subject. He was too busy thinking about what he was going to do to The Doc when they got back.

There was no way that The Doc wasn't involved with Jack's disappearance, and Perry was going to let him have it. If he found out that man hurt Jack…things were going to get very ugly very fast. Like Noah said before, Jack was a part of his family now. There was a connection between them, and even though Perry didn't understand it he understood that Jack was important to him and he was important to Jack. Perry deeply cared for Jack and it seemed to Noah that they would be family in the future. If The Doc was going to meddle with his family, then The Doc was going down; Perry was sure of that.

As he pulled the SUV into an empty spot beside a squad car, Perry turned to Noah and said, "Well, this is it. When I prove The Doc messed with Jack, I'm arresting him and putting him away for life."

"You can't do that," he replied warningly.

"Why not?" Perry demanded. "After everything he's done to you and the people in your life, why wouldn't you want him gone?"

"He's the only person in your group who knows what he's doing," Noah explained. "He's the only one from our world. He's the only one who can find Hara."

"Do you want him to find her?" Perry asked skeptically.

"Of course I do," Noah said, seemingly confused by the question.

Perry stared at him, not sure how to respond.

"How else will we find her?" Noah asked.

Understanding, Perry nodded. "You want to use him."

"Why not? He's using you, isn't he?"

"I suppose so."

"So here's what you're going to do. You go back in there and pretend that you're as stupid as the others. Help him in any way necessary to find her and make sure he has captured her before you take care of him. Once you have her then you're free to do what you want with him. You can use your imagination if you wish."

"Oh, I will," Perry promised, starting to climb out from behind the wheel. Noah stopped him by taking a firm hold of his arm.

"Take this," he instructed, pulling a small, silvery weapon out of his belt and handing it to him. It was the same shape and structure as Perry's own weapon, and the designs looked strangely similar to those on the weapon The Doc had tried to use on Hara before. "It's called an AD Weapon, or an Ability Disarming Weapon. Shoot her in the neck with this as a last resort and she will no longer be able to use her abilities against you. But be very careful. If you hit a regular human with this they will die in a matter of seconds."

"Okay," Perry said uncertainly, examining it quickly before shoving it deep in his pocket. "Thanks."

"Any more questions before we walk into the line of fire?" Noah asked as they both got out of the vehicle.

"I do, actually," Perry replied. "Do you know who Hallie Reifert is?"

Every ounce of emotion was wiped clean from Noah's face and he stared blankly back at Perry. "Sorry…who did you say?"

"Hallie Reifert," Perry repeated, sensing the old man's uneasiness. "Do you know the name?"

For a moment, Noah gazed back at him without blinking, but then he turned away and began walking towards the station's entrance. "No, I'm afraid I don't. My apologies."

Perry finally realized that the name Hallie Reifert had significant meaning to everyone in Hara's world, but the mention of it seemed to be scaring them. It was important yet troubling at the same time. Following Noah, he called, "Aubrey told me I needed to save her just before he died, and I know the name means something to The Doc…"

Rounding on him, Noah's eyes were angry. "That name is harmful to others and poisons the ears! Every time I hear it my heart feels like it's breaking in half! I don't care what Aubrey told you to do! You can't save her, so don't mention her name again!" And with that he turned on his heel and stormed off, leaving Perry behind in a state of confusion.

The harsh tone seemed uncharacteristic of Noah, so as he watched him march to the glass doors, Perry was perplexed and slightly stunned. It was important to him that he find out who this girl was, so even though he knew Noah was upset, he decided to push him further. Hurrying to catch up to him, Perry snapped, "I made a promise to a dying man, Noah. I'm not about to give it up!"

"He was a dying man, Shawn!" Noah cried without facing him. "A dying man who was half controlled by a dead man! He didn't know what he was saying!"

"Yes he did!" Perry protested. "He specifically said Hallie Reifert! What could possibly be so bad about her that you won't tell me who she is so I can help her?"

"You can't save her, Shawn!" Noah exclaimed. "No one can."

"You keep saying that, and I don't care what you think! If you tell me who she is, then there's still a chance I can help her!"

"She's already dead!" Noah snapped, stopping just before the door and turning again.

Perry stopped short to keep himself from slamming into him. "What?" he whispered.

"She's gone," Noah said. "You can't save her."

"But who was she?" Perry asked.

"I can't tell you," Noah whispered.

"Why?" Perry demanded. "What is it with you people and names? You're so secretive about names! You'll tell me some names, and others you refuse to talk about! What's so bad about them? Why do they need to stay a secret?"

"Just let it go, Shawn," Noah ordered, pulling open the glass door and stepping inside.

Shaking his head in disbelief, Perry followed him inside and rushed ahead of him so his colleagues wouldn't be too surprised when they saw him. Perry didn't even get a chance to look around before Agent Long came storming around a corner.

"Where the hell have you been, Perry?" he demanded furiously.

"Well..." Perry started, but he couldn't get more out than that.

"Who's this?" Agent Long asked suspiciously before Perry could come up with a believable excuse.

"This is Noah Travis," Perry introduced, stepping aside so the two of them could get a good look at each other. "Noah, Special Agent Rhett Long, head of field operations."

Noah nodded back at Agent Long and extended his hand.

Stepping forward and taking his hand hesitantly, Agent Long's eyes never left Noah's. "So this is what you were doing, Perry?" he said. "Bringing more people into this?"

"Actually, sir, Noah was in this way before we were," Perry defended. "He's been living with Jack's family for...a while, and he was giving me some valuable information about our investigation. That's what I was doing, sir. Jack sent me there to talk with him."

Agent Long eyed Noah. "So can you throw people through walls too?" he asked.

Noah smiled. "I'm afraid that I have no abilities. I'm just as human as you are, so no need to worry."

"Why should I believe you?" Agent Long demanded. "All anyone involved in this has done is lie, so why should I trust your word?"

Shrugging, Noah said, "Ask him." He nodded to someone over Agent Long's shoulder.

He and Perry both turned and, to Perry's dismay, saw The Doc standing in the hallway, staring back at Noah with a horrified fascination. The Doc clearly knew Noah, and the way Noah had spoken before made it seem like he knew The Doc personally. But there was something else in The Doc's expression that Perry had never seen before. Something that Perry never thought possible from him. It was pain.

"Well?" Agent Long said impatiently. "Is he telling the truth?"

Slowly, The Doc nodded. "Yes," he answered. "He is definitely a human." Watching Noah, he addressed him. "Noah."

"Doc," Noah replied flatly.

Looking back and forth between The Doc's and Noah's stares, Agent Long asked, "You two know each other?"

"Quite well, actually," The Doc mumbled, his gaze never wavering. His mouth seemed to be on autopilot; it didn't seem like his mind was even present there. "But I think the real question is why is he here?"

"I have a message I wanted to deliver to you," Noah replied, stepping forward.

The Doc snickered. "Another message from Hara?"

"No," Noah said. "This one's from me." Reaching out a hand again, he gestured with two fingers for The Doc to come closer.

Just as Agent Long had, The Doc hesitated for a moment before walking forward. He looked surprisingly uncertain.

Noah motioned for Perry and Agent Long to stand aside as The Doc approached, and they obeyed, allowing The Doc to step directly in front of him. He then stood waiting, he and The Doc practically staring into each other's souls. This went on for a while, neither of them speaking. At one point, Perry shot Agent Long an awkward glance, and he received the same look in return.

Finally, Noah spoke.

"Do you want to know a secret?" he asked softly. Something about the way he and The Doc were communicating was beginning to bother Perry. It almost seemed as though The Doc was afraid of Noah, which was just crazy considering the kind of people he had dealt with in the past. After Hara, how could Noah be frightening? What could be so scary about a kind, fragile old man?

The Doc waited for Noah to continue, raising an eyebrow questioningly. He was still uncertain, but it was evident that he wanted to hear what Noah had to say.

Faster than Perry could have expected from such an old man, Noah grabbed The Doc by his hair and yanked his head down so he could speak into his ear. He then whispered something inaudible to the others present, and The Doc's eyes widened in a mixture of shock and fear. When Noah released The Doc's hair, The Doc pulled his head away and stared back at Noah with his fearful gaze. Then the two men repeated what they had done before, staring each other down, knowing something that no one else did.

"And that will be the end of you," Noah said, glowering.

For a man with as many questions as The Doc, Perry was surprised to see him turn and leave the way he came. He must have known what Noah meant with those few words and he didn't remain to press the matter.

Perry and Agent Long watched him leave and Agent Long nodded and said slowly, "Okay."

"Good riddance," Noah muttered.

"What did you say to him?"

"There's a reason I said it in his ear," Noah said. "Because I didn't want the two of you to hear it."

Staring hard at Noah, Perry was stunned by his sudden unfriendly behavior.

"It was between me and him," Noah informed. "It has nothing to do with you." Turning, he started to walk out the door. Agent Long wouldn't allow that.

"Hey!" he called in surprise, his voice firm.

Noah turned back. "Yes?"

"Where do you think you're going?" Agent Long demanded.

Raising an eyebrow, Noah pointed outside. "Out the door. This is a free country, is it not?"

"Yes, it is, but I can't let you leave," Agent Long told him, taking a step closer. "I'm not letting any more of Hara's colleagues just walk out of here."

"Am I under arrest?" Noah asked, gazing back at Agent Long like he was an idiot.

Hesitantly, Agent Long replied, "No."

"Then I'll be seeing you," Noah muttered, turning again.

"Hey!" Agent Long snapped.

"Let him go, sir," Perry requested, stepping between them. "He doesn't know anything about where she is and he didn't participate in any of Hara's work, so there's no point in keeping him here."

Agent Long was furious with the intervention, but he didn't try to fight it either. Turning on his heel, he stalked out of the lobby, calling over his shoulder, "When you're done, get your ass down to the holding cell where Jack was."

"Yes, sir," Perry said, looking back to Noah, who was halfway out the door.

"See you soon," Noah told him, giving him a rather curious look with his bright blue eyes.

"Where are you going?" Perry asked. "Do you have anywhere else to stay?"

"I don't need a place to stay," Noah replied. "Like I said, I'll see you soon." Giving him a stiff nod, he walked out the door and didn't look back.

Perry shook his head and followed Agent Long to the holding cell at the very end of the main hallway. The door was hanging ajar when he arrived, and he was confused to see that his boss was the only person inside. "Where is everyone?" he asked.

"In the offices, trying to find out what happened in here," Agent Long explained in an irritated voice. "The surveillance tapes were destroyed after the incident, so they're trying to hack into the memories of the cameras to figure out what went down."

"Incident?" Perry said, puzzled. But when he looked around at the room, his mouth fell open in shock. "What the hell happened...?"

The room was a disaster. The table at which Jack had been seated was still in the center of the room and the chair was still positioned at it. The right wall was completely blown out, plaster and bricks scattered across the floor. Perry was surprised to see that the table was left undisturbed. He could see the piping on the inside of the wall and also saw that the pipes were undisturbed as well. It confused him; whoever blew up the wall must have only been targeting the bricks and plaster. But how was that possible? It looked as though a bomb had gone off from inside the wall, so how were none of the pipes damaged? Perry thought it must have been Hara, coming back to save her friend. Who else would have destroyed part of the building to save him?

"What exactly happened that led you to discover this?" Perry asked, waving a cloud of dust out of his face as he walked further into the room. "Did you just come in here and find the mess or did you hear something?" He kicked a broken piece of plaster aside with his foot.

"We heard several strange banging sounds, and then the initial explosion that caused this shook the whole building," Agent Long explained. "Of course, our first thought was that The Doc was trying to kill Jack and he put up a fight. Nobody knew where The Doc was so we all assumed that he was killing Jack just like he had Marcus." Agent Long sighed and shook his head, lowering his eyes to the floor.

"Why wasn't anyone guarding the door?" Perry demanded.

"Everyone else was busy contributing to the investigation. Their jobs don't consist of babysitting murderers, even if he was your little brother. Maybe if you had been here, you could have played Nanny!"

Perry flinched. He boss was right. He couldn't just expect someone else to keep watch over Jack when they had a terrorist to find. Clearing his throat awkwardly, he questioned, "So... The Doc wasn't in here when you arrived?"

"Oh, he was," Agent Long said. "But it wasn't what we expected. When we got here, Jack was already gone and The Doc was sitting right there looking rather confused."

Curious, Perry walked to the wall and took a look. He found a small crack that looked to be about two inches long embedded in the plaster. It was located about three or four inches above his head and was shaped like the letter L. Reaching up, he ran his fingers over the crack, thinking.

"You said you found The Doc sitting here and he looked confused?" he asked for clarification.

"Yes."

"How would you describe his state?"

Shrugging, Agent Long replied, "I don't know. It was like he had been hit in the face and was in a daze."

"Huh," Perry said absentmindedly.

"Why?" Agent Long asked curiously.

Perry shrugged and ran his hand over the crack again.

"What are you thinking?" Agent Long recognized the blank stare on Perry's face.

"I'm thinking that The Doc was thrown into this wall, which would explain this crack and also explain why he was sitting here in a daze," Perry said, gesturing for Agent Long to take a look.

"Do you think it was Jack?" Agent Long asked as he came closer and examined the crack.

"No," Perry muttered. "It couldn't have been. He was still cuffed to the chair."

"His hands were cuffed behind the chair," Agent Long reminded. "He may have been able to get up out of the chair and fight The Doc if he was being threatened by him."

"I don't think so. That really doesn't sound like Jack."

Agent Long shrugged again. "Maybe The Doc uncuffed him..."

"No way," Perry said, going over to the blown out wall. There was a pile of broken bricks and plaster in his way and he tripped several times, but he managed to make his way there. As he began to observe the pipes to make sure he hadn't missed any broken piping, he added, "Even if The Doc did uncuff him, I doubt that Jack is anywhere near strong enough to throw someone into the wall with enough force to put that crack in the wall."

"So you think somebody else was here?" Agent Long asked.

"Don't you?" Perry shot a surprised glance at his boss and then gestured to the giant hole in the wall. "The wall was blown into the room. This wasn't an escape attempt. Someone came into the room and took Jack with them, fighting off The Doc in the process."

"Hara?" Agent Long questioned.

"That's my best guess," Perry replied.

"There's something else as well," Agent Long said, pointing towards the chair at the table. "We found Jack's cuffs behind the chair, still locked."

Taking a look himself, Perry saw that he was telling the truth. Resting among the pile of rubble was the pair of cuffs, locked and undisturbed.

"These people can vanish like Houdini," Agent Long commented. "This is the third time we've found a pair of locked cuffs on the ground that had been on one of our fugitives."

"When has that happened?" Perry asked, unable to recall.

"The first time was after the road chase when the mayor first went missing," Agent Long explained. "We found his cuffs lying in the truck still locked. The second time was when Marcus helped him escape. Another pair was found in the parking lot in the direction he had fled. They were still locked."

"Oh," Perry said. "Well, Allan's a teleporter, so that's not too surprising."

"A teleporter?" Agent Long repeated. "Damn, I wish I could do that. It would make transportation so much less of a hassle."

Snorting, Perry assured him, "Trust me, you wouldn't."

"Do you think it was the mayor who took Jack?"

"No. Hara can teleport too, so it still could have been her." Confused by something, he turned back to his boss and asked, "Why didn't you just ask The Doc what happened?"

"He's not talking to anyone," Agent Long said. "He's just been sitting in the conference room muttering to himself ever since we found him. He won't give us anything."

Remembering everything he learned from Noah, he muttered, "I think somebody needs to keep a serious eye on that man."

"Be my guest," Agent Long offered. "What did your friend Noah tell you, anyway? You were gone an awfully long time."

Perry shuddered. "A lot of things. I know what led to Hara's existence, why she's here, and what The Doc has done."

"So he told you why she killed kids?" Agent Long asked hopefully. "And why she's trying to kill Odau's son?"

"Apparently, Jackson is destined to grow into a very bad person that will cause great destruction for her people," Perry explained. "I suppose Jackson is going to end up just like The Doc. Those other kids were killed because they were meant to inspire Jackson's dirty work."

"And how would they possibly know this?"

"There were supposedly millions of people with these abilities, sir. One of them obviously saw it coming."

"How did this so called species begin?"

Perry went on and explained everything Noah had told him. He left out the part about how he was turning into one of them, but he tried to fit in as much as he could. He even explained the video he had seen of The Doc torturing Hara. Agent Long was less than pleased with the information.

"If this is true, then why the hell haven't we heard anything about it? Why did it take a terrorist attack to open our eyes?"

"That's what I've been trying to understand," Perry said. "Noah wouldn't tell me how the secret was kept for so long, so obviously there's a huge conspiracy behind it all."

"This whole thing is one giant conspiracy," Agent Long replied. "And it's ridiculous and unbelievable."

Agent Long turned to leave the room. "Andy was looking for you. He said he found something on the Reifert family."

His stomach leaping with excitement, Perry nodded, "Okay, thanks. I'll be down there soon." Stumbling off of the pile of debris, Perry walked out the door and went straight down the hall that led to the restrooms. He paused for a moment at the door, remembering that room was where Marcus had given him the warning letter. Perry still had it buried deep in one of his pockets. If only he had known that would be one of the last times he would speak to Marcus, he might have been able to do something to prevent his death. Shuddering from the memory of Marcus's dead body, Perry pushed open the door and stepped inside, pulling out his phone as he did so.

He hadn't spoken to his daughter in a long time. With the recent events he wanted to give her a call and make sure she was doing okay. If Noah was telling the truth about the year 2018, then Perry would be the one to take care of Jillian when the outbreak hit.

Standing in the far corner of the restroom, he pulled up Kyra's home phone number on his call list. It was number 1 on the list, and he felt guilty about how many times he had skipped over it. He should have confronted Kyra a long time ago. Now, he was done being pushed around. He was going to talk to his daughter. His finger hesitated over the call button for a moment, but then he took a deep breath and pushed it.

His heart was pounding as the phone rang in his ear. The ten seconds that passed felt like ten years, and finally after the fourth ring Kyra picked up.

"Hello?" she said pleasantly in her sing-song voice.

"Hi, Kyra," Perry muttered slowly, hoping she was in a good mood.

There was a pause. "What do you want?" she demanded, her tone flat.

He didn't expect anything less and was actually surprised she didn't immediately start yelling. Maybe it was because they hadn't spoken in so long and she had a chance to cool down from their earlier encounters.

She wasn't in a terrible mood yet, but Perry had a strong feeling that their conversation was going to end in a shouting match.

"Uh...how are you?" he tried, praying a little kindness would pay off.

"What do you want?" she repeated, her voice rising.

"Is Jillian there?" Perry asked, feeling his face flush in embarrassment. Kyra knew just as well as he did that he didn't care how she was.

Another pause. "It's the middle of the day, Perry," Kyra snapped. "She's at school."

"Right, sorry," Perry said. He felt like an idiot. Of course she was at school; it was two o'clock on a Friday! "Um...what time does she get home?" He decided that he would call back later when he wasn't too busy. He felt like a terrible parent, not even knowing when his daughter was done with school. But it wasn't his fault. Kyra had exiled him from Jillian's life for nearly a year! How was he supposed to know?

"Why do you care?" Kyra muttered rudely.

"I care because I would like to talk to my child!" Perry said in irritation. "Is it so hard to understand that I love Jillian and would like to keep in contact with her?"

"I don't' want you in my life anymore!" Kyra hissed. "You were a mistake! I want you to stop calling me! Just leave me and my family alone!"

"Your family?" Perry repeated. "Jillian may be living with you, but she's my daughter too! I have the same rights as you do to talk to her!"

"Not for long!" Kyra growled. "Riley and I are getting married, and he wants to adopt Jillian. Once the papers are signed then you won't be allowed to come near her or even call my house!"

"What?" Perry cried, and the anger inside him was too fierce to contain. "That will never happen! I won't allow it! I'm never signing my daughter off to that asshole!"

"Oh, you will," Kyra promised him. "If I have to hold the pen in your hand, you'll sign it! Now stop calling me! Just leave me alone!" The line went dead.

Taking a deep breath to calm himself, Perry slipped his phone back into his pocket and turned around to walk out the door. He just about jumped out of his skin when he nearly ran into The Doc.

"Good God!" Perry cried, stumbling back and bumping into the wall. His heart racing from the surprise, he begged, "Will you please stop doing that!"

"Sorry," The Doc replied, not really looking like he cared all that much. "I needed to talk to you, but you were on the phone so I was just waiting for you to finish."

"What is it with you and butting into other people's business?" Perry demanded. "This is, what...the third time today?"

"Actually, I think it's only the second," The Doc corrected, eyeing him curiously like he usually did. "So, your ex-wife is stealing your kid?"

"We were never married," Perry muttered, wrinkling his nose in disgust at the thought of living with her. Brushing past him, he added, "And it's none of your business."

"I wasn't aware you had any children yet," The Doc said to him as he walked out the door.

Turning back, Perry repeated in confusion, "Yet? What do you mean yet?" The Doc started to open his mouth and reply, but then Perry blurted, "On second thought, I don't even care." Shoving through the door, he left the restroom and walked back the way he came. If Hara was trying to kill Odau's son because he was supposed to end up bad and The Doc was here to protect him, then The Doc clearly knew the future as well. Everyone seemed to know Perry's future, and he guessed that The Doc knew something significant about it. Perry really didn't want to know anything else about his future, especially if it involved more children.

"Hey!" The Doc cried in protest, following Perry out the door and down the hall. "Come on, I'm trying to talk to you!"

"Great," Perry muttered, not stopping. "Another highlight of my day."

"Will you stop, please?" The Doc asked, sounding annoyed.

Extremely irritated, Perry halted himself and spun around, scowling at The Doc. "What?" he demanded.

The Doc stopped about five feet away, staring at Perry in a mixture of confusion and amusement. "What is the matter with you? Since when do you not want to talk to me?"

"Oh, where to begin?" Perry said. "Should I start where you tried to kill me last night or where you killed my colleague this morning?"

Smirking, The Doc raised an eyebrow.

"Or maybe I should start at the part where you cut the heart out of a teenage girl while she was still conscious and traumatized her to the point of insanity!"

The smirk immediately left The Doc's face. "What did you just say?" he asked, sounding slightly surprised.

"What, are you shocked that I know?" Perry snapped angrily. "You'd be surprised what you can learn just by talking to people!"

"That was where Jack sent you? He sent you to go talk to Noah so he could tell you all my dirty secrets?" The Doc looked slightly angry.

"He actually sent me there to learn more about the Colicians and how this whole thing began, but we got onto the subject of you."

"So what else did he tell you?" The Doc took an intimidating step forward.

"Enough," Perry growled, holding his ground. He was no longer afraid of him. Now that he knew everything The Doc had done, there were no more secrets that he needed to be afraid of. "I saw the tape of you torturing her, which showed me what you are."

"And what am I?" The Doc asked, walking forward so they were less than a foot apart.

Perry leaned forward. "You're sick!" he hissed. "And I'm done with you!" He turned and began walking away again, but he didn't get very far.

"No, you're not, son," The Doc replied. "There are still plenty of things that you don't know."

"Like what?" Perry snarled, rounding on him. "That in ten years' time there is going to be a huge outbreak of Colicians and everyone in the world with O negative blood is going to get an ability, including myself!"

Taken aback, The Doc gazed at him skeptically.

"Yeah, I know!" Perry shouted furiously. "Do you know what else I know? Jackson Odau is going to grow up and become...I don't know...a follower of you or something, and he's going to end up killing a good majority of the Colicians just like you did, and that's why Hara wants to kill him!"

The silence that followed was almost deafening. Perry's ears were ringing from his anger and racing heart. Neither of them spoke for several seconds, and the hall was so quiet that Perry jumped when The Doc started laughing.

When his laughs finally died away, his expression became very serious. "If you really think that's all the boy is, then you still have quite a lot you need to learn, my friend."

"Why don't you just take your thugs and leave?" Perry snapped. "None of us want you here anymore and we don't want your help!"

"You still need me," The Doc said.

"I don't care!" Perry declared. "I don't want anything to do with you!"

"I'm the only one in this building who can catch Hara," The Doc said with superiority.

"You can't catch her!" Perry shouted in disbelief. "So far you've tried twice and failed both times!"

"I have something that belongs to her," The Doc said. "Something that will bring her to me. She would give her life to protect it, so once we have her in the same room she'll give herself up. Your city will be safe once more."

Perry snickered. "You've already taken away everything she ever loved! There's nothing left in this world that would ever make her give herself up to you!"

The Doc smirked back at him. "You may think I've taken away everything, but you're wrong. I've left a few things behind that she doesn't know about. You'd be surprised how compassionate I can be."

Snorting, Perry snarled, "You're not compassionate! You're just using it to get to her, you sick bastard!"

Chuckling some more, The Doc said, "For a man who has been breaking the law to find this girl, you're rather judgmental."

Pursing his lips as his face grew hot, Perry demanded, "What exactly is this thing you want to threaten her with?"

"Keep me on the team and I'll show you," The Doc said, smiling brightly.

Was this really how The Doc was going to play it?

He didn't want to say it out loud, but he didn't really have much of a choice but to go along with The Doc. Besides, Noah said it was the only way they could find Hara, which was what they needed to do. Perry just had to make sure that The Doc wasn't the one who ended up with her. Turning away again, he took a left down the hall past the holding cells.

"So, is that a yes?" The Doc asked, still following Perry.

"Whatever," Perry muttered. "I'm going to go talk to another agent, and when we're done I'm going to take everyone to the conference room, where I expect you to be. There, you will show us this thing that will supposedly bring Hara to us. Is that understood?"

He could practically hear the smirk come to The Doc's face. "Yes, sir," he replied in mock respect.

Perry tensed but kept walking, hoping that by the time this mess was over he would get an opportunity to shoot The Doc. After everything he had done, Perry would be doing the world a favor.

Suddenly, he stopped, and turned quickly to catch The Doc before he disappeared again. "What did Noah say to you?" he asked. "Before you left, he said something to you. What was it, if you don't mind me asking?"

The Doc hesitated, keeping his back turned for a moment. When he decided to make eye contact, Perry saw that tiny glimmer of fear in his eyes that he had seen before. "He told me that Bo's coming."

"Bo?" Perry said, not recognizing the name. "Who's Bo?"

"He is—or rather, was—Hara's soul mate," The Doc replied.

"Her soul mate?" Perry asked, puzzled.

"To Hara and her people, a soul mate is the equivalent of a husband or wife," The Doc explained. "So, for your sake, I'll call him her husband."

The thought of an eighteen-year-old having a husband had always befuddled Perry, but Hara was far from normal and if he was correct in his recollections she also had five children. Their traditions were clearly very different from those of humans. "Okay, so her husband is coming. Why should that scare you?"

Before The Doc turned away again, Perry saw him swallow hard. "Because he's dead."

✳ ✳ ✳

"Agent Long said you found the Reiferts," Perry said to Martinson after arriving at the desk where his friend was working.

"Yes," Martinson replied, looking up from his computer. "It's a five-person family, consisting of single father John Reifert, who's a history professor at the University of Philadelphia, and his four sons, Tyler, Ethan, Anton, and Walter."

"Wait, did you just say Walter?" Perry asked in surprise. "Walter Reifert?"

"Yeah," Martinson answered, looking confused. "Why?"

"Remember the last time I talked to Jack and he started screaming at me because I hit him?" Perry struggled to recall all the details from that snippet of the conversation. "He said he wasn't going to bow down to me like I was Walter Reifert."

Perplexed, Martinson told him, "Walter Reifert is a kid. An eight-year-old kid. I've seen his school ID. Why would someone bow down to a kid, or anyone for that matter?"

"I haven't a clue," Perry said, sitting down in the extra chair beside the desk. The truth was, he did have a clue, but he wasn't about to share it. The Colicians and everyone who knew about them knew what was supposed to happen in the future, and it seemed as if several children at the moment were going to play a large role in the future after the major outbreak. Perry guessed little Walter would end up being a good person if Jack was talking about bowing down to him.

"What about the mother?" Perry asked. "What happened to her?"

"I was getting to that," Martinson said, a flicker of excitement in his eyes. "She died in a car crash a little over two years ago."

"Okay," Perry said. "But I don't see what that has to do with any of this."

"It doesn't," Martinson said. "But it's her name you'll want to hear. Perry, her name was Hallie. Hallie Reifert."

"Hallie Reifert," Perry repeated, relieved that they had finally found her. But to his dismay, she really was dead, just like Noah had claimed. There was still something about her that Perry felt was important. He was supposed to save Hallie Reifert, like Aubrey had begged him to. He was supposed to save her, and he would. There was something more to Hallie Reifert than they were seeing.

"Have you contacted John Reifert yet?" Perry questioned, pulling out his phone. "There's something else about this woman that we haven't seen. I need to ask him about her."

"I figured you would want to be the one to talk to him, so I decided to wait until you got back," Martinson replied, leaning back in his chair. "Are you sure Aubrey didn't make a mistake? The only Hallie Reifert we could find is dead. I don't see how you're supposed to save a dead woman. The man was possessed by a ghost at the time."

"I don't know. Maybe." Perry thought over what Noah had said when they were entering the building. "Noah did tell me to stop trying to find her because she was already dead. But I can't help thinking there's more to this than just a dead mother. We're supposed to find her."

Giving Perry a bold grin, Martinson said, "Well, Agent Perry, I think we've found our girl."

13

Premonition

Perry was feeling a little too hopeful as he dialed John Reifert's work number. He was expecting that the man's dead wife really was the woman Detective Aubrey had been talking about before he died. But Hallie Reifert was dead, so what was the point in saving a dead woman? How exactly did Aubrey expect him to save a dead woman? Aubrey must have been talking nonsense. After all, his mind had been invaded by another.

"So," Martinson said, clearing his throat awkwardly. "You and Renee, huh?"

Shooting his friend a look that clearly said, "Drop it," Perry put the phone to his ear.

Martinson smirked when Perry didn't deny it. "It wasn't like everybody hadn't already figured it out," he said.

Perry turned to snap something back, but he was interrupted when someone on the other end of the line picked up and said in a not so pleasant tone, "Hello?"

"Hello, is this Professor John Reifert?" Perry asked.

"Yes," John Reifert replied gruffly. "Can I help you?"

"My name is Special Agent Shawn Perry. I'm with the FBI. I was wondering if I might be able to speak with you for a few minutes."

"I'm about to go into a lecture," John Reifert said flatly. "Can this wait an hour?"

"I'm afraid not," Perry said. "This has to do with the attacks of the past few days."

There was a long pause, and then the sound of a door being closed. "What exactly does any of this have to do with me?"

Perry suddenly felt a twinge of guilt for what he was about to request. "I'm really sorry, but I needed to ask you a few questions about your wife, Hallie."

"What about her?" John demanded, his tone sharp.

Feeling like an inconsiderate ass, Perry explained, "You may or may not have heard, but the FBI has been assisting the local police in investigating the incidents in Philadelphia over the past couple days…"

"Yeah, so what the hell does any of that have to do with my dead wife?" John snapped.

"A suspect in the investigation mentioned her name, so it was my job to look into it…"

"Wonderful, and now you've wasted time for both of us," John snapped. "She's dead, Agent! She doesn't have anything to do with these incidents! Now if you'll excuse me, I have to go and describe the effects of the Black Plague on Europe."

"Wait, please!" Perry pleaded. "I know this has something to do with your wife! Please, I need your help!"

"I can't help you," John said harshly.

"I'm just trying to find the girl!"

There was a length of silence on the other line. It was so long and so quiet that Perry was certain John had hung up.

"Mr. Reifert?"

"What did you say?"

Relieved, Perry said, "Did your wife know anyone who was…different?"

"The person you're chasing is a girl? A teenage girl?"

"I just need to know what your wife knew about what's going on," Perry said, not knowing if John had any idea what he was talking about. "Did she ever say anything to you about a girl who could do things that don't seem possible?"

"You're not the only one looking for this girl, are you?" John questioned, not taking notice of anything Perry was saying. "There's another who's trying to find her, isn't there? The doctor. The doctor with gray eyes."

"How do you know all this?" Perry asked.

"I can't talk about this now," John insisted. "We have to meet. Face to face. I have something for you."

"Something for me?"

"A message."

"Why for me?"

"Before she died, someone gave my wife a piece of information that was for her eyes only. Hallie knew she was going to die, because the day before the crash she gave it to me and told me that sometime in the near future a man would be looking for a teenage girl who had caused a lot of damage because of something that had been done to her. She said that I had to give this piece of information to that man who would contact me, because he was the one who could end it all. I didn't believe it because it sounded like a bunch of nonsense. But now that everything is falling into place, I'm starting to think it was all true. And besides, I promised my wife I would deliver it to whoever needed it. So, are you going to meet me or not?"

"Uh…" Perry was bewildered by the story he had just heard, but he didn't have time at the moment to make sense of it all. "Yes. When are you available?"

"Not for a while," John replied.

"Me neither," Perry said.

"I can meet around four. Where do you want to meet? It needs to just be you and me."

"Meet me on the third level of the parking ramp across from the hospital," Perry said. That place was where he had spent the majority of his morning anyway.

"Four o'clock," John reminded. "I'll be there." The line went dead.

"Well?" Martinson inquired as Perry hung up the phone. "What was that all about? You're going to meet him now?"

"He knows something," Perry explained, not seeing how it was possible. He sighed and shook his head. "He wants to give me something that might be able to help us."

"Don't you want to go right away?" Martinson asked. "If whatever he has can help us end this…"

"I'm not so sure that it's something that important," Perry said. "He didn't even seem that certain of it himself. Besides, I've got other people I need to worry myself over."

"Like The Doc?" Martinson muttered.

"Exactly," Perry replied.

"I really don't like him."

"I don't think anyone does. Speaking of which…" Perry looked behind him towards the door. "I can't believe he hasn't come snooping around in here. He always seems to be wherever I am."

"I think he likes you," Martinson said, winking and elbowing Perry in the arm.

"Let's hope not," Perry said grimly.

Despite what the two agents thought, The Doc had been snooping on them. He sat in a chair in the adjacent room, ear buds in his ears attached to a wireless microphone that could pick up the voices of anyone within two hundred feet of him. It didn't take long for him to find Perry and Martinson in the next room and block out all the remaining chatter. What he heard had deeply fascinated him. Perry was going to figure things out much faster than anyone originally anticipated. Even as an agent, the man was still quite bright. But not bright enough. The Doc's plan to secure Hara had failed, but now that he knew where and when to find the Reiferts, getting his girl to come to him would become much easier. He smiled to himself, thriving in Perry's stupidity. The agent was leading the unsuspecting family into a trap, one that they wouldn't have much chance of getting out whole. Once he finished off the Reiferts and had his girl back in his possession, he could finally finish off Perry as well. It would have made his day had he actually killed Perry in the chase that night. The Doc finally had the chance to cause Perry as much pain as Perry had caused him, and he wasn't going to let that opportunity slide. Besides, there would be no future for the Colicians if there was no Shawn Perry to guide it. The future may have been foreseen, but nothing was set in stone. Once Shawn Perry died, the future would die with him.

✳ ✳ ✳

"Well, we're all here, Doc," Perry grumbled when everyone gathered in the conference room. "Now maybe you can explain to us your new and ingenious plan to capture Hara."

The Doc was standing at the head of the table closest to the door, glancing down at the seven others that were seated. None of his guards were with him, something that Perry hadn't expected. "As I was telling Agent Perry, I have something that belongs to Hara, and when she realizes I have it she will come straight to me. I know that my past attempts have failed, but I can assure you all that this will work."

"How can you be so sure of that?" Hersh demanded. "You seemed to be sure about your other plans before, and so far it's appeared as if you don't have a clue what you are doing."

"I know it will work because Hara will give herself to me to protect what I have," The Doc explained, giving Hersh a fake smile.

"What is it?" Perry asked, growing frustrated with The Doc's unnecessary suspense.

"My guards have gone to retrieve it," The Doc told him reassuringly. "They'll be back in a few minutes, so you can relax, Perry."

Perry scowled at him.

"If you're so sure that this will work, then why didn't you just use it in the beginning?" Agent Long demanded.

"Yeah," Renee agreed, her eyes angry. "Why wait so long and cause all this chaos?"

"This is a last resort," The Doc said. "I was only going to use this against her if nothing else worked."

"Why?" Finchly asked, and when Perry turned to look at her he saw the pain in her eyes. If The Doc had just caught Hara right away instead of fooling around then her partner would still be alive.

"It's a last resort because I knew that no one in this room will approve of what I'm about to bring in here," The Doc explained, and then he looked at the door. "Ah, here we are."

Everyone stared at him, wondering just what else he could do to top everything else he had done. They got a slight hint when they heard a strange noise that sounded peculiarly like a shrieking animal coming closer and closer to the room.

"What is that?" Odau asked, raising himself up in his seat to get a better view of the door.

491

The Doc smiled at him. "Ladies and gentlemen, say hello to Dreyson."

The odd shrieking was not from an animal as Perry first suspected. He gawked in horror as two guards came in dragging a young boy with them. The kid looked to be no older than three or four years old, with a thick layer of dark brown hair covering his head and bright green eyes lighting up his terrified face. His eyes looked strangely similar to Hara's, like Jack's had been to Perry's, but Perry knew that everyone in her family was dead. He was barely three feet tall, and the way the guards were dragging him it was surprising that he wasn't being lifted clean off his feet. He couldn't have been much more than forty pounds considering how thin he was. He was wearing a light blue hospital gown, and it looked like it hadn't been washed in months. There were several dark stains all over it, and the left leg of the pants was torn at the knee. The boy's face was also smeared with something that resembled a combination of dirt and vomit. But when Perry squinted he realized what it was. It was multiple bruises and large cuts that had scabbed over to form an unpleasant terracotta color. His eyes were tear-streaked and red, and Perry saw the pain in the toddler's eyes. Perry's heart melted at the sight of him. The boy would be an adorable child if not for the bruises and cuts and fearful expression. What had The Doc done to him?

"What...what? What the hell?" Perry sputtered.

Both guards gave the kid a shove, and he fell flat on his face directly at The Doc's feet. The boy's screams stopped when he hit the floor, and Perry heard a dull whimper come from him as he planted both tiny palms on the carpet to push himself up.

Sighing, The Doc gazed down at him for a moment before reaching down and grabbing him. He pulled the boy upright and right off the ground, setting him down on his feet. Keeping a firm grip on the boy, The Doc glared at him, and the boy began to scream again. "That's enough," he said in a deadly voice, and the boy shut his mouth immediately.

"What the hell is this?" Martinson demanded as everyone gaped at the little boy.

"Dreyson, say hello to all the feds," The Doc instructed, ignoring Martinson.

Little Dreyson just looked from one face to the other as tears streamed down his face and his lips began to tremble. His hands were covering his ears tightly as if afraid that there was going to be a loud sound that no one else knew about.

"Hey!" The Doc snapped. "I told you to say hello, Fortune Teller! Be polite!"

Dreyson whispered in a shaky, pathetic voice, "Hullo."

"What the hell is wrong with you?" Renee cried, jumping to her feet. "That's a little kid! What happened to his face?"

The Doc tilted Dreyson's head back so he could take a look. "Hmm," he muttered. "I don't know. To be completely honest with you, I don't really care either."

Renee's mouth fell open.

"Who is he?" Finchly's eyes were filling up at the sight of Dreyson's condition.

"He's one of them," The Doc answered.

"Does that really give you the excuse to treat a child like this?" Odau snapped. "Especially one this young!"

"He's extremely dangerous," The Doc growled back. "I'd like to see how you would deal with him."

"I'm sick of you and all your senseless excuses!" Renee shouted, walking around the table towards The Doc while glaring at him the whole time. "A three-year-old cannot be dangerous to the point where it is necessary to treat him like this! Now step away from him and give him to me!"

"Or what?" The Doc challenged, holding her gaze.

"Or I will kick you so hard that you'll be singing kindergarten songs for a week!" Renee hissed.

The Doc laughed. "Renee, Renee," he chuckled. "You really wouldn't want me to hurt you in front of your boyfriend, would you?"

With nothing left to say, Renee whipped her fist at him and knocked him one right in the jaw, causing him to stumble backwards and fall to the floor. His hand released Dreyson, but his fall caused Dreyson to lose his balance and fall backwards as well. But before he hit the floor, Renee scooped him up in her arms and cradled him like a baby, backing quickly away from The Doc as he began to climb back to his feet. Both guards drew out their weapons and aimed them at Renee, and in alarm Perry jumped up and whipped out his weapon as well.

"Whoa!" Agent Long, who hadn't said a word since the boy had been brought in, said. "Can everybody please calm down?"

As he gazed at Renee with a very angry, threatening glare, The Doc took a few menacing steps forward and raised his hand, gesturing with two fingers for her to come back to him.

Perry aimed his gun at The Doc to tell him to back off. The Doc stopped and gave him the same furious look he gave Renee, but he waved his hands at his guards and they lowered their weapons. Perry lowered his when Renee was back in her seat with Dreyson.

"Do the two of you want him?" The Doc asked Perry. "Well, you can keep him! Just so long as we catch Hara first."

Glaring back at him, Perry sat back down and turned towards Renee. She was still cradling Dreyson and he was gazing back up at her with his adorable toddler eyes, his expression a slight pout that was fading into a tired look of content. Renee's kindness seemed to be a surprise and a relief to the boy.

"He's so thin," Renee whispered to Perry. She held the little boy tightly in her arms and rocked him gently as he curled into a ball and nuzzled up against her. "It feels like he hasn't been fed in months!"

"Who is this boy?" Hersh demanded.

"Just a Colician I had lying around in my lab," The Doc replied, leftover anger still in his voice.

"Are these people just objects to you?" Agent Long asked him in a very quiet voice, one that Perry recognized as intense rage. "This boy is a living thing. A person."

"And how is this little boy going to cause the girl to give herself up?" Odau snapped.

"He's one of her kind," The Doc said. "one of the last. She'll do anything she can to protect the remaining members of her species. Especially a child."

"So what do we do?" Finchly asked. "How will she know that we have him and he's alive?"

"I have a way," The Doc assured. "When we arrive at our desired location I can tell the boy to call her, and when he does she'll come running."

"How exactly does he call her?" Perry asked curiously.

"With his mind," The Doc explained, tapping the side of his head. "All Colicians have a subconscious mental bond with each other, so if Dreyson cries out for Hara in his head, she will hear him, and she will come to us."

"What did you mean when you said our desired location?" Odau questioned. "Aren't we just going to stay here?"

"No," The Doc said. "You saw what happened the last time she came here. She doesn't care if she causes any damage or hurts anyone because we're in a secure area and no one is around because of the fires still burning. But if we go into a more populated area, she won't cause as much of a struggle. She won't want to make a scene."

"She's made quite the scene already!" Agent Long snapped. "She doesn't care if she makes one now!"

"She doesn't want the world to know about her and her kind just yet," The Doc told him. "She won't make as much of a fuss if there will be a crowd full of eyewitnesses."

"What if someone gets hurt, like Dreyson?" Renee demanded. "We can't risk going to a crowded area!"

The Doc stared back at her with a look of boredom. "No one will get hurt, except possibly me. And maybe Hara."

"How do you know this will work?" Perry asked.

"It will work," The Doc promised him.

"But how do you know for sure?"

Sighing, The Doc nodded to Dreyson. "I know because he told me."

"He's a child!" Renee snapped. "How would he know if she'll come or not?"

"Because Dreyson can see the future," The Doc told her matter-of-factly.

Renee's face turned bright red. "Oh," she muttered, lowering her eyes back to Dreyson, who had fallen asleep like a baby in her arms. The poor kid was exhausted.

"Did you have a specific place in mind where you wanted to wait for her?" Agent Long asked.

"Yes," The Doc answered, looking back to him. "St. Mary's Hospital downtown."

"What?" Perry said in surprise. That was a little too close for comfort because he was meeting John Reifert there later. But that was beside the point. "Do you know how many people are in that building right now?"

"That's exactly my point, Agent Perry," The Doc replied. "We'll be able to take her out quietly with so many people there. It may be crowded, but it will be less of a hassle for us."

"The hospital has double the usual number of patients due to the blast!" Perry protested. "We don't need to be getting in everyone's way!"

"If I am not mistaken, there would seem to be a section on the top few levels that is off limits due to construction," The Doc said, seeming quit certain about everything. "We can be close enough to the other people that she won't risk making too big of a scene, but we'll still have our privacy. Then your precious children and city will be safe, and I can go home."

Everyone at the table groaned and shifted in their chairs. What The Doc was saying made perfect sense. They could catch Hara with less trouble and then Perry could take down The Doc and get Hara to speak with Noah. It seemed to be the perfect setting, but Perry still didn't want to take the risk of getting already injured people caught in the middle of it all.

"I am not going to risk…" he started to argue.

"I think it's a great idea," Agent Long interrupted.

Everybody turned and stared at him. The Doc's eyes widened in surprise.

"I mean, think about it," Agent Long continued. "The Doc is right. Hara killed those kids for a reason. She has no desire to kill innocents. And the Colicians have remained a secret this whole time because they've wanted to stay a secret. She won't risk being exposed to any more people than she already has. She's going to be extra cautious with her abilities because of how many people there will be, giving us the extra advantage." He stared back evenly at Perry's confused gaze.

His eyes landing on The Doc, who was watching him with a look of triumph on his face, Perry sighed and shook his head in frustration. "Please don't make me regret this," he said.

"This had better work," Odau growled. "I just want this girl caught so my son can be safe. If she figures out he's in that hospital..."

"She knows," The Doc told him.

Odau's eyes widened with panic. "Then why hasn't she gone for him?"

"She's not through with me yet," The Doc muttered. "When she is, then she'll go for the boy."

"Well, if the two of you can promise me that she'll come to us first, then I'm with you," Odau told them.

Nodding, Agent Long looked back at The Doc, who was watching him suspiciously. "Well, we're all agreeing, so tell us what you want us to do," he said expectantly.

Staring at him for several more seconds, The Doc said to everyone, "Alright, we'd better get going before we lose too much time."

"I'll call Wesley to let him know we're coming," Odau volunteered, immediately jumping to his feet and making his way out.

Everyone else rose to their feet and began muttering to their neighbors. Perry grabbed his jacket and turned to Renee, who was gazing down at Dreyson once again. "How is he?" Perry asked her.

"I'm no doctor," Renee whispered, hugging Dreyson to her. "But he doesn't look or feel alright to me."

"I think we need an actual doctor to tell us what he thinks," Perry replied.

"Well, I'm a doctor and I can tell you he will be fine," The Doc said from behind them.

They both turned and saw that he was standing far too close behind them, eyeing them both with a look of disapproval. Everyone else, including The Doc's guards, had left by then, so it was just the three of them. Renee's eyes narrowed and she took a step back, gripping Dreyson even tighter in her arms. "And I'm supposed to take your word for it?" she snarled. "Because it hasn't been too reliable so far!"

The Doc's expression didn't change. He just kept staring her down with that nagging look of desire, like an animal planning to attack its prey. It wouldn't surprise Perry if he wanted to kill her at the moment, but that wasn't going to happen.

"Is there something you want?" Renee snapped, not at all intimidated by The Doc's close proximity. "If not, we would appreciate it if you would get out of our faces!"

Raising his eyebrows in an irritated manner, The Doc stretched out his arms. "May I have him back?"

"No, you may not!" Renee said angrily, taking another step back. "I'm never going to leave you alone with him ever again!"

"We need him to catch Hara," The Doc told her, the patience in his voice wearing thin.

"We're all going to the same place!" Renee reminded him. "He can ride with Shawn and me!" And with that said she hurried out the door, making sure to bump into him on the way.

Giving her a glance as she left, The Doc turned back to Perry and grinned. "You know, you really need to learn to control your woman," he said.

"I'm not the kind of guy who feels he needs to control his woman," Perry said flatly. "And just so we're clear on things, she's not my woman."

"She could get hurt with that mouth of hers, you know," The Doc muttered, his gaze following her.

"Are you threatening her?" Perry demanded angrily.

The Doc shot Perry a sideways glance. "Where I come from, people who mouth off to their superiors are often shot."

Wrinkling his nose in disgust, Perry took a step forward so they were eye to eye. "Well, we're not there, are we?" he said firmly. "Thank God. And you are definitely not superior to us." Just to prove his point, he gave The Doc the same shoulder bump that Renee had before he walked out the door as well, following the same path the others had taken to the lobby and then to the parking lot. When he left the building he saw that the two remaining officers and his FBI colleagues had all gone except for Renee, who was loading herself and Dreyson into the passenger side of his SUV. He was halfway from the entrance to his vehicle when he was stopped yet again by The Doc.

"I was dead serious when I told you to control her," he called, his expression serious but sly. "She should really learn to put a cap on it, or she may end up dying sooner than she's supposed to."

Perry stared after him as he turned and walked to his semi. He repeated the line over and over in his mind: *Or she may end up dying sooner than she's supposed to.* Did that mean Renee was meant to die soon? Was The Doc serious, or was he just screwing with Perry? He wanted to ask The Doc what he meant, but Renee shouted at him through his window, "Shawn, let's go!"

Horrified by the comment, Perry turned and walked absentmindedly to the driver's side and climbed in. After he started the car, he gripped the steering wheel in both hands and stared at the dash for a few moments, attempting to calm himself down. It only made him feel worse.

"Shawn, are you alright?" Renee asked, peering over at him. When he didn't reply, she placed a comforting hand on his tensed arm. "Shawn, what's the matter? What did he say to you?"

Slowly looking back up at her, Perry felt tears threatening to spill from his eyes.

✳ ✳ ✳

Dr. Bennett was not pleased when they arrived at the hospital. He yelled at Odau and then at Agent Long. He said it was careless and rude of them to put the patients and staff and risk with their operation and to just barge in and expect him to give them access to the unfinished section of the third floor, as Odau so politely requested. Finally, The Doc stepped in and for some reason Bennett immediately backed down, looking utterly terrified of him. This struck Perry as odd, considering there was no way Bennett could possibly know anything about The Doc.

The Doc noticed the odd behavior as well, and when they were all heading up to the third floor he asked Perry so no one else could hear, "Did you tell him who I am?"

"Of course not!" Perry replied, wondering what bothered Bennett so much that he would give in so suddenly.

They gathered in a room that was still under construction. The room was almost finished, except for the paint job. Bennett had lent them a spare gurney and full set of body restraints for when Hara was caught. He wasn't happy about what they were using the equipment for (but then again he wasn't happy about anything they were doing). There was no other furniture or equipment in the room, which was rather convenient. They could set up the gurney in the center of the room and nothing else would get in their way when Hara finally arrived. The plan was to have Dreyson "call" Hara and then keep him on the gurney for Hara to find. Everyone else would be hiding until she found the bait, at which time they would come out and The Doc would confront her. He instructed the others to draw their weapons on her but not to shoot no matter what happened. "We can't risk shooting each other," he explained when he saw Odau's frustrated face.

"Could you make sure that nobody comes in here?" Odau requested of Bennett when the doctor started to exit the room. "No matter what they hear, we can't have someone walk in here by mistake."

"What's going on?" Renee asked, stepping back in the room with Dreyson in her arms again, resting on her hip. Dreyson had awakened from his nap when they arrived and said he was hungry, so The Doc allowed her to take him to the cafeteria to get something to eat. Now they were back, and Dreyson was sucking on a juice box. For the first time since Perry saw him, the boy was smiling, and he was looking at

Renee with a loving gaze, as if he were looking at his own mother. It wasn't all that surprising. The boy probably didn't have a mother anymore.

Bennett turned towards her when he heard her voice. But when his eyes landed on little Dreyson, they widened in shock and his mouth fell open.

"Is something wrong?" The Doc asked carefully, eyeing Bennett suspiciously.

Gaping at Dreyson like he was an alien, Bennett stuttered, "I...I need to go." As quickly as he could, he rushed out of the room, leaving the others staring after him in confusion.

"Hey, Doc, are we going to get started any time soon?" Agent Long demanded.

"Yes, we should get started right away," The Doc replied.

Perry walked over to Renee, who sat Dreyson down on the edge of the gurney and examined the bruises on his face.

"How's he doing?" Perry asked her, smiling down at Dreyson when the toddler gave him a shy grin.

"He's a lot better now that he's eaten something," Renee said, running a hand through the boy's thick hair. He gave her a toothy grin like he had given Perry and she smiled back at him. Taking Perry aside, she told him seriously, "I never knew that a three-year-old could eat so much in one sitting!"

"I'm not surprised," Perry replied, looking down at Dreyson who was gazing out the window and sipping his juice box. "You've seen how skinny he is! He looks like he hasn't had a decent meal in months!"

"Well, when this is over I'm going to make sure that changes!" Renee declared, stepping back to Dreyson and rubbing his back tenderly. Her maternal instincts were taking over. "If we can't find who his real mother or father is, then I want to adopt him," she said, confirming Perry's thought.

"You're prepared to take in a child with special needs like this?" Perry asked her. "This little boy can see the future. You're ready to live with him telling you exactly what path your life is going to take?"

"Why not?" she whispered, smiling as Dreyson let out a big yawn. "Nobody else knows about these people, so we couldn't let just anyone adopt him. Besides, I've always wanted a kid. It doesn't matter to me if he can tell the future or not."

"Really?" Perry said in surprise. "I didn't know you wanted kids."

"I never mentioned it to anyone before because I never thought that I would meet the right person," Renee explained, glancing up at him. Her eyes appeared mystified, content. "But that was a long time ago. Now..."

"What?" Perry asked, eager to hear her next words. "What about now?"

Swallowing hard, Renee asked him, "Do you believe in soul mates, Shawn?"

"Soul mates?" Perry repeated. "Sure. Why do you ask?"

"Sometimes you meet a person and you know they're the one for you," Renee whispered, gazing back at him.

"You think you found yours?" Perry asked, his heart beating in excitement.

Her face fell. "Don't you feel it too?" Dismay filled her voice, but she didn't realize just how much Perry felt it.

Taking a step closer to her, he murmured, "When this is all over..."

"I want you to be there with me," Renee told him, staring deeply into his eyes.

"I'll always be there with you," Perry whispered to her. "If you really want to take in Dreyson, then I'll still be there with you."

"No matter what trouble he'll be?" Renee asked hopefully.

"You're worth any kind of trouble," Perry promised her. Like he had in the SUV early in the morning, he suddenly became aware of everything about her. Her shining blonde hair, the never ending ocean of her beautiful blue eyes. He could see every detail of her face, every flaw. But in the end, he saw no flaws. He only saw her, and she was perfect. Was this how soul mates were supposed to feel about each other? Such a powerful love that he only saw the beauty in her? That was really all he needed to see. He didn't need the love to see the beauty in her; it had always been there right in front of his face. The beauty of any person was always out there for everyone to see; some people just didn't know how to look.

The urge to kiss her was overpowering, and he found himself actually leaning towards her. She seemed willing to return the kiss, but before their lips met she looked over his shoulder and her eyes widened. Stepping away from him, she scooped Dreyson off the gurney and held him close to her, moving back to the wall.

Turning to see what had spooked her, Perry saw that The Doc was standing directly behind him. He was holding something questionable in his right hand; it was metal and looked like a helmet of some sort with buttons on the side. Whatever it was it couldn't be good, because when Dreyson saw it his face filled up with fear and he clung tightly to Renee.

"Don't come near him!" she warned.

"I just need to activate him," The Doc said impatiently.

"Perry," Agent Long said, his expression telling him to stay out of the way.

Looking from Renee's angry face to The Doc's waiting one, Perry stepped back, giving The Doc a clear path to Renee. Renee was going to be very angry with him for this, but he needed The Doc to think that he was in control.

"Shawn, what are you doing?" she demanded, squeezing Dreyson tighter as The Doc walked past Perry and set the object down on the gurney.

"Agent Michaels, give him the boy," Agent Long ordered.

"No!" she started to fight, glaring at The Doc.

"Renee," Perry said, making his eyes plead with hers.

Her face falling when she realized that he wasn't going to back her up, Renee allowed The Doc to take Dreyson out of her arms. She gazed back at Perry with heartbreak in her eyes, making him feel even worse. But there was nothing he could do. Dreyson was the only thing left that could get them to Hara, and Renee needed to understand that.

When The Doc took Dreyson, the toddler screamed and tried to cling to Renee, but his frail limbs couldn't hold on. He kept screaming and crying and kicking as The Doc held him down on the gurney. He attempted to hop off, but The Doc then pushed him down flat and picked up the helmet. Dreyson screamed again and clamped his hands over his ears like he did before.

"Hold still," The Doc muttered at him as he began to squirm. Placing the helmet on top of Dreyson's head, he pushed three of the buttons and they all lit up with a bright red light. Immediately, Dreyson's body went limp. Both his arms dropped to his side and every muscle in his body relaxed. A surprised expression hung on his face for a few seconds, but then the muscles in his face began to slacken as well. He heaved a big sigh for such a small child, and his eyelids drooped.

"What did you do?" Renee demanded, starting to rush to Dreyson. Perry caught her by the arm and she struggled to break free, but gave up quickly. "What the hell did you do?" she cried.

"The Colicians all have a mental connection to each other," The Doc told her, stepping away from the gurney. "It allows them to know when another one of their kind is near them. It took me a long time to understand, but I finally found a way to suppress the bond. Before I put the helmet on him, his bond with the others was broken. When I turned the helmet on, the bond was brought back. Now Hara will be able to hear him and she will come."

"You cut him off from the rest of his people?" Renee whispered in disgust. "That's sick!"

"Yes, and apparently everything else I do is too," The Doc said, not even bothering to look at her. "Now, we need to act quickly. She'll be coming very soon once she discovers where he is, and we need to be fully prepared when she does. FBI agents will stay in the bathroom. Officers will be with me in the next room. Agent Perry, a word, please." He gestured for Perry to step aside with him.

Following him to the doorway, Perry saw the look of disgust on Finchly's face. She obviously didn't like the idea of working up close with The Doc.

"I need to ask a favor of you, friend," The Doc said to him, dropping his voice so none of the others could overhear them.

"Oh, boy," Perry replied sarcastically.

"There's no need for that tone, now," The Doc scolded.

"How about you do me a favor first," Perry suggested. "Don't ever call me 'friend' again."

Smirking, The Doc told him, "If we just leave Dreyson lying out in the open like that, there's nothing to stop Hara from just running in here, grabbing him, and teleporting out before we have time to react. We need a roadblock."

"What are you suggesting?"

"We need someone to stand by the boy, just out of sight until she enters. Then, the person can step out in front of him and block her way."

"Let Renee do it," Perry volunteered for her. "She'd be more than willing to stand guard for Dreyson. I mean, look at her!" He nodded at Renee, who was standing by Dreyson's side and brushing back his hair like she did before.

"Yes, I've seen how attached she's become to the boy," The Doc assured him, not turning to look. "But Agent Michaels does not matter at all to Hara. We need someone she wouldn't dare risk fighting for fear of what would happen if he were killed." He nodded to him. "Someone like you."

"Oh, great," Perry muttered. "What do you want me to do?"

"The builders have already installed a curtain where the bed will eventually be situated," The Doc explained, pointing to the large white curtain that hung from a semi-circular rod and stretched all the way to the floor. "Our girl is going to enter through this doorway in which we're standing, and she will not be able to see you if you hide behind that curtain. Just stay there until she arrives, and when she starts to go for the boy, simply step out and stand between the two of them. Hara won't risk hurting you."

"Is Dreyson related to Hara?" Perry asked him abruptly.

"I'm sorry?" The Doc said, blinking in surprise.

"I don't think Hara would put her life on the line for just anybody, even if he is a Colician," Perry told him. "I thought about it on the way here, and I think that Dreyson is family to Hara, or she at least knows him in some way. So, what is he? Her brother? Cousin? Nephew? Or is he just the son of a family friend?"

The Doc sighed and smirked at him. "You think you know everything, don't you? Well, what I can tell you is that it doesn't matter what the boy is to her. All that matters is that he will bring her to us. What more could you possibly want?"

Perry opened his mouth to object angrily, but The Doc interrupted. "I have to go somewhere for a few minutes, but I'll be back shortly," he said. "Just stay here until I get back and don't do anything stupid."

"Wait, where are you going?" Perry demanded as The Doc started to leave.

"I'll be back shortly after she gets here."

"What the hell am I supposed to do when she gets here?"

"Keep her talking," The Doc replied, shrugging nonchalantly. "She won't leave without the boy, so if you just stay in her way until I return, everything will go well."

Staring at him in disbelief, Perry asked him, "Why do I have a feeling that this is going to end badly?"

Grinning at him reassuringly, The Doc patted his arm. "Because you're paranoid." He turned to leave again.

"Why would you decide to leave us the second we set the bait for Hara? I thought you really wanted to catch her!"

"We will. You are the only one with permission to use a gun on her. Shoot her if you have to, but she is not leaving this hospital unless it's in my semi." He turned and left Perry, leaving him to wonder what had interested The Doc so much that he would leave when they were so close to catching Hara.

✳ ✳ ✳

When Allan Brown finally awoke from his slumber, it took him several long moments to fully grasp the memories that Hara had inserted into his mind. His brain was still healing from overusing his ability, and Dr. Bennett told Hara it would still be another day or so until he would be able to function properly again. To Hara's dismay, it seemed as though her friend wouldn't be able to understand that Daniel Marcus was dead. But as the heaviness of sleep started to leave him, the memories snapped into place and he understood. His reaction was stronger than she anticipated. Hara heard the gears clicking together as he realized what had happened. He started to scream. He screamed and screamed and couldn't stop.

Hara felt that Allan was in pain. Not only because of the forced memories of Daniel's dead body, but because his brain was not prepared for him to be conscious just yet. She desperately tried to calm him as he screamed and thrashed, but her own emotions were too powerful for her to overcome. Dr. Bennett was forced to sedate him for fear that he might hurt himself. The sight of her friend lying helpless on the bed once more sent her into tears.

"He's going to be alright," Bennett promised her, rubbing her shoulder soothingly. "Please don't cry. He'll be back to normal once the antidote fully heals him."

She was grateful for Bennett's company in that moment. A part of her still didn't want to trust him, even though he had proven himself trustworthy in several different ways. He was a good man. He understood her in a way that not many others could, and he could comfort her in a way that she barely understood. He was very smart and he didn't lie to her, no matter how terrible the truth was. So when he said that Allan would be okay, Hara knew he was telling the truth.

Dr. Bennett had been gone for a long time. After he was sure that Allan was asleep and would stay that way, he left them so he could go tend to other patients. "I really wish I could stay with you, but I've been absent from my work long enough and there are many others who need me right now," he apologized. Hara told him she didn't mind even though she did. She really did not want to be alone.

She couldn't stand the silence. It was too much for her, brought back too many horrible memories. For the first ten minutes or so she paced around the room, but then she became light headed. Bennett said that if she did she should insert the IV in her arm again, and she hesitantly did, her heart pounding the whole time. The bag of solution was still hanging above her bed, so she sat back down and hugged her knees to her chest, rocking back and forth while her heart continued to pound faster and faster. Eventually, she lay down flat and stared wide-eyed up at the ceiling, her breathing fast and shaky. As the minutes ticked past slower and slower, she began to hear the voices.

They began as whispers, so soft that she thought it was just her mind playing tricks on her. But they soon grew to low murmurs, and she knew she wasn't imagining things. At first, she assumed that she accidentally tuned into the thoughts of random people in the building, but then she started to recognize some of the voices. She was crazy, that was why she was hearing them. The voices she was hearing couldn't be real, because every voice she was hearing belonged to someone in her family who was dead.

They started out as inaudible, jumbled words tangled with the sounds of screaming and crying, but as time moved on the voices began to form words that she could actually understand, and she let out a sob when she realized what they were accusing her of.

"This is all your fault!" a woman's voice hissed at her in the loud silence. "If you had just been a normal child with a normal ability, then The Doc wouldn't have killed me! You did this to me!"

"I'm sorry, Mom!" Hara whispered, hurt by her mother's harsh words.

"It's too late for you to apologize now!" her brother Flint snapped somewhere inside her head, his voice that had never been firm now so cruel. "I died trying to protect our dad, and then you went and got him killed anyway! I died for nothing because of you!"

"I tried to turn myself in!" Hara squeaked, wrapping her arms around herself as a shiver swept up and down her whole body. "I didn't want anyone else to die, but The Doc wouldn't take me! He would let me turn myself in..."

"That's no excuse!" her father growled in her ear. "You should have fought him harder, made him take you! I tried to protect our people but was murdered by him before I could do much of anything! It was all because of you..."

"The war would have started with or without me!" Hara said, trying to defend herself. "He just chose to target our family..."

"Because of you!" he snarled. "Damn you, I wish you were never born!"

"Dad!" Hara cried, tears streaming down her face from the horrible comment. To have her own father who had loved her tell her that he wished she had never been born...it was heartbreaking.

"He's right," Hara's second older brother Malcolm said. "I never really considered you a part of my family, yet I still died for you! If you had never existed, then our family would still be alive!"

Hara and her brother Malcolm had never gotten along, but it hurt her when he said that. "It's not my fault..." she tried to deny, even though she knew it was.

"Of course it is!" her older sister Katherine accused. "You got us all killed because of your stupid ability! Even when you were little, everyone was fascinated by you. Everything was always about you! Now look what your notoriety has gained us!"

Whimpering, Hara rolled onto her right side and hugged her knees to her chest again. Her older sister had been one of her best friends. She had never blamed Hara for the war when she was alive, so why would she when she was dead? "I'm sorry..." she whispered. "I'm sorry..."

"Stop apologizing!" Kyle, her younger brother ordered. "It's not going to change anything! We're still all going to hate you!"

"No!" she sobbed, more tears rolling down her face. "Don't hate me! Please! I'm trying to fix everything! I'm going to kill Jackson Odau before he can grow up!"

"That won't change anything, stupid!" her little sister Alice cried in disgust. "The future is still going to happen, with or without Odau! Your feeble efforts are stupid and pointless!"

Sobbing again, Hara buried her face into her hands. "I'm trying to help our future and you!" she screamed, angry at their accusations. "Why are you tearing me down when you know my intentions are only for the greater good of our world?"

"Why did you leave us in the house?"

Gasping in surprise, Hara's eyes went wide and she looked out in front of her. This voice wasn't coming from her head, it was coming from the bed next to her. "No...no! What are you doing here?" she stuttered in horror, staring over at her three dead daughters sitting on the bed.

"Why didn't you take us with you?" Grace demanded, glaring at her as she cradled Baby Lizzie. Her blonde hair was in tangled mats on her head, the tips of it burned black. Her white shirt and shorts had holes burned into them and Hara could see her blackened skin through them. Her blue eyes shown like sapphires in the middle of a crisp, molten face. Lizzie's face was hidden in Grace's chest, but Hara knew she was burned as well. Her blanket was completely black and the back of her head had burns similar to the ones on Grace. She started crying in Grace's arms, and Hara started shaking as she forced herself to keep her sobs in. What kind of cruel torture was this?

"I didn't take you with me because I wanted you to be safe," she told Grace softly, wishing her child would understand. It was killing her to listen to her daughter accusing her of not doing enough to save her life. There was nothing Hara could have done to stop the explosion that killed her three daughters.

"The house wasn't safe!"

Her second daughter, Katie, appeared beside Grace, scowling at her along with her sister. It was shocking to hear her speak, for Hara had barely heard Katie speak two words her whole short life (Katie's telepathic capabilities were so strong that she rarely had a desire to speak, so she was—for the most part—mute). The poor girl also had terrible burns covering her body, barely any of her light brown hair left on her head. "You left us in the house and as soon as you left that bad man blew it up!" she shouted angrily. "The house wasn't safe! You left us in there to die, so you could focus on keeping yourself safe!"

"I would never do that to you, I swear!" Hara promised, her emotion audible in her words. "If I had known it was safer outside, I would have taken you with me!"

"But you didn't!"

"I didn't know what was going to happen! I love you all! I would never have done anything to purposely put you in danger!"

"Why did you let go of my hand?"

Hara snapped her head further to her left as her first son Colin appeared, sitting on the floor with his legs crossed. His face was mud streaked and there was a great big bullet hole in his chest, blood staining his shirt all around the wound.

"You bit and scratched me!" Hara reminded him, not willing to let him blame her for his death, which was clearly his own fault. "I held onto you to keep you with me, but you hurt me and purposely ran out in the open to help your father! That was your own fault!"

"No!" Colin yelled. "You should have held onto me! You didn't do your job as a mother!"

"How dare you!" Hara screamed at him. "This was..."

"He's right, honey."

"No!" Hara cried in terror, turning to look up at her soul mate, Bo, who was standing over her and gazing down softly at her. "Leave me alone!"

"I wasn't there to protect our children and you failed to do so every time," he told her, his brown eyes gentle as he reached down and brushed a strand of hair out of her face. She shivered from the touch she shouldn't have felt, and Bo placed a comforting hand on her shoulder. "They were your responsibility and you couldn't even keep them alive."

"I tried," she whispered, wishing they would all just leave.

She heard Bo sigh above her as she buried her face in her sheets. "It wasn't enough," he told her quietly, stroking her hair the way he always used to.

Unable to take the pain anymore, she let out a terrible, inhuman cry. "Stop it!" she shouted. "You're all dead! I'm sorry I couldn't save any of you, but I'm going to fix it! Stop blaming everything on me!"

Bo sighed again. "You really need to end this right now," he told her.

"I am!" she replied breathlessly, pushing herself up on her hands and looking at him with her red, tired eyes. "I told you! I'm going to fix it!"

"That's not what I mean," Bo said, kneeling down in front of her and putting his face very close to hers. Everything about him was so real. His dark brown eyes, wavy black hair, bronze colored skin...it all looked so real, so exact. But what made her hallucination seem even more real were the smells and feelings; his sweet smelling breath on her face and his special scent that she could never fully describe. He stared into her eyes and reached up to brush her hair out of her face again, but she pulled away from his hand that time. Giving her a reassuring smile, he placed his hand on the side of her face, his touch once again sending a shiver up her spine. "You need to stop causing so much damage and chaos to both our worlds. You should not be in either world anymore."

"What are you saying?" Hara whimpered in dismay. She knew what he was going to say.

"Shh," he shushed, stroking her hair again. "Everyone you've ever loved is dead. Why don't you just come join us?"

"You're asking me to kill myself?" Hara demanded in horror.

"Shh," he said again, firmer that time. "Why not? What is left in the world to keep living for?"

"M-many things!" Hara stammered.

Bo just snickered, and it sounded cruel. "Come on, babe. Nothing in the living world can be any better than your whole family waiting for you in the deceased world. Come be with us. Come be with me."

"I can't!" she whispered urgently. "I need to finish what I came here for!"

"Finish it by killing yourself!" Bo snarled harshly. "The rest of our world will come to an end and no one will ever know about it! You know you want to do it! Just end the pathetic excuse you've been calling a life and let yourself fall away. It will be so much easier..."

"No!" Hara yelled, curling herself up in a ball again. "I won't! You're dead, but I'm not, and I'm going to change everything! So go away and leave me alone! All of you! Just go away!"

"Hara."

Startled, she blinked up at Daniel Marcus, who was gazing down at her with the soft expression he always had. He looked exactly as he had before he was murdered, except that his eyes appeared concerned, urgent.

"Stop arguing with yourself," he told her gently, gesturing with his hand around him. "Nobody's here. Nobody was ever here."

"What..." she whispered, looking around but seeing nothing. "But...they were here..."

"No," Daniel corrected. "It was all in your mind. This war was not your fault, so stop trying to convince yourself of that."

"They all just told me it was my fault..." she began, another sob escaping her throat.

"No one was here," he whispered, pushing her back onto the bed as she started to sit up. "You just want to believe that this was your fault, so you created it all in your head to make you feel even more guilty. But you need to stop it now. Don't listen to them. They're dead. They can't blame you for anything."

"You're dead too," Hara reminded him. "Why should I listen to you?"

"Because I'm really here," he explained softly. "I only died a few hours ago; my mind is still wandering. And you need to listen to me now, okay?"

"Uh...okay," she said hesitantly, not knowing what else to say.

"You need to wake up," he told her, staring deep into her eyes. "Your son is still alive, and you need to wake up so you can save him. Wake up now, sweetheart."

"What are you talking about?"

"Wake up," Daniel repeated firmly. "Now."

A terrible scream erupted inside her head, causing her to sit up straight and start screaming as well. The scream only lasted in her head for about three seconds before dying away to a weak whimper, and she sat shaking and gasping for breath on the bed. Looking around frantically, she saw that nobody was with her but Allan.

The scream had sounded strangely familiar, but it was just part of her hallucination like Daniel said. She was beginning to calm down; her breathing and heart rate were slowing, and she rubbed the sleep from her eyes. She was glad her conversations weren't real, yet they still left her deeply saddened from everything that was said. There was one person in her family who she hadn't heard or seen, and she was disappointed that he didn't show up. "Your son is still alive," he said. She hadn't spoken to Dreyson, so was he somehow alive and Daniel knew? He couldn't be; she had felt him die. There was just no way he could still be living. She felt his soul leave her and the rest of the world, and he was gone forever, just like the rest of her family.

Another scream erupted inside her head, and she cried out in pain and clamped her hands over her ears. It was so familiar! She knew whose mind the scream belonged to, but it was impossible! Dreyson was dead!

MOM! he yelled to her in terror, starting to scream again. MOMMY, GET HIM AWAY!

Screaming in fear, confusion, and horror, Hara jumped to her feet and ran for the door. The IV in her arm held her back for an instant, but without thinking she ripped it out and took off out of the room. She took a left as soon as she was out the door and ran to the closest stairwell, shrieking, "Dreyson!" the whole way. Her son was alive, and she felt that he was in the building. She was going to find him and kill anyone who got in her way.

Something she didn't take into consideration while she rushed to the aid of her child was that she was being set up, and that the whole thing was a trap. She had also left Allan completely alone and defenseless. She was so preoccupied with thoughts of her son that she didn't even notice The Doc standing just to the right of the door, waiting for her to leave so he could get Allan alone.

Watching her bolt out the door and down the stairs towards her fate, The Doc shook his head at the girl's foolishness. How easy it was for him to corner her; her emotions always got the better of her and therefore constantly gave him the advantage. When her screams finally turned to silence and he was sure she was gone, he stepped forward and pulled the door open just enough for him to slip inside. Looking around quickly to make sure no one besides Allan Brown was in there, he landed his gaze upon Allan, who was sleeping soundly. Smiling as he realized just how easy it was going to be, he let the door swing closed behind him.

✳ ✳ ✳

He felt different. He always did after going through a treatment. But this time he felt strange, as if a part of him that wasn't there before had suddenly appeared. Then he remembered the memories Hara had forced upon him, and it took all of his self-restraint to keep himself from screaming again at the image of Daniel's dead body. His life was going downhill so fast since Hara had come back. Part of him wished she had never come back, and then they could have continued living their simple little lives they had built, never again having to worry about their past. Until the major outbreak in ten years, of course. But he knew that hiding like a coward in the human world would not have lasted for very long. Somebody would have noticed, and he should have foreseen that Hara would eventually come back for them. After all, she was the one who originally sent them here.

Allan blinked his eyes open and gazed up at the ceiling. An odd tugging at his right arm had awakened him, and when he tried to move his arm he found it was being restrained. Confused, he started to call for Dr. Bennett to figure out what was wrong with him, but then he realized that there was something soft and odd tasting in his mouth, completely gagging him. What was going on?

Something was really wrong, and Allan knew that immediately. Nothing felt right to him, and as his heart started to beat faster and faster he rolled his head to his right to see if he could see anything that would explain his situation. At first, he feared that his overuse had paralyzed him slightly, but as his eyes landed on a certain someone standing beside his bed, he soon understood that wasn't the case. The Doc had found him.

His cold gray eyes left Allan frozen for a few moments, the shock of seeing him paralyzing his body. But then the panic took over, and he started to scream. He was immediately muffled by the cloth that had been shoved into his mouth, so he tried to jump from the table but remembered he couldn't move. Glancing down quickly told him that The Doc had strapped him down with a full set of body restraints. He bucked and struggled against the straps and tried to yell for help again. It was evident in The Doc's merciless eyes that his time had come. There was no way Allan could get away, and there was no way anyone could come to his aid. He was going to die.

The Doc was loading a large syringe with a thick brown substance from a vile, and Allan understood all too well what it was. The Doc was going to inject that substance into the IV of the solution used to heal him and use it to kill him. Allan had seen The Doc use the drug on many people in the Lab, and he knew that once injected it was fatal. There was no cure. It would stop his heart and there was nothing he could do to keep it from happening.

"Are you afraid?" The Doc asked him, gazing down in curiosity.

Allan didn't answer. He couldn't, but what did The Doc expect him to say?

"You don't need to be afraid," The Doc told him quietly as Allan continued to struggle against the restraints holding him down. "Your friend Daniel wasn't."

Letting out a defeated sob, Allan gave up against the straps and laid there helplessly, gazing up at him with wide, terrified eyes. It wasn't a surprise that Daniel hadn't been afraid; he was always the brave one.

"You really shouldn't have run," The Doc said flatly, looking down at him in disapproval. "Things may have actually ended up better for you." He injected the drug into the IV.

Allan stared in horror as the thick brown liquid mixed in with the treatment and started slowly moving towards his arm. He knew that once it was inside his body there would be no hope for him. In his fear, he tried to call out for Hara with hope that she would hear, but his head began to throb with the effort. His mind was still weak. The Doc had chosen the perfect time to get him, when he was semi-conscious and when his mind was too damaged to fight back.

"Say hi to your family for me," The Doc sneered, smirking at his terrified expression.

If Allan had been able to speak, he would have had a few choice words for him in that last moment. Glaring up at the monster who had murdered everyone he ever cared about, he waited for the pain he was certain would come.

What happened next surprised both of them. A loud, angry cry sounded from behind The Doc, and then someone pounced on his back and wrapped their arm around his neck in a headlock. The Doc's eyes widened in shock and he stumbled backwards, clawing at the arm around his throat. Whoever was attacking him was still screaming in fury, and as The Doc swung around in an attempt to throw the person off, Allan saw a flash of long brown hair and a thin, feminine body. His first thought was that Hara had come to his aid, but when the woman threw The Doc to the floor and spun around, he realized that his life had been saved by a miracle. Meg Hopper had shown up exactly when Allan needed her most, and it didn't look like she was going to give up the fight until she won.

A ferocious, terrifying expression on her face, Meg threw The Doc to the ground and he went down hard. Breathing heavily, she rushed over to Allan's side and ripped the IV out of his arm moments before the drug entered his bloodstream. "Allan," she whispered, pulling the cloth out of his mouth. As she began to undo the straps holding him down, she told him. "I felt something was wrong. I saw one of his guards watching me in the parking lot and I knew something wasn't right. I'm so sorry I didn't get here sooner…"

"Meg, look out!" Allan cried as his right arm was freed.

The Doc had recovered from his fall and attacked Meg from behind. Only this time, he was armed. Clamping a hand over her mouth to keep her from screaming any more, he jabbed the same syringe deep into her chest. It was reloaded, and he injected the entire dose straight into her heart.

"No!" Allan screamed as Meg's eyes widened and she let out a muffled yelp. Quickly unfastening the strap on his left arm, he started to work at the ones over his ankles.

Meg's eyes fluttered closed and The Doc let her body fall to the floor. Glowering at Allan as he attempted to free himself, The Doc started to come toward him again. "How many more of you do I have to kill before you will finally just die?" he demanded angrily.

A loud thump echoed through the room, and The Doc's stunned face froze for a moment before he too dropped like a stone. Confused, Allan peered up at Dr. Bennett, who stood panting over The Doc's now unconscious form, in his hand a brass doorknob left in a pile of construction materials. Dropping it, he went to Allan. "I'm so sorry," he stammered, helping Allan with the final straps. "I tried to get back to you as soon as I realized that he was here, but they wouldn't let me get away. And then people kept pulling me aside…"

"I think that's the least of our concerns right now," Allan said shakily, tears streaming down his face as he hopped down from the bed. His knees buckled and he collapsed to the floor beside Meg. "Meg," he whispered, placing a hand on her shoulder.

She was gasping for breath, her eyes barely open. Her chest was heaving up and down and Allan could tell that she was struggling to stay alive. Her heart was failing, and there was nothing anyone could do.

"You shouldn't have done that!" Allan told her as his tears started to spill out onto her face. "You should have just let him kill me!"

"Allan…" Meg choked out, her body jerking as she fought to stay conscious.

"Don't talk," he instructed, wishing he could do something to help her through it. He knew she was in a lot of pain, and it broke his heart to know that she did it to save him.

"Daniel…" she breathed, her eyes focusing on something above his head.

"What?" Allan asked in bewilderment. "Meg, you're hallucinating…"

"He wants you to help me," she whispered, focusing back on his face. "He says you can help me…" Her eyes fluttered closed again.

"No, no, no!" Allan cried, gripping her shoulder as a sob escaped his throat.

"Allan," Bennett said, kneeling beside him and taking hold of his arm. When Allan didn't respond to him, he shook him hard. "Allan, I think I can help her."

"No one can help her!" Allan sobbed. "There's no antidote for that drug! It's fatal! There's nothing that can reverse what has already been done!" Allan suddenly realized the irony in his own words. There really was no way to reverse anything that had already happened.

"There is one thing," Bennett corrected, pulling Allan away from his dying friend and positioning himself in front of her.

"What are you talking about?" Allan demanded, wiping away the tears from his clouded eyes. He watched as Bennett pulled a smaller syringe out of his coat pocket and held it out for him to see. Allan's mouth dropped open when he realized what the crimson red liquid inside was. "Is that…?"

"Hara's blood," Bennett finished, his expression determined.

"You have to inject it directly into her heart," Allan instructed, moving aside so Bennett could do his job of saving lives. "Otherwise she won't have a chance."

Pulling Meg's shirt halfway down her breast, Bennett stabbed the needle straight down into her heart. "Let's hope to God that this works," he muttered as he injected the blood into Meg.

"How the hell did you manage to get Hara's blood?" Allan asked, staring down at Meg as she gasped for her final few breaths.

"She gave it to me," Bennett replied.

Allan looked at him skeptically. "I don't know how you did it, but you must have really proved yourself trustworthy for her to do something like that for you."

Bennett shrugged. "I was a bit surprised myself."

They both jumped as Meg sat up abruptly and began coughing and wheezing heavily. Her hand shot out and she grabbed Allan's arm.

"Meg, are you alright?" Allan demanded, holding her weak body as her breathing returned to normal. "Just…just try to relax."

"Allan," she blurted, blinking up in a daze at him.

"Shh," he told her, forcing a smile to his face. "You're going to be fine. You should go to sleep now."

Nodding in agreement, Meg sighed deeply and rested her head against his arm. She closed her weary eyes, and just before she lost consciousness she mumbled, "Allan, we need to go to the church. We have to turn on the machine."

Allan's heart skipped a beat at what she said. Only three people in the entire world knew about the church and the machine, and not a word had been spoken of it for more than two years. Now that it had finally been brought up, Allan realized she was right. It was time they turned on the machine.

"Allan?" Bennett asked in confusion, looking from him to Meg. "What was she talking about? Which church? What machine?"

"I need to go now," Allan told him quietly, carefully rising to his feet with Meg in his arms.

"You're in no condition to leave just yet," Bennett protested disapprovingly, blocking his path to the door. "And neither is she."

"Well, staying here won't make my odds any better," Allan replied and nodded to The Doc, who was beginning to stir.

Bennett glanced down at The Doc's unconscious body and wrinkled his nose in disgust. "We'll kill him, and then your war will end for good."

"No," Allan said firmly, glaring at him. "This is not how this is going to end. I am not allowing anyone else to resort to murder. You should know better than that! I didn't pull you into this war to become a murderer!"

"You didn't pull me into this war," Bennett reminded. "Why don't you want him dead? He killed your family."

"Yes, he killed my family!" Allan snapped back. "And that's precisely the reason why I'm not going to kill him! It would just prove that I'm as bad as he is! No, when this war is over, I'm taking him back with me and he's going to pay for everything that he's put us through. Now come on, help me!" His knees buckled again from the extra weight.

"You're never going to make it out like this!" Bennett told him urgently, shooting The Doc a nervous glance.

He was right. Allan was too weak to carry himself and Meg out of there fast enough. But there was something they could do to fix that. "Give me an adrenaline shot," Allan ordered, propping himself up on his knees again.

"What?" Bennett said.

"If you pump me full of adrenaline then I'll be strong enough to get us out of here," Allan explained. "You need to give me a large dose of it, considering my tolerance is significantly higher than yours. Now hurry! We have to be long gone before he wakes up."

Bennett did what Allan said, giving him so much adrenaline that Allan began to shake and his ears started to buzz. He helped him up and they were halfway to the stairs before he stopped them again.

"He came here for Hara, you know," Bennett said quietly. "He's already lured her into his trap. Once he has her..." His voice trailed off. He didn't need to say any more.

"You have to help her," Allan told him urgently. "She can't go through another round with The Doc. Whatever she went after, it can't be important enough to take that risk."

"It's her son," Bennett replied in concern. "Dreyson. He's alive. I've seen him. That's what she went after."

Allan felt like his heart had stopped. So Dreyson really was alive after all. He knew he should be happy for Hara, but he also knew that there would be no possible way for Bennett to convince her not to walk into the trap. It was her child, and she would allow no more harm to come to him. "If she gets caught, you need to help her escape," he said firmly. "The Doc never saw you, and no one knows you're on our side. You'll be able to break her out of there without anybody realizing what you're doing. But this is the final straw for you. Once this is over, they're going to realize what side you're really on. Then, you will truly be a part of this war."

"How am I supposed to help her escape?" Bennett asked.

"I don't care how you do it, just don't kill anyone," Allan replied, continuing on his way to the stairs. "We really need to leave now. He's going to be waking up any moment now."

"Allan," Bennett called. "Please be careful."

Nodding, Allan started to make his way carefully yet hastily down the stairs. "Goodbye, Dr. Bennett. And thank you so much for everything."

✳ ✳ ✳

Regretfully, Bennett watched Allan hobble down the first flight and then disappear around the corner. There was so much more he wished he could do. He didn't understand why Allan didn't want The Doc dead. Bennett knew the best thing to do would be to kill him before he awoke, but then he thought back to what Allan had said. Murdering a man in cold blood would just prove him to be a savage as well. Maybe it would be better to keep him alive. Allan said he wanted The Doc to pay for everything he did, and Bennett realized that that was what he deserved. He still wished he could do more to help Allan. Allan was still terribly weak and he would have to take care of himself and Meg alone. There was only so much help Bennett could actually give. Allan asked him to help Hara, and that was what he was going to do.

"Dr. Bennett," a low voice said from behind him.

Bennett's heart skipped a beat and he jumped around in surprise. His first thought was that The Doc had already awakened, but to his relief it was someone that would cause less of a problem for him, or so he thought.

"Agent Long," he replied, his voice shaking slightly. "What are you doing on this floor? It's off limits and I doubt your fugitive is going to be up here."

Shrugging, Agent Long asked, "If it's off limits then why are you here? I doubt you have any patients on this floor."

That's what you think, Bennett thought to himself. What was Agent Long doing up here in the first place? What interest could this floor possibly have for him?

"So this was where Allan Brown was hiding?" Agent Long muttered, looking in the direction of the room they had been in.

Surprised, Bennett stared at the lead FBI agent, wondering if he had followed him up there and discovered them. He must have been the one who told The Doc where he was. "This…this isn't what it looks like…" he started, afraid of what Agent Long was going to do now that he realized whose side he was really on.

"Oh, this is exactly what it looks like," Agent Long declared, watching his expression carefully. "I know what you've been up to. It's very clear whose side you're working on."

Swallowing hard, Bennett waited for whatever Agent Long had planned for him.

Reaching out, Agent Long put a soft but firm hand on Bennett's shoulder. "The Doc is going to walk out of that room in less than thirty seconds. Is there some place private we could go to talk? I have to tell you something."

* * *

Panic: a high, intense state of fear. That was all Hara could feel while she ran down several flights of stairs and onto the third floor of the hospital. Doctors, visitors, and other patients gave her curious looks as she glanced around frantically, trying to figure out where her son was. His frightened thoughts had died away as soon as they had started, and Hara could no longer hear his young mind calling out for help. So she clung on to the only thing of his she could hear: his heart. It was barely audible among all the other noise, just a light patter as soft as a cat's footsteps. But Hara was on alert, her body pumping adrenaline. She could hear every little sound the world around her had to offer; she heard the air moving through the vents, and even the tiny insects that were burrowed deep inside the walls. None of those sounds mattered to her. She was trying to block out all the unimportant noise and focus only on the soft heartbeat she was so desperate to find.

It was becoming difficult for her to separate the various sounds, so she bumped up her search a notch. She could in fact hear her son's heart, and although there was too much happening for her to directly locate him, there was something else she could do. Thinking only about that specific heartbeat, she exhaled very slowly and gazed around, looking for the vibrations she knew it would give off. There were several more sound vibrations she saw as well, but she knew Dreyson's would be very small and light. It took her about three seconds to find

Dreyson's location, the vibrations like ripples in a lake after a stone was dropped in. He was at the far end of the hall. She saw the vibrations of several other hearts beating in close proximity to his, and they were all beating rapidly. It's a trap, she realized when she saw the anxiety in the beats of the other hearts, and knew she should have been anticipating as much. The Doc is setting a trap, and I'm about to walk into it willingly. What was wrong with that man? He would seriously use her own son against her?

"Is everything okay, hon?" an RN asked her, concern in her eyes.

"No," Hara replied, her anger steadily growing. Pointing down the hall towards where Dreyson was being, held, she declared, "There's a terrorist down in one of those rooms. Call the cops now."

"No, there were some officers and FBI agents down there the last I saw," the RN stated, looking confused.

"They're all terrorists!" Hara cried. "One of them is very dangerous and he has a three-year-old boy as his hostage. Call the cops now!"

"What's your name?" the RN began to ask, but Hara had already taken off down the hall.

Near the end, there were large plastic sheets that hung from the ceiling and divided that section from the rest of the hall. It reminded her of a human horror movie she once saw. Hara knew she was most likely going to be attacked by The Doc once she stepped around the sheets, so she would have to stay alert until she figured out exactly where he was and what he was up to.

She could still hear the several heartbeats surrounding Dreyson, but none of them had started beating faster yet. They obviously didn't know she was there. Wanting to keep it that way, she moved to the wall and as gently as she could brushed the sheet aside. It still made the crinkling noise that plastic items always made (those people were still using plastic!), but she didn't think it was loud enough for anyone to hear. Once again, the heartbeats remained at the same pace, so she assumed she was fine. Unless the people with her son were the mindless zombies The Doc had for guards, which she knew they weren't, their heartbeats were bound to skyrocket once they realized she was there.

The heartbeats were coming from behind the third door on the left, and there were six others besides Dreyson's. Only one was next to her son, and her first thought was The Doc but she immediately sensed it was someone else. It was someone good. Her mind was still too damaged to reach out and discover who it was, but she felt it was somebody good.

When she reached the door, she used her mind to very gently push it open. Had she pushed it with her hand it would have creaked and her presence would have been immediately announced. As it slowly swung open, she realized that it wouldn't have made a difference whether or not she pushed it with her hand; she heard two of the heartbeats begin to thump loudly off to the right. Her improvised element of surprise had already failed. But no one was making a move on her just yet. Hara sensed the fear and apprehension coursing through their bodies, and she knew by their hesitance that they did not intend to kill her. They were too afraid to make any type of attempt on her. She understood this, and knew it would be safe for her to enter, for a while anyway.

Stepping inside, she turned her head in the direction of the pounding hearts. There was another door that was open a few inches, most likely leading into a closet of some sort. She saw only darkness behind the door, but she knew that two people were in there. She could feel the hate radiating off of one of them, and she had a feeling who it might be. Raising a hand, she curved two of her fingers in a sideways motion and the door creaked open, revealing a vulnerable looking Lieutenant Odau and the woman detective named Finchly. Both cops stared at her with their guns level with her head, terrified expressions on each of their faces.

Amused that they were a part of the operation, she grinned and gave them both a little wave. Finchly waved back uncertainly and Odau sincerely gave her the finger. Hara snickered at the realization that he actually thought that was insulting to her. Turning her head to the center of the room, her breath caught in her chest when her eyes landed upon her son, the only member of her family still alive. Her heart leaped for joy at the sight of him, but it only lasted for a second. When she became aware of the condition of her son, her fury returned. The urge to kill everyone in the room became intense. Her baby boy lay on a gurney against the side wall. She could tell just by looking at him that he was malnourished and had been beaten repeatedly. His breathing was off slightly, and Hara was left to wonder if one of his ribs was broken.

The Helmet was on his head, something she had prayed he would never have to endure. The Helmet was an advanced technological version of anesthetic, something only used in her world for pregnant women and emergency operations. They completely paralyze one's brain when activated, taking away all forms of pain but also taking away all forms of self-control. A person wearing The Helmet would be unable to move, which meant that Dreyson was completely helpless and susceptible to The Doc. His eyes were half open and he was forced to stare up at the boring white ceiling. Hara knew how horrible it was to be at the mercy of The Helmet; she was forced to wear it during the bonding phase of her first pregnancy, when the mind of the child begins to develop and its thoughts meld with the mother's. Grace's thoughts were so powerful at first and Hara had been so unprepared for the connection that her mind screamed in agony and the doctors had to paralyze her to keep her from hurting herself. The feeling of being unable to move was unbearable, and most girls had to endure the Helmet at least once during their first pregnancy. The fact that The Doc had used it on her son enraged her, and she looked around, hoping he would show his face so she could kill him.

There was a heartbeat coming from behind the curtain beside the bed. The curtain was pushed all the way to the wall, but from her angle she was unable to see who was on the other side. Three more heartbeats were behind another door across the room, all of which had started to beat faster. The one behind the curtain had started to go a little faster, but whoever it was seemed to be unsure if she was actually there or not.

Eager to get rid of everyone involved in this, Hara's fingertips sparked and hot flames erupted from her hands. All the doors in the room slammed shut in her anger, and she heard the people on opposite sides of them shout in protest and begin to pound on them. Planning to quickly take out whoever was hiding behind the curtain and then grab her son and leave, Hara marched forward and raised her hand to take a swing as the man jumped out and raised a gun. But she stopped short when she realized she couldn't kill him. "Perry?" she said in disbelief, the fire still burning on her palms.

"Hello again," Perry replied as he held the gun up at her chest. He still seemed hesitant, like he knew he should be on her side.

"You're working for The Doc now?" Hara demanded angrily, her patience quickly running out.

Perry shrugged. "Not exactly."

"I save your life repeatedly and this is how you repay me?" The flames expelling from her hands grew larger and brighter.

Seeing this, Perry swallowed and proceeded cautiously. "I just want this to be over."

"This is never going to be over!" Hara snapped. "It's a cycle and it's never going to end! This is only the beginning for you! Don't you understand by now?"

"Maybe if you'd explain everything to me I would understand," he shot back.

"Why are you doing this to me?" Hara asked, forcing her eyes to plead with him. "What did I ever do to you?"

Perry stared at her in bewilderment. "How many people did you kill in the past few days?"

"I did that for us," Hara blurted breathlessly. "To protect us."

"You did it to satisfy your own anger," Perry growled, but Hara could see in his eyes that he now knew she was telling the truth.

"You know that's a lie," Hara told him, praying he would take her side. "You just don't want to believe that killing can be a good thing."

"It isn't!" Perry snapped. "It never will be!"

"Where's The Doc?"

"Who cares? He's probably pissing someone else off!"

"I am only going to say this once," Hara said very quietly. "Get away from the kid and let me take him."

"I'm not letting you leave here unless it's in my custody!" Perry told her.

"You don't understand how much he means to me," Hara replied desperately.

"I don't understand a lot of things."

"You don't know how much danger he's in!" Hara insisted. "If you manage to arrest me, The Doc will take him and do horrible things to him!"

"He's not going anywhere with The Doc," Perry assured. "I'll take him and make sure he lives a safe life."

Hara could barely contain herself. "Did you really think you could just walk in and replace me?" she screamed. "He's mine, damn you! He will never be yours!"

"What?" Perry said in shock, realizing what she was saying.

It didn't surprise Hara that The Doc didn't tell him who Dreyson really was. "Perry, step away from my son," Hara warned, the energy in her mind about to explode out of her.

A horrified look in his eyes, Perry turned quickly and glanced down at Dreyson. It was all the time she needed.

Lurching forward, she swung her hand at his and knocked the gun to the floor. Before he could react, she grabbed him by the front of his jacket and gave him a shove. He lost his balance and skidded across the floor, coming to a halt when his head collided with the wall. In a daze, all he did was lay there. Hara knew The Doc had put Perry in between her and her child because it would be more difficult for her to get past him. But her child came way before Shawn Perry, especially if he was siding with The Doc.

In her struggle with Perry, she had lost her concentration on the doors and everyone came bursting out with their guns ready. Hara could move much faster than any of them, and before they had gotten more than a few feet she had disabled the Helmet, ripped it off her son's head, and picked him up. But with the disabling of the Helmet came something she had not anticipated. Gasping as she felt the presence of Dreyson's mind leave hers, she held her son in front of her and stared at him in horror.

"Don't shoot!" a woman's voice was shouting, but she wasn't even aware of it. "Don't shoot! You might hit Dreyson!"

"What is wrong with you?" Hara whispered to her child, reaching out with her mind to try and find his somewhere. "Where did you go?"

Blinking as his brain was able to function again, Dreyson's eyes started to focus on her face. Considering the circumstances, he seemed alright on the outside. But Hara couldn't feel him anywhere.

"Put the boy down now!" Lieutenant Odau ordered forcefully. "Put him down or we will shoot you!"

"What did he do to you?" Hara sobbed, unable to find her three-year-old's consciousness no matter how hard she looked.

Finally able to see his mother in front of him, Dreyson's face lit up and he reached out his arms. "Mommy!" he whispered in delight, unaware of everything that was going on around him.

"Dear God!" she cried, wrapping him in a tight embrace. For some reason, she had thought he would hate her like everyone in her hallucination did. But he was just as happy to see her as she was to see him.

He hugged her tighter than she thought he could, and he said in her ear in his little baby voice, "I saw you come get me in my dream, so I waited for you. I love you, Mommy."

"I love you so much!" Hara breathed. "What did The Doc do to you to make you like this?" Turning and glaring at everyone surrounding her, she snarled, "What did you do to make him like this?" Letting go of Dreyson with her right hand, a new flame exploded from her.

Her plan was to roast all the people threatening her, but she found herself unable to after something struck her on the side of the neck. Gasping for breath, she almost dropped Dreyson as she fell to her knees. Crying out, her son wrapped his arms around her neck and clung to her with his legs. The fire in her hand winked out, and she turned to see who had shot her.

Perry sat where he had fallen, aiming an AD Weapon at her. Just before she felt all her abilities slip from her, she heard Perry's silent apology.

I'm sorry, but I had to do this.

Of course you had to, you bastard! she wanted to shout. "You didn't have to do anything!" she choked out, pulling the dart out of her neck. Her hands shook as she touched the spot where the dart had struck, her blood trickling out into her palm The tiny cut didn't heal, and it wouldn't for a long time. All of her abilities were gone. She was defenseless.

"Well, well, I see you fell for my bait quite easily," The Doc said from behind her, the smirk audible in his voice.

"No, no!" she whispered in terror, hugging Dreyson close to her as she turned to look her nemesis in the eye.

The Doc stood in the doorway with his hands in his pockets, grinning down at her as he enjoyed finally capturing her. He took comfort in her fear. "Didn't you stop to think this would be a trap?"

"I knew it would be," she muttered, struggling to climb to her feet.

"Yet you still came," he taunted, turning toward Perry as he stood up. "Where in God's name did you get that?"

Perry didn't reply, and while The Doc was distracted Hara made a feeble attempt to break for it. But the suppression of her abilities left her dizzy, so her attempted sprint was more of an awkward stumble. She couldn't catch herself when The Doc swung his fist at her and struck her in the side of the head. Her knees buckled and she went down hard, trying her hardest to avoid hurting Dreyson on the way down.

"Nice try," The Doc said, grinning down at her again.

Hara had fallen just beside the exit door, and while holding her son in one arm she kicked her feet and pushed herself out the door.

"Where are you going?" The Doc asked in amusement, following her. "Do you really think you have any place to go?"

He was right. Without her abilities, she had no chance of getting away from him. Her head was too clouded and confused for her to walk more than a few steps. But the lives of her and her child were on the line, and she was going to put forth every effort she had left in her.

"You're caught this time," The Doc told her as the cops and FBI agents came out after them. "You're not getting out of this one, I'm sorry to tell you."

Hara gripped Dreyson as tight as her weak muscles would allow as The Doc came towards her. He reached down and grabbed Dreyson by the back of the shirt and tried to pull him away from her, but Hara wasn't going to have that. Her child screamed in protest and clung to her while she yelled, "No!" and hugged him tighter.

"Listen to me," The Doc said and dropped his voice to a low whisper. His words were not harsh, but they were strong and pressuring. "You need to let him go."

"What did you do to him?" Hara demanded furiously. "I can't feel him anywhere!"

"That's the whole point," The Doc replied with a smirk. "You were supposed to believe he was dead."

"What did you do?" she repeated louder.

"You remember that 'light' you told me about? The light that connects one to everyone else in the family?" Grinning again, he put his hands on his knees and leaned towards her. "Yeah, I turned it off."

Gaping at him, Hara cried, "You took away his soul?"

The Doc shrugged. "If you really want to put it that way, then fine."

"What is wrong with you?" she shouted. "How could you do that to him?"

Shrugging again, The Doc said, "Why don't you give him to me?"

"Are you nuts?" she snapped. She already knew the answer to that.

"I want you to listen to me very carefully," The Doc murmured, his voice dropping down again. "You need to give him to me right now."

"I just got him back!" Hara cried, tears spilling down her face. She held her son to her and he hugged her back. It was a mutual love they had, and The Doc wasn't about to break it up a second time.

"I am taking you back to my lab whether you like it or not," The Doc told her quietly, the others behind him trying to listen intently. "We can leave with or without Dreyson, but I can tell you right now that if we leave with him I will kill him before we reach our destination. But, since I'm in a strikingly good mood right now I will be kind and make you a deal. If you give him to me I will give him to Agent Perry and he will live a full, normal life. Perry and his girlfriend can raise him and you won't ever have to worry about him getting into trouble with this war again. But, hey, it's your decision."

"Why?" Hara whispered, grief tearing apart her heart. "Why would you want to give him a normal life? Why would you let him live after everything you've done?"

Raising an eyebrow, The Doc answered, "Because now that I have you back, I don't care about anything or anyone else. I just want to focus on you. So, if you don't mind..." This time, The Doc used two hands and picked Dreyson up by his underarms. Hara tried to hold on but she couldn't, and she knew it would be best for her son to just let him go. Dreyson screamed and cried, reaching his arms back towards his mother and trying to kick free of The Doc. "Agent Michaels, did you want him?" The Doc asked a young blonde agent, holding the toddler out to her.

Agent Michaels looked from Dreyson, to Hara, and then to The Doc, confusion and regret in her eyes. "She's his mother," she whispered.

Rolling his eyes, The Doc turned to Perry. "Perry? What about you?"

Perry stared at Dreyson's sobbing face.

"Perry, please!" Hara begged from the floor, pushing herself off her stomach and onto her elbows. She tried to make herself look as desperate as she felt. "Just take him! Get him out of here!"

Gazing back at her in bewilderment, he replied, "He's your son."

"And I'm begging you to take him!" she cried, her face streaming with tears. "Please, for his sake, just take him and go!"

"Does anybody want this?" The Doc asked in an annoyed voice, looking around at everybody. It was as if he was auctioning off a piece of old furniture. Nobody spoke up. "Anybody?" He looked around again. "Going once?"

"Give him to me."

Everyone's head swiveled towards the sound of the man's voice. Hara recognized him from before in the interrogation room. He was the lead FBI agent and he had been watching her from the observation room. Hara suddenly realized that he hadn't been with the others waiting in the trap. Agent Long came marching down the hall towards his colleagues, a stony expression on his face.

"Where have you been?" The Doc demanded suspiciously.

"Looking for you!" Agent Long snapped back, still walking closer. "If Perry and Michaels have changed their minds, then give him to me. I'm not letting that kid go anywhere with you ever again." Without The Doc's consent, he took Dreyson from his arms and cradled him in his own, trying to stop his cries.

"No!" Hara squeaked, pushing herself clumsily to her feet again. She didn't know this man, and she wasn't going to allow her son to be given to just anybody. She could trust Perry to raise him properly, but no one else.

"No, what?" The Doc said in irritation, turning to her.

"It's Perry or no one else!" Hara growled, finally gaining her balance and glaring at him menacingly.

Staring at her in amusement, The Doc asked, "And whose decision is it to choose where he goes?"

"Mine!" Hara snarled. "He's *my* son!"

"He'll be alright," Agent Long assured her as he held her son, whose cries had finally died away. His eyes were sympathetic for her, and they looked like they held more words than he was letting out, but both Hara and The Doc were ignoring him.

"Well, if you're his mother, then why don't you come protect him?" The Doc challenged.

Sick and tired of his taunts, Hara pursed her lips and held her ground. She was going to put up as much of a fight as her weak, currently crippled human brain would allow her.

"Come on then," The Doc commanded, taking a threatening step forward. "Let's see how tough you are without your abilities." He gave her a light push backwards, but it was enough to make her stumble. "Let's see you fight me fairly." He gave her another push, harder this time. "Come on, fight me!" Giving it one last shot, he shoved her so hard that she fell over backwards and slid back several feet. "Give it your best shot! After all, I murdered everything you ever loved!"

Screaming in rage, Hara leapt to her feet and charged at him. Her body struck him full force in the chest and he stumbled a bit, but when he caught himself he was wrestling her back. She hit and clawed at him, but in the end he had her pinned against him and she was unable to move. It took her a moment to realize that The Doc was no longer fighting her; he was holding her. And what scared her was that he was holding her in the same way that her father had when she was upset. He was trying to comfort her. She began to bawl all over his shoulder as she gave in to her defeat. She was completely disgusted with herself. There were seven other people looking on at this awkward moment as the soft sides of both of them came out. The Doc didn't even seem to take notice of them. He let her sob into his shoulder for a while before whispering into her ear, "Are you done? Hmm? Have you had enough of this?"

Gripping the front of his jacket tightly in her hands, she nodded shakily. "Yes," she choked out, swallowing hard as she tried to keep her fear from becoming too intense.

"Good girl," The Doc said, releasing her and taking her arm. "Let's go. We've done enough damage here."

As Hara gave up and let herself be taken, she looked back at her son. He was gazing at her from Agent Long's arms, his big round green eyes curiously calm. He didn't look scared, and he almost looked as if he were having one of his premonitions. Leaning against Agent Long's chest, he raised his hand and opened and closed his fist repeatedly, waving goodbye. "See you soon, Mommy," he called as she was dragged back into the unfinished hospital room, with more horrors still to come.

14

Depression

Now that the hardest part of the operation was over, Perry could relax. Hara was in custody, and because her abilities were repressed there was no way for her to escape. She had put up a hell of a fight at first, but in the end it seemed as if she was too weak to keep going any longer. It might have had something to do with what The Doc had whispered to her, but Perry couldn't know for certain.

Once she gave herself up completely, The Doc took her back into the vacant hospital room and strapped her down to the gurney where Dreyson had been lying. She didn't move while The Doc was restraining her. It was strange behavior for her, but maybe she really was to the point where she had had enough.

Things had been settled down for about twenty minutes, and when The Doc was preoccupied with Lieutenant Odau, Perry took the opportunity to sneak a quick message to Hara. When no one was paying attention he walked over to the gurney and bent down to whisper in her ear.

"Don't worry," he told her as softly as he could. "Everything's going to work out fine. We're not going to let that asshole hurt you anymore. We'll take you somewhere where you can get help." Lifting his head up so he could see her reaction of relief or maybe even excitement, Perry was confused to see her blank stare. Her eyes were aimed directly at the ceiling, yet they didn't move to focus on him and she never blinked. Waving his hand in front of her face, Perry asked her uncertainly, "Can you hear me?"

"She's not responding to anybody," The Doc explained, stepping up to the gurney as well. "I doubt she even knows what's going on right now." Just to confirm his assumption, he leaned over Hara as Perry had. He got about three inches from her face and hovered there, trying to see if she would break and make eye contact with him. But after several uncomfortable moments, The Doc shook his head and stood up straight again. "Nope," he said. "Her mind is elsewhere. She's not even here. You might as well forget about whatever you were trying to say to her."

"Why?" Perry asked as The Doc started to turn away. "Why is she gone? I mean, shouldn't she be scared?"

The Doc glanced down at Hara again and gave her a resolved look. "She's giving up."

A deep, compassionate part of Perry reached out to Hara and felt her pain. He gazed down into her dull eyes that had once burned with such rage. They had once blazed with her anger, spirit, and determination, but now Perry saw nothing. There was nothing looking back at him anymore. He was staring into black, never-ending holes of pain and misery, no will to live left inside them. He was no longer standing beside a person; he was standing beside a body stripped of its soul, left behind to take in the rest of Hara's sufferings. People had repeatedly said that she couldn't die, but Perry realized now that they were wrong. They were so wrong. The Doc had taken every last bit of light and hope from her after their final encounter. After everything she had lived through, all the horrible experiments and tests, The Doc had finally killed her. She may still be breathing, but Perry saw nothing left inside her. She was really gone.

"Nice work, by the way," The Doc told him, clearly not caring about Hara's condition.

"Excuse me?" Perry replied, puzzled by what he was saying.

"You saved the lives of everyone in here," he explained, praising him as if he were a new disciple. "If you hadn't shot her with that dart, she would have killed everyone in this room. Nice work."

"Oh," Perry muttered, not really feeling like he had done something worthy of praise.

The Doc cocked his head, the first time in a long while. "Are you alright? You seem…discontent."

Perry shrugged, wishing he would go away and bother somebody else. He continued to gaze down at Hara's lifeless form.

"You're having second thoughts," The Doc concluded, the smirk surfacing in his voice once more. "You don't want to let me take her, do you?"

Looking up, Perry glared at his amused expression. He had truly had enough. So what if he was having second thoughts about everything? The Doc was not yet aware of their plan to arrest him and take Hara themselves, but did he really feel the need to pick at him because the sight of the poor girl struck a nerve? "What do you want from me?" he demanded. He had asked that question so many times before, but now it was his anger talking.

Still smirking, The Doc asked him, "Where did you happen to get that weapon you used against her? That is clearly not contemporary technology, and it is not something a typical FBI agent would just carry around."

"How do you know I didn't steal it from you?" Perry snapped.

"Ha!" The Doc laughed. "You act so tough, Perry, but you're not willing to risk stealing from me. So where did you get it?"

"Who cares? I caught her, so what more could you possibly need?" He hoped his last question would shut the man up, but no; The Doc was too persistent.

"Noah gave it to you, didn't he?" The Doc looked very certain about it.

"So what if he did?"

Perry was pleased to finally see a confused expression on The Doc's face. For once, Perry controlled the flow of information. "Why would Noah give you something like that?"

"Why not?"

The Doc stared at him curiously, trying to read the answer in his face. He was very good at it. "Noah wouldn't have given you that weapon unless he wanted you to catch her."

Perry shrugged again, growing annoyed. "Maybe he did."

Eyeing Perry suspiciously, The Doc growled, "Do you and Noah have some little operation going behind my back? Are you two plotting something against me?"

"Of course not!" Perry lied, scowling back.

Taking a step forward in an attempt to further intimidate him, The Doc demanded, "Why did Noah want her caught? What are you two doing?"

"There is no plan. He just wanted everything to be over. He's too tired to keep this going any longer."

Once again, The Doc saw right through him. Narrowing his eyes, he accused, "You're lying to me again."

"She's in custody," Perry reminded, forcing any fear out of his voice and replacing it with anger. "If there was a plan, don't you think I would have done something already?"

Still watching his reaction carefully, The Doc muttered, "We'll see." He turned and started walking towards the door. Everyone else had moved out. "Come. We're going to discuss how this will end. My apologies for destroying your city."

Perry looked back down at Hara when the room was clear. "I'm sorry things had to end this way," he whispered, really meaning it. "Maybe if you had explained everything to me sooner I could have helped you. We could have resolved things a bit...differently. You and your people say that I'm one of you, and if that's really true then you should have trusted me. You could have gotten help from me and we could have stopped him before he did all this." Staring down at her while waiting for some sort of response, Perry felt his own anger begin to build up. But when all she did was continue to stare straight up with no signs of life whatsoever, Perry demanded, "Why didn't you come to me for help? Why didn't you just explain things to me right away instead of going around on your own?"

A thought suddenly struck him, something that had made him very angry before. It was a three word sentence that was spoken to him by everyone on Hara's side at least once. "I wouldn't understand," he whispered, finally realizing that they had been correct all along. "You knew I couldn't take it in all at once, and you were completely right. I wouldn't have believed any of it at the time. I had to experience it, be a part of it. Just like you said."

Noticing he was really only talking to himself, he sighed. "I really wish you had dealt with this some other way. I want you to know that I'm very sorry about your family and people, and I'm disgusted by what The Doc did to you. He made you into what you are now. I understand now that this is not your fault. But I can promise you now that we will never let that sick bastard hurt you ever again. I will never let him. You can trust me when I say that. I haven't a clue if you can hear me right now, but if a part of you is still left inside I want you to know that you're safe now. I'm going to help you get through this." Sucking in a deep breath, he told her softly, "I'm so sorry that I let him use your child against you. It was a horrible thing to do. I'm so sorry about everything." Regret hardening like a concrete block in his chest, Perry reached out and patted her shoulder gently. "My heart goes out to you."

For a brief second, Perry could have sworn he saw her eyes light up. It wasn't much, but he had a feeling that his words may have sent a spark of hope through her. There was definitely a part of her still there; one ounce of life left inside her to keep her soul alive. She wasn't gone just yet. The spark was only there for a moment, but it gave him hope that there was at least something left worth saving. Smiling down at her, he said, "Hold on for me. This will be over soon." Giving her shoulder another pat, Perry left her, silently promising that he would come back to save her.

* * *

Perry wasn't the only one who decided to pay a personal visit to Hara. In fact, the person she least expected came to talk to her, entering several minutes after Perry left.

She was vaguely aware of Perry's presence in the room with her, and she knew he was talking to her, but her mind was too far gone to register anything that was going on around her physical self. Hara was appalled by her failure. Not just as a member of a fallen society, but also as a mother. Her child, her beautiful, innocent child, had still been alive without her realizing it. He had been taken from her, and she hadn't been able to protect him. She should have been able to sense Dreyson, even if her bond with him was severed. He was her son, her baby; her love for him should have been enough to keep them connected. Just knowing that she hadn't been around to care for him through the time that they were separated made her hate herself, but what was worse was that she hadn't been there for him after the bond was broken. Hara knew very well the kinds of things The Doc must have done to him. A child so young going through the things he had was bound to live a very troubled life, even more so than Hara.

For a brief moment, Hara had rescued her child from the clutches of The Doc, only to have him taken away from her once again. The humiliation was terrible. She was a failure as a parent. She was pathetic, weak. She was worse than a human. At least Dreyson would live a life away from The Doc and the war. That was what Hara kept telling herself. It was the only thing she could do to ensure that her brain wouldn't implode on itself.

Knowing that Dreyson was safe, Hara allowed herself to slip away, for her mind to dissociate from her body. She knew what was in store for her once The Doc came back for her and took her home. That notion was an immediate invitation for panic and serious apprehension, two things that Hara just didn't have enough energy to survive. So she just let herself go. It wasn't so bad, really. It was peaceful, easy, much more tolerable than the place her body was in. She found that she was able to live in moments of pure happiness from her past. Not actual scenes, just moments. Her first stop was a moment that had captured her heart forever. It was the first time she ever laid eyes on her firstborn child, Grace, in the hospital after she had given birth. Her beautiful brown eyes, the same as Bo's, gazed up at her with such a wonder in them, as if she were saying to her, "You're my mother. I've waited such a long time to finally meet you." Her bald head was soft and smooth, just a short layer of peach fuzz covering it. Her pink lips were so tiny. She stared up at her for the longest time, that same look of wonder in her eyes, until finally her little lips parted to form a smile that showed her pink, toothless gums. She was so beautiful. It brought tears to her eyes seeing the gorgeous little girl she had brought into the world. That feeling of pure love had stuck in her heart forever.

The next place she visited was the countryside. There were small hills all around her, covered in tall grass that swayed and whistled in the light breeze. She was lying on her back halfway up one of the hills, looking up at a beautiful blue sky. The sounds of her three oldest children laughing as they played could be heard somewhere near the bottom of the hill. She jumped when something turned over inside of her. A light, fluttery movement beating against the inside of her belly caused her to look down. She was pregnant with Dreyson. Very pregnant, in fact. She would always remember the light, fluttery movements, almost like a little bird, that Dreyson made during the three months he spent inside her. Recognizing that moment suddenly, she turned her head to her left. Bo was lying beside her on his side, his head supported by his hand, his arm resting on the ground at the elbow. He had been watching her while she dozed. She was so pregnant with the baby, and considering how long they had been running, she must have been sleeping for hours on end. She needed to build up enough energy for the birthing process, a very stressful and upsetting experience. When Hara's gaze landed on him, Bo smiled at her lovingly. He didn't say it this time, but Hara would remember what he said to her next. "Did Jack ever tell you that you're absolutely beautiful when you sleep?" She would always remember that moment because that was when she realized just how much she truly loved him.

Third stop, Grandpa's house. It was right after her father and siblings had convinced her to bring her family back to the capital city and live with him. Her father and Bo were sitting beside each other on the living room floor, grinning at each other as all five of her children climbed all over them while laughing hysterically. Although her father had said he would accept Bo as part of the family because he was Hara's soul mate, Hara never believed him until that moment. The expression in his eyes said it all.

The final place she visited was a moment that had started out filled with grief but had ended with her happy in Bo's arms. It was the day after her brother Malcolm was killed in a nuclear blast targeted at their capital city. So far she had lost him, her oldest brother—and best friend—Flint, and her mother, Shauna. She didn't realize that losing the three of them was nothing compared to what she was about to lose. She never thought that life could be so hard, so painful. Before the war, she had always concerned herself with things that now seemed so trivial. Never had she anticipated such a calamity. Never had anyone anticipated it.

Hara had been sitting alone in her father's house, mourning the loss of yet another family member, when Bo came in and practically ordered her to dance with him. She had never been much of a dancer. She couldn't recall a time after she was six that she had even danced at all. But Bo was insistent. "I'll teach you," he told her. "I'll lead, then think. You listen, then follow." They had danced to a song by a human woman from Ireland called Enya. Hara never had an attraction to human music, but there was something about that song that made her feel comforted. It made her feel that there was something else in her world besides pain: a peace that she had finally found. She listened to Bo counting and thinking the moves inside his head, and they had managed to create a memorable routine from that song. "Caribbean Blue." What a beautiful name. The dance was not the moment she went back to, however. What she went back to was the moment after the dance was over, where she was pressed up against Bo's gentle body, and being held in his arms. She felt at peace, something she hadn't felt in a long time. Even if was only for a brief moment, she was going to savor it. Hara held herself in that moment for as long as she could. She was held by her mate, his soft breath lightly touching her hair, always there to comfort her, never going to leave her...

He had left her, in the end. He died along with everybody else. But Hara didn't think about that. She held onto that moment with all the strength she had left. For all she knew, hours passed and she was still resting in Bo's arms. It was awhile before she finally remembered what he whispered to her in that room, while holding her. He sighed wearily and rubbed a hand up and down her back in a soothing manner. He tilted his head down so he could murmur into her ear. "This isn't your fault."

This isn't your fault.

This isn't your fault.

This isn't my fault!

It wasn't her fault. She couldn't keep blaming herself. She had to stop torturing herself. She had to listen to what everyone kept telling her. She had to pull herself out of this fantasy and keep on fighting. She had to kill Jackson Odau. She had to get her son back. Because it wasn't her fault.

Hara didn't know how, but the soft patter of footsteps on the tiled floor brought her back to reality. The images of Bo faded, leaving only the ominous white ceiling looming above her. She was back in the hospital. She was back on Earth. She was back with The Doc. Someone was crossing the room to get to her, but she sensed that it was not The Doc. She was ever so thankful for that. Her abilities were still restrained and there would be no way to keep him away from her.

She found that she was not quite able to move her muscles; she was still trying to fully grasp where she was and what she needed to do, and therefore couldn't quite control herself yet. Because of that, she couldn't focus her eyes on the person that came to her side and gazed down upon her. Straining to identify him out of the corner of her eye, she recognized him as Perry's superior officer, Agent Long. Out of all the people who could have come, why him? What could he possibly want? The only interest he had ever expressed was capturing her, so what did he come to say? Did he want to boast about how his team had won and how his city was now safe? Well, he could go right ahead, because she had a feeling she wouldn't be running around blowing things up for a long time. Most likely never again if she got her way. She was going to get rid of the boy, get her son, and go home.

"You really shouldn't have done this, you know," Agent Long told her quietly, his hands burrowed deep in his pockets. "There were so many better ways to handle the war."

Dear God, she thought. If this guy pretended like he knew diddly-squat about the war, she was going to throw up in his face.

"What's worse is that you're getting your friends hurt," he continued in his annoying drawl. "Daniel is dead, and Allan, Meg, Jack, and Noah aren't far behind."

Please go away.

"You murdered innocent people," he added solemnly. "Something you swore you'd never do after the things you had seen."

Get out of my face...wait, what?

"Your father was a great man and a great leader, and you were supposed to follow in his footsteps."

How the hell do you know all this?

Agent Long sighed. "Of course I know about this," he said. "I was a part of it."

Who are you? And how can you hear me?

He sighed again. "You don't remember me, H?"

Finally willing herself to move, Hara rotated her gaze to focus on the tall figure standing over her. Was she supposed to remember him from somewhere? He didn't look familiar, but she did recall someone calling her "H" at some point in her life. Agent Long stared back into her eyes for what felt like minutes, never once blinking. It struck her then. His eyes! His skin was black, but his eyes were hazel. She had only met one person with black skin and hazel eyes, but it couldn't be him! The last time she saw him, he was a boy just a few months older than her. What happened to him in the past four years? Was it one of The Doc's experiments?

Rhett?

"H," he whispered, and his mouth broke into a friendly smile. "HR."

Oh my God, it is you!

"Of course it's me," he said with a chuckle. "It's been me all along."

Hara couldn't believe it. The man in charge of the FBI agents pursuing her was actually her childhood buddy Rhett Simco. *What happened to you? You're old!*

"I...I made a mistake," he explained, lowering his eyes. "I needed to escape from there for a while, but then this happened. I feel like a coward. Until you came back I just sort of...forgot about it, I guess."

How could you forget? Hara demanded furiously, wishing she could kick him in the teeth. *You're a Colician too, remember? You will always be a part of this war, no matter how far you run!*

"I know, and I am so, so sorry."

How long have you been trapped here?

"A long time. I can't even remember anymore."

You've been working on The Doc's side this whole time! she accused. *After everything he did to us! He just killed Daniel!*

"I've only been playing along," Rhett assured. "I've been faking so I could get to you and help you."

Help me with what? If you really wanted to help, why didn't you just kill The Doc right from the start?

"I knew that he had Dreyson," he said. "I was planning on killing him as soon as I realized it was him, but I sensed he had something twisted hidden up his sleeve like he always does, so I burrowed deep into the brains of his guards and guess what I found? I was just waiting until you were caught and I knew Dreyson was safe. Plus, I needed to keep an eye on Perry. Somebody had to. Now, my plan for your escape is being set into motion."

Where the hell is my son, Simco?

"Don't call me that," he scolded. "It's Rhett Long now. And don't worry about Dreyson. I gave him to Dr. Bennett."

I love that man so much, Hara said to herself.

"Now here's how this is going to work," Rhett began as he pulled a jet black syringe out of his pocket. "This isn't a very good, fast-working dose, but it should work with enough time to spare."

"What are you doing?" Hara tried to shout, squirming away from him as he attempted to inject her. The muzzle over her mouth muffled her, so she sounded ridiculous.

"*Shh, shh, shh,*" Rhett hushed, putting a finger to his lips urgently. "It's alright. This is just to give you your abilities back. It will start working in ten to twenty minutes, so it would be better to inject you as soon as possible. Right now would be a very good time. You can escape, get your son from Dr. Bennett, and I'll take care of The Doc for good this time. He won't be able to hurt anyone else anymore."

Please be careful, Hara begged him, allowing him to inject it into her upper arm. *I really don't want anyone else to get hurt. You've been living here for all this time, and I don't want you to get hurt or killed because of me.*

"Don't worry about me right now," Rhett told her. "You should be focusing on getting your son back and then getting the hell out of here."

What am I supposed to do once I get out of here?

"Finish what you started."

Staring at him in disbelief, Hara cried, *You just told me that I was hurting too many people!*

"Yes, but killing the lieutenant's boy will end this and prevent the future catastrophes," Rhett explained, taking her hand and squeezing it. "I'll take care of The Doc and you can take care of Jackson." He turned to leave.

Hey! Where are you going?

"I have to act like I'm still on their side," Rhett said.

Can't you let me go first?

"No," he told her regretfully. "They'd know right away it was me, and then I wouldn't be able to get rid of our big problem. And your abilities won't return for another quarter of an hour at least. You wouldn't be able to get very far before they caught you again. We'd both be screwed then. I have to go now, but I should see you soon, okay? Just do me a favor and don't hurt any of my agents on the way out."

You'll come back with me, won't you? Hara asked hopefully. *Maybe we can reverse what's been done to you...*

"You can't reverse this," Rhett chuckled, heading for the door again. "Besides, I doubt I'll be welcome there after what I've done."

If they'll welcome me back after everything I've done, then they will most certainly welcome you back too! We see this through together! That's what friends do!

Rhett turned at the door and sighed. "I'm not sure I even belong in your world anymore, H," he told her softly. He left the room then, leaving Hara to wonder how she was supposed to escape and get to her son. When he met up with the other agents at the end of the hall, Perry stopped him.

"Where's the boy?" he asked curiously.

"He's safe," Agent Long promised him. Looking around uncertainly, he asked, "Where's The Doc?"

"He and Lieutenant Odau went to let Dr. Bennett know that the problem is over and that we'll leave shortly," Martinson reported. "I would assume they will be back momentarily."

"What about Detective Finchly?"

"Right here, sir," Finchly spoke up, pushing aside the plastic curtain and stepping in to join them.

"None of The Doc's guards are out there listening, are they?" Agent Long asked warily.

"No, why?" Finchly was confused, and so were the other four.

"Perry and I need to tell you our plan that we've unfortunately been keeping from you," Agent Long explained.

"What are you talking about?" Hersh demanded skeptically.

"We're not going to let The Doc take Hara, are we?" Michaels asked, understanding immediately. "You were never just going to let him walk out of here with her."

"Of course not," Agent Long said. "What kind of animal do you think I am?"

"Shouldn't we wait for the lieutenant to come back and be a part of this?" Finchly asked hesitantly.

"No," all five FBI agents replied quickly in unison. Agent Long added, "As you all have noticed, the lieutenant has pretty much offered The Doc anything he wants. He is completely against Hara, and he doesn't care what happens to her. So no, we will not even hint to him that we are taking down The Doc. Is that understood?" He shuddered, knowing that Odau felt his connection to The Doc.

"Yes, sir," five voices chimed.

"Good," Agent Long said approvingly. "Now, this is how it will work. Whenever he comes back, I'll distract him and when he has no guards around to protect him I'll get him in cuffs and get him out to the SUVs." He decided to leave out the part where he planned to kill The Doc and claim it was in self-defense. "Perry and Finchly, you two take care of Odau and the guards. If any of them figure out what's going on, this will end badly. The rest of you will take Hara down the back stairwell when everyone else is occupied and get her out of here."

"What are we supposed to do with her after that?" Martinson asked uncertainly. "Where are we supposed to take her? We don't know how to control her."

Agent Long paused. "The station," he answered. "We'll figure out what to do with her once The Doc is dealt with."

"What if Hara gets her abilities back before we get back to the station?" Hersh asked nervously.

"She won't," Agent Long promised. "The Doc told me the effects of the drug lasts for several hours."

"Why didn't you tell us about your plan before?" Michaels demanded.

"We thought if too many people knew then The Doc would get suspicious," Perry explained apologetically. "We didn't want to keep it from the rest of you, but we had no choice."

Agent Long said, "Alright, if there are no other questions or comments, let's get back to work and act normal until our operation is set in motion. We don't want The Doc or Odau to get suspicious."

Without another word, everybody hurried away to various places, uneasy about what they were doing. Everybody except for Perry.

"Where exactly is Dreyson?" he asked when the others were all out of earshot.

"If it was something you needed to concern yourself with, then I would tell you, Perry," Agent Long said.

"I just want to know that he's safe and he's going to be okay," Perry explained, flinching at Agent Long's tone. "I know that I said I would take him, but Renee and I were talking and neither of us have the heart to take him. Hara is his mother, and I saw the love in his eyes when he saw her and that could never be replaced. He belongs with her and no one else."

"He's fine," Agent Long promised. "I took him to a place where he'll be safe until this all blows over."

"Okay," Perry said, giving him a relieved smile. "That's all I need to know."

Agent Long nodded to him. "Get back to your duties, Perry."

"Yes, sir," Perry replied, brushing past the plastic curtain to join the others.

After he was certain that Perry and everyone else were gone, Agent Long walked back to the room where Hara was being held and stopped in the doorway. He gazed upon her still form and wondered to himself if she would have enough strength and self-motivation to escape. He only doubted her for a moment. Then he reminded himself that she would do anything for her child, especially now that he was the only living family. She would most definitely have enough strength to get out, and she would put up the biggest fight yet. Agent Long just prayed she wouldn't injure or kill any of his agents. They were not only his colleagues but his friends. They were messing with an angry, protective mother, and even Agent Long couldn't protect them from that. It was up to Hara what would happen to them. There was no way to warn them of her escape, so they would be caught completely off guard. Any hint he gave them would immediately lead to his incrimination and then he wouldn't be able to take care of The Doc. He just prayed Hara was feeling merciful.

Sighing as he dwelled on the thought that he couldn't keep all of his friends safe, Agent Long followed Perry into the populated section of the hospital and prepared for his final and most deadly battle against The Doc. It would be his last stand in the war, and he didn't know how it would end. All he knew was that the fight would start with two and end with one. One of them wasn't going to leave the hospital alive.

✳ ✳ ✳

The Doc and Lieutenant Odau arrived back about ten minutes later, and Odau automatically went to speak with Perry about something that appeared urgent. To Agent Long's relief, Finchly quickly walked over and joined the conversation. Glancing up, he saw The Doc eyeing him with his ice cold eyes and approaching him suspiciously. Agent Long knew he was coming to speak with him, so he turned his head and made eye contact with Michaels, Martinson, and Hersh for a split second before turning back to The Doc again. He saw the three of them walk back down into the divided section of the hall out of the corner of his eyes, each leaving at a different time as to not look too suspicious.

The fact that Agent Long could not reach his mind into The Doc's disturbed him. Never before had a human been able to block his thoughts from the prying mind of a Colician, especially one as talented and experienced as him. For the time being, there was no way to determine the reason for that, so he would just have to deal with the discomfort. "Is something wrong?" he asked through his teeth as The Doc reached him. He found it very difficult to speak to him now. After everything The Doc had done to his people, it was not easy to pretend to be human and act like he had no clue what the man had done. He could no longer act like the others working with him that thought they knew but were really only imagining. It was so much worse than any of them could ever understand. The war was something that one had to witness with one's own eyes. Agent Long could no longer pretend to be something he wasn't. This had to end now.

"I searched every floor of this building and not once did I see Dr. Bennett," The Doc informed, sounding irritated yet also curious.

"Well, that's unfortunate," Agent Long replied sarcastically, already impatient.

"But do you know what else is interesting?" The Doc asked, not waiting for an answer. "Very few people have seen him in the past few hours. Those who have, say that he was quite distant and always hurrying off to somewhere else."

"Is that supposed to mean something to me?" Agent Long demanded when The Doc waited for him to respond.

Shrugging, The Doc continued to stare at him in that strange, suspicious way. "I don't know. Is it?"

How that man could see right through people, Agent Long would never know. He was surprised that The Doc hadn't already figured out he was a Colician. Maybe he did, but Agent Long would never know because of his empty mind. If there was something—anything—going on in The Doc's head, even just a single thought, Agent Long might be able to understand him slightly and predict what he was plotting next. The Doc's body language and curiosity showed that he still didn't know what Agent Long was or what he had done. It was a good thing; he could announce who and what he really was right before he killed The Doc and then he could stride out of that hospital with his middle finger proudly raised at humanity. But it was quite clear that The Doc was already suspicious of him because of his oddly timed disappearance. The way The Doc stared into his eyes and seemed to look directly at his soul made Agent Long wonder how the man didn't know exactly what was going on yet. It was obvious that he would be more wary and it would be difficult to get him alone.

"Where did you go before?" The Doc asked when Agent Long didn't answer. "You disappeared for some time from what I heard."

Courtesy of Lieutenant Odau, Agent Long thought in irritation, mentally rolling his eyes.

"Did you really come looking for me?" The Doc questioned. "Or were you going to meet somebody else?"

His cold, soulless eyes made Agent Long shiver. He had encountered some pretty intimidating people in his lifetime, but The Doc went off the charts. Agent Long thought back to the very first time he had seen him, just a few hours earlier. When he had lived among the Colicians, The

Doc had only been a name; a scary story that had been told to children to warn them of the danger humans posed to their kind. The few unfortunates who were able to put a face to the name were either murdered or used as science experiments and weapons against themselves. Now that Agent Long was able to match the face and name, he was pleased that he would have the honor of looking the murderer of his species in the eyes before he died. If Agent Long lived long enough to get back to his people, he would always live with the honor of killing the man who killed his kind, his family, and the soul of one of his oldest friends. He told Hara he wouldn't be able to go back with her, but now that he let himself think about the past, he realized he couldn't bear to live another moment among the evil that created The Doc and everything like him. He would go back with Hara and try to help her through the consequences she would face once she returned.

For a few moments, Agent Long let The Doc stand there, waiting. He was busy running over the past in his mind, and thinking of what he could maybe do for the future. He realized he could start by ridding the world of the newest Adolf Hitler. The Doc had managed to survive for so long while being the most wanted target in history, and no one had managed to kill him yet. But Agent Long knew he couldn't be allowed to hurt anyone else. It all had to end. So he used The Doc's thirst for knowledge and insight against him, and took the opportunity while it still stood.

"Actually, I was going to meet someone else," Agent Long told him, knowing The Doc would take the bait. "And I believe we may have a problem."

"Really?" The Doc said, immediately interested. "And what might that be?"

"Are any of your guards around?" Agent Long asked while looking around quickly, praying the answer was no.

"Why?" The Doc demanded suspiciously.

"Because what I'm about to say has to be done face to face. Just you and me." Agent Long raised an eyebrow, implying that he was dead serious. Gesturing with his head towards the crowded hall, he said, "Come, let's talk. I've needed to speak with you about this for a very long time."

As he led The Doc down the hall towards his fate, Agent Long smiled to himself, wondering how it could be so easy.

✳ ✳ ✳

Every second that went by felt ominous like the seconds counting down on a time bomb. The only thing she could hear when she strained herself were the distant voices of the hospital in the next hallway, but other than that there were no sounds at all around her. Hara felt her time slowly running out and her fate bearing down on her like a charging bull. She had one slim chance to escape, and if she made even one wrong move it would end very badly for her and many of her people as well. The FBI agents would be coming for her any minute now, and her abilities still were not functional. It had been just over ten minutes since Rhett had given her the injection and even though he had said it may take up to twenty she felt like it wasn't going to work. Trying to relax and wait patiently for her brain to start working properly again, Hara thought back to something an old friend of hers had once told her.

"At times, you will become aware that a certain event will occur in the not-too-distant future. You will not know when or how long it will take even though that is your utmost desire. Paranoia will become your life, but it is not healthy to live your life fearing what is to come. Patience is a virtue, child, and although I know you fear the future, you must not. Wait patiently and what you are searching for will find you."

Well, it sure as hell found me alright! Hara thought to herself, finding the statement ironic. Good old Clyde.

Clyde Stetzer had been the most widely known and the most feared prophet of the Colician race. There were always several prophets among them, such as Hara's son, but only one per generation had the gift as powerful as Clyde. He could see everything, and in quite the literal sense. Unlike most prophets, he didn't have dreams or visions or flashes of the future. It was almost as if he was "born" knowing every event that was going to play out in his lifetime. (All Colicians who were born human and were changed later in life considered the change their "birth.") Clyde was nearly fifty when Hara first met him just over a year ago, so that would have made him about twenty, just two years older than her father, when he first developed the ability to see forward in time. For a few years, he lived among the Colicians in their isolated little world. But his predictions were always accurate, to the precise detail, and when he began preaching about certain disturbing things that were going to happen, people started to become very afraid of him and his prophecies. There was also the part about how Clyde was a tad insane; knowing everything that would happen must have driven him over the edge. Deciding that it would be in everyone's best interest if he lived on his own where he couldn't scare anyone with his premonitions, Hara's father and his government asked Clyde to leave the populated area. Clyde wasn't upset. In fact, he was thrilled that he would be living alone. Leaving behind his home and pretty much everything he owned, he moved far up north into the snowy region where it was freezing all year round and built his home in a large cave made out of ice. He stayed there in exile for quite a long time, as happy as anyone could be. For nearly twenty-five years he lived his life in peace. That is until the Colician government grew wary of his warning.

Hara first met Clyde after she had gone to visit her brother in the hospital after The Doc's first attack. Once her father convinced her to stay in their capital city for a while, he told her about a prophecy that had been foretold by Clyde. Hara had only heard stories about the great Clyde Stetzer, and she was very surprised when her father told her that Clyde wouldn't give them any more information until they brought her to him. Apparently, the prophecy spoke of their world coming to an end and Hara's father wanted more details so he could find a way to prevent it from happening.

Hoping a trip to the far north together would help to mend their broken relationship, Hara agreed and they made the week-long journey to Clyde Stetzer's ice cave. She was puzzled by the man she encountered; like The Doc, she had difficulty hearing anything going on inside Clyde's head and it frightened her. He was also a very jumpy, schizophrenic man, always hopping about in a twitchy manner and talking to himself constantly. But to everyone's surprise, Hara, her father, Daniel, Allan, Meg, and the few others who accompanied them—including Shawn Perry—Clyde actually made a great effort to tone down his frantic actions in an attempt to keep Hara calm. "You will need a very calm, open mind for what I'm about to show you," he said when her father asked him about it. That was very much the truth. The things that Clyde showed them were so disturbing that they all had trouble sleeping for several weeks. What he showed Hara—and only Hara—left her scared out of her mind.

For the first time since the war started, Hara allowed herself to think back to Clyde's predictions, and how it came to pass exactly as he described. While the two of them were left alone together for only a few minutes, he showed her everything that would happen to her up to the end of the year. He showed her the death of everyone she loved, and how the events would play out. He showed her how she would retaliate. He showed her the horrible experiences she would eventually have with The Doc. He showed her mind slowly slipping away. He showed her how she would leave their world behind to try to find a solution. Unfortunately for her, Clyde never showed her what would happen after she left, so she didn't know how the events that were to come would play out.

When Clyde had first shown her those visions, Hara had no intention in believing him. She had never in her life lost someone she loved to death, and it was impossible for her to imagine that very soon every single friend and family member would succumb to the same fate. So at first she dismissed Clyde's claim, but then he showed her and her father's council the events that would lead up to the death of nearly their entire species. They all saw the humans invading, taking control, and destroying their major cities. They all saw the humans butchering their people like cattle and using the rest as science experiments.

But above all the destruction, they saw two faces that would always be at war with one another: The Doc, labeled "The Beast" or "The Bringer of Death," and Hara, the one who was supposed to slowly lose her soul but also leave the world she knew in order to find a way to reverse everything that had happened. Even though she didn't want to believe him, she did, and now that she let herself think back to the prophecies, she realized that everything Clyde predicted came true. Down to the very last detail. Maybe if she had allowed herself to think back to it earlier, she would have been able to prevent many of the things that had happened. It had all been right there in front of her, but she just kept trying to deny it. Clyde had been absolutely right about her soul; it was almost completely gone. The only part of her left was her son, and she supposed he was the only thing that had ever—even subconsciously—allowed her to hold on. Very, very deep down a part of her must have known Dreyson was still alive even though she couldn't feel him, and that was what must have allowed her to keep living.

It suddenly struck her. Of course! She had always known her son was alive! Even though her mind couldn't feel him and she was tricked into believing he was dead, there had been that small part of her subconscious that refused to listen to her beliefs. It knew her son was still with her, and it forced her to keep pushing forward. Thinking back to when Clyde first showed her the path her future would take, he showed her the deaths of all her family members, except for Dreyson. The images had all been flashes, not even a moment long. It would have been easy for her to make a mistake and automatically assume that Dreyson had been in the images as well. Not to mention that she had forcibly inserted the memories into the back of her mind so she wouldn't have to think about them. The part of her memory storing the vision must have picked out that Dreyson wasn't going to die and held onto that. The Doc had always been trying to understand how her mind worked, but there were parts of her mind that even she didn't understand. The Colician race would continue to surprise even its own people for generations to come.

Hara hadn't been the only one completely horrified by the prophecies. The families of everyone present were predicted to die in the massacre. They were all frantic and desperate to know when these events were expected to begin. It was crucial that they found out when the war would start happening.

Snickering to himself, Clyde had answered, "It's already begun."

Thank you, Clyde, Hara thought to herself as she lay strapped to the gurney. *You saved my life even though I didn't realize it. Thank you so much for keeping me alive long enough to save my son.* She had only encountered Clyde once more after the first time, so she had no idea if he was still alive, but if he was, she prayed he would hear her and know how grateful she was.

Startled out of her thoughts as three people entered the room, she forced herself to stay completely still so none of them would suspect anything when her abilities finally become available to her again. She stared blankly up at the ceiling like she had before, not blinking. She slowed her breathing and made herself remain calm. She needed to be under complete control if she planned to make a successful escape.

"Do you think she's awake?" the FBI agent called Andy Martinson asked.

"No," replied the agent called Jaz Hersh. "I overheard The Doc saying that she's totally catatonic. No movements or responses at all. We should be fine."

"I just get the feeling that she's going to jump up and attack us," said the agent Renee Michaels, the bitch who had tried to steal her kid.

You bet your sweet little blonde ass I will! Hara thought in disgust, planning to go for her throat first.

"Somebody should go and check though, just to be safe," Martinson told the others uncertainly.

Hersh sighed. "Must you always be so chicken shit?" she asked him. Hara heard her approach, and she was careful to not give her any type of response as she came into view and leaned over her. Hersh raised a hand above her face and snapped her fingers several times to see if she would react. But when Hara gave no response at all, she shook her head. "See? Completely catatonic. We'll be fine. Now will you come help?"

"Shouldn't somebody go out to the SUV and make sure it's secure?" Martinson asked, the hesitance still in his voice.

"It'll be fine!" Hersh cried in exasperation. "Let's just go before somebody catches us!"

Just get me the hell out of here.

"Did you hear that?" Michaels said in surprise.

"What?"

"I don't know," she muttered, her voice wary. "I just thought I heard something…"

It took a minute for Hara to realize that Michaels had heard her thoughts. Hara's abilities must have been coming back to her, and she must have been thinking too loudly. Keeping her mind quiet so she wouldn't startle anyone else, she waited as patiently as she could for her abilities to completely return. The three agents were futzing with the locks on the wheels and arguing in hushed tones while she slowly began to feel the energy flow through her bit by bit. It felt good as she started to feel normal again, and to her surprise her self-confidence came back ever so slightly.

When they finally figured out how to unlock the wheels, Hara sensed that she was just about back to her full functioning capacity, but she wanted to wait until she was one hundred percent. It was crucial that she strike at the perfect time, or else she would be right back where she started. Only instead of The Doc as her captor, she would have a bunch of curious, clueless cops prodding her and acting like they knew everything about her when they really knew absolutely nothing. So she waited for her moment as the agents began to push her towards the door, sensing every sound, thought, sight, smell, and feeling around her. The wait was almost worse than the wait during childbirth. It was taking the agents way too long to move her. When she felt her abilities were back entirely, she tightened her fist in anticipation. It was a wonder that nobody could hear her heart pounding in her chest. Her moment had come.

✳ ✳ ✳

"Who was this person you went to see?" The Doc asked curiously once they stepped into an empty stairwell, about one hundred yards from Hara's current position.

As Agent Long closed the door behind him when he was certain no guards were keeping watch, he forgot that The Doc was speaking to him. He was busy thinking about his past. Ever since he came to Philadelphia, he had blocked out his memories of his home. But now he felt it was time he let them soak back in; he wanted to remember everything in crystal clear detail so he would know why he was going to kill this man.

The first thing that came to his mind was his family. His parents, his brothers, his nieces and nephews. Rhett Simco had been the youngest of six boys, and each of his brothers had a soul mate and at least two children. His father had served as a member of the Cabinet for a number of years, until he felt he was too old to continue. His mother had worked as a secretary in the capitol building, and she too had been great friends with Hara's father. That was how Rhett first met Hara.

While the members of the Cabinet worked, the children would play sports and games together. This was, of course, when they weren't attending two hours of classes every day. Unlike human schools, children didn't attend classes for seven hours in large groups. Instead, each child had their own designated "teacher" who gave them a two-hour lesson each day until the big tests every six months. The teachers were actually computers that taught them at the child's basic level, challenging them enough but not to the extent of frustration. At the mid-year tests, the children of each city would gather together in City Hall to test not only their knowledge, but their leadership skills and their ability to work as a team.

Rhett and Hara used to play a human sport called "tennis" with Jack and their other friend Davey. Rhett's older brothers had all moved out once they found their soul mates, so he hadn't seen much of them as he was growing up. They had all found their mates and had children before they were seventeen, and their constant absences left Rhett lonely and desperate for company. He spent more time with his friends than with his family, and he always felt that Hara, Jack, Davey, and his other companions were his true family. But even his friends chose to leave because of their soul mates.

Unfortunately for him, he would be the one forced to say goodbye the next time. His parents retired from the Cabinet when he was about fourteen, and decided to move down to the tropical region and wanted Rhett to go with them. Ever since then, Rhett had stayed detached from the rest of the world so he wouldn't be forced to say any more goodbyes.

Hara was never around much after she met Bo and started having his children. Everyone had always assumed that Hara and Jack would end up together. They had struggled to keep it a secret, but love that powerful is always impossible to hide. So when people found out that Hara's mate was actually Bo Rockwell, one of their biggest enemies, it came as a huge shock. The guy was a Caiten, but he was still her mate and she had to deal with him and the issues he soon brought.

The war first came when the capital city was attacked by humans and nearly a dozen Colicians were killed. The incident started to draw Rhett out of the hole he had dug, and that was when he realized just how uneasy the attack had made everyone, no matter how far away from it they were. His parents were very upset about the brutal deaths of a few of their own, and their race found it disturbing that humans could invade, attack, and then disappear without being detected or stopped. If two dozen humans could enter their world and hurt them as easily as they did, then what was to stop an entire army from invading? Eventually one would.

Rhett's parents were killed in one of the early attacks, so he was on his own right from the start. He fled for months to the snowy mountain region, where very few people lived due to the freezing temperatures. It was to be assumed that since few lived there, the humans wouldn't bother looking for anyone up there. About two hundred thousand survivors had the same idea. On the way up, Rhett encountered several families that had been broken by the war, and even in that time of great sorrow they all managed to pull together and make it up into the mountains. It was in those mountains that Rhett finally met his soul mate, Emily.

Emily Rogers was a beautiful young woman. Humans claimed that all Colicians appeared physically beautiful, but Rhett didn't believe that to be true. For all of his kind to be beautiful, that left no one to be different, special. They were all different. Not everyone was beautiful. But Emily was. Her silky blonde hair flowed halfway down her back in golden waves, and her sapphire blue eyes were as pure as her soul. She had a smile that lit up Rhett's world the first time they met. She had even saved him from committing the unthinkable. She was two years older than him, so she would have been celebrating her twenty-first birthday sometime after Rhett decided to leave.

One thing that always happens after two soul mates meet for the first time is the conception of their first child. Emily was pregnant with their firstborn—a girl whose name was yet to be chosen—when their camp was attacked. It had been mid-December, and the frigid temperatures were unbearable, making it difficult for anyone to fight back. Of the twenty thousand people in his camp, forty-seven were taken to the labs and the rest were murdered. Rhett wasn't really sure how he survived; it all happened so fast that he couldn't keep track of who was Colician and who was human. Someone hit him over the head before he could act to defend himself and his mate. When he awoke, he was surrounded by twenty thousand bodies—his friends and people he had begun to think of as family. He looked and looked for hours, pushing aside a disgusting number of bodies. But he never found his mate, and he had known from the start that he wouldn't. Emily was pregnant; they wouldn't kill a pregnant Colician. It was a disturbing fact that The Doc took interest in those who were pregnant.

It was still unclear how the Bonding Effect—the Soul Mate System—worked, even to the Colicians. The Doc wanted to be the first to figure it out. How was it that two Colicians could simply touch and they immediately knew they were meant to be together? How was it that the woman would then become pregnant, without any sex involved? How was it that the baby knew exactly when to come out, and would then instruct its mother to start pushing? Any pregnant woman was a prize to The Doc. Emily had been taken to one of the labs on the southeastern coast, the same one—as he discovered later from a refugee he encountered—where Hara had been taken. Rhett knew right away that he would never see Emily again. He knew that he would never get to see his baby, his daughter. The Doc was going to dissect them both. Once again, Rhett's family was being destroyed by that bastard. Only this time, they were going to suffer first.

I have to get out of here...

The pain was too much for him to bear. He had lost everything he loved and there was nothing he could do to save his mate and unborn child. He was at the breaking point; he had to get away from the world of war, at least for a while. So he ran as far away as he could from his camp. He ran away from all the dead bodies and he ran away from his life. He ran until he had no more energy to go on any farther.

And then he found the machine.

There were rumors that there was another camp less than fifty miles to the west that was building a machine. The machine could transport people to the human world and they could live a normal life with no one ever knowing they existed. Word had it that only a select few were allowed to go through to try and silently change things, but he had also been told that Hara was the one running the operation, and after she heard what he had been through Rhett was certain she would understand and let him leave. After all, they were friends. He traveled in the direction of the next camp for days, feeling one last shred of hope living inside of him. But when he finally arrived, and he saw that Hara's camp had been entirely wiped out, that last bit of hope died as well. The stench of death was everywhere, and no matter where he ran he couldn't escape it.

For some reason, however, he didn't completely give up. A piece of him still felt there was a way out for him, and he was desperately searching for it. He made it this far and he wasn't dead or captured yet, so there must have been something waiting for him somewhere. The Colician race believed in "destiny," that each person had a specific path they would inevitably follow, and if Rhett hadn't died from any of the massacres already, then didn't that mean he was destined for something more? Maybe he would somehow help H end the war. He prayed his destiny rolled along smoothly, wherever it led. If he did help H win the war, then he could get his mate and child back. Even if he died helping, he knew H would not stop until she killed the Odau boy. His mate and child would survive whether he lived or not, and that, he realized, was why he had lived on in the first place, for this last battle to save his family. It was funny how Colicians' subconscious kept them all alive even after they had lost everything. There was always that one little spark of hope, of life, that pushed them forward even when all seemed lost forever. It was an amazing gift. It had kept him, H, and so many more from committing the unthinkable.

Rhett thought about everything he had lost, and everything he was about to get back. He didn't realize, however, that he had been thinking everything over while staring down at a certain spot on The Doc's right shoulder.

He must have been staring into space for some time, because he was startled back into reality by The Doc's fingers snapping loudly in his face. "Hello? Agent Long? Would you mind waking up, please?"

Blinking in surprise, Rhett raised his eyes to meet the crazy doctor's. He tried to think of something logical to say, like an apology or an explanation, but no words came to mind.

Gazing back at him with a kind of sideways expression, The Doc asked him uncertainly, almost suspiciously, "Are you feeling alright?"

Since when do you give a shit about anyone other than yourself? Rhett wanted to blurt out, but instead he bit his lip and muttered, "I will be. Soon." And it was true. His attention shifted for a moment to the gun in his belt. He would most certainly use it before they left this stairwell, and once The Doc was dead he would be at peace.

Raising an eyebrow, The Doc gave him a half grin. "You seemed pretty urgent earlier. Is there really something you needed to talk to me about or am I just wasting my time here?"

Rhett continued to stare at him, to stare at the man who had murdered his race. How easy it would be to kill him right now. But he couldn't kill him quite yet. Not before he revealed himself to him. So he just stared at him, for so long that The Doc, who made everyone else uncomfortable just by looking at them, shifted his weight uneasily and stuck his hands in his pockets. His expression never wavered, but Rhett could see it in his ice cold eyes. He knew something wasn't right.

"Do you know how many people you killed in the war, Doc?" Rhett asked him finally, his voice soft but chilling.

The half-smile left The Doc's face for just a second, and then it was back, and he snickered loudly. "Oh, Agent Long. You're not turning into Perry, are you?"

"Do you know how many people you killed in the war?" Rhett repeated.

Smirking back at him, The Doc asked coldly, "Do you know how many people I killed in the war?" His eyes no longer matched his face. They were colder.

"Yes," Rhett whispered, nodding slowly. "You killed at least two point one billion people. I'm sorry, Colicians. I forgot you don't count them as people. Who knows how many *people* you've killed too?" Shaking his head in disgust, he repeated, "Two point one billion. How can you live with that?"

Taking a few steps forward so he was in Rhett's face, The Doc demanded, "What exactly is it that you want from me? Do you want an explanation? An apology?" He laughed scornfully. "Do you want me to apologize to her? To all of them? Well, let me tell you something, Agent Long. I'm not sorry for what I did, so I won't be making any apologies, and I don't need to explain myself to anyone."

Sighing, Rhett stared at his enraged face. "I don't want you to apologize."

"Oh, well that's jolly good news," The Doc said sarcastically.

"And I don't need you to explain anything," Rhett continued. "Because I already know."

"Do you?"

"Yes, I do."

"And how would you know?"

"Tell me, Doc, since when can you not sniff out a Colician that's sitting right under your damn nose?" Rhett demanded harshly.

Taken aback, The Doc's anger was replaced by utter confusion. "Excuse me?"

"You've been studying us for what, a decade? Two? Even longer than that? And you couldn't even tell you were working with one this whole time. I thought you could pick one of us out of a crowd with your eyes shut?"

"Who are you?" The Doc asked, actually taking a step back. Rhett saw that he really seemed afraid, but that was because he hadn't been able to see it before. Now he could.

"I think you know," Rhett replied, narrowing his eyes at him.

"I've never met you before today," The Doc declared, his voice shaking slightly. His eyes were searching Rhett's face desperately, trying to find his answers there.

"No, you haven't," Rhett agreed, and added with clenched teeth, "But you've met my mate."

Cocking his head as he had so many times before, The Doc stared hard at him as he thought, trying to place him among the many women he had encountered. "I'm going to need a little more help than that, my friend."

"I am not your friend," Rhett growled.

"Okay," The Doc acknowledged, raising his hands apologetically and taking another cautious step back. "I can see that you don't like me very much—"

"What makes you think that I would?" Rhett demanded furiously.

"Nothing," The Doc said quickly. "Absolutely nothing." Staring hard into Rhett's hazel eyes, he asked carefully. "I can see that you have a hate for me almost as strong as Hara's. Was your mate one of my patients?"

"Patients?" Rhett repeated in disbelief. "Patients? I think you meant to say experiments! Or guinea pigs!"

"Who was she?" The Doc asked, trying not to upset him any more than he already was.

"Emily Rogers!" Rhett cried, clenching his fists and breathing hard.

Mouthing the name a few times, The Doc's face suddenly lit up. "Blonde hair," he said as if reminding himself. "She was pregnant with a little girl."

"Yes," Rhett hissed, not liking the way he used the word was.

The Doc looked back up and a sick, twisted grin came to his face. "Simco."

His ears ringing as The Doc spoke his name, Rhett said again, "Yes."

"That's right," The Doc murmured, nodding slowly as he searched Rhett's face once more. "She told me about you. Beautiful girl. Beautiful baby, too. Nice work."

Rhett's heart skipped a beat. "She…she had the baby?"

"Yes," The Doc answered casually, still grinning. "I induced her ten weeks in to see what the effects of prematurity would be. I'll tell you." He chuckled to himself, clearly enjoying it all. "That baby put up a hell of a fight. She just refused to come out for the longest time, but eventually, she did. Like I've said before." His grin broadened. "I can be very persuasive."

Rhett was not prepared for the amount of rage he was experiencing. His heart started pounding in his chest, and his breathing was sharp and heavy. Clenching his fist even tighter and glaring even harder, he set his jaw and ground his teeth together. It was an unpleasant feeling, but he was far beyond caring. How dare that bastard induce his mate so he could torture their child! He couldn't even feel the babe's bond! Rhett was so close to murder it was surprising The Doc didn't see it. Maybe he did, but he was no longer afraid.

"Oh," The Doc said with fake surprise. "That struck a nerve." Snickering, he pushed Rhett even further, not seeming to be fearful of his approaching death. "Did you know that premature Colician babies have a weakened bond with their parents, which is why you had no idea she had already come into the world? Their abilities show up within days of their birth. Your kid's a pyro, by the way. Difficult to handle, that one. Her ability irritates her so badly that she throws up every time she uses it, which makes her cry and only use the ability more. The only way I can stop her from tormenting herself is by sedating her. Did you know that she's also developed food allergies, something I'm sure you have never heard of in your history…?"

"Shut up!" Rhett snarled, taking a few menacing steps forward. "Just stop talking before I—"

"Before you what?" The Doc asked, allowing Rhett to get right in his face. "What are you going to do, Simco? Get inside my head? You can't, can you?"

"Why can't I?" Rhett demanded, feeling the empty space inside The Doc's head again. "Is it because there's nothing there? Is it because you have no soul? Your poor little family died and you just became nothing?"

His eyes narrowing for a fraction of a second, The Doc growled, "Leave my family out of this."

"Why?" Rhett snapped. "You brought mine into this."

Eyeing him, The Doc said, "Which brings me to asking, why is there such a huge age difference between you and Emily? She was supposed to be older than you, wasn't she?"

"I came here thanks to you and your damn war!" Rhett accused. "I was supposed to be nineteen, and now look at me!"

"It's not my fault you're a coward and chose to run from death," The Doc challenged. "How long have you been hiding, huh? Twenty years? Thirty?"

"I don't know and I don't care either."

"What do you care about?"

"Getting rid of you."

The Doc snorted. "So you brought me here to kill me? Is that it?"

"That was the plan, I suppose," Rhett mumbled, not quite sure where to go from there. "I just thought there were some things I needed to tell you first."

"Then tell me this, Simco," the Doc instructed, crossing his arms over his chest. "If you're a Colician, and you know I've hurt your mate and baby, then why have we been working together this whole time? Why didn't you just kill me right away?"

That was something Rhett had been dying to tell him. "Those poor souls you have as guards? The ones who seem to have been lobotomized? Well, they don't exactly like the way you've made them into mindless drones. Deep down, they're screaming for help, and along with that they're screaming your secrets out to the world."

"And I'm guessing you found something worth keeping me alive for?" The doc muttered, putting on a bored expression.

"Well, actually, most of it just made me want to kill you even quicker. Like the fact that you're planning on killing Perry once you've finished toying with him. Which will be when, by the way? How much longer are you going to sit and laugh while Perry makes a fool of himself and leads the others on fantasy goose chases, looking for things that don't even matter? When were you planning on telling Perry who Hallie Reifert really is, huh? Never? Because he just thinks she's some college professor's dead wife, but both of us know she isn't dead. So did you ever intend to tell Perry the truth, or were you going to make him look like an ass until you got bored and wiped him out of history?"

The Doc didn't respond. He just continued staring at Rhett with those cold gray eyes. Back in his world, Rhett had heard stories about how The Doc wasn't human but was actually a Colician, his power to look into one's eyes and see their soul (Others said that he was actually the Devil coming to swallow them all and send them to hell for what they had become). But they were just rumors. The way The Doc looked at people with eyes so piercing, looking right through them...well, it got to people and messed with their heads. Rhett knew the truth. The Doc was just a regular human with freaky eyes. He was a nut job, after all.

Deciding to let his question go unanswered, Rhett sighed. He could feel himself getting closer and closer to the moment when he would kill The Doc. He had to wait for the perfect moment to do so. He wanted The Doc to know that his Hara was getting away. He wanted The Doc to die with that look of fury in his eyes, knowing that his prized possession would escape and carry out what she had come to this city to do. "I also discovered that you were holding Dreyson hostage long before you decided to tell anybody," he explained. "There was no way I could get him out safely with all the security around your semi, and I needed to find H as well. I figured I'd let you live a little longer to make sure I could get both of them out of this alive, and to see if you had any other sick shit stuffed in your jacket."

The Doc raised an eyebrow at the comment. "And how exactly are you planning to do that?" he demanded. "You may have taken the boy, but I have a transport about ready to take the girl, and I will tell you right now that I will kill you if you try to intervene."

It was Rhett's turn to snicker. "Too late," he whispered.

"What are you talking about?" The Doc asked, concerned but not losing his cool.

"I think you know," Rhett said again, smirking.

"You disappeared before," The Doc recalled, as if finally remembering why they had left to talk in the first place. He was starting to get nervous. "Where did you go? Who did you go see?"

"Why should I tell you?" Rhett said, enjoying that he was now the one withholding valuable information. But he figured he might as well, just to enjoy The Doc's horrified expression once he realized what was really going on. "I went to see Dr. Bennett."

Raising his eyebrow again, The Doc said in surprise, "So you found the good doctor. Where was he hiding all this time?"

"It wasn't where he was hiding, it was where his patients were hiding," Rhett corrected. "You were the one who stumbled across them in the first place. Which leads me to wonder; how did you even find that place?"

"I knew Allan would be weak after all the hops," The Doc replied, his eyes wide as things began to finally click into place in his head. "I figured he'd need a safe place to hide while he got well again. So I searched all the rooms still under construction." He paused as he thought the new information over. "It was Bennett helping them this whole time?"

"Wow. You are slower than I thought you were. He's been on their side since before you attacked Jack's motorcade."

Then why did Hara still fall for the trap?" The Doc demanded growing frustrated.

"She's stubborn, we both know that," Rhett reminded flatly. "But you shouldn't be worried about that right now. What you should be worrying yourself over is the injection I gave H just over ten minutes ago."

The Doc's face actually turned white. Rhett was loving it. "What injection?"

"The injection I gave her to allow her to regain all her abilities."

For a moment, The Doc just stared at him. Then he breathed, "You're bluffing."

Rhett smirked and snickered again. "Am I?"

* * *

Hara waited to make her move until the FBI agents had her in the side stairwell. It was hidden and quiet and if there was a struggle, The Doc's guards wouldn't be able to detect it. Once all three agents were inside the stairwell and the door was closed, Hara let out a pulse that caused them to drop like stones but ultimately wouldn't hurt them. The three were in a debate about how Lieutenant Odau would handle the matter when she hit them. Michaels and Hersh dropped to the floor above the first step, but Martinson tumbled down the first flight and lay splayed out at the bottom. That had been unintentional, but Hara was sure he would be fine. She focused on mentally undoing the straps and pulled the gag out of her mouth once her arms were freed.

"Sorry about that," she apologized to the three of them, pulling the strap off her forehead and mentally undoing the ones over her legs and midsection. When she hopped off the gurney, the muscles in her arms and legs cramped up from how tightly The Doc had fastened the restraints. The skin on her forehead felt tight as well, but she didn't have time to think about what parts of her were uncomfortable. Glancing down at Michaels, who was lying at her feet, she rubbed her wrists and thought about what she should say. The FBI agent's eyes were still open, and they were wide with fear. Hara saw that Michaels was breathing in fast, sharp gasps, as if she was waiting for Hara to attack her. But she wasn't planning on hurting any of them; she was just unsure of what she should say to the woman who had tried to steal her child. She had so many things, nasty things, which she had planned on saying, but now that she was in this situation she was drawing a blank. Should she apologize? Yell at her? Biting her lip, Hara finally said, "You should have just taken my son. This mess would have at least been over." She shook her head down at Michaels' frozen expression of terror. "Tell Perry I said to watch out for The Doc. I have to go now."

Running down the first flight of stairs, Hara was delayed momentarily as Martinson attempted to stop her by grabbing at her leg. Kicking his hand away, she continued on her way. She went down two floors before she reached the first floor and as she pushed out of the door to step into the lobby she suddenly realized how relieved she was to actually be free. After the deal with her son, she hadn't really cared what happened to her. Now that she really was free, she was surprised at how happy she was. She could finally be with her son again, and she could finally finish this war.

Her newly found freedom, unfortunately, left her distracted and she didn't stop to check that the lobby was clear. Walking right out into the open towards the large sliding door exit, Hara's eyes wandered over the people in the large crowd and landed on one individual. It took her a moment to realize he was one of The Doc's guards. By that time he was already speaking into his radio. "She's in the lobby," he said in a low monotone.

Ever since she had first been captured by The Doc, Hara had given up on thinking before acting. It took too long to think of a plan when she was panicking and only had a few seconds to react. When she would finally react she would get shot or tackled or something worse. What she had learned over the many months in captivity is that when facing a human with a weapon, the best thing to do is strike and run. If she tried to think of a way out of it all, she would just end up getting captured again. So she did what she had done many times before.

As the guard was reaching towards his belt, Hara raised her hand and quickly expelled as much fire as she dared at him and immediately began to run. The people in the lobby scattered away from the flames and cries of surprise erupted from all around the room. Changing her course from the sliding doors to the window a few feet to the right of them, Hara dove at the glass, waving her hand and making it shatter before impact. She tumbled through the waterfall of tiny shards and landed hard on her face on the sidewalk outside. Feeling the little cuts on her arms and face heal quickly, Hara jumped to her feet and sprinted past the doors and toward the next parking lot. As she did so, the fire alarm sounded from inside the building and the sliding doors opened, allowing everyone from the lobby and all non-patients from the first floor to come spilling out. A panicked human ran into her and knocked her to the ground. Somebody's foot collided with the side of her head and she clamped her teeth together in pain.

There was so much noise around her; the screaming, the fire alarm, her pounding heart; that her ears started to ring and she cringed from the agony her entire body was experiencing from the sudden blows. She expected that at any second The Doc's guard would grab her by the hair and dragged her away, but when she couldn't sense him around she turned and peered back through the doors into the lobby. Lying in a flaming, burning heap in the center of the room was the guard, already dead. Her aim had been particularly good.

"I'm sorry," she whispered, finally feeling the regret she wanted to feel after taking a life. After all, she knew perfectly well that he had only been a mindless slave, forced to do whatever Master wanted him to do. That's what all of The Doc's guards were.

Without wasting any more time, Hara leapt to her feet once again and dashed around the side of the building. The entire police force would arrive shortly, bringing Herv the Perv and his friends, and she didn't want to be there when that happened. Besides, she had to get to her son. Slowing down her run to a jog, Hara let her mind expand as she searched for her son's. But then she remembered what The Doc had done, and how she would most likely never feel her son's presence again, and she felt the agony once more. Turning her search to the mind of Dr. Bennett, she discovered that he was waiting for her in the center of a large plaza beside a fountain about two blocks directly ahead of her. Her heart soaring, she picked up her pace once again, running towards the last thing she had left to fight for. The last thing she had left to live for.

Only a Colician could have heard it, but a commotion inside the building on the third floor directly above her caused her to come to a halt and stare up in shock. As she stood as still as a statue, she watched in horror as a third floor window was smashed and yet another one of her friends came tumbling to his end.

✳ ✳ ✳

It hadn't been more than ten seconds after Rhett told The Doc about what he had done that one of his guards radioed in to him.

"Sir, the girl is gone," he said in a soulless voice.

Glaring at Rhett furiously, The Doc turned and sprinted out the door and back down the hall towards the room where Hara had been held. Rhett stood staring after him. His hand lay on his gun, which he had been about to take out when The Doc took off. His moment had come, and it had passed, but now The Doc would be in a frantic state due to Hara's escape. He would be distracted, and in his fluster Rhett would take him down. It would be quiet, and to Rhett's dismay it would be quick. The Doc would not get to suffer as he had hoped, but at least he wouldn't be able to cause damage to either of their worlds anymore.

Exhausted from all the disasters of the past few days, Rhett walked out the door and started following The Doc's path back to the restricted section of the floor. The Doc was no longer in his line of sight; he had bolted out of there in quite a hurry. Picking up his pace a little, Rhett hoped that Hara wouldn't hurt any of the other agents during her escape. They may be humans, but he had worked with them for years and he didn't want anything to happen to them. After all his time among them, Rhett learned that there were, in fact, good humans in the world.

A loud roar erupted from below him causing the entire building to shake. Throwing out an arm to catch himself on the wall, Rhett looked around him in surprise. Hara was clearly on the move. Judging from the shockwave that had gone through the entire hospital, she had encountered a few roadblocks. Rhett could only pray that it was one of The Doc's guards and not one of his agents. It sounded like things were getting rough down below.

Most of the people around him had either stumbled or fallen to the floor from the sudden, unexpected quake, and now they were all looking around in fright and talking in loud, worried voices. Some people had actually started screaming. To add even more to all the ruckus, the fire alarms spread out across the floor sounded, and that sent everyone into a wild panic. People began running and screaming through the hallways, some shoving into him in order to find the nearest emergency exits and causing Rhett to fall back into the wall.

Any regular human would not have been able to hear it from where he stood, but Rhett was just able to hear The Doc's voice from the opposite end of the hall. He was shouting about something, and he sounded very angry. Fearing that he had caught the other agents in the act of stealing Hara, Rhett started to sprint the rest of the way. He ran into several panicked people as they attempted to flee the building, but he didn't stop. When he finally reached the plastic sheets dividing the section from the rest of the floor, he brushed them aside and stepped through, immediately keeping an eye out for The Doc. Rhett had arrived just in time to witness The Doc screaming death threats at Michaels, Hersh, and Martinson before dashing back into the room where Hara had been held.

"Agent Long!" Hersh cried when she saw him, hurrying over to him. "Sir, I don't know what happened! We were evacuating her just like you said, and then she paralyzed us or did something to us with her mind so we couldn't move…"

"She got away from us," Martinson interrupted grimly, staring down at the floor in shame.

"There was nothing we could have done to stop her," Michaels added defensively, her eyes showing her fear of failure.

Ignoring them, Rhett asked, "Where's Perry?"

Stammering in surprise, Michaels said, "He…uh…he's one floor below with Finchly and Odau…"

"Go find him," Rhett ordered, moving towards the door where The Doc had entered. "I need to deal with something."

"Sir, I wouldn't—" Martinson began, following him.

"I'm not you, son," Rhett replied, turning on him. "And that's why you are going to find Perry, and I'm going to deal with The Doc."

Martinson and Hersh immediately obeyed, going back to the side stairwell and heading down to the second floor. But Michaels hesitated, appearing extremely worried. "Sir, I don't think you understand—"

"I understand perfectly," Rhett replied impatiently.

"You don't know the state he's in right now!" Michaels declared, her eyes pleading with his.

"Don't worry about me," Rhett instructed her, turning away once more.

"Agent Long, you don't know what he said he was going to do to us!" Michaels cried desperately.

"Go find Perry!" Rhett ordered, stepping inside the small room and closing the door behind him. Right before it clicked shut, he added quietly, "I know what I'm doing."

"No, no, NO!" The Doc was screaming in a rage, slamming his palms furiously against the glass of the window.

Turning to face him, Rhett thought of how easy it would be to kill him in that instant. His back was turned, and he was too angry and distracted to notice him. But Rhett wanted to look in his eyes as he died. He wanted to see him leave this world. Putting one foot in front of the other, Rhett silently walked right up to The Doc until he was only a few feet away.

"God damn it!" The Doc shouted, slamming his fists on the glass once more. The window was making a dangerous quavering noise as if it was about to shatter. Michaels had been right; he wasn't in a pleasant mood.

Sensing H's presence down below, Rhett smirked, knowing that The Doc was being allowed to see his most precious experiment escaping before he died. "I've never really been much of a bluffer," Rhett said quietly, holding his ground as The Doc rounded on him.

His eyes crazed and filled with a rage that would frighten the most intimidating men, The Doc bared his teeth and snarled, "Do you have any idea what I'm going to do to you and your agents when I get that girl back?"

"Yes, I do," Rhett replied calmly, allowing The Doc to get right up in his face again. "And that's why I'm not going to let you get her back." Making sure he had clear eye contact with him, Rhett snapped his hand to his gun and whipped it out. He hadn't expected the Doc to have such quick reflexes.

Catching Rhett by the wrist holding the gun, The Doc pushed his arm away and kneed him hard in the stomach. Rhett, caught by surprise and getting the wind knocked out of him, dropped the gun and lost his balance. The Doc held onto him and swung him around towards the window, reaching for his belt in the process. He pulled an object out of it, but Rhett was only able to catch the glint of something metallic before The Doc shoved it into his throat.

The pain was to be expected, but not at such a high level. He tried to cry out for help, but he found he was unable to make a sound. Tasting the blood and feeling it begin to fill up in his mouth and throat, Rhett stared into The Doc's cold eyes in shock. He was gazing back at him with a mixture of disgust and amusement. How ironic it was that Rhett had planned to look The Doc in the eyes when he killed him. The pain overwhelming, Rhett's eyes started to flutter.

His lips forming into a tight smirk, The Doc pulled the knife out of Rhett's windpipe. "Nice try," he whispered. He shoved him backwards.

Unable to catch himself, Rhett felt the window shatter upon impact. The shards nipped at his exposed skin until he hit the pavement three stories below, falling just in time for Hara to witness his death firsthand.

✳ ✳ ✳

When Rhett struck the ground not six feet in front of her, Hara inhaled so sharply that her breath caught in her throat and a small squeak escaped. She had heard the quarrel between him and The Doc and was so surprised it was Rhett who came crashing through the window that she stood frozen in shock. For the first few devastating seconds she tried to convince herself that it wasn't him and it was in fact The Doc, but she couldn't deny herself the truth for very long. Exhaling slowly as her heart thumped in her chest, Hara reached a shaky hand toward her fallen friend and then closed her fingers into a tight fist. Letting out a sob, she took a few hesitant steps forward before pulling at her hair and moaning loudly through her teeth.

"Oh, God!" she whispered in horror, stepping around to Rhett's side. There was a knife wound in his throat, and dark red blood was pouring out over his chest and forming pools on either side of his head on the pavement. At first, Hara assumed he had died upon impact with the ground, but she soon saw that he was still alive. His eyelids were fluttering open and closed every few seconds, and his chest was barely rising and falling as he struggled for his last few breaths. Carefully reaching out with her mind to his, she found that he was no longer able to feel any pain. His neck had broken from the fall, severing the nerves in his spinal cord. He could no longer move or feel anything. Wailing in grief for her friend, she cried, "Oh my God!" Dropping to her knees, she placed a hand on his shoulder. "Rhett! What has he done to you?"

H, he thought to her, and Hara could hear him straining to even send a silent message to her. *H, it's okay…*

"I thought I told you to be careful!" Hara sobbed, tears spilling out of the corners of her eyes.

This was inevitable, hon, he replied, and then he groaned and his eyes rolled back in his head.

"Oh, God!" Hara cried again, putting a hand over his forehead and the other over the wound in his throat. "This is all my fault! Let me fix this…"

No! Rhett almost screamed at her, and if he had been able to move Hara thought he might have smacked her hands away. *I don't want you to fix this.*

"But I can!" Hara insisted, knowing he was running out of time. "It will only take a moment."

Just leave me be, Rhett ordered, his eyes closing again.

"But you'll die!" Hara squeaked, slowly removing her hands. Rhett's blood soaked her left palm, and even though she knew it would wash off, she also knew it would leave a stain in her soul forever.

I died a very long time ago, Rhett told her, his eyes remaining closed. *I died the moment I decided to abandon my race and my family so I could run from my own fear of death. This is how I deserve to die; slowly and shamefully.*

"You don't deserve this!" Hara whispered, her tears clouding up her eyes. Placing her right hand on his shoulder, she rubbed it soothingly. "Please let me help you."

I've already accepted this, Rhett said, and opened his eyes. *But will you do one favor for me?*

"Of course," Hara exclaimed, nodding quickly. "I'll do anything for you! I owe you that much."

When you fix everything and you go home, I need you to tell my mate something for me, Rhett explained.

"Okay," Hara said, sniffling. "Who is she?"

Her name is Emily Rogers, Rhett answered, his eyes starting to seem hazy. He was beginning to fade. *We decided that before our first child was born we would decide on a name together. But I wasn't there when she was born, and I have a name I would really like her to be called.*

Hara nodded. "I'll tell her. What name is it?"

Paz.

"Paz?" Hara repeated, puzzled. "I've never heard that name before."

It's Spanish, Rhett explained.

Hara nodded again. She was familiar with the language Spanish. English, Spanish, and French were the dominant languages in the Colician society. She didn't speak Spanish, but she had heard a few words of it spoken before. "Paz. It's pretty. What does it mean?"

A low gurgle started in Rhett's throat, making it sound like he might begin choking at any moment. The sound made Hara wary, but she soon realized that he was trying to speak. The knife wound was making it nearly impossible, but he was trying his hardest to get out one final word. Blood was flowing out of his mouth, and finally Rhett formed a single syllable with his lips and croaked it out ever so quietly. It was barely audible, yet Hara managed to catch the simple yet complicated word.

"Peace."

Just after Rhett managed to say his last word, his normally bright eyes went dark and she felt him fade away completely. She couldn't feel any part of his soul left behind. All that was left of him was his stiff, lifeless body. He was gone, just like Daniel.

More sobs began to escape her throat. She had lost yet another friend, and again it was her fault. When would everybody learn that helping her was suicide? But she wasn't only crying for Rhett's death. She was also crying because she hadn't realized how noble a heart Rhett really had. Even after everything they had been through, Rhett still wanted peace between both worlds. It finally dawned on her how much he really wanted peace when he asked her to name his baby Paz. Hara hadn't been able to fully appreciate how brave and compassionate Rhett was until he was dead, and she would never forget it.

I still have time to fix this, she told herself. *It doesn't have to end this way. This can still be reversed. I can still save him.*

"I'm so sorry!" she cried to Rhett's body, staring into his dull, glossy eyes. "I *will* fix this! I *will* change history! I *will* save you!"

She could almost hear Rhett's reassuring voice in her head. Maybe she really was.

"Oh my God!"

Jerking her head up from the sudden shout, Hara saw Perry running towards her from the sliding door entrance. He had a horrified expression on his face that physically showed how Hara was feeling at the moment. His gun was in his hand, but it was swinging down by his side instead of being aimed at her head like it normally was. Dropping to his knees beside her, he covered his mouth with a hand.

"Jesus!" he cried, staring down at his dead boss. "Dear God! He's dead! Oh my God! What happened?" He looked up at her, and for once his eyes weren't accusing. He finally understood that she was not his enemy. He finally understood that he belonged with her, on her side.

Meeting his eyes for a split second, Hara saw the Perry that she remembered. He was finally coming back to her. She didn't have time to focus on that, though. She had to focus on the real problem, the real killer. Looking up to the broken window where Rhett had been pushed, she saw The Doc standing there, peering at her through the shattered glass. His expression was neutral, calm. She had seen that look before, and bad things always came with it. He was angry now, and he was going to hurt a lot of people to get to her this time. Hara wondered how long he had been standing there watching her, but it was pretty obvious that it had been the whole time. Why hadn't he come after her? She knew why. She had declared war on him by running, and he was determined to pull her down even further to a point where she absolutely would not fight any longer. She knew it would mean killing Dreyson, and she would not allow that. When he came for her son, she would kill him without hesitation.

"That son of a bitch," Perry said, and Hara could sense the pain he was experiencing over the loss of Rhett.

"This is only the beginning," Hara whispered, keeping her eyes locked on The Doc's. When Perry turned his eyes back to her, she told him, "He'll keep killing until one of us finishes off the other. Hopefully, I can stop him before this becomes a bloodbath."

"This already is a bloodbath!" Perry snapped, and as Hara shifted her gaze to his she found that his eyes showed hopelessness. "How exactly do you plan to stop him?"

"By killing Odau's son," Hara explained, nodding to him with hopes that he would finally understand. Before she could catch his reaction, however, an angry shout from the entrance made them both turn their heads.

Lieutenant Odau, who was followed closely by Detective Finchly, was sprinting towards them with an intense rage in his eyes. He was glaring at Hara with such a hate that it actually terrified her. His gun was in his hand, and she didn't have to read his mind to know that he would shoot her.

Hara grabbed Perry by the arm. She left a smear of blood on his jacket, but she was thinking too quickly and her heart was pounding too fast for her to even notice. There was something she needed to tell Perry, and she didn't have much time.

"Make sure you keep everyone away from The Doc, yourself included," she instructed urgently, mentally inserting the message into his mind as well to make sure he didn't try to do anything foolish.

"Why?" Perry asked in confusion.

"Because he'll kill you!" Hara hissed, and without anything more she leapt to her feet and took off in the direction where she knew Dr. Bennett was waiting with her son.

"Wait!" Perry started to cry, but Hara knew he wasn't going to go after her. The other two, however, most definitely would.

"Stop now!" she heard Odau shout as he raced after her. "Stop, God damn it!"

But Hara wouldn't stop. She would never stop.

✳ ✳ ✳

She did stop, however, when she reached the plaza where Dr. Bennett and Dreyson were waiting. Bennett was sitting on the ledge of the large fountain he had mentally described to her when explaining how to get there. Dreyson was sitting on his lap, resting his head against Bennett's chest with his eyes closed. He had dozed off in Bennett's arms, but he stirred awake when Bennett spotted Hara and rose to his feet. When Dreyson saw his mother running up to him, a toothy smile crossed his face and he stretched out his arms toward her.

Reaching out and taking her son from Bennett, she breathed a sigh of relief that she finally had him back for good. She held him close and buried her face in his thick dark hair. "You knew I would come back for you," she whispered to him, remembering what he said when The Doc took her away. "You knew you would see me soon."

"I saw you fighting the bad guys," Dreyson said in his sweet baby voice. "You're my mommy. You always come back for me."

"Yes," Hara breathed, and squeezed her eyes shut as she felt a great swell of regret for her past actions, or in this particular situation her lack thereof. "That's right. I'm so sorry I didn't come back for you when we were stuck with The Doc."

"That's okay, Mommy," Dreyson replied softly, taking her face in his tiny hands. "I saw you in my dreams. I knew you would always come get me, even though it took a long time."

Staring into her child's lively green eyes, Hara couldn't help the tears that came flowing down her cheeks once again. She was so happy that someone was finally forgiving her for the mistakes she had made; it was almost more than she could bear. Part of her didn't even want him to forgive her. "I'm so sorry," she said again, her voice barely a murmur.

"I love you, Mommy," Dreyson told her, wrapping his arms around her neck and hugging her as tight as his frail body would allow.

Stifling the sob she so desperately wanted to let loose, Hara replied, "I love you too, baby. And The Doc will never keep us apart or hurt either of us ever again. I promise."

"He won't hurt us anymore," Dreyson agreed, and clung to her neck.

Hara prayed that Dreyson's statement was a premonition and not just an acknowledgment of her promises, but she couldn't know for sure and she wasn't about to ask him. He had been through enough stress and trauma. He didn't deserve any more.

As she continued to hold her son tightly in her arms, she finally noticed Bennett standing in front of them, smiling lightly at their emotional reunion. He appeared tired, and Hara couldn't blame him. Aiding her and her kind was difficult work. Hara knew that he deserved some serious recognition for what he was doing for her, but she didn't know what to do or say. A thank you would not cut it. He had selflessly risked his life to help her and her son, and Hara would never be able to repay him for it. Taking a deep breath, she struggled to find the right words to express her gratitude.

"Thank you so much," she said as more tears streamed out of her eyes. "You have no idea how much I appreciate what you've done for us."

Bennett continued to smile at her warmly. "It was my pleasure," he told her softly, nodding to Dreyson. "He's a great kid. Very well behaved and polite. He has a great mother."

Biting her lip, Hara felt her face flush red. She was having difficulty forming words, and she felt stupid for not having something more to say to him. So instead, she extended her hand toward him, hoping it would be enough for him to understand.

Eyeing her hand in surprise, Bennett slowly extended his as well and took hers. His hand was warm, and as they shook Hara finally saw that there really was a better side to humanity. It was in people like him.

"I don't know how I could ever repay you..." Hara whispered as they dropped their hands back to their sides.

Bennett chuckled. "Don't worry about it," he assured her. "I did it for you, not so I could get something in return."

"Why?" Hara asked, bewildered. "Why would you help me? Especially when you knew what I've done and the risk involved."

Gazing back at her, Bennett shrugged. "Because you needed it. And I thought maybe—just maybe—if someone showed you some compassion, then maybe you would be able to find yourself again."

Biting her tongue to keep from completely breaking down, Hara nodded gratefully to him. "Thank you," she repeated shakily, taking a step back.

"My speculation is, you still need it," Bennett said, following her movement to keep the same distance between them. He may not have wanted anything in return for helping her, but he didn't want to lose her just yet.

Shaking her head, Hara retreated back another step and started to turn away. "I need to go now."

"Where will you go?" Bennett asked her, trying in any way possible to keep her with him so he would know they were both safe.

Pausing, Hara shrugged. She hadn't thought that far ahead. "I'll find someplace."

"I have an apartment," Bennett said quickly as she continued to back away. "It's nothing special, but it's enough for the two of you to stay with me for as long you need."

"Thank you, Dr. Bennett, but you've done enough for us," Hara told him. "I can't intrude upon your home. I've already intruded into your life."

"No," Bennett said, shaking his head with a sad expression on his face. "I'm glad I got to meet you. It would honor me if you would stay with me."

Hara couldn't accept such a kind offer. He was offering too much. "I can't..."

"When's the last time you ate?" Bennett asked as concern crossed his eyes. "When's the last time you slept?"

Hara couldn't recall an answer for either question. When she didn't reply, Bennett pressed further.

"You've been through a terrible ordeal these past several months," he told her, as if it were news to her. "And these past few days have been very rough on you and your child. You need to rest, get a good meal, and you need somewhere where you can clean yourself up." He nodded to her hands, which Hara suddenly recalled were covered with dried blood from Rhett's fatal wound. "Please, come stay with me for a while to allow yourself to rejuvenate. For Dreyson's sake."

Suddenly hardening, Hara grew angry that he was trying to tell her what was best for her son. She would decide what was best for him. Glaring, she growled, "I don't put my trust in humans! Especially doctors!"

Sighing, Bennett said, "I'm not a human. I'm one of you now. And you already do trust me, honey. I can see it in your eyes, no matter how much you try to deny it."

"I can't trust you!" Hara hissed, backing away.

"Yes, you can," Bennett insisted, taking another step forward. "Please come with me now. The police will be patrolling this area to look for you shortly. Come, you can rest while I look after your son." He extended his hand to her like she had to him earlier.

Even though she didn't want to, she knew Bennett was right about everything. He was a doctor, after all. She did need to rest, and she did trust that he would take care of her son while she regained her energy. And if she continued to sink deeper into this depression, she would need somebody to help her through it. She believed that someone could be Dr. Bennett. Reaching out, she took his hand and let him lead her out of the plaza.

After a moment of silence between them, Bennett asked her, "What's your name? Your real name? I know you said it doesn't matter anymore, but I would really like to know." When Hara refused to respond, he looked down at her and gave her hand a gentle squeeze. "You can trust me, remember?"

Sighing, she supposed it wouldn't hurt if she told one person her true name. He already knew too much about her and where she was from. "My name is Hallie," she said. "Hallie Reifert."

15

Caribbean Blue

Even though Hara had mentally inserted her order to avoid The Doc inside Perry's head, Perry didn't obey. The Doc had killed his head of operations, and Perry was ready to put him away for good.

When he first planned to confront him, Perry had no idea what he was going to say to him. There really wasn't much to say, and there was no question about what he needed to do. The Doc couldn't be allowed to hurt anyone else. Perry was going to do what he should have done when he first met him. He was going to arrest him and make sure the world found out about what he had done to the Colicians, the race the world didn't know ever existed. People deserved to know the truth about the biggest government cover up in human history, and Perry was going to be the one to expose it. He didn't care what road blocks he came across or who tried to stop him. The world would know the truth.

Odau and Finchly went after Hara when she took off again, but Perry knew they would never catch her. The lieutenant called in reinforcements, and Perry knew that he didn't have much time to get The Doc. It would have to be before the cops arrived, or else they might ask too many questions. Odau would have to tell them about Marcus and Aubrey eventually, and when he did they would all want the man responsible to pay. But Perry had other plans for The Doc, and it didn't involve cops.

Now that Agent Long was dead, Perry was fully in charge of the operation. When he told the remaining three members of the group that they were still going through with the original plan, they all supported him. They, too, wanted The Doc out of the picture.

Perry asked Renee to stay in the lobby and wait for the cops and try to get in contact with Odau. They needed to make sure the lieutenant would keep his mouth shut about what had transpired until they were ready to blow the secret out of the water. Finchly wouldn't be a problem at all, but Odau was already furious about Hara's escape, and things with him would get even uglier when he found out it was the FBI's fault. Perry also wanted Renee away from The Doc in case things got out of hand, and he had a feeling they might. Martinson and Hersh accompanied him up to the third floor, but the initial plan was for them to stay back while Perry confronted The Doc. Perry assumed The Doc would not hurt him, but he should have listened to Hara.

"Are you sure you want to go in alone?" Martinson asked uncertainly. "You saw what he did to Agent Long…"

"I'll be fine," Perry told him as they approached the room where The Doc had pushed Agent Long. Nobody had seen him leave since the most recent incident, so that was where they were going. Patting his friend's arm, Perry reassured, "If anything goes wrong, then I give you both permission to come in and shoot on sight."

Hersh grinned at him. "Gee, thanks Perry. That makes us feel so much better."

"Our goal is to detain him alive, Jaz," Perry reminded her. "This will only involve bullets if he draws a weapon on me."

"Well, then, let's hope he draws a weapon on you," Martinson replied.

Glancing at him, Perry smirked, even though his stomach was churning nervously. "Thanks, Andy. It's good to know how much you care."

"You know I love you, man," Martinson told him, smiling boldly and rubbing Perry's shoulder with mock affection.

Nodding in return, Perry halted as they reached the plastic sheet dividers to the restricted section. "Well," he sighed, "the two of you should wait here while I deal with this. See you in a few minutes."

"I'll see you when he pulls a weapon on you," Martinson told him, grinning. "Just give a shout if you need us."

"Please be careful, Perry," Hersh begged. "Too many good people have died today."

Perry smiled. "I always am," he promised, stepping into the separate section as he brushed the curtain aside. His heart began to beat a little faster as he approached the room containing The Doc, and for the first time in several hours he noticed the headache that had been bothering him since the previous night. Remembering what Noah told him about gaining an ability early, Perry began to finally wonder about when that ability would show and what he would be able to do. The headache was getting worse, and Perry prayed that it wouldn't get in the way of his job.

Reaching the doorway, Perry paused and stared inside, familiarizing himself with his surroundings. He wanted to be aware of what was in the room, because if there was any sign of danger he would not enter alone. The Doc was still standing at the window looking out where Agent Long had fallen, his hands in the pockets of his white lab coat. He was standing as still as a statue, the shards of window still attached to the frame reflecting his blank expression back at Perry. Perry shuddered, wondering if The Doc had been staring out at Agent Long that whole time or if he was just gazing out at nothing, completely lost in thought. It was hard to tell what he was looking at; it was hard to tell if he was even there. He was so still that the only way Perry knew he was actually a living thing was when his hair would blow back in the light breeze.

Agent Long's body hadn't been moved since his fall, and now Perry kind of wished they had moved him. People who had fled the building due to the fire in the lobby had gone to investigate shortly after Odau took off after Hara. Many of them tried to contact the police. Perry and his colleagues told everyone to stay back from the body, but there was nothing they could do until the police arrived. Once the cops arrived, they could all deal with the mess and then Perry would be able to call headquarters and inform them of Agent Long's death. That was going to be very frustrating. All four of them would have to go through a separate debriefing, and then the other heads of operations would want to further investigate The Doc. They would all have to explain what had happened to the city and who and what Hara was. It was not going to be pleasant in any way, but they were all just going to have to deal with it.

Something peculiar that Perry noticed was that there were no guards in the room with The Doc or anywhere nearby. It was unusual for him to go about unprotected, considering how many people wanted to kill him. But Perry could sense by The Doc's strangely calm behavior and also from the atmosphere of the room that something was off. The Doc appeared so calm, but Perry had a strong feeling that inside he was a volcano about to blow its top. Ever so cautiously, Perry took a step inside.

He thought he was being quiet, but he should have learned by now that it was nearly impossible to sneak up on The Doc. After all, he was the one who had always been sneaking up on Perry. "Close the door," he ordered almost immediately after Perry entered.

It was still unclear whether or not he would be safe in there alone with the doctor, but wrapping his hand around his nine-millimeter in his holster, Perry quietly pushed the door closed behind him. Keeping his hand on his weapon, Perry took a few more steps in. He made sure to stop several feet away, keeping a safe distance between them.

The Doc hadn't turned around or even shifted his weight when he spoke, and once again he remained frozen when asking his next question. "Why don't you come closer?"

His eyes glued on the back of The Doc's head, Perry gritted his teeth. He didn't reply, and waited as patiently as he could for him to turn around.

But The Doc didn't turn around. He still didn't move a muscle. "It almost appears as if you're afraid of me," he said quietly.

"You killed my superior officer," Perry said, scowling at him in contempt.

"So you are afraid of me," The Doc said, continuing to gaze out the window.

Perry snorted. "No," he answered, wishing it was the truth. His heart was beating faster and faster in his chest, and his head was pounding harder with the anxiety. "I'm not afraid."

"You know, Marcus told me the exact same thing before I killed him. I truly believe he wasn't afraid to die. But you..." He slowly turned around to peer across the room at him with those terrifyingly calm, cold eyes. "I'm not so sure I believe you when you say that."

The man had finally admitted his crime of murder, and even though Perry knew he was guilty, he suddenly felt apprehensive now that The Doc actually confessed. Something had changed. The Doc was going to do something that no one would be able to predict. He wouldn't have admitted his crime if he wasn't. "Well, I don't plan on dying anytime soon," Perry stated firmly.

Smiling lightly at him, The Doc kept his hands in his pockets, which was beginning to seem a little suspicious. "Plan all you want, son. Death can creep up on you when you least expect it." He took a single step forward.

His heart rate quickening, Perry's grip tightened on his weapon. "Why did you kill Agent Long?" he demanded, side-stepping toward the wall as The Doc advanced another step.

"His name wasn't Agent Long," The Doc replied softly, his cold eyes continuing to make Perry squirm in his shoes.

"What are you talking about?" Perry asked skeptically.

"The man you knew for so many years as Rhett Long was actually called Rhett Simco," The Doc explained calmly, like that was all old news to him.

"Who is Rhett Simco?" Perry asked, not having a clue what he was talking about.

"He was a Colician," The Doc said, raising his eyebrows at him as if he expected a dramatic reaction.

Staring at him in bewilderment, Perry demanded, "Are you expecting me to believe that I've been working with a Colician for ten years? Did you really think I'd buy into that?"

"Oh, I'm sure you never knew about him at all," The Doc replied sarcastically, advancing several steps. His body language suggested to Perry that he keep back.

Retreating several steps so he was almost bumping the wall, Perry said, "I would have noticed something that extreme about someone I worked with for so long."

"I'm sure that you did," The Doc said in a pressuring manner.

"I don't believe you," Perry said, glaring stubbornly.

Staring into Perry's dark eyes, The Doc told him, "I know that you and your FBI agents were planning to steal Hara from me and then arrest me. She left them lying helpless and stupid in the stairwell when she escaped."

"Whoops," Perry muttered. "You caught us."

"You paralyzed her abilities when you shot her with that dart."

"Well, clearly she got them back."

The Doc shook his head. "A dose like the one you gave her would have left her defenseless for at least three hours." He waited for Perry to put the pieces together.

His brow furrowing in confusion, Perry demanded, "What are you saying?"

"What do you think I'm saying?" The Doc asked, but then answered Perry's question. "Simco used to be a good friend of Hara's during the Colician Empire. I'm saying your superior officer gave Hara an injection to allow her to regain her abilities and escape from us once again. To escape from *me* once again."

"That's absurd!" Perry exclaimed, angry that The Doc was insulting Agent Long's memory in such a way.

"I'm only repeating what he told me," The Doc insisted.

"Agent Long would never do such a thing!" Perry snapped. "He died in an attempt to protect Hara from you!"

"My point exactly!" The Doc said with exasperation. "Where do you think he kept disappearing to?"

Perry opened his mouth to defend his dead colleague, but The Doc's comment caused him to pause and ponder over it. Where had Agent Long disappeared to before? He had claimed it was to find The Doc, but now that Perry stopped to think about it, Agent Long's story was full of holes.

The Doc saw Perry's uncertainty and smiled triumphantly. "Whoops," he said. "I caught you."

"That's impossible," Perry whispered, but it all made sense. He really didn't know anything about Agent Long's past before the FBI. Nothing about high schools, parents, or any type of family for that matter. Nobody had ever bothered to ask, and maybe there was a reason for that. Maybe Agent Long made sure nobody asked about it. Maybe he pushed the thought out of anybody's head who had any curiosity about him.

"You never would have thought a person as ordinary as him would be hiding the biggest secret in the history of the world, would you?" The Doc asked him softly. "Especially if he was somebody you knew. That's what they do. They assume identities that engender trust. Nobody who knew Daniel Marcus, Allan Brown, or Meg Hopper had any suspicions either."

"But…I've known him for ten years," Perry whispered, shaking his head. He was still unable to believe it.

"You've been operating under his orders since you brought him into this," The Doc said, his eyes narrowing suspiciously. Perry sensed a sudden change of mood throughout the room. "What was Simco planning to do with Hara once he helped her escape?"

"He...he wasn't planning anything!" Perry sputtered, eyeing The Doc nervously. "We were just trying to get her away from you so we could get her some help!"

Snorting, and then laughing scornfully, The Doc took another step closer. His face changed back into a menacing glower. "And I'm sure you were going along with that plan," he growled, baring his teeth. "After all, you've been such a trustworthy colleague so far."

"Oh, you're going to accuse me of being untrustworthy?" Perry snapped, glaring back. "If you expected me to be completely honest with you from the start, then maybe you should have been more honest with us!"

"There were too many things that you wouldn't have been able to understand," The Doc claimed, his voice still calm and eerie. "There are still too many things that you won't be able to understand."

"I think I've already uncovered the biggest secret you've kept from us," Perry said.

"Not all of them," The Doc declared with a smirk. "There's still the grand finale which you have left to uncover."

Perry wondered how long The Doc was going to keep him talking. Maybe The Doc was doing it on purpose, knowing it was all over for him.

"The point is, I had a logical reason to keep my secrets," The Doc said, and a single muscle in his lip twitched, showing Perry that he really was irritated. "Dr. Bennett was working with Simco. The two of them were working together to aid Hara's escape."

"Oh, really?" Even if The Doc was telling the truth, Perry wouldn't have cared.

"That's why nobody could find him. He's been helping Allan Brown ever since he escaped from police custody, and he was helping Simco with his plan to reunite Hara with Dreyson."

"This is all very interesting," Perry grumbled. For the first time since Agent Long's death, Perry wondered what his boss had done with Dreyson, and what would happen to him. "But I don't see how any of this supports your accusation of my involvement."

"Dr. Bennett was involved in this," The Doc repeated blankly, moving closer still. He was now close enough to make Perry uneasy. "He was someone we all least expected, along with Agent Long. Who's to say that you wouldn't be involved in this too?" He narrowed his eyes again. "You've been called one of them. Why wouldn't you be involved in this?"

Staring at him in disbelief, Perry snapped, "You know, if you're so certain that Dr. Bennett's a traitor, then why don't you go interrogate him about Hara's whereabouts?"

The Doc snickered, a dry sound that made Perry shiver. "I won't need to bother tracking him down thanks to you, my friend."

"What are you talking about?" Perry said.

"Do you remember John Reifert, the college professor you spoke to on the phone earlier?" The Doc cocked his head.

"How did you know about that?" Perry demanded, inching his way along the wall away from the door in an effort to keep enough space between them.

I was listening in on your conversation in the next room," The Doc replied boldly. Shaking his head in disappointment, he added, "I told you to forget about Hallie Reifert, but you didn't listen to me. I told you that it wasn't important, that it would be a waste of your time to look for her, yet you still insisted on trying to find her."

"Of course I was still trying to find her!" Perry cried. "Aubrey's dying words were his plea for me to save her!"

"And thanks to Simco, you have saved her," The Doc said in exasperation.

"Excuse me?" Perry said, puzzled by the remark.

"You know, you really shouldn't have planned that meeting with John Reifert," The Doc told him coldly. "Now I know exactly where and when to find him. And his kids."

It was becoming difficult to keep up with the dramatic subject changes. "What would you possibly want with the Reifert family?" Perry demanded sharply. "Especially since they're not important."

"Oh, they are important," The Doc said, inching closer. "If I can no longer use Dreyson against her, then I'll just have to use them against her."

"Why would they matter to her?" Perry questioned curiously.

"Well, of course you wouldn't know. They're her family, after all!" The Doc raised his eyebrows. "That's why they matter to her."

"Her family is dead!" Perry snarled. "You murdered them!"

"She lied to you," The Doc insisted. "There's still some out there, and she'll fight to keep them safe. That's why I've been fighting to keep the lieutenant's boy safe."

His jaw dropping in amazement, Perry stuttered, "You...you're related to the Odau's?"

Cocking his head again and smirking, The Doc said, "I suppose you could say that."

"How...?" Perry stared at him, the new information startling and unexpected, just like many of the things he had recently learned. But it all made sense. Why else would The Doc want to keep Jackson alive? Why had Odau claimed that he knew the Doc from somewhere but couldn't quite place him? Whether the Reiferts or the Odaus knew it or not, they were in this mess because they were the last remaining family of two opposing forces, both of which were struggling to keep their last rays of hope alive.

Grinning wickedly at him, The Doc crooned, "Come on, Perry. I can hear the gears grinding in your head. Come on. It's not too hard. I know you can figure this out."

Gazing at him as he thought through the various possibilities, Perry asked, "This is something big, isn't it? Something bigger than the outbreak. Something too big to even imagine being possible."

Nodding slowly, The Doc replied, "You're on the right track. To figure this one out, Agent Perry, you're going to have to think beyond what is possible. As you said, this is greater than genetically altered humans."

"I'm not going to allow you to use the Reiferts against her," Perry said.

Snorting, The Doc asked, "How are you going to stop me? Did you really think I was going to just let you walk out of here after what you've done?"

"What are you saying?" Perry demanded, but then he realized what The Doc had been doing while they were talking. The steps he had been taking forward were not to get closer to Perry; they were to get between him and the door.

"I'm afraid this is the end of the line for you," The Doc said solemnly, eyeing Perry's uncertain expression.

"You're not going to hurt me," Perry declared, although his heart was beginning to pound in his chest. "If I yell, my colleagues will come running through that door and will fire on sight."

"Well, you're not going to yell," The Doc promised, this time taking an intentional step toward Perry. "You're going to remain very quiet."

"Don't come any closer to me," Perry ordered as his voice shook. Hearing sirens sounding from outside the broken window, he shot a glance toward the street and then back to The Doc. Maybe, just maybe, he could keep The Doc talking long enough for the cops to get to him. Or at least long enough for his colleagues to come to his aid.

The Doc saw the hope in his eyes. "They won't arrive in time for you, I'm afraid."

"What do you want?" Perry demanded, wondering if it was just another game of his to get him to talk. The Doc's next comment clearly proved him wrong.

"For you to not fight me while I kill you," he answered, his cold eyes narrowing to slits. Seeing Perry swallow his fear back down, he reassured, "Don't worry. It will hurt, but I'll try to make it as quick as possible." Finally taking his hands out of his pockets, Perry saw that The Doc held in his right hand the six inch blade that killed Agent Long, still stained with his blood.

Quickly drawing his weapon, Perry leveled it with The Doc's chest. "Drop it now!" he commanded, his voice quavering.

Smirking, The Doc gazed back at him in amusement, not seeming the least bit fazed by the loaded gun aimed at his heart. "I wouldn't even bother with that," he jeered. "I emptied out all your bullets before we captured Hara."

His heart skipping a beat, Perry dropped his eyes to his gun, certain it was a bluff but still having a moment's hesitation. That was probably the biggest mistake he would ever make.

In the moment that Perry was confused and distracted, The Doc used his free hand to knock the gun out of Perry's grip, causing it to clatter to the floor. Startled, Perry started to raise his arms in defense. But his reaction wasn't fast enough, and before he could fight back, The Doc clamped his hand firmly over Perry's mouth and shoved him backwards into the wall. Then, causing Perry's eyes to grow wide in surprise and agony, The Doc plunged the knife deep into his stomach.

His eyes began to tear up from the excruciating pain in his abdomen, and in a moment of sheer hope he imagined that none of it was real. He wanted to cry out, to scream for help from his colleagues, but because of The Doc's hand over his mouth, the only sounds he managed to get out were muffled and pathetic. Grabbing at The Doc's wrist in an effort to pry his hand off, Perry found that he couldn't quite control his movements anymore. His hands bumped each other awkwardly and his fingers fumbled aimlessly over The Doc's arm. Black pinpricks were popping up in front of his eyes, and when he tried to blink them away his vision only became worse. The sting of iron and the taste of blood in his mouth was clear evidence that he was dying. It wouldn't matter if The Doc stabbed him again or not; he would be dead in a matter of minutes.

If you die, our future dies with you. Hara's words suddenly popped into his head, and if he had remembered them earlier, he might not have been in this situation. If The Doc killed Perry, then there would be no future for the Colicians. That was what Hara claimed. The Doc set out to destroy the very existence of the Colicians. Why Perry thought The Doc would want to preserve him, Perry had no idea. The Doc probably planned to kill him all along. Now that Perry remembered Hara's words, it was obvious that The Doc would want him dead. If killing Perry destroyed any chance of a future for the Colicians, it was surprising that The Doc hadn't killed him sooner. Hara tried to warn him, but thanks to Perry's stubbornness, it was all over. The Colicians had no chance to survive now.

As Perry gripped The Doc's arm and struggled to inhale, his eyes, which were shifting in and out of focus, landed on The Doc's tranquil face. How he could be killing someone and keep a calm expression, Perry would never understand. But now that he was focused on him again, The Doc leaned closer to Perry so he could whisper in his ear.

"Do you know why I told you that looking for Hallie Reifert was a waste of your time?" he asked. "I told you that because Hallie Reifert is Hara's real name." Tightening his grip on the handle of the knife, he wrenched it upward, leaving an eight inch slice from his belly button to his diaphragm. Perry tried to scream again, but by that time there was so much blood rising in his throat that it was nearly impossible to breathe. If The Doc didn't remove his hand from his mouth soon, Perry was going to choke to death on his own blood. Grabbing at The Doc's arm again, Perry desperately attempted to keep his eyes focused. There was so much pain. Getting closer still, so that their noses were nearly touching, The Doc hissed, "You've been wasting your time looking for a girl whom you've already found." Pulling the knife out of Perry's chest, The Doc kept his hand over Perry's mouth as Perry's knees buckled and he collapsed to the floor. As Perry, who was still in agony and barely able to keep conscious, slid down the wall, he tried one last time to summon help. The only sound he was capable of making, however, was a muffled moan that was immediately hushed by The Doc. "Shhhh," he whispered. "You've only got about a minute left. Your friends can't help you now."

Perry began to cough up blood into his mouth and all over The Doc's hand, his entire body heaving up and down. Sliding down the rest of the wall, Perry's upper body landed on the floor and his head thumped down as well. The Doc finally removed his hand. Turning his head, Perry started spitting out blood. It flowed out of his mouth and covered his face and neck, the rest of it forming large pools on the floor beside him. He didn't want to look down at the gaping wound in his torso; placing his right hand on it and feeling it was enough for him to know that it was not a pretty sight. Peering up and blinking rapidly to keep his vision clear, Perry watched as The Doc stood up and took out a white cloth from his jacket pocket to wipe the blood off his hand and the blade. Once The Doc cleaned most of it off his hand, he replaced the cloth and knife in his pocket and stooped down to scoop up Perry's gun, which had dropped to the floor a few feet away.

"I don't know why you believed me when I told you I removed your bullets, even if it was for only a moment. You've been an agent for ten years; you should be able to feel when your weapon is empty." Aiming the gun at the floor, he fired one round and then raised the weapon towards the door.

Struggling to hang on to life, Perry's eyelids started to droop as he gazed up in confusion. He didn't understand what The Doc was doing until his colleagues burst into the room with their guns at the ready. Martinson started to scream, "Freeze!" and Hersh looked ready to shoot, but surprisingly The Doc fired Perry's weapon first. The first round struck Martinson squarely between the eyes, and the second hit Hersh just above her heart. Both of them dropped like stones, surprised expressions locked on their faces. Neither Andy nor Jaz had fired their weapons, and when their bodies hit the floor their weapons clattered away from them.

Completely horrified, Perry stared at his two dead friends on the floor beside him, both killed by his gun because they were trying to protect him. Perry shouldn't have gone in alone. Now, all three of them were dead, and it was his poor judgment that led them there. Worse yet, Perry knew that Renee would come up to the third floor after the sound of gunshots.

As if he was reading Perry's mind, The Doc stated, "I'm going to kill your girlfriend whether she comes up here or not."

Spitting up more blood, Perry dropped his head to the floor and squeezed his eyes shut in agony and helplessness. His head was feeling so light that he knew he would pass out at any moment. He was done for; he could no longer do anything to fight. He prayed that Renee wouldn't come up there, but he knew she would. When she did, he wouldn't be able to do anything to protect her.

"I don't want you to take this too personally," Perry heard The Doc say to him, patting his shoulder gently. "Your death will provide a better future for the humans. And for me."

But not for the Colicians, Perry thought in growing dread. As faint as he felt and as much pain as he was in, a new pain was beginning to make the gash in his chest feel like a paper cut. Perry's head began to pound, and he could feel his heart beat in his temples. It felt like he was slowly being shot in the side of the head, able to feel every excruciating moment of it. His eyes watering again, he let out a low groan. Whatever was making him hurt so much, it made Perry wish he would just hurry up and die.

Hearing the door being kicked open once again and a loud gasp echo through the room, Perry's eyes shot open and they landed on a horrified, dumbstruck Renee. Seeing her there in the doorway, knowing she was about to die, gave Perry renewed strength. It must have been his love for her, because he didn't know what else it could have been. He actually managed to fight back the pain and sit up slightly, causing more blood to flow out of his wound.

Fear for Perry in her eyes, Renee raised her gun at The Doc as her hands shook dangerously. "Drop it!" she cried desperately.

"You drop it," The Doc replied smoothly, raising Perry's gun slightly so it was aimed at Perry's head.

Perry tried to tell her to run, but there was so much blood in his mouth that he ended up just spitting it all over himself. He was going to die whether The Doc shot him or not, and he wanted her to be as far away from The Doc as possible when he stopped breathing. When Renee looked back down at Perry, with an expression of heartbreak on her face, Perry tried to tell her with his eyes that she needed to turn and run as fast and as far as she could. He guessed that she took his expression to be one of desperation. She lowered her gun slightly while keeping her gaze locked on Perry.

Standing back up slowly, The Doc took careful steps towards her, making sure that his gun stayed level with Perry. "Put it down," he said firmly, cocking his gun warningly.

Renee's lower lip trembled, and she looked as if she was about to start crying. Her eyes apologetic, she slowly lowered her weapon.

"Good," The Doc said, and he reached out his free hand to her. "Now give it here."

Perry shook his head furiously at Renee, hoping she would take the hint and run, but she was no longer looking at him.

"What are you going to do if I give it to you?" Renee demanded shakily, but Perry saw in her eyes that she had already given up.

"Give it to me or I will splatter his brains all over the floor," The Doc threatened coldly. It was clear that was his final warning.

Hesitating, Renee began to hold out her gun to The Doc. Perry knew what was going to happen once she was defenseless, but he wasn't going to let that happen. He needed something to distract The Doc long enough for Renee to get out of there. Looking around him frantically, he saw that Martinson, whose body lay only feet from him, had dropped his weapon when The Doc killed him and it had come to rest by Perry's side. For a moment Perry's hopes soared.

"You're almost as stupid as Perry was," The Doc said as he took Renee's gun from her. "You should have just shot me. There's no way Perry will survive the wound I inflicted on him. Now you both have to die." Tossing Renee's gun aside, he raised Perry's gun up to her.

As the pain in his head exploded to a new level of agony, Perry felt a tingling sensation in his abdomen where the knife wound was. It almost felt to him as if the pain from the wound was lessening, and as the strange sensation heightened in intensity, he found a new strength inside him he never thought possible. Rolling onto his side so he could snatch Martinson's weapon off the floor, he whipped the gun around and fired at The Doc without aiming. The shot echoed through the room and The Doc cried out in pain before firing himself. Renee screamed and clutched at her right arm, collapsing to the ground as blood seeped through her fingers. Her face showed her pain, but from where Perry was lying it looked as if the bullet had gone straight through. She would be alright.

As he went down to his knees, The Doc's free hand shot to his left calf where he had been hit. Unfortunately for everyone, it seemed as if The Doc's wound would not be life threatening; however it was clear that his injury was worse than Renee's. More blood was flowing from his leg, and his hand was once again becoming covered with blood, only this time, it was his own. Turning his head toward Perry, his eyes expressed a fury that Perry hadn't ever seen in him. The Doc turned the gun on Perry once more, and this time he fired.

Perry felt the bullet strike him in the shoulder, and the blow left him so shocked that the little breath he had remaining left him in a rush before he fell back against the floor. Gazing back at The Doc as the gun was cocked once again, he prayed The Doc would make it end quickly, like he promised. The pain and exhaustion was becoming too much to fight any longer.

Something happened then that caused The Doc's finger to freeze on the trigger. Perry didn't know what it was at first; he just knew that it was enough to leave the man utterly bewildered. His eyes slowly went from furious, to amazed, and to horrified, in barely a few seconds and his mouth fell open in awe. Staring at Perry with a dumbfounded look on his face, The Doc whispered, "That's impossible!"

Confused by what was happening, Perry realized that his wound hardly hurt any longer. Looking at Renee, he saw that she was gaping at him with the same look as The Doc. But then he realized that they weren't looking at him, they were looking at his stomach. Dropping his eyes as well, Perry was thoroughly repulsed by what he saw. The skin around the gash seemed to be moving, or more accurately stretching. Each side was stretching towards the other, as if reaching out to latch together. The two sides stretched until they met and began to fuse together. It was like two pieces of metal being welded together. Only when his skin finally melded back into itself, there was no mark left. There was no evidence, other than the blood soaking his torso, to suggest that there had ever been an injury to begin with. Glancing at his shoulder, Perry saw that the same thing was happening with the bullet wound. His skin stretched until both sides were able to melt together, leaving no scar behind. The process felt strange, like something was tugging at his skin, but it didn't hurt him. However, the fact that his own body had done a thing like that left him baffled, and he gazed back at The Doc hoping to get some answers.

The Doc lowered his gun and observed Perry with the same look as when he watched Hara. An unpleasant feeling began to develop in the pit of his stomach because of what that might mean. It was clear that

Perry was about to be unwillingly added to The Doc's human guinea pig list.

"Wow," The Doc murmured, nodding in approval. "Hara gave you quite the defense mechanism, didn't she?" Shoving the gun into his jacket pocket, he limped over to Perry, bent over, and grabbed him by the arm. "Get up," he ordered, practically dragging Perry to his feet.

His wounds were completely healed, but Perry was still weak from the massive blood loss. He stumbled and swayed unsteadily, his head spinning as the room tilted underneath him. Attempting to find his balance, Perry tried to shake The Doc's firm hand off. "Let go of me!" he snapped, finally able to find his voice. Much of the leftover blood spilled out of his mouth and down his front once again.

"You can either come with me now, or I'll kill her," The Doc threatened, gesturing at Renee, who was still cowering against the wall beside the door.

Staring into The Doc's eyes, Perry finally found some truth buried in them. The Doc was so interested in what was occurring inside of Perry that he was willing to let Renee live in exchange for Perry's cooperation. Whatever was in store for Perry was not good, but if it meant Renee's safety and survival, he would do anything. Giving her a single look of regret, Perry allowed The Doc to drag him out of the room. As Perry was led away to his fate, he wondered if Hara had felt the same dread that he was feeling the first time she was taken away by The Doc.

✳ ✳ ✳

In front of Hara, there was a door standing ajar, inviting her inside. It was almost beckoning for her to enter. Inside the door, she could see a long sofa against a side wall, its blue and red patterns faded from time. A few feet in front of the sofa sat a coffee table, with three different remote controls sitting on top of it along with a newspaper and several different magazines whose covers Hara didn't even bother reading. On the opposite wall from the sofa was a large, flat television embedded into the wall. A DVD player and surround sound system sat beneath it in a small wooden cabinet whose doors sat wide open on either side. It was funny seeing TVs everywhere she went. There were very few TVs in the place where she came from. Televisions were considered primitive. Her people had much more advanced technology they used in place of them. On the wall opposite Hara, she saw a wooden bureau with many different drawers, the top scattered with pictures of a beautiful woman with flowing blonde hair and bright blue eyes as well as several young children Hara recognized to be Bennett's children and grandchildren.

Her eyes paused for a moment on a photo of a young, smiling Danny Bennett, who couldn't have been more than four years old, and she wished she could tell Dr. Bennett just how much the boy had helped her and her family. One end of the bureau held a CD player, and behind it rested a rack holding dozens of different CDs. That was one of the things Hara so desperately missed from before the war: music. To the left of the bureau was a doorway that led to the kitchen. She could see a table with three chairs seated around it, almost as if he had predicted the company, and a window behind the table looked out toward the next apartment block. There was a doorway just to the left of the entrance that led to a dark bedroom, but Dr. Bennett stepped in her line of sight before she could see any more. Inside the room, there was a place for her to rest and feel safe. Inside was safety. If that was so, then why was she still hanging back? What was she waiting for? Outside was dark and loud and filled with many bad things, but for some reason she felt at home amongst it all.

Watching her carefully, fearful that she may run, Dr. Bennett asked quietly from just inside the door, "Are you going to come in?"

Looking down at Dreyson, who had fallen asleep, nestled in her arms, she wondered if she really should. They both needed the rest, but The Doc and the cops were still looking for her. It might not be the best time for sleep.

Dr. Bennett, however, was not going to take no for an answer. Taking her arm, he began to slowly coax her forward. "Come on," he said gently, and he pulled the door closed behind them once she inched her way inside. Taking another step into the room to give her some space, Bennett gazed back at Hara as she peered around nervously. "You don't need to be afraid," he told her, smiling reassuringly. "This is a safe place. There's no one here but us. There's no one here to hurt you."

Hara nodded absentmindedly, but she couldn't seem to shake the ever-present feeling of uneasiness in her stomach. She had gone so long without a place of asylum, a place where she really was safe, that she was going to have difficulty calming down enough to relax and sleep. Her entire mind and body was going to be on alert the entire time she was here.

"Are you hungry?" Bennett asked her.

Thinking about it, Hara decided that she really wasn't. She hadn't eaten in days, but she had no hunger pains. There were much stronger things providing her energy. Shaking her head, she looked back down at her son's sleeping face. She had forgotten how much she loved watching her children sleep. They always appeared to her as little angels.

"Here, let me take him," Bennett said, stepping forward and reaching for Dreyson. When Hara pulled away in alarm, he smiled again and placed a comforting hand on her shoulder. "No one's going to take him from you," he promised her. "I was just going to take him to the spare bedroom. I have a bunk bed in there for when my grandkids stay over."

"He'll be alone," Hara whispered, gripping her son tightly.

"He'll be safe," Bennett assured. "No one will be able to find us. At least not for a while." He tried again as Hara's uncertainty didn't subside. "Your little boy needs to get some sleep, and so do you. But you need to do it separately, otherwise you'll be constantly fussing over him and you won't get any rest. You have nothing to worry about. He'll just be in the next room." Reaching towards the toddler again, he asked, "Can I please take him?"

Regrettably, Hara hesitantly passed her son to Dr. Bennett, remembering the day back home when The Doc had taken him from her with no hope she would ever see him again. Taking a deep breath, she stared at the floor as she felt hot tears pricking the corners of her eyes.

She could feel Dr. Bennett watching her. "He'll be alright," he promised again in his soft, soothing voice.

Nodding, Hara forced a smile but kept her gaze on the floor. "I know," she replied, and she suddenly realized how tired she was. Bennett was right; she really did need the sleep.

"I'll go put him to bed and then I can show you to your bed," he told her. "I'll just be a moment."

"Actually, I think I'll sleep on your couch if you don't mind," Hara said softly, convincing herself to meet his gentle gaze. There was no way she would be able to sleep anywhere unless it was in that room. She had to be able to see the door, to know her way out, especially if it meant that she would be between an intruder and her child.

Pausing, Bennett looked as if he might argue with her over it. She thought he was going to lecture her on how she needed to relax and get decent sleep in a decent bed, but instead he nodded understandingly. "I'll bring you a pillow and some blankets."

"Thank you," Hara said gratefully, glad he understood.

Giving her another nod in return, Bennett turned and walked to the door leading to the kitchen. Once inside the kitchen, he took a sharp right and disappeared from sight.

Sighing as a wave of exhaustion hit her, Hara wandered over to the CD rack across the room. Some soft music would really help her relax. There had to be at least fifty different CDs, and although much of humanity's music was unpopular among her people (all that screaming and electronic instruments...how could humans enjoy that stuff?), there had to be something she would recognize. After all, Bennett seemed like a man with good taste.

The CDs were in alphabetical order, and after fourteen CDs she began to grow disappointed. But her eyes stopped halfway through the E's, and her heart skipped a beat. Pulling the CD out of its slot, her spirits soared as she read the title. Grinning boldly yet remorsefully, she turned the case over to see if the song she was looking for was labeled on the back. The CD was *The Best of Enya,* Hara's one and only favorite human singer. Enya was probably the only human singer that most of her people thoroughly enjoyed, and there was one song she sang that Hara absolutely loved. When she discovered that "Caribbean Blue" was in fact on the CD, she quickly slipped it into the top of the player and fumbled with it until she managed to turn it on. Turning the volume knob to put it at a softer level, Hara pressed the forward button to get to "Caribbean Blue." Taking several steps back until she was in the center of the room, she closed her eyes as the soft, beautiful music began to play.

"Caribbean Blue" was the song playing when Hara first learned to dance. Bo had taught her a short and simple partner dance just months before his death. It was right after her brother Flint was killed, and because he and Hara were so close, she was having a difficult time coping. Bo thought it would help if he did something to take her mind off of her brother, so he decided to teach her a small dance. It did take her mind off of Flint, for a while at least. The music that Bo introduced to her was probably what kept her sane for so long.

As the song went on, Hara kept her eyes closed and swayed gently from side to side, mouthing the words as they were sung. It made her so happy yet so sad at the same time. A familiar memory soothed her, but it reminded her too much of Bo. The memory of his soft features and kind face smiling down at her broke her heart, and remembering how his left hand had slid around her waist while his right hand held hers brought tears to her eyes once again. His body had felt warm against hers while they danced, and the pressure of his mind over hers kept her calm enough to focus. Hara wished he could come back for just three minutes, so they could have one last dance.

"Hallie…" a familiar voice whispered, one she shouldn't have heard.

Her eyes shot open, and she stared in shock at Bo standing not three feet in front of her. He looked exactly as he did before his death. His thick black hair sat in light curls on top of his head, one lock falling out of place and dangling just above his left eye. His dark brown eyes were warm and inviting, but they seemed sad, as if he knew what Hara had become. It would be painful for Hara to see him in a state like that if their positions were reversed, but Bo was dead, so how could he feel her pain, or his own pain for that matter? Was he really dead? This was the second time he had appeared to her, and both times everything seemed very real. His flawless, bronze skin, the corners of his mouth tuned up in a gentle smile…none of it could be a hallucination. She knew hallucinations, and they were never as real as this.

"Hey, baby," he said, his smile widening and his eyes becoming sadder. His voice was warm and deep, just like his eyes. He was too real to just be in her mind this time.

"What are you doing here?" Hara demanded breathlessly, her voice cracking. His appearance was too much for her to handle right now. Trying to fight back her raging emotions, she took a hesitant step backwards. She could no longer take the pain and pretend she was alright. Keeping her eyes on the floor as she felt herself about to burst, Hara prayed her mate would leave before she had a complete emotional breakdown.

"I needed to be with you," Bo replied softly, taking a step forward to keep the same distance between them. "Even if it will only be for a few minutes."

"You're dead," Hara whispered, her words causing her agony as the song—their song—continued to play.

"No," Bo said, coming another step closer. "I'm alive in you."

"That's not the same." Raising her eyes to meet Bo's, she struggled to contain her sobs. "You're not really here."

"Of course I am," Bo told her, trying to keep his smile convincing. "And I'll be here whenever you need me to be."

"I need you all the time!" Hara cried. "Now and forever!"

Shaking his head slowly, Bo sighed. "No you don't, Hallie. You've been doing fine without me so far."

Staring at him skeptically, she demanded, "Do you call this fine? I can barely function without you! Do you know how hard it is to live day to day knowing that you're dead and you can't be with me?"

"Hallie," Bo started soothingly as several hoarse sobs escaped Hara's throat.

"Don't call me Hallie!" Hara snapped, tears spilling out all over her.

"Why?" Bo asked quietly, and Hara could finally hear and see his pain for her.

"Because she died with you!" Hara sobbed, biting her lip and covering her mouth with her hand.

"I'm not dead, sweetie," Bo tried to soothe.

"Yes, you are!" Hara insisted, retreating again.

"We can still be together," Bo said.

"I don't even know who I am anymore!" Hara whispered.

"Well, I know who you are," Bo assured her, once again trying to close the space between them. "And I can show you if you need me to."

"Please leave," Hara begged him, wishing Dr. Bennett would come back to wake her up from this nightmare and tell her it was all in her head. Covering her whole face with her hands, she blurted, "I want you to leave *now!*"

"No, you don't," Bo whispered, and Hara sensed him reaching for her.

"Don't touch me!" Hara warned, trying to pull away. Bo already had her by the arm.

"Come here, honey," Bo murmured, pulling her in.

"Stop it!" Hara cried, shocked by his touch. If he wasn't real, then how could she feel him? She again tried to wrench her arm out of his grip.

"Come here," he repeated, and caught her in a tearful embrace. He held her tightly but lovingly. One hand was around her back so he could hold her in, and the other was holding her head against his chest. She could hear his heartbeat. How could she hear his heartbeat? His lips pressed against the top of her head, and he breathed softly into her hair. Hara wasn't sure if he was crying too, but by the way he was holding her she wouldn't have been surprised.

Hara gave up against him, and she gripped in her fingers the black t-shirt he was wearing. It clung loosely to his abs, and no matter how long she gripped him and no matter how long he held her, she still couldn't get it in her head that he was really there. She let herself sob into him, and she let him shush her and stroke her back comfortingly. "You told me that everything was my fault!" she balled, remembering their earlier encounter. "You told me I should kill myself!"

"No," Bo replied firmly. "That was you."

"I miss you so much!" Hara gasped, finding it difficult to breathe.

"I miss you too, baby," Bo whispered into her hair, continuing to rub her back. He listened to "Caribbean Blue" as it came to an end, and then he said, "This is our song, Hallie. Will you dance with me?"

Pulling away from him slightly so she could gaze into his compassionate brown eyes, Hara nodded. She knew the song was what brought Bo back to her in the first place.

Stepping back to the CD player, Bo hit the repeat button so the song would start over. Then, he took Hara's hand in his and slid his other hand around her waist. When the song began again, they started their dance.

It felt like it had been forever since Bo taught her the dance, but she remembered it with such precision that even Bo was impressed with her. "You didn't forget it," he whispered in praise.

"Of course I didn't," Hara murmured back. "How could I?"

They danced for about a minute without speaking, and Hara was lost in the feeling. Her depression lifted in the ninety seconds they were dancing, and she really missed the old times when she was always happy. She really missed Bo being with her all the time. The song and the dance calmed her internally, and as it came to an end, she wished that that moment would last forever.

Bo stopped the dance early. On the last spin, instead of lifting her, he pulled Hara into him once again and gripped her in another tight embrace. Swaying from side to side slowly, he kissed the top of her head tenderly. She felt how sorry he was that he had left her, and how sorry he was that she had turned into a monster, but she also felt his relief that she was still fighting and his joy at being able to spend just a few moments with her. He was really there. Feeling her sharp intake of air at the sudden realization, Bo laid his cheek on her hair. "Hallie," he breathed. "My Hallie."

"I feel you," Hara said, her fingers tightening around him. "You're really here."

"You can't change the past, honey," Bo told her, his voice filled with regret.

"I've already changed it," Hara whispered, breathing in his scent.

"You can't change what's already been set in stone," Bo insisted, running the tips of his fingers lightly over the skin on her arm. "You can only set a better course for the future."

"That's what I've been doing," Hara declared, resting her head against his chest and sighing heavily. "That's why I came back."

"Please come home," Bo pleaded. "I need you back home with me. I miss you. I love you."

"I will come home," Hara promised, closing her eyes. "But not until I finish this." Just then, the song ended, and she felt her arms wrap around air and her fingers grasp at nothing. Blinking her eyes open in surprise, she stared frozen at the space directly in front of her where he had stood. There was no one there. There was no sign that anyone had been there. There was no way for her to really know if Bo had in fact been with her or if it was all in her head. "I love you too," she whispered to the air around her, praying that wherever Bo was now, he could hear her. Her knees buckled beneath her, and she collapsed to the ground in a heap and allowed herself to cry. It was too much for her to bear. She loved Bo so much, and each time he appeared to her a little bit more of her died when he left. Would they ever be able to be together again as mates? Was Bo right when he said the past was set in stone? Maybe the past was, but their future certainly wasn't. That must be what Bo was talking about. She couldn't change what had happened to the Colicians, but maybe she still had a chance to save them all. She could bring them back somehow.

As she thought about it, she realized that Bo was wrong. She could change the past. She was, in fact, already changing things. If she hadn't changed anything, then they would never have danced together. She would kill Jackson Odau, and she would save her family and her people. There was nothing she wouldn't do for them.

Suddenly realizing she was being watched, Hara looked back up to the doorway leading to the kitchen. Dr. Bennett was standing there with a white pillow and a thick red blanket in his arms, staring at her in concern and uncertainty. Hara wasn't sure if he had seen the entire episode or had just walked in on her, but she knew that he had seen enough. Words such as delusional and hallucinations and desperation were running through his head, and upon hearing them, her cheeks flushed red in embarrassment.

Now that his presence was known, Dr. Bennett stepped into the room and walked over to the CD player. "I see you've found my CDs," he said, pressing the stop button and turning it off. The sudden silence made Hara squirm on the floor.

"I like Enya," Hara apologized, sniffling and wrapping her arms around her knees.

Nodding, Bennett kept his eyes locked on her. "What were you doing just now?" he asked quietly.

"Dancing," Hara replied, gazing at the gray carpet beneath her.

"Oh," he said, continuing to stare at her. "By yourself?"

"No," Hara muttered, blushing even more. If anyone could understand what she was experiencing, it would be him. "I was dancing with Bo."

Pausing, Bennett told her gently, "There was no one else here, honey."

Looking up into his soft, concerned eyes, Hara said, "You just couldn't see him."

Bennett bit his lip uncertainly. "Hallie...you just imagined him. I was watching you and you were talking to yourself. I'm sorry, but Bo was never here."

"He was here," Hara whispered insistently, feeling her eyes tear up again. "I could feel him."

"Hallie..." Bennett started again, but Hara cut him off angrily.

"My name isn't Hallie!" she cried, pounding her fist on the floor. "Who's Hallie? I don't know a Hallie! She's dead! She died a long time ago! My name is Hara!"

"No," Bennett told her firmly, setting the blanket and pillow down on the sofa and fixing his gaze on hers. "Your name is Hallie. There's a part of her still alive in you, just like there's a part of Bo that's still alive in you. As time moves forward, I see more and more of her beginning to come out. You may deny her existence, but she's there inside of you, and I think that before this is all over, she's going to come back completely. I think Hara is going to die by the end of this, and everything will go back to how it was."

Wincing, Hara wished he was right. If everything went back to how it was, it would be a miracle. "Don't hold your breath," she muttered, lowering her eyes to the floor.

There was an awkward silence, and Hara heard Bennett sigh heavily. "Come on, honey," he said. "You need to get some rest if you plan to confront The Doc again."

Suddenly feeling very weary, Hara slowly rose to her feet and walked over to Bennett's couch, where Bennett was adjusting the pillow and spreading out the blanket. When Bennett seemed to feel that it was sufficient enough for her, he stepped aside and gestured for her to take a seat, but she refused to sit. Staring hard at him, she said through her teeth, "I'm not crazy."

Bennett stared back evenly at her. "I never said that you were."

You've been thinking that, she wanted to say, but she bit her tongue and lowered herself to the couch. Dropping her head into her hands, she shook her head in frustration. She wasn't crazy. Bo had been with her; he had really been with her. Something she had done had obviously altered what had happened, because Bo really was alive, or at least his mind was. Had it been the children she killed? Was telling the truth what changed things? Was it a little thing she had done that she wouldn't have expected to make a difference? Whatever it may have been, it wasn't enough for her. She meant what she said to Bo before he left. She would go home, but not until she destroyed the final thing standing in the way of a good future for her people. Jackson Odau was the only thing that could bring down the Colicians, and she owed them that much. She had promised them all that she would save them, and she planned to keep her promise.

"Lie down," Bennett told her, gently pushing on her shoulder.

She did, lying on her side and resting her head on the pillow. Pulling her knees up to her chest, she wrapped her arms around her legs. She really wanted to sleep, but there were too many things on her mind. Her son, Bo, The Doc, and Jackson Odau were all distractions that would keep her mind busy until she could finally fix the catastrophe. She doubted she would be able to get any decent sleep until she was able to go home. And even then, it might take time.

Bennett pulled the blanket up to her shoulder. It was soft and had a musty smell to it, like it had been folded in a closet for years. Despite the strange smell, the blanket was warm and comforting and made her relax ever so slightly. Bennett, however, was beginning to make her feel uneasy. "Here," he said, taking four pills out of his white jacket pocket. Two of them were translucent blue caplets, and the other two were oval shaped and white. "I want you to take these."

"Why?" Hara demanded, eyeing him suspiciously.

"They'll help you sleep," Bennett replied, holding them out to her. He was determined to make sure she took them.

"The blue ones will, yes," Hara replied, narrowing her eyes as she read his mind. "But what about the white ones?"

Bennett clamped his teeth together, knowing that it was futile to try to lie. Sighing, he answered, "The white ones help patients with schizophrenia to relax."

"That's very interesting," Hara muttered, glaring at him. Bennett didn't reply or avert his eyes. He really though that taking those pills would be in her best interest, but Hara knew she wasn't crazy. Bo had really been there with her. Bennett just wouldn't be able to understand because he was human, and Hara had learned over the past few days that humans refused to believe in anything they couldn't understand. She decided that even though Bennett was trying to drug her, she really did want to sleep, even if just for a little while. Taking the two blue pills, she popped them into her mouth and swallowed hard to get them down, gazing back stubbornly at Bennett.

Realizing that she was refusing to take the white pills, Bennett tried again. "Please take these," he begged. "You'd be surprised how much better they can make you feel..."

"I'm not crazy," Hara repeated, firmer than before. She had had enough of everybody judging her.

"I don't think you're crazy," Bennett assured her breathlessly, and by his exasperated thoughts, Hara could tell he was growing frustrated.

"You're trying to get me to take pills that will stop these recurring delusions I'm having," Hara accused, repeating his exact thought. "Well, I'm not having any delusions, so I don't see a point in taking them. Bo was really here with me. I know he was."

"Hallucinations seem real while you're having them..."

"You've seen the tapes The Doc made. You've seen what types of drugs he used on me. I know hallucinations. I've had plenty of them. This was no dream. He was real."

"Hara..." Bennett sighted, finally switching back to her preferred name. "I can't help you unless you let me."

"You want me to trust you, right?" Hara asked, trying to get him to understand.

Blinking in confusion, Bennett nodded. "Of course I do."

"Then you need to trust me as well," Hara declared, wrapping her blanket around her and closing her eyes.

For several long moments, Hara sensed Bennett remaining frozen where he was beside her. Then, he drew his hand away and put the pills back in his jacket pocket. Sighing again, he murmured, "I do trust you, kid." He turned to walk back into his kitchen. "I'll be in the next room if you need anything."

Smiling to herself, Hara allowed her exhaustion to take control of her mind and body. It felt to her as if only seconds passed before the depths of unconsciousness enveloped her. She just prayed she would be able to stay under for a little while.

✳ ✳ ✳

"Caribbean Blue." Perry had heard the song before, but not for a long time. It was a nice song, sure, but he had never been much of a music person. An old friend of his had been playing it on a stereo and Perry had listened, but after that he had never heard it again. So why was he dreaming about it? Why was the song being played in the far corners of his mind?

Something was choking Perry. That was the first thing he became aware of as he slowly awoke. There was something soft and thick and bitter shoved in his mouth to the back of his throat. He bit down on it and tried to swallow, but gagged and attempted to spit it out. He found that he was unable to move his arms, or any part of his body for that matter, and was unable to pull the object out of his mouth. Blinking rapidly to unstick his eyelids, he peered into blackness. A hood covered his head, and as he became more and more conscious of what was happening to him, his heart began to pound in his chest.

Breathing hard through his nose, Perry struggled to remember what had happened to him. He had blacked out in the stairwell before he made it down to the second level. Just before he lost consciousness, he heard The Doc calling for backup on his radio. Then Perry remembered; The Doc had stabbed him in the stomach, but then the wound healed over. Noah's prediction had come true; Perry had gained his ability ten years early. Now that Perry had an ability, and The Doc was there to witness it, what was The Doc going to do to him? What had The Doc already done to him? Whatever he had planned, it couldn't be good.

Even though he couldn't see anything and he couldn't move, Perry could tell he was in a vehicle. He was sitting upright and could feel every bump in the road. He could also hear a soft whirring sound that told him the vehicle was traveling at a pretty high velocity. There were no voices, and no sounds to indicate that anyone was with him, but Perry knew better. He could feel his mind on alert, and he found that he was now able to sense the malevolent force that was threatening his very existence.

As Perry predicted, his hood was pulled off moments later and he squinted up at The Doc's smirking face. There was a single florescent light bulb above them on a high ceiling, casting a dim glow over them and the equipment around them. His wrists and ankles were cuffed to the uncomfortable metal chair in which he was sitting. Despite knowing that he was in a vehicle, he stared down the extended room he was in. It was narrow and long, and the end opposite him was lost in the darkness. To Perry's left, there were dozens of control boxes with colorful flashing lights set upon cabinets that appeared embedded somehow into the metal walls. Each cabinet was a dull blue color and had two doors with white button-shaped handles, and each cabinet also had two boxes on top. Perry couldn't even speculate what the boxes were for, and frankly, he didn't care. What he did care about was what was on the other side of him. He wasn't able to feel anything, but his heart leapt in his chest when he saw the thick IV jutting out of his arm. His jacket sleeve was rolled up and a pouch full of a cloudy liquid hung from a metal hook just above his left shoulder, draining down through a tube into his arm. The substance was preventing him from moving.

Behind the pouch, on the right wall, there were shelves with trays stocked with vials of different colored liquids. They appeared to be just the proper size to fit into a syringe. The shelves stretched all the way down into the darkness before him, lit up with florescent blue lights that were positioned on the bottom of each shelf and illuminating the shelves beneath them. There were four shelves stacked one above the other and on a section of the second shelf from the floor there were trays filled with several different sized syringes. Perry's stomach churned at the sight of them.

He could see that there was much more equipment spread out in front of him and probably behind him as well, but it was too dark and he was too wary and terrified to focus on what they could be. It was clear he was in a vehicle; the floor beneath him was bouncy and unsteady and it sounded as if they were on a highway; but it seemed way too big. There was enough space to go running through it. Perry then remembered that The Doc didn't have any ordinary vehicle. This was the answer to the mystery of what was in The Doc's semitrailer. The Doc had kidnapped Perry and brought him to the one place where he could escape yet still conduct experiments.

"Rise and shine," The Doc said cheerfully, tossing the hood aside. His eyes searched Perry over with that sickly curious air about them. Perry pictured himself as Hara, and The Doc was staring him down like a wolf staring down a rabbit. Whatever had happened that gave Perry this newfound ability, The Doc wanted to dissect him and find out how he worked. Perry wished he could move, because he had never felt so terrified in all his years as an FBI agent and wanted desperately to get out of there, but he couldn't even wiggle his fingers. The Doc could read the fear on Perry's face. "Sorry about the paralysis inducer," he apologized. "I couldn't have you fighting while I do this." Turning slightly, he took one of the larger syringes from the tray and came towards Perry.

Gasping through his nose, Perry gagged on the object in his mouth again. He couldn't understand why he wasn't able to move; his heart was pounding so fast that it felt to him as if his heart could propel his movements. He willed himself to move, but he was forced to watch as The Doc rolled up his left sleeve to expose his arm. An elastic band was tied around his bicep. Perry tried to plead with the doctor, but his words came out as a muffled mess.

The Doc was quick to silence him. "Don't worry about a thing," he said. "I've seen what you've done for the Colician race. You're a tough bastard. You can handle this just fine." Patting the side of Perry's sweating head, The Doc stuck the needle into the vein in the crook of Perry's left arm. Blood back flowed into the syringe, and it took Perry a moment to realize that The Doc wasn't injecting him with anything; he was extracting a blood sample.

Perry watched as The Doc filled the syringe with blood. He saw that he was still covered in blood from The Doc's knife assault. His white shirt was completely soaked red, and there was a slit in the middle where the knife had penetrated. Blood was covering the skin underneath his shirt as well, but there was no visible wound. It was more difficult to see the stain on his black jacket, but it was still visible. Perry suddenly noticed that The Doc was still hurt. The right leg of his pants was splattered with his blood and Perry could see the wound through the slit. He was still bleeding, and Perry realized why The Doc was withdrawing his blood. If he still wanted to catch Hara, and Perry knew he did, then The Doc would need to be in his best shape to do so. A bullet wound in his leg was not going to allow him to get very far. When the syringe was full, The Doc pulled out the needle and limped backwards a few feet. Reaching behind the chair Perry was strapped onto, he took out a metal stool and seated himself on it. For the first time since Perry had met The Doc, he saw him wince in pain as he rolled up his pant leg and exposed the bullet wound. The bullet had passed all the way through his calf, so all The Doc had to do was inject himself with Perry's brand new regenerative blood and his leg would be in pristine condition. That was exactly what The Doc did. Injecting the entire dose into the area just above the injury, he watched as his own wound healed itself in less than twenty seconds. Just like with Perry's wound, there was no scar or even a mark to suggest he had ever been injured. The only evidence remaining was the blood still left on his leg, shoe, and pant leg.

Setting the syringe back on the tray, The Doc stretched out his leg, as if testing it to make sure it would really function correctly. When he appeared satisfied, he rose to his feet and approached Perry once again. "Thank you for that," he said. Whether his gratitude was real or not was unclear. "Consider us even now. I spared your girlfriend's life and you healed the wound you inflicted on me." The Doc grinned somewhat triumphantly.

Perry glared at him, hoping he could look as intimidating as The Doc. If he seriously thought they were even, he wasn't just crazy. He was stupid.

Snickering to himself but continuing to search Perry with his eyes, The Doc went on. "You do know that you weren't supposed to get this ability for another ten years, don't you?" he asked, but didn't wait for a response. "Everyone who knows about you understands that. It's a key point in history. It hasn't happened yet, but everyone knows what's supposed to happen on April 4, 2018." The Doc shook his head thoughtfully. "Hara must have activated you by accident while healing your head injury, which means that she altered your future and your history. That silly girl should have thought that through before she tried to be noble." Narrowing his eyes at Perry, he continued. "You know how the Colician abilities spread, don't you? When the chemical weapon first escaped the laboratory, it only spread to the few miles surrounding that area. Those who were affected spread the disease to other O Negatives through touch. Hara is a second generation O Negative, so she can't spread the disease through touch, but the energy exchange must be what caused your early onset."

He stared at Perry for a few moments, waiting for Perry's look of surprise or understanding, but when all he gave him was a blank expression, The Doc blinked and asked, "You already knew it was coming early, didn't you? Yes, I can see it in your eyes. Someone warned you about what was going to happen to you, but who could have known…?" He paused again to think. "Ah, it was Noah, wasn't it? He figured it all out and told you before you went back to the station. A smart old man, he is." He stared off into space thoughtfully for some time. "Nothing like this has ever happened before," he went on, still gazing at Perry with that fascinated expression of his. "This is…impossible. Well, it is possible, but this was not supposed to happen now. Ten years, Perry. You have your ability ten years early. Hara really screwed things up. This was not the way it was supposed to happen."

For a while, Perry had been under the impression that The Doc was just talking to himself, speaking his thoughts aloud to come to his own conclusions. At the end of his speech, Perry finally felt the need to be a part of the conversation. "Says who?" he tried to snap, but he could barely get the sounds out. He gagged again, and remembered to breathe through his nose or he would choke to death.

Smirking at Perry's pointless attempt, The Doc said, "Could you speak up, please? I'm having trouble hearing you."

Perry tried to furiously shout something at him, but he started gagging before he had even taken a breath. Dropping his chin to his chest, he felt his eyes water and he made an unpleasant retching sound from deep in his throat.

The Doc seemed to understand what was wrong. "Oh, I'm sorry. Is that choking you?"

Hearing The Doc step up to him again and seeing his feet enter his line of sight, Perry was quite surprised when The Doc grabbed the object in his mouth and started to take it out. He was so surprised, in fact, that he chomped down with his teeth on The Doc's fingers before the object was fully out of his mouth.

Crying out in pain but mostly in surprise, The Doc snapped his hand away and took a step back. It couldn't have been too painful because Perry didn't even bite down that hard.

Even though The Doc hadn't pulled the gag out all the way, Perry was able to spit it out onto the floor. He glared back at The Doc's stunned expression. In hadn't been intentional, but Perry wanted to let The Doc know that he didn't feel sorry for it.

Perry could see the hint of amusement on his face as he raised his eyebrows, sighed, and said, "Agent Perry, that hurt."

"Yes, well, stabbing me in the gut didn't feel too great either!" Perry snapped back, finding his voice raspy and his throat sore.

An emotion that Perry could not identify flashed across The Doc's face. "No hard feelings," he replied softly.

"Forgive me if I have a few!" Perry snarled, trying with every ounce of strength in his body to move. Even if it was a finger or a toe, it would give him one small shred of hope that he wasn't completely immobile and helpless. To his dismay, not a muscle twitched. "What the hell did you do to me?" he demanded.

"It's only temporary," The Doc assured. "I don't need you kicking and clawing as well as biting."

"What do you want from me?" Perry asked, just wanting a straight answer. "Why didn't you just leave me there?"

Cocking his head ever so slightly, The Doc said quietly, "I think you know the answer to that, son."

"What do you want from me?" Perry shouted.

His expression blank, The Doc stated, "You're something new."

Perry swallowed hard. The way The Doc was staring at him with that sick fascination, the same exact way Perry had seen him stare at Hara or Allan Brown or even Jack, was very unnerving. The Doc had gone from being homicidal to being completely enthralled by Perry in just a few seconds, but his interest was not a positive thing. Perry did not intend to be dissected. The Doc found him so fascinating now, but he had just tried to kill him. The Doc may not have known what Perry was at first, but he knew what he was going to become. "Why did you try to kill me?" Perry asked, even though he had a feeling he didn't need an answer. The Doc didn't seem like a man who was afraid to alter the course of history.

Smiling lightly, The Doc replied, "I think you know the answer to that too."

"I told you," Perry said shakily. "I didn't know anything about Agent Long or what he was doing, and I still don't believe your story!"

"Believe it," The Doc said curtly.

Perry still had doubts about The Doc's explanation. Sure, Agent Long had disappeared a few times and Hara's escape had been rather suspicious, but it was a big jump to assume he was a Colician and had been on the opposing side the whole time. The Doc had been lying to his face since the beginning, so why should Perry believe anything the man said now?

"Even if you didn't know about Simco's plan, I still would have tried to kill you," The Doc informed. "In the future, you are one of the main reasons the Colicians survive, and probably the Caitens as well."

"How do I help the Caitens?" Perry asked in surprise, hearing that news for the first time.

"You'll help them in the same way you'll help the Colicians," The Doc replied. "You'll end up becoming the savior of both races."

"But how do I help them?" Perry demanded, hoping for one straight answer.

"I can't tell you that," The Doc said softly. "Evidently, the future needs you so badly that it would change your destiny in order to keep you alive." A strange expression passed over his face. "Unless…this was always supposed to happen." He laughed suddenly, making Perry jump. "That's it! I think I've finally figured it out!" Giving Perry a very serious look, he explained, "Agent Perry, as much as Hara denies it, history is in fact set in stone. She claims she can change what happened to her people and alter future events, but she can't. Just like I can't kill you now. Even though I know everything that is going to happen for the next several decades, I can't change anything that I want to. You play a very important role in the future's history, and I can't change that. I can't wipe you out of history, because history won't let me. Hara was always meant to accidently give you this ability ten years early and we were always meant to interfere with current events. Forgive me for being so surprised; I was never informed that you received your ability in 2008."

"Will you do me a favor?" Perry begged. "Just this once, will you answer my question, and with the truth?"

The Doc smiled at him. "I suppose that would depend on the question," he replied smugly. When Perry refused to ask his question, The Doc sighed. "I suppose that I do owe you that much. I'll do my best to answer truthfully."

"Thank you," Perry said gratefully, although he had a feeling he wouldn't get the truth anyway. "I can understand how Hara knows what's supposed to happen in the future, but how do you know everything? The last time I checked, you weren't predicting catastrophes. Not on your own, anyway."

For a moment, The Doc just stared at him. Then, both corners of his mouth turned up in a grin. Placing one hand on each of Perry's wrists, he leaned in so close that Perry turned his head away as he became uncomfortable. "I torture and experiment on Colicians. Trust me." He grabbed Perry's chin and forced him to look at him, "You learn things."

Pulling away in disgust, Perry wished he'd never asked. "How the hell do you enjoy your job so much?" he demanded.

Bending down to pick up the object he had used to gag Perry, he replied, "When you've been through as much as I have, you'd be surprised what you find enjoyable."

Perry was about to make a comment, but he stopped when he recognized the object The Doc was now holding. "Is that my sock?" he asked, suddenly feeling very sick to his stomach. Glancing down at his foot, he saw that his shoe had been replaced, but his left sock was missing.

The Doc gazed down at Perry's sock in his hand and looked back at Perry. "Yes."

Wrinkling his nose, Perry cried, "You gagged me with my own sock?" He made a mental note to use a different laundry detergent, preferably one of better taste, should a situation like this ever happen again.

"Well," The Doc began, raising his eyebrows, "I could have used your boxers, but that would have made us both uncomfortable."

Gaping at him in disbelief, Perry decided to not press the matter. The Doc was clearly not in the mood for serious responses. Instead, Perry asked hesitantly, "So…what now?" When The Doc cocked his head questioningly, Perry said, "I mean…what are you going to do to me?"

The blank expression held on his face for some time. "I'm going to dissect you," The Doc answered calmly, intently watching Perry's reaction. "I'm going to find out how exactly Hara triggered your ability, because, my friend, this is scientifically… impossible."

"I thought abilities were triggered by touch?" Perry said.

"As I said earlier, second generation Colicians can't spread abilities," The Doc explained. "It's been proven in several studies."

"Well, Hara isn't exactly normal," Perry reminded. "Even for a Colician. And if the first generation is the one that spreads abilities through contact, why wasn't anyone affected by Marcus, Brown, or Hopper?"

"They were very careful," The Doc told him. "They used their minds to suppress their own abilities as a method of hiding as well as a method of keeping the contamination contained. I'm sure they were also avoiding physical contact with any non-contaminated O negative. Now, I've really been enjoying our conversation, but if you don't mind…" Stepping forward once more, The Doc grabbed Perry by the jaw, forced his mouth open, and shoved the sock back in.

Pushing his tongue to the back of his throat so the sock wouldn't choke him again, Perry attempted to bite The Doc's fingers again. The Doc was predicting that, and made sure to keep his fingers clear of

Perry's teeth. Perry glared back at his amused face, but it was pointless. He couldn't intimidate The Doc if he was unable to move and was strapped to a chair. He couldn't intimidate a mouse in his position.

"Unfortunately for you, most of these tests are going to hurt," the Doc informed him, pulling his stool up closer to Perry and sitting back down. Locking eyes with him, The Doc added quietly, "So try not to scream too loud." Cocking his head again, his eyes narrowed. "How's that for a serious response?"

Perry blinked in surprise. Had The Doc somehow heard him think that earlier? How could he? He wasn't a Colician...or was he?

Smirking, The Doc muttered, "I suppose you'll never know, will you?"

16

Changing Sides

Jerking awake with a gasp, Hara stared down at the blue sofa she was lying on. Once again, she was glad to be back to the horrific reality, because it took away the even more horrific dreams. When her slumber first began, she believed that everything she could see through Perry's eyes was all just another bad dream. Unfortunately, as the dream went on, she realized that everything occurring was real. It was all too real. Perry was about to go through a round with The Doc because she had accidentally set off his ability. He was about to fully understand just how much pain Hara had endured over her few months in captivity with The Doc, and it was all her fault. She wanted Perry to understand her pain, but not in the way he was about to.

Hara wanted to stay with Perry until The Doc began his tests, at which point she planned to duck out. She thought she owed it to Perry to suffer with him, but she knew she wouldn't be able to emotionally handle it. But once she realized that The Doc could hear Perry's thoughts, she panicked and immediately pulled out of the dream.

She lay as still as she could, breathing hard from the sudden shock. It was horrifying to think that The Doc actually had an ability, but to think that so much time had passed without her knowing about it was even worse. How could The Doc have an ability? He wasn't a Colician or a Caiten, and he had murdered his father, who was helping the Colicians during the initial outbreak. The Doc had B positive blood, and that was a known fact. Had he developed a new strain that gave him an ability? If he loathed the Colician race as much as he claimed, then why would he want to make himself into one? Was it just an accident? Was his ability the reason why no Colician or Caiten could ever hear his thoughts? The questions were endless, and Hara had a feeling they weren't about to be answered anytime soon.

Suddenly sensing the presence of another, Hara raised her eyes to the person watching over her. Dr. Bennett pulled over one of the chairs from the kitchen table and sat in it beside her. His concerned eyes were searching her face carefully, like they had after her latest encounter with Bo, and his hands were folded neatly over his knee as he patiently waited for her to fully come back down to Earth. When she met his eyes, he smiled at her. "Are you okay?" he asked softly.

"How long have you been sitting there?" Hara asked uneasily. The only person who ever watched her sleep was The Doc, and as her time with Bennett ticked by, Bennett was beginning to remind her more and more of The Doc.

"A minute or so," Bennett replied, shrugging nonchalantly. "You cried out a few times in your sleep, so I just wanted to make sure you were alright."

Nodding, Hara sighed and lay her head back down on the sofa. She had struggled to keep herself quiet while The Doc was speaking to Perry, but evidently she had problems controlling herself while she was sleeping.

Bennett peered down at her troubled expression. "Are you alright?" he repeated, eager for an honest answer.

"I doubt I'll be alright ever again," she responded, sighing again.

"What were you dreaming about?" Bennett asked curiously, leaning forward ever so slightly.

"I wasn't dreaming," Hara declared, pushing herself up so she could rest her back on the arm of the sofa. "I was observing what Perry was up to."

His forehead furrowing in confusion, Bennett asked, "Is there something wrong?"

Shrugging, Hara replied, "Perry was abducted by The Doc, and The Doc is going to torture him, but Perry will be okay."

"How can you be sure?" Bennett demanded, his expression becoming thoroughly worried.

"I made sure he would be," Hara whispered, even though triggering Perry's ability had been a complete accident. "Besides, the future wants him, so his safety is guaranteed."

"Yes, but I thought you were changing things?" Bennett said, his confusion back.

"I'm not sure that I have changed anything," Hara muttered, thinking over everything The Doc had told Perry. "I'm not sure that I can change anything."

"How do you know you can't?" Bennett asked, and he sounded almost as desperate as Hara felt. They both wanted to be able to alter the course of the future.

"I don't," Hara said, and she felt herself harden again. Narrowing her eyes, she told Bennett, "And I'm not going to stop until I'm sure."

Nodding, Bennett knew Hara was completely serious. "I know you won't."

"What time is it?" Hara wondered curiously, unsure of how long she had been sleeping.

"It's close to four," Bennett answered. Peering at her, he asked. "Do you want something to eat?"

"No," Hara said, feeling her exhaustion overwhelming her once more. She was disappointed that she had only been asleep for a little more than an hour. Pushing herself back down so she was lying flat on the couch again, she said, "I think I'm going to try to sleep some more."

Bennett nodded again, and his eyes suddenly looked sad. "Is there anything I can get for you? Is there anything you need?"

"No, thank you," Hara whispered, her heart turning into a knot in her chest. The way Bennett cared for her was exactly how Daniel had cared for her back at the hideout, but now Daniel wasn't around to care for her anymore. It was difficult for her to find people that cared that much for her ever since her family was murdered. "I think you've done enough for me."

Lowering his eyes, he told her, "I know you probably don't want to hear this now, but I thought you had better know."

Her heart skipping a beat, Hara pushed herself up on one elbow. "What happened?"

Glancing back up to her panicked gaze, Bennett bit his lip nervously. "After you left your room to retrieve your son, The Doc found Allan and tried to kill him."

"Oh, God!" Hara breathed, thinking only the worst possible things. With all the negative emotions she had been experiencing while trying to get her son back, it would have been very possible for her to have missed sensing Allan's death. Why hadn't she remembered Allan's condition earlier? She had completely forgotten that he was in Bennett's care, and she hadn't thought about it when Bennett left his duties at the hospital to care for her and Dreyson. How could she have forgotten about Allan? He was one of the few Colicians left in the fight, and on her side. Most of all, he was her friend. He had stuck with her since the beginning, and he deserved so much from her. It was sad that she had forgotten he was gravely ill and possibly dying.

"Don't worry," Bennett reassured quickly, and Hara sighed in relief. "Meg stopped him, but…"

"No…" Hara whispered, her eyes growing wide with horror. Allan hadn't been the one to die.

"The Doc injected her with a substance that very nearly killed her," Bennett explained. "She would have died if I hadn't stopped The Doc and if you hadn't given me your blood. You were right." He nodded to her and smiled. "It came in handy."

"Is she okay?" Hara asked hesitantly, not sure if she wanted to hear the answer.

"I don't know," Bennett replied. "Allan took her and they both fled the hospital."

"Where did they go?" Hara was worried. Allan wouldn't be able to make it far in his state. She heard in Bennett's mind that he had given Allan a shot of adrenaline so he could keep going, but Allan would crash eventually and Hara feared for his safety when that happened. Also, Meg was going to be weak after going through what she did. The Doc had most likely injected her with the same substance that killed Daniel, and Hara had seen many people injected with it back in the labs. It painfully killed anyone in under a minute. Hara wished she had known when her friends were in trouble. She might have been able to help them and prevent what happened to them, but she knew in her heart that she wouldn't have gone back for them. She had been too determined to get her son back. Maybe Meg had blocked the incident from Hara because she knew how horrible a choice it would have been for Hara. She prayed that was the reason why she hadn't remembered they were in trouble.

"They didn't tell me. Before they left, however, Meg said that they had to go to a church and turn on 'the machine.'" Bennett squinted at her curiously.

Realization striking her, Hara inhaled sharply. One thing she didn't take into consideration when she chose to come back to Philadelphia was how she was going to get home when she finished her mission. Now that Bennett told her what Allan and Meg planned to do, Hara realized that they already had a solution to that problem. They had already built the machine that would get them home. They were going to turn it on and wait for Hara to finish the job so they could all go home together.

"Do you know what that means?" Bennett asked hopefully.

"Yes, of course," Hara whispered. It took a moment for her to catch on to what Bennett had meant by "church." Allan, Meg, and Daniel chose the one place that held meaning to all of them to build the machine. The church was the same one where Hara first made contact with Daniel the day before. It was old and run-down and abandoned, but it was the Colicians' symbol of a new beginning.

"If you know where they are, you should tell me so I can go help them," Bennett insisted anxiously. He was worried for Allan and Meg. "They won't be able to defend themselves on their own..."

"If they're at the church and they've turned on the machine, then they're safe," Hara assured him, lying her head back down. "Nothing can hurt them in that place."

Bennett's expression told her that he wanted to argue further, but instead he just said, "Well, if you think they're safe, I suppose I trust your judgment."

Ignoring Bennett's uncertainty, Hara asked him before she forgot about the others too, "Have you heard about Jack or Noah at all?"

"I'm afraid not," Bennett apologized. "But I suppose that's a good thing. If nobody knows anything about them then they aren't in custody and The Doc hasn't captured them either."

"Let's hope you're right," Hara murmured, trying to find her four friends with her mind. She couldn't feel any of them. She was slowly losing her connection with her own species. If she couldn't change past events or the course of the future, Hara prayed that she would die when the fight was over. She wouldn't be able to go on living as completely broken as she was. "I'm going to try and sleep some more." Her voice cracked with emotion as she spoke.

Bennett's brow furrowed in concern. "Are you alright, honey?" he asked, leaning in a little closer to her as tears spilled out of her eyes and onto the couch.

"No," she croaked, squeezing her eyes closed. "No, no, no…"

"What's the matter?" Hara could tell by Bennett's voice that he had no idea what had upset her, but he deeply cared. "What's wrong?"

"I can't feel them anymore!" Hara cried, letting out several sobs but keeping her eyes tightly shut. "I can't feel their presence anywhere!" Reaching out to her son, she found that even her bond with him was hazy. She was becoming less and less Colician and more and more human with every passing moment, with every breath. She was losing her own power. "I can barely feel Dreyson anymore! I can't go on like this! I have to fix the past, or I'll…I'll…I'll end it all!"

Pausing as what she was saying sank in, she heard Bennett whisper, "You can't kill yourself."

"Says who?" Hara demanded, wanting to glare at him. Her eyelids were already beginning to stick shut. "I can do whatever I want to, and if I can't fix this, then death is the only escape." *At least then I'll be with my family!* she wanted to say, but she couldn't. It was too painful to think about.

"Your son needs you," Bennett said angrily. "You can't just abandon him here on Earth! Not with what's coming!"

"I'm going to sleep now," Hara snapped, wanting Bennett to leave. She wanted the discussion to end, because she knew he was right. She couldn't just abandon Dreyson, not with 2018 rapidly approaching, drawing closer and closer as they spoke. How could she be so selfish?

She thought once again that Bennett was going to press the matter, but all he did was sigh. He then reached out and placed a comforting hand on the side of her head for a few seconds before standing up and leaving the room. The gentle touch reminded her of Bo, and had Bennett remained for only a few moments longer, he would have seen the single tear trickle down her cheek.

Her memories left behind only pain.

❉ ❉ ❉

As Bennett left his den to let Hara sleep some more, he thought over everything the poor girl had said. She was broken, and not just in two, but in many different pieces. The loss of her family and nearly everyone she ever loved had sent her over the edge a long time ago. Now that

Allan and Meg were out of the fight, Hara was the last Colician standing against The Doc. She was alone. On a planet of billions, she was completely alone.

Bennett understood why she said she would end her life if the past and future couldn't be altered. There would be nothing left for her to live for other than her son, but even Dreyson wouldn't be enough to sustain her after all she had lost in that war. Bennett was finally beginning to understand just how hard losing someone was for a Colician. In losing her family, she had lost her soul. In losing her soul, she had lost her sanity. In losing her sanity, she had lost her sense of morality, therefore losing every last shred of who she was. Bennett could still see that a small part of Hallie was clinging to life, but if Hara was pushed over the edge one more time, any remains of Hallie Reifert would be lost forever. Hara had lost so much, and Bennett felt that it was his duty to prevent Hallie from being completely destroyed. He would protect Dreyson and anyone else Hara cared about, whether or not he died in the process.

Upon entering his kitchen, Bennett turned when he heard something moving off to his left. His heart skipped a beat when he saw the door of his refrigerator hanging open, the light from inside shining out over the rest of the kitchen. A shadow of somebody rummaging around inside could be seen on the floor. The first thought that crossed his mind was that someone had broken into his apartment. He expected The Doc to suddenly appear around the corner with a weapon in hand. Glancing around the room a few times, Bennett slowly approached from the side of the fridge before cautiously peeking inside. Images of a bomb exploding or another horrible attack filled his mind, but as he looked inside, he saw that the only invasion was that of Dreyson.

The boy was standing on the bottom shelf and was stretching up on his tip-toes as he reached for something on the top shelf. Bennett had given the toddler one of his grandson's t-shirts to wear. It was large on Dreyson and billowed out around him, but Bennett knew that underneath the baggy shirt was the child's boney body. The poor boy had been starved and beaten over a period of months. Bennett knew because he had seen the bruises and his ribs poking out of his chest when he helped Dreyson change into the clean shirt. It was remarkable that the child was still able to walk! He got his strength from his mother. Just like Hara, Bennett figured that Dreyson too would fight until the very end, no matter how small and young he was.

As Bennett cast his shadow over the boy, Dreyson turned and looked up at him with his big green eyes. He looked just like his mother with those eyes and his curly brown hair. Bennett wondered if Dreyson was just as troubled as Hara after what he had been through. The child hadn't spoken a word in Bennett's presence, so it was unclear just how traumatized he was. Bennett prayed he wasn't as angry or lost as Hara. There wasn't enough room in the world for two Hara's.

"What are you looking for?" Bennett asked as Dreyson climbed down out of the fridge.

Giving Bennett an uncertain look, as he had several times since Agent Long handed him over, Dreyson pointed at the top shelf. He didn't say a word to answer, and Bennett was beginning to wonder if the boy was even capable of speech.

Stepping closer, Bennett examined the items on the top shelf of his fridge. There were a few different things that Dreyson could have been trying to obtain. Reaching up his hand, Bennett grabbed the handle of the half-empty gallon of milk. "This?"

Dreyson shook his head hard, his eyebrows coming together and his tiny mouth frowning. He jabbed his finger at the top shelf again, his little expression impatient.

Looking back again, Bennett wished that Dreyson would just say what he wanted, but he knew how young children could be; after all, he had raised three of his own. Plus, Dreyson had been through a great ordeal, and he most likely had trust issues like his mother. Bennett would cut the boy some slack. Pointing to the unopened half-gallon jug of orange juice, he asked, "Is this what you want?" As he looked to check Dreyson's reaction, he saw that the toddler was smiling a toothy smile and nodding his head eagerly.

Glad that he had figured out what Dreyson wanted, Bennett smiled back and took the jug out of the fridge. After everything the kid had been through, all he wanted was a cup of juice. Sometimes, it was the simple things that could be missed the most. Setting the jug on the counter, Bennett started to close the door, but Dreyson reached out and grabbed it to keep it from shutting.

"What's wrong?" Bennett asked, looking back down again. Dreyson was jumping up and down and pointing urgently at something else on the top shelf. His expression seemed almost pained, as if he felt he was going to die if Bennett didn't get it for him. Bennett, not understanding what the boy wanted, stared at the jar of pickles Dreyson was pointing at. "You want pickles?" he asked skeptically. He didn't need to look at Dreyson to know that wasn't what he wanted. Pickles and orange juice? No, Dreyson was pointing at what was behind the pickles. It had slipped Bennett's mind that the boy could foresee future events, and maybe that meant he knew what was behind the jar. Reaching up again, Bennett pushed aside the pickle jar and found that there was a small jar of strawberry jelly. Holding it up, Bennett gazed down at Dreyson's beaming face. "Is this what you were looking for?" When the boy nodded, Bennett asked him, "PB&J?" Dreyson nodded again. Bennett gestured to his kitchen table. "Take a seat."

Obeying, Dreyson walked over to the chair facing away from Bennett and carefully climbed up on to it, resting on his knees so he could see over the top of the table.

Bennett set the jelly on the counter beside the orange juice and opened the cabinets above him, taking out a small plastic plate, cup, and the bag of bread. He poured the orange juice into the cup about halfway and then took a lid out of the cabinet to make a sippy-cup for the toddler. Neither he nor Dreyson spoke as he prepared Dreyson's sandwich, and once he finished and cut the sandwich into two triangles, he walked over and set the plate and cup in front of Dreyson. The boy picked up one half delicately in his little hands and took a bite so big that Bennett was surprised he didn't choke. Pulling out the chair beside Dreyson's, Bennett took a seat and watched the boy eat for a moment. The toddler was avoiding his prying gaze, so Bennett decided to speak to get his attention.

"How are you doing?" he asked quietly. Dreyson glanced up curiously, so Bennett clarified, "Are you okay?"

Nodding, Dreyson went back to his sandwich.

Unsure of how the boy planned to deal with his traumatic past, Bennett asked hesitantly, "Do you...do you want to talk about anything that happened?"

Without looking up, Dreyson shook his head, a dark lock of hair falling over his face.

Sighing, Bennett nodded impatiently. He wanted Dreyson to say something—anything—to prove that he really was okay. Bennett had seen The Doc's tapes of Hara; if Dreyson endured half of what his mother did, then he was not okay. He didn't have a desire to toy with the child's emotions, but as a doctor, Bennett felt it was his duty to try and help Dreyson. "Do you miss your sisters and brother?"

At first, it appeared as if Dreyson was ignoring the question, but after a moment he nodded again. He continued to eat his sandwich without looking up. It was difficult to see if he was experiencing any emotion.

"And your daddy?" Bennett said softly.

Finally, Dreyson looked up. He stared into Bennett's eyes with such intensity that he appeared to be saying a thousand words without saying anything at all. The harsh stare that came from such a small child made Bennett shudder as Dreyson nodded once again.

"Your mommy misses him too," Bennett told him, unsure how a three year old could make him so uncomfortable. Peering down at him, he was uncertain whether Dreyson understood the meaning of death. "You do understand that he's gone, don't you? You won't see him again."

Dreyson cocked his head to the side, in the same familiar way that The Doc always did.

Bennett wasn't surprised by Dreyson's confusion. He was just hesitating because he didn't feel like the right person to explain it to the boy, but somebody had to, and his mother was certainly not in the proper state to be the one to do so. "Your dad is dead, son," Bennett explained softly.

A bewildered expression crossed Dreyson's face. Slowly, while staring at Bennett as if he was crazy, the boy shook his head.

Bennett sighed again, knowing the boy was too young to fully understand and accept the loss of his family. Rubbing his eyes, it suddenly crossed his mind how exhausted he was from the past few hectic days. "Your mommy's very sad, do you know?" he asked, hoping Dreyson would at least understand that.

"She's sick," Dreyson replied.

Startled by his sudden voice, Bennett blinked several times. Dreyson's voice was small and high-pitched, as most toddlers' voices were, but his voice also sounded older and more mature than any three-year-old that Bennett had ever encountered before. He sounded very intelligent, but Bennett supposed that was how most young Colician children were. They were much more advanced biologically and intellectually than humans, and the children developed and learned much quicker than human children. It must have had something to do with the short incubation period of the fetus. From Hara's quick explanation and his observations of The Doc's tapes, Bennett gathered that a Colician pregnancy was shortened to three months rather than nine, and within a few months after birth the babies were talking and walking and learning. They developed quicker because sometimes two Colician soul mates would meet at a very young age, like Hara and Bo. As soon as two soul mates made contact, the girl fell pregnant, so Colicians had to develop quickly in case their time came early.

"She misses your daddy," Bennett said when he finally found his own voice.

"She'll be with him again soon," Dreyson said between bites. He didn't seem the least bit fazed by that.

Bennett's heart skipped a beat. "Is your mommy going to die soon?" he asked, unsure of whether or not he really wanted the answer.

Once again, that perplexed look crossed Dreyson's face. His stunning green eyes were utterly confused. "My mommy can't die."

Peering down at him, Bennett himself was very confused. He hadn't really believed before that Hara was capable of changing past and future events, but what Dreyson was beginning to say would fall right into place with what Hara was trying to do. "Is your mommy going to stop the bad things that happened from ever happening?" he questioned, knowing it would be better if that war never played its part in history.

Dreyson stared at him dubiously. "No," he said slowly. "She can't."

"Then how are your mommy and daddy going to be together again?" Your daddy's dead. He can't be with your mommy anymore."

"My daddy's not dead!" Dreyson insisted, starting to become angry. "He's alive! Stop saying he's dead!"

Sighing, Bennett chose his next words carefully as to not upset the boy any further. "When are they going to be back together again?"

"Tonight," Dreyson declared, taking a long drink of his juice.

"Tonight?" Bennett repeated skeptically.

"Daddy's going to help Mommy save everyone," Dreyson explained. "Then we can go back home."

Thinking over what the boy was saying, Bennett couldn't understand how that would work. "If your mommy isn't going to change what happened, then how is she going to get back with your daddy?"

"He's going to come and help her," Dreyson repeated impatiently.

"How is he going to help her?" Bennett demanded, becoming just as impatient.

"You'll see," Dreyson promised, popping the last bit of sandwich in his mouth.

Rubbing his forehead, Bennett decided against asking any more questions on the subject. Instead, he asked, "How do you think your daddy will feel when he sees how sad your mommy is?"

"He already knows that she's sad," Dreyson claimed, pushing his plate away from him. "But Mommy's really sick, and Daddy's going to make sure she gets better."

"How is he going to help her get better?" Bennett asked curiously.

"Whenever Mommy gets sick, Daddy always takes her to Dr. Perry," Dreyson explained, drinking the last few drops of his juice.

"Dr. Perry?" Bennett repeated in surprise.

"Uh-huh," Dreyson said, nodding in assurance. "Dr. Perry will help her get better."

"Your dad's going to take her to Dr. Perry?" Was Dreyson talking about Agent Perry? If so, many more things were beginning to click into place.

"Yes, but Dr. Perry's a good doctor," Dreyson promised. "He helps Mommy. He's not a bad doctor like The Doc. He's not mean. He's good. He's nice."

Bennett nodded. He was finally starting to comprehend why Perry was so important to the Colicians and their future.

"How come you don't have a big house?" Dreyson asked him suddenly, his eyes quite curious.

His brow furrowing, Bennett peered down at him. "Why would I?"

"You're a doctor too, right?" Dreyson questioned. "A good doctor?"

"I'd like to think so, yes," Bennett answered slowly, not sure what the boy was expecting for the second question.

"Dr. Perry is a good doctor, and he had a big house," Dreyson explained, appearing confused. "You should have a big house too if you help people like me and my Mommy."

"I don't need a big house," Bennett told him, understanding what Dreyson was inquiring. "I live by myself."

"Don't you have kids?" Dreyson asked in confusion, looking over to the variety of pictures hanging on the refrigerator door.

"Yes, but they moved out a while ago," Bennett explained. "They're all grown up now."

"They don't live with you?"

Bennett wondered if Colician families lived in the same house together forever. If his kids still lived with him, he probably would have gone insane a long time ago. "Not anymore."

"But don't you get lonely?" Dreyson asked, his eyes full of sadness for Bennett.

Forcing a smile to his face, Bennett tried not to think about just how lonely he was. After his wife died, and he was left alone, his old house didn't really feel like home anymore. He moved into a smaller apartment, even though he very well could have afforded better. In the small place where he wasn't surrounded by open space, he felt less alone than he did in his big house. However, when he recalled the memories of his wife or thought about how much he missed her, he would go into a depression lasting from a few days to a few months. He tried his best not to think about the thing he had loved the most in his life, the one thing that always kept him going, but he couldn't just forget the greatest thing that had ever happened to him. When he thought long and hard about all he had lost, he did feel lonely. He felt so lonely that sometimes he felt as if the world would fall out from beneath his feet and everything would just disappear forever. Nothing would ever be the same without Amanda. The world would never be the same. His heart would never be whole ever again.

Shrugging, Bennett looked away from the boy's prying eyes. "Sometimes," he admitted quietly, folding his hands on the table and looking down at them. He didn't want to discuss it any further.

To his surprise, Dreyson didn't push the subject. There was a long silence between them, and Bennett sensed that Dreyson was pondering over the various possibilities for why Bennett was alone. After a little while, Bennett saw Dreyson reach out a hand out of the corner of his eye and place it on Bennett's in a comforting manner. "I was alone for a long time, too," Dreyson said softly. The boy seemed to understand Bennett's pain better than any human ever did. It was probably because of how difficult death was for Colicians, and also because they had all been stripped of everything during the course of the war.

Dreyson's soft green eyes were full of sympathy, something Bennett found surprising coming from a toddler. Young children didn't understand the meaning of death, and most certainly didn't understand how it affected others. This boy knew how to comfort people who had lost someone they loved. Giving him a small smile, Dreyson explained, "When I was in the lab with The Doc, and my brother and sisters and daddy were all dead, I was lonely and sad too. I wanted to be with Mommy, but The Doc is bad and wouldn't let me see her ever. But everything got better. I'm with my mommy now, and I'll see my daddy soon, too. Daddy will help Mommy save everyone, and then I'll be with Colin and Grace and Katie and Lizzie, too. Things are bad sometimes, and sometimes we're lonely for a while, but everything always gets better. Things will get better for you, too."

Bennett smiled appreciatively down at him, but he felt something tearing at his heart. "I'd like to say you're right, son, but I don't think there's any way I can save my wife."

"She died?" Dreyson asked sadly, even though Bennett was certain that he already knew that.

"Yes, a long time ago," Bennett whispered, struggling not to think about the day he lost the greatest thing in his life. That day would haunt him forever...

"You'll see her again," Dreyson told him, almost sounding hopeful.

Chuckling, almost sarcastically, Bennett asked, "When?"

"Soon," Dreyson said.

Puzzled, Bennett pondered over that thought. Colicians seemed to have a deep connection to the afterlife and believed in life after death. Would Bennett reunite with Amanda in the afterlife? He prayed that he would, but what did Dreyson mean when he said they would see each other soon? Was Bennett going to die soon? He thought back to the conversation with Hara in the hospital, about how Bennett might go crazy if he knew his future. He decided to ask the boy, even though he didn't really want to know. "Am I going to die soon?"

Bennett saw Dreyson's expression harden. He had said too much. Avoiding the question, he said, "Everybody sees their families when they die."

"How do you know?" Bennett asked, truly fascinated.

"Because I've seen it," Dreyson declared, and he smiled. "It's beautiful."

Breathing a sigh of relief, Bennett beamed from ear to ear. His greatest fear was that he had lost Amanda for all eternity, but she was safe, and she was waiting for him in a place of beauty, as Dreyson described. "So there is a heaven."

"It's not heaven," Dreyson corrected. "It's love."

"Love?" Bennett repeated in confusion.

"Love binds people together," Dreyson explained, beginning to sound even older. "If you loved someone while you lived, you'll find them in the afterlife. Love will always bring people back together. When you die, you can be with Amanda for all eternity."

Bennett didn't even ask how Dreyson knew his late wife's name; he didn't care. All he could think about was how glad he was that Amanda was in a good place where she absolutely deserved to be, and how he couldn't wait to be there with her. Taking a deep breath in an attempt to calm his racing heart, Bennett closed his eyes. "You say you've see this place? You know it's a good place?"

"It's beautiful," Dreyson said again, with a quiet sort of fascination.

"And you know for sure that my wife is there?" Bennett asked, wanting to be completely certain that what Dreyson described was real.

"All good people go there," Dreyson assured. "Even humans go there, too. That's where my sister and brother are, and my grandpa and grandma, and Uncle Flint, and Aunt Katherine, and Daniel, and Mommy's friend Rhett, and Detective Aubrey."

"How do you know they're all there?" Bennett asked curiously, interested to know how Dreyson communicated with the world of the dead.

"I talked to them," Dreyson said, looking down at his empty plate. He suddenly appeared uncomfortable, as if it were a touchy topic.

"When did you talk to Daniel and Rhett and Detective Aubrey?" Bennett asked in surprise, not realizing that any of those three had died. It must have all happened earlier that day, and Agent Long must have just died in the past hour, because Bennett had spoken to him at the hospital before departing. But if they had all died in the past day, Bennett didn't understand how or when Dreyson could have communicated with them.

"When I was sleeping," Dreyson explained quietly, fidgeting with his hands in his lap. "They talked to me for a while."

"Do you always talk to people when you sleep?" Bennett asked him, leaning towards him. His doctoral instincts were beginning to kick in.

Dreyson nodded slowly, like he didn't want to discuss it.

"What did they talk to you about?" Bennett didn't want to make the boy uncomfortable, but he really wanted to know.

"Mommy," Dreyson murmured, raising his eyes to meet Bennett's "And The Doc."

"What about them?" Bennett was anxious for an answer, but it didn't appear as if the boy was going to give him one.

"They told me not to tell," Dreyson said quietly, looking back down.

Bennett sighed, but he didn't try to pressure the boy. Instead, after a moment's pause, he asked, "Have you talked to my wife at all?"

Dreyson seemed glad that Bennett changed the subject. "Yes, she's really pretty and nice."

Bennett smiled at his memories of Amanda. "Yes, she was very pretty and nice."

"She still is," Dreyson told him, smiling back.

After more than twenty years, Bennett had trouble thinking about his wife in the present tense. He couldn't feel her like Colicians could feel their loved ones, and it didn't feel to him like she existed anywhere now. When Amanda died, Bennett thought that she was going to be wiped out of existence. He thought she would be forgotten like every other lost soul in history, and that was how he had always viewed someone's passing. He believed that people lived for a certain amount of time and then died, and their existence was lost in time forever. But that wasn't true. Nobody was lost in time. Everyone went to a good place to spend eternity with the people they loved, and his wife was there waiting for him. She wasn't lost. "What did you two talk about?"

"She misses you and the kids," Dreyson said, and quickly added, "But she's waiting for you, and she says she has eternity, so she'll wait for you for as long as it takes." Dreyson waited for a response, but when Bennett didn't say anything, he whispered, "She told me to tell you that she loves you."

That last bit made Bennett crack. Swallowing hard to keep the tears and emotions back, he choked out, "Well, the next time you see her, tell her I love her, too."

"Why don't you tell her?" Dreyson suggested, and for a moment Bennett believed the kid was toying with him.

"How am I supposed to tell her that?" Bennett demanded when he realized that Dreyson was serious. "I can't communicate with the dead like you can!"

"Yes, you can," Dreyson replied insistently, nodding his head quickly several times. "Anyone can, so long as they know how."

"How?" Bennett was leaning forward intently, resisting the temptation to shake the boy to get his answer. "How do I do this?"

"You have to believe that you can do it," Dreyson explained with a dramatic tone. "Do it when you sleep. It's easier to do when your mind is open. You just have to believe that you can do it, and your wife will find you." The toddler appeared excited that Bennett would get to communicate with his long lost love. Dreyson was one of the few who could commiserate with Bennett's loss.

If it hadn't been for the various duties he had to fulfill, Bennett would have been nearly overdosing on sleeping pills just to have a conversation with Amanda. There were too many things he needed to complete and too many people he needed to look out for, so the nap would have to wait. He would just have to wait for Hara to get back on her feet and save her people and go home. He hadn't a clue how she was going to do that or how long it was going to take, but the few Colicians in the city kept implying that something big was going to happen tonight, so his opportunity might not be too far away.

"My mommy did bad things after she got out of the lab, didn't she?" Dreyson asked suddenly, and when Bennett gazed down at him in surprise, the boy was staring down at the table with a melancholy expression.

Bennett put a comforting hand on the toddler's shoulder, returning the kind gesture from before. "Yes, she did, but she only did them because she loved you and was trying as hard as she could to get you back." When Dreyson's face didn't lighten, Bennett struggled to find a way to explain. "Sometimes, people do bad things to serve a higher purpose." He wasn't certain if the boy understood what that meant, but he was certain of the irony in his own words. Not only had Hara been doing bad things for a good cause, but The Doc, too, insisted that he was hurting people for the benefit of the human race. Maybe The Doc was, in his own eyes, but Bennett wasn't the only person who had trouble believing that.

"I don't like seeing my mommy sick," Dreyson muttered, heaving a huge sigh for such a small boy.

There was a pang in Bennett's heart for that poor child. How awful it must have been for Dreyson to watch his own mother destroyed from the inside out. "Neither do I, bud, but you say she'll get better, right?"

"Not for a really long time," Dreyson whispered softly, and the crack of emotion in his voice was just barely audible.

Biting his lip, Bennett decided to use Dreyson's own line to try and cheer him up some. "Everything will get better," he promised.

A look of surprise crossed Dreyson's face as his own words filled his head, and he looked up at Bennett curiously. When Bennett smiled down at him reassuringly, Dreyson forced a smile in return. Then, reminding Bennett that he was still only three years old, Dreyson let out a huge yawn. His expression made him look so little that Bennett couldn't help but laugh. It was difficult to comprehend that this boy was as young as he was.

"I think maybe your nap isn't quite over yet," Bennett chuckled, standing up and carefully picking up Dreyson. He was worried that he might damage the boy's fragile body. Bennett tried to convince Hara to allow him to examine her child, but Hara refused, insisting her son would be fine until a Colician doctor had a chance to take a look at him. He tried to take no offense and let Hara have her way. If she didn't trust a human doctor to make a proper examination of her child, then he wasn't going to argue with her. A mother could be one of the most dangerous people that Bennett would ever encounter.

Walking back to the spare bedroom where Dreyson would continue resting, Bennett glanced at Hara as he passed by the doorway to the den. She was sleeping soundly and peacefully on the couch where she had been the whole time. Bennett knew, however, that her dreams were not peaceful or sound in any way. Even when she slept, the poor girl couldn't escape the horrific nightmare in which she was trapped.

※ ※ ※

It couldn't have been more than twenty minutes before Hara awoke again. For the first time in nearly twelve months, she had slept without any dreams. Even better, there were no nightmares. The realization was so amazing that she nearly forgot to breathe. If only every time she slept could be like that. She felt a smile cross her lips at the sudden sense of peace. She felt great, completely rejuvenated. She could get used to that feeling. Hope began clinging to her soul; maybe things would turn out okay after all. Maybe it was a sign that she really had a chance to change things.

Her good feelings didn't last, however. She was forced to wonder, if she had been sleeping so peacefully, then why did she awaken so soon? Her eyes had remained closed since she regained consciousness, and she didn't open them just yet. She allowed her senses that were rapidly increasing to expand all around her. As she did so, she thought back to when she first awakened, and tried to remember if something occurred around her to cause her to subconsciously wake herself. She thought hard, and then she recalled the ever so quiet sound of a door slowly creaking open. Her first thought was that Dr. Bennett opened a door to a different room, but as her senses expanded she suddenly felt the presence of an unwelcomed guest in the apartment, and he was standing right above her.

Her eyes shot open. Hara blinked away the haze and stared up in shock at Lieutenant Odau looming over her. Hara was so stunned that she didn't react as the cop's hands wrapped around her throat and tightened to the point of extreme pain. She gazed up in horror into Odau's furious eyes, clueless as to how he had found her. He was angrier than she had ever seen him before, and as she felt the air being squeezed out of her, she didn't feel the strength required to fight him off.

"I can't let you live to kill my son," Odau hissed at her, tightening his grip even more. "You don't belong in this world, anyway!"

Finally finding the will to fight back, Hara grabbed his wrists and dug her nails into his flesh as hard as she possibly could. Opening her mouth to try and get just a small amount of oxygen into her lungs, she found that her airway was completely cut off and Odau had no intention of releasing her. Unable to make any sort of verbal communication, she sent her words to him mentally.

You're right, she told him, trying her best to keep calm as her oxygen supply began to dwindle. *I don't belong in this world. I promise you that I will leave this world and never come back as soon as I…*

"Murder my son!" Odau snarled, lifting Hara up off the couch and then slamming her back down again. "Get your sick, messed up mind out of mine!"

Forcing herself to ignore her pain as she had so many times before, she stared up into the gray eyes that had haunted her nightmares for so long. They would haunt her for as long as she lived. *As soon as I finish what I came here to do,* she clarified, but Odau understood what that was.

"I'm not going to let you kill my son!" Odau shouted, his fingers beginning to feel like hot knives against her neck.

Hara wondered where the hell Bennett could be. She could really use his help. *He's not the boy you think he is! He's not good!*

"You don't know my son!" Odau yelled angrily, his teeth bared ferociously at her.

Neither do you, Hara whispered, pleading with his eyes.

"He's a great boy!" Odau said firmly through gritted teeth. "He's going to grow up to be an even better man!"

He won't grow into a good man, Hara told him, wishing Odau would just accept that she could see what was coming.

"You don't know that for sure!" Odau cried. "How could you possibly know that for sure?"

I know because I've seen what he becomes, Hara said grimly. *He's not going to be good. He could never be good. It's not his destiny.*

"He could if you'd let him!" Odau glared even harder into her eyes. "I keep hearing from you people that my son's going to turn into a bad person, but maybe if you gave him a chance, you'd see that he has a greater potential! You don't get to decide who lives and who dies! My son deserves a chance, just like yours!"

Knowing there was nothing more she could do to convince Odau that she was doing the right thing, Hara gave his mind a push.

A startled expression crossing his face, the lieutenant released her throat and then stumbled backwards before falling over.

Hara sat upright and clutched her throbbing neck, coughing heavily to regain her breath. The fresh air burned her windpipe on the way down. Although her vision was beginning to blur, she was as alert as ever and was glaring over at Odau as he breathed hard on the floor not six feet from her. Rising to her feet as Odau started to stir, she continued to rub her throat. She took a step towards Odau so she could look into his eyes again. Just a moment before his eyes narrowed in anger and hatred once more, Hara caught the helpless look of desperation from his soul.

To her surprise, Hara herself couldn't help feeling a swell of pity for the man. She couldn't believe that she actually felt sorry for him, but she did. It actually struck a nerve in her heart that Odau was denying what she claimed about his son, because he was finally beginning to believe it himself. The thought of it was so horrible to him that he didn't want to believe it could be true.

Shaking her head gently, she gazed sympathetically into his desperate, enraged eyes. For a single moment she was reminded of herself; she had been in the same position as him several times before. "I can't take the risk of allowing him a chance," she said softly.

"We gave you a chance!" Odau blurted, but even he knew that wasn't true.

Hara couldn't help but laugh scornfully. The humans had never given them a chance, and they never would either. "You humans tried to wipe us out," she told him, shaking her head again out of disappointment rather than sympathy. "After we resettled in our share of the world, Colicians who were left behind were butchered or used as lab experiments rather than being allowed to peacefully relocate to our haven. When I was fifteen, my father and my mate's father attempted to sign a peace treaty with human leaders from around the world, and the American, British, and German presidents attempted to assassinate them at the signing. Colicians who stepped onto human soil to try to rescue our people were executed.

"Several years ago, an innocent man—who we now know as The Doc—lost his family and then tried to take the daughter of another innocent man." She raised her eyebrows to let him know that she was referring to herself and her father. "When my father refused to give up part of his family, he and the rest of our species were killed in what was the biggest genocide in all of history."

Crouching down beside him, she told him forcefully, "You have never given us a chance! And you never will. Anything that is different from you or anything you don't understand, you destroy. Humans are frightened, narrow-minded, selfish, cruel, and they don't care who they hurt as long as they get their way. You're all blind. That's all you will ever be."

"How do you know that this future of yours will come true?" Odau demanded, continuing to glare at her but remaining on the floor. "There's a chance I could keep him from becoming whatever it is he's destined to become."

"I know the future will come true because I've seen what your boy will become," Hara replied softly. "And so have you."

"You're insane!" Odau cried, pulling his gun out of his holster.

Taking several anxious steps back as the lieutenant leapt to his feet and pulled out his weapon, Hara put her hands in the air to show him that she didn't want a struggle. "That may be true, but you know that I'm telling the truth," she pointed out hesitantly. "Even you—of all people—are beginning to believe it."

"I'm not going to let you kill my son," Odau repeated, his entire body quivering and his arm twitching dangerously.

Backing up until she was in the doorway of the kitchen, Hara tried to reason with the angry cop—and father. "Believe me, Lieutenant, I know what you think of me, but I am a good person. I never wanted to kill children, and I don't want to kill your son because I'm sure he is a very good kid, but killing him is the only option I've got…"

"Stop talking!" Odau cried ferociously, raising his weapon and aiming it at her. Hara's attempts to reason had failed. Odau was once again the furious, defensive father that Hara had first met in Jackson's bedroom.

Milliseconds before the lieutenant fired, Hara took off in the direction of the bedroom her own son was in. Bennett was clearly not going to be of any help, so she was going to have to protect her son and fend off the angry cop on her own. She felt the heat of the bullet as it grazed her bicep, and then heard the shattering of glass as it blew through the kitchen window, but she didn't pause to see the mess it made. The rage radiating from Odau was enough to send wolves running away with their tails between their legs.

Dreyson's bedroom was the next room over, so it only took her a moment to reach it. As soon as she was inside, she slammed the door closed just as Odau followed her and fired another round. It penetrated the wooden frame of the door but didn't come all of the way through. Quickly rounding on her son's sleeping form on the bottom bunk, Hara scooped up her child in one fluid movement and rushed around the side towards the window. She would have to jump; there was no other way out of the apartment. Dreyson still had not moved since her entrance, but she didn't have time to worry about him, because Odau was kicking the door in.

With a cry, Hara closed her eyes and dove headfirst through the window, making certain to protect her child's fragile body in the process. She heard the glass break and felt the shards tearing at any exposed skin as she went through. The pain was barely noticeable as she tumbled out of the six-story window; she was too busy bracing herself for the deadly impact. Her eyes were squeezed shut and the cool April air was whistling through her ears as she fell, but she never struck the ground. For several seconds she kept her eyes closed and held Dreyson tightly, and it wasn't until she was spoken to that she finally realized that she wouldn't hit the ground.

"Hallie!" a cheerful, giggly, and amused voice chirped off to her right.

Her heart skipping a beat at the sound of the familiar voice, Hara opened her eyes again and looked to her right. She could never forget that voice. Gazing into the lively blue eyes of Clyde Stetzer, Hara gasped. His curly black hair was still sticking out wildly around his head, and as he had the first time they met, he was wearing a thick, raggedy, blue parka. The coat wasn't really appropriate for the temperature of Philadelphia, but Hara supposed that this was all just another dream of hers. She hadn't escaped the nightmares after all.

"I was hoping to speak to you under better conditions, but this should do just fine," Clyde said, and grinned his ever-present toothy grin. He hadn't changed since their previous meeting; Hara probably created him in her dream based on his original appearance. He most likely wasn't really communicating with her, but considering how many times Hara had spoken with the dead in the past day, maybe he was.

The two of them were sitting on the silver metal pole holding a large green sign above a highway. Cars rumbled down the road beneath them at high speeds, not seeming to notice the two people sitting high above them. There was a heavy wind whistling through Hara's ears, which made her think that she was still falling from the window. Surprised by the sudden change of scenery, Hara lost her balance and started to fall backwards.

"Whoa!" Clyde cried, snapping out a hand and catching her by the upper arm before she could fall.

Gripping the bar tightly in her left hand to balance herself better, she attempted to hold onto her son as well, but she suddenly realized that Dreyson was no longer in her arms. She panicked, fearing that she had dropped him by mistake and he had plummeted to a gruesome death below. Frantically peering down at the steady flow of traffic, her heart began pounding even faster in her chest. She had lost her son yet again. She really did fail as a parent.

Clyde could see her anxiety and immediately jumped in to reassure her. "He's fine," he promised, patting her shoulder. "He's sleeping, as are you."

Heaving a loud, exasperated groan, Hara threw her head back in distress. "I'm dreaming again?!" It was less of a question and more of a frustrated cry. She already knew she must be dreaming; she just needed clarification.

Peering at her curiously, Clyde asked, "Is that a problem?"

Hara turned to him, a hopeless expression present on her face. "Of course it's a problem!" she cried shrilly. "I can't ever escape them!"

"It's your subconscious, dear," Clyde stated matter-of-factly. "There's no escaping what's locked away in there."

Gazing helplessly at him, Hara wondered how her dream was going to end up torturing her like all her others did. She prayed that Clyde would just say what he needed to say and get out of her head quickly. Her sanity over the past few days had deteriorated to a point where it wouldn't take much to send her into a totally catatonic state, and she would be lost in her own damaged mind forever. "Are you dead too?" she whispered, inferring that the humans had gotten to Clyde's isolated ice cave.

"Oh, no," Clyde said, shaking his head and appearing slightly offended. "Nope, the humans haven't come far enough north to find me. They all think that everybody lived down south in the warmer regions. How wrong they are!"

"How are you here then?" Hara demanded, eyeing his nonchalant body posture and wondering how someone as deranged as him could be so careless at a time such as this.

"I needed to speak with you, dear," Clyde replied, watching her with a look that suggested that he thought that he was doing something wrong. "Do you not want me here?"

"No, that's not what I meant!" Hara clarified quickly. "It's great to see you." It surprised her just how much she meant that. "It's just…I didn't believe that anyone would be able to find me. After all, I'm so far from home."

Clyde continued to watch her inquisitively. "Bo found you."

Remembering their emotional dance to "Caribbean Blue" a little while earlier, Hara closed her eyes once more and held back everything that was threatening to burst forth from her. "That's different," she whispered. "He's…"

"Not dead," Clyde finished for her. Before Hara could try to protest against his impossible claim, he asked her, "You've been speaking to the dead a lot recently, haven't you?"

"Just with Daniel," Hara answered quietly, feeling another pang of regret at his memory. "And my family. And Bo."

Clyde didn't argue with Hara about Bo any further, but he did press the matter about communicating with the dead. "Didn't I tell you that would happen? You wouldn't believe me when I said that you eventually would be able to."

"It seemed absurd at the time," Hara told him, remembering how naïve she had been about everything when she and Clyde first met. "Only damaged people and people who had seen death are able to communicate with the afterlife."

"Everything I told you is beginning to unravel, isn't it?" Clyde asked, smiling at her like his prophecy had been a game. He had no idea just how terrified Hara had been once he told her his predictions. It was never a game to her. "You lost everything, you've been suffering when you never deserved it, and The Doc made a big mess of the world, didn't he?"

Hara sighed in defeat. "Yes, he did."

"But most importantly of all, you're fixing what's happened," Clyde chimed, gazing at her with a pleased smile. "You're almost there. You can almost go home."

"How do I fix everything?" Hara asked eagerly, realizing that if Clyde could have predicted the war and everything that went with it, he would also be able to predict how Hara would finish the war. "How do I put an end to this?"

"You want to know how to save our people?" Clyde asked her, his voice and expression abruptly becoming very serious. "I'll tell you how." Leaning closer to her so he was staring into her eyes and their faces were inches apart, he murmured quietly, "You need to listen to Bo."

Growing more frustrated, Hara cried, "I have listened to Bo! Do I have to kill Jackson Odau? How do I change what has happened?"

Giving her an amused look, Clyde snickered. "Who said anything about changing things?" Taking hold of her arm once more, he gave her a hard shove forwards and she slipped off the pole, plummeting to the ground below.

✳ ✳ ✳

The sudden, unexpected fall caused Hara to jerk awake and gasp as the shock of reality hit her. Sitting straight up and breathing hard and fast, she looked around at the familiar surroundings of Bennett's apartment and let out a scream of fury. "No!" she cried, punching the arm of Bennett's sofa. She thought she heard a crack and wasn't able to distinguish whether it was the couch or her hand, but she couldn't register anything in her mind other than her anger.

"No, no, NO!" How could Clyde have forced her out of her own dream like that? Not only was it extremely rude—invading her subconscious and then kicking her out of it—but it was also enraging since he held all the answers to how the future would unfold and he wasn't telling her what to do about it. If he wanted to talk to her about altering events, and he obviously did since that was all he really said to her, then why didn't he clearly tell her how to do it instead of talking in riddles? Falling back against the sofa, she covered her face with her hands and let out an angry wail that sounded like the cry of a wounded animal.

She heard Bennett rush in a moment later, breathless and concerned. She could sense him looking around uneasily before asking anxiously, "What is it? What's wrong?"

"Why, why, WHY?!" Hara yelled angrily, wanting to knock a building down or start something on fire. She struggled to contain her abilities that were begging to be set free.

In that instant, Bennett understood, and he came to her side to comfort her. Kneeling beside the couch, he rubbed her back gently. "It's okay. It was just another dream. Nothing here is going to hurt you now. You're safe. The Doc can't hurt you."

Sucking in several deep breaths to calm herself, Hara rocked back and forth as she clutched her knees to her chin. She didn't bother telling Bennett that—for once—her dream wasn't about The Doc. She didn't feel like explaining it. Sighing heavily, she held back her tears of frustration and looked over to Bennett's worried face peering down at her. There was no way that she would be able to get back in contact with Clyde in her weakened state, so she decided to just let it go, as much as it angered her. She could save her people in her own way if Clyde wasn't going to help her. "How's Dreyson doing?" she asked, trying hard to keep her voice level as she spoke.

Looking frustrated himself, Bennett sighed as well. He was probably disappointed that she wasn't going to share her dream with him. Hara didn't want to go through a therapy session with him. "He's fine," Bennett replied softly, his eyes expressing more concern for her than for Dreyson. "He was up for a while to get something to eat, but he's sound asleep again." He paused, his gaze still worried. "Are you hungry at all yet?"

Hara shook her head in response, her mind not really registering whether or not she was hungry. Staring off just past Bennett's left ear, she thought about what Clyde told her during their short meeting. He told her that she needed to listen to Bo. She had listened to Bo, for the short time in which they were together anyway. She listened to every beautiful word he said. What else did Clyde want her to do? Was there some hidden meaning in Bo's words?

She suddenly realized that it wasn't Bo whom she had misunderstood the first time; it was Clyde. Clyde didn't mean for her to only hear Bo's words, he wanted her to obey and believe in Bo's words. Bo claimed that he wasn't dead, but how could that be? Hara heard and felt him die, and if he was alive then she would have been able to feel his presence no matter where she was. Their bond was too powerful to be obscured. Was Hara's mind so damaged that she couldn't even feel her own soul mate's existence?

Bo had also told her that she needed to come home. Could she somehow save everybody by going back? Was the answer to salvation in her world instead of the humans'? No, that was impossible. The only way to save her people was by killing Jackson Odau. The boy's death was the only way to safely guarantee the revival of her kind, but Bo needed her to go home and Clyde specifically instructed her to go back. Was returning to her destroyed world the only way to truly fix things?

"Hey."

Blinking in surprise as Bennett's curious face lit up her line of sight, her internal debate was left behind in the corners of her mind. "What?" she asked, irritated by the sudden distraction.

"Are you alright?" Bennett asked carefully, continuing to peer at her pryingly. "Where did you just go?"

"Nowhere," Hara replied, suddenly feeling cornered. Something was wrong. It wasn't something with Clyde, or with Bo, or Bennett, or Dreyson, or even with her. It was something around her, something around all of them. Something was encroaching on their space, and Hara didn't like it at all. "I was just..." Her head snapped up towards Bennett's front door, and she stared at it so hard that she nearly blew it open with her mind.

Seeing how agitated she was, Bennett looked to the door and then back to her. "Honey, what's the matter? What's bothering you?"

There was somebody just outside the door, somebody who was trying to invade their space. Hara would not have that. She nearly knocked Bennett over as she leaped off the couch and ran at the door. Something made her hesitate right in front of it, and she stared at the door handle that was slowly and silently turning as someone tried to break in from the other side. It might have been the fact that she was having difficulty hearing what the interloper was thinking that caused her to pause. Ever since her last encounter with The Doc, she was having trouble connecting her mind to the minds of others. She was still able to detect emotions, but it would be more helpful for her to be able to fully comprehend the thoughts of others. The emotions of the intruder were not threatening; in fact, they seemed almost friendly, but anyone trying to sneak in on her and her child was no friend to her. After her dream of Lieutenant Odau attacking her, she wasn't going to let anybody catch her off guard. The dream had felt remarkably real to her, so maybe it was another premonition.

Whatever the situation, Hara was feeling threatened and cornered, and that was not a good combination.

"What is it?" Bennett asked cautiously, understanding her odd behavior. "Who's here?"

Shushing him with a wave of her hand, Hara waited until the intruder picked the lock on the other side of the door and was slowly pushing it open before she sent out a burst of energy to throw it open all the way. She caught the look of surprise on the intruder's face half a second before she made him slam back against the wall of the hallway. Hara held her hand toward him like she was holding his throat tightly, causing the man's breath to come out choked and strangled. His feet were three inches off the ground, and he kicked his legs and grabbed at his throat, the look of desperation on his face almost amusing. It took longer than it should have for Hara to recognize the intruder. The man had Perry's face, but it wasn't Perry.

"Hallie!" Jack choked out, his eyes pleading with hers. "I'm sorry..."

Her eyes widening in horror, Hara dropped her hand and Jack collapsed to the ground. "Oh my God, Jack! I'm so sorry! I didn't realize..."

Coughing and sputtering, Jack shook his head and managed to smile up at her. "Don't worry about it. It was my mistake."

"Are you okay?" Hara demanded, grabbing his arm and pulling him to his feet. "Did I hurt you?"

"Don't worry about me," Jack reassured, even though his voice was hoarse and he was still trying to catch his breath. "I'm fine. Sorry I snuck up on you like that..."

Jack didn't even finish his sentence before Hara nearly knocked him off his feet once again as she grabbed him in a tight embrace. She was so relieved to see that he was alright and out of police custody. She hadn't been thinking about him much lately, but since he was back with her she realized just how much she really missed him, and how much she really needed him. As she hugged him as tightly as she could, she first sensed his surprise and then his hesitation before he finally hugged her back.

"I'm so sorry I didn't try to break you out of there!" Hara whispered, regretting how he hadn't even crossed her mind while she was in the police station with The Doc. "I know I said I'd come back for you..."

"You had more important things to concern yourself with," Jack tried to convince her, but Hara could sense his feeling of betrayal deep down inside.

"No," Hara said firmly, pulling away from him and looking fiercely into his exhausted eyes. "The people I love are the most important things right now. That's what I'm fighting for."

"It's okay," Jack told her sadly, his eyes full of sympathy.

"Daniel's dead," Hara said, her voice cracking with her grief.

"I know," Jack whispered with just as much grief.

"How did you get out of that station without being killed by The Doc?" Hara asked, amazed that The Doc didn't at least try to finish him off.

"He tried to kill me," Jack explained. "But I was saved by Davey."

"Davey?" Hara repeated in disbelief.

"He survived the war, and he somehow managed to find us here through my dad," Jack said, his expression becoming angry. "My dad knew that the war was going to happen because of our interference with history, yet he didn't tell any of us."

"Of course," Hara breathed in realization. "Our interference is a part of history. He knows the course that history is supposed to take! He was always supposed to know!" As much as she wanted to, she couldn't concern herself with Jack's father. There were bigger things that she had to worry about. "Where is Davey now?"

"Getting Perry," Jack replied flatly, still angry at his father. He most likely would be angry at his dad for a very long time after discovering that he hadn't warned the Colicians about the war that would annihilate them all. Hara most definitely would be angry. "The Doc nabbed him. I picked up his thoughts not too long ago." He stared hard at her. "You somehow activated his ability, because now The Doc is running experiments on him in his tractor-trailer as they're driving very quickly towards New York."

"I know," Hara whispered, recalling her all too real dream about Perry and The Doc. "This wasn't supposed to happen..."

"Maybe it was," Jack said quietly, gazing at the floor.

Her mind too busy with other matters to think about how strange and unpredictable the flow of history could be, Hara shrugged off Jack's comment and asked him, "How did you know where to find me? Could you hear my mind while I slept?"

Jack shook his head. "The rest of our people that are here are in hiding, so I thought that if there was one person in this hostile world that you could trust—and it wasn't Perry—who would it be?" He looked over her shoulder and nodded. "A Bennett."

Turning, Hara saw Dr. Bennett watching them patiently from a few feet behind, waiting to be introduced to the intruder in his apartment. Taking it upon herself, Hara stepped to the side to allow Jack to enter before closing the door behind him. Gesturing to Dr. Bennett, she told Jack, "This is Dr. Wesley Bennett, Danny Bennett's grandfather."

Have you told him anything? Jack sent the mental question as Dr. Bennett took a few steps forward.

Yes, but it's irrelevant to his personal future, Hara answered right before she said, "Dr. Bennett, this is my best friend Jack. He's helped me through a lot of stuff, including The Doc's experiments." Shooting a glance at Jack, she explained to him, *He saw the tapes The Doc made of me and his experiments.* Dr. Bennett asked some questions about his future earlier, but Hara didn't answer him for a reason. Sometimes, Hara really wanted to just spill everything about her people and her future to him as he asked, but she couldn't put such a horrible truth on his shoulders. She knew just as well as Jack that Bennett wouldn't live to see 2018. He would never witness the rise and fall of the Colician Empire.

Extending a hand, Dr. Bennett smiled warmly at Jack.

Jack hesitated, staring at his hand for several long moments before shaking it. He seldom came into physical contact with humans other than Noah before the war, and when he did it was never in a good way. Considering Dr. Bennett was a doctor and a human, Hara was surprised that Jack let him stand so close, let alone touch him. *He knows about what happened between the two of us,* Jack told Hara with great disapproval.

Yes, I told him, Hara explained, praying that Jack wouldn't be too angry with her for sharing their personal past with a human she barely knew. She was glad that Jack didn't have anything else to say about it, because she didn't really want to think about the time when she once loved him and then broke his heart to be with someone else. She could kill children, but she didn't have a heart black enough to cause Jack any more pain.

"It's nice to meet you, Jack," Dr. Bennett said, still smiling at him.

Jack nodded and pressed his back up against the door to remain as far from Bennett as possible. "Sorry for intruding on your home like this," he mumbled, lowering his eyes to the floor uncomfortably.

Bennett started to respond by insisting that it wasn't a problem, but they were all distracted as they heard a quick shuffling from the next room. A moment later, Dreyson popped in the doorway from the kitchen in his baggy borrowed clothes. He was dragging a long blue and red Spiderman blanket behind him. His face was exhausted and his eyes were red and sleep-deprived, but when he saw Jack he made a dopey smile and gave a little wave.

"Hey, bud," Jack said, beaming at him like he was his own son.

Dreyson trotted over to Hara before reaching up his arms to be picked up. When she scooped him up into her arms, he gave Jack's shoulder a friendly little pat and rested his tiny head on her shoulder. Hara could tell that her child was still worn out and weak just by holding his fragile body, and by feeling how thin he was she knew that he wouldn't be his springy self again for a very long time. Sighing sadly, she rested her head on the top of her boy's head. "You knew that Jack was coming, didn't you?" she asked him. He knew when to wake up so he could see Jack. "You just wanted to say hi." Reaching out, she took Jack's hand in hers and when he looked up in surprise, she smiled at him. "I'm glad you're here," she told him. "Thank you for finding me."

Jack shrugged and squeezed her hand as he smiled in return, but he looked away from her. It pained him to feel such love for her that he couldn't express. "You know I'd do anything for you," he murmured, and Hara knew it was true. He would even go to the ends of the human world and back for her. "I think I've proven that much."

Hara heard tension in Jack's voice, but Bennett cleared his throat awkwardly at their small moment, reminding them that he was still there. "Do you need me to give you a minute?" he asked them uncertainly.

Hara quickly became uncomfortable, knowing that Bennett was thinking that she and Jack's past relationship together might be rekindling. "No, thank you," she replied, rubbing Dreyson's back as she realized that her son hadn't moved in her arms for several moments. He had drifted back to sleep on her shoulder. "Somebody is still completely wiped," she murmured, smiling at her baby boy's sleeping form in her arms. She missed being able to hold her children while they fell asleep. It was a nice, familiar feeling that made her feel warm inside. When the time came that she would be able to hold all of her children in her arms once again, her life would finally be complete, and the chaos and carnage of the war would finally be behind her.

"I'll put him back down," Bennett offered, still seeming to think that she and Jack needed a moment to themselves.

Hara didn't want a moment alone with Jack, because she could sense that Jack was extremely stressed and from past experiences she knew that while under stress he tended to act without thinking, but she allowed Bennett to take Dreyson from her. She figured it would be more awkward if Bennett was alone with Jack than if she was alone with him.

As soon as the sound of Bennett closing the door to Dreyson's room was heard, Jack turned on her. He had a very uncomfortable expression, as if he were trying to hold something back. To Hara's dismay, he wasn't able to hold it back. "Forgive me, but I just really have to do this," he apologized. Stepping forward, he put his hands on either side of her face and kissed her hard. He only kissed her for a couple of seconds before pulling away, but it was enough to really bother her.

Gazing at him blankly, she turned away from him and walked away into the kitchen. She was really regretting not taking her son to bed herself and leaving Bennett with Jack. At least Jack wouldn't have kissed him.

＊ ＊ ＊

If The Doc ran any more tests, Perry was sure he would die. The doc had only performed two tests, but they had been so painful it seemed like many more. He started by taking a sample of spinal fluid, picking up a very long, thick needle and sticking it into Perry's back to extract a thick white liquid. Perry struggled to keep quiet throughout the painful process, but in the end he couldn't contain his screams. After that was over, The Doc decided to test Perry's ability further by shooting him in several places on his body to see if he could heal an injury anywhere. He shot Perry once in the arm, the leg, the stomach, the chest, and the neck to see how his body reacted to trauma. Unfortunately for Perry, the bullet fired into his chest became lodged between two of his ribs instead of going all the way through, so The Doc was forced to dig the bullet out with a pair of large tongs to allow Perry to regenerate. All of that was performed while Perry was fully conscious and without anything to reduce the pain.

Another large needle was in the vein in Perry's right arm, draining out so much of his regenerative blood into a bag that he could barely focus on anything around him. His head was foggy and his vision was hazy, but he could see well enough to make out The Doc as he came forward with a needle bigger than the one for the spinal fluid.

"Please," Perry choked out, barely managing to make a sound. He was breathing hard and heavily, but there was so much blood being taken from him that his efforts weren't enough to sustain him. Perry could feel himself beginning to go under and wasn't about to stop himself, but he was afraid of what The Doc would do once he was unconscious and couldn't scream any longer. "Please, I've had enough…"

His vision was blackening at the edges and he embraced the depths of unconsciousness, but just before he went all the way under he felt The Doc take out the needle extracting his blood. The Doc then slapped his face several times until Perry's eyes fluttered open and focused on his irritated expression.

"Come on, boy, stay with me," The Doc said as Perry struggled to clear his weary mind and focus. "You need to feel this."

"Why?" Perry mumbled, his eyes fluttering again.

"You wanted to understand Hara," The Doc replied informatively. "Now you can." Grabbing Perry firmly by his hair and forcing his head back, The Doc leveled the giant syringe with Perry's left eye.

"Stop! Stop!" Perry screamed in terror, barely stopping The Doc in time.

Sighing, The Doc lowered the needle slightly so he was able to look Perry in the eye. "Perry, I know you're scared," he said softly, and to Perry's surprise he didn't seem amused. "But after a minute this will all be over."

Before The Doc could stick the needle through Perry's eye, the trailer suddenly slammed to the side and The Doc was knocked clean off his feet. Perry's chair tipped over and his head struck the metal floor. Clamping his teeth together, he squeezed his eyes shut as the truck was thrown from side to side and the shrill sound of tires squealing could be clearly heard. Then, the truck was flipping several times, and Perry was trying not to cry out in pain as he struck the floor, walls, and ceiling many more times. He was spinning so fast that he couldn't keep track of how many times he bounced hard. The equipment inside the trailer was breaking and everything made from glass was shattering, small shards biting his skin. His head was so jumbled and he thought that they would never stop flipping, but then suddenly the truck struck something hard and it slammed to a stop.

Perry's entire body collided with what he thought was the ceiling, and as he held back the pain coursing through him, he slowly opened his eyes to see the damage surrounding him. The single light had been destroyed, so he was now in complete darkness. He couldn't hear any movement from The Doc, and Perry prayed that he had died in the crash. It couldn't have been more than a few seconds, but it felt like a very long time passed before Perry summoned up the courage to attempt to move. He moved his shoulder and cried out as a massive wave of agony shot through his body, and then a loud roar erupted from all around him. Water was suddenly filling up the trailer, and in a matter of seconds the water level was over Perry's trapped body. He was still strapped onto the chair, and he ignored the horrible pain consuming him as he struggled desperately to pull free of the cuffs. A horrible pounding noise was sounding from all around him, and as the thick, slimy water filled his nose, mouth, and throat, he feared that there would be no way out for him.

His panicked thoughts were proven wrong as he felt someone touch him. Two arms wrapped around his shoulders from behind, and then his head began to spin rapidly before he felt himself miraculously break free from the chair. Things didn't go as he anticipated after that. He felt the chair pull away from him, or maybe it was him being pulled away from the chair. Then he suddenly felt his back slam into a hard wood floor. A loud splash echoed around him, and there was no longer any water pouring in on him. Coughing up mouthfuls of water as the air surrounding him caressed his skin, he blinked up at a white ceiling.

"Oh my God!" a familiar female voice cried close to him.

Gasping as the shock of the new surroundings overwhelmed him, Perry lifted his head slightly before being forced to drop it back to the floor. He coughed heavily again and groaned in pain. Every part of his body ached from the crash, combined with being suddenly transported to wherever Hara was only added to his confusion. He saw a glimpse of where he was when he raised his head. He was in a kitchen in what appeared to be an apartment. Hara and Jack were standing over him while a third person lay on the floor beside him. Perry suddenly remembered that Allan Brown was a teleporter, and he wondered if that was who rescued him from The Doc. The new, unfamiliar voice he heard proved otherwise.

"That was exhilarating!" someone with a British accent squealed in delight.

Perry's next thought was that it was Noah, but Noah was human and the new man sounded much younger and more energetic.

"What the hell happened?" Jack demanded in confusion.

"Things got pretty intense!" the British man replied breathlessly as he stood up and peered down at Perry. Perry managed to get a good look at him. He looked to be about Jack's age, with dirty-blonde hair, blue eyes, and a grinning face. The boy must have been a teleporter as well. He was soaking wet, too, so it was obvious that he had been the one to grab Perry and get him out of that trailer. He didn't seem the least bit concerned for Perry's health or sanity as he declared, "I figured I might as well take out The Doc while rescuing him. The truck ended up flipping into a river."

"You could have killed him!" Jack said angrily, kneeling beside Perry's shivering body and placing a hand on his shoulder to see if he was alright.

"No, he couldn't have," Perry heard Hara reply solemnly.

"You didn't kill The Doc," Perry told the British boy, finally managing to find his voice. He didn't hear any noise from The Doc after the crash and before the trailer was flooded, but his gut told him to still be wary. A man like The Doc wouldn't go down that easily. "He's still out there somewhere."

"Are you okay?" Jack asked, peering down at him with troubled eyes.

Flinching away from the boy's touch, Perry looked up at him accusingly. Everything was his fault. If he and the other Colicians had just stayed wherever they belonged, Perry wouldn't have become a freak as well. Perry didn't want to have an ability. He only discovered he had it a short time ago, and he already hated it. What did Jack care if he was alright? It was because of Hara that he was covered in his own blood and looked like he had been through hell, which indeed he had been. If Jack cared about Perry, then he would have stopped Hara from changing him. Perry had a little something that he needed to scream at Hara...

"What the hell is going on out there?" a strikingly familiar voice snapped from another room off to Perry's left. "I'm trying to put this kid to sleep..."

Turning his head slightly, Perry saw the legs and shoes of another man, the rest of his body blocked from view by a small kitchen table and four wooden chairs. Perry didn't need to see the man's face to know it was Dr. Bennett. The Doc had been telling the truth the whole time. Bennett really was a spy for the other side, which meant that Agent Long had really been a Colician. It was too much for Perry to accept all at one time.

"Sorry," the British boy said to Bennett, his face changing from being cheerful to apologetic. "Do you have a mop?" Perry assumed that Bennett didn't appear too pleased about his soaking wet kitchen. The British boy pulled at his wet shirt clinging to his body. "And maybe a towel?" He glanced down at Perry, who was attempting to sit up. "You'd better make that three."

As Perry pushed himself up onto his elbows and groaned again, Bennett walked around his table to see his unexpected visitor, his feet splashing in the water on the floor. "Dear God, Agent Perry, what happened to you?"

Perry's furious eyes locked onto Hara, who was standing behind Bennett. Guilt was written all over her face. Perry pulled away from Jack and stumbled to his feet. When he could stand well enough that his legs were no longer buckling, he lunged at Hara and caught her around the throat with both his hands. "This is your fault!" he snarled, shaking her hard as Bennett and Jack peeled him off of her. "You did this to me!"

"Easy!" Bennett said soothingly as he and Jack pried Perry's hands from Hara's neck and forced him back into one of the chairs at the table. Observing the blood and various holes in Perry's clothing, he started to pull up Perry's shirt. "Let me take a look."

Glaring at Hara as he struggled to catch his breath, Perry realized just how bad the girl really did feel. He noticed that she didn't fight him while he tried to choke her, something any other person would have done to protect themselves. Her eyes were terribly sad and apologetic, and she hadn't moved an inch since Perry's arrival, even when he attacked her. Shaking her head remorsefully, she whispered, "I'm so sorry." She already knew exactly what she had done.

"There are no wounds!" Bennett exclaimed in confusion, staring at Perry's blood-smeared chest. He pulled Perry's shirt back down and fumbled with the huge knife slash through the front of it. "You were stabbed!" he said as he realized what the slash was from. "How is that possible?"

"He's one of us now," Hara explained softly, gazing back at her new creation with a deep regret.

If Perry wasn't so angry, he would have forgiven her for what she did. She had only been trying to save his life. She didn't intentionally change him, but now that he was changed, she was really very sorry for it. She could see in his eyes what he had been through in that trailer. Even though she was regretting what she did, Perry was too furious with her to forgive her. She may have saved his life, but in the process she had completely destroyed it. She had turned him into something he had no desire to be. "You should have let me die in that street!" he growled.

Hara shook her head again, an unbounded emptiness in her eyes. "You know I couldn't do that."

"Why?" Perry demanded, attempting to stand to emphasize his rage. He was quickly pushed back down by Bennett. "Because I'm too damn precious to your future?"

"And to me," Hara said, her expression offended. "You won't understand me when I tell you this—because right now you're so different from the Perry I once knew—but in a strange way, I love you."

"I'm not one of you!" Perry snapped, breathing hard as he glowered across the room at her.

Nodding, Hara gazed evenly at him. "Yes, you are, Shawn Perry," she declared, taking a step through the doorway behind her. "You always will be." Turning away from him and everyone else, she slowly walked to a sofa in the next room and seated herself, putting her face in her hands. Perry could almost feel her remorse radiating from her. Despite what he may claim, biologically, Perry was now a Colician. Maybe he really could feel Hara's remorse. If he could, then Hara was certainly expelling quite a lot of it.

Bennett seemed to understand without any further discussion what had happened to Perry, but he was still confused about how it happened. "How is it possible for you to have an ability?" Bennett asked. "Were you exposed to something?"

"She did this to me," Perry hissed, scowling at Hara in the next room. He wanted to strangle her for it, but it wouldn't make him feel any better because she wouldn't stay dead. But then again, that always gave him the opportunity to choke her more than once...

"Sir, Davey can explain it to you," Jack cut in, pulling out another chair and sitting across from Perry. "He understands what happened, and he can explain it if you wouldn't mind just giving me a few minutes with my...with Perry."

Looking from Perry to Jack—two completely different men with the same face—Bennett sighed. He knew that Jack would be the only one who could calm Perry down. Giving a stiff nod, Bennett walked towards a door to the right and gestured for Davey to follow him. "I'll bring you a towel," he called back to Perry.

"Hey, Mr. Perry?" Davey said, cautiously approaching Perry from the side. "I'm really sorry abut flipping the truck over..."

"Davey!" Jack insisted impatiently, pointing after Bennett. Davey regretfully left, leaving Jack and Perry alone in an uncomfortable silence.

Perry didn't think that Jack would have any luck comforting him, but he decided to humor the boy. Maybe Jack actually had something to say that could ease Perry's mind.

"Are you alright?" Jack asked softly.

Glancing back at him, Perry muttered, "I was just stabbed, shot half a dozen times, and tortured for an hour. On top of that, your buddy flipped over the vehicle I was in and dumped it in a river where I very nearly drowned. The only thing about that is, now I can't die because I'm a fucking Colician! So thank you for caring, Jack, but no, I will never be okay again!"

Forcing a smile to his face, Jack replied, "I doubt this is comforting, but that was the only experiment you will ever be put through. No one will ever hurt you like that again."

Neither of them spoke as Bennett reentered the room and handed Perry a towel before quickly exiting again. Shivering as he realized how cold he was, Perry wrapped the towel around his shoulders and hugged it tightly to him. It wasn't warm, but it did help to comfort him. Something that had been bothering Perry for a while was stirring in his mind once again. Jack was gazing at him with a hint of passion in his eyes, a sort of admiration that Perry had only seen one other person give him, and that was his daughter. Jack was giving Perry the same look of adoration that Jillian had given him several times before. It was the look a child gave to a parent, the look of love and loyalty. Was it possible that Perry was Jack's father? No, Jack was twenty-two, so Perry would have been thirteen when he was born. Were they really brothers, and Jack was just admiring his older brother?

"What is my relationship to you?" Perry blurted.

The question seemed to catch Jack off guard. "What?" he stuttered, taken aback.

"You told me that we're brothers, but I know that's not it." Perry stared hard at him, trying to will the answer out of him. "I can see in your face that I'm important to you, but not in the way you originally claimed. What am I to you?"

Jack stared back at Perry. He desperately wanted to tell him the truth, but something bigger than the two of them was holding him back. Perry understood in that moment why Jack refused to share his information. It wasn't because he didn't want to; it was because he had made a promise not to share, a promise to someone more important to Jack than Perry could ever be. Curse that girl!

"More than you will ever know," Jack whispered painfully, looking down at the wooden floor that was still covered in water. "Even when we knew each other, you never knew just how much you meant to me, and now you never will."

"Please just tell me what you've been dying to tell me since the moment we met," Perry pleaded. "How do we—or did we—know each other?"

"You know that I promised Hara that I wouldn't tell you that." Jack was reading Perry's mind.

"What, you can't trust me?"

Giving him a sideways glance, Jack repeated Hara's words. "You're so different than the Perry I once knew."

"I'm still the same man, aren't I?"

"I suppose, but…"

"But what?"

"I…I can't tell you. I'm sorry. If I were you, I wouldn't want to understand our relationship."

"Why?"

"It's too weird."

Sighing in frustration, Perry wondered if Jack was just expecting him to guess so he wouldn't be forced to say it aloud. Deciding to forget about it for a while, Perry shivered again and hugged the towel around him tighter.

Peering at him hopefully, Jack asked, "Are you going to be okay for now?"

Staring into Jack's mahogany eyes, into his own mahogany eyes, Perry asked hopelessly, "Am I going to be like this forever?"

Nodding, Jack answered, "Yes, I'm afraid so."

Perry sighed again, more from exhaustion than anything, and shook his head. Jack knew he didn't want the ability. The universe hated him. His parents both died when he was young, he never got married, he had a child he could never see, and now he had this horrible thing forced on him! He wished that he had never come to Philadelphia. What more did the universe have in store for him?

"It will grow on you," Jack promised, giving another small smile. "Once you're only around people like us and you don't have to hide it anymore, you'll learn to appreciate the gift you've been given. You'll come to use it for good things. Everything will get better."

"I hope you're right," Perry grumbled. "Because after what I've been through today and after everything that I've witnessed, I'm not sure how much more of this I'm physically and mentally able to take. I just want this to all be over."

Snickering, Jack replied, "This will never be over."

✳ ✳ ✳

Hara had been feeling a lot of regret lately, and a whole new load of it had been dumped on her when Davey appeared with an angry Perry. She didn't have time to reunite with Davey before Perry was blaming her for everything. She knew it was her fault; she was the one to trigger the ability, and she could never reverse what she'd done. Perry was stuck with his ability ten years earlier than he was supposed to be, but after Hara sat down and had a chance to think everything over, she figured that it was all for the best. He was one of the most important leaders in the rise of the Colician Empire, and if he had ten years to prepare for what was coming, then he could be several steps ahead of the humans. Perry might think the ability was horrible, but he would thank her for it later. Unfortunately, she wouldn't be around for him to thank. Hara knew that they wouldn't meet again for a very long time.

Perry and Jack had been talking for a few minutes in the kitchen when Hara sensed movement out in the hallway again. Her mind was still fuzzy and she wasn't able to get into the minds of the three people out there, but she already knew who they were. She had been expecting them to show up. Aware that things may not go as well as she would like, she sighed and rose to her feet to let them in. When she pulled the door open, she stared up at Lieutenant Odau's puzzled expression, his hand raised in a fist as if he was about to knock. He stared back at her; for once his face was not completely enraged. Maybe it was due to Hara's calmness, her placidity at a level never seen by him.

"Hi," she said quietly.

"Hi," Odau replied gruffly, although his attitude didn't seem quite as venomous as it normally was.

Instead of waiting for Odau to get into his sermon of how he won't ever let her kill his son, Hara got right to the point. "I don't want to fight anymore."

After a moment's pause, Odau's face, which had been hardened in her general direction, softened in a way that Hara hadn't imagined possible from him. "Me neither, kid."

An image from the previous night flashed into Hara's head, of how she had been holding a gun to his son's head while he aimed a gun at her head. For her to stand there before Odau and no longer feel blind hatred towards him was unreal. Now, the two of them were about to have a civilized conversation. "You should probably come in before somebody notices you," Hara said.

"I brought some friends with me," Odau informed, pointing to his left.

"I know," Hara replied as Detective Finchly and Agent Michaels both cautiously stepped into view. They hung back near the opposite wall, eyeing Hara nervously as she gazed back at them. Finchly appeared just fine, but Agent Michaels was another story. Her right arm was wrapped in bandages and was in a sling. Her face was pale and her eyes were dull, but they seemed eager. She came in hope of finding out what happened to Perry, because, and Hara could sense it, she thought that he was either dead or still with The Doc. Michaels had been working to stop Hara along with the others, but after what went down in the hospital, she knew that she had been fighting for the wrong side the whole time. She and her colleagues were about to change sides.

Hara was still pissed at Michaels for trying to steal Dreyson, but she decided to let her off the hook. Hara stepped aside so the three of them could see deeper into the apartment, and told Michaels, "There's somebody here I think you want to see."

Squinting to see who Hara was referring to, Michaels' eyes suddenly went wide. "Shawn!" she cried in relief, rushing into the apartment and running to Perry.

"Renee?" Hara heard Perry say in surprise. She could hear the two of them having an emotional reunion, but she wasn't focusing on them. The lieutenant still hadn't budged from his place just outside the door, and Hara had a feeling that Finchly wasn't going to enter unless Odau entered first. Odau still appeared uncertain about Hara's sudden change of personality, and Hara wanted him to enter before someone saw him and came to investigate. That was the last thing she needed: anyone else getting involved.

Odau finally stepped inside and was quickly followed by Finchly. She shut the door and glanced over to Michaels and Perry to see what they were up to. Perry was still sitting in his chair across from Jack, and Michaels was examining the holes in his bloody shirt. Hara didn't pay attention to what they were saying to each other, because as Odau and Finchly entered Bennett's living room, Bennett appeared from the doorway to the kitchen.

The look of astonishment on his face matched Odau's when Hara first opened the door. Bennett stopped in his tracks and stared at Odau. He looked frightened, as if he had just been caught.

"So you've been with her this whole time?" he demanded in a growl, narrowing his eyes. "When I was trusting you to keep my son safe, you were setting out to destroy him?"

Observing the body language between the two men, Hara realized something. They were friends. She had turned two friends against each other.

His nervous eyes hardening, Bennett muttered back, "I've seen what's happened and what's going to happen. Believe me, if you knew the whole truth, you would view this whole situation differently, and you would most definitely view your son very differently."

"I trusted you!" Odau exclaimed in betrayal. "And you were playing me this whole time!"

"I was aiding the people who needed me most!" Bennett said defensively.

"Then why didn't *you* just kill my son?" Odau demanded. "What was stopping you? You had plenty of opportunities!"

"His life isn't mine to take," Bennett answered, and he turned his eyes to Hara. "I think she's earned the right to be the one to do it."

Hara kept her eyes on the floor. She could feel Odau's eyes burning holes through her soul. Finally, he asked her, "Are you still going to kill my son?"

Grinding her teeth together as she pondered over that question, she glanced up into the lieutenant's prying gray eyes and shuddered at their familiarity. "I'm not so sure that I can," she told him quietly.

* * *

After she explained to Odau and the others the recurring theory of how the flow of time could not be altered even the slightest, Hara separated herself from the group. The lieutenant went to the kitchen with Finchly to check on Perry. After she gave him a look, Bennett left her as well. She took her place once again on the sofa. She didn't move a single muscle for nearly fifteen minutes. Perry and Odau were discussing new information that Perry learned from The Doc from his time in captivity, but Hara didn't listen in on that conversation. Her thoughts were preoccupied with the matter at hand. If she formed an alliance with Odau and the others, then she couldn't kill Jackson Odau, and if she didn't kill the boy, then what was she going to do? Did she really want to let her friends die in vain? She spent so long devising her plan; was she really going to change her mind now? She couldn't turn back. She had to change what happened to her world. She had to save Daniel and Rhett, her friends who died here for her. Once the boy was dead, none of the calamities—on earth or on her world—would have ever occurred. Wasn't one life worth all of that? People kept telling her that she couldn't change anything, but why couldn't she? The flow of time couldn't stop her! Nothing could stop her from saving her race! Clyde said that she had to listen to Bo, and Bo was saying that she had to go home to save everybody. Bo planned for her to save the others, but would it be as effective as killing the boy? She had to do what she knew was right; she had to do it for her people, for her friends, and for her family.

But was it the right thing to do?

Suddenly realizing that somebody was sitting beside her, she turned and made eye contact with Lieutenant Odau. For the first time since she met him, she saw that his eyes were soft. She was startled by his sudden appearance and by the fact that she didn't sense him coming, but when she inhaled sharply it wasn't because of that. Looking into his face in that moment caused her to doubt what she initially thought was the right thing to do. Maybe Bo was right; the only way to save everyone was to go home. Hara was seeing something in Odau that she never saw before: a soul. She could finally see a soul in that man, and it made her think about his boy's soul as well. Despite what she was led to believe, humans really did have souls. It was just hard to see them. And it all made sense; Colicians evolved from humans, and even though Hara had mostly seen humans at their worst, there were, in fact, good people in the world. Maybe it was time for her to start viewing them all differently. Maybe, if he tried hard enough, Odau could actually alter the course of his son's destiny himself. The thought crossed her mind for the moment that she gazed into Odau's eyes, but she knew that after tonight, he wouldn't be able to change it. He would be too horrified to look at his son the same way again.

"What were you thinking about?" Odau asked her quietly.

It was a strange question coming from him. She was dumbstruck that he had any interest in what was going on in her damaged mind.

"I was trying to figure out what I'm supposed to do next," she answered honestly, watching the lieutenant's icy gray eyes and wondering whether he was ever going to make the connection between himself and The Doc.

Odau stared intently at her, and his expression and tone of voice didn't change when he asked, "You still want to kill him, don't you?"

"Of course," Hara replied bluntly, looking away from him. "You don't understand what he's done to me, or what he's going to do to me. You won't either until you learn the truth."

Turning his head so he could see her face, Odau asked her, "When am I going to learn the truth?"

Raising her eyes back to him, she answered, "Before I leave tonight."

Blinking in surprise, Odau sputtered, "You're...you're leaving tonight? How? I thought you had other things you needed to complete here?"

Hara shook her head. "Everything that I'm going to do, I need to do before midnight. I've already decided that I'm going back to my world before this night is over."

"Why? What's the significance of tonight?"

Bo's face popped into Hara's head. "Somebody's calling me home. I have to go home tonight and help him."

"Help him do what?"

"Help him bring back everyone who was killed. He claims that I can save everyone if I go home."

"Then why are you still here?"

The abrupt comment left her stunned. Staring back at him, she replied, "Because I have to figure out what I'm going to do."

"What exactly are you here to do?" That was the first time Odau could ask that question and expect a straight answer.

Growing irritated, she told him what she had been trying to explain to everyone since the very beginning. "I came here in the first place to kill the three boys I've already killed and your son, and to bring back the people who came here before me. You and your people keep asking me why I'm here and why I'm doing what I'm doing, and I've explained it several times. Will you actually listen to me when I tell you this time? Your son is going to murder all the Colicians in the future when he's an adult, and I have to stop that from happening again. That is why I'm here to kill your son. Do you understand me now?"

Nodding slowly, Odau said, "Yes."

"And you have to understand that giving up on my mission after coming this far and losing so many people is very difficult for me." Lowering her eyes again, she sighed heavily. "I have to decide whether or not turning back now will be worth it in the end."

Odau allowed Hara to sit and ponder for a few minutes before he asked another question. "Is The Doc really related to me?"

Her heart skipped a beat as she looked back at him in amazement. He really was figuring it out on his own! What made him suddenly change the way he looked at things?

"Perry told me that The Doc said we're family," Odau explained.

She was disappointed that it was Perry who found out first and told the lieutenant. "You know, you shouldn't listen to everything Perry tells you. The Doc's a liar." She wanted the lieutenant to figure out the mystery so he would stop fighting her and accept the truth about everything. Until he did, he wouldn't fully understand what was really going on, which was why Hara tried to shield the truth yet again. The truth couldn't just be told; it had to be experienced.

She shuddered when Odau cocked his head in the same way that The Doc always did and replied, "That may be true, but from what I've witnessed, much of what he's said is the truth, is it not?" He peered at her as intently as ever. When she remained silent, he asked, "Is he related to me? He must be, right? He looks familiar to me, but I've never met him before."

"Yes, you have," she replied softly, gazing back at him evenly. He would figure it out quite soon, but she couldn't tell him before then.

"How is he related to me?" Odau asked again, a hint of frustration and irritation in his voice.

Sighing, Hara told him, "You wouldn't believe me if I told you."

Odau sighed too, but to Hara's surprise he looked down at the floor and didn't ask any more questions about The Doc. Instead, he asked questions about her people. "Is it true that we tried to kill you all within a few months of your creation?"

"Yeah," Hara said, sighing in disappointment at the history that the Colician and human races shared together. "Things got pretty gruesome."

"And then when your father tried to make a peace treaty, the president tried to assassinate him? When he was trying to bring peace?"

"Yes." Hara paused. "Wait. How did you know that? I didn't tell you that!"

Odau's brow furrowed. He was just as confused as she was. "Yes, you did."

"No, I didn't…" Remembering her dream encounter with Odau, she said, "Oh." She had dreamed the encounter with Odau, but they really did have the conversation.

"We had an entire conversation about this," Odau reminded, staring at her oddly. "Don't you remember?"

"I didn't realize we actually had that discussion," Hara explained, massaging the sides of her face with her hands. "I assumed that I was dreaming the whole confrontation."

"No, you were definitely talking to me," Odau insisted. "I don't know how, but you were. When I first felt you in my head, I wanted you out, but then I thought it would be better if I got some things said that needed saying. You tried to push me out shortly after that, but I hung on. I'm glad that I did. After hearing what you had to say, I started looking at this whole situation differently. It hit me that you really were doing it all for a reason, and a good one. Like I said before, I can't let you kill my son, but I will help you hunt down The Doc." He turned his head again to get a better view of her face. "You are going to go after him before you go home, aren't you?"

"I have to," Hara told him softly. "There's no way I can go home knowing that he's still in either of our worlds." She sighed wearily. "I refuse to go home if that man is still breathing. Either I kill him, or I die trying."

"Then I'll help you," Odau promised. "Once you kill him, you can go home and help your friend save your people. You don't have to kill my son."

Hara bit her lip. "You do understand that it won't be the same unless your boy dies?" She didn't want to elicit another outburst from the lieutenant, but she needed to get the facts straight in his head.

"And why not?" Odau asked, and Hara saw that look of anger in his eyes again.

Feeling a lump rise in her throat and tears forming in the corners of her eyes, she explained, "Because if I kill him, then nothing that happened would have happened. I want him to be erased from my life forever!"

"I still don't understand how killing Jackson now will change something that has already happened."

"It's complicated," Hara said.

There was a question hanging on the tip of Odau's tongue. Hara could see that on his face. It took him a few moments to put it into words. "When you go home, and you fix everything, you're not ever going to come back, are you?"

Hara blinked at him in sarcastic innocence. "Don't you want me to?" she flouted sweetly.

Odau said slowly, "I know we're about to work together, but forgive me when I say that after tonight, I don't want to ever see you again."

Forcing a smile, Hara told him, "After tonight, I will have no reason to ever come back here. Whatever goes down tonight, it will be the last you ever see of me. That's a promise."

Breathing a sigh of relief, Odau smiled, which was something else that Hara had never expected. "Good."

Hara raised her eyebrows and smirked at him. "I honestly never believed you were physically or emotionally able to smile."

Odau chuckled and lowered his eyes to the floor again. "Yeah, that's not the first time I've heard that." His smile faded from his lips and he suddenly looked lost in thought. "You know, Marcus said that to me once, and I thought it was so funny because he was always so afraid of me. Now, I realize why that was." He sighed again. "He said my son is going to destroy his people—your people—and he knew it from the beginning of our careers together. Marcus died because he was peacefully trying to stop it from happening, and I never fully understood what he died for. It seems to me that all peaceful people are killed for being peaceful, because they're the easiest to destroy." He sighed with regret. "I never realized just how great of a man he was. Now I do. How could he stand to work with me for as long as he did? Why didn't he try to kill my son himself?"

Smiling lightly at the memory of Daniel, Hara said, "Because he was better than that. He thought there was always an alternative to killing, and I suppose he's right. He never killed a person in his life, and look at how far he managed to get."

"How are you going to kill The Doc?" Odau asked her, quickly changing the subject. "You know he's not going to make it easy for you, don't you? He has been one step ahead of you this whole time."

"Yes, I know," Hara replied grimly. "But I have an advantage over him. I don't need to fire a gun to hurt him."

"Finding him won't be easy either," Odau muttered.

"Sure it will," Hara assured him. "He may be hiding from the cops, but he won't try to hide from me. He's still after me, and he'll keep coming for me until one of us is dead; hopefully it will be him."

"Is there any place you can think of that he would go?"

"Like I said, I don't need to look anywhere for him. He'll come to me."

"Is there anyone else out there that he could use against you?" Odau asked hesitantly. "Are there any more people important to your future out there?"

"Oh, several. But I highly doubt that The Doc will try to bring anyone else into this mess."

Odau started to ask another question, but he stopped when Dreyson ambled into the room, dragging behind him a toy Optimus Prime semi. The truck was almost as big as him, but he had no trouble pulling it along with only one hand. It rattled loudly as it banged along the floor, and Hara feared it would break. If it belonged to Bennett's grandchildren, then breaking it was the last thing she wanted. When Dreyson reached the center of the room, he plopped down on the floor and pulled the truck onto his lap. He must have sensed them watching him, because he glanced up and when he made eye contact with Odau, his gaze didn't shift.

"It's okay, honey," Hara reassured him as she sensed his hesitation. "He's our friend now."

Giving Odau an uncertain look, Dreyson glanced over at Hara and nodded once before returning to his truck.

For a few moments, Hara and Odau silently watched him play with the truck in his lap. Watching her son made her smile as a sense of peace swept over her.

"He's a beautiful child," Odau told her quietly. There was something else in his voice, and Hara knew exactly what it was. She experienced the same sense of peace every time she watched a child playing.

"He is," Hara replied. She wasn't sure how to say what she needed to say. "I understand...how you feel."

Confused, Odau looked back to her. "Excuse me?"

"Well...I'm not in your situation right now, but...I've been there."

"What are you talking about?"

"I understand how angry you must be about this situation," Hara tried to explain to him. "I've been where you are now. I know the feeling of dread you had when you thought I was about to kill your son. I tried so hard to save my children from The Doc, but in the end The Doc won. He killed four of my beautiful children, and I lost my fifth to him as well." She looked back to Dreyson, her baby boy. "I never thought I would ever see him again."

"Why would The Doc want to kill your children?" Odau asked her softly. "I understand that he hates your race, but why was your family a target?"

"He started by killing people close to my father to try to tear him down emotionally so he would give in to his demands," Hara told him. "But in the end, The Doc realized that my father was stronger than that and wasn't going to give up. He killed my father and then went after me to try to do the exact same thing so it would be easier to catch me. As you heard him say before, he wanted somebody to understand him, so he was trying to tear me down to his level so I would know his pain. It's twisted, but that's why he did this to me."

"I'm sorry," Odau said quietly. "That's awful."

"Yeah," Hara muttered. "I guess what I'm trying to say is that I know how you feel about me trying to kill your son, and I'm sorry. I had to endure losing children, and I had no right to try and take the life of one of yours."

He nodded at her. "Apology accepted," he replied, holding out his hand.

Hara shook the lieutenant's hand. She was reconciling with a human and forming the alliance that her father had been trying to achieve with the humans for a very long time. Now, in her darkest hour, she was able to do something good for the benefit of both their species.

* * *

The arrival of Odau, Finchly, and most of all, Renee, was totally unexpected. It was still unclear to Perry where he was, although he was fairly certain that it was Dr. Bennett's apartment. He did know that it was a safe place. After everything that happened in the past hour, he was just hoping for things to tone down for a while.

When he glanced over Jack's shoulder and saw Hara open the door, his heart started pounding. His first assumption was that Odau was going to open fire on Hara once again, but to his and Jack's bewilderment, they started talking to each other. Was Hara inside his head to keep him calm? No. Somehow, and Perry would never understand why, the two of them had a change of heart. Neither of them wanted to fight any more. They were done. The lieutenant was switching sides to oppose The Doc, but there was only one way that the two of them could come to terms, and that was if Hara was willing to give up killing Jackson Odau.

Perry's thoughts were distracted as Hara stepped to the side and he made eye contact with Renee. His heart skipped a beat and the next thing he knew she was running to kiss him. Perry managed to catch the combination of disgust and malcontent on Jack's face before he turned away from them. It felt odd kissing Renee in front of Jack, but Perry didn't tell her to stop until Bennett and Davey came out of the bathroom with two more towels and a change of clothes for him.

They showered and changed after Perry told the lieutenant everything he learned from The Doc. Once Perry and Renee left, Odau went to speak to Hara while Bennett, Jack, Davey, and Finchly remained in the kitchen to give everyone their own space.

It felt amazing for Perry to get out of his blood and water-soaked clothes. He had been feeling absolutely disgusting ever since his knife wound healed over. Once he was in the shower it was like a rebirth for him. For fifteen minutes he did nothing but enjoy the steaming water with his eyes closed, soaking up the good feeling while his mind lingered on recent events. He was struggling to avoid thinking about his time with The Doc, but the memories were so vivid they refused to leave his mind. He never believed something so horrible would ever happen to him. Nothing was ever going to look the same to him ever again. For the time being, however, he was going to have to push his emotions aside in order to do his job. The pain in his head would have to be dealt with later. He had to be strong like Hara and the others fighting alongside her. He had to be strong like his own people.

Turning off the water, he brushed the curtain aside and stepped out. His towel was sitting on the counter beside the sink. He rubbed it against the fogged-up mirror, forming a circle just big enough so he was able to see his exhausted face. He knew it wasn't going to be very attractive after what he had gone through, but he wanted to see if there were any noticeable physical changes after his recent biological changes.

To his surprise, his reflection didn't appear all that bad. He didn't look as tired as he anticipated, although his face was a nasty shade of gray, probably from the blood loss. He supposed his ability couldn't regenerate that part of him quite as quickly. Other than that, there wasn't really anything noticeably different except for his eyes. There was something off about them, and at first Perry couldn't place it. He leaned forward, getting himself closer to the mirror so he could get a better look. After several seconds of thoroughly studying his irises, he managed to identify the difference. His eyes were extremely bright. The deep, dark shade of mahogany was now even more vivid. There was a new light shining in them, making him seem more alive. It was the light that he had seen in the eyes of every Colician he encountered.

There were two doors that led into the bathroom; the one to Perry's right came from the kitchen, and the one to his left came from Bennett's bedroom. The one connecting to the bedroom suddenly clicked open, and Perry quickly fumbled with his towel to wrap it around his waist before anyone saw something they shouldn't.

"Shawn?" Renee called as she started to step inside, but when she saw that she had caught him at an awkward moment she looked away and said, "Oh, sorry."

"That's okay," Perry replied as she closed the door so it was only open a crack.

"How are you doing?" she asked through the crack. She knew he was troubled. Any fool could have seen that.

"Fine," he lied, and quickly tried to change the subject. "Are you sure you don't want a shower?"

Renee saw right through that. "Stop trying to avoid talking about it," she whispered, her voice irritated but sympathetic. "You're going to have to whether you want to or not."

Perry set his towel back on the counter and started changing into the shirt and pants that Bennett had lent him. Perry hadn't told Renee what had happened after he was taken by The Doc, but she would have to assume the worst. She could see how different he was, and it wasn't because of the change from human to Colician. The Doc had changed him emotionally, and it wasn't at all hard to see.

"How did Hara change you?" Renee questioned.

"She triggered the change when she healed my head injury," Perry answered.

"And after you healed the injury The Doc inflicted on you...what happened?"

Unable to bring himself to talk about it, Perry pulled his shirt on and hung up his towel. He then emptied out the contents of his old jacket and pants pockets to see what was salvageable before throwing all his bloodstained clothing into Bennett's wastebasket.

"Shawn," Renee said stubbornly.

"Why do you want to make me relive this so badly?" Perry demanded angrily. "Can't you see it was hard enough the first time?"

Renee marched right up to Perry and kissed him. As she did so, she slowly wrapped her arms around his neck and ran a gentle and passionate hand through his hair.

Perry's first reaction was to pull away because he knew she was only doing it to elicit a response from him, but when he realized she was also doing it as an apology he gave in and wrapped his arms around her back. It was nice to finally show some of their feelings for each other without having somebody watching over their shoulders, and if Hara really did end everything tonight they would finally be able to begin their life together.

Pulling away, Renee gazed lovingly yet sorrowfully into his eyes. "I'm sorry," she whispered. "I'm just trying to help you. Holding it in will only make it worse."

Gritting his teeth to keep his emotions back, he stepped away from her. "I just want to act as if none of it ever happened," he said, his voice cracking. "I just want to forget."

Renee shook her head remorsefully. "Bottling everything inside you isn't going to help you heal." She reached up and held his face in both her hands, her eyes full of pain for him.

Perry pulled her hands away from his face and held them in his own. He held her gaze for as long as he could before his eyes overflowed and tears began trickling down his cheeks. As his knees began to give out, he sat down on the toilet seat and covered his mouth with his hands in a feeble effort to suppress his sobs.

Renee ran her hand through Perry's hair again as he cried. She knew it was going to be very difficult for him until he had a chance to come to terms with what had happened to him. "Shawn, I love you," she told him quietly. "You know you can trust me, don't you? I'm going to be right here by your side while you cope with this. If you really don't want to talk about it now, we don't have to, but we need to talk about this later. *You* need to talk about this later."

Nodding slowly as his entire body shook, Perry took her hand when she offered it to him. He was grateful that she wasn't going to continue forcing the memories on him, but he wasn't looking forward to the talk they were going to have later.

"You just need to stay strong for a few more hours so we can put an end to this," she said soothingly. "It's almost over."

Trying to get hold of himself, Perry breathed in and out slowly several times and managed to stop his tears from coming. He wiped his eyes and glanced up at Renee's concerned face. "How did you find me here?" he asked.

"Somehow, the lieutenant knew Hara was here. I don't know how, but I think they were communicating." She waved a finger at her head to explain that it had been telepathic communication. "Anyway, he said this was where she was and that we had to come here."

"Well, I'm glad you did," Perry replied, forcing a smile.

Renee smiled back, but Perry could see another question burning in her eyes. A moment later, she asked him, "How did you manage to escape?"

"I didn't," Perry explained. "Jack's friend Davey teleported me out."

"It's strange that this affected people in different parts of the world," Renee muttered, but then her brow furrowed in confusion. "I thought this happened in Philadelphia and nowhere else?"

"He's too young to have been affected by the initial outbreak," Perry said. "His parents must have been affected first, just like Hara's parents. They were probably just in the wrong place at the wrong time."

"That's exactly how I feel about this case," Renee replied.

"That's how I feel the future is going to go as well," Perry murmured.

"What do you mean?"

"There's going to be another outbreak. In ten years, everyone in the world with O negative blood will gain an ability. No one will escape it."

Renee's brow furrowed. "How do you know this?"

"Noah, the man Jack had me go see, told me about it."

Pausing, Renee whispered, "I have O negative."

Sighing, Perry said, "I know. My daughter has it too. Thinking about what's going to happen makes me think so much about her, how much she's going to go through when this happens. I tried calling her today, just to talk to her, but her damn mother never lets me get a word in!" He shook his head angrily. "Is it asking so much to want to talk to my daughter?"

"No," Renee said, pulling her phone out of her pocket. "It's not much to ask at all. That's why you're going to talk to her. Right now."

Perry was grateful for what she was trying to do, but it was useless. "Kyra always answers the phone. There's no way she'll give the phone to Jillian if I call."

"That's why you're not going to call," Renee replied, raising an eyebrow deviously. She held out her phone to him. "Dial the number. Let me handle the rest."

Smiling, Perry took the phone and quickly dialed the number. He then handed it back to Renee, watching anxiously.

He heard the phone ring a few times before it was answered. "Hi, my name is Miss Renee Michaels. I'm a teacher at your daughter Jillian's school and I was wondering if I could have a quick word with her?" There was silence on both ends of the line for a few seconds before Kyra asked Renee something. "Oh, it's just regarding an assignment that's being done outside of class. I was just calling to check up on her progress." Silence again. Kyra said something short before Renee's mouth turned up in a triumphant grin. "Here," she said in a whisper, handing the phone to Perry. "She fell for it. She's getting Jillian."

Relieved, Perry took the phone and put it to his ear. He waited for a little while until he heard a young voice ask hesitantly, "Hello?"

"Jillian," Perry breathed, the sound of his daughter's gentle voice melting his heart.

Jillian gasped, but Kyra must have still been listening, because Jillian answered, "Hi, Miss Michaels. I'm doing fine, thank you. How are you?"

Perry was proud of his child. She was a pretty good actor for a five-year-old. "I'm fine, baby. Are you really doing okay?"

"Yep. Everything's going great."

"Good." Perry found himself beaming. Just hearing his daughter's voice made him feel remarkably better.

"Daddy!" Jillian hissed suddenly. Kyra must have left the room. "Why haven't you called in so long?"

"I've been trying, honey," Perry promised her, feeling tears in his eyes. "I really have. But your mom doesn't want me to talk to you."

"Ugh!" Jillian said in disgust. "She's such a witch!"

Perry laughed. "Yep. That she is."

"I wish I could come live with you," Jillian said softly, a hint of sadness in her voice. "You're way nicer than Riley."

"This Riley character, what's he like?" Perry asked. "Is he good to you? He hasn't hurt you, has he?"

"No, but I still don't like him. He and Mom yell a lot, and he makes me get beer for him all the time."

Rolling his eyes, Perry said, "That sounds like someone your mother would marry."

"I don't want him to adopt me!" Jillian whispered fiercely. "I don't want him to replace you! He's not my daddy! You're my daddy! Promise me you won't let him adopt me?"

"I promise you that I will do whatever I can to get you to come up here with me. You'd like my friend, Renee. If you do get to come up, you'll probably see her a lot."

"She's probably a lot nicer than Mom," Jillian grumbled.

"Oh, she is," Perry assured. "Trust me."

"Riley can't adopt me if you don't want him to, can he?" Jillian asked nervously. "You're my real daddy, so you can say no, can't you?"

"Don't worry about it right now," Perry said, not wanting to think about what might happen. "We'll see what happens when the time comes. Until then…just hope that things work out for us."

"I will," Jillian promised. "Oh, no. I have to go. Mom's coming. I love you, Daddy. Call again soon."

The line went dead before Perry could say, "I love you, too." The conversation had been brief, but it was more than he had gotten in nearly a year. He sighed, feeling a wonderful sense of peacefulness from having the chance to talk to his sweet little girl. The feeling was taken from him quickly when Renee's eyes suddenly lit up.

"Oh, before I forget again," she said. "Somebody called and left a message on your cell phone." She reached into her pocket and pulled out his phone, which now had a large, jagged crack across the screen. It was a miracle that it still worked. "It fell out of your pocket after you were taken by The Doc. A man named John Reifert left you a message about two hours ago."

As his breath caught in his chest, he stared up at Renee. "Oh, God," he whispered in growing dread. "I completely forgot!"

"What?" Renee asked in confusion. "Forgot what?"

"What did the message say?" Perry demanded urgently, jumping to his feet and grabbing Renee's arms so she could see it was important.

"He said he was going to be about ten minutes late to your meeting. Something was going on with one of his kids at school."

"Oh, God," Perry repeated. "Oh, no." Looking Renee in the eyes again, he asked her, "What time is it right now?" He already knew it was going to be too late.

Flipping open her own cell phone, Renee responded, "About 4:15."

"Shit!" Perry cried in anger at himself, immediately shoving past her to get out the door to the kitchen.

"Shawn, what's wrong?" Renee cried, catching his arm as he grabbed the door knob. "What's going on?"

"I have to talk to Hara right now!" Perry insisted quickly. "The Doc's going after her remaining family hiding among us! I think he's going to kill them!"

✳ ✳ ✳

An awkward silence followed Hara and Odau's handshake. They both sat staring at the floor for several minutes, thinking over the compact their handshake had created. Odau finally broke the uncomfortable silence. "We should probably find Perry and see if he's ready to get back to work again. We shouldn't wait too much longer to get started on our search…or whatever it is you're planning on doing."

Nodding, Hara agreed, "Yeah, okay."

They both rose to their feet, and Hara had just started for the kitchen when Perry came bursting through the doorway, followed quickly by an uncertain Renee Michaels. It only took Hara a second after seeing Perry's expression to make the connection.

"What's wrong?" she demanded, her heart rate beginning to quicken.

"I'm so sorry I forgot to tell you," Perry apologized, his eyes full of fear and regret. "But you have a serious problem."

"What is he doing now?" Hara asked in dread, knowing it had to do with something The Doc had told him.

"He's going after your family!" Perry cried.

"He already killed my family," Hara replied sternly as she felt her insides knotting up.

"No, your human family!" Perry said in a desperate attempt to clarify. "John Reifert!" He stared at her helplessly. "And Walter."

"He's going after Walter Reifert?" Jack demanded, marching up behind Perry and staring at him in horror.

"Oh, dear God!" Davey moaned as he followed Jack.

"Who's Walter Reifert?" Odau asked in confusion.

"The last person in our world that Hara still needs to protect," Bennett replied, gazing back at Hara with a look of fear in his eyes.

"Is he related to Hallie Reifert?" Odau asked, remembering Perry's eagerness to find her earlier that day.

"*I'm* Hallie Reifert," Hara said.

Looking at her in surprise, he mumbled, "Oh."

"What are you going to do?" Jack asked hesitantly.

"Let me think!" Hara snapped, her heart pounding faster and faster. She was really scared. If The Doc got his hands on little Walter…bad things were going to happen. Very bad things.

"Who is he?" Perry asked breathlessly. "Why is he so important? Tell me, and maybe I can help you fix this!"

"Do you remember how we explained that you're crucial to our survival?" Hara asked, monitoring her breathing in a careful attempt to keep herself calm. "Well, forgive me when I say that you're not the most important person to our future."

"Walter's going to help Shawn save all of you," Michaels said, looking to Hara to see if that was correct.

"No," Hara replied. "Perry is the one that helps Walter save us all."

Jack explained, "Walter Reifert is going to be the father of the Colician movement."

"Yeah," Davey piped in. "He negotiates the terms for our relocation, and he saves us all by getting us to our new home safely. He is a great man."

"Boy," Perry reminded, raising an eyebrow at him. "He's just a boy."

"Right. Boy." Davey looked down.

"Where exactly is your home?" Odau asked Hara.

"I can't explain that to you right now. I don't have the time." Turning back to Perry, she demanded, "How in the hell did The Doc find out where they were?"

Guilt flaming in his eyes, he whispered, "He overheard me scheduling a meeting with John."

Exhaling slowly, Hara asked softly, "Where is this meeting?"

"In the parking ramp across from the hospital."

"And at what time was this meeting supposed to take place?"

Pausing, Perry breathed, "Right now."

Before Hara could let out her cry of rage at Perry for not telling her about this earlier, Davey wailed loudly and collapsed to his knees. "We're all dead!" he yelled up at the ceiling with a defeated look on his face. "Oh God, we're so screwed!"

"No, we're not," Hara said calmly.

"Yes, I'm quite sure that we are," Jack replied, his fear shown very clearly in his dark eyes.

"We are not screwed until I say we are screwed!" Hara informed him sharply. "We have not lost until I am dead! If The Doc is going after Walter, then we are not going to sit around waiting! We are going to him, and we're not leaving the fight until either he or I am dead! The Doc is done stepping on us like we're nothing! He cannot keep threatening our very existence like this! This war ends tonight, right here and right now! Davey, get up!"

Fat, pathetic tears were streaming down both sides of his face as the fear of extermination overtook him, but Davey managed to rise anyway. He stared at her angry expression and stammered, "How are you going to stop him? We're already too late!"

"You can get us there," Hara told him, placing a comforting hand on his shoulder and trying to calm his panicked mind. For what she would need him to do, he would need to be very focused. "And you can get us there much faster than it would take to drive."

"Not all of us!" Davey protested. "I can only transport a few people at once!"

"You're only going to need to take Jack and me," Hara replied reassuringly. "But we need to go now."

"We don't have any weapons!"

"We are weapons!"

"Do you think he'll really kill Walter?" Bennett asked nervously.

"He can't," Hara said, but deep down she really wasn't sure. "If he kills him, our side won't be the only side with a great loss. He'll lose something too."

"What?" Odau asked in bewilderment.

"Me." Hara made eye contact with him for a split second before turning back to Bennett. "Watch after my child for me while I'm gone," she instructed, and then looked at Jack and Davey. "We need to go right now." She took one of Davey's hands and Jack did the same with Davey's other hand.

"I don't know where I'm going!" Davey whimpered helplessly.

"I'll guide you," Hara promised in a whisper. "Don't worry about a thing."

"Let us help you," Odau requested, taking a hesitant step toward them.

Without looking at him, Hara told him, "If you want to help, then meet us there." Nodding to Davey, she placed the image of the hospital in his head as she felt him begin to teleport them away. She hadn't gotten a good look at the parking ramp when she had been there before so he couldn't transport them directly, but if they landed back at the hospital and then teleported into the ramp from there, they might be able to get to the Reiferts in time.

17

Prisoners of War

Throughout the course of that school year, John Reifert had been contacted three times by the principal of the elementary school to deal with his youngest son Walter. That afternoon, the principal actually called John in to discuss the consequences of Walter's latest outburst. Each time there was a problem with Walter at school it was because he had gotten into a fight with another boy in his class, and today was the same. Unfortunately, troubled eight-year-old Walter refused to explain why he had attacked the boy. He would never explain his actions, and John was becoming very frustrated. His wife had died just a year earlier, and it was clear that much of Walter's anger was coming from his grief for the loss of his mother.

"Are you going to tell me what happened?" John asked quietly as he pulled his Prius into the parking ramp across the street from the hospital. He didn't want to take any of his children to his meeting with Special Agent Perry, but he was already late and he didn't have time to take Walter home after the meeting with the principal. The girl who had given his wife the letter for Agent Perry had warned her to be careful while delivering it because there was going to be a man with him that would want to do him harm. Now that the letter was in John's possession and was his responsibility, he was the one that needed to be wary of whoever would be waiting for him. As long as Walter stayed in the car, he felt that everything would be fine.

When Walter refused to explain himself, John sighed angrily. "You do understand what your principal wanted your punishment to be this time?" he demanded. "He wanted to have you expelled, but I managed to talk him out of it. If you pull one more stunt like that, I won't be able to get you out of it. One more time, and you're going to be expelled. You won't be able to go to that school anymore!"

"Good," Walter muttered under his breath as John pulled the car into a stall on the second level.

"What did you say?" John snapped, taking the keys out of the ignition and glaring down at his son.

Walter's head was down and his green eyes were obscured by his wavy brown hair, but John knew that he was glowering down at the floor. His hands were clenched into tight fists and his shoulders were tensed. The poor boy was so angry, and as John looked on at this he suddenly felt very sad and helpless.

Sighing again, John said, "Walter, I know you miss your mom. I miss her too, and I want to help you through these troubles you're facing, but I can't if you don't start talking to me." He waited for his son to speak a few words or to just look up at him, but he received absolutely no response. Pursing his lips in frustration, John replied through gritted teeth, "Fine." Turning, he pushed his door open and stuck a leg out. "Stay in the car. I'll only be a few minutes." As he got out and started walking towards the interior of the large concrete structure, he clicked the locks of his car shut with the remote lock on his key chain. He knew his son wouldn't be foolish enough to leave the car in a place as unfamiliar as this, but he was worried about people getting in rather than out. The atmosphere around him was too quiet and still for comfort. Nobody was anywhere to be seen, despite how many cars were parked in the stalls.

The woman who gave the letter to his wife had known something bad was approaching, and that paranoia had been wearing off on him. John had managed to get a bit of information out of Hallie about the approaching apocalypse. Hallie told him that she was going to die very soon and then it would be up to him to protect their children from the calamities to come. Only a year after she died, a man would contact John and ask about her. That man would be the recipient of the letter, because he was the man who was already fighting the war and the letter would greatly help him in his effort. Along with that man there would be another man, a man with cold, gray, unmistakable eyes. That man would be the one who wanted to harm him. Another thing John learned was that after the letter was delivered, he would meet a young girl who he had never met before, but he would know her. He had no idea what that was supposed to mean, but since everything else was unfolding as Hallie had described, he assumed that he would understand soon enough.

At first, John didn't believe her, but when she died unexpectedly a few years after the encounter, he realized that she had been telling the truth all along. Now, as John cautiously walked past several rows of cars, he had the nervous feeling that what was left of his wife's prophecy would soon be realized. There was an itch in the back of his mind that told him someone would attempt to stop the delivery of the letter John had stored in the inside pocket of his jacket. He also felt, however, that his late wife was somehow there to protect him.

Suddenly feeling very cold, as if an icy wind had enveloped him, John shivered and wrapped his arms around himself. Looking at every car he passed to see if anybody was waiting for him inside, he called out hesitantly, "Agent Perry? Hello?" When no one answered, John grew even more wary. Part of him wanted to get back to his son and drive away and forget all about the letter, but he had made a promise to Hallie.

Continuing on his way, he opened his mouth to call out again, but he slowed to a halt when he suddenly spotted a man at the very end of the level. The man was in between a black SUV and a silver Mercedes, and he was leaning against the concrete beam while gazing out at the city. His back was turned to John, but John saw that he was wearing what appeared to be a white lab coat. He didn't really look like he was with the FBI, but John figured he should try anyway just to be sure.

"Hello?" John called again as he cautiously approached the man from behind.

At first, it seemed as if John had gone unheard, but then the man slowly turned to peer curiously back at him. It turned out that the man was indeed wearing a lab coat, and he wore a white shirt underneath and white pants as well. He couldn't have been much older than John, but there was something about him that made him look older. There was intelligence in his eyes that told John this man knew things he never would. And the man's eyes...they were so cold and gray that they alone made John's soul freeze over. Gray eyes...the man with gray eyes will seek to harm you, Hallie had said all those years ago. Now that John was aware of this physical trait, he became more aware of the things that weren't right about the man. His right pant leg was torn with blood stains around the ankle. The front of his jacket also had flecks of blood on it, his undershirt was soaked, and his sandy brown hair was tossed about on top of his head like he had just gone swimming.

Peering at the man inquisitively, John asked uncertainly, "Agent Perry?"

The man shook his head solemnly, and what appeared to be a smirk crossed his face. "No, but I'm a friend of his." Cocking his head slightly, he asked, "You're John Reifert, aren't you?"

Suspiciously, John answered, "Yeah, who are you?"

The man didn't answer; he just watched John with that jeering smirk and started toward him slowly. "I've been waiting for you," he said softly.

Quickly becoming uncomfortable, John started to back away. He only retreated a few steps before he felt his muscles freeze up on him. He was paralyzed, and he could hear a soft voice whispering in his head, telling him to keep quiet and hold still. "Please don't come any closer to me," he warned shakily.

"*Shh, shh, shh,*" the man whispered, raising a finger to his lips. "Let's try not to make too much noise with this."

John was frozen in terror, and the whisper in his head grew louder. He finally allowed himself to believe what he already knew. "Are you here to kill me?"

The man's gray eyes narrowed on him, and he nodded. "Yes."

Swallowing hard, John wondered what he should do. In his fear, he would either run, or attempt to plead with the man to let him live. John was a single father with four children; wouldn't the man understand that and have pity on him? Something told John that he wouldn't. That left option number one...

Seeing the instinct of flight in John's terrified eyes, the man warned, "Please don't try to run."

The voice in John's head was saying the exact same thing, only it was more forceful. It took John a moment to realize that the whisper was coming from the man. He didn't listen to either voice. Without speaking another word or waiting around for what the man had planned for him, John turned and started sprinting back towards his car. If he could just get back to Walter and then get out of there, everything would be fine. But the man knew his name, so would he come after him at his home? Would his children be in danger from this man as well?

He didn't get very far when a gunshot echoed through the air and he felt an excruciating pain in his back before he collapsed to the ground. Gasping for breath as his vision turned white and the agony he felt caused him to cry out, John automatically snapped a hand behind him and clutched at the wound in his back. Blood covered his hand and he felt it drip to the ground.

As his vision cleared, his mind went to Walter, who was locked in their car alone with nothing to defend himself. Fighting through his pain, John pushed a shaky hand into his pants pocket and drew out his keys. He aimed it at his car and clicked the locks open, but he was too late to help his son. A moment after the lights of his Prius flashed to say it was unlocked, John heard a click and a peculiar whirring sound behind him before a long and narrow object belching smoke shot in the direction of his vehicle. As the device shattered through the back window, a huge explosion erupted through the silence and the Prius blew into pieces, flames licking at the air above the remnants of the car.

"No!" John cried in horror and pictured his youngest son helpless as the bomb flew through the window. "Walter!"

He couldn't take his eyes off the horrifying sight of his youngest child perishing, but then John felt a foot roughly nudge his shoulder until he regrettably rolled over onto his back, being careful to avoid resting on the bullet wound. The nose of a gun was pointed at his face, and he felt pitiful lying on the ground, wounded and unable to save himself as he had been unable to save Walter. No words were exchanged at first, and John began to feel a great anger boiling inside him as the realization of his son's death began to take hold of him. Hallie hadn't told him what events would unfold after meeting this man, and he decided that he was going to determine the outcome himself. Gazing up into the man's cold, remorseless eyes, John no longer felt pitiful. His own eyes narrowing in hate, John bared his teeth and snarled, "Do you want what Perry was coming for?"

The man only cocked his head at him again, his expression remaining blank.

"Do you want it?" John demanded, his voice cracking and eyes watering in his agony. Reaching inside his jacket pocket to fetch it out, he continued to glare furiously. "Did you really just murder my child so you could get your hands on this? Well, take it! I have no use for it! Take it, you son of a bitch! Take it and leave!" Causing himself even more pain, he flung the envelope at the man.

It fluttered to the ground at the man's feet, but he barely even glanced at it. He was too busy studying John's face. "Are you scared?" he asked abruptly, his expression unchanging.

"What?" John cried in disgust, staring up at him in bewilderment. His vision was starting to fade, but he was going to make one last effort. "Just take what you came for and leave me here!"

"I'm not here for whatever it is Perry wanted from you," the man said sharply, holding the gun level with John's head. "I'm here because I needed to get your son out of my way."

"Out of your way for what?" John demanded, his head dropping back down to the concrete.

"I'm sorry," the man said, but there was no mercy in his eyes. He cocked the gun. "This wasn't your fault."

A sudden ding off to John's right caused them both to look over in surprise. He was lying about six feet from the elevator, and the up arrow above the door was lit up. The door opened then, revealing a girl; her dark brown hair fluttered about her face, and her brilliant, intelligent green eyes—which appeared strikingly familiar—held a rage as deep as hell. She was giving the man standing over John a murderous glare, and John heard him inhale sharply at the sight of her.

"How are you still..." he started, but his voice broke off as confusion overcame him.

"Here?" the girl asked in a silky sweet voice, sneering at him. "Well, dear man, I beat you to Walter."

At first glance, John couldn't see anything dangerous about her. Her eyes were scary enough, but she had no weapons and she was too thin to really pose much of a physical threat. She left him dumbfounded when she raised both of her hands and a huge, roaring flame erupted from her. The fire flowed from her—seemingly being created from nothing—and struck the man square in the chest. John saw him go down and his lab coat set ablaze.

The fury was not only burning in her hands but her eyes as well. When she turned on him, she changed. Her eyes held deep love and concern for him, and she herself looked as if she were in pain. Rushing to him, she knelt beside him and gently helped him to his feet. Once he was on both feet he struggled to keep from collapsing again. He found himself incapable of standing erect, and when his knees began to buckle beneath him, the girl slipped under his arm and kindly guided him back to the elevator. As they stepped inside, John panted, "Who are you?"

"A friend," the girl promised softly, pressing the close button and helping John sit in the back corner.

That much was obvious. "Did you say that you saved my son?" he asked hopefully. He gasped and clutched his back in his agony.

"Yes," the girl assured him. "Walter's just fine." She crouched down beside him again as the doors closed. Her eyes held even deeper worry for him than before. "You're the one that you should be worried about."

"Who was that man?" John asked as she gingerly touched the area surrounding the bullet wound.

"He's a very disturbed man who's been after our family for a long time now," the girl replied, intently focused on his injury.

"Our family?" John was sure he had never met her before. "Ow!" he cried as she poked him right where the wound was.

"I'm sorry!" she apologized, and then placed her palm entirely over the wound.

"Is he dead?" John asked hopefully.

"I'm afraid he won't go down so easily," the girl answered regretfully. And then she said, as if to read his mind, "But not to worry; he's not going to go after you or your other children."

"It wouldn't matter if he came after me again," John whimpered, knowing that his breaths were numbered. His vision was beginning to fail and the pain was too much for him to bear. He knew it was the end. "I'm done…"

"It's not your time yet," the girl murmured softly. "Now please try to hold still."

"What are you…*aaaarrrrrhhhhh!*" John screamed as a new, internal pain began. The girl held his shoulder firmly to keep him down and spoke to him in a soothing whisper. It felt as if she were sticking a knife straight into his wound. It was worse than the initial shot and was the worst pain he had ever experienced. And then, as abruptly as it began, it was over. There was no more pain; not even from the gunshot. The girl removed her hands from him and peered at him expectantly. Puzzled, John reached back and cautiously touched where his injury had been. The blood was still there, but there was no wound to account for it. Staring back at her in shock, he stammered, "What …what did you do?"

Holding out her hand, she showed him the blood covered bullet in her palm. "I saved your life," she replied quietly.

The elevator made another dinging sound, and as the doors slid open the girl snapped to her feet in alarm. As if she had foreseen it, the man with the gray eyes was waiting for them on the other side of the doorway, his smirk still present on his face. In his hands he held a device which looked oddly like a leaf blower. When he saw their looks of fear, his smile widened. "Boo," he whispered smugly.

John's eyes automatically closed as the flames burst forth from the nozzle of the device, but he managed to see the girl turn her head away and raise her arms in defense. He felt the heat from the fire, and for an instant he feared that the man had scorched the girl and was going for him next. The air suddenly began to get cooler, and after a loud crashing noise was heard, the heat stopped altogether. Snapping his eyes open, he saw the girl poised over him with her fists clenched while she stared in fury at the man who was now laying spread eagle on the concrete several feet away. After a moment, however, the man rose to his feet and glared back at the girl. Their expressions were so fierce that it made John extremely uneasy. The sound of squealing tires broke their concentration, and the man took off running in the opposite direction of whatever car had just entered the lower level.

The girl turned back to him, her gaze soft once again. She extended a hand to him.

This girl was special, whoever she was, and she clearly cared for John by the way she was treating him. John knew in his heart that she posed no threat to him. "Who are you?" John repeated hesitantly.

The pained look returned to the girl's eyes. "Can't you see?" she whispered as he took her hand and stood up.

John was starting to wonder why the girl's eyes resembled his and Walter's so much, but he was distracted as a black SUV squealed to a halt in front of the elevator and four people leapt out.

"Let him go!" the girl yelled to the two men who had started after the man with the gray eyes. "Just let him go."

"Are you alright?" the younger man with dark hair and eyes demanded urgently as he rushed over to them.

"We're both fine," the girl assured him calmly as the man gawked at John's blood-stained shirt. "I healed his wound. He's fine."

The young man searched John's face with concern. "John Reifert?" he asked.

"Agent Perry!" John breathed a sigh of relief when he realized who the young man was.

"I'm so sorry about all of this!" Agent Perry apologized hurriedly. "I should never have put you at risk like that…"

"It doesn't matter anymore," John replied curtly.

"Was there something you were going to give me?" Perry asked uncertainly, sensing John's agitation.

Oh no. Recalling how he had thrown the letter at the man with the gray eyes, John felt his face go white. "I...I lost it," he admitted in shame.

"No, you didn't." The girl reached into her back pocket and took out the envelope. She handed it to Perry, who had a look of relief on his face. "I hope this was worth risking John's life for," she told Perry flatly.

"Hey!"

All six of them turned as a young man a few years older than the girl came running towards them, Walter clinging to his hand.

"Davey, you got Walter!" the blonde woman, who John assumed was also an FBI agent, said.

"Walter!" John cried in relief, catching his son in a tight embrace as he ran into his arms. "Oh God, I'm so sorry!"

"I'm sorry I keep fighting, Dad," Walter said shakily, fear in his eyes as he gazed apologetically into John's eyes. "I won't do it anymore, I promise!"

"Don't worry about that right now!" John told him, hugging him tighter. "Are you okay?"

"Yeah," Walter said, pulling away from John and staring in awe at the young man called Davey. "He saved me, Dad!"

Staring at Davey, John extended his hand. "Thank you," he whispered as Davey shook it and nodded back to him in respect.

"We have to go," the girl said, taking Walter and Davey by the hand and starting to lead them away. "We're running out of time."

"Wait!" John yelled in protest, catching his son by the arm. "You can't just leave with my son!"

The girl turned on him in a way that made John think she would strike him, but she had only the look of compassion and love. She released Walter, and so did John. She took a step closer to him so she was looking right up into his face. Then, her whisper barely audible, "Do you trust me?"

For a third time, John asked her, "Who are you?"

She stared unblinking into his eyes for several long moments, and at first John didn't realize what she was doing. She wanted him to look back into her eyes as well, and not just into them, but also at them. Now that John was so close to her, he could see that her eyes were identical to his and Walter's. Those eyes were a genetic trait from John's side of the family. Every fourth child received those exact green eyes, so how was it that she also possessed them? She had said "our family", so was she his family? After pondering over that, John did something he never thought possible. He actually looked through the girl's eyes and into her soul. He saw things—horrible things—about her that explained not only who she was but what she was. As he looked into her and saw everything, he gasped and took a step backwards. "Hallie," he whispered in amazement, unable to take his eyes off of her. She was beautiful. Nodding quickly to answer her question, he said, "Yes, I trust you."

Smiling, it appeared as if she knew what John had seen. "I promise you that I will bring him back to you," she said. "But right now I'm the only person who can protect him from The Doc."

"Take care of him, Hallie," John said, and he nodded to her to show his respect.

She stopped—half of her body ready to bolt and the other half wanting to linger with him—and smiled her pained smile. "You know I will," she breathed.

Reaching out to her, John gently brushed his hand across her cheek, making her inhale sharply. He needed to touch her just once, just so he could be sure she was really there. His greatest fear was that she wasn't real. Sighing heavily as a great peace swept over him, he murmured, "You look like her. You look like me, too."

Young Hallie reached up as well and took John's hand in her own. She was glad they had met, as was he. "I can't stay here," she whispered.

John nodded. "Thank you," he said gratefully, smiling at her one last time.

"You know I didn't have a choice," Hallie replied, pulling away to start running again with Walter and Davey.

"No!" John protested, squeezing her hand so she couldn't leave quite yet. As she turned back in surprise, he clarified, "I didn't just mean that for saving Walter. I also meant thank you for giving me the chance to meet you."

The sadness in Hallie's eyes increased and she turned away from him as tears began to flow. "I have to go," she whispered, her misery traveling to John.

"I know," John said, regretfully releasing her hand.

Hallie gestured for Davey and Walter to start running, and she followed them. The older man with Agent Perry, who was dressed in a police uniform, called out sharply, "Where are you going?"

"I'll be back in a moment!" she answered, and the three of them disappeared around the corner.

Agent Perry was still holding the unopened envelope in his hands. He was staring at John curiously. "Do you know her?" he asked quietly. "You seemed to recognize her."

Shrugging, John replied, "I've never met her before if that's what you're asking."

"Yet you let her take your eight-year-old son?"

John bit his lip, knowing that he shouldn't tell Perry what he knew. "I don't exactly know how to explain to you what she just showed me. She...I don't know. I suppose she showed me who she really is."

"And who is she?" Perry asked eagerly. John could see he felt so very close to a long desired answer.

Shaking his head apologetically, John took a step back. "I don't think I should say."

When Perry took a sudden step toward him, John feared he was going to make a threat to get an answer. But Perry didn't seem interested in an answer anymore. He was too concerned with studying John's eyes. "Your eyes," he said in awe. "They're green."

"Yes," John replied uncertainly, his eyes flickering to the other three who were also gazing at him intently.

"The same green as Hara's eyes," Perry murmured.

"You mean Hallie," John corrected, knowing that Hallie used the name Hara when attempting to suppress the emotions that weakened her.

"Yes," Perry replied absentmindedly. He pointed to John's eyes. "Is that a genetic trait?" He was getting closer to his answer.

John nodded. "It comes from my side of the family. Every fourth child has them."

Perry nodded slowly, his eyes remaining ever so curious. "Hara is a fourth child."

Shrugging, John glanced at the ground. "I wouldn't know," he muttered.

"Wait, where is this going?" the blonde agent asked.

"Is Hara your daughter?" Perry asked.

"I don't have a daughter," John said, knowing that Perry realized they were related somehow. "Besides, Walter is my fourth."

"Do any of your siblings have a daughter?"

"My sister Jaclyn has a daughter," John said, but quickly added, "But her name's Maia, and she's only six..."

"Sir, you need to tell me who she is!" Perry instructed in frustration. "I know you know! This is crucial!"

"Shawn, what is going on?" the blonde demanded breathlessly.

"The two of them are related! Can't you see it?" Perry glared hard at John. "I know it, and he knows it too!"

"How much time have you spent with her?" John asked as Perry's colleagues started to argue again. "You should have figured out by now that she's not of this world!"

"Well, of course she's not from around here!" the dark haired woman snapped. "We would have noticed people like her before!"

"I didn't mean she's not of *our* world!" John said in exasperation, trying to get them to open their eyes. "I meant she's not of *this* world!"

The four of them stared at him until Perry's older male colleague spoke up. "Are you...are you saying that she's not from this planet?"

Before John could give his response, a voice erupted inside of his head, causing him to fall to the ground. The others seemed to be experiencing the same phenomenon. He saw that they were on the ground clutching their heads. It wasn't painful; it was just a shock. Then, Hallie's voice spoke up.

"Hey, Doc," she said with a sneer in her voice. "I have something of yours. I want you to see something. Meet me on the Independence Bridge at ten o'clock tonight if you ever want to see it again."

Gasping, John slowly rose to his feet as the others did as well.

"Oh my God!" the older man cried in horror as he stood up, an expression of realization crossing his face. "She's got my son again! She's got Jackson!" Running to the sidewalk just outside of the garage, he screamed into the air around him, "Hara! Hara! HARA!"

"I'm right here, Lieutenant," Hallie said softly as she suddenly stepped up beside John again. Her abrupt presence was startling; she seemed to just appear out of nowhere.

The lieutenant, angry but fearful, marched up to her and snarled, "What the hell do you think you're doing?"

"I have to end this," Hallie answered quietly, staring evenly into his eyes.

"So what are you going to do?" the lieutenant demanded, but his voice was now weak in anticipation.

"This was never going to work," Hallie said, shaking her head apologetically and backing away from him.

"What? Our agreement? I thought we were going to help each other? I thought it was The Doc you wanted! Just leave my son alone—!" The lieutenant swung his palm at her face to slap her, but his hand moved right through her, as if she were only an apparition.

Hallie shook her head again, and she actually appeared sorry. "I'm not really here," she told him. "I couldn't risk you trying to stop me."

"You can't do this!" the lieutenant shouted at her in fury. "I will stop you! No matter what it takes!"

Once again, Hallie shook her head solemnly. "It's too late," she replied. "I've already got him. There's nothing you can do now. I'm sorry." Her form then vanished right before them, without leaving a single trace that she had ever been there.

The lieutenant let out a scream so terrifying it sent shivers through John. He then rounded on John, but his expression wasn't angry. It was desperate. He ran to him and grabbed him by both arms, trying to get him to see the situation he was in. "Please," he begged, his voice cracking with his emotion. "You have to help me! Please, she's going to kill my son!"

John blinked in surprise. He didn't realize who this man was until now. "Your son is Jackson Odau?" He saw the boy when he looked into Hallie's eyes before, and he wasn't anyone John desired to protect.

"Yes!" Lieutenant Odau said hopefully, his grip tightening on John's arms. "Will you help me stop her?"

His brow furrowing in his confusion, John asked him, "Don't you know who your son is?"

Lieutenant Odau released him and took a step back, a hopeless look in his eyes. "Not you too," he whispered in defeat. He turned helplessly to Perry and the two women. "Please, you have to help me! Please! You don't understand what I'm going to lose!"

"She won't kill your son for at least another six hours," Perry reassured him.

"What?" Odau cried. "How could you possibly know that?"

"She was giving a message to The Doc telling him to meet her at ten o'clock," the blonde reminded him. "We all heard it. She wants him to watch, so all we have to do is intercept her at the bridge tonight."

"Do you really think we can stop her now?" Odau demanded. He pointed to John and yelled at Perry, "Get him to answer your questions! If he's really her family, then he's protecting her and he's the only one who knows how to stop her!"

They all turned on John, and John, who was feeling extremely vulnerable by that point, started taking several steps back. He raised his hands defensively. "I'm not the enemy here. I only just met her!"

"Yet you seem like you know more about her than we do," Perry said accusingly.

"Look, I'm sorry about this situation you're all in," John told them nervously, inching to the side. "But I really have to get home. I have three boys alone at my house..."

Perry grabbed John by the front of his shirt as he tried to walk away from them and slammed him back into the elevator door, staring stubbornly at him.

Gazing uncertainly back at the agent, John glanced down at the still unopened envelope poking out of Perry's breast pocket. "You haven't opened your letter yet," he told him.

His gaze not shifting, Perry said quietly, "Before I open it, answer me this. Your wife was Hallie Reifert, correct?"

"Yes."

"And our Hallie Reifert...is she your wife?"

"Excuse me?" John raised his eyebrows incredulously, feeling insulted.

Shrugging, Perry released John. "I just thought I'd ask." He took the envelope out of his pocket and started to open it.

"What kind of a question was that?" the blonde demanded, wrinkling her nose. "What was the point of that?"

"Hara can't die so I thought maybe she doesn't age either," Perry replied.

"If Hara is the real Hallie Reifert then why does his wife have the same name?" Odau asked in perplexity.

"Obviously there are two of them," Perry replied.

"Well, which one did Aubrey want you to save?"

Perry looked at the lieutenant with his mouth half open. "I would assume the one that's still living." He unfolded the letter and stared at it intently.

His colleagues, along with John, crowded around him to look on as he read. John knew he wasn't supposed to read it, but he figured that since he knew far too much already it really didn't matter anymore. To his and everyone else's surprise, the letter only had a few words typed on it. On the very top of the page, it read in bold print, "Can't you see?" Beneath that, a close-up of a smiling ten-year-old boy with sandy brown hair and piercing gray eyes was taped to the page. If John wasn't mistaken, it was Jackson Odau. Beneath the picture, at the very bottom of the page, were four more words.

"Do you see now?"

Odau groaned in frustration. "I don't have time for this crap!" He sprinted away to the outside and rounded a corner, following the direction that Hara, Davey, and Walter had gone. John had a feeling he wouldn't be seeing him again.

"Oh, wow," Perry muttered, staring wide-eyed at the paper. "Oh no."

"What?" the two women asked him.

"I see it now," Perry whispered, staring back at John who returned the gaze calmly.

"See what?" the blonde asked him quickly, looking from him to the picture and back at him again. "What do you see?"

"You know what this means?" Perry asked John, holding up the letter and pointing to Jackson Odau's picture.

John nodded.

"Agent Perry, what does it mean?" the dark haired woman demanded impatiently.

"The answer to all our questions, the answer to this entire investigation, has been staring us in the face this whole time," Perry declared, waving the message at all of them. "All this time, we've been overlooking everything! It was all right in front of us!"

"What are you talking about?" the blonde said in confusion. "Will you please just explain to us what is going on?"

Turning to John again, Perry lowered his voice and asked, "Will you come with us to help me explain this to Odau?"

"Sure," John replied, even though he knew he should get home to his older boys. "I'll need to borrow a phone to make a call, though."

"That can be arranged," Perry promised, taking John's arm and guiding him to the SUV. "We need to go now," he called to his colleagues. "We have to find Odau so we can explain everything to him."

"What are we explaining?" the blonde demanded.

"Get in the car," Perry ordered. "I'll explain everything while we drive, but we have to leave now!"

✳ ✳ ✳

Two hours after everyone left, Bennett received the knock on his front door. He was mopping up the remaining dirty water from the mess Davey had made on his kitchen floor when the sharp rap caused him to look up in surprise. He wasn't sure if it would be wise to open the door, but glancing towards the bedroom where Dreyson was sleeping, Bennett reckoned that if there was going to be a problem, the boy would have been up and ready for it.

Setting the mop up against the kitchen table and drying his hands on his pants, Bennett slowly approached the front door. He didn't have a gun, and he debated whether he should go back to the kitchen for a knife. He remembered Dreyson, and tried to assure himself that things would be fine.

He didn't bother to ask who was outside before he pulled open the door, and as he felt the nose of a gun being pressed against his forehead, he cursed himself for not doing so first. He didn't need to look at the man's face to know who it was.

The Doc said, "Dr. Wesley Bennett. I don't know how I could have overlooked you the first time." He pressed the gun harder into Bennett's head, a hint for him to start backing inside.

"You're alone?" Bennett asked him and cautiously raised his hands. There was a gun to his head, but he wasn't afraid.

A muscle in his jaw twitching in either annoyance or anger, The Doc replied distastefully, "I'm not sure if you've met David yet, but he has a habit of sabotaging my vehicles. My semi and all my men are at the bottom of the Delaware River."

"It's a shame you're not down there with them," Bennett said as emotionlessly as he could.

Snickering, The Doc told him, "You're a bit cocky for a man who's got a gun to his head."

"What do you want?"

"Where's the boy?"

Bennett's heart skipped a beat. "What boy?" Somehow, The Doc knew he was protecting Dreyson.

"Oh, gee, I don't know," The Doc mumbled sarcastically at him. "How many toddlers are you hiding in this dump of yours?"

Bennett spoke through gritted teeth. "Why can't you just leave the poor child alone? Haven't you caused him enough pain?"

"Let's just say that our Hara is having a bit of a mental breakdown, and I need something that will help calm her down," The Doc said smugly.

"I don't think you have the right to diagnose her with anything," Bennett snapped, already quite irritated with the man.

"We're both doctors," The Doc pointed out flatly. "We both know there are many things wrong with her."

"Well, there are plenty of things wrong with you too," Bennett challenged.

Narrowing his eyes, The Doc asked again. "Where's the boy?"

"Did you really think that I would just allow you to walk out with a helpless child?" Bennett demanded angrily.

The Doc blinked at something that seemed to be puzzling him. For a short time he curiously studied Bennett's face and appeared to be lost in thought. Then, he asked quietly, "Would you really die for that boy?"

Bennett barely needed to think that question over. "Yes," he answered confidently despite the gun still being held to his head.

Cocking his head to the side, The Doc appeared quite amused. "Why?"

This time, Bennett had to think of exactly how to word his response. "Because his cause is much greater than yours."

A furious expression crossed The Doc's face, and in a rage he lifted his arm holding the gun and brought the weapon down on Bennett's head. The blow caused Bennett to collapse to the floor, and he prepared himself for the next attack. Bennett heard The Doc's gun being cocked, and he closed his eyes as he prepared for the worst.

"Don't pretend to know my cause!" The Doc snarled furiously. "You think you know me from my actions, but you don't know me, my cause, or my motives! Now where's the boy? Tell me, or I'll kill you right here on your floor!"

"Go to hell," Bennett muttered helplessly, resting his head on the floor.

There was a pause. "Fine."

Bennett was so certain he was going to die that when he heard the sudden cry he jumped in surprise.

"No!" a tiny voice screamed.

Horrified, Bennett snapped his eyes open and tilted his head toward the kitchen doorway so he could see Dreyson standing there. "Dreyson, run!" Bennett cried, knowing he wasn't going to be able to protect the boy. Bennett didn't want the child to watch if The Doc decided to pull the trigger.

Ignoring his cry, Dreyson stared at The Doc while poised in a way that expressed defiance. His head was held high and his expression was stubborn. "I'll go with you, but you have to promise that you won't hurt him!"

"No, Dreyson!" Bennett shouted as he began to panic. "Just go! Get out of here!"

"Dr. Bennett, if you don't be quiet I'm going to have to shoot you," The Doc told him calmly, but with a hint of annoyance.

"You won't shoot him," Dreyson said softly, almost sounding like a challenge. Bennett really hoped the child wasn't purposely antagonizing The Doc.

He looked back at The Doc from his place on the floor, and saw The Doc's intense desire to prove Dreyson wrong. "You knew I wouldn't before I even got here, didn't you?" Dreyson must have nodded, because The Doc then sighed in disappointment. "Okay, fine. Let's go."

The Doc still didn't lower the gun, and Dreyson refused to move. "You have to promise that you won't hurt him," he repeated sternly. Bennett would have sworn he saw a smirk beginning to play at the boy's lips. Dreyson knew he was toying with The Doc, and he was enjoying it.

The Doc was having difficulty meeting Dreyson's terms. "I promise that I won't hurt him," he said in a long, sarcastic drawl to emphasize his impatience.

"And put your gun away," Dreyson commanded, folding his arms stubbornly.

Pursing his lips, The Doc shoved the gun into his lab coat. "I cannot believe I am actually negotiating with a three-year-old," he grumbled angrily.

Placing his little hands on his hips, Dreyson gave The Doc a sassy shake of his head and stuck out his tongue. It would have made Bennett laugh if he had not been lying injured on his floor. The boy got his attitude from his mother, without a doubt.

"Now get over here!" The Doc ordered with a wave of his hand and a grouchy look on his face.

"Yes, ma'am," Dreyson replied cheerfully, starting to go to him. He got halfway past Bennett before he stopped and went to his side. Kneeling down so he could whisper in his ear, he cupped his hands over his mouth so The Doc could not hear. "Wait here until my daddy gets here. He'll help you."

"Your daddy's gone," Bennett whispered back softly.

"He'll help you," Dreyson repeated insistently.

"Will you be okay?" Bennett asked.

Nodding, Dreyson answered, "Yes, and so will you." He pointed to where The Doc had struck him. Rising back to his feet, the toddler waddled over to The Doc. "Bye!" he said, giving Bennett a small smile and wave.

"Yes, goodbye," The Doc muttered, glaring at Bennett as he picked up Dreyson and walked out.

Remembering the promise he made to Hara to protect her baby while she was gone, a pang of guilt stabbed Bennett in his chest. Ironically, Dreyson was the one who had to protect Bennett. Bennett tried to rise so he could go after The Doc. Unfortunately, he found that he could barely push himself up on one elbow.

He couldn't get up. The Doc had really hurt him.

✳ ✳ ✳

He was only three years old, but Dreyson knew things that many adults did not. Many human adults, anyway. Dreyson was a very complex child. He was quiet, but he knew things that would shock his own mother. No one knew it, but speaking to people in the afterlife was his real ability. Everyone thought that he could see into the future, but that wasn't the truth. The souls who were still thirsting for life came to him and told him what was to come. Those poor souls wanted to hang onto anything they could in the world of the living, and Dreyson allowed them to speak to him and in return they gave him information regarding his future and the future of those closest to him.

Now that so many people he knew had passed on to the afterlife, Dreyson had been communicating with the dead much more than the living. His family had spoken to him numerous times and told him many terrifying things, most of which had already come to pass. Recently, Daniel Marcus came to him to warn him of what was coming. Thanks to him, the boy knew exactly how the following events would unfold, and that was why he had decided to go with The Doc. Daniel told him to. Everything that would happen in the next several hours was already foretold by Daniel, and although things would get ugly, it was the most acceptable route to take, considering the consequences any other path would hold. Dreyson was able to see anything he wanted to, even his entire future, but there was one thing that no one had the answer to, and it was the one thing that he absolutely needed to know: Why did The Doc hurt his mommy?

For the first time since The Doc took him from Dr. Bennett's care, Dreyson looked up and made eye contact with him. The Doc brought him into a diner and actually bought him food. They were sitting in a booth in the far corner of the restaurant away from everyone else.

Several minutes passed since their food arrived, but Dreyson hadn't touched his yet. He watched The Doc eat his basket of food.

The Doc must have been watching him, because when Dreyson looked up it was almost as if he was waiting to meet the boy's gaze. As he chewed, The Doc stared into Dreyson and narrowed his eyes before ordering, "Eat."

Gazing back silently for a moment, Dreyson's thoughts didn't drift in the slightest towards the plate of food in front of him. "Can I ask you a question?" he asked quietly.

"No," The Doc replied sternly, frowning at him.

"Why are you giving me food now and you never did while me and my mommy were in your lab?" Dreyson asked, ignoring The Doc's attitude.

Looking extremely annoyed, The Doc snapped, "Just shut up and eat your food."

Blinking, little Dreyson decided it was time to ask his big question; the question no one could find an answer to in all their searching. "Why did you do all that bad stuff to my family just to hurt my mommy?"

The Doc stopped chewing and slowly raised his eyes to meet Dreyson's awaiting expression. Swallowing, he cleared his throat and folded his hands neatly upon the table. Clearly, it was a question that he felt deserved an honest answer. It was probably because deep down, he knew what he had done was wrong. So, so wrong. "It wasn't my initial goal to hurt your mom," he explained softly, managing to hold Dreyson's small yet powerful gaze. "I didn't set out to hurt her. That wasn't how it started."

"You just wanted to hurt my grandpa," Dreyson accused, remembering his grandpa talking about that fact before.

The Doc's eyes hardened. "Your grandpa was a bad man," The Doc replied harshly. "He hurt me. He hurt me badly."

"Then why did you hurt Mommy like that?" Dreyson demanded, growing angrier. "If you knew how painful it was to lose your family, then why did you make Mommy suffer?"

The Doc continued to stare at Dreyson while he was lost in thought. Maybe The Doc didn't even understand why he had chosen Hallie. "I didn't want to hurt her," he said in a whisper. "I just...needed someone to understand me, and I felt like that person was her." He looked away.

Dreyson remained silent for a few seconds to allow The Doc to dwell on his past wrongdoings and realize what he had done to Hallie was cruel and selfish. After feeling that the truth had sunk in far enough, Dreyson asked another question. "Do you love her?"

This time, The Doc didn't look back up. "You wouldn't understand," he muttered. It was his way of saying yes.

"I understand much more than you give me credit for," Dreyson replied.

"Of course you do," The Doc growled, glaring back stonily at him. "You're three years old, yet you speak better than many adults do. That alone shows that you understand things. But then there's your gift that allows you to know everything." He narrowed his eyes even more. "You know how things are going to end tonight."

Dreyson just stared back at The Doc's penetrating eyes.

Cocking his head, The Doc asked very quietly, "So how is this whole thing going to end? Is she going to kill the boy? Am I going to die?"

Raising his eyebrows, Dreyson replied in the same tone of voice, "One can only hope." Reaching out to his plate while keeping his eyes locked on The Doc's, he pulled it towards him and started nibbling on some French fries. For once, Dreyson was the one with all the information, but how was The Doc going to get it out of him? He couldn't in front of all these people. Dreyson, despite his young age, was in complete control. And he loved it.

* * *

Walter Reifert had never met the girl who had taken him, but just like his dad, he felt like he knew her. She was kind to him and had a warm smile, and her eyes were exactly like his and his dad's, giving her a sweet familiarity. There was something else inside of her eyes though. A secret. Something was locked away in those eyes of hers that might hold the answer to their mysterious connection. It was obvious that she felt it too, and she most likely already knew what the connection was. Whatever it may be, it was clear that she had come to protect him from something.

After the girl called Hallie—just like his mom—and the young man named Davey took him from his dad, they went across the street to the hospital and climbed into the back of an ambulance waiting for them. Another man named Jack was driving it, and in the back there was also a boy, a few years older than Walter who was tied up with duct tape. Hallie didn't like the other boy. Walter knew by the way she snapped at him that she hated him. Walter wondered what the boy did, causing such a sweet girl to hate him so, but when he asked Hallie about it she told him that it didn't matter.

There was a thick piece of tape over the boy's mouth, but Walter saw that he was scared. Fat tears kept streaming down his cheeks, and he continuously pulled at the tape around his wrists. Walter decided that he would talk to the boy when he got a chance to try to comfort him. At school, Walter got into many fights, but he wasn't a bad kid. When he wasn't fighting he was actually very polite to others. Most of the kids in his class liked him and he was very good at helping others when they needed it most. This boy needed his help, and Walter was going to give it to him.

They drove around for a while—seemingly to nowhere at all—and after a few hours Hallie told Jack to "pull in here." She then turned to Walter and said, "You're hungry, right?" Walter was surprised; it was like she had read his mind. He then nodded and she bought him a Cheeseburger Happy Meal from McDonald's. They parked the ambulance in an alley somewhere so they wouldn't attract attention, and Hallie and Davey jumped out of the back to go speak to Jack at the wheel. By the tones of their hushed voices, it sounded as if Hallie was frustrated and it didn't seem like they were going anywhere anytime soon. Peering through the small gap between the passengers' and driver's compartments, Walter made sure the other three were distracted and would stay that way for at least a few minutes. Holding his cheeseburger in one hand, Walter quickly got off of his bench and sat down on the bench next to the other boy.

The boy's eyes went wide with fear as Walter gently peeled the tape off of his mouth. When Walter offered him his cheeseburger, the boy shook his head quickly and whispered fearfully, "She'll kill me!"

"No, she won't," Walter said.

"She tried to last night!" the boy insisted, shooting a nervous glance at Hallie at the front of the ambulance.

"I can't believe that!" Walter scoffed. "She and her friends saved my life."

"She likes you," the boy muttered, looking down.

"She's a good person," Walter assured him.

"She's a horrible person!" the boy hissed. "Do you know how many people my dad told me she's killed?"

"If she were a horrible person, then why would she have saved me?" Walter demanded.

The boy thought about it, then shrugged helplessly and tugged at the tape binding his hands.

"Everything will be okay," Walter promised him, smiling reassuringly. "Don't worry, I'll protect you. What's your name?"

The boy smiled back weakly. "I'm Jackson," he said.

"I'm Walter. How old are you?"

"Ten. You?"

"Eight." Walter peered at him, trying to see if he could recognize Jackson from school. "What school do you go to? I haven't seen you at mine."

"I'm in middle school now," Jackson told him, and appeared to blush. "I skipped a grade."

"Oh." Looking down at his cheeseburger, Walter offered it up a second time.

Jackson looked over at Hallie before taking a bite, making sure she didn't see. He was really worried that she would hurt him, which Walter still found to be ridiculous. How could someone as kind and gentle as Hallie want to hurt a child?

"So what did you do?" Walter asked him curiously as he chewed.

Swallowing and taking another bite, Jackson managed to explain between chews, "I didn't do anything. She just came into my house last night and kept saying that it was all my fault and that she was going to kill me, and then my dad shot her..."

"Your dad shot her?" Walter repeated in shock.

Jackson nodded. "Twice. He's a cop. But she's okay now, and she's back to get me for good this time!" Leaning closer, he whispered, "She has freaky X-Men powers! She can heal herself like Wolverine!"

"Whoa," Walter said in envy and wonder. "I want an X-Men power too!"

"No, you don't," Jackson told him. "Because then you get chased around by my dad and get shot at." He winced and tugged at the tape around his wrists again.

"Are you okay?"

"It's really tight," Jackson complained.

"Here, I'll take it off," Walter said, trying to tear it apart.

"No, don't!" Jackson cried, attempting to pull away.

"Walter!" a sharp voice snapped from behind him.

Whipping around, Walter stared wide-eyed at Hallie, who had suddenly appeared at the open doors. She was frowning up at him from the ground, and she told him in a growl, "Get away from him."

Suddenly scared of the way her penetrating eyes were glaring at him, Walter backed away from Jackson and sat back down on his own bench. He could now understand why Jackson had such a fear of her, and Walter prayed he wouldn't have to be afraid of her as well.

In a single, graceful movement, Hallie jumped up into the back and turned her hateful gaze on Jackson. She scowled down at the terrified boy for a few moments, and then suddenly started for him with her hand raised in a fist.

"No!" Walter cried, leaping to his feet and running in front of Jackson to shield him from her. Throwing his arms out to the sides to show her that he wasn't going to let her hurt him, he stared back at her, fearful she might hurt him too.

Stopping, she warned him, "You stay away from him! Don't even look at him!"

"Why?" Walter demanded, dropping his arms and narrowing his eyes at her. He knew now that she had no intention of hurting him, even though her expression was stern. If she wanted to hurt him, she would have done so already. Besides, he could see in her eyes that she cared for him.

"He's bad news," Hallie replied quietly, with a tone of voice that could freeze a person's soul. "He'll poison your innocence."

"He's not bad!" Walter protested, remembering how scared Jackson was. "He's just like me!"

Bending down so she could look into his face, Hallie whispered fiercely, "He is nothing like you! He's not good like you!"

"How would you know?" Walter snapped. "You don't even know me!"

Hallie looked confused. She remained silent with her mouth halfway open for a few seconds before she asked him, "Why are you defending him?"

"Because he's just a kid like me!" Walter declared angrily. "He didn't do anything! He's nice. You're scaring him and telling him you're going to hurt him! Why would you want to hurt him?"

Standing straight up and setting her jaw, Hallie muttered, "You'll understand someday." Biting her lip as she pondered over the situation, she gestured to the front of the vehicle. "Why don't you go sit in the front? You can ride up there with Jack."

"Do you promise you won't hurt him?" Walter asked cautiously, refusing to move just yet.

Pausing, Hallie gave a slow nod.

Turning to give Jackson a reassuring smile, Walter brushed by Hallie and hopped out of the back.

✳ ✳ ✳

Hara was in shock. She had just witnessed something that took her breath away, and it would be something that would haunt her memory for as long as she lived. She witnessed Walter Reifert comforting Jackson Odau. Walter Reifert, the savior of the Colicians, was defending Jackson Odau, the destroyer of worlds. It was the most ironic thing the world had ever presented her. When they became adults, the two boys would be mortal enemies. If Walter knew what Jackson would become, would he have still comforted him?

Hara closed the back doors of the ambulance and took a seat across from Jackson where Walter had been sitting. She could hear Walter talking cheerfully to Jack and Davey in the front seats. Folding her hands in her lap, she stared sharply across at Jackson. Walter had taken off the tape covering his mouth, and Hara decided against replacing it. She had witnessed an act of compassion from Walter Reifert, and she decided that it was time she did the same. Maybe it would do her some good.

Jackson knew that she was watching him, and he was trying his hardest to avoid her eyes. Every few seconds he would glance up, and when he made eye contact he would quickly look away. He shifted in his seat uncomfortably and pulled his knees up to his chest. His expression was frightened and exhausted. It was so pathetic that it made Hara actually feel a small swell of pity for him.

Hara decided to give him a tiny bit of consolation. "Your dad loves you very much. Did you know that?"

Surprised by her soft voice, Jackson glanced up and stared at her. Hesitantly, he nodded.

Leaning forward and making the boy cower in fear, she asked him, "Do you know why I'm doing this?"

Swallowing hard, the boy shook his head slowly.

She raised her eyebrows. "Would you like to?"

Uncertainty flickering in his eyes, Jackson watched her carefully. "Sure," he said quietly.

She gestured to Walter in the front seat. "You know the boy that was just here with you? Do you know who that was?"

Jackson blinked in confusion and shook his head.

"That's the boy you're going to murder in forty years," Hara hissed at him causing him to shrink away in fright. "And he won't be the first. He's one of millions that will die at your hands."

Tears welling in his eyes, Jackson choked out weakly, "What?"

"I've seen the future," Hara growled. "Do you believe that?" When Jackson nodded, she continued. "In the future, you're a very bad person. You kill millions of people like me and cause many others so much pain. I've seen all of this, and that's why I've come to kill you. I can't let you hurt all those people when I have the ability to stop it from happening."

Horrified, Jackson squeaked, "I don't want to hurt anyone! Why would I ever hurt anyone?"

Narrowing her eyes, Hara said through gritted teeth, "Because you're sick!"

Shaking his head quickly, Jackson's eyes pleaded with hers. "I would never hurt Walter! He was nice to me! I wouldn't hurt a nice person like him!"

"You would, and you will!" Hara snapped, sitting back and folding her arms across her chest firmly.

Fat tears started pouring down his face again and he whimpered, but he didn't argue with her anymore. Continuing to cry, he looked down and hugged his knees to him.

Hara was so angry, and she wanted so badly to kill Jackson Odau right there. Despite her hate for him, she was also a mother, and seeing the child cry gave her a pang of guilt. She had an epiphany then; the boy really was innocent. His future may not be so bright, but at this moment in time he was guilty of no crimes. Maybe she should try to make his last living memories at least somewhat comforting.

Her gaze softening, Hara sighed in sudden remorse for what she was about to do. He was only a child. He couldn't understand how horrible a person he was going to become, because he wasn't a bad kid. Odau had been serious when he said that, and Hara could finally see its truth. It was strange to picture Jackson as good and gentle, because Hara had only seen the destruction he would cause. Maybe Odau was right; maybe it was possible to push the boy in the opposite direction from where he was going to end up. Maybe he did have a potential greater than she could see. Maybe there was a hope that Jackson's future could take a lighter path. Hara's hesitation started to get the better of her, and before it could completely take hold she shook it off. She couldn't take the chance of allowing Jackson to live. Besides, as she had reminded herself before, if she turned back when she was so close to success, then Daniel and Rhett and the rest of her people would have died for nothing, and her past would never change. She needed it to change. If she had to live another day remembering what happened to her and her family, she would lose it for good. She would never be able to recover. Her mind was set. She was killing the boy.

However, Hara decided that a simple act of kindness was not beyond her limits. Raising three of her fingers, she aimed them at Jackson and let out a small portion of her energy. The tape around his wrists and ankles unraveled. Surprised, the boy stared up at her.

Hara couldn't bear to look at the boy for a moment longer. Those cold gray eyes that were haunting her memories were staring at her from the face of a child. Even in this child's face, those eyes still gave off that darkness, that hint of evil. Hara shivered. She shook her head and whispered, "I'm so sorry," before lowering her eyes to the metal floor. It was true. She really was sorry, but she doubted it would be of any comfort to Jackson. After all, he knew as well as she did that he didn't have long to live.

✳ ✳ ✳

It was 9:30 before anyone found Dr. Bennett. He had been lying on his living room floor ever since The Doc left with Dreyson. He was unable to get up or even move much. His door had been left slightly ajar, but no one else in the building had walked by in the past several hours. He was too weak to call out for help, and after The Doc left his home with that innocent child, he honestly wouldn't care if he died right there on his floor.

While he was lying there, he had some time to think over the events of his life. He found that the only thing he regretted was not spending enough time with Amanda before she passed. There was so much more time he could have set aside for her in the happy years they had together.

At the time he assumed they had forever. Had he known that their happiness would have ended so soon, he would have made every moment count. He supposed there isn't a way of knowing when the end is coming. Holding his memories of Amanda in his heart and mind, Bennett sighed and closed his eyes. As the hours passed, he figured he would die in the night and someone would discover his body the next morning.

Just after 9:30, he heard his door slowly creak open. His heart began to pound, but he couldn't summon the strength to raise his head to see who was entering. Light footsteps began to cautiously approach him from behind, and before long Bennett saw two feet enter his line of sight. All he could see were the pair of black boots as the figure came to a halt and loomed over him. Bennett managed to turn his head towards the ceiling just enough so he could see the man.

The man wore black pants, a black sweatshirt, and a black ski mask that obscured his entire face except for his mouth and eyes, which were a bright, sapphire blue. They gleamed with such intensity and power that Bennett knew the man was a Colician. His eyes were also soft, so despite his condition, it didn't appear as if he had any intention of hurting Bennett.

Bennett was expecting Bo, but this man would do just fine. He could tell the newcomer was not Bo by the color of his eyes. Bennett had seen Hara's family photo and he recalled that Bo had dark brown eyes. Gazing up at the man in wonder, Bennett waited for him to explain his presence.

After about a minute of them simply staring at each other, the man finally said, "Hello." His voice was soft, but it had a very flat tone which suggested displeasure. Dreyson had told him that Bo was coming for him, but who was this man and why was he here?

Slowly dropping down to one knee, the man explained, "I'm not Bo, and I understand that you're expecting him. My name's Flint. I'm Hallie's brother."

Flint was telepathic and he had read Bennett's mind. It was strange for Bennett to contemplate. If Flint was really Hara's brother, then wasn't he supposed to be dead?

"I hear you," Flint told him softly. "But I can't explain everything just yet."

"Where's Bo?" Bennett managed to murmur, his remaining strength fading.

"He's on his way," Flint assured.

"I'm here now." More footsteps reverberated around the room, and then another man about the same height and girth and dressed like Flint appeared beside him. He knelt down as well. The only visible difference was his eyes. They were a deep dark brown. It really was Bo. He smiled warmly at Bennett, and his eyes showed kindness. "Hello, Dr. Bennett," Bo greeted quietly. "I understand you've been waiting for me."

"Your son told me you'd come," Bennett slurred, his eyelids fluttering. The doctor faintly recalled he had something to tell Bo, but at the moment he was finding himself unable to remember what. If Bo wanted information from him, he'd have to ask his questions quick. There was no way Bennett would be able to recover from this.

Nodding gently, Bo reached into a hidden pocket in the side of the sweatshirt and pulled out a syringe filled with a dark crimson liquid. "I have something for you. It will make you feel better."

Bennett already knew what it was. "Hallie's blood?" he asked, just to clarify.

Nodding again, Bo injected Bennett in his right arm. "I need your help with something," he said. "Will you help me?"

"Anything for you," Bennett breathed, not even feeling the needle in his arm.

"I need to find my mate," Bo explained, replacing the syringe in his pocket. "She's very sick, and I'm unable to find her here. Do you have any idea where she's going?"

"No," Bennett muttered, but then grabbed Bo's arm as he recalled the reason he was immobile on his floor. "The Doc took your son…"

"I know," Bo murmured. "Dreyson will be just fine. It's Hallie we need to find right now. Are you sure you don't know where she's going?"

"I don't…" Bennett was beginning to feel some of his strength returning, and he thought of something that might be of some help. "Allan Brown said he was taking Meg Hopper back to 'the church' to turn on 'the machine,' so she might have gone there. I think she's going to kill the boy."

"What boy?" Flint asked, suddenly very interested.

"The lieutenant's son," Bennett replied. "Jackson Odau."

Flint and Bo looked at each other. "That's the reason she came back here," Bo whispered to his colleague.

"This is going to be more difficult than we thought," Bo muttered, shaking his head. "I may actually have to shoot her."

"If you really want to stop her, then you'll have to do it fast," Bennett told them, able to push himself up into a sitting position. He didn't understand why they would want to stop her, but that's what it seemed like they were going to do. "Whatever she's got planned, I have a feeling it's going to happen very soon."

"Will you come with us?" Bo asked him hopefully. "We could really use your help."

Nodding, Bennett accepted Bo's hand to help him rise.

673

✳ ✳ ✳

Perry and the rest of his crew were unable to find Lieutenant Odau. By the time 9:00 came around, they gave up and figured they would meet him at the bridge anyway. If Hara allowed them a few minutes, they may even be able to explain to Odau what was really going on.

Perry drove the SUV to the bridge where they were supposed to wait for Hara. It was 9:30 when they arrived. Perry got out almost immediately and rested himself against the hood, and Renee joined him not long after. Neither of them spoke. At 9:50, Finchly joined them; John Reifert remained in the car. He seemed too timid to get involved in the confrontation, and Perry didn't blame him. Once he got in, there would be no way for him to get back out again.

At 9:56, they all leaned forward eagerly as they saw the first set of headlights coming at them. Most of that part of the city had been evacuated due to Hara's threat, so the likelihood that it was someone outside their small circle was remote. As the headlights drew closer, Perry saw that they belonged to a large white cargo van that was slowly coming to a halt not far from the SUV. The windows were tinted and it was impossible to see the occupants, but Perry knew right away that it wasn't Hara. He had new senses now, and he could feel a familiar evil residing within the truck.

Finchly started to take a few steps towards the van, but Perry quickly threw out his arm to stop her. She gave him a confused look. "What's wrong?"

"Don't go over there," Perry instructed, watching the vehicle closely as the headlights remained on and the engine continued to run. Carefully, he extracted his replacement weapon from his holster and kept it at his side, just in case.

Moments later, the headlights blinked out and the engine died down. The driver's door opened to reveal The Doc, nervous yet composed. He stepped out, and to everyone's surprise, Dreyson was tucked under his arm. Little Dreyson appeared calm considering the circumstances, and he didn't struggle to escape. In The Doc's other hand was a gun. When he got a good look at Perry, Renee, and Finchly and started to walk in their direction, he gave them a smirk and said, "Look here. It's my favorite group of people in the whole world."

Perry's gun hand twitched. It would be so easy to just shoot him right there.

Glancing around hopefully, The Doc frowned. "No sign of her yet, I presume?"

"Clearly," Perry replied curtly, glaring at him.

"How did you get Dreyson?" Renee demanded, taking an angry step forward.

Perry heard the maternal concern in her voice, but somehow he knew that everything was okay. Taking hold of her arm, he pulled her back to him. He really didn't want a firefight right now. "Just let it go, honey," he told her softly. "Everything will be fine."

Rounding on him, her eyes pleaded desperately with his. "He's going to hurt him!"

"No," Perry whispered soothingly, shaking his head gently. "He's going to be fine."

She must have seen the truth in his eyes, because Renee pursed her lips and didn't argue any further. Renee, however, wasn't the only one that needed to be reassured.

Perry heard one of the SUV doors pop open and then a very frantic John Reifert was running at The Doc. Perry ran to John and caught him around the shoulders before he could get very far. "Easy!" Perry said, tugging John back to the SUV. "You don't know what you're getting yourself into..."

"Let me go!" John commanded, fighting against Perry's firm hold.

"Just relax!" Perry ordered, shoving him back inside. "Dreyson will be fine!"

"I have to get him back!" John insisted breathlessly. "He's my—"

"I know!" Perry assured him, placing his hands on John's shoulders to keep him from bolting again. "I know what he is to you. But if you want to keep him safe, you have to leave him where he is. He'll be just fine, okay?"

"How could you know?" John asked in a whisper, his expression distraught.

"I just do," Perry told him, smiling lightly. "Now please, stay here until we've sorted through this mess."

Hesitating, John nodded in defeat and sat back in his seat. He looked at the floor as Perry closed the door and locked the vehicle.

Perry turned back towards The Doc, expecting to see a bold smirk on his face. It was quite surprising for Perry to see that he had a very solemn expression and an aura of extreme anxiety about him. Then it hit Perry; The Doc was under a great deal of pressure. Hara seemed quite certain about killing Jackson Odau this time, and if he couldn't stop her then he was going to lose the most valuable thing in the world to him. It wasn't a time for his sense of humor to be out and about. For the first time since Perry met him, The Doc was actually afraid. Comforted by that fact, Perry stared back into his empty gaze and wondered how it must feel to be in The Doc's position. It was sad to know that Jackson was the only thing in either of their worlds that The Doc truly cared about. It just proved that his life was empty and no one else was of any value to him.

Three impossibly long minutes passed. For two of the three, he and The Doc had a stare down contest. Neither of them blinked or shifted their gaze. Normally, it would have made Perry uncomfortable, but he had gained a new confidence that wouldn't let him falter easily. He was the one with the ability and the remarkable new power, so it was his turn to be the intimidating one. There wasn't anything The Doc could do to him that he hadn't already done, so why should Perry fear him any longer? No, it was Perry's turn to be feared; it was The Doc's turn to be afraid.

Keeping his firearm at his side, Perry marched across the distance separating them and came to a halt several feet from The Doc. It was close enough for them to have a private conversation, but also gave him enough space to react if The Doc attacked him again. He glared at The Doc, and The Doc's gaze wasn't much kinder. It was challenging for Perry to remain calm as he stood in such close proximity, but he had to let The Doc know that he knew everything. "I know your secret," Perry growled.

"Do you?" The Doc replied in a low voice, not appearing convinced.

"I finally know why it is Hara wants to kill Jackson so badly," Perry said quietly. "I understand why you want to keep him alive as much as you do, and why you're afraid of what the consequences will be if he does die."

The Doc gave a dry laugh. "So you've finally figured it out. After all this time, the reality of this situation has finally hit you." Cocking his head to one side, he asked suspiciously, "Did it have something to do with the envelope that your Reifert friend wanted to give you?"

Nodding slowly, Perry added, "And do you know what else? I doubt I would have ever been able to figure it out without help. You were right, as much as I hate to admit it. The answers to all my questions were right before my eyes."

The Doc's expression didn't change. "Do you understand now why no one told you the truth at the beginning of all this?" he asked.

Perry nodded again. "Because I wouldn't have believed it."

Snickering, The Doc replied, "People of this time just don't believe that anything of this magnitude could ever be possible. They're all so narrow-minded." He chuckled, a dry, hoarse sound.

"They'll see," Perry agreed, snickering as well.

"You're not going to tell him, are you?" The Doc asked quickly as Perry started to turn away. There was a slight hint of agitation in his voice.

Raising his eyebrows, Perry said, "Who, Jackson?"

"No," The Doc grumbled, and with great difficulty said, "The lieutenant."

"Of course I'm going to tell him," Perry replied, and upon seeing The Doc's unnerved expression, it dawned on him. "That's it," he whispered. "You're ashamed of what you've done! You're ashamed and you don't want Odau to know the truth!"

The muscles in his face twitching, The Doc hissed through gritted teeth, "I just don't want to deal with him right now."

Laughing scornfully, Perry demanded, "Are you afraid of what he might think?"

Trying to contain his fury, The Doc growled, "This conversation is over."

Shaking his head and smirking, Perry started to turn to leave again.

"Oh, and Perry?" The Doc called, and when Perry turned he whispered, "You might want to watch your back."

Catching the threat, Perry's own fury arose inside him. "You can't hurt me any more than you already have!" he snapped. "I don't need to be afraid of you!"

"Then why are you still keeping your distance from me?" The Doc taunted.

Glaring, Perry said, "I truly hope that this is the last conversation we ever have!"

"Oh, trust me," The Doc chuckled. "You and I both know we have many more to come."

Scowling in disgust, Perry turned and started back to his colleagues. He knew he had nothing to fear, but nevertheless he still felt uneasy with his back turned. There really wasn't anything more The Doc could do to hurt him, was there? His instincts told him that The Doc had one last surprise waiting for him. Perry would have to be extremely cautious as to what—and who—he left vulnerable.

The sound of a car rapidly approaching from behind caused Perry to snap around. The Doc turned also, and he lowered Dreyson to the ground but kept a firm hand around his wrist. As everyone gazed at the headlights and the flashing emergency lights, Perry relaxed slightly. It was Lieutenant Odau. He was speeding; that was clear by the roar of the engine as it quickly approached. When he got fairly close to the group, Perry thought that he was just going to fly by them without stopping. But the brakes on the squad car sounded, and it squealed to a halt beside the SUV, leaving black tire marks on the road and the smell of burning rubber in the air. Perry glanced at his watch as Odau jumped out and left the car running and the lights flashing. It was 9:59. One more minute.

Panting breathlessly, Odau looked around frantically and began running over to Perry's group. "Where is she?"

"She hasn't come yet," Perry answered, glancing to his colleagues uncertainly. Their expressions were urging and insistent. They knew the truth, and they knew that it was time Odau learned the truth as well.

Turning his head to The Doc, who had insisted that Perry keep the truth from Odau, Perry saw him shake his head as a reminder.

"It's ten o'clock!" Odau protested, the pitch of his voice rising dramatically.

"We still have a minute," Perry reassured him. "Relax. We're not going to miss anything."

"Yeah," Odau snapped. "That's so easy for you to say because it isn't your child's life on the line!"

"And you won't be the only one who has sacrificed something!" Perry shot back angrily.

Looking to Perry, Renee whispered, "Shawn, it's time. He has to know."

Staring back into her blue eyes, Perry nodded. He gazed at Odau's furious face and sighed. "We know the truth now."

"The truth about what?" Odau demanded, not appearing as if he wanted to listen.

"About everything," Perry said. "Where the Colicians are from, why Hara wants to kill Jackson, and who Jackson really is."

Shaking his head hard, Odau took several steps backwards. "I don't want to hear it," he stated firmly.

"Please, you really need to…" Perry insisted, but Odau cut him off quickly.

"I've already decided that I don't care what Jackson is going to become!" Odau shouted. "He's my son, and I'm not going to just let some bitch murder him out of some sick sense of self-righteousness!"

"Lieutenant, please!" Perry pleaded desperately, wishing the stubborn man would listen to him. Just once.

"Perry," The Doc said warningly, raising his eyebrows. He wasn't going to fight Perry, but he really wanted his secret to remain a secret.

Ignoring him, Perry told Odau, "I think once you understand the severity of—"

"I don't care about the Colicians or why one of them went crazy!" Odau cried in a rage. "All I care about is my son!"

His jaw tightening, Perry shook his head. "If that's all you truly care about," Perry started quietly, "then you really are your son's father."

Turning back on him as he started to move away, Odau snarled, "What did you just say to me?"

"She's coming!" Finchly declared as Perry began to reply.

Both men peered around the SUV in the direction where Finchly was pointing. They were surprised to see the back end of an ambulance slowly and steadily approaching. The brake lights were on and it took a little while for it to reach them. Perry's watch read 10:00 exactly; Hara was right on time, and things were about to become very interesting.

Odau drew out his gun when the ambulance slowed to a halt between Perry's SUV and Odau's squad car, and out of the corner of his eye, Perry could see The Doc taking out a weapon as well. The lights of the ambulance flickered out, and the back doors suddenly burst open. Perry gasped as Jackson was practically thrown out of the back. As the boy struck the ground with a yelp of pain, Perry wished he had gotten the chance to explain the situation to Odau. It would have been a little easier for the lieutenant to handle the events which followed.

※ ※ ※

Immediately after jumping out of the back of the ambulance, Hara whipped out a gun from her belt and aimed it at Jackson's head. As she gazed around and breathed in the cool night air, she was surprised to see only one gun pointed in her direction, Lieutenant Odau's. Finchly, Michaels, and Perry held theirs lightly at their sides, and as she turned her eyes on The Doc she saw that he had a gun aimed at Dreyson's head. Dreyson was standing in front of The Doc, his wrist being held firmly by the vile man, but he appeared to be composed and unharmed. The toddler smiled when they made eye contact and with his free hand he gave a little wave of greeting. Hara inhaled sharply and her eyes narrowed harshly when they met The Doc's again.

The Doc's response was what it always was; a smirk. Only this time, it was masking his own fear. "Hello, Hallie," he said pleasantly.

Reaching down quickly, she dragged Jackson to his feet and put the gun to his temple. The boy whimpered in pain, but Hara was too angry to care.

"I wouldn't do that if I were you," The Doc told her calmly, but his eyes said that he was anything but calm.

"Well, I'm not you," Hara hissed, keeping her finger on the trigger.

Cocking the gun pointed at Dreyson's head, The Doc's eyes narrowed. It was time for him to make his final stand before everything he worked for was destroyed. He was no longer afraid. "Maybe we should talk this over," he suggested quietly, his finger resting on the trigger as well.

"We've had our share of talks," Hara growled through her teeth. "We have nothing left to talk about."

"Okay, I'll try to make this a little clearer for you," The Doc snarled, glaring at her. "I will kill your son if you don't put that gun down now!"

"If you kill him, then I'll kill Jackson," Hara replied smoothly, not feeling at all worried about the threat. She had the upper hand in this. The Doc was in an impossible position. He was doomed either way.

Thinking it over, The Doc's nostrils flared as a flash of panic crossed his face. His voice shaking, he tried again. "And if you shoot him, then I'll kill your son for sure!"

"If I shoot him, then you won't be able to pull the trigger," Hara reminded him smugly.

He couldn't pretend to be tough anymore. There was no point. In the end, The Doc allowed one girl to see into him. Despite everything he had done and everything he appeared to be, an angry, frightened man was all he ever was. "Please," he whispered. He had come to his last resort: begging. "You know what will happen. You can't change the course of history like this."

Taking comfort in his fear, Hara gave him a smirk. "Watch me," she said quietly. She shoved Jackson back to the ground, raised the gun, and cocked it.

A variety of noises erupted around her. Jackson cried in fear and covered his head with his arm where he lay. The Doc let out a fearful cry and Odau screamed, "God, no!" But above all of it; Hara stopped when she heard Perry's voice.

"Hara," he called softly.

Keeping her gun level with Jackson's head, Hara turned at the sound of Perry's gentle voice. He was gazing at her solemnly with his hands raised to her. His gun was replaced in his holster and he took a few careful steps in her direction.

"Please," he begged, his eyes pleading. "Let us explain to the lieutenant what is really going on here."

Hara looked to The Doc in shock, searching for some answers in his eyes. Perry knew? How could he have learned the truth? Did the letter John gave him explain everything? The Doc's face was stony. He was offering her nothing.

"I told you before!" Odau snapped furiously. "I don't want to hear it! I don't care!"

Looking back at Perry's pleading gaze, Hara hardened herself again. As she felt Jack and Davey linger several feet behind her to watch, she told him, "If he chooses to listen, you can explain it once I'm gone." Ignoring Perry's pained expression, Hara turned back to Jackson.

"Wait!" Odau cried suddenly, and as Hara glanced over impatiently, he did something nobody was expecting him to do. Tossing his gun away, he dropped to his knees. He was going to beg, just like The Doc. His face filled with grief, he pleaded, "I'll do anything! I'll help you put those who are guilty in prison. I'll help you rebuild what was destroyed. Just please, don't do this!"

Hara felt evil like The Doc when she narrowed her eyes mercilessly at him, but once again, she didn't care. "Mark this day," she said. "Mark this day as the day that the Colicians made their stand. No longer will we stand by and allow the humans to spit on us and treat us like animals. No longer will we pleasantly try to work through your threats and attacks peacefully. Now, the Colicians will be the ones holding all the cards. We will kill anyone who threatens to jeopardize our peaceful existence, starting with this boy."

"Hallie, please," Odau whispered helplessly, tears wetting his face. "Do you remember what you said to me in Bennett's apartment? You told me that you had lost your children, and that you never wanted to put another parent through that. Please, don't make me suffer as well. Don't do this to me."

"This isn't about you and me," Hara told him softly. "This is so much bigger than just you and me."

"Look at my son," Odau instructed desperately, stalling for a few more seconds. "And then look at yours. Do you see? They're the same. And so are we."

"Our sons are not the same!" Hara snapped angrily, refusing to look.

"They're both children," Odau said quietly.

"And how are we the same?"

"We're both parents fighting to save a child," Odau whispered, his tears glistening in the dim light of the headlights. Shaking his head slowly, he pleaded, "Please don't kill my son. It will only prove you to be just as bad as The Doc. Don't let anyone else suffer. Please!"

Hara looked down at Jackson cowering beneath her with a terrified expression. Then, she looked at Dreyson being held by The Doc with a gun to his head, the boy still as calm as ever. Looking back at Jackson, Hara suddenly recalled a memory that she had placed in the back of her mind for a reason. Right before her soul mate Bo had been murdered, their eldest son Colin had been shot and killed as well. Hara was forced to watch in agony, and she could never forget the fear and desperation in her baby boy's eyes. She now saw Colin beneath her, holding onto his last few living moments like they were treasure. For a moment, just a moment, Hara's gaze softened at Jackson lying helpless on the ground. Could she really murder a child in cold blood while looking him in the eyes? Hara looked the boy in the eyes and saw the cold grayness in them, and remembered what—and who—he was going to become. Her gaze still soft, she stared into Jackson's cold eyes and said not just to him, but to everyone, "I'm sorry."

She pulled the trigger.

18

Saving Hallie Reifert

Things started happening very quickly. Perry saw Hara squeeze the trigger, but it wasn't her gun that fired. The first shot struck her in the arm and caused her to release her weapon with a gasp of pain. The next several shots struck her in the chest and stomach and then she was on the ground. Perry was able to witness the agony and surprise on her face before she went down. After she did, she didn't move. Perry was both relieved and furious. Who shot her? He turned to see.

Odau let out a horrifying scream at the sound of the first shot, jumped to his feet, and scrambled over to his son. Jackson clung to him and sobbed. Hara hadn't pulled her trigger fast enough to put a bullet in him. The boy was okay. The lieutenant's weapon wasn't in his hand at the first shot, so it couldn't have been him that saved his son.

Looking at The Doc, Perry saw that he was still holding Dreyson by the arm and the gun was still aimed at the toddler's head. The only change was his dumbfounded expression. He had been so close to his end.

Neither Finchly nor Renee had shot her, and Jack and Davey hadn't moved since they came out of the ambulance. Perry looked around frantically, but no one he looked at had a weapon raised or an expression showing anything but shock.

Then came the squealing tires and the roaring of car engines. Perry looked in both directions and saw two large trucks coming from either direction. Their headlights pierced the blackness of the night as they came barreling towards the group.

Perry jumped as he heard one of the doors of his SUV slam shut. Turning his head, he tried to react fast enough to catch John Reifert by the arm as he ran past, but he was unsuccessful. "John!" Perry cried out as he ran to Hara's side, but he had bigger things to fret about than John Reifert. His heart started to beat faster with anticipation as the vehicles drew closer.

"Hey!" a small voice said, and then young Walter rushed over to his father to peer down at Hara's motionless form as well. "Is she okay?" he asked.

As his father answered him in a voice too low for Perry to hear, Jack and Davey finally dared to approach their friend, cautiously stepping around the Reiferts to get a better look.

Perry looked around quickly again as both trucks squealed to a halt, boxing them in on the bridge. For a few seconds, both trucks sat with their engines running. Then the high beams on both of them were turned on and Perry was blinded for a moment. Blinking, Perry's sight returned in time to see several men jumping out of both trucks and running towards the group. In a sudden flash of fear, Perry started to raise his weapon, but before he knew what was happening he was on the ground and staring up at the starry sky in a daze. He had absolutely no idea what caused him to collapse, but his head was spinning uncontrollably and his chest was rising and falling quickly with his rapid breathing. There were at least three men standing over Perry; he was aware of that much. Panic pounding through his veins, he tried to sit up and raise his gun, but he found that his weapon was no longer in his possession. Several strong hands pushed him back down.

"Just take it easy, Dr. Perry," a firm voice ordered, but the tone seemed almost friendly.

Squinting up at the man, Perry attempted to ask him, "What did you just call me?" He found that he was unable to speak.

As Perry's vision stopped spinning, he saw that the man gazing into his face had brilliant blue eyes, with a light in them that could only mean one thing: he was a Colician. There was a kindness in the Colician's eyes that Perry could not explain. Somehow this man whom he had never met knew him just like Hara and her colleagues had.

"Sorry about that," the Colician apologized. "But I didn't want you to shoot me."

Rolling his head around, Perry saw that Renee and Finchly were also lying on the ground, several men standing over each of them and handcuffing them. Looking back into the man's kind eyes, Perry found his voice again. "Who are you?"

The man slowly reached up and pulled off his mask. He was a few years younger than Perry and had a head full of curly blonde hair. Peering down at Perry, he sighed in disappointment. "I suppose you wouldn't know me yet."

Perry started to resist when he felt his own wrists being cuffed, but the blonde Colician put a hand on his shoulder to stop him. "We're not going to hurt you," he promised in a soothing voice, smiling gently once more. "Please don't take this personally."

"You wouldn't believe how many times I've been told that today," Perry muttered at him, but he obliged.

Chuckling, the blonde helped him to his feet. "I'd believe it," he told him.

Perry glanced down at the cuffs in disapproval, but didn't fight against them. What was the point? All the men in the trucks were Colicians, and the Colicians would never hurt him if everything Hara claimed was the truth. Perry gratefully accepted the hand that was extended to him to help him rise.

Another man stepped in front of Perry, and he was different from the first. He had a light in his deep brown eyes as well, but it was a different light. He didn't gaze at Perry with the same kindness as the first, but there was a great amount of respect in them. The new man made Perry uneasy and he started to take a step back nervously, but the blonde Colician was somehow comforting him. He could feel the slight pressure of the man's mind on his own and immediately felt calmer. The blonde clearly had some form of telepathic ability.

"Thank you," the second man said. He didn't say anything more, but those two words spoke thousands more. Even though his eyes were not as compassionate as the blonde's, there was an emotion in them that was far more powerful. The gratitude and grief expressed in just those two words were being broadcast through his eyes as well as his voice.

At first, Perry was puzzled as to what the man meant by "Thank you," but it quickly began to sink in. From the man's pure emotion, Perry started putting the pieces together. He had never met the man before and could only see his eyes, but he suddenly knew who he was.

"Bo," Perry whispered. He had never seen a picture of Hara's soul mate, but he knew it was him. Bo was expressing gratitude to him for saving Hallie. Not just from The Doc, but from herself. Perry's group had managed to keep her from killing Jackson just long enough for Bo to miraculously return. Had she killed the boy, she would no longer have any trace of Hallie Reifert left inside of her. If that had happened there would be no way back for her.

Nodding, Bo started to turn away. "You were doing good even when you thought you weren't," he told him. "Thank you for saving my girl."

Perry nodded in return and watched curiously as Bo walked away from him and approached The Doc. He could only imagine the amount of rage Bo had for the man.

Half a dozen men from the truck farthest from Perry surrounded The Doc and took a threatening stance. None of them had weapons, and Perry figured they didn't need them. As he already knew, Bo was not a Colician but a Caiten, and Caitens had a telepathic ability that could outmatch half a dozen Colicians. It seemed most likely that Bo came back with a group of Caiten colleagues to rescue Hara and the other Colicians trapped on Earth. It would make sense. The Colicians and Caitens shared a world and had fought in the war together, so it wasn't peculiar that the Caitens would come to assist their brothers and sisters. It was amazing for Perry to see two species so very different fighting alongside each other. Humans were separated by countries and races and would never be able to work with another species because they couldn't even get along with their own. For the first time since his transformation, Perry felt glad for the change. He could see by the way the two races were working together that living in the Colician society would be so much better than living among the humans. It would be a more peaceful existence.

There was the question of how Bo was there, though. Bo was dead, and Hara hadn't been capable of changing the past. It was impossible for him to be there. If one lost soul could be brought back and made whole again, then the same could be done for the billions who were lost in the battle. If only Hara had known this sooner, she wouldn't have suffered the loss of her fallen colleagues on Earth, and she wouldn't have come back to fix things. Or would she still have?

Bo stopped not three feet from The Doc. After staring into his eyes for several long moments, he reached up and took off his mask. He was taller than The Doc and carried himself with the rage he must have been feeling, making him appear more intimidating. The Doc's face was nervous and surprised, and his grip tightened around Dreyson's arm. Upon seeing Dreyson's father standing before him—who was supposed to be dead—The Doc lowered the gun pointed at the boy's head. "Bo?" he asked warily.

"Get your hands off of my son," Bo replied quietly, and then punched him in the face. The force of the blow knocked The Doc clean off his feet and sent him sprawling. Luckily, he had released Dreyson so the toddler didn't go down with him. Exhaling slowly as if to calm himself, Bo reached down to his beaming son and scooped him into his arms. Dreyson hugged him around the neck and Bo lovingly returned the embrace. Turning, he finally permitted Perry to see his face. He was much older than Hara—six or seven years at least—but that wasn't what Perry noticed. The pain on the young man's face would have been unbearable even to the toughest of men. Tears were pouring from the corners of his eyes, and the eyes themselves screamed a thousand agonized words. Bo was grieving; he was suffering. He must have known exactly what The Doc had done to his family, and now he was feeling their pain.

Perry had a feeling that if he were still human, he wouldn't hear what Bo and Dreyson were whispering to each other. "I'm sorry I was gone so long," Bo told his son.

"I knew you would come back," Dreyson replied, nuzzling his head into his father's shoulder.

"Bo?"

Hara's voice was weak and confused. She still hadn't moved since her collapse, but as Bo turned at the sound of her voice, she began to stir. Her body was weary from major regeneration, and she was having difficulty sitting up. She tried several times to push herself upright onto her elbows, but her arms were shaking and she repeatedly fell back against the ground.

As Bo watched this, more agony flashed across his face. Keeping Dreyson curled up in his arms, he walked over to where his mate lay wounded. His footsteps were heavy, and Perry knew by the way he was carrying himself that Bo could feel her pain. Stopping at her side, he looked up at John Reifert who rose at Bo's approach. The two men stared each other down, and then smiled with recognition. John knew Bo from the vision Hara had given him, and Bo clearly recognized John. An aura of trust burned about them as Bo carefully handed Dreyson to John. After another moment John took Dreyson and Walter back towards Perry's SUV so they could give Bo and Hara some space.

Stiffly, Bo crouched down so he could be closer to Hara. He smiled gently. "Hey," he whispered softly, reaching out to allow a strand of her hair to fall through his fingers.

Forcing herself to raise her head, Hara squinted at her soul mate in stunned silence. Her eyes were red and surrounded by purple circles. Breathing with great difficulty, she started to push herself up again. "Bo," she whispered with determination. It was no longer a question.

"Don't stress yourself," Bo told her, placing his hand on her shoulder to steady her.

"You're really here," she breathed, ignoring his advice. Gaping at him in awe, she sputtered, "How are you...you can't..." She looked at Jackson Odau, who was still crying in the sheltered arms of his father. "I didn't kill him!" Looking back at Bo in desperate confusion, several tears trickled out of her eyes. Reaching out, she cautiously extended a hand towards his face, as if he might bite her. Seeing her hesitation, Bo took her hand in his own and rested it against his cheek, his eyes softening at her touch. Hara gasped at the feeling of his warmth beneath her fingertips, and more tears flowed as she gave him a small smile. "I didn't change anything," she sobbed.

"You didn't have to, Hallie," he replied mournfully. With an even greater sadness than before, he placed both hands on either side of her head.

Perry couldn't tell what Bo was doing, but whatever it was, it was causing Hara pain. Her eyes widened and her hands snapped to his before her face scrunched up and she let out a pained cry. "Stop!" she managed to scream, but she was weakening once again.

"I'm sorry, sweetie," Bo murmured as Hara's expression calmed and became peaceful. Her eyes drifted closed, and Bo carefully lowered her until she was lying flat on the ground. He gazed down at his beautiful, damaged mate for a long while before standing up and rounding on The Doc. His expression beyond rage, he growled, "How I wish I could kill you for what you've done to her!" His entire body was heaving up and down with his fury. "Luckily for you, there's somebody back home who wants you unscathed!" Looking to the rest of his Caiten comrades, he ordered, "Cuff him! Put him in the van with the others and meet me at the church." Bending down, he effortlessly scooped up his mate and started for his truck.

"Hey!" Jack said in protest, rushing up and catching Bo by the arm. "What are you going to do with her?"

Giving Jack a glare that could freeze magma, Bo snarled, "What you couldn't!"

Stunned, Jack stared at Bo's back as he continued with Hara to his truck. It was easy to sense that Jack knew he had done wrong by Hara. He had urged her to commit the heinous act that would have ultimately destroyed her. Bo yelled back at him, "If you really loved her, you would have tried to save her, not push her deeper into the dark hole she was already stuck in!"

Jack turned toward Perry and made eye contact with him for a split second, and Perry saw the regret. He nearly destroyed the girl he was trying to help.

As Bo reached the truck, he turned and called, "Mr. Reifert? Will you come with me? And bring our sons."

John Reifert took Walter's hand and brought him and Dreyson to the truck. He lifted Dreyson into the back and then helped Walter up before climbing in the back himself. Bo was still holding Hara in his arms as he called out, "Flint, you'll want to come as well."

The blonde stepped away from Perry's side and jogged over to the truck. He climbed in the driver's side and started the truck while Bo put Hara in the back with the rest of her family and then jumped in the back as well. Just before he closed the doors, he made eye contact with Perry one last time and nodded again in respect and gratitude.

The truck drove past all of them and began speeding off in the direction Perry's SUV had come. The rest of Bo's comrades stopped what they were doing and watched as the Reiferts left. All of the others—Perry, Finchly, Renee, Lieutenant Odau, and Jackson—looked on as well. Perry thought it was a mutual peace they were all beginning to feel. His heart felt like it was folding in on itself. It was beautiful to see a broken family being put back together again.

Gazing at the people surrounding him, Perry felt like he had accomplished a great thing. It seemed like months ago to him, but that morning he made a promise to a dying man that he would save a dying girl named Hallie Reifert. After much struggle, pain, and death, he lived up to his promise. Special Agent Shawn Perry saved eighteen-year-old Hallie Reifert. He didn't save her from The Doc. He didn't save her from the human race. He saved her from herself.

If Perry couldn't be at peace with anything else, he could be at peace with that.

Someone took Perry's arm and brought him back to reality. Another masked colleague of Bo, with Bo's same brown eyes, was gesturing for him to come to the remaining truck. Renee and Finchly were being helped inside, and several other masked men were already inside with the Doc and Dr. Wesley Bennett. Three of the masked Caitens and Colicians were trying to coax Odau and his boy into the truck as well. They were all going to the church with Bo and his family. Maybe, just maybe, they were finally going to get the whole truth. It was time for answers. Staring at the familiar brown eyes, Perry realized that Bo hadn't brought just anyone to help him reunite with his mate. Bo had brought his own family. It was one big family reunion. Whether or not it was going to be a happy one was still to be decided.

Bo's brother smiled at Perry under his mask. "It's time to go, sir," he said softly, taking his arm to help guide him into the truck.

✳ ✳ ✳

Hallie didn't know how much time passed before she woke to a series of steady bumps and jolts. She tried to unglue her eyelids, but just thinking about performing such a task was extremely difficult. When Bo had taken her head in his hands, he had healed her mind. Somewhat, anyway. He found the evil that had taken hold of her inside her mind and destroyed it. He found Hara and killed her. Hara—her counterpart, her parallel—was gone. Now that Hara was gone, Hallie felt quite relieved. She could finally think rationally and begin to comprehend the horrible things she had done. She was in complete control of her actions.

Along with the relief came other emotions as well. She was horrified at everything she had done under Hara's driving rage. Hallie would have never killed children willingly, even if they were guilty of crimes greater than anyone's comprehension. She wanted to scream about what Hara had made her do. Now that Hara was gone, many things that had been suppressed were beginning to come back to kick Hallie in the gut. Hara had been so eager to complete her mission that she had suppressed many of Hallie's needs, such as food and sleep. Hallie could feel her stomach cramping up so painfully from her lack of nutrition that she felt sick. Her exhaustion from the pain and stress she had endured was also finally catching up to her. Every muscle in her body ached and she was so tired that she could barely open her eyes, let alone move her body.

After she pushed her physical pain to the side, she embraced more of her mental pain. Hallie, unlike Hara, felt more loss for her dead friends. She had lost Daniel and Rhett in the last day, and now she was in her right mind to properly mourn for them. She had gotten them killed for a lost cause, and she could never forgive herself for that.

Bo was back, and that itself caused her agony. It made her remember the rest of her family who had perished in this damned war because of her. She should have forced The Doc to take her when she first tried to give herself up. Nobody else would have had to die. The Doc...that son of a bitch had been the creator of Hara! He was the cause of everything! He killed Rhett and Daniel and all of her family. He had transformed her into a monster! Would that psychotic bastard ever pay for what he had done?

Hallie forced her eyelids open a crack. She was in one of the trucks that Bo and his array of Colician, Caiten, and human helpers had arrived in. She was in the back, and a few others were there with her. It was barely possible for her to make out the silhouettes of John Reifert, Walter, Dreyson, and Bo around her. Walter was sitting on John's lap to her right, and Dreyson was asleep in Bo's arms to her left. It was a sweet sight to see her son finally reunited with his daddy. Seeing her family being slowly put back together made her want to be a part of it as well. She didn't want to be alone any longer.

With great effort that caused her to groan softly, Hallie made her eyes open all the way. Hearing her beginning to wake, Bo looked down into her troubled eyes and smiled. Even though he hadn't been there to see her suffer through everything The Doc had done to her, he knew what she had gone through. She didn't need to read his mind to know that; everything he was feeling was being expressed through his eyes. He was feeling her pain. That was how the soul mate system worked.

Hallie tried to smile back at him, but it was already taking every ounce of strength just to keep her eyes open. So she took everything in that she possibly could. Bo's deep, dark brown eyes, his smooth, chestnut colored skin, his shining, silky black hair...he looked exactly as he did before his death. The only thing different about him was his sorrowful eyes. It was almost as if he never died. How was it possible? How could he be alive if she didn't change anything? If there had been any other way, Hallie would have taken it to save her species and spare the children. But, as she thought about it, it didn't matter. Hara still would have taken this path of violence. Vengeance was Hara's only motive.

Trying to summon the strength that Hara had provided, Hallie started to lift her head. It was one of the most physically draining things she had ever tried to do. But she was determined. She wasn't about to give up completely. Not yet anyway.

Bo must have seen the strain on her face, because he reached out his hand and gently pushed her head back down. Hallie let him have his way and kept her head down. His smile still there, Bo smoothed back her hair in the delicate manner he always did. "Just try to rest, sweetie," he murmured, and Hallie could feel the light pressure of his mind on hers again. Only able to take so much, Hallie went under again quite quickly.

A few minutes later she woke again. Feeling slightly stronger, her eyes blinked open and she gazed up at Bo, who was carrying her in his arms and jogging at a fairly quick pace. Looking in the direction they were headed, Hallie gasped when she saw the church. It was the church where she had first reunited with Daniel Marcus. It was the church where Allan Brown and Meg Hopper had sought refuge after their close encounter with The Doc. It was the same church that held the answers to many of their secrets.

Bo heard her gasp, and he glanced down at her startled expression as he nudged the front door open with his shoulder. "I was really hoping you would be asleep for this," he said quietly.

"What are you doing?" Hallie asked nervously, looking around at the rows of empty pews. She was still too tired to hear what her mate was thinking, but she knew that something was about to happen. When he didn't answer her, she demanded, "Bo, where are you taking me?"

Pushing through another door, Bo carried her into the sanctuary, and she got her answer. Hallie gaped at what she saw. Near the altar sat a device that would appear strange to anyone except her people. It was a large silver metallic platform about six feet in diameter held up a few inches off the floor by three curved legs. On either side of the platform there were long metal posts that stretched out ten feet in the shape of a V. The posts were attached to a circular belt that went all the way around the outside of the platform, allowing them to rotate in circles when needed. At the front inside the belt was a stand supporting a small control board for punching in a time and destination. A transparent, glowing sphere enveloped the machine above the platform, and the entire contraption was making a steady, pulsing whir. Hallie saw it and knew immediately what it was. It was the only thing that could get them all home. Allan had really done it. He had really recreated the machine.

The device she saw off to the side caused a knot in Hallie's stomach. It was at least twelve feet tall and cylindrical in shape. The top and bottom were black, and in between was a compartment of glass. The floor of the compartment was a thin sheet of glass with several large holes in it over the top of something that was flashing an ominous orange light. There was a small door giving access to the inside of the compartment, but there was only a handle on the outside. To complete the strange looking device, a thin metal antenna stretched several feet above it, making it appear as if it were going to broadcast something.

Realizing that was where Bo was taking her, Hallie began to frantically squirm in his arms. She had no desire to be placed inside that compartment. She knew all too well what was going to happen once she was inside. She had only seen this machine once, but seeing its effects had haunted her.

Bo's hold around her tightened and his pace quickened as he tried shushing her. "Please just keep still for me," he pleaded, his voice filled with remorse for what he was about to do.

"Bo, put me down!" Hallie cried in fear, her struggles becoming more intense as Bo approached the compartment door.

Allan suddenly appeared from behind Bo and grabbed the handle of the door. He looked at Hallie, his eyes exhausted and apologetic.

"Allan, help me!" Hallie begged him, kicking against Bo's firm grip.

He paused, and there was a moment's hesitation on his face before he regretfully opened the door.

"No!" Hallie screamed, thrashing wildly as Bo forced her inside. She was pushed to the opposite side of the compartment against the glass, and when Bo released her and pulled back she scrambled back to the door in a desperate attempt to escape. Before she could get out, Bo slammed it shut and clicked the handle into place. Hallie slapped her palms against the glass and cried pleadingly, "Let me out!" She stared desperately into Bo's sad eyes and was terribly confused. He knew how claustrophobic this cage would make her feel, so why would her mate who loved her with every ounce of his heart and soul want to torture her like that? He was upset seeing her as scared as she was, so what was the purpose of putting her in there?

"Don't do this to me, please!" Quickly rising to her feet, she pounded her fists on the glass higher up. "Let me out!" Panic coursing through her body, she placed her hands flat against the side and attempted to shatter it. She was unsure if she was capable of using an ability just yet, but she let forth a burst of energy anyway. The stress of it knocked her over backwards into the glass on the opposite side, and she slid to the floor as she began to sob. Peering out of her prison through her clouded eyes, she looked at the people who were all there to watch. Allan and Bo stood together beside the compartment door. She saw Meg sitting uncomfortably in a pew at the opposite end of the sanctuary. John Reifert, Walter, and Dreyson had entered with them and taken a seat in the fifth row. The boys were both falling asleep on John, but John was watching intently.

Bo pressed his finger on something near the bottom of the device and told her, "Please don't try to get out, sweetie. You'll only hurt yourself." He drew back his hand and turned to say something to Allan, but Hallie couldn't hear anything through the soundproof glass.

"Let me out! Please!" Hallie was too weak to try anything else. She sat sobbing on the floor of her prison while Bo and Allan fiddled with something on the lower section. She was so scared and all she wanted was for Bo to let her out and hold her.

A man stepped out from behind Hallie and gazed in at her. His presence made her stop abruptly. The man was thirty years old, had curly blonde hair and gleaming blue eyes, and while he didn't look too much like Hallie he was her family all the same.

"Flint," Hallie whispered as he smiled reassuringly, and she placed her hand on the glass. He was her big brother, and one of her truest friends. He had been brought back from the afterlife as well.

Flint put his hand to hers on the opposite side of the glass.

"Help me, big brother," she begged, pressing her forehead to the glass.

His eyes apologetic as Allan's had been, Flint silently mouthed, "We are, little sister."

As he backed away from the glass, the floor beneath Hallie began to vibrate and produce a deep humming sound. The floor stopped flashing but remained the violent orange color. Fear made her heart and head pound and her breathing approach hyperventilation. She leapt to her feet once again and danced around in terror on top of the ferociously vibrating platform. Her head snapped up as she heard a high pitched whirring sound. She saw that the ceiling was comprised of a vent covering a large fan-shaped object that was spinning very, very quickly. What was about to happen was not going to be very pleasant.

"Let me out! She screamed again, her fists pummeling the glass. Why would her family stand there and watch her in that cage when they knew it was torture to her? "Let me out!"

A hand suddenly came out of nowhere and wrapped around hers softly. It was warm and comforting, but the fact that Hallie was supposed to be alone made it frightening. Her eyes wide, she looked to see whose body the hand belonged to. To her surprise, she was looking into the soft baby blues of Daniel Marcus.

Daniel looked better than he had in months. It didn't have anything to do with how he was physically, but there was something about him that made him appear almost happy. He seemed to be grateful, as if now he could finally be at peace with his death. As Hallie stared at him with a mixture of horror and amazement, he smiled down at her, and almost looked as if he would laugh. Maybe her disbelief was amusing to him.

Hallie slowly turned and looked at the machine near the altar. She saw that Daniel's body had been brought to the church as well and laid to rest peacefully beside it. She turned back to Daniel's spirit beside her.

Still beaming at her, Daniel gave her a squeeze of the hand that made her shiver. Then, his voice just a whisper inside her head, he said, "Thank you."

It was unclear to Hallie what he was thanking her for, and she didn't have time to ask him about it. A thick, yellow-brown gas that smelled of sulfur began pouring out of the floor and steadily rose up through the compartment. As Hallie looked down in horror at what was about to consume her, she felt Daniel's hand leave hers and any sense of his presence was gone. That was Daniel's final goodbye to the world of the living, and a knot formed in Hallie's heart when she realized she would never see nor hear from him again.

She wished she could take more time to mourn his last farewell to her, but at the moment she was having issues of her own. The putrid gas was permeating the compartment very quickly, and she had absolutely no desire to suffocate in it. In an attempt to escape it, she tried putting her feet in front of her on the glass and her hands behind her so she could push herself up and out of the billowing cloud, but the glass was too slippery and she kept sliding back down. As the gaseous cloud was nearly over her head and Hallie's terror was in control of her, she pressed her face against the glass one last time in a final act of desperation to get some answers. John Reifert was holding Walter and Dreyson close to him and was covering their faces with his hands while he himself looked away. Allan joined Meg and they sat down in the front row pew together. Allan's arm was wrapped around Meg and they were both staring at the floor, almost in shame. Flint was standing in front of Hallie only a few feet from the machine, but he was covering his face with his own hand and shaking his head repeatedly.

There was only one person there who was actually watching. Bo stood beside Flint, his hands in his pockets, his jaw set, and his eyes agonized. No one in that sanctuary wanted to put her through this, because it hurt them to see her in such a state of fear. Bo was the only one who forced himself to watch every horrible moment.

Once the gas was over her head and she could no longer see out, she gave up completely. She was too weak to use an ability and too exhausted to scream any longer. Her knees were just about to collapse when suddenly the floor vibrated so hard that it sent an electrical current through her entire body. Crying out in pain, she fell to the floor and curled up in a ball. As she gasped for her breath to come back to her, she was shocked again.

And again.

And again.

And again.

Each time was worse than the last. Hallie was no longer able to scream. It felt to her as if the shocks were draining every ounce of energy she possessed. Every last bit was being sucked out of her by the machine. The spinning of the fan increased in speed. There was so much noise around her. Finally, the shocks ceased, the pulsing died away, and the fan stopped spinning.

All was quiet for about three seconds before a deafening roar sounded overhead. Hallie was relieved that the pain was finally over, but she was mistaken. With the roar, the gas in the machine dissipated, but a new violent blue light exploded around her. She wasn't able to move as the entire machine shook and pulled everything out of her. She could feel it all being taken from her, and when it all finally stopped, she could hardly believe her body was still intact. The gas was gone, and she was just barely able to see the blue light flowing through the top of the machine to the antenna before being shot to the other machine near the altar in a streak of blue lightning. The light penetrated the blue sphere, and the two V-shaped beams began to spin in rapid circles. That was all Hallie saw before her eyes fluttered shut.

Whatever Bo had done to her, and whatever he had sent back to their world, she prayed it would be worth it. For as much strength as Hara had given Hallie in her time of existence, it wasn't enough to sustain her now. She could feel herself falling into a deep pit of blackness. She couldn't hold on any longer.

She thought she heard someone calling her name in the far corners of her mind, but she was already too far gone. Without understanding what was happening, Hallie Reifert died.

✳ ✳ ✳

The awkward silence in the back of the truck during the ride to the church made Perry nervous. He still didn't have an answer as to why he was cuffed, but he was too intimidated by the masked men to ask.

The Doc had been forced into the very front of the cargo bay so there would be no possible way for him to escape. He was seated across from Dr. Bennett, and for the entire twenty minute ride they glared at each other. So far, neither of them appeared to be wavering.

A masked man sat beside both of them. Finchly and Renee sat across from each other with their eyes lowered and expressions exhausted. Two men sat on the other side of Renee by Perry. Across from him were Davey and Jack. Davey was as jittery as ever, his head twitching around in every possible direction, but Jack just stared at the floor with a look of self-pity in his eyes. Lieutenant Odau sat with intense pain on his face. The group of Bo's men had tried to cuff Odau and get him into the truck, but the cop had fought viciously against them. Because of his struggles, Odau's cuffs were pretty tight. Across from him was Jackson. The boy sat nervously, wringing his hands and looking back and forth between all the men. Perry could see that he really wanted to be sitting by his father.

Perry noticed that his Caiten and Colician friends were glancing at him every so often. No one had spoken yet during the ride, but it was clear that something needed saying. Finally, the man between Jack and Odau reached up and pulled off his mask.

He shook out his wavy blonde hair before meeting Perry's gaze, revealing very light green eyes. This man, apart from his eye color, looked very similar to Allan Brown. He was a few years younger, but the biological relationship was definitely visible.

After the man allowed Perry to take a look at him, he asked, "Do you recognize me?"

"You're Allan Brown's brother," he guessed.

Nodding and smiling, the man said, "I'm Eric Brown."

"What are you doing, Eric?" the man to Perry's right demanded. His voice was lower and sounded much older than Eric's.

"I trusted this man back home and I sure as hell can trust him here!" Eric snapped and then looked back at Perry. "Do you know why we're here?"

"For God's sake!" another man said incredulously.

"You know as well as I do that this is a good man!" Eric shouted as an uproar of protests started from his colleagues. "He has the right to know the whole truth if he doesn't already!"

"I know where you're from, if that's what you're wondering," Perry told them. "I know where you're from, why you're here, and why Hara—I mean Hallie—is here. It's okay. I won't tell anyone. None of us will."

Since Perry had told Finchly and Renee everything he had uncovered, it turned out that Odau and Jackson were the only two who still didn't have a clue what was going on. Perry prayed the truth would be kept from poor Jackson, but Odau needed to know why the Colicians wanted his son dead. Perry planned to tell Odau everything once they arrived at their destination.

Finally, the man to Perry's left said, "Screw it, then." He ripped off his mask and shifted in his seat so he could get a good look at Perry. He was the young man who looked like Bo; same black hair, brown eyes, and chestnut skin, but slightly older. "Hi, Dr. Perry, I'm James Rockwell. Bo is my little brother." He looked around at the rest of his colleagues. "I don't think it matters anymore whether we hide ourselves or not."

Nobody moved for a moment, but then the two men on either side of Renee took off their masks as well. The one between her and The Doc spoke first. "I'm Jeff Robinson, personal advisor to the President of the Caitens."

The second man then said, "I'm Vincent Lobner, Secretary of Defense and brother-in-law to the President. My younger sister, Miriam, is Bo and James' mother."

Both of them leaned forward so Perry could see them. Jeff was much older than Perry. He had to be in his mid to late sixties at least. His face was old and tired, his gray eyes wise and challenging. Vincent, on the other hand, looked much younger and seemed more ready for action. He looked to be in his mid-forties, closer to Odau's age, and looked a lot like James and Bo. His hair was jet black with a crew cut, and his eyes were the same dark brown. The Rockwell boys clearly got their looks from their mother's side.

With an irritated sigh, the man beside Perry took off his mask as well. He was around the same age as Vincent, but there was something about him that made him different from all the others. It wasn't his deep, navy blue eyes or his graying sandy-colored hair or even the fact that he seemed to be the most tired and tense in the whole group. It was the way he held himself. This man may have been exhausted, but he still held his head high, in the same way that Agent Long had when he was still alive. He was the one in charge, and Perry didn't need three guesses to figure out who he was.

"I'm Austin Rockwell, President of the Caitens, father of James and Bobby, and husband to Miriam Lobner."

"She's not your soul mate?" Perry asked him curiously. That was the only thing he could come up with to say to the leader of another species.

Eric, James, Jeff, and Vincent all snorted and President Rockwell raised an eyebrow. "That's a Colician thing," he muttered distastefully.

Perry felt like a fool. He could sense the dissatisfaction coming from the President. Clearing his throat awkwardly, Perry said, "Well...I just assumed since Bo has a soul mate..."

"It's understandable," Rockwell replied quietly, looking away and leaning back against the wall. "But Bobby's always been a little...different."

Bobby. That would take some getting used to.

James started laughing, and looked at Eric with a huge smirk. "He's a freak!" He was cackling with laughter, but he shut up after his father glared at him in disapproval.

Perry looked at Eric. "Are you the only Colician here?"

He nodded. "Apart from Flint, yes. The others here are all Caitens and humans."

"Humans?" Perry said in surprise. "Where? I didn't know you worked with humans."

Rockwell chuckled. "We don't. If humans want a better life, then they work for us and we let them live among us. Most of the time, the humans that live in our world were exiled. They help us in exchange for protection."

"Protection?"

"Neither one of our species much appreciates them after what they've done to us. It's not safe for them to walk on the streets. But humans that help us, like the three brave men up front who are escorting us, are recognized for their loyalty and therefore have respect among the community. They usually accompany us whenever we visit America, because they're better drivers than most of us. And even after they help us, it can still be dangerous to be out in the open. After all, the humans have hurt us terribly. You would understand that, wouldn't you, Dr. Perry?"

Perry gazed at him uncertainly. He tried to not think about his time spent with The Doc. A question was nagging him, but he wasn't sure if he should ask any more just yet. He knew the answers to most of the big questions about the Colicians, but there were still a few facts about himself that he didn't quite understand. "You call me Dr. Perry…"

Nodding, Rockwell stated, "Because you are the most brilliant doctor and scientist of all three of our species." Turning towards the front, he said, "I hate to disappoint you, Doc, but you'll always be second best."

Perry cringed at Rockwell's words, not wanting to have The Doc's pride threatened by him. He didn't bother to look for The Doc's reaction. Once again he cleared his throat awkwardly, and he asked Rockwell, "Are there humans who help you who still live among their own kind?"

"Yes, several," Rockwell replied, almost boastfully. "Like our friend here." He pointed to the man between Bennett and Finchly, the only one who hadn't removed his mask. "He's our finest, most trusted human ally in all our short history. He was the first to volunteer to help on this mission. After Bobby and Flint, of course."

"Who is he?" Perry asked curiously, peering over and wishing the man would take off his mask so he could see. The only part of his face that was visible was his eyes, which were light brown, like Bennett's.

Rockwell looked at his human colleague, who was evading everyone's gaze, and paused. "It looks as if he doesn't want his identity to be revealed just yet," he told Perry.

"Does he care that we're talking about his species in a…not so polite fashion?" Perry was hesitant as he spoke, knowing that the man could in fact hear every impolite word they were saying.

Shrugging carelessly, Rockwell replied, "If he did I would hope that he would have said something by now."

Perry looked to the human apologetically, but he was still avoiding everyone's eyes.

"Where exactly are we going?" Perry asked

"Home," Rockwell said, and then quickly specified, "Well, we are. You're not."

"Wait, so are you taking us—" Perry wasn't quite sure whether or not Rockwell was implying the remarkable.

"Please, no more questions," Rockwell ordered impatiently. "Just have some patience and you'll find that all the answers will soon come to you."

Perry kept his mouth shut, but there were many more questions he wanted to ask. He decided to obey Rockwell and pray he was telling the truth.

The truck halted abruptly and the engine turned off. There was only silence outside the metal walls, and as Perry opened his mouth to ask another nervous question, Rockwell turned to him again.

"I really don't think these are necessary anymore, do you?" he asked, taking the chain of Perry's handcuffs and pulling Perry's hands up to him.

"I'm not going anywhere," Perry replied, but Rockwell was already pressing his thumb down on the cuff below Perry's right palm. The metal of the cuffs flashed blue before they clicked open and fell into Rockwell's hands.

Jeff and Vincent removed the cuffs from Finchly and Renee as well, neither of them apparently a threat. It was Odau they were concerned with.

"What about you?" Rockwell asked sharply, nodding to Odau. "Can we un-cuff you too, or are we going to have a problem?"

Odau didn't give a verbal response, but he replied by glaring harshly at the president. Perry thought they might indeed have a problem.

Rockwell was ready for that. "Just so you are aware," he started in a disapproving, dangerous voice. "If you carry out any of the little schemes going on in that head of yours, I will personally kill your son, and trust me." He leaned forward. "It would be my pleasure."

Setting his jaw, Odau turned away in defeat.

"I'm glad we understand each other." Nodding to Eric who then undid Odau's cuffs, Rockwell stood up and kept his head bent to avoid bumping it on the low ceiling. "Time to go get your answers," he told Perry softly, and gestured for him to rise as well.

The doors opened and Odau and Jackson were quickly pulled out into the still night. The others soon followed, and Perry did what he was told just to keep the tension in the air from getting any worse. He wanted to ask where they were and what they were doing there, but Rockwell seemed on edge and Perry didn't want to be the one to push him off.

The Doc was the only one still cuffed. Perry took a look around. They had pulled off the highway into a parking lot beside the other cargo truck. There were a few orange lamps spread out around the lot, cutting through the darkness. In front of Perry was the church.

The church's windows were boarded up. There were two white doors hanging open before them, and the dim glow from inside made the church appear as if it were the gates of hell beckoning for all of them to enter.

Perry swallowed nervously, and as he stutter-stepped, Rockwell put his hand on his back and gave him a gentle push forward. He glanced back uncertainly and received an encouraging smile from Rockwell.

"You're not going to get any of your answers out here," Rockwell told him.

Nodding in agreement, Perry led the group inside. As they walked into what appeared to be the Fellowship Hall, a low-pitched pulsing sound came from the other side of the door just ahead. A hand slipped into his suddenly and startled him, but he heard Renee's shaky breathing beside him and he relaxed. She was just as terrified as he was. The pulsing on the other side of the door was not inviting, and it made his heart beat faster and faster in his chest. He gripped Renee's hand tightly and pushed forward. When he reached the door and carefully nudged it open, he saw something that changed his world forever.

"Whoa!" he and Renee said in unison, gaping at the altar in awe. A huge platform held a tall, strange looking device that was surrounded by a glowing, translucent blue sphere. It took him a moment to understand that the tall structure was one machine while the platform itself was another. The platform with the blue sphere was the origin of the pulsing sound that was filling Perry with such anxiety.

The whole thing was so foreign and complex to Perry that he didn't realize he had stopped in the middle of the doorway until Rockwell cleared his throat behind him. Still mesmerized by the peculiar beauty of it all, Perry remained frozen and looked around at the array of people in the church. Allan Brown and Meg Hopper sat off in the left section in the front pew while John Reifert, Walter, and Dreyson were seated in the middle section in the front row. Flint had his hand inside the blue sphere near the altar and was pressing what looked like buttons on the V-shaped beams of the platform. Below Flint, sitting on the step to the altar, was Bo holding a limp and lifeless Hara in his arms.

"Oh my God," Perry said, letting go of Renee's hand and starting to rush up the aisle. He didn't see Noah Travis approaching him and nearly knocked him over.

"You really don't want to go up there," he warned grimly, catching him by the arm.

The church, the Colicians' sanctuary, must have been Noah's haven since their last encounter. "I have to see if she's okay!" Perry protested, trying to pull away.

Noah held on. "You really ought to give them some space," he advised sternly.

Rockwell had already brushed by to get to Bo, and Perry wasn't going to hang around for someone to announce what had happened. Pulling away from Noah, Perry, followed by most of the others, hurried up the aisle to find out what was going on.

He made it to Bo just in time to hear his father ask him, "Did the extraction work?"

"As far as I know, yes," Bo replied, his voice cracking with emotion. His eyes were red and he was crying softly, cradling his beloved mate close to him. "We're still here, after all."

"Is she okay?" Perry asked quickly. When Bo looked up at him, his face showing grief, the horrifying truth began to dawn on him. "She isn't..."

"She's dead," Bo said quietly, his voice cracking again.

"But...she can't die!" Perry felt stupid for saying that, but he didn't care. It was the truth.

"If she doesn't have enough energy to regenerate, she can!" Bo snapped, pulling Hara closer to him.

Perry couldn't believe it. After everything she had done and how far she had come, how could it end so abruptly, and right when she was about to go home? "What happened?"

"The Colicians were all but wiped out," Rockwell explained, taking over as his son was overwhelmed with emotion. "We couldn't continue to let our brothers and sisters die. We heard that their best scientist had escaped the apocalypse and was building something that could bring back all of those who had perished." He turned and pointed to the tall machine on the platform. "Does it look familiar?"

Raising an eyebrow, Perry demanded, "Why would it look familiar to me?"

Peering at him, Rockwell replied, "Because you're the one who built it."

Perry stared at him in perplexity, but before he could say anything, Flint called, "Eric, grab the escorts! I need you all to take the machine back home."

"Did it work?" Eric asked hopefully from his place halfway up the aisle.

"It worked," Flint promised, not looking all that relieved.

Laughing triumphantly, Eric ran back to the Fellowship Hall.

"I've never seen this before in my life!" Perry said to Rockwell once the commotion was over.

"Perry, I thought you knew everything," Rockwell said, the hint of a smile playing at his lips.

Eric ran back into the sanctuary and up to the altar, followed by the three humans who had been driving the truck. They still hadn't taken their masks off, so Perry wasn't able to see their faces.

"Are we all going to fit?" Eric asked, peering up at the machine which was taking up most of the available space on the platform.

"There should be room for the four of you."

"Eric?"

Allan heard his little brother's voice and stood up to see him. He stared in shock, his eyes wide and his mouth half open. It was then that Perry understood that Eric had also been brought back, just like Flint and Bo.

"Allan!" Eric cried joyfully, and the brothers grabbed each other in a tight embrace. Both of them were laughing and there may have also been some tears involved.

"You were brought back before...?" Allan was just as confused as everyone else about the men who had been miraculously been brought back to life.

"I love you, man, and they'll explain everything but right now I really have to go!" Eric pulled away regrettably and rushed up onto the altar. He stepped through the blue sphere and hopped onto the platform where the three masked humans were waiting. Smiling at his shocked brother below, he waited for whatever was going to happen next.

"Let my father know we'll be there shortly," Flint instructed, pulling down a lever on the beam.

The two beams began to spin in circles, faster and faster, until the pulsing stopped and the blue sphere radiated a blinding light so bright that it left blue spots imbedded in Perry's retinas. He covered his eyes for a moment and blinked rapidly to regain his vision, and then everyone who had been inside the sphere was gone.

Perry and his colleagues stood gaping at the platform where everyone had disappeared. The V-shaped beams were right back where they started, and the light of the blue sphere reduced in intensity to its previous level.

"Where did they go?" Odau asked slowly after several long moments of stunned silence. It was the first time he had spoken since the near catastrophe at the bridge.

"Home," Perry heard James reply smugly.

"And...where is home?"

"Well, maybe if you had allowed Perry to explain it instead of insisting that you didn't care, you would know."

Perry tried to change the subject. "How did that machine bring back all of those who died, and why did it kill Hara...I mean Hallie?"

"The machine is designed to extract the energy of specific abilities from a Colician," Bo said, having gained back some of his composure. "In this case, it extracted Hallie's ability to regenerate as well as her ability to communicate with the afterlife. After sucking every last drop of energy from her, we sent the payload home using the transporter and it was released into our world. The bodies of everyone who died in the war over the past year were completely regenerated, and the souls from the afterlife were then pulled back into our world and put back into the proper body."

701

"That actually worked?" Perry asked skeptically, thoroughly confused.

"Yes, it worked," Bo answered flatly. "It took a long time for the machine to be perfected, but in the end we managed to get it to work."

"Then how are you here if you just sent the payload?" Perry demanded.

Bo paused. "I'll get to that, but first, I think you all have some questions about our existence. I think it's time you learned the whole truth."

✳ ✳ ✳

"Hallie."

Hallie opened her eyes when she heard her name. She gasped. Daniel was standing in front of her, his eyes soft but worried. He looked well, as well as he had before his death. The question to ask was; why was she standing before him?

"Hallie, what are you doing?" he asked her quietly.

"I…" Hallie looked around in confusion. There was nothing around her. An infinite horizon of nothing. She was nowhere. But then she saw two men standing behind Daniel, and she knew what had happened to her. She understood. Behind Daniel stood Rhett and Detective Aubrey. Looking at Daniel in horror, she breathed, "I died."

Daniel forced a small, sad smile. "Yes, you died."

"How?" she whispered. "I should have healed…"

"I don't think this is a matter of your anatomy anymore, sweetheart," Daniel told her gently, reaching out and putting a comforting hand on her shoulder. "I think this is a matter of what you choose to do next."

"This was my choice," Hallie whispered, nodding as she began to understand it all. "I chose to die."

"No," Daniel said. "You died because you couldn't help it. What you do next is your choice."

"What do you mean?" Hallie whispered, but she knew.

Rhett moved up beside Daniel. "You choose where you go next, H. You just saved our race. You brought everyone back. Everyone is alive. You can go back to them. You can be with your family again. But if you're tired, if you're done fighting, then you can come with us." He stepped aside, and beckoned for Daniel to do the same.

A bright, white light landed on Hallie's face, and she shielded her eyes at first from its harshness. But when she blinked and looked into the light, her eyes widened and she gasped with a mixture of amazement and awe. "My God," she breathed, stunned by the beauty of it. She knew where she would be going if she followed her friends, and it was a beautiful place. It was Heaven.

"It's up to you," Detective Aubrey said, walking up to her as well. "But if I were you, I would go back. You have your family waiting for you."

Hallie was still staring wide-eyed and open-mouthed at the place she had been so afraid of for the longest time. There was nothing to be afraid of. It was beautiful. It was peaceful. It was where she wanted to be.

"It's your choice, Hallie," Daniel told her again, drawing his hand away from her and taking a step back. He, Rhett, and Aubrey began taking slow, hesitant steps backwards. "It's up to you where you choose to go next. But you need to choose now. We have to go."

Mesmerized by the light and what lay beyond it, Hallie nodded absentmindedly. It was her choice. Live or die. Die or live. Peace or chaos. Hallie already knew where it was she wanted to go.

Hesitantly, she took a step forward. She took a step towards the light.

19

Parallels

"First, I want to know why Hallie's dead!" Perry said stubbornly, not realizing how hard Bo was handling his mate's death.

"Let him finish!" Rockwell told him, irritated.

"I can't..." Bo replied, shaking his head as many more tears came to his eyes. "I can't, Dad!"

Pausing as he realized just how difficult the death of his mate was for Bo, Rockwell placed a hand on the top of his son's head. "Everything will be okay," he promised, but he didn't sound very convinced himself. Turning back to Perry, his expression became stony. "The extraction was so stressful that it killed her, and if she doesn't gain back enough energy soon, she'll stay dead."

"So there's still a chance that she'll come back!" Perry asked. If there was still a chance that Hallie would live, no matter how small, then Perry knew that she would be okay. He had witnessed what that girl had been through and how strong she was, and no extraction could destroy her. It would take something much more powerful—even more powerful than The Doc—to bring her down. Perry was beginning to believe that the only thing capable of bringing Hallie Reifert to an end was herself.

"A very slim chance," Rockwell replied grimly.

"Will my blood help her?" Perry asked quickly, ignoring Rockwell's negativity. When the President peered at him curiously, Perry explained, "Hallie changed me. I can regenerate, so can I help?"

"Regenerative blood can't heal a damaged mind, Perry," Rockwell said, gazing at him as if he should already know that. "But that's very kind of you."

Perry said, "Trust me, she's not about to give up just yet."

"I hope you're right," Flint muttered hopelessly, his eyes pained as well.

"She has to be okay!" Bo cried suddenly, unable to contain his grief. "She has to be! I can't live without her!" Several hoarse sobs escaped his throat, and James sat beside him to try and comfort him.

With that said, Hallie's eyes popped open and she gasped as she struggled to take a breath. Her body didn't move, but her eyes roamed the room to take in where she was and to observe the new arrivals. Bo's need for Hallie and Hallie's need for Bo brought her back. She was so lost that if her soul mate hadn't needed her so badly, she would have given in to death and left for the afterlife. Love is a truly powerful thing. It saved Hallie and brought her back to her family.

"Oh God, Hallie!" Bo whispered as he cried, except now it was out of joy rather than anguish. He kissed her forehead as she gazed around in confusion. "I didn't think you would be able to make it back!"

"She came back for you," Perry told him softly, and he smiled down at Bo when he glanced up.

"I know what heaven looks like," Hallie breathed, staring up at the ceiling in wide-eyed awe. She looked—miraculously—like she was finally at peace with herself.

"I know what it looks like too," Bo said, smiling down at her. "It's beautiful."

"I don't know why I was so worried about you," Hallie whispered, and her eyes were accusing as she made eye contact with Bo. Her weak voice barely audible, she demanded, "Why did you do that to me?"

Choking back his sobs, Bo explained, "You saved everybody, just like you were trying to. The extraction brought everyone back. You don't have to kill any more people, Hallie."

Her eyes wandering over the ceiling again, Hallie looked like she was in an entirely different place. "They're all okay," she said softly. "I can feel them." Her eyes landed on Bo's again. "I can't move."

"That's okay," Bo assured her, holding onto her as he rose and stepped over to the front pew. He set her down so she could rest, her feet just inches from where John Reifert was seated. "It will take a little while for you to gain back all your strength. The only thing that matters now is that you're alive, and everybody else is alive too."

"Not everybody." Hallie had managed to turn her head towards the altar, and she was gazing at something up there.

Perry turned and saw the body of Daniel Marcus resting beside the platform. His skin was pale and gaunt, as it had been when his body was first discovered in the police station all those hours ago, but the fact that he was still dead struck Perry as odd. If the Colician race had just been brought back from the dead, then why wasn't Marcus alright? Perry half expected him to sit up and look around at any second, but the body remained still. Perry looked to Rockwell for an answer.

The President shook his head solemnly. "It only worked for those who died on our own home world," he explained sadly. "The connection couldn't work unless the death occurred on our soil. Anyone who died here...well, we can't bring them back."

"What if we take him back home?" Jack chimed in hopefully.

"That wouldn't change a thing," Rockwell grumbled.

"Why not?" Meg demanded.

"We don't know!" Rockwell glared at anyone who cared to look at him. "We don't know why we have to tell Marcus's family that he's one of the few that can't be brought back. It's just how the machine functions. Believe me, if Perry knew of a way to bring everybody back, he would have done it already."

All eyes landed on Perry, and Perry felt his face flush. It was on his conscience that Marcus was dead for good. He wondered if he should apologize, but Hallie was speaking again before he could even open his mouth.

"So Rhett…and the detective who died…none of them can be brought back either?" Hallie's eyes were glistening with tears for the few that were truly lost forever.

"I'm afraid not," Rockwell murmured, lowering his gaze to the floor.

Hallie brought her eyes back to Bo, who was kneeling beside her, and her expression became absolutely furious. "You should have let me kill the boy!" she shouted. "Then I could have saved everyone!"

"We can't risk the flow of time being changed," Bo told her, worried by her outburst. "It would cause even worse disasters than what we've been through. Besides," he brushed a strand of hair off of her face, "you're not that kind of person."

"You have no idea what kind of a person I've become!" Hallie snarled fiercely, and then her eyes rolled back and her head lolled to one side.

"I've seen what that man has made you into," Bo assured her softly. "But I know that you're better than that." He looked up at his father. "We need to get her back so we can get her help."

"No!" Hallie said, blinking as she tried to focus again. She stared pleadingly into her mate's eyes. "Please, I promised Perry he would get an explanation from me, and I'm keeping my promise."

Hallie, Bo, Rockwell, and Flint all looked up at Perry, but Perry was already shaking his head. "I think Lieutenant Odau needs the explanation more than I do."

Lieutenant Odau was still standing halfway up the aisle with his son clinging to his side. He looked ready to run for it, and Perry doubted anyone would try to stop him. Everybody turned to look at him, but he too was shaking his head. "I've already figured it out," he declared.

"I highly doubt that," James retorted.

"You're from a parallel universe," Odau said, ignoring James. "It makes sense because no one here has ever heard of the Colician strain and something that big couldn't be kept a secret for so long. You need this strange machine to travel back and forth, and in your alternate reality, Perry is a scientist and he's one of you and that's why he doesn't know any of you…"

"Lieutenant!"

The sharp and irritated voice of Finchly made everybody jump. Perry looked at her in surprise. Finchly's face was tired and frustrated, and she was glaring at Odau in contempt. She couldn't contain her frustration with her commanding officer any longer, and she had finally found her voice to stand up to him. "For once in your life, will you stop acting like you know everything and listen to someone else!"

His face turning bright red, Odau swallowed and licked his lips. To everyone's surprise, he nodded and whispered, "Okay." The events and emotions from the past two days had even changed this stubborn man. He looked at Rockwell and waited for the explanation.

When he had Odau's attention, Rockwell began. "You're partly right. We're from a parallel world, but we're not from an alternate reality. When the Colicians were first created, it was clear that the humans were not going to share the earth with them willingly, so with their combined abilities they created a second earth that could be reached through a rift in space. They crossed over and when we Caitens were created they shared their world with us. We've been in a cold war with the humans since the birth of our two species, and we knew it was only a matter of time before a trigger happy human decided to attack us. We're from a parallel earth, but I'm guessing that doesn't quite explain everything, like how we know Perry while he doesn't know us and why Hallie tried to kill your son and killed those other children."

Pausing, Odau shook his head.

Looking at Perry, Rockwell said, "Maybe Perry would like to explain it since he knows this part."

Perry looked down at Hallie's waiting gaze. Taking a deep breath, he declared, "You don't know the future because you've seen the future. You know the future because you're *from* the future."

Hallie smiled and nodded once.

"You're...*from* the future?" Odau said in disbelief.

Perry nodded at him. "Noah kept saying that the Colicians were created thirty years ago, but it was thirty years ago for them. The Colician outbreak that created the race is the same outbreak that will happen ten years from today. There was only one outbreak, and there will only ever be one. The outbreak that changed all of the Colicians occurs on April 4, 2018, and if the outbreak happened thirty years ago for them, then that makes them from the year 2048. Am I right?"

"Very much so," Rockwell replied, grinning with approval. "Please continue."

"Hallie came back in time from the war to try and change what had already happened to all of you," Perry said, hoping that Odau would figure the rest out on his own. "She thought if she killed the future problem before it became a problem, then the war would have never begun in the first place."

"Correct again," Rockwell said, glancing at Odau.

"That was also why those who were dead, like Bo, were able to come back," Perry continued. "They came after Hallie had already saved them so they could make sure that she saved everyone and didn't alter the course of history." Perry glanced at Noah across the room. "This also explains why the times people gave me were off. Meg, Allan, and Daniel all came back here two years ago to escape the war, while Hallie came here and it had been only weeks since she had last seen them. I never would have believed it before, but it all makes sense to me now."

Odau was beginning to make some connections, but not the ones he needed to make. He looked at the Reiferts and then looked at Hallie, seeing the distinguishable features that the three of them shared. "If you're from the future, then Walter's..."

Hallie smiled at the lieutenant as he and Jackson came to the end of the aisle to join the rest of them. "He's my father. Our father." She lifted her finger and pointed at Flint. "That was why I needed to protect him so badly, and that's why John recognizes me."

"He recognizes you even if he hasn't met you before?" Odau asked in confusion.

"She looks like my Hallie," John said from his place on the pew, letting them all know that he was listening.

"He can see the resemblance," Hallie explained. "But I also showed John who I really am."

The truth of Hallie's statement finally dawned on Perry, and he took a moment to recognize one of his relationships that needed clarification. He glanced at Jack, who was gazing back almost as if he had been waiting for Perry to say it aloud. "You're not my brother," Perry said.

Hallie smiled again. "He's your son."

Jack forced a half smile before looking away awkwardly. Perry couldn't believe that he would actually have a son one day. Two sons, because Jack had a little brother. It was strange yet incredible to meet Jack. Somehow, he was going to become a brilliant scientist, save the Colicians and the Caitens, and then save them all again when the war came for them, all within the next forty years. He would meet The Doc again someday, and would have to endure grief, pain, and loss at a level that he couldn't fathom. April 4, 2008, was just a prep day for what was really coming in his future.

"Wait," Odau said suddenly, and when Perry looked at him it was clear that the truth was finally dawning on him. "If you're from the future, and you came to the past to erase the future problem, then...my son..." He was unable to finish as his voice caught in his throat. He stared at the floor to avoid the intense gazes of everyone and to try and come up with an alternative explanation for Jackson's involvement in everything.

John saw what was going on and knew that Jackson didn't deserve to hear the horrifying truth. Standing up and nudging Dreyson and Walter towards the aisle, John walked past Odau and took Jackson by the hand. "Let's go sit back here while your dad talks to the grown-ups," he said, and led the children to the very back pew.

Odau allowed his son to be led away, because he didn't want Jackson knowing the truth either. The lieutenant's shoulders began to shake and he covered his hand with his mouth, not wanting to believe any of it. "My son...the one destined to destroy the Colician race." He slowly raised his eyes to The Doc, who was standing cuffed at the altar between Jeff and Vincent, watching with his cold gray stare.

"Jackson."

After a single, silent second, The Doc muttered, "Hi, Dad."

"Oh God, no!" Odau cried, taking a horrified step back. He couldn't take his eyes off The Doc's emotionless expression. "Please, no! Jackson, what happened to you?"

Snickering, Dr. Jackson Odau replied smugly, "Don't act so surprised. You're the one who made me what I am now."

Taken aback, Odau squeaked out, "What?"

"Don't listen to him," Rockwell ordered. "He's full of crap and he won't accept responsibility for his own asinine mistakes."

The Doc rolled his eyes.

Odau turned toward Hallie and said, "You told me that he was going to kill me in ten years. Why?"

"Because when the Colician strain is set loose, you're going to lose your wife and both of your daughters to it," Hallie told him. She sighed at Odau's heartbroken expression. "He's going to kill you because you try to help the Colicians to protect your family, and he didn't like the fact that you were helping those who Jackson blamed." Upon seeing Odau's distraught expression, she whispered, "I'm sorry. I'm so, so sorry."

It took the lieutenant a while to find his voice, but nobody spoke to allow him some time to process it all. After taking several deep breaths, Odau spoke very quietly. "Why am I the one who's going to lose everything?" He looked back at The Doc, and his expression hardened. "You're not my son!" he hissed, shaking his head and taking many steps back.

"Lieutenant, it's okay," Perry told him in an attempt to comfort him.

"No!" he shouted furiously. "No!" Turning, he ran out through the door and disappeared from sight.

James started to go after him, but Hallie ordered, "Let him go. Just leave him be. He deserves that much."

"Perry," Allan said, taking a step towards him. "How did you figure it all out on your own?"

"I didn't," Perry insisted, pointing at John Reifert in the back. "John gave me a photo of young Jackson along with a note asking me if I could see it now. Whoever wrote the letter could see the future and knew I would need it to finally understand."

"How did it make you understand?" Meg asked.

"His eyes," Perry explained, knowing that anyone who had met either Jackson or The Doc would know exactly what he was talking about. "When I got the picture, I took a good long look at it. Those eyes are unmistakable. Even as a child, his eyes have an icy glow to them." He shot a stern look at The Doc. "I think the boy is already becoming The Doc. I can see him in Jackson's eyes." He looked back at Hallie. "I'm sorry it took so long for me to figure it out. If I had just looked at the two of them long enough, I might have been able to see it."

Hallie shook her head gently. "You wouldn't have believed it," she told him softly.

Perry knew she was right, but he didn't want to admit it. Suddenly remembering something that he had forgotten to ask about earlier, he turned to Bo. "What about the other children, the three that were killed? Who were they supposed to be? Wouldn't their deaths change the future as well?"

Shaking his head and sighing, Bo explained, "Those kids were people who The Doc claimed gave him knowledge and insight. They were supposedly the three who began The Doc's plan to wipe out the Colician race."

"I looked up their files just before I was killed," Flint chimed in, his voice grave. "I read that all three of them had died on the night of April 3, 2008. They had all been killed by the same group of assassins. The Doc made up the entire story about them. He used their deaths as an excuse to create the plan himself."

"You were always supposed to come back here," Perry realized. "The reason they were dead was because Hallie was always meant to kill them. Their deaths were set in stone, just like your visit here."

Hallie let out a wail so awful that everyone cringed. Forcing herself to raise her head, she glared furiously at The Doc's calm expression. "You bastard!" she cried. "You lied to us all, and you made me kill three innocent kids! What the hell is wrong with you?"

His expression unchanging, The Doc shrugged carelessly. "I'm not the one who pulled the trigger."

Hallie stared hard at him, but she didn't fight it further. The Doc wasn't lying that time. Dropping her head back down to the pew, Hallie stared in anguish at the crumbling ceiling.

There was a long, awkward pause that followed, and everyone seemed to be waiting for someone else to speak first. Finally, Allan cleared his throat and asked uncertainly, "What do we do now?"

"We go home," Rockwell replied, glad to be on a different topic. "I don't know about you, but I've had a long day and I need some serious sleep. Oh, somebody go get the lieutenant. Perry's entire crew is coming back with us, including the Reiferts."

"Wait, what?" Perry said in confusion. "Why are we going back with you?"

Rockwell stared at him. "We have to wipe your memories. We can't allow you to live your lives fearing what the future will bring."

"What?" Perry repeated, taking a step back but being caught on the arm by James. He really didn't like what he was hearing, and shooting a nervous glance at Renee and Finchly, he saw that they were just as terrified as he was.

"Nobody's memory is getting erased, Austin, and don't argue with me on that!" Hallie's voice was still soft and weak, but it was the voice of an authority figure. She was now able to push herself up on her elbows, and she stared hard at the Caiten president. "After all, Perry is the only one who will be able to warn us of what's coming." She gazed at Perry. "You have to warn us, Perry. You're our only chance for change."

Perry nodded quickly as James released him. "I will," he promised.

Rockwell looked around at everybody. "Well, then, we're making two trips home. First trip is Marcus's body, Jeff, Vincent, James..."

"Uh, Austin?" Jeff said uncertainly. "Don't you want us to bring this back with us?" He jabbed a thumb at The Doc.

"I think I can handle him," Rockwell informed them, smirking at The Doc. "So...Marcus, Jeff, Vincent, James, Davey, Allan, Meg...oh, and Danny too."

Everybody turned to the hooded human still standing beside Bennett—who had finally removed his hood—and Perry could finally see it. The human called Danny was Danny Bennett, Dr. Bennett's grandson. They had the same kind eyes, the same facial shape, and they both held themselves with a sort of modest pride.

Danny must have been about forty-five and he was several inches taller than Bennett, so when he looked at his grandfather he had to look down. Seeing Bennett's stunned expression, Danny smiled kindly. "Thanks, Grandpa," he said with a deep voice, giving Bennett a quick, slightly awkward hug before rushing up to the platform.

Perry managed to glimpse the joyous smile on Bennett's face before he turned away. He smiled to himself, having a feeling that Bennett wouldn't live to see the Colician outbreak or the heroic acts of his grandson.

Rockwell brought the others back to the matter at hand and was taking charge again. "Alright, those I listed, get onto the platform," he ordered. "The rest of us are taking the second ride."

✳ ✳ ✳

While those taking the first trip prepared themselves to go home, Perry saw his chance to try and speak with Jack before he disappeared into the future forever. Determined, Perry made his way towards Jack as Jack walked with Davey to the platform to see him off. Reaching out his hand, he tried to catch Jack by the arm but just missed him as somebody else caught him and pulled him back.

Turning in surprise, Perry saw that it was Bo and he had a very serious expression on his face. Gesturing with his head towards the aisle, Bo said in a low voice, "I need to talk to you."

Glancing back at Jack as he said his farewell to Davey, Perry saw that Renee was already approaching Jack and calling his name. "Can't it wait just a minute?" Perry asked impatiently, hoping Bo would understand.

Bo shook his head stubbornly and gave Perry's arm a tug. "This cannot wait any longer."

Sighing in frustration, Perry unhappily followed Bo halfway down the aisle so they would be out of earshot of the rest of the group. Perry didn't understand what was so urgent that he had to hear it immediately. He had already uncovered all the important facts. It turned out that Bo wasn't trying to fill him with more information; he was making a request.

"I know what Hallie told you," Bo said in a low voice. "But you can't say a word to anyone about what's coming. No matter how much you feel you must, you can't tell anyone, or even hint at it."

"Why?" Perry demanded in surprise. Did Bo want the war to happen? "I could make sure that everybody is prepared so we can make a stand..."

"No," Bo told him forcefully. He sighed and rubbed his eyes. "I hear you, and I don't want the war to happen, but we don't have a heck of a lot of options here. We have to maintain a steady stream of time, because if we change something, even something as small as warning Walter Reifert about a future war, then something far worse than The Doc's war could happen."

"What are you talking about?"

"The humans were bound to attack our planet sooner or later. It wouldn't make any difference whether Hallie killed The Doc as a child. Somebody else, maybe even worse than The Doc, would have come along and destroyed our world, and the problem is that there would be different results. In the end, we managed to bring back everyone lost with the exception of the few unfortunates who died on Terran soil. If we wiped this war out of history and a new war came later, then there is the chance that you would never be allowed to complete the extraction machine and Hallie could never restore life to our planet. The war is our destiny, and it will take place one way or another. Do you understand?"

Perry understood just fine. He just wished there was some way he could save Marcus, Agent Long, and Aubrey and prevent the war. "Perfectly," Perry muttered, looking down at the floor.

With a heavy sigh, Bo put a comforting hand on Perry's shoulder. "I know," he said quietly. "It's hard, but this is the right thing to do. I've thought long and hard about it, and this is the only way we can ensure the safety of our people."

Nodding slowly, Perry said, "Okay. I trust your judgment, so I'll keep my mouth shut."

Smiling, Bo replied, "Thank you. If anyone asks you, tell them you'll provide a warning, but you have to keep quiet about this until after the war is over."

"Which is now?" Perry asked.

Bo nodded. "Now that the Colician race has been restored, the Caiten Armada will drive the humans back onto the mainland and through the rift while the Colicians wipe out the labs throughout the big cities. It shouldn't take more than a few days."

"Good luck," Perry muttered, already beginning to dread his future.

"Just a fair warning for you," Bo added quickly. "When we all go home, quite a few of us are going to be unhappy with future you because you didn't tell. I just want you to be prepared for how your son is going to feel about you once he goes back."

"He's going to hate me," Perry concluded grimly.

"I just thought you should take some time to prepare yourself for what your future family will become. After all, you've got forty years to sit on this."

"I can't imagine having children when I'm so old," Perry told him, grimacing at the thought of himself with gray hair.

Bo snickered. "You don't look a day older than you do right now," he replied.

Startled, Perry realized that along with the regeneration, he must be unable to age as well. Becoming immortal had not been his goal in life, and he was curious as to whether or not Hallie would suffer the same fate as him.

Patting Perry's shoulder, Bo said, "Thank you for everything. Now, if you'll excuse me, I have to speak to John Reifert."

"Wait!" Perry protested, catching Bo's arm as he began to walk away. "When am I going to see you again?"

"In the year 2043," Bo answered immediately. "The first time Hallie and I ever meet, but I won't remember you, so don't act like you know me."

"Don't worry," Perry assured, grinning. "I'll keep my mouth shut if it means the protection of my people."

"Our people," Bo corrected, raising an eyebrow. "I really have to go now. Go talk to your son. Goodbye, Shawn Perry."

Perry watched Bo Rockwell walk away towards John Reifert in the back pew, and he wondered if he would really be able to keep the truth a secret. It would be difficult to lie to the faces of everyone he held dear while he watched them suffer and perish at the hands of a monster that only he had the power to stop.

✳ ✳ ✳

It was a disappointment for Jack that he and Davey were going to be separated, but he knew Rockwell had done that on purpose. Davey had been sent by Jack's father to stop Hallie from killing The Doc as a child, but when they all learned that The Doc was going after young Walter Reifert, Davey panicked and jumped to the opposite side to help Hallie. Jack had been a part of Hallie's violent plot to drastically change the course of history, and he knew that he was going to be punished for pushing her on. He would have to face his father yet again, and that was going to be the worst part. His father had kept the war a secret after he knew the horrors it would bring, and if he tried to judge Jack for his sin, Jack was going to have some serious words with him. There would be serious words between the two of them whether his father judged him or not. Everything was Perry's fault, and if it was true that the flow of time had not yet been altered, then Perry knew about everything yet refused to say a word.

As he bid his farewell to Davey, Jack had a feeling that he wouldn't be seeing his friend for a very long time. He watched Davey climb up onto the platform with the others who were leaving first and turned in surprise when he heard Renee Michaels calling his name. The FBI agent hurried over to him, and Jack groaned internally. It had really irritated him to see her with his father. He wasn't used to seeing him with another woman, and whenever he saw her he became really angry and annoyed. Although as Jack looked at her, he remembered a story his father had once told him when he was almost fourteen. His father had told him about his first wife from before the Colician outbreak. Her name had been Renee Perry, and if Jack recalled correctly she was supposed to have blonde hair and blue eyes. Her description matched the Renee in front of him, and Perry had also described his first two children which they had raised together. His first daughter, Jillian, who had already been born, and Perry and Renee's daughter named Hallie had been raised by the two of them in the time before the strain began to spread. Perry only talked to Jack about it that once, and Jack knew that he never talked about it with anyone else because it hurt too much for him to remember. After he was told that story, Jack spent a lot of time thinking about what his older sisters might have looked like, or what their personalities might have been like. He spent a while wishing that he could have just once met them, but eventually he forced himself to forget about Jillian and Hallie. It wasn't worth causing himself pain for things he couldn't control. The past was the past, and there was nothing he could do to change that. He finally allowed that to sink in.

"Jack!" Renee said as she reached him, eagerness and excitement in her voice as well as her head.

Raising his eyebrows, Jack waited for her to ask the question he was sure she was going to ask.

"Shawn really is your father, isn't he?" she asked, a bright smile lighting up her face.

Jack stared at her. "Yes," he replied, continuing to wait for it. He found it amusing that she called his father by his first name. Jack's own mother rarely called him that.

"And you know the future," Renee added, getting even more excited. "So will you answer me something? Do Shawn and I get married?"

"Yes," Jack answered immediately, feeling the question beginning to boil.

Renee sighed in relief and her smile widened even more. "Do we have kids before you? I never thought it would happen, but it's always been a dream of mine to have a daughter."

Chewing on his lip, Jack told her, "My dad's daughter Jillian will be adopted by the two of you, and in 2012 you will give birth to another daughter."

A joyful laugh escaping her throat, Renee thoroughly surprised Jack by wrapping him in a tight hug. "You have a little brother, right?" she asked, pulling back. "Four kids are a little more than I was planning on, but that's good enough for me!"

Beginning to feel upset that he had to be the one to tell her and crush her joyful spirit, Jack gazed back at her with terribly sad eyes. He regretted judging her before he'd even had a chance to talk to her. She was a very nice woman, and Jack could see why his father felt such grief for her in the future. She was going to make Perry a very happy man for the next ten years.

The smile slowly faded from her face, and the realization in her eyes was unmistakable. "I...I am your mother, aren't I?" she asked, and Jack heard her praying in her head that she was. "If Shawn's your father, then that makes me your mother...doesn't it?"

Jack sighed and shook his head. "My mother's name is Denise. She would only be a child right now."

Renee's face fell and it was clear that she was about to start crying. "We're soul mates, though! I can feel it! We're supposed to be together!"

"I can see that now…" Jack said quietly, his sadness for her increasing. "But… something happens."

As she thought about it, her eyes suddenly lit up with a new realization. "We get separated during the outbreak, don't we?"

Sighing again, Jack nodded apologetically.

Renee nodded as well, and she took a deep breath. "What happens to me?" When Jack looked away, she snapped, "Don't try to spare me! I want to know!"

Jack knew that he shouldn't tell her, but she was a nice woman and he felt sorry for her. "My dad poses as a double agent to help our people, and he gets caught. The government kills you and both daughters when they find out you're all Colicians as well." He couldn't keep his eyes on her because of her devastated expression. "I'm so, so sorry."

There was a pause, but then Jack saw Renee nod out of the corner of his eye. "It's okay," she whispered, in a surprisingly calm voice. "It's okay. We've still got time together."

Jack nodded. "Ten years is a long time."

As she started to pull away from him, Renee murmured, "Thank you for not lying to me about it. I really appreciate it."

"Renee," Jack called, not really sure what he was doing. When she turned, he asked her, "Will you do me a favor? Don't tell my dad anything. It would kill him if he found out the truth. He really loves you."

Renee smiled lightly. "He does, doesn't he?"

"He told me about you once when I was a kid," Jack told her softly, and then he returned her smile. "I really wish I'd gotten a chance to know you."

"Well, your dad can tell you all about me when you go home," Renee replied.

"I'll be sure to ask him about you," Jack promised as she turned away. He started to think about his older sister, Hallie. It had always been ironic that his sister shared the same name as Walter Reifert's mother and daughter, but his father had claimed that it was just a pretty name that he and his wife had chosen for her. Jack now knew the truth. His father had named his daughter after Hallie Reifert, after his life changing encounter with her. He had named his child after the goodness in a damaged mother's cracked soul. Hallie was the parallel—the goodness—of Hara, and after the secret that Perry was keeping from his people, he named a part of him after that goodness. Maybe, at the time, Perry had felt that his daughter was the goodness in himself.

✳ ✳ ✳

716

Despite everything that was certain to happen in the near future, John Reifert felt strangely at peace. His life was going to end in ten years along with his three oldest boys, but that didn't faze him quite yet. He'd had his time, and he didn't have any regrets. When it would be time for him to go, he wasn't going to be afraid. At least he got to meet two of his future grandchildren. His first three boys would not make it to a very old age, but his family would indeed go on. That was why he was at peace. One Reifert child would live through the terror of the outbreak, and he would be the one to carry on the family legacy. He was not afraid of dying, like he used to be. He couldn't spend the rest of his life in fear anymore, because there wasn't anything to fear.

He was sitting in the back pew far from the commotion, and he was keeping a careful eye on the children that were playing two rows up. It was ironic to watch his son playing with the boy that would grow into the man who would ultimately destroy him and most of his people. Neither Walter nor Jackson knew who they would become and what would happen when they did meet again, but it was still a peculiar sight. Seeing Dreyson playing along with them was even more mind-boggling. The toddler was young, but he was smart and he did know who Jackson was. For some reason, the little boy chose to be a friend to the boy who would eventually murder his family and torture him and his mother. Dreyson must have known that even the darkest of hearts could have a shred of light in them. Ten-year-old Jackson would become The Doc one day, but at the moment he was just as innocent as Dreyson and Walter. Dreyson was a child, but the boy knew that much.

John had been so distracted by the children that he didn't realize Bo had approached him until he sat down beside him. Bo had been reborn out of the ashes of the present calamity, and because he had come back to save John's granddaughter, John considered him family as well. But he didn't look at Bo, even when he felt the pressuring weight of his stare. John knew why Bo was there. He didn't know how, but he knew, and no matter what he would have to do, John wasn't going to allow Bo to do what he wanted to do.

When Bo seemed to realize that John wasn't going to acknowledge him and was purposely ignoring him, he asked quietly, "How are you doing?"

Refusing to respond, John stared straight ahead and continued to watch the children, He could feel Bo probing around inside his head to find his own answers. It was kind of irritating, but John forced himself to continue ignoring his grandson-in-law.

As Bo sighed, he scooted a little closer to John. "You know, I really should wipe your memory," he said softly.

John finally willed himself to look at Bo. "You won't," he whispered.

Bo's expression was very serious, but John could see the sadness in him as well. He didn't want to take John's memories. "What makes you so sure?" he asked.

Narrowing his own eyes, John muttered, "Because you don't even want to."

Bo looked away. "It's not fair that you should be forced to live knowing what you know. I can't allow you to live with such a burden."

"Please," John said, determined to make sure that Bo gave up on it. "I'm going to die in ten years. There are six grandchildren and at least eleven great grandchildren I will never get to meet, but I have their faces locked away in my head. Don't take away the only part of them I will ever get to have."

Shifting his eyes back to John, Bo sighed sadly again. "I never met you, but I always knew that Walter got his greatness from you."

Without knowing what to say to such a compliment, John turned his gaze back on his son. He never could have predicted what Walter was going to become, but he always knew deep down that his youngest boy was going to grow into someone spectacular. Unfortunately, John would never get to see that happen, but living long enough to be sure that it would was good enough for him.

"You raised him well," Bo told him respectfully as John felt his cheeks blush bright red. Bo leaned forward so he could see John's face. "I'll let you keep your memories as long as you promise me one thing."

John looked at him. "And what's that?"

Shaking his head solemnly, Bo replied, "You can't ever tell your son what's coming."

"I wasn't planning on it," John responded. "He needs to have an easy childhood without dreading the day that everything's going to come crashing down. He can't have me there making him so paranoid that he screws up. He has to do this on his own." His eyes suddenly left Bo's and moved to Flint, his oldest grandson that he still hadn't had a chance to talk to. Even when John made eye contact with him, Flint avoided anything to do with him. John didn't know why that was, and it made him sad. It was also sad that Flint would be born so soon after John's death. John would miss the birth of his first grandchild by less than five months.

He saw that Bo was watching Flint as well, and John murmured, "I keep hoping that he'll come talk to me, but I'm starting to think that he doesn't want anything to do with me."

"He does," Bo reassured quickly. "It's just...difficult for him. He's been through a lot, and he has a lot of emotion for you that he doesn't know how to express."

"Why?" John asked.

"Because you saved his father's life," Bo told him softly.

Up on the altar, where Flint was pressing the final buttons to send his people back home, Flint suddenly made eye contact with John. It was only for a quick second before Flint looked away, but it was long enough to see the admiration in his eyes.

"He wants to talk to you," Bo explained. "He just doesn't know how."

"Well, then I suppose I'll just have to go talk to him," John declared.

"I think he would like that," Bo chuckled.

John glanced at him. "You say I'm going to save Walter? How will I do that?"

Giving him a small smile, Bo replied, "You already have."

John wasn't sure what Bo meant by that. He supposed it was something for Bo to know and for him to figure out.

"Where did you get that note from?" Bo asked suddenly. "The note that you gave to Shawn Perry. Who gave it to you?"

"Oh," John said in surprise, trying to remember the name of the woman who had given his wife Hallie the envelope so many years before. "Well, she was a young, very pretty woman. She had blue eyes and dark red hair. I think her name was Angela...no, it was Angelina. Now I remember. Her name was Angelina Skyler." Peering at Bo's astonished expression, John asked, "Why, do you know that name?"

"That's Hallie's grandmother," Bo said softly. "She's the mother of Walter's future soul mate." He smiled suddenly. "I suppose that Hallie's whole family is just brilliant, even those who never survived the outbreak. They always seem to know what's coming."

John smiled in return.

Patting his shoulder, Bo stood up and started to exit the pew. "I need to get my son so we can go home. I'm glad I got the chance to meet you, John Reifert."

"My granddaughter's a very lucky girl to have you," John told him, smiling as a harsh blue light erupted from the machine near the altar and sent the people on it back to the future.

Bo turned and smiled. "I'm a very lucky guy to have your granddaughter."

* * *

Perry finally managed to talk to Jack, but it wasn't quite the reunion he had hoped for. As he left Bo to his conversation with John Reifert, Perry walked up the aisle to the altar and Renee turned away suddenly from Jack and hurried away. Her eyes were cloudy and she looked rather upset, but she didn't look at Perry when she brushed past him. Confused, Perry glanced at her as she walked away, and then he turned to Jack. "What did you say to her?"

"Nothing," Jack lied quickly, swallowing hard. "I think the stress of the whole day just finally caught up with her."

His eyes narrowing on his son, Perry let it go. He could always ask Renee about it later. Instead, he brought up a different problem between the two of them. "Why didn't you just tell me the truth?" he asked even though he already knew the answer.

"That I'm really your son?" Jack said skeptically, raising his eyebrows. "Would you have believed me?"

Perry grinned. "No; definitely not." His grin faded when Jack's expression didn't brighten. "What's the matter? Your people are saved, and you get to go home to a fresh start! Isn't that a good thing?"

"My life has been meaningless ever since Bo took Hallie from me," Jack muttered, looking at the floor. "Sure, our kind gets a fresh start, but I don't." Sighing, he grumbled, "I guess the stress of the day has finally caught up with me, too."

"Hey, Hallie just wasn't who you were meant to be with. Don't worry, you'll find you soul mate someday."

"Bo made you promise not to tell anyone about the war, didn't he?" Jack asked abruptly.

Perry lowered his eyes out of guilt. "Look, I'm sorry," Perry apologized desperately as Jack started to turn away. "But Bo..."

"Yeah, I know," Jack said curtly. "Bo made a really good point. He always does."

Perry's heart sank at Jack's look of betrayal. "Jack, I can tell by how our conversations have gone that we're not that close in the future, but when I see this, I know it has to change. I promise you that I will do whatever it takes to give the two of us a good relationship this time around."

"You say that now," Jack muttered sharply. "But when my time comes you won't be the same man that you are now."

"Jack, please!" Perry begged hopelessly. "I can change something as insignificant as this!"

"Insignificant?" Jack repeated in furious disbelief.

Damn it. "That's not what I meant!" Perry exclaimed quickly at the sight of Jack's enraged glare.

"I know exactly what you meant!" Jack snapped. "And I'm going to tell you now to forget it! Our relationship is set in stone! The whole flow of time is set in stone! Nothing is ever going to change! This war is going to be a repeating cycle of pain and misery, and it's never going to end!"

"Nothing is set in stone," Perry said quietly, hoping his son would calm down.

"Forget it, Perry!" Jack growled angrily.

Taken aback, Perry whispered, "You know, you can just call me 'Dad.'"

Shaking his head hard, Jack glared at him. "You're not my dad yet!"

"Everyone else, say your goodbyes and get on the platform!" Rockwell suddenly called loudly.

Jack muttered, "I'll see you in forty years. You'll see me in eighteen." Turning on his heel, Jack made his way towards the machine.

It felt like Perry's chest was going to explode. He had made an effort to reconcile with his son, but Jack was convinced that they could never have a decent father-son relationship and clearly had no interest in reconciling. The future for the Colicians might have a valiant light to it, but Perry's future really didn't seem all that bright. But, as the seconds seemed to suddenly slow to a halt, he realized that there were worse things that he had to worry about than Jack.

Perry didn't have a telepathic ability, but he must have had the mental father-son connection with Jack because something happened that he couldn't explain. Jack was hearing a vision that Dreyson was seeing, and Jack must have been unintentionally projecting the images inside Perry's head. Everything began happening in slow motion. At first, he was only aware of the people moving steadily around him. Flint, Jack, and James were standing beside the machine near the altar, chatting in low voices. Rockwell and Finchly were standing beside Hallie where she lay on the pew as they spoke to her. The Doc was standing casually at the bottom of the steps to the altar, handcuffed and unguarded. Bennett had taken a seat in the pew behind Hallie and was talking to her as well. Jackson was sitting alone where he had previously been playing with Walter and Dreyson. John was now holding Walter's hand and leading him up the aisle, most likely going to say goodbye to Hallie. Bo was carrying Dreyson in his arms several feet ahead of the Reiferts, and they were almost to the end of the aisle when the following events were set in motion.

Finchly called Renee over to ask her a question, and as Renee walked by Perry once again, Perry saw little Dreyson's pupils dilate and his eyes get very wide. Not half a second later, Bo gasped and threw himself and his son down behind the front pew, yelling, "Everybody get down!"

As all of those things began to happen, Perry found that he had to make a difficult choice. He had to choose between Renee and Walter. He had to choose between the woman he loved and the boy who would become the father of their future. Cursing himself a thousand times and praying for the best possible outcome, Perry ran down the aisle.

He wasn't watching it, but Perry knew what was happening. As Renee froze in surprise from the sudden cry, The Doc, who was standing not three feet behind her, lurched forward and snatched the gun from her belt. Renee began to turn and her entire body went on the defense, but The Doc had fired on her before she even got all the way around. The bullet struck her square in the chest and she started to go down hard.

The Doc then turned the gun on Rockwell, but as he fired, Finchly gave the president a shove and the bullet struck her instead. Rockwell was knocked to the ground and he rolled under Hallie's pew while Finchly collapsed beside Renee. Bennett ducked down beside Rockwell, and Jack, Flint, and James took shelter on the other side of the machine behind one of the wide beams.

Time slowed even more for Perry as he kept moving towards the Reiferts, and he could feel his heart pounding as he sensed The Doc aiming the gun at Walter. Perry couldn't have been more than a few feet from the startled Reiferts as The Doc fired one last time, and for a horrible, fleeting moment he was sure that he had made his move too late. But with everything he had left in him, Perry threw himself forward and collided with John as he felt the bullet strike him in his lower side. Fighting the familiar pain, Perry shoved John down toward the shelter of the pews. John grabbed Walter as he went down and pushed him in first, and when Walter lay frozen on the floor and Perry realized that the bullet had gone right through his own side, Perry feared that Walter had suffered a wound as well from the same bullet. To his tremendous relief, Walter was just stunned from the fall and he quickly scrambled to where his father was guiding him. John quickly followed him as time resumed at its normal pace, leaving Perry sprawled injured and helpless in the center of the aisle. Thankfully, he was the one person that—no matter how many times he was shot—would never be able to die.

"Agent Perry," The Doc said in his smug voice, and Perry could hear him coming closer. "Or should I call you Dr. Perry?" Snickering, he told him, "You may be the best doctor, but I'll always be the best shot!"

Feeling his wound beginning to close, Perry carefully rolled over and squinted at him. The Doc was standing about two yards from him, his gun still raised in a firing position.

His eyes narrowed in distaste, The Doc demanded, "Why is it always you that gets in my way?"

"I'm the only one you can't kill," Perry said evenly despite his pain. Glaring at The Doc's angry expression, he hissed, "I'll always be there to stop you! I'll take a thousand bullets before I let you kill that boy!"

A corner of his mouth turned up in a smirk, and something changed in The Doc's eyes. "Well, if you won't let me kill him, then I suppose you'll have to."

"What?" Perry cried. "Are you insane?" He didn't know why he bothered asking that question; the answer was quite obvious.

His eyes narrowing even more, the smirk left The Doc's face. "Take out your gun Perry," he growled quietly.

"Ha!" Perry laughed sarcastically. "You're not just crazy, you're stupid!" Even as he said it, he felt his hand begin to reach for his belt. It wasn't intentional, but he wasn't stopping himself either. When he realized what he was doing, he attempted to put his arm back down, but he wasn't moving his arm with his own free will. He tried grabbing his wrist with his other hand, but he found that the left side of his body was completely useless, as if someone had given him a large dose of anesthetic and had numbed that half of his body. As his rebellious hand wrapped around his weapon, he stared up in horror at The Doc. "What are you doing to me?" Perry had a feeling that their situation wasn't going to end well.

The Doc didn't reply at first; he just kept staring at Perry with his merciless eyes which clearly held more secrets than anyone realized. How was it that The Doc was a human yet had the ability to control Perry? Why couldn't anyone get inside of his head? If Perry was lucky, then someone would figure it out in the next few moments and stop The Doc before he could make Perry hurt Walter.

"How do you think your people will take it when they find out that you were the one who brought their reign to an end?" The Doc asked icily as Perry drew out his gun. "Dr. Shawn Perry, the savior and destroyer of the Colician race."

"Stop it!" Perry pleaded. "You don't have to do any of this!"

"Point it at Walter," The Doc instructed coldly, his dark expression still unchanging.

"Jackson, stop!" Perry cried.

His lip curling up in a snarl, The Doc fired his own weapon and hit Perry in almost the exact same place as before. "Don't call me that!" he roared.

Even in his pain, Perry's arm was still moving steadily towards the gap between two of the pews, right where Walter and John were sheltered. "Listen to me," he begged. "Stop this now, and we can help you. You don't have to be like this!"

"Ha!" The Doc snickered, imitating Perry's earlier amusement. "My father may have made me into what I am today, but you and your people helped!" His amusement replaced by disgust, he growled, "There's nothing you and your people could do to help me. Aim your gun at Walter!"

Moaning in his effort to stop his arm, Perry aimed his gun at the helpless boy and his father.

"Perry, fight him!" Rockwell shouted from his hiding place. Perry could see him on the floor underneath the pews. His face was desperate. "Don't let him control you!"

"Push him out of your head, Dad!" Jack's voice echoed throughout the church.

"If he's not welcome, then force him out!" Bo yelled, knowing that if Walter was killed, then Hallie would never be born.

"You can't let him die!" Flint cried pleadingly.

723

Somebody must have tried to come out of their hiding place, because The Doc's eyes snapped away from Perry's for a split second and he fired at one of the pews, but then his eyes were right back on Perry's. There wasn't the sound of a body falling, so Perry prayed that meant The Doc had missed.

When The Doc's concentration shifted from him for that fleeting moment, Perry had suddenly felt under his own control again. If someone could divert The Doc's attention just once more, Perry would have enough strength to raise his arm and shoot The Doc or at least throw his gun away from him. Perry had a feeling he wasn't going to get that chance. His arm was already pointed at Walter, and his finger was on the trigger. The Doc wouldn't give him enough time to make that move.

"Shoot him," The Doc whispered.

Perry felt the trigger beneath his index finger, and he felt the iron weight forcing his finger down. He used every ounce of his own power to keep his finger from coming down, but even that wasn't going to be enough. He wanted to push The Doc out of his head like everyone was yelling for him to do, but unlike when others had been inside his head, Perry couldn't feel a presence this time. The Doc was nothing. Nobody could control him, and nobody could stop him either.

Looking desperately at John Reifert's horrified expression as the father shielded his son with his own body, Perry said through gritted teeth, "Move!"

"Perry, you have to stop," John told him, his voice and face full of fear. "Don't let him control you. You of all people have the power to stop him."

Apologizing with his eyes, Perry shook his head helplessly. "I can't!" Feeling his control beginning to slip, Perry squeezed his eyes shut. He couldn't watch what was about to happen. Just before his finger came all the way down, a soft voice hissed inside his head from somewhere in the sanctuary.

"*Stop.*"

The pressure on Perry's fingers lessened, and he found that he was able to move under his own free will again. Wrenching his arm away from the Reiferts and opening his eyes again with a gasp, Perry whipped his gun over his head and heard it clatter to the floor several yards behind him. He looked at The Doc to see who had distracted him, and was shocked to see that his expression had become strained, and his face was red while his hands began to shake violently. He still managed to hold onto the gun, which was still pointed at Perry. Sitting up, he looked around and saw that order hadn't been for himself. Hallie had been the one to take a stand against The Doc. It would always be her.

She swayed dangerously on her feet in her weakened state, but the determination in her eyes told Perry that she wasn't going down just yet.

Her gaze remained locked on the side of The Doc's head, and Perry was certain that the slightest distraction would take away her impossible control over him. It was unclear as to how she had managed to get inside his head to get him to stop, but it didn't surprise Perry that it had been her to be the first to figure it out. After all, she had been with him for months and most likely knew him better than anyone else.

Her left eyelid twitched slightly, and then her eyes slowly began to narrow. Her chest was heaving up and down, and her face was very pale and gaunt.

The Doc made a grunting noise, and then his hands began to rise, the gun being aimed away from Perry. Then, his hands aimed the gun at his own head. "You're going to kill me?" he demanded with great effort, and he tried to sound doubtful but it was clear that he was scared.

"I can't give you the chance to hurt any more people," Hallie whispered coldly as the nose of the gun pressed up against The Doc's temple. "You need to be gone from this world and face your judgment on the other side."

"You could never bring yourself to pull the trigger before!" The Doc said, desperately trying to shame her out of it. "What makes you think you can do it now?"

"Because I won't be the one to pull the trigger," Hallie replied smugly. "You will."

"You can't kill me!" The Doc shouted, the fear in him exposed to everyone. "Bo just took the killer out of you! Do you really want to make the good part of you bad as well?"

"The only way I can really be rid of my darkness is to be rid of you," Hallie whispered. "You're a part of me, but you're the bad part of me. You were right, my friend. We are parallels. Hara wasn't just a part of me; she's a part of you." She sighed regretfully. "I have a feeling that wherever you go next, I'll find you there again someday." Her eye twitched again.

Perry saw The Doc's finger start to come down on the trigger, and he couldn't believe that Hallie was really going to force The Doc to kill himself.

"Hallie," Bo begged her, poking his head up from behind the front pew. "Hallie, don't do this. He's not worth it. You're better than that."

Hallie's expression changed, but she didn't stop right away. It was easy to see that she was dying to get The Doc out of her life, but at the same time she wanted to listen to Bo's words. He was right, after all. Hallie Reifert was better than that. Finally, with much difficulty, she let The Doc go. Almost instantly afterwards, she fell forward in a heap on the floor, the effort it took to get inside The Doc's head taking every bit of energy she had.

Gasping in shock as he found he could control himself again, The Doc quickly lowered his cuffed hands in front of him. He stood still for a moment to catch his breath, but then his expression hardened once again and he furiously rounded on Hallie's limp, helpless form. Aiming the gun at her head, he snarled, "Regenerate this, bitch!"

It sounded like everyone else but Perry screamed, "No!" Perry would have been devastated to see poor Hallie killed by The Doc, but somehow he knew that The Doc wouldn't be able to bring himself to do it, for a reason entirely different from Hallie's. Hallie didn't kill The Doc so she could save herself even though she hated him. The Doc wouldn't kill Hallie; not to preserve himself, but because he loved her. Jackson Odau loved Hallie Reifert and wouldn't try to kill her even though she had tried to kill him.

His expression was still hard, but he didn't shoot her. He just stood glaring at her for a long time while everyone else anxiously looked on. At one point, The Doc looked almost certain that he would shoot her, but then his expression softened and he gazed down at her with deep sadness.

Hallie struggled to raise her head and look up at The Doc. Her eyes pleading with his, she whispered, "Go ahead. Kill me."

Slowly lowering the gun again, the pain on The Doc's face intensified. Shaking his head, he said, "I can't."

"It's me or you," Hallie breathed, her head dropping to the floor with an unpleasant thump. Sighing, she forced out, "One of us has got to go, Jackson."

"I could never let it be you," he told her softly.

Perry watched as The Doc stared down at Hallie's weak, crumpled body. A single tear fell from his eye, and it was enough to make Perry smile. The Doc was right; the Colicians couldn't cure his insanity. If anyone could help him, it was Hallie. She was already changing him. She was beginning to heal a grieving man with a hate-driven vengeance.

"Please get up," he said, cocking his head to one side.

Moaning in pain, Hallie was having trouble forming words. "I can't!" she whimpered.

"Can I help you?" he asked her, peering down at her helplessly.

It seemed to everyone as if The Doc had been calmed enough to the point of surrender, and Bo made the mistake of moving around the pew and approaching him. His hands raised to symbolize that he wasn't a threat, Bo asked quietly, "Will you put the gun down, please?"

Snapping out of his emotional reverie, The Doc's head raised towards Bo and his expression hardened again. Maybe he was just angry or maybe he just wanted Bo out of the way, but whatever the reason, The Doc pointed his gun at Bo and fired.

Somebody fired at The Doc at the same time, his gun flew out of his hand, and he cried out in pain as he collapsed to the floor with his hands clutching his chest. Blood began staining his lab coat. Someone had precise enough aim that they had managed to shoot the gun right out of his hand. The bullet that would have struck Bo in the head struck the pew beside him instead. Bo stood with his mouth agape, relief flooding his face. There was only one person with good enough aim to do that.

Turning towards the back of the sanctuary, Perry saw Lieutenant Odau standing in the aisle. He had picked up Perry's gun and shot The Doc. His teeth were bared, and his expression was furious. Now that Perry knew that The Doc was Odau's son, it was easy to see the resemblance when both of them were angry. The cold gray eyes the two men shared were unmistakable. Keeping the gun locked on The Doc, Odau walked briskly up the aisle, passed Perry, and stopped at his son's side, making sure to kick Renee's gun away from The Doc as he tried to grab for it.

Glaring up at him as he grimaced in his pain, The Doc growled, "Kill me! You heard her; one of us has got to go!" When the lieutenant didn't respond, The Doc let out an angry yell and shouted, "Kill me! I killed you!"

As Perry came forward, Odau bent down, grabbed a handful of The Doc's hair, and pulled him closer so their faces were only inches apart. Then, he hissed, "I *never* would!"

"Why?" The Doc demanded angrily, and he repeated, "I killed you!"

"Because you're my son," Odau whispered, releasing The Doc and standing up straight again. "And I love you no matter what you did or what you'll do."

Perry barely had a chance to see the look of shock on The Doc's face before Flint was jerking The Doc to his feet and uncuffing him. "I knew we should have just sedated him," Flint grumbled, spinning The Doc around and cuffing his hands behind his back. Shoving The Doc down into the front pew, Flint snapped, "Don't move!"

His heart pounding, Perry rushed around the corner to where Finchly and Renee lay bleeding. Bo tried to stop him while on his way to Hallie by asking, "Are you alright?" but Perry pushed him out of the way and told him, "Don't worry about me right now!" He knelt beside Renee, who had blood running out of her mouth and the wound in her chest. Her eyes were pained and scared. Picking up her head and setting it gently in his lap, he gazed down at her agonized and confused expression and whispered, "*Shhh*, everything's going to be fine." He looked over at Austin Rockwell, who was holding Finchly in his arms, and asked hopefully, "How is she doing?"

"Damn it, Maggie!" Rockwell said in a murmur, gazing softly down at her and ignoring Perry. "Why did you do that? You shouldn't have done that."

Finchly was in worse condition than Renee—the bullet was centered just below her left breast and her breathing was labored—but she managed to choke out a few words. "Your life is worth more than mine."

Rockwell shook his head gently. "No life is worth more than another," he replied, interlacing his fingers with hers.

Giving his hand a squeeze as she managed a small smile, she added, "And I wanted you to know that there *is* a shred of goodness in the human race." Her eyelids drooped and her head fell back into Rockwell's lap.

Rockwell took a deep breath and whispered, "I *know* there is."

Another pang stabbing his heart, Perry asked, "Is she going to be alright?"

Rockwell looked up at him slowly, his eyes full of regret. "She's gone."

Before Perry could express his own loss for Finchly, Renee's body began jerking up and down and she started throwing up blood, making a horrible gagging sound in her throat. "Oh, God!" Perry cried as Renee's eyes rolled back in her head. "Somebody help her, please!"

"There's nothing we can do for her here," Jack told him, kneeling beside him and putting a comforting hand on his shoulder.

"Then take her back with you!" Perry begged them, staring down at one of the few things he couldn't stand to lose as she slowly slipped away. "Just help her!"

"There won't be enough time," Rockwell said, placing Finchly's body on the floor and moving over to join Perry, Jack, and most of the others who had approached as well.

Looking pleadingly into the sad faces of everyone around him, Perry's eyes landed on Hallie. She was still face down on the floor and she remained motionless, but Perry knew that she would push herself for something as important as that. "Hallie!" he called quickly. "Hallie, you have to help her!"

"She can't," Bo told him apologetically, placing his hands on her shoulders defensively.

"She has to!" Perry protested desperately. "She's the only one who can save her!"

"Perry, I'm sorry!" Bo said firmly. "She's unconscious, and even if she wasn't she wouldn't be able to. She's too exhausted to do something like that."

As tears fell from his eyes, Perry looked back down at Renee as she slipped closer to death. Suddenly, he had another idea. "I can save her," he said aloud. "Does anyone have a syringe? My blood is the only other thing that can save her."

Nobody answered, and there was an awkward tension within the group. Glancing up at Rockwell, Perry saw that he was gazing at Flint and they were most likely having a mental conversation. When Rockwell turned back to Perry, his expression was serious. "Your blood will save her, yes, but…" He hesitated. "There will be side effects."

"What kind of side effects?" Perry asked.

Rockwell opened his mouth to answer, but he seemed unable to do so. Looking to Flint helplessly, he gestured to Perry with his head. Flint then knelt down as well and tried to explain it as gently as he could. "Since Renee is an O Negative, if your blood mixes with her, then she will get her ability early like you."

Nodding, Perry began to panic as he thought that over. "Is it a one hundred percent guarantee?"

"Most likely," Flint replied apologetically.

"I'll take that chance," Perry whispered fiercely.

His eyes narrowing, Rockwell said, "I don't think that's your decision to make."

"Who else is supposed to make it?" Perry snapped impatiently.

"The change is life altering," Flint said seriously. "You should know. Would you have wanted somebody else to make this decision for you if you were in her place?"

"I *have* been in her place!" Perry exclaimed.

Before anyone could respond, Renee's raspy voice spoke up. "Do it," she said, her breaths numbered. "Do it."

Perry looked from face to face again. "Well?" he demanded.

Sighing, Rockwell shook his head. "If that's what she wants, then I have no objections."

"I need a syringe," Perry said urgently.

"I have one," Dr. Bennett offered, stepping forward and handing Perry a syringe from his jacket pocket.

Perry took it and then handed it to Rockwell. Rockwell pulled Perry's arm toward him, snapped the vein in the inside of his elbow twice and then withdrew his blood. Before he injected it into Renee's arm, he warned Perry, "Her ability could be much more noticeable and uncontrollable than yours."

Narrowing his eyes, Perry asked suspiciously, "Don't you know?"

A muscle in Rockwell's face twitched. "I might," he replied. "But it's not my place to say." Looking back down, he injected Renee with the regenerative blood.

"Can I help Finchly too?" Perry asked, praying that there was still a chance for her.

"I'm afraid not," Rockwell said quietly. "She's already gone. Once someone's truly gone there is no way to bring them back with this method."

"This is all your fault!"

Everybody turned in surprise to see who had made the accusation. Jack stood up and rounded on Bo, who was still trying to wake Hallie. When Bo looked up and saw the declaration had been directed his way, his eyes narrowed as well. "Excuse me?" he demanded sharply.

"This is all your fault!" Jack repeated harshly as Bo stood up to face him.

"My fault?"

"Yes, *your* fault!" Jack marched up to him and shoved him backwards. "If you had just let Hallie finish what she was here to do, then none of this would have happened and nobody would have had to die!"

Bo gave Jack a harder shove. "Do you know why I'm her soul mate and you're not? You only try to give her what she wants to try to please her, but you don't know shit about what she needs!"

"Is this what she needs?" Jack demanded, pushing Bo again.

"Give her up, Jack!" Bo shouted, taking a step back instead of retorting. "She hasn't loved you for years! I'm the one who knows her better now!"

Letting out an enraged cry, Jack launched himself at Bo and slammed into him, his fists punching any part of his body that he could.

In unison, both Perry and Rockwell scrambled to their feet and ran to their sons. Perry grabbed Jack around the shoulders to pry him away from Bo, and Rockwell stepped in between his own son and Jack to keep them from attacking each other again. Bo wasn't going to fight back despite his cross glare, but his father kept a firm hand on his chest nevertheless.

"I'm going to kill you!" Jack yelled, trying to break away from Perry.

"Enough!" Rockwell said loudly, glaring at Jack as well. When Jack stopped fighting, Rockwell declared, "We're all on the same side! How are we supposed to fight the real enemy if we're fighting each other?"

"There are more than two sides in this war!" Jack replied curtly.

"There can only be two sides in this war," Rockwell snapped angrily. "You're creating your own personal war!"

"Stop it," Hallie said quietly from her place on the floor. She slowly and shakily raised her head to move her eyes between the four men. Pleadingly, she told Jack, "Listen to them, Jack. No more fighting. Stop defending me. It isn't your job anymore. It hasn't been for more than five years."

Swallowing back his tears as Hallie looked away from him and accepted Bo's hand to help her up, Jack gave up and slumped against Perry.

"We have too many problems we need to deal with," Hallie whispered, gesturing to The Doc. "We don't need to be creating any more."

"I know there are issues we need to sort out here," Perry said, "but did I miss something? How the hell does The Doc have the ability to control people? He's not a Colician!" He looked to Bo. "Is he?"

As he slowly coaxed Hallie to her feet, Bo looked back at Perry with a very serious expression. "He's not a Colician," he replied. "Nor is he a Caiten. This is the result of what he did to Hallie."

"And what exactly did he do to Hallie?" Perry asked hesitantly, every second he spent pondering it causing him to dread the answer even more.

"I've only seen into his mind once," Bo said. "The only one who has any real access to it is Hallie, so I was startled when I managed to catch a glimpse inside while he was killing Hallie's father. When I saw into his mind, I saw his plan. He wanted her to understand him, so he put a part of himself inside her."

"That's how Hara began," Perry realized. He glanced at Hallie as Bo helped her sit down on the step to the altar, and he saw that she was trying not to listen in order to mask her pain.

"That's not all, though," Bo said, leaving Hallie's side and taking a few steps closer to Perry. His eyes were distraught as he explained, "In order to put a part of himself in her, he also had to take a part of her and put it inside him."

"What?" Perry cried in disgust. "Why would he do that?"

The muscles in his face twitching in his contempt for The Doc, Bo growled, "Because he loves her."

Perry shot a glance at The Doc, but The Doc wasn't paying attention to them. He was in the same position that Flint had put him in and was sitting so still that he didn't even look alive.

"That's how he has these abilities to control people and block us out and know what other people are thinking or planning to do," Bo muttered. "He stole a part of Hallie and put himself in its place."

"How could that give him an ability, though?" Perry asked in confusion. "If he doesn't have the right blood type…"

"This is about more than just blood types, Perry," Bo replied sharply. "It has to do with one's mind as well. When he stole that bit of Hallie, it changed his mind. It changed him. She changed him." Turning away, Bo went back to Hallie's side.

Perry released Jack as things calmed down finally and stepped in front of him. "You called me Dad," he told him softly.

Jack looked up at him and his brow furrowed in confusion. "What?"

"Before, when you were near the altar," Perry explained, unable to keep a grin from forming on his face. "You called me Dad."

His face turning bright red, Jack shrugged and looked away. "Old habits die hard, I suppose."

"I meant what I said, you know," Perry told him, smiling at him when he looked up again. "I'm going to try and make this work for us."

"Well, don't hold your breath," Jack muttered in reply.

Before Perry could respond to that, Bo suddenly appeared beside them with tension on his face. "Jack," he said, and sighed as Jack's face hardened. "Listen, I'm really sorry that things didn't turn out the way you wanted them to. It was never my intention to take Hallie from you. I don't want to fight anymore. I don't want to be your enemy." He held out his hand.

Raising an eyebrow, Jack looked from Bo's face, to his hand, and then to his face again before brushing past him and joining the others at the altar. He didn't care for anything Bo would ever have to say. He would never shake hands with Bo.

Perry saw the exhausted look of defeat in Bo's eyes. Bo was tired of fighting, but Jack was never going to let Hallie go.

Giving Bo an apologetic look, Perry followed Jack to the altar.

"We really need to go," Flint was saying insistently as Perry approached. "My father's becoming extremely concerned and he's getting ready to send a rescue party after us. We all know how badly things will progress if that happens." He looked from face to face, a way of communication Perry was finding common among their kind. Turning to Perry, Flint said, "Mr. Perry, a word, if you will."

Following Flint off to the side where they were joined by Rockwell, Perry asked, "What's this all about?"

"We need a favor from you," Flint explained. "Once we leave, we need you to burn the church down."

"Burn it down?" Perry questioned.

"You have to dispose of this evidence for us," Rockwell persisted as he came to join them, pointing at the glowing transporter near the altar. "We can't allow anyone of this time period to get their hands on this time machine and rift generator. They're not that hard to operate, and if somebody discovered their purpose, very bad things could happen. So we're asking you to please burn this church down once everybody leaves."

"Okay," Perry agreed, nodding.

"Here." Rockwell pulled two keys out of his pocket and tossed them to Perry. "There's a container of gasoline in the back of each truck as well as a box of matches. After this building and everything in it is destroyed, you're free to take the trucks to get back home."

Perry stared at him. "So that's it?"

Both Flint and Rockwell blinked in confusion.

"What about everything that's happened here today?" Perry demanded. "Am I just supposed to forget about it all until the global apocalypse arrives in ten years?"

"Of course not," Rockwell replied. "Just don't tell anyone about what's coming."

"What am I supposed to tell the FBI and police about what happened to their officers?" Perry asked, looking at each of their calm faces and wondering how they could contain it all. "What am I supposed to tell my superior officers? I can't just pretend that they died for nothing!"

"They didn't die for nothing," Flint promised him. "Nobody here will know what they died for, but when we go home, we will remember those who lost their lives while fighting for us: Daniel Marcus, Rhett Simco, Andrew Martinson, Jazlyn Hersh, Maggie Finchly, and Garrick Aubrey. None of them will be forgotten, Perry. They didn't die for nothing."

"What am I supposed to tell the city about what happened downtown and to their mayor?" Perry demanded angrily, not at all comforted by Flint's promise. "What am I supposed to tell the parents of the children that were murdered?"

"Hey, hey," Flint said soothingly, putting his hand on Perry's shoulder. "Just calm down. This doesn't have to end up being a huge government conspiracy."

"But that's what it is!" Perry cried. "We're covering up all of this, but what am I supposed to tell all the people who need answers?"

"Tell them what they want to hear," Hallie said as Bo helped ease her over to the group. She put her hand on Perry's shoulder just as Flint had. Her eyes were filled with hesitation, but they also showed that she felt she was doing the right thing. "Everybody who died or was taken back home, I killed them."

"What?" Perry whispered in horror. "No...no! I won't lie about you like that! This wasn't you! The Doc..."

"Cannot be brought into the picture," Hallie said firmly. "You were working with him in secret, and it has to stay that way. We have to keep this all under the radar."

Shaking his head, Perry said, "After everything you've done and everything you've been put through, I can't blame the death of our friends on you. I can't do this to you!"

"That's the way it has to be," Hallie murmured, her exhausted face showing deep sadness. She didn't want to take the blame for it all, but she was right. The people of Philadelphia wouldn't accept anything else, and that was the only way that Perry could explain to the authorities what had gone down on April 4, 2008. "Hara was a crazy teenager who killed a lot of innocent people. You and your colleagues finally cornered her here in this church and in the struggle, a fire started. She perished in

733

the flames along with a young female detective named Maggie Finchly. Many of the bodies of the dead were never found, but that was fine with you so long as the killer was dead." She sighed heavily. "Case closed." At Perry's disagreeing expression, she insisted, "Hara was a criminal who came into the world without any warning, and left the world with a bang just as quickly. I know you want to tell the truth, Perry. The Doc was the killer, but as soon as he comes into the picture this whole thing will become far too complicated and people will start asking questions that you can't answer. I know it's hard for you, and believe me when I say it's hard for me too, but you have to promise me that you'll tell the world that it was me."

Remembering the promise he had already made to her that he couldn't keep, Perry glanced at Bo. Bo nodded, and Perry sighed. "If that's how you want it."

Hallie smiled lightly. "Thank you. Now, we all have to leave. Goodbye, Shawn Perry. I can assure you that we'll meet again someday."

Perry smiled back as Bo helped lead Hallie towards the altar. Gripping the keys tightly in his palm, Perry looked over at Renee, whose wound was fully healed and was being helped to her feet by James. Relieved, Perry walked over to her and wrapped her in a tight embrace.

As Renee hugged him back, she whispered in his ear, "Thank you."

"I don't want to live forever unless you'll be there with me," Perry whispered back. He felt her tense up when he said that, but the others around him were bustling about and distracted him before he could say anything about it.

"We are leaving right now!" Bo informed the group as he helped Hallie up the steps to the altar. "Those who are coming, get on the platform."

James and his father quickly climbed onto the platform, followed shortly afterwards by Flint and The Doc, who both appeared rather unhappy. Flint began punching in his code for the machine, and the blue sphere began to glow brighter. Jack started up the stairs after Bo and Hallie, but then he stopped and turned suddenly, a confused expression on his face.

"Noah, are you coming?" he asked hesitantly.

Everybody looked at Noah, who was lingering back at the head of the aisle. He was leaning against one of the pews as he peacefully watched the others gather on the platform. The old man carefully limped over to him. "I'm staying here," he replied, patting Jack's shoulder gently. "This is where I belong."

"You belong with us!" Jack protested desperately.

Noah shook his head and smiled. "I have cancer," he said softly. "I told your father that I didn't want it cured, and he said that I would die within a decade. I'm old, Jack. I've lived a great life with you and your family, but this is my home. I'd like to spend my final years here while I can."

His eyes agonized at the thought of losing his friend. Jack opened his mouth to try to argue more, but then he nodded. "I understand," he whispered.

"Tell your dad I'm sorry," Noah requested, and then turned towards Perry with a twinkle in his eye. "Then again, I suppose he already knows."

Perry nodded at him.

Jack hugged Noah and said as his voice cracked with emotion, "I'm going to miss you!"

"And I you, my boy," Noah told him, pulling away and pushing him towards the altar. "Now go home. You've earned that much."

With much difficulty, Jack left Noah and went to join the others.

"Noah," Hallie called from the base of the machine. Her face was tormented as well. "I'm sorry about everything that I said before. I wasn't talking about you..."

"I understand exactly what you were talking about," Noah promised her, smiling. "Don't worry, sweetheart. You have nothing to apologize for."

"Thank you for everything you've done for me," she told him, her eyes tearing up. "You will be truly missed by my family as well as Jack's." She started to go with Bo onto the platform, but then she realized that she was forgetting something. "Come on, Dreyson," she called. "It's time to go home, honey."

Dreyson had been walking with John and Walter to the front, and after giving John's leg a quick hug he rushed over to Dr. Bennett on the other side of Renee and Perry, close to where the body of Finchly rested. Hugging him as well, he said three small words that didn't make a whole lot of sense, but seemed to hold great meaning to the two of them.

"When you sleep," he said quietly before scrambling to join his parents on the platform.

The people who Perry had been trying to stop were finally going home, and it was hard for Perry to believe that he had ever been against them. After all, he was one of them now. As Flint punched in the final numbers for the code and the two beams began to spin in circles, the people on the platform bid their final farewells to the others remaining below. There were so many silent goodbyes and thank you's being exchanged, but the one that would remain extraordinarily vivid in Perry's mind forever was the goodbye he received from Hallie.

When she was finished waving to her young father and grandfather, Hallie looked up and made eye contact with Perry. For a moment, her gaze and light smile remained gentle, and Perry knew that if she could, she would be telling him thank you without using any words.

The beams spun faster and faster, and the blue sphere shone brighter and brighter. Perry nodded to Hallie and smiled, but as the machine was seconds away from transporting them all home, the smile was wiped clean off of his face. In the final moments that they gazed upon each other, Hallie suddenly changed. Her green eyes let off a radiant emerald light. Right before the blue light became too unbearable for the naked eye, Perry saw Hallie's sweet smile transform into a twisted grin. But it wasn't just twisted; it was evil. Perry wasn't looking at Hallie anymore. He was looking at Hara.

Horrified and confused by how that was possible, Perry's gaze shifted to The Doc's. The Doc had finally raised his eyes and seemed like he had been waiting for Perry to realize what was happening. When Perry did look at him with a terrible fear in his heart, The Doc smirked back and gave him a wink. Somehow, The Doc knew that Hara was still living, and then Perry understood what was really happening.

"Wait!" he started to yell, but before he could warn Bo or anyone else, the light exploded into a violent supernova. When the light ceased, everyone on the platform was gone.

Hallie's earlier words crossed Perry's mind, about how Hara wouldn't be truly dead until The Doc was gone for good. Perry now knew how right she had been. Hara was a part of The Doc as well as Hallie, but that wasn't all. The Doc had taken a part of her and replaced it with part of himself, and because of that, even if The Doc was killed or locked away, he would always be in the Colicians' lives, unless of course the truth about Hallie's horribly troubled mind was uncovered.

Perry stared in horror at the platform, knowing that the war wasn't over yet. Hara was still alive, and would be for as long as Hallie had The Doc inside of her. They didn't realize it yet, but the Colician race would very soon face a problem that could potentially become much worse than the war itself. Because of that, Perry was forced to ask himself a crucial question that he wouldn't receive an answer to for more than forty years:

Did Hallie know what was still inside her?

20

What Now?

As Perry watched the church burn, he stepped over to where Lieutenant Odau was standing with his son. He patted Odau on the shoulder, and when the officer looked blankly back at him, Perry told him, "Don't be hard on your son because of what he's going to become. There's still a chance he could be that great man you want him to be."

Odau looked like he really wanted to say something in response, but the lieutenant kept his mouth shut and just continued to stare blankly back. When he looked away from Perry and Perry started back for Renee, Perry glimpsed Odau taking his son's hand in his own and giving it a squeeze. It made Perry smile. At least Odau wasn't going to shun his child after meeting The Doc.

Perry told the Reiferts, Bennett, and Noah that it wasn't safe for them to be at the church when the police force arrived, so the four of them would take one of the trucks and flee the scene. Walter and John were already inside, and Perry decided to take a detour to get one last chance to speak to Bennett and Noah before they departed as well.

"Dr. Bennett!" he called as he jogged over to their truck.

Bennett turned at the sound of his name, and his face was still as withdrawn as it had been after Dreyson had spoken his final words to him.

"Are you alright?" Perry asked in concern, nervous about what was bothering the doctor.

Shrugging, Bennett started for the passenger side. "I will be," he muttered as he walked away.

"It's a difficult thing to take in all those secrets at once," Noah said. "I think he's exhausted from everything that's happened today."

"Do you think he'll be alright?" Perry asked uncertainly.

"I'm sure he'll be fine," Noah replied, smiling from his place at the driver's side door.

"What about you?" Perry said. "What are you going to do? Where are you going to go?"

Noah shrugged. He didn't look the least bit concerned about that. "I have an idea, but I'm not worried. After what I've lived through, nothing that I'll face in the future could scare me."

"I have an extra bedroom in my apartment," Perry told him. "You're welcome to stay with me in Pittsburgh until you can get back on your feet."

Laughing, Noah shook his head. "That's very kind of you, but I've lived with you and your family long enough. I'm not going to be a burden on you any longer. Don't worry, sir," he insisted upon seeing Perry's protesting expression. "I've lived on earth in the mid twenty-first century. There is nothing in this world that I can't handle on my own."

Respecting the right to make his own decision, Perry nodded at him. "Alright, but promise me that you'll call me if you ever need anything?" He pulled out his card from his pocket and handed it to Noah.

"Fair enough," Noah replied, taking the card and opening the driver's door. "I'm fairly certain that I'll see you before I die, anyway."

"Take care," Perry said as Noah started the vehicle and drove off into the night. Sighing as the only sound around him was once again the roaring flames, Perry walked back over to Renee.

She was waiting for him. "What now?" she asked as he reached her. "Where do we go from here?"

Perry sighed again and shrugged. "I don't know," he answered truthfully. "I suppose we'll just have to sit back and see where life takes us."

Renee smiled. "Together, right?"

"I wouldn't have it any other way," Perry whispered, leaning forward and kissing her forehead The two of them continued to watch the church burn to the ground until the fire department arrived. As a police car pulled off the highway and into the parking lot, Perry felt Renee's hand slip into his, just as Odau's hand had slipped into Jackson's.

God only knew where Perry's life would take him, but he realized that none of that mattered. As long as he had the people he loved, the hardships he endured would all be worth it in the end. Taking a deep breath, Perry squeezed Renee's hand.

Perry let the church burn for thirty minutes before he called it in. He explained to an officer everything that had "happened" inside, and five minutes later the sounds of sirens could be heard above the roar of the fire. In a matter of minutes, the police force arrived along with the fire department, and within a matter of hours, more FBI agents showed up. Perry explained to them that the three agents who died were killed by Hara, along with all the others who had perished over the course of the past few days. After he was debriefed, he and Renee could return home to Pittsburgh. As Hallie had said, "Case closed." It was going to be difficult for him to lie about the case after what he had experienced, and it was definitely going to be difficult to cope, but he had made a promise to Hallie that he was going to keep.

Epilogue—2049 A.D.

The sun was just beginning to rise over Reifert City. The streets were silent as the citizens got their final hour of rest before going back to work to continue restoring the city.

There was a hill about a mile outside the city that provided an excellent view. It overlooked every part of the town. That was where Hallie Reifert and her colleagues arrived when they came home to the future. The silence and beauty of her home world stunned Hallie. No more Earth, no more humans, and no more death.

Her son squirmed in her arms and she set him down as she continued to gaze at her city. She had forgotten what it looked like, and she was glad that it was so beautiful. There were voices off to her right, and she looked over to see who was in the welcome party. There were only a few family members of those returning, and Hallie was grateful for that. The group that had come ahead of hers was already gone, and she didn't blame them. After everything she had been through, all Hallie wanted to do was go home.

Bo was holding Dreyson's hand as they, James, and Austin walked over to greet Bo's mother, Miriam. She beamed brightly and embraced each one of them for a long time, glad they were all okay. Hallie's mother Shauna joined the happy reunion as well.

Flint dragged The Doc behind him to proudly present him to Walter. Walter stared hard into The Doc's cold, defeated eyes, letting The Doc know that he was in serious trouble. The Doc stared back with a sort of uncertain fear in his eyes, knowing that Walter had been the one who wanted him brought back alive and that the Colicians had something special planned for him. Walter looked back at Flint and gestured with his head to take him away. As Flint led The Doc away, they passed by Dr. Shawn Perry, who had come to see his son's return.

Jack started for his father. Perry smiled at his son as he approached, but Jack wiped the smile off of his face with a single punch. He glared harshly at his father before shoving past him and starting after Flint.

Perry didn't look shocked. In fact, he looked rather ashamed. He kept his eyes lowered in guilt while the rest of the reunion continued.

Hallie felt the same as Perry, ashamed. She kept her own eyes lowered and refused to acknowledge her family that had gathered. She would never be able to forgive herself for what she had done. She was grateful to her parents for not bringing her children with them; she didn't want to see them just yet. Hallie didn't want to frighten them with her appearance or her thoughts. They would be able to see in her head exactly what she had done, and she knew that the images would scare them. Sighing in regret as she realized that she would never be able to take back the horrible acts that she had committed, she blinked the tears away that were clouding her eyes. As the tears struck the grass beneath her weary feet, something began to sprout out of the ground. Surprised, Hallie watched as a single, beautiful white carnation bloomed from her devastated tears. She had no idea how something so beautiful could come from her. She didn't think there was enough good left in her to create life.

Her father startled her when his hand touched her shoulder. She hadn't seen him approach and when her eyes snapped to his she was afraid of what she would see in them. She feared that his eyes would tell her that he was ashamed of her, or furious with her, or that he never wanted to see her again, or worse, that he pitied her. His eyes didn't say any of those things. His eyes said that he was proud of her. For what? Hallie had a few ideas. She had fought for her people until the very end, and although Hara had made her do terrible things, Hallie chose the right path several times. Her father was proud of her because she had been strong enough to fight the evil in herself as well as the evil surrounding her.

Walter was smiling down at her gently, and his green eyes caused an image of young Walter to flash through her head. Hallie wondered if her father remembered the day that his future daughter came to the past and saved his life, but she had a feeling that he wouldn't. He had been young, and he probably hadn't really understood what was happening.

Hallie didn't want to make eye contact with her father for very long for fear that he would see into her and see everything that she was feeling, but she forced herself to anyway. She wished that he could see the shame in her eyes, because she didn't want him to be proud of her. Looking away finally, she choked out, "I'm so sorry!"

Chuckling, Walter shook his head and then wrapped his arms tightly around her. He whispered in her head, *You have* nothing *that you need to apologize to me for.*

As more tears welled in her eyes and her emotions choked her, Hallie hugged her father back. She didn't want to let go for a very long time. It was a long hug, because she hadn't seen him alive in more than six months. It was well needed. When she pulled away, her father brushed a stray tear from her cheek. "What now?" she asked him hopelessly. "Where do I go from here?"

Glancing down at the carnation that she had created from her tears, Walter smiled again. "We start over."

Hallie looked at the carnation as well, and then she understood what it symbolized. The Colician race had been reborn, and it was time for them all to begin again. The carnation was Hallie. Out of the carnage and destruction of the war, she could completely change herself if she chose to. She could transform herself into something beautiful even after what she had done, if she could just let go of it all and—as her father had said—start over. But did she have enough strength left for that?

As her father's hand slipped into hers and Bo and Dreyson came to her side as well, Hallie gazed out at Reifert City as it was being rebuilt. She realized that as long as she had the people she loved, anything was possible. If there was one place to start over, it was home. Bo took her other hand and kissed the side of her head, and Hallie gripped his hand tightly in hers. She knew that she would be okay as long as she had him. Smiling as she gazed out at the place where she would be reborn, Hallie prayed that the rest of her life with Bo would be nothing but sheer happiness.

The war with The Doc was finally over, but as she gazed out at her beautiful home, Hallie had no idea that the worst of everything was still to come.

ABOUT THE AUTHOR

Author photo by Amber Blanchard Photography

Ms. King resides in Southern Wisconsin with her family. She enjoys writing, reading, long walks, and spending time with friends and family. To contact the author visit CSJ King Publishing at www.repeatproductions.samsbiz.com.

www.ingramcontent.com/pod-product-compliance
Lightning Source LLC
Chambersburg PA
CBHW070533030726
47505CB00001B/26